Santa Montefiore was born in England in 1970 She has written seven novels which have been translated into over twenty-five languages and sell all over the world. She lives in London with her husband, the historian Simon Sebag Montefiore and their two children. To find out more about her novels, visit Santa's website at www.santamontefiore.co.uk

Praise for Meet Me Under the Ombu Tree

'An enjoyable tale of heat, dust and lust that maintains the tension to the very end.'

The Mail on Sunday

'All the ingredients of a classic romantic read — thwarted love, exotic locations and lifestyles of the rich and famous.'

Daily Mail

'Ambitious . . . contains all the basic ingredients of a satisfying saga. It is impossible not to root for Sofia.'

Sunday Telegraph

'The descriptions of Argentina are fascinating, there is enough of a sprinkling of politics to keep readers on their toes and, as ever, the predicament of star-crossed lovers is the stuff of delicious escapism.'

Sunday Times

SANTA MONTEFIORE

MEET ME UNDER THE OMBU TREE

HODDER

Copyright © 2001 by Santa Montefiore

First published in Great Britain in 2001 by Hodder & Stoughton
A division of Hodder Headline

This paperback edition published in 2007

The right of Santa Montefiore to be identified as the Author of
the Work has been asserted by her in accordance with the
Copyright, Designs and Patents Act 1988.

A Hodder Paperback

6

A CIP catalogue record for this title
is available from the British Library.

ISBN 978 0 340 89806 2

Typeset in Centaur by Hewer Text Ltd, Edinburgh
Printed and bound in the UK by
CPI Group (UK) Ltd, Croydon, CR0 4YY

Hodder Headline's policy is to use papers that are natural, renewable and recyclable
products and made from wood grown in sustainable forests. The logging and
manufacturing processes are expected to conform to the environmental regulations of
the country of origin.

Hodder & Stoughton
A division of Hodder Headline
338 Euston Road
London NW1 3BH

To my beloved Sebag

THE SOLANAS FAMILY TREE

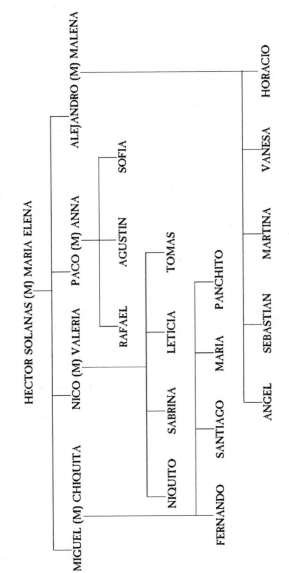

AUTHOR'S NOTE: For ease of reading, accents on Spanish words – except in spoken Spanish – have been omitted.

ACKNOWLEDGEMENTS

I would like to extend my heartfelt thanks to my Argentine 'family' who embraced me into their world. They shared with me their home and their country, and inspired me to love both. Without them, this book could never have been written.

I would also like to thank my friend Katie Rock, my agent Jo Frank and my editor Kirsty Fowkes for their invaluable advice and support and my mother for her memories.

Chapter One

When I close my eyes I see the flat, fertile plains of the Argentine *pampa*. It is like no other place on earth. The vast horizon stretches out for miles and miles – we used to sit at the top of the ombu tree and watch the sun disappear behind it, flooding the plains with honey.

As a child I was unaware of the political chaos around me. Those were the days of General Perón's exile; turbulent years from 1955–73 when the military ruled the country like incompetent school-children playing Pass the Parcel with political power. They were dark days of guerrilla warfare and terrorism. But Santa Catalina, our ranch, was a small oasis of peace, far from the riots and oppression taking place in the capital. From the top of our magical tree we gazed lovingly down onto a world of old-fashioned values and traditional family life punctuated with horse riding, polo and long, languorous barbecues in the dazzling summer sunshine. The bodyguards were the only indications of the trouble that simmered on our borders.

My grandfather, Dermot O'Dwyer, never did believe in the magic of the ombu tree. That's not to say he wasn't superstitious, he used to hide his liquor in a different place every night to fool the leprechauns. But he just didn't see how a tree could possess any kind of power. 'A tree is a tree,' he'd say in his Irish drawl, 'and that's all there is to it.' But he wasn't made from Argentine soil; like his daughter, my mother, he was an alien and never did fit in. He didn't want to be buried in our family tomb either. 'I came from the earth and to the earth I'll return,' he was very fond of saying. So he was buried on the plain with his bottle of liquor – I guess he was still anxious to outsmart those leprechauns.

I cannot think about Argentina without the craggy image of that tree, as wise and omniscient as an oracle, rising to the surface of my thoughts. I know now that one can never recapture the past, but that old tree holds all the memories of yesterday and the hopes invested in tomorrow within the very essence of its boughs. Like a rock in the middle of a river the ombu has remained the same while all those around it have changed.

I left Argentina in the summer of 1976, but as long as my heart beats, its resonance shall vibrate across those grassy plains, despite all that has happened since. I grew up on the family ranch or *campo* as they say in Spanish. Santa Catalina was set in the middle of that plain which is part of the vast eastern region they call the *pampa*. Flat as a ginger nut biscuit, you can see for miles in every direction. Long, straight roads cut through the land, which is arid in summer and verdant in winter, and in my day those roads were little more than dirt tracks.

The entrance to our farm resembled the entrance to those spaghetti western towns; it had a large sign that swung in the autumn wind saying *Santa Catalina* in large black writing. The drive was lengthy and dusty, lined by tall maple trees planted by my great-grandfather, Hector Solanas. In the late nineteenth century he built his house, the house I grew up in. Typically colonial, it was constructed around a courtyard and was painted white with a flat roof. At the two front corners stood two towers; one housed my parents' bedroom, the other my brother Rafael's. As the firstborn he got the nicest bedroom.

My grandfather, also called Hector just to make everyone's lives

2

more complicated, had four children – Miguel, Nico, Paco (my father), and Alejandro – and each one built a house of their own when they grew up and married. They all had several children, but I spent most of my time in Miguel and Chiquita's house with Santi and Maria, two of their children. I liked them the best of all. Nico and Valeria's and Alejandro and Malena's houses were always open to us as well, and we spent as much time there as we did at home.

At Santa Catalina the houses were built in the middle of the plain, divided only by large trees – pines, eucalyptus, poplar and plane trees mostly, which were planted equidistant from each other in order to resemble parks. At the front of each house were wide terraces where we would sit and gaze over the uninterrupted fields that stretched out before us. When I first arrived in England I remember how the houses in the countryside delighted me, their gardens and hedges were so neat and groomed. My Aunt Chiquita loved English gardens and tried to emulate them, but it wasn't really possible at Santa Catalina; beds of flowers simply looked out of place due to the vastness of the land. My mother planted bougainvillaea and hydrangeas and hung pots of geraniums everywhere instead.

Santa Catalina was surrounded by fields full of ponies; my uncle Alejandro bred them and sold them all over the world. There was a large swimming pool set into a man-made hill screened by bushes and trees, and a tennis court that we all shared. Jose managed the *gauchos* who looked after the ponies and lived in houses on the farm called *ranchos*. Their wives and daughters worked as maids in our houses, cooking, cleaning and looking after the children. I used to yearn for the long summer holiday, which lasted from the middle of December to the middle of March. During those few months we wouldn't leave Santa Catalina. My fondest memories are of that time.

Argentina is very Catholic. But no one embraced the Catholic religion as fervently as my mother, Anna Melody O'Dwyer. Grandpa O'Dwyer was religious in a sensible way – not like my mother, whose life was inhibited by the need to keep up appearances. She manipulated religion to suit herself. Their arguments on the Will of God used to keep us children amused for hours. Mama believed that everything was the Will of God – if she was depressed God was punishing her for something, if she was happy then it was a reward. If I gave her trouble, which I managed to do most of the time, then God was punishing her for not bringing me up right.

Grandpa O'Dwyer said she was simply shirking responsibility. 'Just because yer testy this morning don't go blaming it on the Good Lord; it's the way you look at the world, Anna Melody, that makes you want to change it.'

He used to say that health is a gift from God while happiness is up to us. To him it was the way you saw things; a glass of wine could be half full or half empty depending on the way you looked at it. It was all about having a positive mental attitude. Mama thought that was blasphemy and used to go quite pink in the face if he ever mentioned it, which he did often as he enjoyed tormenting her.

'Slap me with a kipper, Anna Melody, but the sooner you stop putting words into God's mouth and take responsibility for yer moods the happier yer gonna to be.'

'May you be forgiven, Dad,' she'd stammer, her cheeks clashing with her sunset red hair.

Mama had beautiful hair. Long red locks like Botticelli's Venus, except she never looked serene like Venus, or poetical. She was either too studied or too cross. She had been unaffected once – Grandpa told me she used to run barefoot around Glengariff, their home in Southern Ireland, like a wild animal with a storm in her eyes. He said her eyes were blue but sometimes they were grey like a drizzly Irish day when the sun's pushing through the clouds. That sounded very poetic to me. He told me how she was always running off up the hills.

'In a village of that size you just couldn't lose anything, least of all someone as lively as Anna Melody O'Dwyer. But once she'd

4

been gone for hours. We searched those hills, calling for her to the skies. When we found her she was under a tree by a stream, playing with half a dozen fox cubs she'd found. She knew we were looking for her, but she just couldn't tear herself away from them cubs. They'd lost their mother and she was crying.'

When I asked him why she had changed, he replied that life had been a disappointment. 'The storm's still there, but I can't see the sunshine pushing through no more.' I wondered why life had so disappointed her.

Now my father was a romantic figure. His eyes were as blue as cornflowers and his lips curled up at the corners even when he wasn't smiling. He was Señor Paco and everyone on the farm respected him. He was tall, slim and hairy. Not as hairy as his brother Miguel – Miguel was like a bear and so dark-skinned they called him *El Indio* (the Indian). Papa was fairer like his mother and so handsome that Soledad, our maid, would often blush when serving around the table. She once confessed to me that she was unable to look him straight in the eye. Papa understood that as a sign of humility. I couldn't tell him it was because she fancied him, she would never have forgiven me. Soledad didn't have much contact with my father, that was Mama's department, but she didn't miss a thing.

In order to understand Argentina through the eyes of a foreigner I have to cast my mind back to when I was a child, riding along in the horse-drawn cart called a *carro*, with Grandpa O'Dwyer commenting on things that to me were commonplace and mundane. Firstly the nature of the people. Argentina was conquered by the Spanish in the sixteenth century and ruled by the viceroys who represented the Spanish crown. Independence from Spain was won on two days – 25 May and 9 July 1816. Grandpa used to say that having two dates to celebrate was typical of the Argentines. 'They always have to do everything bigger and better than everyone else,' he'd grumble. I suppose he was right; after all, the avenue in Buenos Aires called Avenida 9 de Julio is the widest in the world. As children we were always very proud of that fact.

In the late nineteenth century, in response to the agricultural revolution, thousands of Europeans, mainly from Northern Italy and Spain, immigrated to Argentina to exploit the rich land of the *pampas*. That is when my ancestors arrived. Hector Solanas was the head of the family, and a fine fellow he was too; were it not for him, we might never have seen an ombu tree or the ginger nut plain.

When I cast my thoughts to those fragrant plains it is the rough brown faces of the *gauchos* that emerge with all their flamboyance out of the mists of my memory and cause me to sigh from deep within my being, because the *gaucho* is the romantic symbol of all that is Argentine. Historically they were wild and untameable *mestizo* (people of mixed Indian and Spanish blood) – outlaws who lived off the large herds of cows and horses that roamed the *pampas*. They'd capture the horses and use them to round up the herds of cows. They would then sell the hides and tallow, which was very profitable, in exchange for *Mate* and tobacco. Of course, this was before beef became an exportable commodity. Now *Mate* (pronounced 'matay') is the traditional herbal tea they sipped from a decorated round gourd through an ornate silver 'straw' called a *bombilla*. It's quite addictive, and according to our maids it was also good for weight loss.

The life of a *gaucho* is on horseback – his skill as a horseman is possibly unmatched anywhere else in the world. At Santa Catalina the *gauchos* were a colourful part of the scenery. The *gaucho* attire is showy as well as practical. They wear *bombachas*, baggy trousers with buttoned ankles that go into their leather boots; a *faja*, a woollen sash they tie around their waists which they then cover with a *rastra*, a stiff leather belt decorated with silver coins. The *rastra* also supports their backs during the long days on horseback. They traditionally carry a *facón*, a knife which is used for castrating and skinning as well as for self-defence and eating. Grandpa O'Dwyer once joked that Jose, our head *gaucho*, should have been in the circus. My father was furious and thankful that his father-in-law didn't speak any Spanish.

The *gauchos* are as proud as they are capable. On a romantic level they are part of the Argentine national culture and there have been many novels, songs and poems written about them. Martin Fierro's epic poem 'El Gaucho' is the best example of these – I know because we were made to memorise large portions of it at school. Occasionally when my parents entertained foreign visitors at Santa Catalina the *gauchos* would put on fantastic displays for them. This would involve rodeo, the breaking-in of horses and much riding around at terrific speed with their lassoes snapping the air like demonic snakes.

Jose taught me how to play polo, which was rare for a girl in those days. The boys hated me playing because I was better than some of them, and certainly better than a girl should be.

My father was always very proud of the fact that the Argentines are indisputably the best polo players in the world, even though the game started in India and was brought to Argentina by the British. My family would go and watch the top tournaments played in Buenos Aires in the summer months of October and November at the polo ground in Palermo. I remember my brothers and cousins using those tournaments to pick up girls, rather like at Mass in the city where no one paid too much attention to the priest because they were far too busy eyeing each other up. But at Santa Catalina polo was played almost all year round. The *petiseros*, stable-hands, would train and care for the ponies and we had only to call the *puesto* to let them know when we'd be playing and the ponies would be saddled up and ready, snorting in the shade of the eucalyptus trees, for when we wanted them.

In those days, the 1960s, Argentina was ravaged by unemployment and inflation, crime, social unrest and repression, but it hadn't always been like that. During the early part of the twentieth century Argentina had been a country of vast wealth due to the exportation of meat and wheat, which is where my family had made their fortune. Argentina was the richest country in South America. It was a golden age of abundance and elegance. My grandfather, Hector Solanas, blamed the ruthless dictatorship of President Juan Domingo Perón for the decline, which resulted in Perón's exile in 1955 when the military intervened. Perón is still as hot a topic of conversation today as he was in the years when he was dictator. He inspires extreme love or extreme hate, but never indifference.

Perón, who rose to power through the military and became President in 1946, was handsome, charismatic and clever. Together with his wife, the beautiful though ruthlessly ambitious Eva Duarte, they were a dazzling, charismatic team disproving the theory that to become 'someone' in Buenos Aires you had to belong to an 'old' family. He was from a small town and she was an illegitimate child raised in rural poverty – a modern-day Cinderella.

Hector said that Perón's power was forged in the loyal following of working classes he had so carefully cultivated. He complained that Perón and his wife Evita encouraged the workers to rely on handouts instead of working. They took from the rich and gave to the poor, thus draining the country of its wealth. Evita famously ordered thousands of pairs of *alpargatas* (the traditional working-class espadrilles) to give to the poor and then refused to pay the bill, thanking the unfortunate manufacturer for his generous gift to the people.

Among the working classes, Evita became an icon. She was literally worshipped by the poor and the downtrodden. My grandmother, Maria Elena Solanas, told us a gripping story of the time she went to the cinema with her cousin Susana. Evita's face appeared on the screen as it always did before the film and Susana whispered to my grandmother that Evita obviously dyed her hair blonde. Once the film had finished Susana was dragged into the ladies' room by a mob of angry women who brutally cut off all her hair. Such was the power of Evita Perón; it drove people to complete madness.

Still, in spite of her power and her prestige the upper classes considered her little more than a common tart who had slept her way out of poverty to become the richest, most famous woman in the world. But they were a minority; when she died in 1952 at the age of thirty-three, two million people turned out to witness her funeral and her workers petitioned the Pope to grant her a sainthood. Her body was embalmed for ever like a waxwork by a Spanish specialist called Dr Pedro Ara, and after being buried in various secret places all over the world for fear that it would inspire a cult, it was laid to rest beside the 'oligarchs' she hated in the elegant cemetery of La Recoleta in Buenos Aires in 1976.

After Perón had fled into exile the government changed countless times due to the intervention of the military. If the present government wasn't satisfactory the military stepped in. My father said they chucked out politicians before giving them a chance. In fact, the only time he was pleased the military interfered was in 1976 when General Videla ousted the incompetent Isabelita, Perón's second wife, who had taken over the presidency when her husband died during his comeback in 1973.

When I asked my father how come the military had so much control, he told me that it was partly due to the fact that it was the Spanish military who conquered Latin America in the sixteenth century. 'Consider the military like school prefects with weapons,' he once said, and as a child this seemed to make sense. I mean, who's more powerful than that? I don't know how they did it with all the chopping and changing, but my family was always canny enough to stay on the right side of whichever government was in power.

During that dangerous time, kidnapping was a real threat to a family such as mine. Santa Catalina crawled with security. But to us children the men hired to protect us were just part of the place like Jose and Pablo and we never questioned their existence. They'd wander about the farm with their fat bellies bursting out of their khaki trousers and their thick moustaches twitching in the heat. Santi would imitate the way they walked – one hand on their guns, the other scratching their groins or wiping their sweaty brows with a grubby *pañuelo*. If they hadn't been so fat they might have looked menacing, but to us they were there to make fun of, or as part of our games; it was always a challenge to get the better of them.

We were also accompanied to school. Grandpa Solanas had survived a kidnap attempt so my father made sure that in the city we were accompanied everywhere by bodyguards. My mother would have been delighted if they had kidnapped Grandpa O'Dwyer instead of *Abuelo* Solanas. I doubt they would have paid the ransom for him, though. Mind you, God help the kidnapper who'd be foolish enough to take on Grandpa O'Dwyer!

At school in the city it was natural for children to turn up with bodyguards. I used to flirt with them at tea break. They'd loiter around the school gates in the midday heat guffawing at stories about girls and guns. If there had been a kidnapping attempt, those sloths would have been the last people to notice. They enjoyed talking to me, though. Maria, Santi's sister, always cautious, would anxiously beckon me to retreat back into the playground. The more she flustered the more outrageous my behaviour would become. Once when my mother came to pick me up because Jacinto the chauffeur had been taken ill, she nearly keeled over because they all greeted me by name. When Carlito Blanco winked I thought she'd burst with fury; her face was as red as one of Antonio's tomatoes. After that, tea break was no fun any more. Mama had spoken to Miss Sarah and I was forbidden to hang around the school gates. She said the guards were 'common people' and I wasn't to talk to those who weren't from my class. When I grew old enough to understand, Grandpa O'Dwyer told me stories that made me realise just how ridiculous that was coming from her, of all people.

I didn't understand the fear or 'the dirty war' as it was called when the military set out to destroy anyone who opposed their power during the mid–1970s, after the death of Perón. It was something I only learned about later when I returned after many long years to find it had slipped through the gates of Santa Catalina to claim one of her own. I hadn't been there when those closest to me had been torn apart and our home violated by strangers.

How strange life is, and how unexpected. I, Sofia Solanas Harrison, look back on the various adventures I have played out, and think how far I am now from the Argentine farm of my girlhood. The flat land of the *pampa* has been replaced by the undulating hills of the English countryside, and in spite of all their beauty I still long for those hills to open up and to see that vast plain rise out of the fields and settle beneath an Argentine sun.

Chapter Two

'Sofia, Sofia! *Por Dios!* Where has she got to now?'

Anna Melody Solanas de O'Dwyer paced up and down the terrace, looking out over the arid plains with weary irritation. An elegant woman in a long white sundress, her flame-red hair pulled back into an untidy ponytail, she cut a cool figure against the Argentine sunset. The long summer holiday that stretched from December to March had been a drain on her patience. Sofia was like a wild animal, disappearing for hours, rebelling against her mother with a rudeness that Anna found difficult to deal with. She felt emotionally depleted, used up. She longed for the hot days to recede into autumn and for the school term to begin again. At least in Buenos Aires the children were shadowed by security, and thank God for school, she thought. Discipline would be her teacher's responsibility.

'Jesus, Mary and Joseph, woman, give the girl some rein. If you pull her in too hard, one day she'll seize her opportunity and run off altogether,' growled Grandpa O'Dwyer, shuffling out onto the terrace with a pair of secateurs.

'What are you going to do with them, Dad?' she asked suspiciously, narrowing her watery blue eyes and watching him lurch across the grass.

'Well, I'm not going to chop yer head off, if that's what yer worried about, Anna Melody,' he chuckled, snipping at her.

'You've been drinking again, Dad.'

'A bit o' liquor never hurt anyone.'

'Dad, Antonio does the garden, there's nothing for you to do.' She shook her head in exasperation.

'Yer dear mother loved her garden. "Them delphiniums are crying out to be staked," she'd say. No one loved delphiniums like yer mother.'

Dermot O'Dwyer was born and raised in Glengariff, Southern Ireland. He married his childhood sweetheart, Emer Melody, when he was barely old enough to earn a living. But Dermot O'Dwyer always knew what he wanted, and nothing and no one could ever persuade him any different. Much of their courtship had taken place in a ruined abbey that stood at the foot of the Glengariff hills, and it was there that the couple were wed. The abbey had lost most of its roof and in through the gaping holes twisted and turned the greedy fingers of the ivy plant, determined to claim what it hadn't already destroyed.

It rained so hard on the day of their wedding that the young bride wore rubber boots down the aisle holding her white chiffon dress above her knees, followed by her fat sister Dorothy Melody clutching a white umbrella with unsteady hands. Emer and Dorothy had eight brothers and sisters; there would have been ten had the twins not died before their first birthday. Father O'Reilly shielded himself against the rain under a big black umbrella and told the large gathering of family and friends that the rain was a sign of luck and that God was blessing their union with holy water from the Heavens.

He was right. Dermot and Emer loved each other until the day she was taken from him, a dull February morning in 1958. He didn't like to think of her lying pale and cold on the kitchen floor so he remembered her the way she was on their wedding day thirty-two years before, with honeysuckle in her long red hair, her generous, mischievous mouth and her small smiling eyes that sparkled for him alone. After she had passed on, everything in Glengariff reminded him of her. So he packed his few belongings – a book of photos, her sewing basket, his father's Bible and a bundle of old letters – and spent every penny he owned on a one-way ticket to Argentina. At first his daughter believed him when he said he would only stay with her for a few weeks, but as the weeks rolled on into months she realised that he had come for good.

Anna Melody was named after her mother, Emer Melody. Dermot loved her 'tuneful' name so much that he wanted to call their baby simply Melody O'Dwyer, but Emer thought Melody on its own sounded like the name you'd give a cat and so the child was christened Anna after her grandmother.

After Anna Melody was born Emer believed that God decided they didn't need any more children. She would say that Anna Melody was so beautiful God didn't want to give them another child to live in her shadow. Emer's God was kind and knew what was best for her and her family, but she longed for more children. She watched her brothers and sisters raise enough children to populate an entire city, but her mother had always taught her to thank God for whatever He saw fit to give her. She was lucky enough to have one child to love. So she poured the love she had inside her for a family of twelve onto her family of two and suppressed the nagging envy she felt in her heart whenever she took Anna Melody to visit her cousins.

Anna Melody enjoyed a carefree childhood. Spoilt by her parents, she never had to share her toys or wait her turn, and when she was with her cousins she only had to whimper if she didn't get her way and her mother would come running over to do whatever was necessary to make her smile again. This made her cousins suspicious of her. They claimed she ruined their games. They begged their parents not to have her in their houses. When she did appear they'd ignore her, tell her to go home, tell her she wasn't wanted. So Anna Melody was excluded from their fun. Not

14

that she minded. She didn't like them either. She was an awkward child, happier out on the hills by herself than in a claustrophobic group of shabby youngsters running about the streets of Glengariff like stray cats. Up on those hills she could be anyone she wanted to be and she dreamed of living the fine life like those movie stars she saw at the flicks, all shiny and glossy with beautiful dresses and long, sparkling eyelashes. Katharine Hepburn, Lauren Bacall, Deborah Kerr. She would look down onto the town and tell herself that one day she'd be better than all of them. She'd leave her horrid cousins and never come back.

When Anna Melody married Paco and left Glengariff for ever, she barely cast a thought to her parents who suddenly found themselves alone in a home with only her memory to comfort them. The house became cold and dark without their beloved Anna Melody to warm it with her laughter and her love. Emer was never the same after that. The ten years that she suffered without her daughter were empty and soulful. Anna Melody's frequent letters home were filled with assurances that she would visit, and these promises kept her parents' hope alive until they knew in their hearts that they were shallow words written without thought or indeed, intention.

When Emer died in 1958 Dermot knew that it was because her heart, sapped of its juices, had finally broken. He knew it was so. But he was stronger than she was and more courageous. When he set off for Buenos Aires he wondered why the hell he hadn't done it years before; if he had, perhaps his beloved wife would still be with him today.

Anna (only Dermot O'Dwyer called his daughter Anna Melody) watched her father rummaging around in the flowerbed and longed for him to be like other children's grandfathers. Paco's father, named Hector Solanas after his grandfather, had always been beautifully dressed and cleanshaven, even on weekends. His sweaters were always cashmere, his shirts from Savile Row in London, and he possessed a great dignity, like King George of England. To

Anna he had been the nearest thing to royalty and he had never fallen off his pedestal. Even in death he loomed over her and she still longed for his approval. After so many years she still yearned to feel a sense of belonging that had somehow, in spite of all her efforts, eluded her. Sometimes she felt she was watching the world about her from a place behind an invisible glass window – a place where no one else seemed able to reach her.

'Señora Anna, Señora Chiquita is on the telephone for you.'

Anna was abruptly drawn back to the present and to her father who like a mad botanist was snipping away at anything green.

'*Gracias*, Soledad. We will not wait for Señorita Sofia but eat as normal at nine,' she replied and disappeared inside to talk to her sister-in-law.

'*Como quiera*, Señora Anna,' replied Soledad humbly, smiling to herself as she padded back to the hot kitchen. Of all Señora Anna's three children, Soledad loved Sofia the most.

Soledad had been employed by Señor Paco since she was seventeen years old. The newly married niece of Chiquita's maid, Encarnacion, she had been instructed to cook and clean while her husband Antonio had been hired to look after the estate. Antonio and Soledad were childless, although they had tried to have children, but without success. She recalled those times when Antonio had slipped into her anywhere and everywhere, by the stove, behind a bush or tree – whenever an opportunity arose, Antonio had taken care not to miss it. What a pair of young lovers they had been, she mused proudly. But to their bewilderment, no child had ever been conceived. So Soledad had consoled herself by embracing Sofia as her own.

While Señora Anna had given all her time to her sons, Soledad had rarely been without the little Sofia wrapped in her apron, nestled against her foamy breasts. She even took to carrying the child to her bed – she seemed to sleep better that way, enveloped in her maid's womanly scent and soft flesh. Anxious that the child wasn't receiving enough love from her mother, Soledad asserted herself in the nursery in order to make up for it. Señora Anna didn't seem to mind. In fact, she seemed almost grateful. She never was very interested in her daughter. But Soledad wasn't there to put the world to rights. It was none of her business. The tension between Señor Paco and Señora Anna wasn't her concern and she only discussed it with the other maids in order to justify why she spent so much time with Sofia. No other reason. She wasn't one to gossip. So she cared for the child with a fierce devotion, as if the little angel belonged to her.

Now she looked at her watch. It was late – Sofia was in trouble again. She was always in trouble. She seemed to thrive on it. Poor lamb, thought Soledad as she stirred the tuna sauce and cooked the veal. She's starved of attention, any fool can see that.

Anna marched into the sitting room shaking her head with fury and picked up the receiver.

'*Hola* Chiquita,' she said curtly, leaning back against the heavy wooden chest.

'Anna, I am so sorry, Sofia has gone off with Santiago and Maria again. They really should be back any minute . . .'

'Again!' she exploded, picking up a magazine from the table and fanning herself in agitation. 'Santiago should be more responsible – he'll be eighteen in March. He'll be a man. Why he wants to muck around with a fifteen-year-old child I cannot imagine. Anyhow, this is not the first time, you know. Didn't you say anything to him last time?'

'Of course,' the other woman replied patiently. She hated it when her sister-in-law lost her temper.

'*Por Dios*, Chiquita, don't you realise there are kidnappers just waiting out there to prey on children like ours?'

'Anna, just calm down a little. It's quite safe here, they won't have gone far . . .' But Anna wasn't listening.

'Santiago is a bad influence on Sofia,' she ranted. 'She is young and impressionable, so she looks up to him. And as for Maria, she's a sensible girl and should know better.'

'I know, I will tell them,' Chiquita conceded wearily.

'Good.'

There was a brief, uncomfortable silence before Chiquita tried to change the subject.

'The *asado* tomorrow, before the match, can I help with anything?' she asked, somewhat strained. 'Anything at all?'

'No, I'm fine, thank you,' replied Anna, softening a little. 'Oh, I'm sorry, Chiquita. Sometimes I don't know what to do with Sofia. She's so headstrong and thoughtless. The boys give me no trouble at all. I don't know who she gets it from!'

'Neither do I,' replied Chiquita dryly.

'Tonight is the most beautiful night of the summer,' sighed Sofia from one of the highest boughs of the ombu tree.

There is no tree in the world like the ombu tree. Gigantic with low horizontal branches, its enormous girth can often exceed forty to fifty feet. Its thick roots radiate out over the ground in long bumpy tentacles, as if the tree itself has begun to melt, spreading like wax over the earth. Besides its peculiar shape, the ombu is the only tree indigenous to those dry plains. The only tree that truly belongs. The native Indians had seen their gods in the boughs and it was said no *gaucho* would sleep beneath it, even in Sofia's day. To the children brought up at Santa Catalina it was a magic tree. It granted wishes where it saw fit, and being tall it was the perfect look-out tower allowing them to see for miles around. But above all, the ombu had a mysterious allure that one simply couldn't put one's finger on, an allure that had drawn generations of children to seek adventure within its branches.

'I can see Jose and Pablo. Hurry up, don't be boring!' she called down impatiently.

'I'm coming, be patient,' shouted Santi to his cousin as he busily tended to the ponies.

'Santi, will you give me a leg-up?' Maria asked her brother in her soft, husky voice, watching Sofia climb higher into the spaghetti of thick branches.

18

Maria had always admired Sofia. She was brave, outspoken and sure of herself. They had been best friends all their lives, done everything together – plotted, conspired, played and shared secrets. In fact Maria's mother, Chiquita, used to call them *'Las Dos Sombras'* (the Two Shadows) when they were smaller, because one was always the shadow of the other.

The rest of the girls on the farm were either older or younger, so Sofia and Maria, being of the same age, were natural allies in a family dominated by boys. Neither had a sister so they had decided years ago to become 'blood sisters' by pricking their fingers with a pin and pressing them together to 'unite' their blood. From then on they had shared a special secret that no one else knew. They had the same blood and that made them siblings. They were both proud and respectful of their clandestine bond.

From the very top of the tree Sofia could see the whole world – and if not the whole world then at least her world, laid out before her under an awesome sky. The horizon was a vast cauldron of colour as the sun had almost set, flooding the heavens with splashes of pink and gold. The air was sticky and the mosquitoes hovered menacingly about the leaves.

'I've been bitten again,' winced Maria, scratching her leg.

'Here,' said Santi, bending down and taking his younger sister's foot in his hands. With a swift movement he lifted her up so she could lean on the first branch with her stomach. After that she could make it on her own.

Santi then scaled the tree himself with a lightness of step that never ceased to amaze those who knew him well. As a small child he had suffered a polo accident that had left him with a slight limp. His parents, desperate that this handicap might hinder him in later life, flew him to the United States where he saw every possible specialist. But they needn't have bothered. Santi had defied doctors' predictions and found ways around it. As a little boy he had managed to run faster than all his cousins, even those a couple of years older than himself, even if he had run in a slightly odd way, one foot facing inwards. As a young man he was the best polo player on the ranch. 'There is no doubt about it,' said his father proudly, 'young Santiago has a rare courage not often seen these days. He'll go far. And he'll have earned every step of the way.'

'Fantastic, isn't it!' beamed a triumphant Sofia, when her cousin joined her. 'Do you have the penknife? I want to make a wish.'

'What are you going to wish for this time? It won't come true,' Santi said, sitting down and swinging his legs in the air. 'I don't know why you bother.' He sniffed. But Sofia's hand was already running over the trunk, searching the bark for traces of their past.

'Oh yes it will, maybe not this year, but one day when it's really important. You know the tree knows which wishes to grant and which wishes to ignore.' And she patted it fondly.

'Now you're going to tell me the damn tree thinks and feels,' he scoffed, pushing his thick blond hair off his forehead with a sweaty hand.

'You're just an ignorant fool, Santi, but one day you'll learn. You wait. One day you'll really need a wish to come true and then when no one's looking, you'll sneak up here in the dark to carve your mark in this trunk.' She laughed.

'I'd rather go and see *La Vieja Bruja* in town. That old witch has more chance of directing my future than this silly tree.'

'Go and see her then if you like – *if* you can hold your breath long enough not to smell her. Oh, here's one,' she exclaimed, finding one of their latest wishes carved into the wood. Like an old wound, it had left a tidy white scar.

Maria joined them, flushed and hot from exertion. Her tawny brown hair fell about her shoulders in wispy curls, sticking slightly to her glistening round cheeks.

'Look at the view, it's magnificent!' she gasped, gazing about her. But her cousin had lost interest in the view and was busy scanning the bark for her artistry.

'I think that one was mine,' she said, stepping onto the branch above Santi's so she could study it a little closer. 'Yes, definitely mine – my symbol, you see?'

'It might have been a symbol six months ago but it's a smudge now,' said Santi, pushing himself up and settling on another bumpy arm of the tree.

'I drew a star – I'm quite good at drawing stars,' she replied proudly. 'Hey, Maria, where's yours?'

Maria edged her way up her branch with unsteady steps. After orientating herself a moment she crossed over Santi's and sat down on a lower branch close to the trunk. Finding her scar she fingered it nostalgically.

'My symbol was a bird,' she said, and smiled at the recollection.

'What was that for?' asked Sofia, jumping confidently down to join her.

'You'll laugh if I tell you,' she replied bashfully.

'No, we won't,' said Santi. 'Has it come true?'

'Of course not, and it never will, but it's still worth wishing for,' she said.

'Well?' urged Sofia, intrigued now that her cousin was reluctant to tell them.

'Okay. I wished for a beautiful voice so I can sing with Mama's guitar,' she said, then raising her hazel eyes saw that they were both laughing.

'So, the bird symbolises "song",' said Santi, grinning broadly.

'I suppose so, although that wasn't exactly why I drew it.'

'Then why did you, dopey?'

'Because I like birds and there was one in the tree as I made the wish. It was really close. Adorable. You know, Papa always said that the symbol doesn't have to have anything to do with your wish. You just have to make your mark. Anyway, my bird's not that funny – and it was a year ago. I was only fourteen at the time. If mine's so funny what was your wish, Sofia?'

'I wished for Papa to let me play in the *Copa Santa Catalina*,' she replied haughtily, waiting for Santi's reaction. As she had expected he exploded into exaggerated laughter.

'The Santa Catalina Cup? You can't be serious!' he exclaimed in amazement, narrowing his pale green eyes imperiously and pulling a face to show his disbelief.

'I'm very serious,' she replied challengingly.

'So what was the star for?' asked Maria, brushing her shoulder where some of the moss had soiled her shirt.

'I want to be a polo star,' Sofia told them both casually, as if she had just declared she wanted to be a nurse.

Mentirosa! Chofi, it's probably the only thing you can draw – Maria's the only artist in this family.' And he lay back on the branch chuckling. *La Copa Santa Catalina.* You're only a child.'

'Only a child, you patronising oaf?' she retorted, pretending to be cross. 'I'll be sixteen in April. That's only three months away, then I'll be a woman.'

'Chofi, you'll never be a woman because you've never been a girl,' he said, referring to her tomboy nature. 'Girls are like Maria. No, Chofi, you're not a girl at all.'

Sofia watched him flop down over the bough of the tree. His jeans were loose and worn, hanging low on his hips. His T-shirt had ridden up his chest revealing a flat brown tummy and hipbones that stuck out as if he needed feeding. But no one ate more than Santi. He devoured his food with the urgency of someone who hasn't eaten in a very long time. She wanted to run her fingers over his skin and tickle him. Any excuse to touch him. They mobbed around most of the time and the physical contact excited her. But she hadn't touched him for an hour or two, so the desire to do so was irresistible.

'Where's yours then?' she asked, demanding his attention again.

'Oh, I don't know and I don't care – it's rubbish anyway.'

'No it isn't,' insisted the girls in unison.

'Papa used to make us carve our wishes every summer, remember?' said Sofia wistfully.

'They used to do it as children, too. I'm sure their scars are still here if we look for them,' added Maria enthusiastically

'They'll be long gone, Maria. They disappear within a year or two I think,' said Santi knowledgeably. 'Anyway, you'd need a lot of magic to make Paco let Sofia play in the *Copa Santa Catalina.'* And he began to laugh again, holding his stomach with his hands to show how ludicrous her ambitions were to him. Sofia jumped lithely from her branch to his and then ran her hand over his lower belly until he shrieked with pleasure and pain combined.

'Chofi, don't do that up here. We'll both fall off and be killed!' he gasped between gales of laughter as her fingers skipped across the line that separated his tan from the secret white skin that hid from the sun beneath his shorts. He grabbed her by the wrist and squeezed it so hard she winced. Santi was seventeen years old, two years older than his cousin and sister. It excited Sofia when he used his superior strength to dominate her, but pretending she didn't like it was all part of the game.

'I don't see that it's such a long shot,' she argued, nursing her wrist against her chest.

'It's a very long shot, Chofi,' he replied, smirking at her.

'Why?'

'Because girls don't play in matches.'

'Well, there's always a first time,' she told him defiantly. 'I think Papa will let me play in the end.'

'Not the *Copa Santa Catalina.* There's a lot of pride riding on that match, Chofi — anyhow, Agustin's the fourth.'

'You know I can play just as well as Agustin.'

'No, I don't — but if you *do* end up playing it will have nothing whatsoever to do with magic. Foul play, manipulation — they're more your style. Poor Paco's wrapped around your little finger and he doesn't even know it.'

'Everyone's wrapped around Sofia's little finger, Santi,' laughed Maria, without the slightest hint of envy.

'Except Mama.'

'You're losing your touch, Chofi.'

'With Anna, Sofia's never had a touch.'

The Santa Catalina Cup was the annual polo match played against the neighbouring *estancia*, La Paz. The two *estancias* had been rivals for many years, generations even, and the year before, Santa Catalina had been beaten by only one goal. The cousins at Santa Catalina, and there were many, played polo most afternoons during the summer months, in the same way that Anna's cousins used to play hurling back in Glengariff. Sofia's father Paco and his elder brother, Miguel, took the most interest and bullied the boys in order to refine their game. Santi already played a six-goal handicap, which was excellent as the best handicap was ten and one had to be a very accomplished player to qualify for a handicap at all. Miguel was fiercely proud of his son and did little to hide his favouritism.

Fernando, Santi's elder brother, was only a four-goal handicap. It irritated Fernando that his younger brother beat him at everything. It was even more humiliating that not only was he a superior athlete but he was superior *and* lame. It hadn't escaped his notice, either, that Santi was not only the apple of his parents' eye, but the entire fruit bowl. So he willed his brother to fail, he ground his teeth together at night from willing so hard, but Santi seemed invincible. Now the bloody dentist had given him an ugly mould to wear in his mouth at night to save his teeth – another nail Santi had happily hammered into his coffin.

Sofia on the other hand had two elder brothers, Rafael and Agustin, who made up the four players of the team. Rafael also played a four-goal and Agustin a two. Sofia, much to her fury, was not considered.

Sofia wished she had been born a boy. She hated girlie games and had grown up following the boys around hoping to be included. Santi always allowed her to join in. He often took the time to help her with her polo and insisted she practise with the boys, even when he had had to withstand fierce opposition from his brother and cousins, who hated playing polo with a girl, especially as she played better than some of them. Santi claimed that he only let her join in to keep the peace. 'You could be extremely demanding, it was easier to give in,' he told her. Santi was her favourite cousin. He had always stuck up for her. In fact, he was a better brother to her than Rafael and the hapless Agustin could ever be.

Now Santi threw Sofia his penknife. 'Go on then, make your wishes,' he said lazily, pulling out a packet of cigarettes from his breast pocket. 'Do you want one, Chofi?'

'Sure, why not.'

He pulled one out, lit it, then after taking a long drag passed it down to his cousin. Sofia climbed up to the higher branch with the expertise of a Venezuelan monkey and sat cross-legged, revealing her brown kneecaps through the frayed slashes in her jeans.

'Now, what do I wish for this time?' she sighed, and opened the knife.

'Make sure it's attainable,' advised Santi, casting his eye over to where his sister was sitting quietly, watching her cousin with undisguised admiration. Sofia sucked on the cigarette before blowing the smoke out in disgust.

'Hey, give me back my fag, if you're not going to smoke it properly. Don't waste it,' he said irritably. 'You can't imagine how difficult it is to get my hands on these.'

'Don't lie, Encarnacion gets them for you,' replied Sofia casually as she began to carve into the bark. The soft wood came away quite easily after the initial cut, the little shavings falling off like chocolate.

'Who told you that?' he asked accusingly.

'Maria.'

'I didn't mean . . .' began Maria guiltily.

'Look, who cares, Santi. No one gives a damn. Anyway, we'll keep your secret,' said Sofia, more interested now in her wish than the squabble that she had ignited between brother and sister.

Santi inhaled deeply, holding the cigarette between his thumb and his forefinger as he watched Sofia drawing on the bark. He had grown up with her and had always considered her to be another sister, along with Maria. Fernando wouldn't agree; he had always found Sofia trying at the best of times. Her face was fixed into an expression of intense concentration. She had beautiful skin, Santi decided. It was smooth and brown like Encarnacion's milk chocolate mousse. Her profile revealed a certain arrogance, perhaps it was the way her nose turned up at the end, or was it in the strength of her chin? He liked her character; she was defiant and difficult. Her almond-shaped brown eyes could change from soft to imperious in a blink, and when she was angry they darkened from chestnut to a rich red-brown colour he had never seen in anyone else's eyes. No one could say she was a pushover. He admired that quality; she had a charisma that drew people to her even though sometimes they burnt their toes on her coals when they got too close. He enjoyed watching them burn from his unique position of special status. He was always there to run back to when her friendships went awry.

After a while Sofia sat back and smiled proudly at her work of art.

'Well, what is it then?' asked Maria, leaning into the tree to see better.

'Can't you tell?' replied Sofia indignantly.

'I'm sorry, Sofia, but no,' she replied.

'It's a love heart.' She caught Maria's eye, who frowned back enquiringly.

'Oh?'

'Bit of a cliché, isn't it? Who's the lucky guy?' asked Santi who had flopped back onto his branch and was dangling his arms and legs in the air lethargically.

'Not telling, I'm wishing,' she replied, lowering her eyes coyly.

Sofia rarely blushed, but in the last few months she had begun to feel differently about her cousin. When he looked into her eyes in that intense way, her face coloured and her heart hopped about like

26

a cricket for no apparent reason. She admired him, looked up to him, adored him. Oddly her face had taken to blushing. It had nothing to do with her, she hadn't been consulted, it just happened. When she complained to Soledad that her face turned red when she talked to boys, her maid laughed and said it was all part of growing up. Sofia hoped she'd grow out of it just as quickly. She reflected on these new feelings with curiosity and exhilaration, but Santi was miles away, exhaling smoke like a Red Indian. Maria took the knife and carved a small sun.

'May I be blessed with a long, happy life,' she said.

'That's a bit of an odd thing to wish for,' scoffed Sofia, screwing up her nose.

'You must never take anything for granted, Sofia,' said Maria seriously.

'Oh God, you've been listening to my raving mother. Are you going to kiss your crucifix now?' Maria laughed as Sofia pulled her face into an expression of piety and crossed herself irreverently.

'Aren't you going to wish, Santi? Go on, it's tradition!' she insisted.

'No, it's girl's stuff,' he replied.

'Please yourself,' said Sofia, throwing herself back against the trunk. 'Mmm. Can you smell the eucalyptus?' A satin breeze brushed softly over her hot cheeks, carrying with it the unmistakable medicinal scent of eucalyptus. 'You know, of all the smells in the *campo*, this is the one I love best. If I were lost at sea and smelt this smell I would cry for home.' And she sighed melodramatically.

Santi inhaled deeply, blowing the smoke out of his mouth in rings.

'I agree, it always reminds me of summer.'

'I can't smell eucalyptus. The only scent coming my way is Santi's Marlboro,' complained Maria, waving her hand in the air.

'*Bueno*, don't sit downwind then,' he retorted.

'No, Santi, don't *you* sit upwind from me!'

'*Mujeres!*' he sighed, his sandy blond hair falling about his head

27

like one of those mysterious auras that *La Vieja Bruja* raved on about in the village. Apparently everyone had one, everyone except the very wicked. The three of them draped themselves like cats over the branches, searching in silence for the first stars through the dusk.

The ponies snorted and stamped wearily under the ombu, changing their weight every now and then to rest their feet. Tossing their heads they patiently fought off the cloud of flies and mosquitoes that gathered about them. Finally Maria suggested they begin to make their way back.

'It'll be totally dark soon,' she said anxiously, mounting her pony.

'Mama is going to murder me,' Sofia sighed, already envisaging Anna's fury.

'I'll get the blame again, I suppose,' groaned Santi.

'Well, Santiago, you're the adult – you're meant to be looking after us.'

'With your mother on the warpath, Chofi, I don't think I want the responsibility.' Anna was well-known for her temper.

Sofia jumped onto her pony and with an experienced hand guided it through the darkness.

Back on the ranch they gave their ponies to old Jose, the most senior *gaucho*, who had been leaning against the fence sipping *Mate* through an ornate silver *bombilla*, waiting with the patience of someone to whom time means very little. He shook his grey head with gentle disapproval.

'Señorita Sofia, your mother has been calling us all night,' he chided. 'This is a dangerous time, *niña*, you must be careful.'

'Oh, dear Jose, you shouldn't worry so much, you know I'll get away with it!' And laughing she ran after Maria and Santi who were already walking off towards the lights.

As predicted, Anna was outraged. Like a jack-in-the-box, the moment she saw her daughter she sprang up, her arms waving about as if she had no way of controlling them.

'Where on earth have you been?' she demanded, her red face clashing horribly with her hair.

'We went for a ride and just forgot the time, I'm sorry.'

Agustin and Rafael, her older brothers, both stretched out on the sofas, smirked ironically.

'What are they grinning about? Agustin, don't eavesdrop! This has nothing to do with you.'

'Sofia, you're a lying toad,' he said from the sofa.

'Rafael, Agustin, this is not a joke,' their mother snapped in exasperation.

' "Off to your room, Señorita Sofia",' added Agustin under his breath. Anna wasn't in the mood for his jokes and looked to her husband for support but Paco returned to his sons and the *Copa Santa Catalina*. Grandpa O'Dwyer, who wouldn't have been any help at all, was snoring loudly in the armchair in the corner. So Anna, as usual, was left to play the autocrat. She turned to her daughter and with the sigh of a well-practised martyr, sent her to her room without any supper.

Sofia left the sitting room unfazed and wandered into the kitchen. As she had hoped, Soledad was prepared, ready with *empanadas* and a bowl of steaming *zapallo* soup.

'Paco, why don't you support me?' Anna asked her husband wearily. 'Why do you take her part every time? I can't do this on my own.'

'*Mi amor*, you're tired. Why don't you get an early night?' Paco looked up at her grim face. He searched her features for the soft young girl he had married and wondered why she was afraid to come out and show herself. Somewhere along the line she had retreated and he wondered whether he would ever get her back again.

Dinner was awkward. Anna wore a pinched expression on her face in an act of defiance. Rafael and Agustin continued to talk with their father about the polo match the following day as if she wasn't there. They forgot that Sofia was absent. Her empty place at the dinner table was fast becoming a regular occurrence.

'Roberto and Francisco Lobito are the ones we've got to watch out for,' said Rafael, talking with his mouth full. Anna watched him warily, but at twenty-three years old he was too grown-up to be told what to do by his mother.

'They'll be marking Santi heavily,' said Paco, looking up from under his serious brow. 'He's the best player on our team – that means you boys will have more responsibility. Do you understand? Agustin, you're going to have to concentrate. *Really* concentrate.'

'Don't worry, Papa,' replied Agustin, shifting his small brown eyes from his father to his brother in a bid to show his sincerity. 'I won't let you down.'

'You'd better not, or that sister of yours will be playing in your place,' said Paco and watched Agustin scowl into his veal. Anna sighed loudly and shook her head, but Paco didn't notice her. She pursed her lips and continued to eat in silence. She had accepted that Sofia played polo with her cousins, but that was a private thing within the family. Over my dead body will she play in a match in front of the Lobito family from La Paz, she thought angrily to herself.

Sofia meanwhile lolled in a warm bath filled with glittering white bubbles. She lay back and allowed her mind to focus on Santi. She knew she shouldn't think of her cousin in that way. Padre Julio would give her twenty Hail Marys if he knew what lascivious thoughts gripped her loins with longing. Her mother would cross herself and say that an infatuation of that sort wasn't natural. To Sofia it was the most natural thing in the world.

She imagined him kissing her, and wondered what it would feel like. She had never kissed anyone. Well, she had kissed Nacho Estrada in the school playground because she had lost a bet, but that hadn't been a proper kiss. Not the way two people who really loved each other kissed. She closed her eyes and pictured his hot honey face an inch away from hers, his full, smiling lips opening slightly before resting on her lips. She imagined his tourmaline-green eyes gazing into hers lovingly. When she couldn't go any further than that because she wasn't really sure what would happen next, she rewound the tape and started again until the bathwater had turned cold and the pads of her fingers resembled a wrinkled old iguana.

Chapter Three

Sofia awoke to the soft glimmer of dawn flickering through the gap in the curtains. She lay there a while listening to the first sounds of morning. The singing *gorriones* and *tordos* were a cheerful prelude to the day, hopping from branch to branch in the tall plane trees and poplars. She didn't need to look at her watch to know that it was six o'clock; she always rose at six in the summer. Her favourite time of the day was early morning when the rest of the household were still asleep in their beds. She pulled on her jeans and T-shirt, tied her long dark plait with a red ribbon and slipped into her *alpargatas*.

Outside, the sun was a hazy glow, emerging softly through the dawn mist. She skipped with a buoyant heart through the trees towards the *puesto* and polo field. Her feet barely touched the ground. Jose was already up and expecting her, traditionally clad in baggy *bombachas*, rich brown leather boots and his heavy *rastra*, decorated with large silver coins. Together with his son Pablo she would practise hitting the ball about, called stick and balling, for a couple of hours before breakfast under the experienced guidance of the old *gaucho*. Sofia was happiest on a pony; there she felt a freedom unmatched anywhere else in her life, charging up and down the field while the rest of her family were far away and unaware.

At eight she gave the mare to Jose and made her way back through the trees towards home. As she went by, she glanced over at Santi's house, half hidden behind an oak tree. Rosa and Encarnacion, their maids, in pristine white and pastel blue uniforms, were quietly laying out the breakfast table on the terrace but Santi was nowhere to be seen. He liked his sleep and rarely rose before eleven. Chiquita's house was not like Anna's; it was weathered pink with dusty-coloured roof tiles, bleached from the sun, and only had one floor. But Sofia loved her own house the best, with its gleaming bleached walls, dark green shutters somewhat obscured behind Virginia creeper and large round terracotta pots of geraniums and plumbago.

At home, Paco and Anna were already up and sipping coffee on the terrace, shaded from the sun under a large parasol. Grandpa O'Dwyer was practising card tricks on one of the skinny dogs who, hopeful for a scrap from the table, was unusually compliant. Paco, in a pink polo shirt and jeans, was sitting back in his chair reading the papers through the pair of glasses perched on the end of his hooked nose. As Sofia approached he put down the paper and poured himself some more coffee.

'Papa . . .' she began.

'No.'

'What? I haven't even asked you yet,' she laughed, bending down to kiss him.

'I know what you're going to ask me, Sofia, and the answer is no.'

She sat down and grabbed an apple, then noticing his mouth curve into a small smile she fixed him with her chestnut eyes and grinned back with a smile she reserved for him or her grandfather, childish and mischievous, but utterly charming.

'*Dale* Papa, I never get the chance to play, it's so unfair! After all, Papito, you taught me how to play.'

'Sofia, enough is enough!' scolded her mother in exasperation. She couldn't understand why her husband fell for it every time. 'Papa has said no, now leave him alone and eat your breakfast decently – with a knife!'

Irritated, Sofia stabbed sulkily at her apple. Anna ignored her and leafed through a magazine. She could feel her daughter watching her out of the corner of her eye and her expression hardened with resolve.

'Why don't you let me play polo, Mama?' she asked in English.

'It's just not ladylike, Sofia. You are a young woman, not a tomboy,' she replied steadily.

'Just because you don't like horses . . .' Sofia mumbled petulantly.

'That's has got nothing to do with it.'

'Yes it has. You want me to be like you, but I'm not like you – I'm like Papa. *No es cierto, Papá?*'

'What were you talking about?' asked Paco, who hadn't been listening to their conversation. He tended to lose interest when they spoke English. At that moment Rafael and Agustin staggered out into the light like a couple of vampires, squinting uncomfortably into the sunshine. They had spent the best part of the dawn at the small nightclub in town. Anna put down the magazine and watched tenderly as they approached.

'Definitely too bright,' groaned Agustin. 'My head is killing me.'

'What time did you two get back last night?' she asked sympathetically.

'About five a.m. Mama. I could have slept all morning,' replied Rafael, kissing her unsteadily. 'What's up, Sofia?'

'Nothing,' she snapped, narrowing her eyes. 'I'm going to the pool.' And off she flounced. Once she had gone, Anna picked up her magazine again and smiled wearily at her sons in a manner they were both familiar with.

'Today is going to be a bad day,' she sighed. 'Sofia is very upset that she isn't allowed to play in the match.'

'*Por Dios,* Papa – no way is she going to play!'

'Papa, you're not seriously considering it, are you?' choked Agustin.

Anna was thrilled that for once her capricious daughter hadn't managed to manipulate her father and she smiled at him gratefully, placing her hand briefly on his.

'For the moment I'm only thinking about whether to have butter on my *media luna*, to have toast with *membrillo* or to have nothing but coffee. That is the only decision I feel like making this morning,' he replied and picking up the paper disappeared behind it once more.

'What was all that about, Anna Melody?' asked Grandpa O'Dwyer who didn't understand a word of Spanish. He belonged to the generation that expected everyone to speak English. Having lived in Argentina for sixteen years he had never even attempted to learn the language. Instead of picking up the essential phrases, the staff at Santa Catalina had found themselves having to interpret his gestures or the few words of Spanish that he would attempt in a very slow, very loud voice. When they raised their hands and shrugged in despair he would mutter irritably, 'You'd have thought they'd have picked it up by now!' and shuffle off to find someone who could translate for him.

'She wants to play in the polo match,' replied Anna, humouring him.

'Bloody good idea. Show those boys a thing or two.'

The water was cold against her skin as Sofia cut through the surface. Furiously she carved her way up and down the pool until she sensed she was being watched. Rising to the surface she noticed Maria.

'*Hola!*' she spluttered, catching her breath.

'What's up with you?'

'Don't ask, I'm completely *loca* with irritation!'

'The match? Your father won't let you play?' she said, stepping out of her white cotton shorts and stretching out on the sunbed.

'How did you guess?'

'Call it intuition – you're easy to read, Sofia.'

'Sometimes, Maria, I could quite happily throttle my mother.'

'Couldn't we all,' replied Maria, pulling her lotions out of her tidy floral bag.

'Oh no, you have no idea, your mother is a saint – a goddess from heaven. Chiquita is the sweetest person alive – I wish she were my mother.'

'I know, I'm very lucky,' conceded Maria who was the first to appreciate the good relationship she had with her mother.

'I just wish Mama would leave me alone. It's because I'm the youngest and the only girl,' Sofia complained, climbing up the steps and taking her place alongside her cousin on one of the other sunbeds.

'I suppose having Panchito takes up most of Mama's attention.'

'Wish I had a younger brother instead of those two oafs. Agustin is such a nightmare, he's always getting at me. It's the way he looks at me with that superior expression of his.'

'Rafa's kind to you.'

'Rafa's okay. No, Agustin's got to go. I wish he'd leave and study abroad. I'd love to see the back of him, I really would.'

'You never know, your wish might be granted.'

'If you mean the tree, I've got more important wishes to ask for,' Sofia told her, and smiled to herself. She didn't want to waste one on Agustin.

'So, what are you going to do about the match?' Maria asked, smoothing oil onto her voluptuous thighs. *'Quemada, no?'*

'Yes, you're black, you look like one of the Indians! Hey, give me some. Thank God I haven't inherited Mama's red hair and pale skin – poor Rafa, he just goes as pink as a monkey's bottom.'

'So, come on, what are you going to do?'

Sofia sighed deeply. 'I surrender,' she said dramatically, raising her arms in the air.

'Sofia, that's not like you.' Maria was a little disappointed.

'Well, I haven't devised a plan yet – anyway, I don't know if I can really be bothered. Though it would be worth it just to see Mama and Agustin's faces.'

Just then she was swept up from the sunbed by two very strong arms and before she could work out what was happening, found herself at once in the air and then in the water, sunglasses and all, struggling to free herself.

'Santi!' she gasped happily, coming up for air. *'Boludo!'* Lunging at him, she pushed his grinning head under the water. To her delight he grabbed her in a bear hug around her hips and pulled her down with him where they wrestled together until they were forced to shoot up to the surface to breathe. Sofia wished they could fight some more but found herself reluctantly following him to the edge.

'Thanks a bunch. I was just beginning to cook,' she said at last when she had regained her breath.

'You looked far too hot to me, like one of Jose's sausages. I was doing you a favour,' he replied.

'Some favour.'

'So, Chofi, you're not playing this afternoon?' he goaded. 'You've really wound your brothers up like two clockwork mice.'

'Good, they needed their cages rattling a bit.'

'You didn't really think Paco would let you, did you?'

'If you have to know – yes, I thought I could get around Papa.'

Santi smirked in amusement, the lines around his eyes and mouth creasing in a way that was particular only to him. He looks so handsome when he smiles, thought Sofia to herself.

'If anyone can get around old Paco, then you can – what went wrong?'

'Let me spell it for you: M-A-M-A.'

'Oh, I see. No hope then?'

'None.'

Santi climbed out and sat on the hot paving stones; his chest and arms were already covered in soft, sandy-coloured hair that the young Sofia found curiously intriguing.

'Chofi, you have to prove to your father that you can play as well as Agustin,' he suggested, pushing his dripping blond hair away from his eyes.

'You know I can play as well as Agustin. Jose knows I can – ask him.'

'It doesn't matter what I think, or what Jose thinks – the only person you have to impress is your father . . . or mine.'

Sofia squinted thoughtfully for a moment.

'What are you plotting now?' he asked, amused.

'Nothing,' she replied coyly.

'I know you, Chofi . . .'

'Oh look, we're being invaded,' said Maria as Chiquita and her youngest, three-year-old Panchito, neared the pool surrounded by five or six of the other cousins.

'Come on, Santi,' said Sofia, making for the steps. 'Let's get out of here.' Then as an afterthought she turned to her cousin. 'Maria, are you coming?' Maria shook her head and waved to her mother to join her.

By twelve noon the rich, charcoal smell of the *asado* drifted on the breeze and hung about the ranch causing packs of bony dogs to linger hungrily about the barbecue. Jose had been tending the smouldering wood since 10 a.m. for the meat to be well cooked by lunchtime. Soledad, Rosa, Encarnacion and the maids from the other houses were setting out the tables for the traditional Saturday get-together. White tablecloths and crystal gleamed in the sun-shine.

Occasionally Señora Anna would put down her magazine and wander around in her straw sunhat and long white dress, checking the tables. To the maids she was something of a curiosity with her flame-red hair and pale skin – like the austere Virgin Mary in the little church of *Nuestra Señora de la Asunción* in town. She was firm and direct and had little patience if something wasn't to her liking. Her command of the Spanish language was surprisingly negligent for someone who had spent so many years of her life in the Argentine, and she was the subject of brutal imitation in the maids' quarters.

Señor Paco, however, was much loved by all at Santa Catalina.

Hector Francisco Solanas, Paco's late father, had been a strong-willed, dignified man who believed that family came before business and politics. He believed that nothing was as important as a man's home. His wife, Maria Elena, was the mother of his children and for that he had held her in high esteem. He respected her and admired her and in his own way he loved her. But they had never been in love. They had been chosen for each other by their parents who were great friends and believed the match to be beneficial to both parties. On certain levels it was. Maria Elena was both beautiful and accomplished and Hector was swarthy and dashing with an acute business mind. They were the toast of Buenos Aires, in great demand. They entertained lavishly and were loved by everyone. Put it down to chemistry, they didn't love each other in the way that lovers should. However, in the darkness of the midnight hours they had sometimes made love with such passion, as if they had momentarily forgotten themselves, or each other, only to wake up to their usual formality, to find that the intimacy of the night before had evaporated with the dawn.

Maria Elena was aware that Hector had a mistress in town. Everyone knew. Besides, it was common for husbands to take lovers, so she came to terms with it and never spoke of it to anyone. To fill the void in her life she had given herself entirely to her children, until the arrival of Alexei Shahovskoi. Alexei Shahovskoi had fled from Russia to escape the 1905 Revolution. Flamboyant, dreamy, he had entered her life as her piano tutor. Besides the piano he had taught her to appreciate opera, art and the passion of a man to whom love was in concert with the music he taught. If Maria Elena had ever reciprocated the feelings that were played out in every note he touched and revealed in the silent way he gazed upon her with liquid eyes, she never betrayed herself or her husband. While she enjoyed his company and his instruction, she rebuffed his advances with the dignity of an honourable woman who has made her choice in life. He didn't satisfy her need for love but he gave her the gift of music. In every score there was a country to yearn for, a sunset to cry over, a horizon to fly to . . . Music gave her the means to live other lives in her imagination and it brought her not only an escape from the sometimes stifling constraints of her world but a great deal of happiness. What Paco remembered most of all about his mother was her love of music and her beautiful white hands dancing over the keys of her piano.

At one o'clock the gong was rung from the tower to summon everyone to lunch. From every corner of the *estancia* the family made their way to Paco and Anna's house, following the strong smell of cooked *lomo* and *chorizo*. The Solanas family was large. Miguel and Paco had two other brothers, Nico and Alejandro. Nico and Valeria had four children, Niquito, Sabrina, Leticia and Tomas, and Alejandro and Malena had five, Angel, Sebastian, Martina, Vanesa and Horacio. Lunch was as usual a noisy affair, and the food was rich and bountiful like a splendid banquet. There was, however, one person missing and once everyone had helped themselves from the barbecue and sat down, the gap became noticeable.

'Sofia! Where is she?' Anna whispered to Soledad as she passed with a bowl of salad.

'No sé, Señora Anna, no la vi.' Then suddenly turning her eyes to the polo field she exclaimed, *'Qué horror! Ahí está.'*

With that the whole family turned to look and a shocked silence descended upon them all. A confident, shameless Sofia was galloping towards them, stick in the air, whacking the ball in front of her. On her face was fixed a determined grimace. Anna jumped to her feet, flushed with anger and despair.

'Sofia, how could you!' she shrieked in horror, throwing down her napkin. 'May the Good Lord forgive you,' she added in English under her breath. Santi sank into his chair guiltily while the rest of the family looked on in bewilderment. Only Paco and Grandpa O'Dwyer, who was always stuck at the end of the table blinking down at his food because no one ever bothered to talk to him, grinned proudly to themselves as Sofia galloped with great panache towards them.

'I'll show you I can play polo better than Agustin,' hissed Sofia through gritted teeth. 'Just watch me, Papa. You should be proud – you taught me.' As she thundered across the grass she deftly swung her mallet, sat firmly and competently in the saddle, controlled the ball and the pony, all the while smiling happily without embarrassment. She felt twenty pairs of eyes on her and she relished the attention.

Seconds before crashing into the table she pulled at the reins, drawing her snorting pony to a dusty halt and stood defiantly before her father.

'See, Papa?' she announced triumphantly. The whole table turned their attention to Paco, curious as to what he was going to do. To everyone's surprise he sat placidly back in his chair, picked up his wine glass and raised it.

'*Bien*, Sofia. Now come and join us – you're missing a feast,' he said calmly, and an amused smile crept across his weathered face. Thrilled, she jumped down and walked her sweating pony the full length of the table.

'Sorry I'm late for lunch, Mama,' she said as she passed Anna, who had sat down again for her legs could no longer sustain her.

'I've never seen such a blatant display of attention-seeking in all my life,' she snapped in English, barely able to get the words out she was shaking so much. Sofia tied the reins to a tree, then brushing down her jeans she sauntered over to the buffet.

'Sofia, you will wash your hands and change before you join the table,' Anna said crossly, her eyes darting about the silent faces of her in-laws in shame. Sofia huffed loudly before retreating into the house to do as her mother asked.

Once she had gone, the lunch-party continued where it had left off, except the subject of everyone's conversation was *La sin vergüenza* Sofia. Anna sat tight-lipped and in silence, hiding her face beneath her hat in humiliation. Why was it that Sofia always let her down in front of the whole family? She quietly thanked God that Hector wasn't alive to witness his granddaughter's unabashed behavior. He would have been appalled by her lack of restraint. She raised her eyes to her father who sat muttering to a group of dogs who salivated hopefully at his feet; she knew he admired Sofia more the worse she behaved. Maria giggled behind her hand and watched everyone's reaction in order to give Sofia a detailed account of it later when they were on their own.

Agustin turned to Rafael and Fernando to complain. 'She's nothing but a bloody show-off,' he whispered so that his father couldn't hear. 'Papa's to blame. He lets her get away with everything.'

'Don't worry,' said Fernando smugly. 'She won't play in the match. My father would never allow it.'

'She's such an exhibitionist,' said Sabrina to her cousin Martina. They were both a bit older than Sofia. 'I would never do something like that in front of everyone.'

'Well, Sofia doesn't know when to stop. All that wanting to play polo, why doesn't she just admit she's a girl and stop being so childish?'

'Look at Anna,' said Chiquita to Malena. 'She's so embarrassed, I really feel for her.'

'I don't,' Malena replied brusquely. 'It's her own fault. She's always been too busy admiring her sons. She should have taken more trouble with Sofia instead of palming her off on young Soledad. Really, Soledad was only a child herself when Sofia was born.'

'I know, but she tries. Sofia isn't easy,' insisted Chiquita, glancing sympathetically across the table at Anna who was trying to act normally and talk to Miguel and Alejandro. Her features betrayed her strain, especially around the throat, which was taut as if she were trying to prevent herself from crying.

When Sofia skipped back to the table she had changed into another pair of frayed jeans and a clean white T-shirt. After helping herself to some food she slipped in beside Santi and Sebastian.

'What on earth was that all about?' Santi whispered into her ear.

'You gave me the idea.' She giggled.

'I did?'

'You said I had to impress my father or yours. So I impressed them both,' she said triumphantly.

'I don't think you impressed my father,' said Santi, looking down the table at Miguel who was in conversation with Anna and his brother Alejandro. Miguel caught his son's eye and shook his head. Santi shrugged as if to say 'it wasn't my idea'.

'So you think you'll play in the match this afternoon because of that?' he asked, looking down at his cousin who was devouring her food to catch up with everyone else.

'Of course.'

'If you do, I'll be amazed.'

'I won't. I will have earned it,' she said, scraping her knife across the plate on purpose to make everyone wince.

Once the lunch was over Maria and Sofia disappeared behind the house and dissolved into fits of laughter. They tried to talk but their stomachs hurt so much from laughing that they had to hold them for a while with their hands and concentrate on breathing. Sofia felt very pleased with herself.

'Do you think it worked?' she asked Maria between gasps, but she knew that it had.

'Oh yes,' nodded Maria. 'Uncle Paco was very impressed.'

'What about Mama?'

'Furious!'

'*O Dios!*'

'Don't pretend you mind.'

'Mind? I'm thrilled! We'd better not make too much noise or she'll find me. Shhhhh!' she said, holding her finger against her mouth. 'Not a sound, all right?'

'Not a sound,' Maria whispered obediently.

'So, Papa was impressed was he? Really?' Sofia's eyes were alight with merriment.

'He's got to let you play. It's so unfair if he doesn't. Just because you're a girl!'

'Why don't we poison Agustin?' Sofia sniggered wickedly.

'What with?'

'Soledad can get a potion from that witch in town. Or we can make one ourselves.'

'We don't need a potion, a spell will do.'

'All right, I suppose it's the only way. To the ombu,' announced Sofia decisively.

'To the ombu!' Maria, repeated, saluting. Sofia saluted back. Then both girls ran across the fields together, their voices ringing out across the plains as they concocted their plan.

Anna was mortified. As soon as the lunch was over she feigned a headache and rushed to her room where she fell onto her bed and furiously fanned herself with a book. Pulling the austere wooden cross from her bedside table she pressed it to her lips and muttered a short prayer. She asked God for guidance. 'What have I done to deserve this difficult child?' she said out loud. 'Why do I let her get to me? She only does it to spite me. How come Paco and Dad are blind to her capriciousness? Don't they have eyes? Can't they see? Or am I the only one who can see her for the monster that she can be? I know, it's some sort of punishment for not marrying Sean O'Mara all those years ago. Haven't I made up for that, Lord? Haven't I suffered enough? God, give me strength. I've never needed it more than now. And while yer at it, don't let her play in that ruddy match. She doesn't deserve it.'

La Copa Santa Catalina began on time, which is rare in the Argentine, at 5 p.m. It was still hot as the boys in white jeans and gleaming brown boots galloped up and down the pitch in a frenzied fever of competitiveness. The four strapping youths from La Paz wore black shirts, Santa Catalina wore pink. Out of the four boys from La Paz, Roberto and Francisco Lobito were the best players; their two cousins Marco and Davico were the same standard as Rafael and Agustin. Roberto Lobito was Fernando's best friend but during a match like this there was no room for friendship; for the duration of the game they would be bitter enemies.

Fernando, Santi, Rafael and Agustin had all played together since childhood. Today all were on form – except for Agustin who was still hungover from the night before. Santi played with flamboyance, throwing himself out of the saddle in a cool display of skill. However, the teamwork that Santa Catalina was so famous for was undermined by the fourth link, Agustin, whose reactions were unusually slow as if he were a beat behind everyone else. They were playing six chukkas – six periods of seven minutes.

'You have five more chukkas to pull yourself together, Agustin,' Paco said gruffly during the break at the end of first one. 'If you hadn't been floundering about in the middle of the field, Roberto Lobito wouldn't have had the chance to score – twice.' He said the word *twice* with emphasis as if it had all been Agustin's fault. While they swapped their exhausted, frothing ponies for fresh ones Agustin glanced uneasily across the field at his sister. 'You may well look anxious, son. If you don't improve your game, Sofia will be taking your place,' Paco added before striding off the field. That was enough of a threat to get Agustin through the second chukka, although Santa Catalina was still lagging behind by two goals.

The whole of Santa Catalina and La Paz had come out to watch. Usually they all sat together, but today was different; the importance of this match meant that they sat in groups watching the other camp suspiciously. The boys all stood together like packs of wolves, shuffling their feet nervously, one eye on the match, the other on the girls. The girls from La Paz draped themselves over the bonnets of the Jeeps in short A-line skirts and headscarves, discussing boys and fashion, their dark glasses obscuring eyes that more often than not were lustfully hooked on one of the boys from Santa Catalina. Meanwhile the girls from Santa Catalina, Sabrina, Martina, Pia, Leticia and Vanesa watched the handsome Roberto

Lobito ride his pony like a dashing knight on a charger up and down the field, his pale blond hair flopping over his beautiful face each time he bent his head to hit the ball. Sofia and Maria kept their distance, preferring to sit on the fence with Chiquita and little Panchito, who played around the sidelines with a mini mallet and ball, so that their attention would not be distracted from their brothers and cousins.

'They can't lose!' Sofia protested passionately, watching Santi gallop towards the goal, then pass the ball to Agustin who consequently missed. '*Choto* Agustin!' she shouted in frustration. Maria bit her lip anxiously.

'Sofia, don't use that word, it isn't dignified,' Chiquita said softly, without taking her eyes off her son.

'I can't stand to watch my idiotic brother, he's an embarrassment.'

'*Chopo chopo,*' laughed Panchito, hitting the ball against an unsuspecting dog.

'No, Panchito,' chided Chiquita, running to the rescue. 'That's not a nice word, even if you don't say it properly.'

'Don't worry, Sofia. I can feel the wind of change,' said Maria, catching her cousin's eye.

'I hope you're right. If Agustin continues playing like this we're sure to lose,' she replied, then winked at Maria behind Chiquita's back.

By the fourth chukka, in spite of Santi and Fernando scoring a goal each, Santa Catalina were still two goals down. La Paz, confident that they were going to win, sat back complacently in their saddles. Suddenly Agustin seemed to appear from nowhere, seize the ball and thunder towards the goal unchecked. With hearty encouragement from the sidelines he whacked it.

'Oh my God!' shouted Sofia, cheering up. 'Agustin's scored.' There was an uproar from the Santa Catalina support team, who nearly tumbled off their bonnets with relief. However, his pony didn't stop at the goal but galloped on victoriously before coming to a sudden halt, throwing a delirious Agustin into the air. He landed with a groan and lay inert on the grass. Miguel and Paco rushed to his side. Within seconds he was surrounded. There passed a terrible few moments that seemed to the distraught Anna to last an eternity before Paco announced that he had nothing more than a sore head and a heavy hangover! To everyone's surprise he shouted for Sofia.

'You're on.'

She looked at him, stunned. Anna was about to object but a moaning Agustin diverted her attention.

'*Cómo?*'

'You're on, now get a move on.' Then he added gravely, 'You had better win.'

'Maria, Maria!' cried Sofia in amazement. 'It worked!' Maria shook her head in disbelief and awe – the tree really was a magic tree after all.

Sofia couldn't believe her good fortune as she scrambled into a pink shirt and mounted her pony. She noticed the boys from La Paz laughing in disbelief as she entered the game. Roberto Lobito shouted something to his brother Francisco and they both sniggered scornfully. She'd show them, she vowed. She'd show them all what she was capable of. She had no time to speak to Santi and the others. Before she knew it the game had recommenced. In seconds she was passed the ball and ridden-off by Marco who nudged his pony against hers, pushing her off-course; she could only watch helplessly as the ball whizzed between her pony's legs and out the other side. Furious, she threw herself against him and then against Francisco for good measure before galloping off. She found that Rafael and Fernando were reluctant to pass to her; only Santi used her when he could, but Santi was heavily marked by a sneering Roberto Lobito. In fact, Roberto and Santi seemed to be playing out some sort of private battle as if they were the only two people on the field, knocking into each other, hooking mallets and shouting obscenities.

'Fercho, on your left!' Sofia shouted to Fernando when an opportunity arose. He glanced over to her, hesitated, then passed the ball to Rafael instead who was consequently ridden-off by both Marco and Davico at once in a vicious sandwich. 'Pass it to me next time, Fercho. I had a clear ride to goal!' she shouted furiously, glaring at him.

'Sure you did,' he replied spitefully and cantered off. She noticed Roberto Lobito break their silent rule and shake his head sympathetically at Fernando.

Sabrina and Martina were horrified that Sofia had been allowed into the game.

'She'll cock it up for them,' Sabrina said irritably.

'She's only fifteen, for God's sake,' Martina sniffed. 'She really shouldn't be allowed to play with the big boys.'

'It's Santi's fault, he encourages her,' said Pia, spitefully.

'He's got a soft spot for her – God only knows why. She's spoilt rotten. Look, she's hanging around doing nothing. No one's using her. She might as well pack it in,' complained Sabrina, watching her young cousin floundering in the middle of the field.

At the end of the fifth chukka they were still one goal down.

'Use Sofia, for God's sake! We're a team, and the only way we're going to win is with teamwork,' exploded Santi, dismounting.

'We use her and we're sure to lose,' replied Fernando, removing his hat and shaking out his black sweaty hair.

'Come on, Fercho, don't be childish,' said Rafael. 'She's playing and there's nothing you can do about it. They won't expect us to use her, so make the most of it.'

'We're not going to win as a three-sided team,' shouted Santi, exasperated, 'so bloody well include her!' Fernando scowled at his brother with loathing.

'I'll show you chauvinists that I can play better than that idiotic Agustin. Just swallow your pride and play with me – not *against* me. The enemy's La Paz, remember?' And Sofia cantered confidently back onto the field. Fernando quietly smouldered while Rafael raised his eyes to the sky and Santi chuckled with admiration.

The tension was almost tangible as they cantered onto the field for the last chukka. When the game began, a hefty silence descended upon the spectators. The final chukka was an aggressive display of one-upmanship as each side desperately tried to outdo the other. Santi, who was undoubtedly the best player on the team, was heavily marked, and Sofia, who they all assumed wouldn't get a look in, was hardly marked at all. Time was running out. In spite of their earlier dispute Sofia was hardly passed the ball and spent most of the time angrily covering for the others. At last, Santi managed to even the score.

The spectators were now on their feet unable to remain seated as the battle intensified in the last few minutes of the game. They all knew that if they didn't finish it in time they would have to go on to 'sudden death'. The field resounded with furious cries and impatient commands as Roberto tried to control his team and Santi tried to persuade his brother to play with Sofia. Maria jumped up and down in agitation, unable to keep still, willing Sofia to score. Miguel and Paco paced impatiently up and down the sidelines, without taking their eyes off the match. Paco looked at his watch – one minute to go. Perhaps it had been a mistake letting Sofia play, he thought bleakly.

Suddenly Rafael took possession of the ball, passed it to Fernando who passed it back. Santi snaked his way past Roberto and Marco who galloped after him in pursuit. There followed a burst of fevered shouts, but Rafael managed to pass it to Santi and he flew unmarked down the field. Only Sofia and her opponent, Francisco, stood between him and the goal. He had a choice, he could dare to ride past Francisco and try to score himself, or he could risk hitting it to Sofia. Sure that Santi wouldn't pass to Sofia, Francisco left her side to ride him off the ball. Santi raised his green eyes to his cousin who understood immediately and positioned herself. Just before Francisco crashed into him he whacked the ball to Sofia. 'Go for goal, Chofi!' he shrieked.

Not one to miss an opportunity like that she cantered after it, clamping her jaw together with resolve. She hit it once, twice, then swinging her *taco* in the air with a practised arm she thought of Jose, her father and then of Santi as she struck it straight through the posts. Seconds later the whistle blew. They had won the match.

'I don't believe it!' gasped Sabrina.

'My God, she's done it. Sofia's scored,' cried Martina, jumping up and clapping her hands. 'Well done, Sofia!' she shouted. *'Idola!'*

'Just in the nick of time!' Miguel beamed, slapping Paco on the back. 'Luckily for you, or you just might have been barbecued with the *lomo.'*

'She played well – let down by her own team. There's no question about her ability, though,' he said proudly.

Rafael cantered up to Sofia and patted her on the back. *'Bien hecho, gorda!'* he chuckled. 'You're a star!' Fernando nodded to her without smiling. He was pleased they had won but couldn't quite bring himself to congratulate Sofia. Santi almost tugged her off her pony by grabbing her behind the neck and pulling her towards him so he could kiss her dusty cheek.

'I knew you could do it, Chofi. You didn't let me down,' he laughed, removing his hat and scratching his damp hair.

Roberto Lobito walked up to her as she dismounted her pony. 'You play well for a girl,' he said, smiling down at her.

'You play well for a boy,' she replied arrogantly.

Roberto laughed. 'So, will I be seeing you more often on the field?' he said, his brown eyes tracing her features with interest.

'Perhaps.'

'Well, I look forward to it,' he added, winking at her. Sofia screwed up her nose, before dismissing him with a husky laugh and running off to join her team.

Later that evening, when the first stars sprinkled the twilight with silver, Santi and Sofia sat beneath the sinewy branches of the craggy ombu and looked out onto the horizon.

'You played well today, Chofi.'

'Thanks to you, Santi. You believed in me. I had the last laugh, didn't I?' And she chuckled, remembering Agustin falling off his pony. 'Those brothers of mine . . .'

'Ignore them. They only wind you up because you rise.'

'I can't help it. They're so spoilt – especially Agustin.'

'Mothers are like that with their sons. Just you wait.'

'A long, long time, I hope.'

'Maybe a lot less long than you think. Life is never what you expect.'

'Mine will be, you'll see. Anyway, thank you for trusting me today and for standing up for me. I really showed them, didn't I?' she said proudly.

He looked at her earnest face through the dusk and placed his hand affectionately on her neck. 'I knew you could do it. No one has the determination that you have. No one.' He then went silent for a moment as if lost in thought.

'What are you thinking about?' she asked.

'You're just not like other girls, Chofi.'

'I'm not?' she replied, pleased.

'No, you're more fun, more . . . how can I put it? You're a *personaje.*'

'Well, if I'm a "character", to me, Santi, you're an *idolo!* Do you know that?'

'Don't put me on a pedestal – I might fall off,' he chuckled.

'I'm lucky to have a friend like you,' she replied bashfully, feeling her heartbeat accelerate. 'You're most definitely my favourite cousin.'

'Cousin.' He sighed deeply and a little sadly. 'You're my favourite cousin, too.'

Chapter Four

'Girls are just as good as boys at games,' announced Sofia, absentmindedly flicking through the pages of one of Chiquita's magazines.

'Rubbish!' replied Agustin, breaking away from his discussion with Fernando and Rafael to rise to her bait like a hungry trout.

'Ignore her,' Fernando said testily. '*Callate*, Sofia, why don't you go and find Maria to play with and leave us alone.' Sofia was four and a half years younger than him and he had little patience with children.

'I'm bored,' she huffed, wriggling her brown toes that were stretched out in front of her across the sofa. It was raining. Fat summer drops that rattled against the windowpanes. It had rained all day, hard and constant and unrelenting. Santi had gone into town with his cousins Sebastian, Angel and Niquito. Maria was over at Anna's house with Chiquita, Panchito and their Aunt Malena with her young son Horacio. Sofia didn't share Maria's love of playing with small children, so she had left her to it. She stretched lazily. There was nothing to do and no one to play with. She looked around the room and sighed. The boys were deep in conversation.

'I'm just as good at polo as Agustin, and Papa knows it,' she persisted, waiting for her brother's response. 'After all, he let me play in the *Copa Santa Catalina*.'

'Shut up, Sofia,' said Fernando.

'Sofia, you're being very boring,' said Rafael.

'I'm only stating the truth. There you all are, discussing sport like your sex is the only one that does it well. Girls would be just as good as boys if they were given the opportunity. I'm living proof.'

'I'm not going to rise, Sofia,' said Agustin, rising, 'but what I will say is that I've got more strength than you could ever muster. So don't even compare us.'

'I'm not talking strength. I'm talking wit and skill. Of course I know men are stronger than women – that's not the point. Typical you, Agustin, to miss the point.' She laughed scornfully, pleased that she had provoked a reaction.

'Sofia, if you don't shut up, now, I'm going to personally throw you out into the rain, and then let's see who cries like a girl,' snarled Fernando, exasperated.

At that moment Santi burst in like a wet dog, followed closely by Sebastian, Angel and Niquito. They were all complaining bitterly about the weather, wiping the rain off their faces.

'We could hardly drive back up the track,' he said breathlessly. 'The mud is just unbelievable.'

'It's a miracle we didn't get stuck,' said Sebastian, shaking his dripping dark hair over the tiled floor.

'What's your grandfather doing out in this weather?' Santi asked, turning to Sofia.

'I don't know, what is he doing?'

'Walking around as if the sun's out.'

'Sounds just like Grandpa,' chuckled Sofia. 'Hey, Santi, are girls just as good as boys at sport?'

'She's been a pain all morning, Santi. Do us a favour and take her away,' said Rafael.

'I'm not taking sides if that's what you're angling for, Chofi.'

'I'm not talking about strength or anything like that. Skill, cunning . . .'

'You've got more cunning than most boys.' He agreed, moving her legs so he could join her on the sofa.

'I just said I'm as capable as Agustin,' she explained. She watched Agustin's shoulders hunch irritably. He muttered something under his breath to Fernando and Rafael.

'Well, prove it,' Santi shrugged. 'You could go on about it for hours. You're obviously being annoying.'

'Okay. Agustin, do you want to be beaten at backgammon?' she challenged.

'Play with Santi, I'm not in the mood.' He scowled.

'I don't want to play with Santi.'

'Because you know you'll get beaten,' Santi said smugly.

'That's not the point. I'm not pretending to be better than Santi, or Rafa or Fercho. I'm saying that I'm better than Agustin.'

Her brother suddenly got to his feet and glared at her. 'Okay, Sofia, so you want to be beaten? Go and get the board and we'll see who's better.'

'Leave it, Agustin,' said Rafael, tired of his brother and sister's constant bickering. Fernando shook his head disapprovingly. Sofia was trying at the worst of times, but when she was bored she was unbearable.

'No, I'll play, but on one condition,' said Agustin.

'What's that?' she replied, lifting the board out of Miguel's games drawer.

'If I win, you agree that I'm better than you at everything.'

'All right.'

'Set it up then call me when you're ready. I'm going to get a drink.' And he wandered out of the room.

'Are you really prepared to agree to that?' asked Santi, watching her set up the board.

'I won't lose.'

'Don't be so sure. Luck has a lot to do with it too, you know. You just might be unlucky.'

'I'll win, luck or no luck,' she replied pompously.

* * *

54

When Agustin and Sofia rolled the dice to start the game the others gathered around like crows to watch the match, except Fernando. He sat himself at his father's card table, lit a cigarette, then began piecing together the half-finished puzzle that lay scattered there.

'Santi, you're not to help Sofia. She's got to do it on her own,' Rafael said seriously. Santi smirked as Sofia threw a double six.

'I don't believe it, you lucky cow,' spat Agustin competitively, watching his sister build up a heavy wall of pieces, blocking in two of his players. Sofia felt just as competitive as her brother but tried hard not to let it show. Instead she casually threw the dice, made ridiculous comments and fixed an arrogant smirk onto her face that she knew would annoy him.

Sofia won the first game — but that wasn't enough. It was understood that any game, whether it was tennis or tiddlywinks, had to be the best of three. On winning the first game she couldn't resist but show off about it.

'You see? Poor old Agustin! What does it feel like to be beaten by a girl?' she crowed. 'And I'm younger than you!'

'It's the best of three. I have plenty of time to win,' he said with forced calmness.

Sofia caught Santi's eye and winked at him. He slowly shook his head at her in reproof. He could tell all this bragging was only going to make her fall a harder one.

The second game commenced. Sofia's comments dried up as she seemed only to manage to throw low numbers while Agustin threw fives and sixes. The smile melted off her face leaving a rather unattractive scowl. Santi watched her in amusement. Once or twice he could see her making an unfavourable move and tried to catch her eye, but she didn't look up from the board. She sensed the game slipping away from her. Her cheeks burned scarlet when Agustin captured one of her players and then threw the dice again as there was no free place for her to come on. She could feel his self-satisfied grin, it crawled beneath her skin and made her squirm.

'Hurry up,' she ordered petulantly. 'You're just slowing it up to annoy me.'

'Look who's changed her tune,' he goaded. 'Not smirking any more, are we?'

'Right, one all,' announced Agustin triumphantly. 'Ready for the decider, sister dear?'

Fernando hadn't been listening. In fact, he had been making a big effort not to listen. The puzzle had kept him interested for a few minutes, and his cigarette had been good. He picked up the packet and lit another. When he heard Sofia whining from the other end of the room, he thought things sounded more interesting. Throwing the match into the empty fireplace he sauntered over to see what was happening.

'So, Sofia's being beaten by a boy?' he laughed, taking a look at the state of play. His cousin didn't reply and hung her head. Leaning over like a big bat, he cast a shadow across the board. Sebastian, Niquito and Angel made jokes each time Sofia tossed the dice; Agustin, who was now winning, laughed heartily. Rafael, who had initially wanted his brother to win, typically changed sides to support the underdog. He always relented when Sofia got upset. Santi, of course, wanted Sofia to win. He had always felt like a protective elder brother where she was concerned. He could see she was miserable she was losing and probably wishing she hadn't been so overconfident. He finally caught her eye as she looked at him sheepishly. She had probably only baited Agustin for attention and because it was raining and she had nothing better to do than aggravate everyone. He knew Sofia. He knew her better than anyone.

'I've won!' Agustin proclaimed proudly, placing his last pieces into the leather slot to the side of the board.

'You cheated,' Sofia said, crossly. Santi laughed and rolled his eyes.

'Shut up!' replied Agustin. 'I won fair and square and I've got five witnesses.'

'You still cheated,' she said grouchily.

'Chofi, admit defeat gracefully,' said Santi seriously, wandering out of the room.

'I won't. Not from Agustin. Not from him, ever!' she cried, and flounced out after him.

'Well done, Agustin,' Fernando applauded, patting him roughly on the back. 'That shut her up. Now we'll have a peaceful afternoon.'

'You'll now have a peaceful afternoon,' sighed Rafael. 'We'll have a horrible evening. She'll sulk for days.'

'No one sulks like Sofia,' agreed Agustin. 'But it'll be worth every tantrum. I enjoyed that. Anyone else fancy a game?'

Sofia followed Santi down the corridor.

'Where are you going?' she asked, dragging her hand along the wall.

'You should have better grace when you lose.'

'I don't care.'

'You should – a bad loser is very unattractive.' He knew that would get a reaction. Sofia was very vain.

'I wasn't that graceless. Only with Agustin. You know how he gets to me.'

'I gather you baited him in the first place.'

At that moment the door burst open and in tumbled Chiquita, Maria and Panchito under a large black umbrella.

'It is foul out there,' gasped Chiquita. 'Ah, Santiago, be a dear and help Panchito out of his things, he's soaked through. Encarnacion!' she shouted.

'What's Dermot doing out in the rain?' asked Maria, wringing her hair out with her hands.

'I'm going to see Grandpa,' Sofia announced, rushing past them. 'See you later.'

'It's so unlike summer to rain like this, it just hasn't stopped all day,' said Chiquita, shaking her head.

Sofia ran through the trees shouting for her grandfather. It really was raining hard, and she couldn't imagine what had possessed him to venture out in such a deluge. To her amusement she saw him across the plain knocking croquet balls through hoops, watched miserably by a couple of sodden dogs whose tails hung limply between their legs.

'Grandpa, what on earth are you doing?' she asked as she approached.

'The sun's about to come out, Sofia Melody,' he replied. 'Ah, good shot, Dermot! Told you I'd do it,' he added to the dogs as the blue ball glided easily through the hoop.

'But you're soaking wet.'

'So are you.'

'You've been out here all afternoon. Everyone's talking about it.'

'I'll be dry soon. That sun's on its way out, I can feel it already on my back.' Sofia felt the cold drips sliding down hers and shivered. She cast her eyes up to the sky, expecting there to be nothing but grey mist. But to her surprise she found a resplendent glow beginning to break through the cloud. Squinting her eyes to stop the rain falling in, she could feel the heat on her face.

'You're right, Grandpa. The sun *is* about to come out.'

'Of course I am, girl. Now take a mallet. Let's see if you can hit the yellow through that hoop over there.'

'I'm not in the mood for games. Agustin's just beaten me at backgammon.'

'Oh dear. You weren't a good loser, I'll bet.' He chuckled.

'Wasn't that bad.'

'If I know you, Sofia Melody, you flounced off like a spoilt princess.'

'Well, I wasn't very happy,' she conceded truthfully, wiping a drop off the end of her nose with the back of her hand.

'Charm will only take you half the way,' he said wisely, before trotting off in the direction of the house.

'Where are you going? The sun's coming out.'

'Time for a drink.'

'Grandpa, it's four o'clock.'

'Exactly.' Then turning to her he winked. 'Don't tell yer mother. Follow me.'

Dermot led his granddaughter by the hand in through the kitchen door so as not to bump into Anna. They squelched their way furtively down the tiled corridor, leaving a glistening trail behind them. Casting his eye about him he cautiously opened the linen cupboard.

'So this is where you keep it, Grandpa,' Sofia hissed, as his hand disappeared between the towels then withdrew clasping a bottle of whiskey. 'Don't you worry that Soledad might find it?'

'Soledad is my partner in crime. A fine woman for secrets, is Soledad,' he said, licking his lips. 'Come with me if you too want to be a partner in crime.' Sofia followed him back down the corridor, out through the kitchen door and across the courtyard towards the trees.

'Where are we going?'

'My secret place.'

'*Your* secret place?' repeated Sofia, who loved intrigue. 'I have a secret place too.' But her grandfather wasn't listening. He was cradling that bottle of whiskey to his chest with the care of a new mother carrying her baby. 'It's the ombu tree,' she said.

'I'll bet it is, I'll bet it is,' he mumbled in front of her, almost jogging with impatience. Finally they arrived at a small, wooden shed. Sofia must have walked past it hundreds of times and never noticed it.

Dermot opened the door and led her in. The interior was dark and musty. The windowpane keeping the rain out was small and covered with moss, allowing scarcely any light to enter through it. The roof was like a giant sieve, releasing heavy drops that splashed onto the floor and furniture. Not that the furniture warranted care – the table was clearly rotten and a stack of shelves had already crumbled and hung precariously off the wall.

'This used to be Antonio's shed,' Dermot said, sitting down on the bench. 'Don't stand on ceremony, Sofia Melody. Take yer place.' Sofia sat down and shivered. 'This is Doctor Dermot's cure for a cold,' he added, handing her the bottle after he had taken a large swig himself. 'Ah, it certainly reaches the spot.' He gurgled happily. Sofia put it to her nose and sniffed. 'Don't sniff it, girl, drink it.'

'Strong stuff, Grandpa,' she said before knocking it back and taking a big gulp. As the ball of fire shot down her throat her body convulsed and her mouth opened wide like a dragon, letting out a long, agonising wheeze.

'Atta girl.' He nodded appreciatively, patting her on the back. For a second she was unable to inhale; but then the fire entered her veins and raced through her body causing the pain to turn to exquisite pleasure and she inhaled extravagantly. Turning to her grandfather with burning cheeks she smiled, somewhat vaguely, before taking the bottle for another go.

'That's some secret you've got there, Grandpa. Some secret,' she giggled, putting it to her lips again. After a few swigs she no longer felt wet, or cross with Agustin. In fact, she thought to herself, I love Agustin, and Rafa and Mama. I love them all. She felt dizzy and happy, deliriously happy, as if nothing in the world mattered and everything was funny. She laughed for no reason. Suddenly everything was hilarious. Dermot began telling her dislocated stories of his 'Ireland days' and Sofia half listened to them with a grin that quivered loosely on her glowing face. He then took it upon himself to teach her a few Irish songs.

'I met her in the garden where the praties grow . . .' he began. In Sofia's drunken state he had the most beautiful voice she had ever heard.

'You're like an angel, Grandpa. An *angel*,' she said unsteadily, her eyes misting over.

Neither knew nor cared how long they had been in the shed, but once Dermot had drained the last drop from the bottle they both decided to make their way back to the house.

'Shhhh!' hissed Sofia, pressing a finger to her mouth, missing and finding her nose instead. 'Oh,' she gulped in surprise, withdrawing it shakily.

'Don't make a noise,' Dermot said loudly. 'No noise at all.' Then he laughed a loud belly laugh. 'Good God, girl, you've only had a few swigs and look at the state of you.'

'Shhhh,' she hissed again, holding on to him to steady herself. 'You've had the whole bottle. The whole bottle. I can't believe you're still standing,' she exclaimed as they weaved their way precariously through the dusk.

'I met her in the garden where the praties grow . . .' He began again and Sofia joined in tonelessly, following his lead a word behind him.

As they fumbled with the doorknob it opened all by itself.

'Open sesame!' slurred Dermot, throwing back his arms.

'*Por Dios,* Señor O'Dwyer!' gasped Soledad. 'Señorita Sofia!' She recoiled when she saw Sofia, ruddy-cheeked and smiling stupidly. Gathering them in she hurriedly shuffled Sofia down the corridor to her rooms. Dermot staggered off in the other direction. As he wandered into the sitting room, Soledad heard the cries of horror from Señora Anna.

'Sweet Jesus, Dad!' she squawked. Then there was a crash, most probably the empty bottle breaking on the tiles. Soledad didn't wait to listen, she closed the door to her quarters quietly behind her.

'Dear child, what have you done?' she lamented when they were safely inside her tidy room. Sofia grinned back inanely.

'I met her in the garden where the praties grow . . .' she droned.

Soledad helped her out of her clothes and ran a hot bath. She then forced her to drink a glass of water mixed with a heavy dose of salt. Sofia promptly threw her head down the loo and proceeded to throw up the fire that had made her feel like nothing mattered at all. It had been blissful but now she felt nauseous and sorry for herself. After a warm bath and a cup of hot milk Soledad put her to bed.

'What were you thinking of?' she asked, the frown creasing her plump brown skin.

'I don't know. It just happened.' She moaned.

'You're lucky it only took a few gulps to get you drunk. Poor Señor O'Dwyer, it'll take him all night to sober up,' Soledad said sympathetically. 'I'll go and tell Señora Anna that you're unwell, shall I?'

'Do you think she'll believe me?'

'Why shouldn't she? You don't smell of alcohol any more. You're lucky to get away with it. Can you imagine how much trouble you'd have been in had she discovered you?'

'Thank you, Soledad,' she said quietly as Soledad made for the door.

'I'm used to covering for your grandfather. I never thought I'd be covering for you,' she chuckled, her heavy breasts wobbling beneath her uniform.

Sofia had almost slipped into a deep sleep when the door opened and Anna walked in.

'Sofia,' she said softly. 'What's the matter with you?' Then she walked over to feel her child's brow. 'Hmmm, a bit of a fever. Poor old you.'

'I'll be better in the morning,' Sofia muttered, guiltily peeping out from under the blanket.

'Unlike yer grandfather who'll feel as sick as a dog tomorrow,' she said curtly.

'Is he ill too?'

'Ill? He wishes he was ill, I bet. No,' she said, placing her hands on her hips and sighing wearily. 'He's been drinking again.'

'Oh.'

'I don't know where he hides those damned bottles. I find one, he hides a new one. It'll be the death of him one day.'

'Where is he?'

'Slumped in his chair, snoring like a pig.'

'Mama!' gasped Sofia. She wished he had been nursed back to sobriety by Soledad like she had.

'Well, it's his own silly fault. There are only so many times I can tell him. He won't listen so I won't preach.'

'Are you just going to leave him?'

'Yes, I'm just going to leave him,' she repeated brusquely. 'Why, what would you rather I did?'

'I don't know, put him to bed with a cup of hot milk,' said Sofia hopefully, but her mother only laughed at her.

'He'd be lucky to get anything at all. Now,' she said, and her voice changed. Sofia winced beneath the sheets. 'Agustin tells me you weren't very polite today.'

'Polite? We played a game of backgammon and he won. He should be pleased he won.'

'That's got nothing to do with it, and you know it,' Anna said tersely. 'There's nothing more undignified than a bad loser, Sofia. He tells me you just stalked out leaving a bad atmosphere. Don't let me hear it happen again. Do you understand?'

'Agustin exaggerates. What did Rafa say?'

'I don't want to go into this, Sofia. Just make sure it doesn't happen again. I don't want people to think I haven't brought you up properly, now do I?'

'No,' she replied automatically. Agustin's a sneak *and* a cheat, she thought to herself crossly. But she was too sleepy to argue. She watched her mother leave the room and sighed with relief that she hadn't been caught. She thought of her grandfather asleep in his chair, all wet and drunk and uncomfortable and she longed to go and look after him. But she felt too unwell to get up. Later when Soledad quietly entered her room to check on her she was far away, riding the clouds with Santi.

Chapter Five

London, 1947

It was a cold overcast morning, and yet everything about London enchanted the young Anna Melody O'Dwyer. She opened the large French windows of her hotel room in South Kensington and stepped out onto the small balcony. She pulled her dressing gown tightly around her and imagined that the hotel was her palace and she was an English princess. She looked down at the foggy street, at the bare trees that lined the road, twisted and crippled in the cold and wished she could leave Glengariff for the romance of London. The tarmac glistened like liquorice in the yellow light of the street lamps and a few cars hummed past, like grey ghosts disappearing into the smog. It was early but Anna was so excited she couldn't sleep. She tiptoed inside and closed the windows quietly so as not to wake her sleeping mother and her fat Aunt Dorothy who twitched like a beached walrus in the next-door room.

She wandered over to the marble table and picked up an apple from the fruit bowl. Never in her life had she seen such luxury, although she had often dreamed about it. This was the kind of hotel Hollywood movie stars lived in. Her mother had asked for a suite. A sitting-room, bedroom and adjoining bathroom. The bedroom was really for two but when the concierge was told that this was a very special weekend he made them put a camp bed in so the three of them could all sleep together. Her mother was about to tell them that they couldn't afford a bigger suite, that her family had all clubbed together to give her daughter a grand weekend, but Anna had stopped her. This was the one weekend in her life she was going to be able to live like a princess and she didn't want it spoiled by some snotty concierge looking down his nose at her.

Anna Melody O'Dwyer was getting married. She had known Sean O'Mara all her life and it seemed the natural thing to do. Her parents were pleased. But she didn't love him. At least, she didn't love him in the way she thought that one ought to love one's fiancé. He was no Mr Darcy. Her heart didn't pound when she saw him. She didn't long for their wedding night; in fact, she predicted that it would be something of a damp squib and the thought made her squirm. She'd put him off for as long as she could. But it was what her parents wanted so she danced along in spite of the fact that she found the music somewhat distasteful. There wasn't anyone else in Glengariff for her to marry so Sean O'Mara would have to do. Sean and Anna had been matched from birth. There seemed no way of getting away from it, or from Glengariff. They would live with her parents and Aunt Dorothy until Sean had earned enough money to buy a house of their own. She rather hoped that it would take a while. Her mother had created such a warm home she was in no hurry to move out. The thought of cooking for a husband every night made her eyes water. There must be more to life than that?

Well, now she was in the De Vere Hotel, surrounded by things of such beauty and elegance she couldn't help but wonder what her life might be like were she to marry a count, or a prince. She ran the bath and poured in half the hotel's complimentary bottle of Floris bath oil so that the room filled with the rich scent of rose, then she lay in the hot water until the mirror matched the smog outside and she could scarcely breathe for the steam. She indulged in her favourite fantasies surrounded by marble and gilt, large glass bottles of bath salts and perfume. When she stepped out she covered her entire body with the lotion that went with the bath oil and ran a comb through her long auburn hair before pinning it back into a bun at the nape of her long white neck. She felt beautiful and sophisticated. Never in her life had she felt so pleasing to the eye and her heart literally danced a jig in her chest. When her mother and aunt awoke Anna was dressed in her Sunday best and had painted her nails red.

Emer didn't like painted nails or faces and when she saw her daughter done up like a film star she was about to tell her to wipe it all off. But this was Anna Melody's special weekend and she didn't want to ruin it, so she said nothing. Later when Anna was in the changing room in Marshall & Snelgrove, the grand department store on the much celebrated Oxford Street, she quietly assured her sister that she'd return to normal once she was back in Glengariff. This was her wedding weekend and she could do anything she wanted to. 'Let's face it, Dorothy,' she said. 'Life will be difficult enough for her once she's married with children, the least we can do is indulge her while we can.'

'*Indulge* her, Emer Melody?' wheezed Aunt Dorothy, appalled. 'You and Dermot have given that word an entirely new meaning.'

Emer and Aunt Dorothy had dressed up for their trip. Both marched down the wet streets in solid heels, thick suits and kid gloves. Dorothy had embellished her outfit with a somewhat mangy fox fur complete with paws and head, which she had found in a second-hand shop in Dublin. It was draped over her large shoulder, its jaw resting on the mound of her bosom that had miraculously been contained behind the strained buttons of her suit. They both balanced small hats on their heads with a large number of pins and had pulled the net veils down over their eyes. 'We can't let Anna Melody down,' Emer had said when they had dressed that morning. Aunt Dorothy had painted her lips blood red and wondered how many times she had heard her sister say that. But she didn't disagree. After all, it was Anna Melody's special weekend and it wasn't the moment to speak her mind. But one day she would. By God, she'd speak her mind one of these days.

Weary from shopping but still energised by the excitement of her first visit to London, Anna waited in the lobby of Brown's Hotel for her mother and aunt to finish 'powdering their noses' in the ladies' room before taking tea in the famous tea room. It was there that she met Paco Solanas. She was sitting waiting, her shopping bags scattered about her feet, when in he walked. He was charismatic and turned every head in the room. He had sandy-coloured hair cut very short and eyes of such a vivid blue that Anna thought they might slice right through her if he looked at her; which, of course, he did.

After searching around the lobby his gaze finally settled on the strikingly beautiful young woman reading a magazine in the corner. He scrutinised her for a moment. She was aware of his stare and felt her cheeks burn. Anna never looked her best when she blushed; her face and neck went red and blotchy in spite of her carefully applied make-up. However, he found her strangely intriguing. She looked like a girl playing at being a woman. Her make-up didn't fit, nor did her dress. Yet there she sat with the sophistication of an English aristocrat.

He wandered over to where she was sitting and flopped into the leather armchair next to hers. She felt him beside her and her hands trembled. His presence was so strong it overwhelmed her and the spicy scent of his cologne made her head spin. He noticed her magazine quiver and found himself falling in love with this pale young woman who was a stranger to him. He said something in a foreign language and his voice was deep and commanding. She caught her breath and lowered her magazine. Was he talking to her? When she looked at him he noticed her blue-grey eyes; there was something wild in their expression and he felt the sudden urge to struggle with her and tame her like one of his ponies back at Santa Catalina. She blinked at him apprehensively.

'You are too beautiful to be sitting on your own,' he told her in a heavy accent. 'I am meant to be meeting someone, but he is late. I am glad he is late. I hope he doesn't come at all. Are you waiting for someone too?' She looked at his hopeful face and replied that she was waiting for her mother and aunt to come down for tea. He looked relieved.

'You are not waiting for your husband, then?' he said and Anna noticed the mischievous twinkle in his eyes. He looked down at her left hand and added, 'No, you are not married. I am very happy.'

She laughed and lowered her eyes again. She knew she shouldn't be talking to a stranger but there was an honesty in his expression, or at least she thought she saw honesty and anyway, she was in London, the city of romance. She hoped her mother and aunt would take their time and give her a few more minutes. She had never seen such a handsome man in all her life.

'Do you live here?' he asked.

'No. I'm just here for the weekend. To shop and . . .' She wondered what rich girls might be in London for and added, 'To see the museums and churches.' He seemed impressed.

'Where are you from?'

'Ireland. I'm from Ireland.'

'I'm away from home too.'

'Where are you from?' she asked and his face glowed when he told her.

'I am from God's own country, Argentina. Where the sun is the size of a giant orange and the sky is so big it's a reflection of heaven itself.' She smiled at the poetry of his description. He looked so deeply into her eyes that she felt powerless to turn herself away. She suddenly panicked that he might leave and she would never see him again.

'What are you doing here then?' she asked, feeling her throat tighten with emotion. Please God, don't let him leave, she prayed. Give us more time.

'I'm studying. I've been here since two years, and in all that time, I have not returned home. *Imagináte!* But I love London,' he said, then his voice tailed off. He held her gaze with his before adding impulsively, 'I want you to see my country.' She giggled nervously and looked away, but when she turned to him again she saw that he was still looking at her.

Her mother and aunt stepped into the lobby and looked around for Anna Melody. Then Aunt Dorothy saw her, sitting in the corner, deep in conversation with a strange young man.

'Jesus, Mary and Joseph, Emer, what is she up to now? What would poor Sean O'Mara say if he saw her talking like that with a strange man? Look at the face on her. We shouldn't have left her on her own.'

'Sweet Jesus, Dorothy!' exclaimed Emer hotly. 'Go and get her before she compromises herself.'

Anna saw her aunt approach across the lobby like a Panzer tank and turned to her new friend in despair. He took her hand in his and squeezed it.

'Meet me here tonight at midnight,' he said and the urgency in his voice made Anna's stomach disappear. She nodded eagerly in response before he got to his feet, bowed politely to Aunt Dorothy and made a hasty retreat.

'In God's name, Anna Melody O'Dwyer, what do you think yer doing talking to a stranger, handsome though he is?' she gasped, watching him leave through the revolving door. Anna felt hot and weak, and very excited.

'Don't worry, Aunt Dorothy, this is London. There's no law here against keeping a girl company while she's sitting on her own,' she replied confidently, but inside her nerves buzzed as if they were alive with electricity.

Anna sat dreamily through tea, scraping the silver spoon around her teacup absentmindedly. Aunt Dorothy buttered her third scone. 'These are fine cakes. Fine cakes. Anna Melody, do you have to make that noise? It penetrates my eardrums in the most unpleasant manner.' Anna sighed and sat back in her chair. 'What's the matter with you? Too much shopping?'

'I'm tired, that's all,' she replied and gazed out of the window, hoping that perhaps he might walk past. Just perhaps. She pictured his face and tried to hold it there, afraid that if she allowed it to swim about at the back of her mind it might sink and be lost for ever.

'There, there, dear. We'll go back to the hotel straight after tea. Why don't you try a hot buttered teacake. They're quite delicious,' her mother suggested gently.

'I don't want to go to the theatre tonight,' Anna said petulantly, sulking into her tea. 'I'm too tired.'

'You don't want to see *Oklahoma!*? Good God, Anna, most girls yer age don't get to London, let alone the theatre,' snapped Aunt Dorothy, rearranging the fox that appeared to be clawing its way down her bosom. 'Those tickets were expensive.'

'Dorothy, if Anna Melody doesn't want to go to the theatre then she doesn't have to go. It's her weekend, remember?' said Emer, placing a hand on her daughter's arm. Aunt Dorothy pursed her lips together and snorted out of her nostrils like an angry bull.

'Oh, and I suppose you'll want to stay with her,' she said crossly.

'I can't leave her by herself in a strange city. It's just not fair.'

'Not fair, Emer! We've spent good money on those tickets. I've been looking forward to *Oklahoma!* for ages.'

'Well, let's go back to the hotel and put our feet up for a while. Perhaps after that you might feel a bit better,' said Emer, nodding at her daughter.

'I'm sorry, Emer, I'll put up with a lot, but when it comes down to money, I'm not going to let Anna Melody throw it away because she can't be bothered. It's nothing but sheer capriciousness, Emer, you and Dermot have let her get away with it all her life. It'll do her no good, I warn you.'

Completely oblivious to her aunt's annoyance, Anna crossed her arms in front of her and turned to look once again out of the window. She longed for midnight. She didn't want to go to the theatre. She didn't want to go anywhere. She wanted to sit in the lobby and wait for him.

Anna went to the theatre. She had to. Aunt Dorothy had threatened to send her straight back to Glengariff if she didn't. After all, half the money was hers. So Anna had sat through the musical, ignoring the catchy tunes that would have her mother and aunt singing merrily up the pavements for the next two days, silently working out how she was going to get to Brown's Hotel in the middle of the night from South Kensington when she had no money of her own. He had obviously been under the impression that she was staying at Brown's. She had to be there.

It wasn't long before her mother and aunt were sleeping heavily in their beds back at the hotel. Aunt Dorothy began to snore loudly through her nose as she lay on her back. Once or twice a particularly loud snort nearly woke her; for a second she balanced between consciousness and unconsciousness before drifting back into her secret world of dreams. Emer, more delicate than her sister in both size and sound, slept quietly, curled up into a ball.

Anna stepped silently into her clothes, stuffed pillows down her bed to give the impression that she was there in case one of those snorts woke her aunt or mother, and rummaged around in Aunt Dorothy's purse for some money. The concierge was most helpful; too polite to raise an eyebrow, he did as she asked and called for a taxi. Thanking him for his trouble, as if there was nothing unusual about her midnight outing, she sat in the back like a fugitive and watched the bright city lights pass by her window.

At a quarter to midnight Anna was sitting once more in the armchair in the corner of the lobby. Under her coat, she had on the new dress her mother had bought her in Harrods, and her hair was still pinned at the nape of her neck. The hotel was busy for such a late hour. A group of fashionable young people entered with an explosion of laughter. They must have been out on the town, she thought enviously. No one seemed to notice she was there. She placed her hand on the chair next to hers and ran her fingers over the leather imagining it still warm from when he had sat there with her. He had been so refined, a real gentleman. He had smelt of expensive cologne and came from an exotic land far away. He was cultivated, educated, handsome and obviously rich too. He was the prince she had dreamed of. She knew there was more to life than Sean O'Mara and dreary Glengariff.

Anna sat nervously watching the door. Should she look expectant or nonchalant? She decided she would look ridiculous if she tried to appear casual; after all, what else would she be doing in the lobby of the hotel at midnight? Then she wondered what she would do if he didn't turn up. Perhaps he had played a joke on her. Perhaps he didn't intend to meet her after all. He was probably out with his friends laughing about her. Laughing like her cousins laughed at her back home in Glengariff.

As the clock chimed twelve Paco Solanas stepped in through the heavy hotel doors. He saw Anna immediately and his face creased into a wide smile. He marched over to her in his navy cashmere coat and took her by the hand.

'I am happy you came,' he said, his eyes sparkling under the rim of his hat.

'So am I,' she replied and felt her hand tremble in his.

'Come with me.' Then he hesitated. '*Por Dios!* I don't know your name.'

'Anna Melody O'Dwyer. Anna,' she replied and smiled. He found her smile completely captivating. It made him feel warm on the inside.

'*Ana Melodía — qué lindo.* That is a beautiful name, just like you.'

'Thank you. What's your name?'

'Paco Solanas.'

'Paco. Pleased to meet you, I'm sure,' she replied shyly and he led her by the hand out into the night.

The weather had cleared towards the end of the day and they found themselves walking up the streets under a bright, starry sky.

72

It was very cold; their breath misted in the frosty air, but neither of them felt it. They wandered up the empty back streets towards Soho, laughing and talking like old friends, then made their way down to Leicester Square along the glittering pavements still wet from the drizzle.

Paco held her hand all the time and after a while it no longer felt strange to her but more natural than it had ever felt with Sean O'Mara. He talked to her about Argentina, painting a rich picture in her mind with the enthusiasm and artlessness of a true story-teller. She told him little about Ireland. She felt that if he knew that she wasn't rich like him he might lose interest in her and she couldn't afford that. She had to pretend she came from a life of privilege. But Paco loved the way she was different from all the girls he knew back home and all the sophisticates he had met in the various cities of his travels. She was unrefined and carefree. When he kissed her he did so with the intention of removing her hideous lipstick.

Anna had never been kissed like that before. His lips were warm and wet, his face cold from the night air. He held her close and pressed his mouth to hers with a passion she had only ever seen in the flicks. When he pulled away and gazed down at her face he saw that he had kissed her make-up clean off. He liked her better that way.

They sat on the edge of one of the fountains in Trafalgar Square and he kissed her again. He pulled out the pins from her hair and scrunching it in his hands he let it fall over her shoulders and down her back in wild, rolling curls.

'Why do you tie your hair up?' he asked, but before she could reply his mouth was on hers again, his tongue gently exploring her mouth with a fluid sensuality that caused her stomach to flutter as if the wings of a hummingbird quivered within. 'Please forgive my English,' he said after a while, holding her face with one hand and running the other down the hair that fell away at her temple. 'If I could say this in *Castellano* it would sound more *poetico*.'

'Yer English is very good, Paco,' she replied, then blushed at the sound of his name.

'I don't know you, but I know I love you. *Sí, te quiero,*' he said, tracing his fingers down her cold cheek and looking into her features with incredulous eyes as if trying to discover the nature of the spell that captivated him. 'When do you return to Ireland?' he asked. Anna didn't want to think about that. She didn't want to contemplate never seeing him again.

'The day after tomorrow. On Monday,' she replied sadly, nuzzling her face into his hand and smiling up at him regretfully.

'So soon!' he exclaimed in horror. 'Will I ever see you again?'

'I don't know,' she said, hoping that he would think of something.

'Do you come to London often?'

'No.' She shook her head. Paco moved away from her and sat with his elbows on his knees, anxiously rubbing his face with his hands. At once Anna feared that he was going to tell her their romance had no point. She watched his body expand beneath his coat as he sighed deeply. In the yellow glow of the city lights his face looked melancholic and dejected; she wanted to wrap her arms around him. But she was afraid he might reject her so she stayed where she was, not even daring to move.

'Then marry me,' he said suddenly. 'I cannot support life without you.'

Anna was overwhelmed and disbelieving. They had barely spent more than a few hours together. 'Marry you?' she stammered.

'Yes, marry me, Anna,' he told her seriously. He took her hand in both of his and pressed it fervently.

'But you know nothing about me,' she protested.

'I knew I wanted to marry you the moment I saw you in the hotel. I've never felt like this about anyone. I've dated girls, hundreds of them. You're not like anyone else I've ever met. You're different. I can't explain it. How can I explain what's in my heart?' he said and his eyes glistened. 'I don't want to lose you.'

'Can you hear the music?' Anna asked him, standing up and

suppressing the thought of Sean O'Mara and the commitment they were supposed to be making to one another. They both listened to the soft music that reverberated across the square from a club somewhere.

'*Ti voglio bene*,' he murmured, repeating the words of the song.

'What does that mean?' she asked as he took her in his arms and started to dance with her around the fountain.

'It means, I love you. It means, I love you, *Ana Melodía*, and want you to be my wife.' They danced on in silence, listening to the sleepy music that carried them. Anna was unable to think clearly. Her mind was all in a muddle, like her Aunt Mary's knitting wool, all tangled up. Had he really asked her to marry him? 'I will take you to Santa Catalina,' he said softly. 'You will live in a beautiful white house with green shutters and pass the day in the sunshine, looking out over the *pampas*. Everyone will love you like I do.'

'But Paco, I don't know you. My parents will never allow it,' she said, imagining Aunt Dorothy's reaction with a sinking feeling in her stomach.

'I will talk to them. I will tell them how I feel,' he said, then he looked into her fearful eyes and added, 'Don't you care for me, not even *un poquito*?'

She hesitated, not because she didn't love him, she adored him, he overwhelmed her with an excitement that jolted her every sense into life, but her mother had always told her that love is something that grows. The urgent 'love' of two people attracted to one another was something altogether different.

'I do love you,' she said and the tremor in her voice surprised her. She had never said those words to anyone, not even to Sean O'Mara. 'I feel like I've known you for ever,' she added, as if to justify to herself that the way she loved him wasn't the urgent, irrational 'love' of two people attracted to one another, but something much more profound and real.

'So what is the problem? You can stay in London and we can get to know each other better, if that is what you wish.'

'It's not that simple,' she objected, wishing it were.

'Things are only complicated if you let them be. I will write to my parents and tell them that I have met a beautiful, innocent girl with whom I want to spend the rest of my life.'

'And they'll understand?' she asked apprehensively.

'They will when they meet you,' he replied confidently, kissing her again. 'I don't think you understand, *Ana Melodía*. I love you. I love the way you smile, the nervous way you play with your hair, the frightened look in your eyes when I tell you how I feel. The confident, spirited way you met me in the hotel tonight. I've never met anyone like you before. I admit, I don't know you. I don't know your favourite food, your favourite books. I don't know your favourite colour or what you were like as a child. I have no idea how many brothers and sisters you have. I don't even care. All I know is that here,' he said, placing her hand on his coat, 'is where my heart beats, and with every beat it tells me how I feel about you. Can you feel it?' She laughed and tried to feel his heart beneath his coat, but only felt the quickness of the pulse in her thumb. 'I will marry you, *Ana Melodía*. I will marry you because if I let you go, I will regret it for the rest of my life.'

When Paco kissed her she wanted more than anything a happy ending like in the films she watched at the flicks. When he put his arms around her and hugged her against him she felt sure that he could protect her from all that was unpleasant in the world. If she married Paco she could leave Glengariff for ever. She'd be with the man she loved. She'd be Mrs Paco Solanas. They'd have children as beautiful as him and be happier than she ever dreamed possible. When he kissed her she remembered Sean O'Mara's limp kiss, the fear of her wedding night, the bleakness of the future that stretched out before her like a monotonous grey road leading to nothing but hardship and stagnation, but most importantly a future without true love. With Paco it was different. She desired nothing more than to belong to him, to give herself to him, to allow him to claim her body for himself so he could love her wholly.

'Yes, Paco, I will marry you,' she whispered, overcome with emotion. Paco wrapped his arms so tightly around her she found herself laughing into his neck. He laughed too, with relief.

'I am so happy, I want to sing!' he exclaimed, lifting her off the ground so that her feet dangled in the air.

'Paco, put me down,' she giggled. But he proceeded to dance with her like that around the fountain.

'I will make you so happy, *Ana Melodía*, you will not regret your choice,' he said, placing her feet back on the wet stones. 'I want to meet your parents tomorrow. I want to ask your father for your hand in marriage.'

'I'm afraid they won't let us marry,' she said apprehensively.

'Leave it all to me, *mi amor*. Leave everything to me,' he said, stroking her worried face. 'Let's meet at Gunther's Tea Shop.'

'Gunther's Tea Shop?' Anna repeated, looking up at him blankly.

'Gunther's Tea Shop on Park Lane. Five o'clock,' he said, before kissing her again.

Anna stayed up with Paco until the dawn streaked the sky with gold. They talked about their future together, made plans, sewed their dreams into the fabric of their destiny. The only problem was how she was going to explain it all to her mother and Aunt Dorothy.

'Jesus, Mary and Joseph, Anna Melody, have you gone mad?' her aunt objected when she heard the news. Emer took a deep breath and sipped her tea with a trembling hand.

'Tell us about him, Anna Melody,' she asked faintly. So Anna told them how they had spent the night wandering the streets of London. She omitted the kiss; she didn't feel it was fair in front of Aunt Dorothy who had never married.

'You spent the night alone with him in the streets?' spluttered Aunt Dorothy. 'Good God, girl, what would people think? Poor Sean O'Mara. Sneaking out of yer bedroom like that in the middle of the night, like some tramp from the back streets. Oh Anna!' She patted her sweating brow with a lace hanky. 'You've only known him for a few hours. You know nothing about him. How can you trust him?'

'Aunt Dorothy's right, dear. You don't know this man. I'm only thankful he didn't harm you,' Emer said tearfully. Aunt Dorothy sniffed her approval that her sister was for once seeing sense and agreeing with her.

'Harm me?' Anna cried in exasperation. 'He didn't harm me. We danced around the fountain. We held hands. He told me I was beautiful. He told me he had loved me from the moment he saw me sitting in the lobby. Harm me indeed! He's captured my heart, that's all he's guilty of,' she said, sighing melodramatically.

'What will yer father say?' Emer said, shaking her head. 'Don't think he'll sit back and let you run off to a foreign land. Yer father and I want you near us in Ireland. Yer our only child, Anna Melody, and we love you.'

'Why don't you at least meet him, Mam?' suggested Anna hopefully.

'Meet him? When?'

'Today at Gunther's Tea Shop on Park Lane,' she said breezily.

'My my, you've got this all worked out, haven't you, young lady,' huffed Aunt Dorothy disapprovingly, pouring herself some more coffee. 'What are his parents going to think, I wonder.'

'He said they'd be happy for him.'

'I'll bet he did,' she said, digging her chins into her neck and nodding her head sagely. 'I'm sure they'll be over the moon that their son has fallen in love with a strange girl from Ireland with not a penny to her name. A girl he's met only once.'

'Twice,' interjected Anna crossly.

'Twice if you count the brief introduction in the hotel. He should be ashamed of himself and run after someone from his own class and culture.'

'Perhaps we should at least meet him, Dorothy,' Emer suggested, smiling kindly at her daughter who had pinched her lips together in fury and was glaring at her aunt venomously.

'Well, that's typical. One sniff from Anna Melody and you'll give her anything she wants, like you always have,' said Aunt Dorothy. 'I suppose you think they'll welcome you into their family with open arms, do you? I bet you do. Life is never that simple. His parents are probably hoping he'll marry someone from Argentina, someone with class and connections. They'll be suspicious of you because they'll know nothing about you. You think yer cousins call you horrid names, well how does "gold digger" sound to you – hmm? Oh yes, you may say I'm being harsh and unfair, but I'm only teaching you now what life will teach you later. Think about it hard, Anna Melody, and remember that the grass is always greener on the other side.'

Anna folded her arms in front of her and looked imploringly at her mother. Aunt Dorothy sat stiffly in her chair and slurped her coffee, but without her usual gusto. Emer stared into her tea and wondered what to do.

'What if you could stay on in London – get a job, perhaps, I don't know. Maybe there's a way that will enable you to get to know him properly. Perhaps he can come over to Ireland and meet Dermot?' suggested Emer, trying to find a middle way.

'No!' said Anna quickly. 'He can't go to Glengariff. He can't. Dad can come over here and meet him in London.'

'Afraid he'll no longer want you when he sees where you come from?' snapped Aunt Dorothy. 'If he truly loves you, he won't care where you come from.'

'Oh, I don't know, Anna Melody. I don't know what to do,' Emer sighed sadly.

'Please come and meet him. When you see him, you'll know why I love him like I do,' she said, directing her words to her mother and deliberately ignoring Aunt Dorothy.

Emer knew there was very little she or anyone could do to stop Anna Melody if she was set on something. She had inherited that stubborn streak from her father.

'All right,' she conceded wearily. 'We'll meet him.'

*   *   *

Emer and Aunt Dorothy sat stiffly at the table in the corner of the tea room. Aunt Dorothy had thought it more discreet to sit as far away from the other guests as possible. 'You can never be sure who's listening,' she had said. Anna was nervous. She played with the cutlery and went to the cloakroom twice in the space of ten minutes. When she came back the second time she announced that she would wait for him outside. 'You'll do nothing of the sort!' sniffed Aunt Dorothy. But Emer told her to go. 'Whatever makes you feel more comfortable, dear,' she said.

Anna stood outside in the cold, looking anxiously down the street to see if she could spot Paco among the unfamiliar faces that walked towards her. When she finally saw him, tall and handsome beneath the sharp brim of his hat, she thought, this is the man I'm going to marry, and grinned with pride. He walked with confidence, looking around at the people about him as if they were there to make life comfortable for him. He had the languid insouciance of a dashing Spanish viceroy who believed his supremacy would never be undermined. Money had put the world at his feet. Life had been generous to him. He expected nothing less.

Paco smiled at Anna, took her by her hands and kissed her cheek. After telling her she shouldn't be waiting outside in the cold in such a thin dress they entered the hot steaming tea shop together. Briefly she explained that her father wasn't there, he had had business in Ireland to attend to. Paco was disappointed. He had hoped to ask for Anna's hand immediately. He was as impatient as he was ardent.

Emer and Aunt Dorothy watched them approach the table, weaving their way through the clusters of small round tables that were tightly grouped about the room like lily pads on a pond, laden with silver pots and china cups, pyramids of teacakes and scones around which the most distinguished and elegant people chatted in low voices. What struck Emer immediately was the superior way with which Paco held himself and the loftiness of his gaze. He possessed an air of languorous privilege and easy charm that Emer felt must belong to the enchanted world from which he came. At that moment she feared her daughter had swum far out of her depth and would have trouble keeping up with the strong undercurrents her new situation would bring. Aunt Dorothy thought he was the most handsome man she had ever seen and she experienced a bitter twinge of resentment that her niece, in spite of all her caprices, had won the heart of such a gentleman when fate had removed any such possibility from her own past and without doubt, her future too.

After the initial pleasantries, about the dreary weather and the show they had seen the night before, Paco took it upon himself to tell them a little about his family. 'I understand that this is somewhat hasty for you, but I assure you I am no infatuated cowboy. I am from a decent family and my intentions are decent,' he explained. He told them that he had been brought up in Argentina. Both his parents were of Spanish origin, though his maternal grandmother was Austrian. That accounted for his fair hair and blue eyes, he laughed.

'My father is so dark, you wouldn't know we are related,' he said, trying to alleviate the heaviness of the atmosphere. Emer smiled with encouragement, Aunt Dorothy sat tight-lipped and unforgiving, Anna listened to his every word with more reverence than she would have accorded the Pope. His command and confidence assured her that she would be well looked after when they were married. In him she recognised the manly self-possession she had always admired in Cary Grant.

He had been educated, he told them, at the English boarding school of St George's in Argentina. He spoke English, French and was completely fluent in Italian as well as his native Spanish. His family were one of the wealthiest and most respected families in Argentina. His father owned a small plane. As well as the family *estancia*, Santa Catalina, his family took up most of an apartment building in the centre of Buenos Aires. Once they were married they would live in an apartment of their own in the same building and spend weekends at his parents' house at Santa Catalina.

'I can assure you, *Señora*, your daughter will be well cared for and will be very happy. I love *Ana Melodía*. I cannot describe how I love her, I have surprised even myself. But I do and I believe she loves me too. Sometimes one is lucky enough to be struck by a bolt of lightning. Some people take longer to find love and are unable to understand the bolt of lightning. I was one of those, but now I understand what poets have so often written about. It has happened to me and I am the happiest man in the world.' Emer could understand exactly how he loved her daughter. He looked at Anna in the same way that Dermot had looked at her all those years ago when they married. She wished he were with her now but feared his reaction. He would never let his precious daughter marry a foreigner.

'I don't care much for riches, Mr Solanas, neither does my husband,' said Emer in her gentle voice. She sat with a straight back and looked steadily into Paco's sincere blue eyes. 'What concerns us is the happiness and health of our daughter. She is our only child, you see. I can speak for my husband on this account. The thought of her marrying and living across the seas, so far away, is traumatic for us. But we have always given Anna Melody a certain amount of freedom. If this is what she really wants, we cannot stand in her way. Although, we would feel happier if you could just spend some more time together before you get married. Get to know each other a little. That is all. And, of course, you will have to meet my husband to ask for her hand.'

'But, Mam . . .' protested Anna. She knew her parents couldn't afford to put her up in a hotel and they knew no one in London. Paco silently understood their dilemma.

'Might I suggest that your daughter stays with my cousin Antoine La Rivière and his wife Dominique? They are recently married and living in London for the moment. If after six months we still wish to marry, do we have your blessing?'

'I will have to discuss it with my husband,' Emer said carefully. 'Anna Melody must come back to Ireland with us tomorrow.' Anna looked at her in horror. 'Dear, let's not rush into this. Yer father will want to talk it over with you,' her mother said, patting her hand and smiling sympathetically at Paco.

'Then at least can we spend the evening together,' she said, 'if I'm to go back to Ireland tomorrow? You want us to get to know each other, don't you?' Paco took Anna's hand in his and lifted it to his lips and kissed it, silently telling her to leave the discussion of such matters to him.

'I would be honoured if you would allow me to take the three of you out for dinner tonight,' he said politely. Anna opened her mouth in horror. Emer ignored her sister who kicked her under the table.

'Yer very kind, Mr Solanas,' she replied, drawing her feet in under her chair. 'Why don't you take Anna Melody out on her own? After all, you'll have to get to know each other if you want to marry. You can pick her up from the hotel at seven-thirty.'

'And return her before midnight,' added Aunt Dorothy tartly.

After tea Anna and Paco said goodbye to each other at the door while her mother and aunt waited for their coats.

'Sweet Jesus, Emer, do you think we've done the right thing?'

'All I can say, Dorothy, is that our Anna Melody knows her mind. She'll have a much better life with this young man than she'd ever have with Sean O'Mara, that I can tell you for nothing. I can't bear to think of her the other side of the world. But how can I deny her such a life? If that is what she wants. By God, there's got to be more of a life for her out there than in Glengariff.'

'I hope Paco Solanas knows what a spirited, fanciful young woman Anna Melody is. If she's as cunning as I think she is, she'll play the game until the ring is on the finger,' Aunt Dorothy commented dryly.

'Dorothy, sometimes you are so mean.'

'Not mean, Emer – truthful. I seem to be the only one around here who sees things the way they are,' she said grimly, and walked out into the street.

Chapter Six

The last night in London had been unsettling. Emer and Aunt Dorothy had sat up in their nightdresses until Anna was safely returned to them at midnight. Anna, trapped in her lie about where she was staying, had been forced to take another taxi to Brown's Hotel so that Paco could meet her there as agreed. He had taken her to dinner at a small restaurant overlooking the Thames, where they had later walked and talked beneath the tremulous stars that glittered above them.

Paco was unhappy that she had to return to Ireland and couldn't really understand why. He had hoped she would stay in London. Afraid that she would disappear into the Celtic mists never to be seen again, he had taken great care in writing down her address and telephone number and said that he would call her every day until she returned. He had wanted to walk her back to Brown's, but she insisted that he see her into a taxi on account of the lack of romance in the hotel lobby.

'I want you to kiss me beneath a lamp post in the drizzle. I don't want to remember you in some public lobby,' she said and he had believed her. His kiss had been long and soulful. When she returned to the De Vere in South Kensington her heart was burning through her skin with ardour and her mouth still trembling from where he had kissed her. She was too excited to sleep so she lay staring into the darkness, replaying his kisses over and over again until her thoughts turned into dreams and she drifted into a sensual sleep.

Anna was like a wind-up doll, spinning around the suite in a state of manic excitement. She didn't seem to care much about Sean O'Mara; all her thoughts were for the handsome Paco Solanas alone, and however much Aunt Dorothy tried to impress upon her the gravity of her situation she just didn't seem to want to know.

'Sit down a while, Anna Melody, yer making me dizzy,' wheezed Aunt Dorothy, turning pale.

'But I'm so happy I want to dance,' she replied, breaking into an imaginary waltz. 'He's so romantic – like a Hollywood film star.' She sighed and skipped across the carpet.

'You really must think about this very hard. There's more to a marriage than passion,' her mother said carefully. 'This young man lives in a faraway country. You may never see Ireland again.'

'I don't care for Glengariff. The world is opening up for me, Mam. What is there for me in Glengariff?' Her mother looked hurt and swallowed a sob. She couldn't allow her own feelings to influence her daughter in this choice although she felt an over-whelming desire to fall at her feet and beg her to stay. She didn't know how she would be able to live without her.

'Yer family, that's what,' interjected Aunt Dorothy crossly. 'A family that loves the bones of you. Don't belittle that, my girl. There's more to life than riches. You'll learn that the hard way.'

'Calm down, Aunt Dorothy. I love him. I don't care how rich he is. I'd love him if he were a pauper,' Anna said imperiously.

'Love is something that grows, my dear. Don't rush into anything,' her mother said indulgently. 'We're not talking about London or Paris, Anna, we're talking about a country that is on the other side of the world. They speak a different language. The culture is different. You'll miss home.' She choked, then pulled herself together.

'I can learn Spanish. Look I can already say *te amo* – I love you,' Anna said and giggled. *'Te amo, te amo.'*

'It's yer decision, dear, but you'll have to convince yer father,' Emer conceded sadly.

'Thank you, Mam. Aunt Dorothy's an old cynic,' Anna joked.

'Oh, and no thought at all for young Sean? I suppose you think you'll be able to pick up with him where you left off when it all goes wrong?'

'Aunt Dorothy, no!' gasped Anna. 'Besides, it won't go wrong,' she added firmly.

'He's too good for you.'

'Dorothy, really,' chided Emer nervously. 'Anna knows her own mind, she knows what's best for her.'

'I don't know, Emer. You haven't spared a thought for that poor young man who's been nothing but kind to you. Don't you care what becomes of him? He's looking forward to a future with the woman he loves and you're just callously throwing that back in his face. I tell you, Emer, you and Dermot have indulged this child to the point where she can only think of herself. She hasn't been taught to think of anyone else.'

'Please, Dorothy. This is a happy time for Anna.'

'And a miserable time for Sean O'Mara,' huffed Aunt Dorothy, folding her arms in front of her stubbornly.

'I can't help it if I've fallen in love with Paco. What do you expect me to do, Aunt Dorothy – ignore my own heart and return to a man I no longer love?' Anna said melodramatically, sinking into a chair.

'There, there, Anna Melody, it's all right. Yer aunt and I, we only want what's best for you. This has all come as something of a shock. Better to break it off with Sean now than regret it down the line. Once yer married, yer married for life,' Emer said, gently stroking her daughter's long red hair.

Aunt Dorothy sighed heavily. There was nothing she could do. How many scenes like this had she witnessed? Countless. There was no point trying to put the world to rights. Destiny will do that for me, she thought to herself.

'I'm only being realistic,' she conceded, adopting a softer tone of voice. 'I'm older than you and wiser, Anna. As yer father always says, "knowledge can be learnt, wisdom comes with experience". He's right, of course. I'll leave life to do the teaching.'

'We love you, Anna Melody. We don't want to see you making a mistake. Oh, I do wish yer father had been here. What is he going to say?' her mother asked apprehensively.

Dermot O'Dwyer's cheeks grew redder and redder until his large grey eyes looked like they would pop right out of his face. He paced the room in agitation, not knowing what to say. He wasn't going to allow his only daughter to disappear off to some godforsaken country the other end of the earth, to marry some man she had only known for twenty-four hours.

'Jesus, Mary and Joseph, girl. What on earth has possessed you? London fever, that's what. You'll marry young Sean if I have to drag you there myself,' he said angrily.

'I will not marry Sean even if you put a gun to my head, Dad,' Anna cried defiantly, her pink face wet with tears. Emer tried to intervene.

'He was a fine young man, Dermot. Very handsome and mature. You'd have been impressed.'

'I don't care if he's the bloody King of Buenos Aires, I will not have my daughter marrying some foreigner. You were raised in Ireland, you'll stay in Ireland,' he bellowed, pouring himself a large whiskey and knocking it back in one. Emer noticed that his hands were shaking and his pain tore at her heart. Like a wounded animal he was gnashing his teeth at anyone who approached him.

'I will go to Argentina if I have to swim there. I know he's the man for me, Dad. I don't love Sean. I never have. I only went along with it because I wanted to please you, because there was no one else. But now I've seen the man who is my destiny. Can't you see, God meant us to meet? It is meant to be,' Anna said and her eyes implored him to understand and relent.

'Whose idea was it to take you off to London in the first place?' he asked, looking at his wife accusingly. Aunt Dorothy had gone out. 'I've said my piece,' she had explained as she closed the door behind her. Emer looked around helplessly and shook her head.

'We weren't to know that this would happen. It could have happened in Dublin,' she said and her lips trembled, because she knew her husband well enough to know that he would let her go in the end. He always did give in to Anna Melody in the end.

'Dublin is another matter. I will not allow you to run off to Argentina when you've only known this young man five minutes,' he said, putting the bottle of whiskey to his lips and swigging it straight. 'At least we'd be able to look out for you in Dublin.'

'Why can't I go and work in London? Cousin Peter went and worked in London,' Anna suggested hopefully.

'And who would you stay with? Answer me that. I don't know anyone in London and we certainly can't afford to pay for a hotel,' he replied.

'Paco has a cousin who's married and lives in London. He says I could board with them. I could get a job, Dad. Can't you just give me six months? Please give me the chance to get to know him. If after six months I still love him, will you allow him to ask yer permission to marry me?' Dermot sank into a chair and looked defeated. Anna knelt on the floor and pressed her damp cheek against his hand. 'Please, Dad. Please let me find out if he is the one for me. If I don't I'll regret it for the rest of my life. Please don't make me marry a man I don't love. A man whose caresses will be unwelcome. Please don't make me have to bear *that,*' she said with a special emphasis on the word 'that', knowing how the thought of her being subjected to the sexual advances of a man she didn't care for would be enough to weaken his resolve.

'Go out and see yer cousins, Anna Melody. I want to talk to yer mother,' he said quietly, withdrawing his hand.

'Love, I don't want her to go either. But this young man is wealthy, cultured, intelligent – not to mention handsome. He'll give her a better life than Sean can,' Emer said, allowing the tears to run freely now her daughter had left the room.

'Remember how we prayed for a child?' he said, the corners of his mouth drooping as if they had no strength, or will, in them to sit straight on his face. Emer took her daughter's place on the floor and kissed his hand that rested limply on the armrest.

'She has given us so much joy,' she sobbed. 'But one day we'll be gone and then she'll have a future without us. We can't keep her here just for us.'

'The house won't be the same,' he stammered, the whiskey loosening his tongue and his emotions.

'No, no it won't. But think of her future. Anyway, after six months she might decide that he's not for her at all. Then she might come back.'

'She might.' But he didn't believe it.

'Dorothy says we've bred her to be this wilful. If that's true then it's our own fault. We've raised her expectations. Glengariff isn't good enough for her.'

'Maybe,' he replied despondently. 'I don't know.' The thought of their home without the happy chaos of grandchildren lingered in their minds and their hearts strained against the heaviness that weighed down upon them. 'I'll give her six months then. I'll only meet him after six months,' he conceded. 'If she marries him that's it. Goodbye. There's no way I'll go all the way to Argentina to visit her,' he said, and his eyes filled with tears. 'No way.'

Anna walked along the ridge of the hill, the mist swirling around her like thin smoke from heavenly chimneys. She didn't want to see her cousins. She hated them. They had never made her feel welcome. But now she was leaving them. She might never come back. She'd love to see their reactions when they were told about her radiant future. A shudder of excitement raced up her body and she pulled her coat about her and smiled to herself. Paco would take her off into the sun. 'Anna Solanas,' she said. 'Anna Solanas,' she repeated loudly until she was shouting it across the hills. A new name to signal a new life. She'd miss her parents, she knew she would. She'd miss the warm intimacy of their home and the tender caresses of her mother. But Paco would make her happy. Paco would kiss her homesickness away.

When Anna returned from the hills her mother had closed Dermot's study door to leave him alone with his grief, and so as not to upset their daughter. She told Anna that he had said she could go to London, but that she was to call the moment she arrived to assure them she was safely installed in the La Rivières' flat.

Anna embraced her mother. 'Thank you, Mam. I know you persuaded him. I knew you would,' she said happily, kissing the soft skin that smelt of soap and powder.

'When Paco calls, you can tell him yer father has agreed to you living in London for six months. Tell him, if you both feel the same after that time then he'll go to London to meet him. Is that all right, dear?' Emer asked and ran a pale hand down her daughter's long red hair. 'You're very special to us, Anna Melody. We'll not be happy with yer going. But God will be with you and He knows what is good for you,' she said, her voice trembling again. 'Forgive me for being emotional. You've been the sunshine in our lives . . .'

Anna embraced her mother again and felt the emotion choke her too, not because she was leaving, but because her happiness would bring her parents such unhappiness.

Dermot sat disgruntled until sundown. He watched the shadows creep in through the windows until they dominated the study floor, eating up the last shafts of light. He could see his little girl dancing around the room in her Sunday dress. But after a while her merriment gave way to tears and she collapsed crying onto the floor. He wanted to run to her but when he staggered to his feet, the empty whiskey bottle fell to the ground with a crash and frightened her away. When Emer came to take him up to bed he was snoring loudly in his chair, a sad and broken man.

*　　*　　*

Anna had one last duty to perform before she left for London. She went to tell Sean O'Mara that she couldn't marry him. When she arrived at his house his mother, a cheerful woman with the squat physique of a jovial toad, sprang back into the hallway to shout to her son that his fiancée had taken them all by surprise and appeared as if by magic.

'How was yer trip, dear? I'll bet it was quite something, quite something,' she chuckled, rubbing her flour-covered hands on her apron.

'It was very pleasant, Moira,' Anna replied, smiling uneasily and glancing over the woman's shoulder to watch her son come jumping down the stairs.

'Well, I'm glad yer back, that I'll tell you for nothing.' She chuckled. 'Our Sean has been moping around all weekend. It's nice to see him smile again, isn't it, Sean?' She retreated back into the house, adding happily, 'I'll leave you two love-birds to it, then.'

Sean kissed Anna awkwardly on the cheek before taking her by the hand and leading her up the street.

'So, how was London?' he asked.

'Fine,' she replied, greeting Paddy Nyhan who passed them on his bicycle. After smiling and nodding to various other villagers, Anna could bear the suspense not a moment longer.

'Sean, I need to talk to you, somewhere we can be alone,' she said, her forehead creasing into an anxious frown.

'Don't look so worried, Anna. Nothing can be that bad,' he laughed as they walked up the side streets towards the hills. They climbed in silence. Sean attempted to strike up a conversation by asking her questions about London but she answered him in staccato so after a while he gave up. Finally, away from prying eyes and ears, they sat on a damp bench that looked down the valley.

'So, what's on yer mind?' asked Sean. Anna looked into his pale, angular face and naïve green eyes and feared that she wouldn't have the courage to tell him. There was no way she could say it without hurting him.

'I can't marry you, Sean,' she said at last and watched his face crumble.

'You can't marry me?' he repeated incredulously. 'What do you mean, you can't marry me?'

'I just can't, that's all,' she said and looked away. His face flushed crimson, especially around the eyes that welled with emotion.

'I don't understand. What's brought this on?' he stammered. 'Yer nervous, that's all. So am I. But you don't have to call it off. It'll be okay once we're married,' he insisted reassuringly.

'I can't marry you because I'm in love with someone else,' she said and crumpled into sobs. Sean stood up, placed his hands on his hips and snorted in fury.

'Who is this someone else? I'll kill him!' He spat angrily. 'C'mon – who is he?' Anna looked up at him and recognised the pain behind his rage, which made her cry all the more.

'I'm sorry, Sean, I never meant to hurt you,' she sniffed.

'Who is he, Anna? I have a right to know,' he shouted, sitting back down on the bench and pulling her around to face him.

'He's called Paco Solanas,' she replied, pulling out of his grasp.

'What sort of a name is that?' He laughed scornfully.

'It's Spanish. He's from Argentina. I met him in London.'

'In London. Jesus, Anna, you've known him all of two days. This is a joke.'

'It's not a joke. I'm leaving for London at the end of the week,' she said, drying her face with the sleeve of her coat.

'It won't last.'

'Oh Sean. I'm sorry. It's just not meant to be,' she said gently, placing a hand on his.

'I thought you loved me,' he said, gripping her hand and gazing into her distant eyes as if trying to find the Anna he loved hiding behind them.

'I do love you, but like a sister.'

'A sister.'

'Yes. I don't love you like a wife,' she explained, trying to be kind.

'So this is it?' He gulped. 'This is all there is to it – goodbye?' Anna nodded.

'Yer prepared to run off with a man you've known for two days instead of marrying me who you've known all yer life. I don't understand you, Anna.'

'I'm sorry.'

'Stop saying yer sorry. Yer not sorry or you wouldn't be jilting me.' He stood up abruptly. Anna noticed the muscle throb in his cheek as if he was straining against the impulse to break down and cry. But he maintained his composure. 'That's it then. Goodbye. I hope you have a happy life, because you've just ruined mine.' He looked into her watery blue eyes that were beginning to spill over again.

'Don't leave like this,' she said, running after him. But he strode away down the field and disappeared into the village.

Anna returned to the bench and cried because of the pain she had inflicted on him. But there was no kind way of doing it. She loved Paco. She couldn't help it. She consoled herself that Sean would find someone else in time. Hearts were broken every day, she thought, and hearts were mended every day, too. He would get over her. She spent the next few days hiding in her home, talking to Paco on the telephone, avoiding her cousins and the villagers who, having heard the news, blamed Anna for shattering Sean O'Mara's future. She dared not go out. When she left Glengariff she didn't look back; if she had she would have seen Sean O'Mara's sallow face sadly watching her from his bedroom window.

Anna stayed in London for six months. She lived with Antoine and Dominique La Rivière in their spacious apartment in Kensington. Dominique was a budding novelist and Antoine was already quite successful in the City. Paco had been appalled by the idea that his fiancée would work while in London and had insisted she attend courses instead, one of which was Spanish. Anna had been too embarrassed to tell her parents for fear of hurting their pride so she told them she was working in a library.

Paco wrote to his parents telling them of his plans. His father voiced his concern in an uncharacteristically long epistle. He advised that if, at the end of his courses, he still felt the same way, then he should bring his girlfriend home to see how she fitted in. *You'll be able to tell very quickly if it's going to work,* he wrote. His mother, Maria Elena, wrote that she trusted his judgement. She had no doubt that Anna would fit in at Santa Catalina and that everyone would love her like he did.

After six months Anna told her father that she and Paco still loved each other and were determined to marry. When Dermot suggested that Paco come to Ireland, she insisted that Dermot come to London. Her father realised that she was ashamed of their home and worried for the young couple's future if their present wasn't an honest one. But he agreed to go.

Dermot left his wife and daughter to walk around Hyde Park while he met Paco Solanas in the Dorchester Hotel. Emer could see that her daughter had grown up in the six months that she had been living in London. Her new independent life had been good for her. She looked radiant and Emer could tell from the way they held hands and smiled at each other that the couple were truly happy.

After Dermot had asked Paco the usual questions, he said that he trusted Paco was an honest young man and was assured that his daughter would be well looked after.

'I hope you know what yer letting yerself in for, young man,' he said heavily. 'She's wilful and indulged. If parents can love their child too much we're guilty of it. She's not easy, but life will never be dull. I know she'll have a better life with you than she would have in Ireland. But it won't be as easy for her as she thinks. All I ask is that you take care of her. She's very precious to us.'

Paco noticed that the older man's eyes were moist. He shook

Dermot's hand and said that he hoped he would see her happiness for himself at the wedding at Santa Catalina.

'We won't be there,' Dermot said decisively.

Paco was astounded. 'You won't come to your daughter's wedding?' he said, appalled.

'You write and tell us about it,' said Dermot stubbornly. How could he explain to a sophisticated man like Paco Solanas that he was afraid of travelling so far and afraid of finding himself in a strange country with strange people and a strange language. He couldn't explain, he was too proud.

Anna embraced both her parents affectionately. When she hugged her mother she was sure she had got smaller and thinner than when she had last seen her in Ireland six months before. Emer smiled in spite of the sadness that clawed at her soul. When she told her daughter that she loved her, her voice was dry and rasping; the words got lost somewhere in her throat, which had constricted to prevent them through. The tears tumbled out of her eyes and trickled in thick streams down her powdered cheeks, dropping off her nose and chin. She had meant to remain calm, but suddenly holding her daughter for what could be the last time in a long while, she could contain her emotions no longer. She dabbed her hot face with a lace hanky that fluttered about in her trembling hand like a white dove attempting to fly away.

Dermot watched his wife with envy. The agony of holding back his own tears, of swallowing his own pain, was almost too much. He patted Paco on the back a little too firmly and shook his hand a little too hard. When he squeezed Anna he did so with too much fervour so that she cried out in discomfort and he had to release her much too soon.

Anna cried too. She cried because her parents were so unhappy to lose her. She wanted to cut herself in two so that they could keep one half of her with them. They looked frail and vulnerable next to the tall, imposing frame of Paco. She was sad that they weren't going to come out for her wedding, but glad that her new family wouldn't get to meet them. She didn't want them to know where she came from in case they thought she wasn't good enough. She felt guilty that she had allowed such a selfish thought to enter her head while she was saying goodbye to her parents. They would have been so hurt.

With one last wave Anna bade farewell to her past and welcomed an uncertain future with an assurance that would have been more suitable within the pages of a fairytale.

Chapter Seven

When Anna saw Santa Catalina for the first time she was able to see her future in the tall, frothy trees, the colonial house and the vast, flat plain, and knew that she would be happy. Glengariff seemed like worlds away and she was too excited to have time to miss her family or to think about poor Sean O'Mara.

She had left London in the golden glow of autumn and arrived in Buenos Aires as the city burst into flower, for the Argentine seasons are the opposite to those in Europe. The airport smelt thickly of humidity and sweat that mingled with the strong scent of lily of the valley wafting from one of their fellow passengers who had just visited the ladies' room to freshen up.

Anna and Paco were met by a stout, brown-faced man with small shiny brown eyes and an incomplete smile. He saw to their luggage and led them through a side door out into the hot November sunshine. Paco didn't let go of her hand for a moment but held it possessively as they waited for the car to be brought around from the car park.

'Esteban, this is my fiancée, Señorita O'Dwyer,' he said, as the little brown man loaded the cases into the boot.

Anna, who had learnt a little Spanish in London, smiled at him timidly and extended her hand. Esteban's hand was hot and clammy as he took hers and shook it firmly, leaving his raisin eyes to study her face curiously. When she asked Paco why everyone stared at her and why Esteban had looked at her so inquisitively, he replied that it was due to her red hair. Very few people had red hair and such pale skin in Argentina. As they drove into Buenos Aires Anna placed her head beside the open window to allow the cool breeze to blow through her hair and fan her hot face.

To Anna, Buenos Aires possessed the languid charm of an old-fashioned city. At first glance it resembled the European cities she had seen in picture books. The ornate stone buildings could have belonged in Paris or Madrid. The squares were lined with tall sycamores and palm trees, the parks ablaze with flowers and bushes. To her delight, the concrete itself seemed to blossom with thousands of violet flowers fallen from the rich jacaranda trees. The atmosphere was sensual. The small cafés spilled out onto the dusty pavements where the people of Buenos Aires sat drinking tea or playing cards in the stifling humidity. Paco explained that when their ancestors immigrated to Argentina in the late nineteenth century from Europe they recreated in the architecture and customs reminders of their old worlds to stave off the inexorable home-sickness that rattled their souls. Hence, he pointed out, the Theatre Colon is like La Scala in Milan, the Retiro Station is like Waterloo and the sycamore-lined streets are like the South of France. 'We're a hopelessly nostalgic people,' he said. 'And a hopelessly romantic one, too.' She laughed, leaning over and kissing him affectionately.

Anna breathed in the heady scents of eucalyptus and jasmine that emanated from the leafy plazas and observed the bustle of everyday life meander up the dilapidated pavements in the form of elegant women with smooth brown faces and long shiny hair, watched brazenly by swarthy men with dark eyes and lethargic gaits. She saw the ballet of courtship as couples held hands at the small tables in the cafés or sat on park benches kissing in the sunshine. She had never seen so much kissing in one city. Everyone was kissing.

The car descended into an underground garage on the tree-lined Avenida Libertador where a smiling maid with milk-chocolate skin and eager brown eyes stood waiting to help with the luggage. When she saw Paco her large eyes welled with tears and she embraced him fondly, although she barely reached his chest in height. Laughing he put his arms around her thick body and hugged her back.

'Señor Paco, you look so well,' she breathed, running her eyes up and down the length of him in wonder. 'Europe has done you the power of good, just look at you. Ah!' she cried, shifting her eyes to look at Anna. 'This must be your fiancée. Everyone is very excited. They are dying to meet her.' She extended her chubby hand, which Anna shook in bewilderment. She spoke so fast Anna hadn't understood a word.

'Mi *amor*, this is our dear maid, Esmeralda. Isn't she a delight?' he said and winked at her. Anna smiled back before following him into the lift. 'I was twenty-four when I left and she hasn't seen me for two years. As you can imagine, she's a bit overwhelmed.'

'Your family won't be here?' asked Anna apprehensively.

'Of course not. It's Saturday – we never spend weekends in the city,' he said as if it was the most obvious question. 'We'll just take what we need to the country. We'll leave the rest to Esmeralda.'

The apartment was large and airy. Shiny windows looked out over the park, thick with leafy trees under which dreamy lovers gazed into each other's eyes, laughing and necking in the breezy spring morning. The clamour of birds and children's voices reverberated in the shady street below and a dog barked somewhere not too far away for his bark was loud and constant and unrelenting. Paco showed Anna to a small, pale blue room decorated in a very English style with flowered curtains that matched the bedspread and cushion of the dressing-table chair. Looking out she could see over the rooftops of the city to the glistening brown river beyond.

'That is the Rio de La Plata,' said Paco, wrapping his arms around her from behind and looking over her shoulder. 'Across the water is Uruguay. The river is the widest in the world. Over there,' he said, pointing across the buildings, 'is the area of La Boca, the old port area settled by Italians. I'll take you there as the Italian restaurants are fantastic and the houses I think you'll find rather amusing as they're painted in bright festive colours. Then I'll take you to San Telmo, the old part of the city, where the streets are cobbled and the houses romantic and crumbling and there I will dance with you the Tango.' Anna smiled in delight as she looked over the city that was to be her new home and felt a rush of excitement race through her bones. 'We'll walk along the bank of the river called the Costanera and hold hands and kiss and then . . .'

'And then?' she laughed coquettishly.

'And then I will bring you home and make love to you in our matrimonial bed, slowly and sensually,' he replied.

Anna giggled throatily, recalling those long nights of kissing, when she had resisted her own desire that threatened to overwhelm her when he ran his lips over her skin and felt with his hands the brazen swelling of her breasts beneath her blouse. She had pulled away, her face flushed with lust and shame combined, for her mother had taught her to save herself for her wedding night. No decent girl allows a man to compromise her reputation, she had said.

Paco was old-fashioned and chivalrous, and although his loins ached under the strain of having to resist his impulses to go further than was decent, he respected Anna's wish to remain a virgin. He had suppressed his own longing with brisk walks and vigorous showers. 'We will have all the time in the world to discover each other once we are married,' he had said.

Anna pulled out her summer clothes from her suitcase, leaving the rest of her things for Esmeralda to unpack as Paco had instructed. She showered in the marble bathroom and slipped into a long floral dress. While Paco was busy in his room she took a moment to wander around the apartment, which was on two floors, and look into the black and white photographs of his family that smiled out from shining silver frames. There was one of Paco's parents, Hector and Maria Elena. Hector was tall and dark with remote black eyes and aquiline features that gave him the regal grace of a hawk. Maria Elena was small and fair with melancholic pale eyes and a warm generous mouth. They looked elegant and proud. Anna hoped they would like her. She remembered Aunt Dorothy's warning that they would probably wish him to marry someone from his own 'class and culture'. She had felt so confident back in London; now the thought of stepping into this glamorous new world frightened her. In spite of her airs and graces Aunt Dorothy was right – she was just a small town Irish girl with childish dreams of grandeur.

She heard Paco talking to Esmeralda on the landing. Then he descended the stairs with his suitcase. 'Is that all you're taking?' he asked when he saw Anna standing in the hallway, clutching a small brown case. She nodded. She didn't own many summer clothes. 'All right, let's go,' he said, shrugging his shoulders. Anna smiled at Esmeralda who gave her a basket of provisions to take down to the farm and managed to mumble *'Adios,'* as she had been taught in her classes in London. Paco turned and raised an eyebrow when he heard her say it. 'Said like a native,' he joked, placing their bags in the lift. 'Well done!'

Paco owned a gleaming Mercedes imported from Germany. It was a pale blue convertible and made a loud roaring noise that echoed off the garage walls when he turned the key in the ignition. Anna watched Buenos Aires rush past her and felt she was in a speedboat slicing through the ocean. She wished her horrid cousins could see her now. They'd go mad with jealousy, she thought happily to herself. Her parents would swell with pride and for the first time since she had left them their tear-stained faces rose to the surface of her mind like bubbles. Her heart momentarily lurched with homesickness but then they were on the open road with the wind in her hair and the sun on her face and the bubbles burst and disappeared altogether.

Paco had explained to her that he had three brothers. He was number three. The eldest, Miguel, was like his father, dark with rich brown skin and brown eyes. He was married to Chiquita whom Paco had said she would like very much. Then there was Nico, who was also dark like his father with blue eyes like his mother. He was married to Valeria, who was sharp and not as sweet-natured as Chiquita, but he was sure they would become friends once they got to know each other. After Paco there came Alejandro, the youngest, who was unmarried but apparently very seriously courting a girl called Malena who, according to Miguel's letters, was one of the most beautiful girls in Buenos Aires. 'Don't worry,' Paco advised Anna kindly. 'Just be yourself and they will all love you like I do.'

Overwhelmed by the difference in the scenery, Anna found herself speechless with wonder. Far from the wet green hills of Ireland she looked about her at the dry flat land of the *pampas*. The plain, studded with scattered herds of cows, sometimes horses, stretched out to the ends of the earth like a tawny brown sea beneath a bright blue sky of such an exquisite colour it reminded Anna of cornflowers. Santa Catalina sat like a leafy oasis of verdant trees and glimmering green grasses at the end of a long dusty track. On hearing the familiar purr of Paco's car his mother had left the cool shade of the house to welcome him home. She wore a pair of white pleated trousers with buttons at the ankles that Anna soon learnt were a copy of the traditional gaucho trousers called *bombachas*, and an open-neck white shirt rolled up at the sleeves. Around her waist she wore a thick leather belt decorated with silver coins that caught the light and glittered. Her fair hair was pulled back into a bun at the nape of her neck exposing her gentle features and pale blue eyes.

Maria Elena embraced her son with unbridled affection. She placed her long elegant hands on his face and looked up into his eyes exclaiming in Spanish words which Anna was unable to understand, but knew were exclamations of joy. Then she turned to Anna and with more reserve walked over to kiss her on her pale cheek and told her in broken English that it was a pleasure to meet her. Anna followed them inside to where the rest of the family waited to greet Paco and meet his new fiancée.

When Anna saw the cool sitting-room filled with strange people she felt suddenly weak with terror. She noticed every eye scrutinise her critically to see whether she was good enough for their Paco. Paco dropped her hand and was at once swallowed up into the arms of his family who hadn't seen him for two years. For a brief moment, which seemed to the startled Anna an embarrassingly long time, she felt herself alone, like a small boat cast adrift in the sea. Looking helplessly about her with misted eyes she stood rooted to the spot, feeling awkward and conspicuous. Just when she thought she could take it no longer, Miguel strode up to her and took it upon himself to introduce her to the family. Miguel was kind and smiled at her sympathetically.

'This is going to be a nightmare for you. Just take a deep breath and you'll get through it,' he said in English spoken with a charmingly thick accent like his brother and placed a rough hand on her arm reassuringly. Nico and Alejandro smiled at her politely, but when she turned her back she felt their eyes still on her and heard them discussing her in Spanish although the words still failed to reach her understanding in spite of all the classes she had attended. They spoke so fast. She winced at the imperious beauty of Valeria, who kissed Anna without smiling and looked at her with steady, confident eyes. She was relieved when Chiquita embraced her affectionately and welcomed her into the family.

'Paco's letters said so much of you. I am happy you are here,' she said in faltering English and then blushed. Anna was so grateful she could have cried.

When Anna saw the forbidding figure of Hector approach her she felt the sweat drip down the backs of her legs and her stomach swim. He was tall and commanding and she shrank under the suffocating weight of his charisma. He bent down to kiss her and he smelt of a spicy cologne that lingered on her skin for some time afterwards. Paco looked very like his father, with the same aquiline features, the same hooked nose, except Paco had inherited the gentle expression of his mother, and her colouring.

'I would like to welcome you to Santa Catalina. To Argentina. I take it this is your first time here?' he said in perfect English. Anna caught her breath and nodded lamely. 'I would like to talk to my son alone, would you mind if I left you with my wife?' Anna shook her head.

'Of course not,' she replied huskily, wishing Paco could take her back to Buenos Aires where they could be alone. But Paco withdrew happily with his father and Anna knew that he expected her to cope.

'Come, let us sit outside,' said Maria Elena kindly, watching her husband and son disappear into the hall with an apprehensive look that darkened her pale eyes. Anna had no choice but to allow herself to be swept out onto the terrace with Maria Elena and her family, out into the sunshine where they could see her better.

'*Por Dios*, Paco!' began his father in his deep steady voice, shaking his head with impatience. 'She's beautiful, there's no doubt about that, but look at her — she's like a startled rabbit in there. Is it fair to bring her here?'

Paco's face flooded crimson and his blue eyes flashed violet. He had been waiting for this confrontation. He had expected his father's disapproval from the beginning.

'Papa, are you surprised she's terrified? She doesn't speak the language and she's being scrutinised by every member of my family to see if she's good enough. Well, I know what's good enough for me and I will allow no one to persuade me any different.' He looked at his father defiantly.

'Son, I know you're in love and that's all very well, but marriage isn't necessarily about love.'

'Don't speak about my mother like that,' snapped Paco. 'I will marry Anna,' he added in a quiet, determined voice.

'Paco, she's provincial, she's never been out of Ireland. Is it fair on her to place her in the middle of our world? How do you think she's going to cope?'

'She'll cope, because I'll help her cope. Because *you* will help her cope,' Paco said hotly. 'Because you'll tell the rest of the family to make her feel welcome.'

'That's not enough. We live in a rigid society – she'll be judged by everyone. With all the beautiful girls here in Argentina, why couldn't you choose one of them?' Hector raised his hands in exasperation. 'Your brothers have managed to find suitable matches in this country, why couldn't you?'

'I love Anna because she's different from all of them. So she's unsophisticated, she's provincial, and she's not from our class. So what? I love her the way she is and so will you when you get to know her. Let her relax a little. When she forgets her fear you'll understand why I love her like I do.'

Paco fixed his father with unwavering eyes that softened when he talked about Anna. Hector's jaw was rigid and his chin jutted out stubbornly. He shook his head slowly and breathed in through flared nostrils, without taking his eyes off the face of his son.

'All right,' he conceded. 'I can't stop you marrying her. But I hope you know what you're doing, because I sure as hell don't.'

'Give her time, Papa,' said Paco, grateful that his father had backed down. In the lifetime that Paco had known his father he had never once remembered him backing down.

'You're a man now and old enough to make your own decisions,' Hector said, brusquely. 'It's your life. I hope I'm not proved right.'

'You won't be. I know what I want,' Paco told him. Hector nodded before embracing his son firmly and kissing him on his damp cheek, as was their custom once an argument was over.

'Let's go and join the others,' Hector said, and they both made for the door.

Anna warmed immediately to Chiquita and Miguel, who embraced her into the family with unconditional affection.

'Don't worry about Valeria,' said Chiquita as she showed Anna around the *estancia*. 'She will like you when she knows you. Everyone was hoping that Paco would marry an Argentine. It is a shock, you see. Paco announces that he is getting married and no one has met you. You will be happy here once you are settled.'

Chiquita showed Anna the *ranchos* – the tight cluster of squat white houses where the *gauchos* lived – and the polo field which came alive in the summer months when the boys did nothing but play, and if they weren't playing they were talking about it. She took her to the tennis court that sat nestled amidst the heavy, damp plane trees and eucalyptus, and the limpid pool placed on a man-made hill from where one could see a large grassy field full of pale brown cows chewing the cud.

With Chiquita Anna soon began to practise speaking Spanish. Chiquita explained to her the grammatical differences between the Spanish from Spain, which Anna had learnt in London, and the Spanish spoken in Argentina, and she listened with patience as Anna nervously stumbled through her sentences.

During the week, Anna and Paco lived in Buenos Aires with his parents and although at first the mealtimes were tense, as Anna's Spanish progressed so did her somewhat overwrought relationship with Hector and Maria Elena. Anna voiced little of her fears during these few months of their engagement, sensing that Paco wanted her to cope and fit in. He began to work in his father's business leaving Anna to spend her days studying Spanish and taking a course in Art History. She dreaded the weekends when the whole family gathered together on the farm, primarily because of the hostility she felt in Valeria.

Valeria made her feel unworthy. In her immaculate summer dresses, with her long dark hair and aristocratic features, Valeria made Anna's stomach churn with feelings of inadequacy. She would sit with her friends in a whispering huddle around the pool and Anna knew they were talking about her. They would smoke their cigarettes and watch her like a pack of beautiful, glossy panthers lazily observing a timorous doe and enjoying it when she stumbled. Anna recalled with bitterness her cousins back in Ireland and wondered who were worse. At least in Glengariff she had been able to escape to the hills; here she had nowhere to hide. She couldn't confide in Paco as she wanted him to feel she was fitting in and she didn't want to whinge to Chiquita who had become a real friend and ally. It had always been her way to hide her feelings and her father had once told her to hide her weaknesses from people who might take advantage of them. In this case he was sure to be right and she didn't want to give any of them the satisfaction of watching her fail.

'She's no better than Eva Perón!' Valeria said crossly when Nico confronted her about being so unfriendly. 'An upstart trying to climb up the social ladder by marrying into your family. Can't you see it?'

'She loves Paco, I can see that,' he replied gruffly, in defence of his brother's choice.

'Men are so dopey when it comes to understanding women. Hector and Maria Elena see it, I can tell,' she persisted.

At that time Perón was at the height of his power. He had reduced the population to total subjection. Backed by the military, he controlled the press, the radio, and the universities. No one dared deviate from the party line. Although he had the popularity to implement a democracy he preferred to rule with military precision and total control. Admittedly, there were no concentration camps for those who dissented and the foreign press were permitted to visit the country with complete freedom, yet an undercurrent of fear simmered below the surface of Perón's Argentina. Eva, named Evita by her millions of supporters, used her status and power to act like a modern-day Robin Hood and the waiting room of her office literally vibrated with the queues of people requesting favours – a new house, a pension, a job – to which Eva would respond with a wave of her magic wand. She saw it as her personal mission to alleviate the sufferings of the poor, of which she had first-hand experience, and took great pleasure in quite simply taking from the rich in order to give to her *descamisados* – a name coined by Perón himself which literally means 'shirtless ones'. Many of the wealthy, worried that Perón's dictatorship would lead to Communism, left the country altogether during that time.

'Yes,' Valeria said spitefully, 'Anna is just like Eva Perón. Socially ambitious, and you and your family are going to let her get away with it.' Nico scratched his head and decided her argument was so ridiculous he wouldn't dignify it by discussing it.

'Give the girl a chance,' he said. 'Put yourself in her shoes and then I think you'll be a little kinder.'

Valeria bit her lower lip and wondered why men were so hopeless at seeing beneath the surface of a beautiful woman. Just like Juan Perón.

The decisive moment arose one afternoon when the whole family draped themselves over the hot paving stones around the pool, basking in the glorious sunshine and drinking the abundant fruit juices brought up from Hector's house by maids in pale blue uniforms. Anna was sitting with Chiquita and Maria Elena in the shade when one of Miguel's friends, Diego Braun, finding himself dazed by the Celtic beauty of Paco's fiancée, couldn't resist but flirt with her in front of everyone.

'*Anna, por qué no te bañás?*' he asked from the pool, hoping that she might jump in and join him for a while. Anna understood the question perfectly. 'Anna, why don't you come for a swim?' But she was so nervous, sensing everyone was listening for her response that she muddled up her grammar and translated directly from the English.

'*Porque estoy caliente,*' she replied, wanting to communicate that she didn't want to swim in the cold water because she was comfortably hot. To her surprise everyone disintegrated into laughter. They were laughing so hard they had to hold their bellies to ease the pain.

Anna looked helplessly at Chiquita who, between infectious giggles, told her what she had said.

' "I'm lustful" I think is the correct translation.' Then Chiquita began to laugh again with the rest of her family and friends.

Anna reflected on what she had said and suddenly Chiquita's laughter ignited a tickle in her own belly and she too began to howl with mirth. They all laughed together and for the first time Anna felt part of the clan. Standing up she said in her strong Irish accent, not caring if the grammar was right or wrong, that she had perhaps better take a swim to cool off.

From that moment on she learnt to laugh at herself and realised that a sense of humour was the only way she was going to endear herself to them. The men stopped admiring her quietly from afar and teased her about her poor Spanish and the girls took it upon themselves to help her not only cope with the language but the men as well. They taught her that Latin men have a confidence and shamelessness with women that meant that she would have to take care; she wasn't safe even as a married woman. They'd try it on all the same. As a European and beautiful, she would have to be doubly careful. European women were like red rags to bulls, they said, with a reputation for being 'easy'. But saying 'no' had never been a problem for Anna and, gaining confidence, her strength of character and that familiar capriciousness began to assert themselves again.

As Anna's character emerged out of the fog that had been her fear and the limitations that the language barrier had imposed upon it, Valeria realised that Anna wasn't weak and hopeless, as at first she had suspected. In fact, she had a steely strength of character and the tongue of a viper, even in faltering Spanish. She answered people back and even disagreed openly with Hector one lunchtime in front of the whole family and won her argument, while Paco looked on triumphantly. By the time of the wedding if Anna hadn't won the affections of each member of her new family, at least she had won their respect.

* * *

The wedding was held under an ocean-blue sky in the summer gardens of Santa Catalina. Surrounded by 300 people she did not know, Anna Melody O'Dwyer glowed beneath a misty veil studded with small flowers and sequins. As she walked down the aisle on the arm of the distinguished Hector Solanas she felt she had truly leapt into the pages of the fairytale books she had pawed over as a small child. Through her sheer determination and force of personality she had earned it. Everyone was looking at her, nodding to each other, commenting on what an exquisite creature she was. She felt admired and adored. She had shed the skin of the frightened girl who had arrived in Argentina three months before and emerged like the butterfly she always knew she could be. When she made her vows to her prince she believed tales like these really did have happy endings. They would walk off into the sunset and live happily ever after.

On the morning of her wedding she had received a telegram from her family. It read: TO OUR DEAREST ANNA MELODY STOP ALL OUR LOVE FOR YOUR FUTURE HAPPINESS STOP YOUR LOVING PARENTS AUNT DOROTHY STOP WE ALL MISS YOU STOP. Anna read it while Encarnacion threaded jasmine into her hair and afterwards folded it away with her old life.

Their wedding night was as tender and stirring as she had hoped it would be. Finally, alone together beneath the shroud of darkness, she had allowed her new husband to discover her. Trembling she had let him undress her, kissing each part of her body as it was revealed to him. He enjoyed the fair innocence of her skin, iridescent in the dusky moonlight that entered in shimmering shafts through the gaps in the curtains. He enjoyed her curiosity and her delight as she abandoned herself to him and allowed him to explore those places that had previously been forbidden. With each caress, with each touch, Anna truly felt that their very souls were uniting on a spiritual plain and that her feelings for Paco pertained to another world, a world beyond the physical. She felt blessed by God.

At first she didn't miss her family or her country at all. In fact, her life was suddenly so much more exciting. As the wife of Paco Solanas she could have anything she wanted and respect came with the name. Her new status far outshone the traces of her humble past. She enjoyed playing the hostess in her new apartment in Buenos Aires, gliding about the large, exquisitely decorated rooms, always the centre of attention. She charmed everyone with her poor attempts to speak Spanish and her unsophisticated ways; if the Solanas family had accepted her then so would the Porteños – the people of Buenos Aires. As a foreigner she was a curiosity and got away with almost everything. Paco was deeply proud of his wife. She was different from everyone else in this city of strict social codes.

At the beginning of her marriage, though, she still made mistakes. She wasn't used to servants so she tended to treat them in a manner that was discourteous, believing it to be the way the upper classes treated their staff. She wanted people to think that she had grown up with maids in the house, but she was wrong; her attitude towards them offended her new family. Paco had pretended not to notice for the first few months, hoping that she would learn from watching her sisters-in-law. But eventually he found himself having to take her aside to gently ask her to treat them with more respect. He couldn't tell her how Angelina, their cook, had appeared at the door of his study wringing her hands in distress, claiming that no Solanas had ever talked to her in the way that Señora Anna did. Anna was mortified and sulked for a few days. Paco tried to coax her out of her bad humour. These moods didn't belong to the '*Ana Melodía*' he had fallen in love with in London.

Anna suddenly found she had more money than the Count of Montecristo. In an attempt to show that she wasn't a small-town girl from Southern Ireland and to lift her spirits, she wandered down Avenida Florida looking for something special to wear for her father-in-law's birthday dinner. She found a very glamorous outfit in a small boutique on the corner where Avenida Santa Fe crosses the Avenida Florida. The sales girl was very helpful and gave her a free bottle of scent as a gift. Anna was delighted and began to feel again that inner buoyancy she had felt when she had first set foot in Buenos Aires.

However, the moment she entered the room at Hector and Maria Elena's apartment that evening and saw what all the other women were wearing, she realised to her embarrassment that she had chosen badly. All eyes turned to her and their smiles hid the disapproval they were far too polite to show. She had chosen a dress that was much too low-cut and fancy for this quietly elegant occasion. To add to her shame, Hector walked up to her. His black hair, which was only greying slightly at the temples, and tall frame made him look terrifying. Overshadowing her with dread, he offered her a shawl. 'I don't want you to feel the cold,' he said kindly. 'Maria Elena doesn't like to heat the house, it gives her headaches.' She thanked him, repressing a sob, and gulped down a glass of wine as fast as was dignified. Paco later told her that although she was inappropriately dressed she had still been the most beautiful girl in the room.

By the time Rafael Francisco Solanas (nicknamed Rafa) was born in the winter of 1951 Anna felt she was beginning to fit in. Chiquita, now her sister-in-law, had taken her shopping and she began stepping out in the most elegant outfits imported from Paris, and everyone was full of admiration that she had produced a boy. He was fair and so pale he looked like a fat little albino monkey. But to Anna he was the most precious creature she had ever seen.

Paco sat by her hospital bed and told her how happy she had made him. He held her slender hand in his and kissed it with great tenderness before placing on one of her fingers a diamond and ruby eternity ring.

'You have given me a son, *Ana Melodía*. I am so proud of my beautiful wife,' he said, hoping that a child would help her settle in and give her something to fill her days with besides shopping.

Maria Elena gave her a gold locket studded with emeralds that had belonged to her mother and Hector took one look at the child and said he looked like his mother but cried with the might of a true Solanas.

When Anna telephoned her mother in Ireland, Emer cried for most of the call. More than anything she wanted to be with her daughter at this time, and it tore her apart to know she might never lay eyes on her grandson. Aunt Dorothy took over the receiver and interpreted what her sister was trying to say, repeating her niece's words to all those in the small sitting room.

Dermot wanted to know that she was happy and well cared for. He spoke briefly to Paco who told him that Anna was much loved by his entire family. When Dermot put down the telephone he was more than satisfied, but Aunt Dorothy wasn't convinced. 'She didn't sound herself, if you ask me,' she said darkly, putting down her knitting.

'What do you mean?' Emer was still tearful.

'She sounded happy enough to me,' Dermot said gruffly.

'Oh yes, she sounded happy enough, though slightly chastened,' Aunt Dorothy said thoughtfully. 'That's the word, chastened. Argentina's obviously doing our Anna Melody the world of good.'

Anna had everything she could possibly want in her life, except for one thing that was constantly nagging at her pride. However hard she watched and copied those around her, she could never seem to shake off the feeling of being socially inadequate. In late September when spring covered the *pampas* with long rich grasses and wild-flowers, Anna found another obstacle that wedged its way between her and the sense of belonging that she craved for – horses.

Anna had never liked horses; in fact she was allergic to them. She loved most other animals: the mischievous *vizcachas*, big rodents similar to the hare, which burrowed all over the plain, the *gato montés* or wild cat, which she often spotted sloping lithely through the bushes and the armadillo which fascinated her by virtue of its absurd shape. Hector used the shell of one as an *objet* on his study table, which she found very distressing. But she soon realised that life at Santa Catalina revolved around polo. Everyone rode a horse; cars were obsolete in a place where the roads joining one *estancia* to another were often little more than dirt tracks or simply paths cutting through the long grasses.

Life at Santa Catalina was very sociable; they were always taking tea or enjoying large barbecues, *asados,* at other people's ranches. Anna found herself having to drive the long way around by truck when all the others simply jumped on a horse and galloped their way there in no time at all. Conversation was dominated by polo, the matches they played against other *estancias,* their handicaps, their ponies, their equipment. The men seemed to play most evenings. It was entertainment. The women would sit out on the grass with their children and watch their husbands and sons gallop up and down the field – but for what? To hit a ball between two poles. It was hardly worth the effort, thought Anna sourly. When she watched small children, barely able to walk, playing on the sidelines with a mini mallet she would roll her eyes in despair. There was no getting away from it.

Agustin Paco Solanas was born in the autumn of 1954. Unlike his brother he was dark and hairy. Paco said he looked just like Grandfather Solanas. This time he gave his wife a diamond and sapphire eternity ring. But there was a chill in their relationship that hadn't been noticeable before.

Anna occupied herself fully in the young lives of her two sons. Although she had Encarnacion's young niece, Soledad, to look after them she preferred to do most of the caring herself. Her sons needed her, depended on her. To them she was everything and their love was unconditional. She responded to their affection with blind devotion. The more she doted on her sons the more distant her husband became, until Paco resembled a shadowy character in the background of her nursery life. He seemed to spend more and more time away from her, arriving very late from work most evenings and leaving before she got up in the morning. At weekends at Santa Catalina they spoke to each other with a cool politeness that had crept into their relationship with the subtlety of a prairie puma. Anna wondered where all the joy and laughter had gone. What had become of their games? Now they seemed to talk only about their children.

Paco dared not admit to anyone that perhaps he had been wrong. That perhaps he had been asking too much of Anna to acclimatise to a culture that was alien to her. He had watched the *Ana Melodía* he had fallen in love with disappear slowly behind the remote veneer of a woman trying to be something that she was not. He had watched helplessly as her unbridled nature and defiant independence had turned to sullenness and petulance. She was defensive about everything. She seemed to be struggling to find herself, which only resulted in attempting to emulate those about her in order to become just like them. She sacrificed those unique qualities that Paco had found so endearing in exchange for a sophistication that hung loosely on her like an ill-fitting gown. He knew she was capable of great passion but as much as he tried to kiss away her reserve their nocturnal encounters became nothing more than that, encounters. As much as he might have wanted to discuss his worries with his mother he was too proud to admit that maybe he should have left Anna Melody O'Dwyer on those smoggy London streets and saved them both from this unhappiness.

When Sofia Emer Solanas screamed her way into the world in the autumn of 1956 the chill had turned to a frost. Paco and Anna were barely speaking. Maria Elena wondered whether the separation from her family wasn't beginning to take its toll, so she suggested that Paco fly her parents out to Santa Catalina as a surprise. At first Paco resisted; he didn't know whether it would please Anna to go behind her back. But Maria Elena was firm and determined. 'If you want to save your marriage, you should think less and do more,' she said sternly. Paco relented and called Dermot in Ireland to tell him of his plan. He chose his words carefully so as not to bruise the old man's pride. Dermot and Emer accepted his gift with gratitude. Aunt Dorothy was mortified she wasn't included. 'Don't forget a single detail, Emer Melody, or I'll never speak to you again!' she warned in good humour, fighting her disappointment.

Dermot had never been further than Brighton and Emer was nervous of flying, even though she was reassured that Swissair was a very respectable airline. However, the thought of seeing their beloved Anna Melody and meeting their grandchildren for the first time was enough to expel those fears. The tickets arrived as promised and they began the arduous forty-hour journey from London to Buenos Aires, stopping in Geneva, Dakar, Recife, Rio and Montevideo. They survived the trip in spite of getting lost in Geneva Airport and almost missing their connecting flight.

When Anna returned to Santa Catalina with the two-week-old Sofia tightly wrapped in an ivory lace shawl she found her parents tearful and exhausted waiting for her on the terrace. She handed the child over to the excited Soledad and threw her arms around both her parents at once. They had brought presents for the six-year-old Rafael and little Agustin and Emer's book of old photos for Anna. Paco and his family tactfully left them to be together for a couple of hours, during which they talked without drawing breath, cried without shame and laughed as only the Irish can.

Dermot commented on the 'fine life' that Anna Melody had acquired for herself and Emer went through her closets and the rooms of her home with genuine admiration. 'If Aunt Dorothy could see you now, dear, she'd be so proud of you. You really have fallen on yer feet.'

Emer was encouraged that her daughter asked tenderly after Sean O'Mara. She'd tell Aunt Dorothy that the child wasn't as selfish as she had supposed, or as heartless. Emer told her daughter that he had married and gone to live in Dublin. She understood that he was doing well from what his parents told them. Now she wasn't certain but she seemed to remember someone telling her that he had had a daughter, or a son, perhaps, she couldn't be sure, but a child nonetheless. Anna smiled wistfully and said that she was happy for him.

Both Emer and Dermot doted on the children who warmed to them immediately. Yet when the initial excitement of their presence had worn off Anna wished her parents weren't so provincial. They were both dressed in their Sunday best, a timid couple against this foreign landscape. Maria Elena took tea with Emer and Anna at her house in front of a boisterous fire as it got quite chilly when the sun went down and Hector showed Dermot the farm in the *carro* drawn by two shiny ponies. The whole family joined them for dinner and once Dermot had downed a couple of shots of good Irish whiskey he held forth, telling wildly exaggerated stories of life back in Ireland and embarrassing tales of Anna as a child. His hair that had been neatly combed on his arrival now frizzed out in grey curls and his cheeks glowed with merriment. When he started to sing 'Danny Boy' after supper with Maria Elena at the piano Anna wished they had never come.

Four weeks later Anna hugged her mother goodbye. She could not have known that she would never see her gentle face again. Emer knew. Sometimes one senses these things and Emer Melody had inherited a sharp intuition from her grandmother. She died two years later.

Anna was sad to see them go, but not sorry. The years had weakened the ties that bound them together; she felt she had moved on in the world, while they hadn't moved at all. While she had delighted in seeing them she also felt they had let her down. Having presented herself as a lady she was sure her husband's family would now see her for what she really was. But Paco and his parents had grown very fond of Emer with her gentle Irish nature and enchanting smile, and everyone had adored her eccentric father. It was only in Anna's mind that this shadow dwelt and grew, until it threatened to destroy the very thing it loved.

*   *   *

Two years later, when Anna discovered a hotel bill in Paco's jacket pocket, she suddenly realised where he had taken his love and blamed his betrayal for all her feelings of exclusion and inadequacy. She didn't take the time to wonder who had driven him there.

Chapter Eight

Santa Catalina, February 1972

'Maria, don't you just hate it when you're told that you have to like someone?' moaned Sofia, kicking off her tennis shoes and sitting down on the grass next to her cousin.

'How do you mean?' she asked.

'Well, this Eva person. Mama says I have to look after her and be nice to her. I hate that kind of responsibility.'

'She's only staying for ten days.'

'Ten days too long.'

'I hear she's very pretty.'

'Huh.' Sofia was already bristling at the thought of competition. She had heard nothing for the last few months but how beautiful Eva was. She hoped her parents were exaggerating to be kind. 'Still, I don't know why Mama has to go and ask her to stay.'

'Why has she asked her?'

'She's the daughter of friends of theirs from Chile.'

'Are they coming too?'

'No, worst luck, even more of a responsibility.'

'I'll help you. She might be really nice; we may all become friends. Don't be so pessimistic,' laughed Maria, wondering what Sofia's problem was. 'How old is she?'

'Our age, fifteen or sixteen. I can't remember.'

'When is she arriving?'

'Tomorrow.'

'We can meet her together. We only need worry if she's dull.'

Sofia hoped Eva would be dull – dull and plain. Perhaps she could leave her with Maria, and they would bond. Maria was so accommodating, there was no reason why she wouldn't relieve Sofia of her charge and entertain Eva for her. That's the sort of girl Maria is, thought Sofia happily. She's always eager to please. Suddenly the following week didn't seem so bleak after all. She would be able to spend all her time with Santi, leaving Maria and Eva to amuse themselves.

The following morning Sofia, her brother, and her cousins were lying chatting in the shade of one of the tall plane trees, listening to Neil Diamond's voice resound through the open drawing-room windows, when a shiny car drew up. They all stopped talking and turned their attention to Jacinto, the chauffeur, who climbed out, walked around to the back door and opened it. His face was red and he was smiling. When the beautiful Eva descended, his wide smile and throbbing, swollen cheeks surprised no one. Sofia's stomach shuddered competitively. She glanced at the boys who had suddenly raised themselves onto their haunches like a pack of prairie dogs.

'*Puta madre!*' exclaimed Agustin.

'*Dios*, just look at that hair!' hissed Fernando.

'A filly with better legs, I have not seen,' muttered Santi under his breath.

'Oh, for God's sake, boys, put your tongues in. The hair is blonde – lots of girls have blonde hair,' Sofia snapped irritably, getting up. 'Wipe your mouth, Agustin, you're dribbling,' she added before striding off towards the car.

Anna, who had been sitting on the terrace with Chiquita and Valeria, walked across the grass towards the new arrival who stood shyly beside the hypnotised Jacinto.

'Eva,' she said as she approached. 'How are you?'

Eva floated up to her. She didn't stride and she didn't walk, she floated. Her long blonde hair was loose and flowing about her angular face, framing large aquamarine eyes that blinked up nervously from under thick dark lashes.

Sofia tried desperately to find fault with this creature that had appeared before her like a demon in disguise ready to steal Santi away, but she was perfect. Sofia didn't think she had ever seen anything more exquisite before. She watched her mother embrace her warmly, ask after her parents and give Jacinto orders to take her suitcase into the spare room.

'Eva, this is Sofia,' said Anna, nudging her daughter forward. Sofia kissed her and smelt the fresh lemon scent of her cologne.

Eva was taller than Sofia and very slim. She looked much older than fifteen. When she smiled, a timid smile, the cushions of her cheeks blushed before the colour subsided a little, spreading across the rest of her face. When Eva blushed she looked even prettier; her eyes seemed more blue, more acute.

Sofia mumbled a feeble *'Hola,'* before letting her mother lead their guest onto the terrace. Sofia followed lamely. She glanced across at the boys who were still watching from their lair. But they weren't watching her; they were watching Eva. They were all imagining what it would be like to have her.

Eva noticed their silent appraisal too; she could feel their eyes following her across the terrace. She didn't dare look at them. She sat down and crossed her legs, feeling the sweat behind her knees and on her thighs.

Sofia sat mutely beside her mother, Chiquita and Valeria who fought for Eva's attention like a group of admiring schoolgirls. She wondered whether they'd notice if she just slipped away. No one cared whether she spoke or not, they didn't even look at her. She might just as well have been a shadow.

Soledad came out with a tray of iced lemon and glasses and proceeded to hand them around. When she got to Sofia she frowned at her enquiringly. Sofia pulled a thin smile, which Soledad recognised immediately and understood. She grinned back as if to say, 'You're too spoilt for your own good, Señorita Sofia.' Sofia gulped down the lemon, then retained a cube of ice in her mouth which she swilled around petulantly. Eva's eyes caught Sofia's and she seemed to smile at her through them. Sofia smiled back bashfully but was determined not to like her. She looked over at the boys who moved about restlessly under the tree in their poorly disguised efforts to see as much of Eva as possible. Then Santi stood up, gesticulated to the others as if in response to a dare, and strode confidently over to where the women were sitting on the terrace.

Chiquita beckoned him to join them. 'Eva, this is my son Santiago,' she said proudly, watching her handsome son bend down to kiss their exquisite guest before pulling up a chair. She smiled as she detected a glimmer of attraction cause Eva's pale tanzanite eyes to shine and look away bashfully.

'You're from Chile?' he asked and grinned broadly, giving Eva the full benefit of his generous mouth and large, white teeth. Sofia rolled her eyes. He's smitten too, the fool, she thought irritably.

'Yes, from Chile,' Eva replied in her silky Chilean accent.

'Santiago?'

'Yes.'

'Well, welcome to Santa Catalina. Do you ride?'

'Yes, I do. I love horses,' she told him happily.

'Then I'll show you around the farm on horseback if you like,' he offered. Sofia was about to drown in her misery when Santi reached for her glass of iced lemon and, taking it out of her hand, put it to his own mouth and took a swig. The fact that he had shared her glass so naturally would show Eva that he belonged to her. She hoped Eva noticed.

Santi then sat back; placing his ankle onto his knee and resting the glass on his thigh he rolled it around idly. They continued to talk about horses, her parents' beach house in Cachagua and the long summer mists that sometimes linger over the coast until midday. While they talked Sofia leant over to reclaim her glass. Her hand touched Santi's as she took it from him and proceeded to finish off what was left of the lemon. But Santi barely acknowledged her. He seemed unable to wrench his eyes away from the mesmeric Eva who sat smiling prettily at him.

Once the other boys had watched Santi settle into the group so effortlessly they galvanised themselves and wandered over. Eva saw the group of tanned, hungry predators emerge from the shade into the sun and her pale lips quivered uneasily. But then Santi grinned at her in sympathy as they approached the terrace to sniff the honey pot and she smiled back gratefully.

Maria appeared out of the trees with Panchito and little Horacio, and Paco strode around the corner with Miguel, Nico and Alejandro, followed closely by Malena with her two daughters, Martina and Vanesa. Soon Eva had been introduced to almost everyone on the *estancia*; even the dogs seemed compelled to bask in her aura and sat about her chair meekly. The boys wanted to sleep with her, the girls wanted to be her, and all at once they asked her questions and tried to win her affection. Sofia stifled a yawn and was about to slip away when Grandpa O'Dwyer shuffled unsteadily out of the drawing room.

'Who's this pretty young thing who has appeared among us?' he said when his eyes focused on the lovely Eva.

'This is Eva Alarcon, Dad. She's come over from Chile for a week,' Anna replied in English, hurriedly assessing him to determine whether he had been drinking.

'Well, Eva, do you speak English?' he asked gruffly, hovering over her like a large moth attracted to a beautiful flower.

'A little,' she replied with a strong accent.

'Don't worry about him,' said Anna in Spanish, 'he's only lived here for thirteen years.'

'Not a word of Spanish,' said Agustin, eager for Eva to notice him. 'Ignore him, we all do.' He laughed and took pleasure in watching her smile at his humour.

'You might,' said Sofia grumpily, 'but I never ignore him.' Santi looked at her and frowned as if to ask why she had come over all moody, but she averted her eyes and smiled at her grandfather.

'From Chile, eh?' continued Dermot, taking a chair from Soledad, who had anticipated his thoughts, and making everyone move aside so he could sit next to Eva. They all had to shuffle along and there was much scraping of chairs on the tiles before Dermot was able to squeeze into the small space that had been made for him. Anna shook her head wearily. Sofia smiled in amusement. Let's see how she copes with Grandpa, she thought gleefully to herself.

'What do you do in Chile?' he asked. 'Good girl,' he muttered to Soledad as she brought him a glass tumbler of iced lemon. 'I don't suppose there's a surprise in this for me, is there?' he added, sniffing it. Unable to understand his English, Soledad retreated inside.

'Well, we ride horses on the beach,' replied Eva earnestly.

'Horses, eh?' said Dermot, nodding approvingly. 'We ride horses in Ireland. What do you do in Chile that we can't do in Ireland?'

'Shoot the rapids?' she suggested and smiled politely.

'Shoot the rabbits?'

'Yes, we have the fastest rapid in the world,' she added with pride.

'By God, it must be a fast rabbit if it's the fastest in all the world.' He chuckled.

'It's not only fast but very dangerous.'

'Dangerous too. Does it bite?'

'Excuse me?' she said, looking helplessly across at Sofia, who decided not to rush to her aid like the rest of her sycophantic family and shrugged her shoulders instead.

'Hasn't someone shot it yet?' he asked.

'Oh yes, they shoot it all the time.'

'They can't be very good shots in Chile then, or that damn rabbit must run like lightning,' he said and laughed loudly. 'A rabbit who runs like lightning, well I'll be damned.'

'Excuse me?'

'In Ireland the rabbits are fat and slow, too many carrots, easy targets. I'd like to try my hand at shooting yer fast rabbit.' At that point Sofia couldn't hold her laughter in another minute. She opened her mouth and laughed until the tears squeezed out and caught in her eyelashes.

'Grandpa, she's talking about rapids – you know, those fast-running rivers that people throw themselves down in rubber boats. Not rabbits!' she gasped and when everyone else understood the joke they too laughed. Eva giggled and blushed. When she glanced shyly at Santi she saw that he was looking at her.

After lunch Anna suggested that Sofia and Maria take Eva off to the pool to lie in the sun. Sofia and Maria accompanied her to her room to unpack her things first. The girl was pleased with her room. It was large and light, with two tall open windows that looked out over the orchard of apple and plum trees. The scent of jasmine and gardenia floated up on the heat and filled the air with their heady perfume. There were twin beds covered in blue and white floral throws scented with lavender and a delicate wooden dressing table for her to lay out her brushes and cologne. She also had an adjoining bathroom with a deep enamel bath with chrome attachments imported all the way from Paris.

'This is such a pretty room,' she sighed, opening her suitcase.

'I love your accent,' enthused Maria. 'I love how the Chileans speak Spanish, it's very delicate, don't you think, Sofia?' Her cousin nodded impassively.

'Thank you, Maria,' Eva replied. 'You know, this is the first time I've been to the *pampas*. I've been to Buenos Aires many times, but never to an *estancia*. It's really beautiful here.'

'How do you like our cousins?' asked Sofia, lying back on one of the beds and crossing one brown foot over the other.

'They are all charming,' she responded innocently.

'No, I mean how do you *like* them? They all fancied you – you can have your pick.'

'Sofia, you are too sweet. I don't think they do fancy me, I'm just new, that's all. As far as fancying them, I've barely had time to look at them.'

'Well, they've had time to look at you,' she said, watching Eva steadily.

'Sofia, leave her alone, poor girl, she's only just arrived,' Maria interrupted. 'Now, hurry and put on your swimsuit, I'm dying of heat in here.'

Up at the pool the boys were already lying in the sun like a pride of male lions, waiting for Eva to appear in her swimsuit. With their eyes squinting into the light they watched the trees with shallow breaths and hot bodies. They didn't have to wait long. They hissed a few lewd comments to each other as the girls approached and then pretended to be disinterested, talking to each other about polo. Eva self-consciously dropped her shorts and wriggled out of her T-shirt, revealing the body of a woman with large round breasts, flat stomach, full hips and smooth, brown skin. She felt their stares stripping her of her modesty and fingered her costume with a trembling hand to make sure that it was still there. Sofia threw her clothes onto the ground and walked over to the sunbeds with her duck's walk, bottom out and tummy in, her feet pointing outwards. Santi lay on the sunbed next to hers, watching Eva quietly with the patient arrogance of a man who knows that the woman of his desire will come to him eventually. Sofia noticed his expression and stuck out her lower lip resentfully.

'Do you need some oil rubbed on your back?' shouted Agustin from the water.

'Not with your cold wet hands,' laughed Eva, feeling more confident now she had made friends with the girls.

'Don't trust Agustin,' Fernando said. 'If you need oil rubbing on your back, *I'm* the most reliable.' They all laughed.

'I'm fine, thank you.'

'Here, take my sunbed, Eva,' said Santi, getting up. Sofia noticed Maria had taken the other one.

'No, really . . .' she began.

'I'm too hot here anyway,' he insisted. 'There are only three. I'll bring some more up from the pool house later.'

'Well, if you're sure,' she said, spreading her towel neatly over the sunbed and lying down. Santi sat on the paving stones beside her and chatted to her as if they had known each other for a long time. He had an easy way with women which drew them into his confidence. Unlike the others, he won their trust. Sofia felt jealousy rise from her stomach like bile. Placing her sunglasses over her eyes she lay back in the sunshine and tried to ignore them.

Fernando watched his brother chatting up the new blonde and hoped she wouldn't fancy him. What was it about Santi that made all the girls go for him? He hoped she would notice his limp and that it would put her off. If he were a girl it would put him off, he thought sourly to himself. He decided to wait in the pool. She's bound to get hot at some stage and go for a swim, he thought, and then I'll be ready for her.

Rafael had lost interest and fallen asleep in the shade with a magazine over his sunburnt face. Agustin had dived a few times, he was good at diving, and performed the odd somersault. She had smiled at him. He had impressed her, no doubt. But now she was being monopolised by Santi, keen to get in there too, so Agustin told himself he'd simply have to wait his moment like Fernando and swim about like a shark until she decided to put her toe in. Angel, Niquito and Sebastian had sized up the competition and realised that there was no point getting into the arena; they had no chance. So they sloped off to knock a tennis ball around on the hot court that shimmered like a furnace behind the wire fencing.

When the heat became too much, Eva encouraged Sofia and Maria to take a swim with her; the sharks were too threatening to brave the water alone. When Eva stood up, it was as if an icy wind had blown through the languid confines of the pool waking everyone up from their siestas. Suddenly Agustin was diving again, Fernando was roaring up and down doing front crawl, Sebastian, Niquito and Angel came back to cool down from their game of tennis, and Santi sat on the edge with his feet in the water. Only Rafael continued to snore from his shade, the pages of the magazine flying about on his breath. Sofia sulked in the corner while Maria and Eva tried to swim lengths in the rough, choppy water.

'What's the matter with *you*?' Santi asked, dropping into the water and swimming up to join Sofia in her miserable corner.

'Nothing,' she replied defensively.

'I know you,' he said and smiled.

'No, you don't.'

'Oh, I think I do. You're jealous you're not getting any attention.' His green eyes sparkled at her in amusement. 'I've been watching you all day.'

'Don't be silly. I'm not feeling well.'

'Chofi. You're a liar and a brat, but you'll always be my favourite cousin.'

'Thanks,' she said, feeling a little happier.

'You can't always be the centre of attention. Give someone else a chance.'

'Look, that's not it. I really don't feel very well. It's the heat. I might go and lie in the shade for a while,' she said half-heartedly, hoping that he'd go with her.

'Please yourself,' he replied, turning to watch Eva swimming gracefully like a swan amidst a commotion of playful ducks.

That night the three girls decided to sleep all together. Soledad moved a camp bed into Eva's room and told Sofia that as she was the hostess she had to sleep in it. Typical, she thought resentfully, and I didn't want to share in the first place. But as they chatted away in the pale blue light of the moon that entered through the large open windows with the sweet earthy scents of the dewy *pampa*, her mood lifted and she began to like Eva in spite of herself.

'As I was walking back to the house, Agustin jumped out from behind a tree and threw me against it,' Eva giggled. 'It was *so* embarrassing.'

'I don't believe it!' Sofia exclaimed, amazed at her brother's shamelessness. 'What did he do?'

'He pushed me up against the bark and told me he was in love with me.'

'They all are!' laughed Maria. 'Watch out, soon there won't be a safe tree in the whole of Santa Catalina.'

'Did he kiss you?' Sofia asked hopefully, but she knew Eva would never fancy the outlandish Agustin.

'He tried.'

'Oh God, how embarrassing,' sighed Sofia.

'Then when we were playing tennis he'd only hand me a ball after kissing it first.'

'Oh dear.'

'Sofia, I shouldn't be telling you this, he's your brother.'

'Unfortunately. Maria's brothers are a better pair than mine.'

'Yes, Santi is very attractive,' said Eva, her clear eyes shining with the fever that had captivated her young body.

'Santi?' Sofia's heart stopped.

'Yes, Santi.'

'The one with the limp – tall, fair?'

'Yes, the one with the limp,' she repeated. 'He's handsome yet sweet and his limp just makes him more endearing.'

Sofia wanted to cry. *You can't fancy Santi, not my Santi!* she screamed inside her head. Then more coolly she made a decision. She had to think of a plan, she had to think of a way of preventing a romance that would surely flare up unless she smothered it right now, in these early stages. She had to stop this beautiful temptress from digging her long pink fingernails into Santi. Shame, I was just beginning to like her, she thought dismissively.

Chapter Nine

Sofia spent the following three days making sure that she became Eva's best friend and confidante. Her mother had praised her for being such a good hostess and for her valiant effort to make their young guest feel welcome. They went everywhere together and Sofia didn't need to spy on her when she was with Santi because, having won Eva's confidence, she told her everything voluntarily.

Suddenly the boys began to make a fuss of Sofia too; they saw her as their ticket to getting close to Eva. Sofia enjoyed the attention. No longer in the shadow, she played her part with bravado. But Eva wasn't interested in Agustin, Fernando or any of the others; she was hopelessly attracted to Santi. Every move that he made she recounted to Sofia. He had taken her riding across the plains. Sofia had refused to go, making up a weak excuse about having to help her grandfather rearrange his room. He had then asked her to be his partner in tennis. Eva had confessed she went weak whenever she saw him, but so far Santi had said nothing that might suggest he felt anything more than friendship.

'Don't worry,' said Sofia. 'Santi's my cousin, I'm closer to him than anyone. He tells me everything – things he doesn't tell Maria. I'll find out for you, subtly of course, then let you know. If you want me to do this, don't tell Maria, she can't keep a secret,' she lied.

'All right, but be careful. I don't want to look a fool.'

'You won't look a fool,' Sofia assured her happily.

Later she engineered it so that she was alone with Santi. He was practising his golf swing on the land in front of his house. Sofia left Maria and Eva talking on the terrace with her aunts and mother and strolled over to him with her mission.

'Good swing, Santi,' she said as he hit the ball high into the air.

'Thanks, Chofi.'

'You've been very kind to Eva, taking her riding, showing her the farm.'

'She's a sweet girl,' he said, placing a new ball onto the grass.

'She's more than that. She's adorable and beautiful. In fact, I don't think I've seen anyone more beautiful than her, ever.'

'She's certainly beautiful,' he said absentmindedly, concentrating more on his swing than on the conversation with his duplicitous cousin.

'You know who she really fancies?' she said quietly, choosing her words with the care of a snake sliding through the long grass in pursuit of its prey.

'Who?' he replied, bringing down his club and looking at her steadily.

'Agustin.'

'Agustin?' he scoffed.

'Yes.'

'You're joking, aren't you?'

'Why? He's very attractive – he's a dark horse.'

'Sofia, I don't believe you,' he said and smirked, shaking his head impatiently.

'Well, he kissed her the other night. She doesn't want anyone to know.'

'He kissed her. Sure!'

'I promise – just don't mention it, she'll kill me. We're such good friends now I don't want to ruin it. But you know me, I can't keep anything from you.'

'Thanks for that, Chofi,' he said sarcastically. Then drawing his club up behind his shoulder he brought it down furiously and missed the ball. '*Mierda!*'

'Santi, you missed! That's not like you. What's the matter? You don't fancy her, do you?' she said and tried to hide her smile by playing with a stray piece of hair across her lips.

'Of course not. Now go away, you're distracting me,' he said, dismissing her.

'Okay. See you later.' She walked off with her arrogant duck's gait, smiling to herself with glee.

Santi could not believe that the beautiful Eva could fancy Agustin. He was mystified and furious. Agustin! It simply wasn't possible. He squinted his eyes as he cast them over to the terrace where Sofia now sat cross-legged on the grass with Maria and Eva, their heads together like a trio of plotting witches. What is she up to? he thought, knowing better than to trust her.

'He didn't let on, I'm afraid. He's keeping his cards very close to his chest,' said Sofia later as she and Eva helped themselves from the buffet. 'If I were you I would just wait for him to make a move. I can't recommend anything else. He certainly wouldn't like a woman to make the first move. You know men.'

'Well, at least he didn't say he didn't like me,' Eva said hopefully.

'No, he didn't say he didn't like you,' replied Sofia truthfully.

'Thank you, Sofia, you're a real friend.' Eva kissed her on the cheek. Sofia felt a moment's guilt, but then the feeling passed and she cut into her juicy *lomo* hungrily.

During the next few days Sofia watched Eva float around Santa Catalina like Snow White followed by the drooling dwarfs in the shape of Fernando, Agustin, Sebastian, Niquito and Angel. She noticed to her relief that since their conversation Santi had lost interest. He virtually ignored her. Even Eva had stopped talking about him as if she knew the battle was lost. Sofia basked in her victory.

*   *   *

As Eva's holiday drained away Sofia began to see less and less of her. She would disappear for hours on horseback or go into town with Chiquita. She knew her way around now and began to entertain herself. Sofia was delighted. Her plot had worked. Not only had she deterred her from pursuing Santi but she had also somehow managed to avoid having to entertain her all week. She would have been more delighted if Santi hadn't been equally elusive. However, he claimed to have been over on the neighbour-ing *estancia* hitting a polo ball around. Sofia supposed that he was angry with her for breaking the bad news to him about Eva's secret romance with Agustin. He'll get over it, she thought dismissively.

Eva's last day was spent by the pool and on the tennis court. She said goodbye to the cousins before disappearing into the house to pack and change. Once she had gone, Santi sat down next to Sofia and secretly gave her a note sealed in a plain white envelope.

'Chofi, please give this to Eva just before she goes,' he requested.

'What is it?' she asked, turning it over in her hands curiously.

'One last chance. Make sure Agustin doesn't see, won't you. He'll kill me if he finds out.'

Sofia shrugged. 'All right, if that's what you want, but it won't do you any good,' she said and smiled at him sympathetically.

'It might,' he replied hopefully.

Sofia ran back to the house. She had just enough time to steam open the letter before Eva left for the airport. She rushed into the kitchen and boiled the kettle. Poor Santi, she thought, he hasn't got a clue. She couldn't imagine anyone fancying Agustin over Santi. It was just inconceivable. Still, she had convinced him. She chuckled to herself as the steam bellowed up against the seal, enabling her to carefully peel it back. Leaning against the counter she opened the neatly folded paper and read the short, handwritten message.

Next time, mind your own business, Chofi.

She was stunned. Blood flooded into her face until it throbbed with embarrassment. She read it again slowly. Again and again in disbelief. Then she tore it into tiny little pieces and threw it in the bin. She then paced the kitchen in panic, not knowing what to do next, not wanting to face Santi or Eva.

Finally she realised she had no choice but to walk out with her head held high and act as if nothing had happened. Eva was saying goodbye to Maria, who tearfully embraced her new friend and swapped telephone numbers and addresses. Sofia looked about for Santi but to her relief he wasn't there. She smiled the smile of a good actress and hugged Eva, breathing in once again the fresh lemon smell of her cologne. She promised to spend the following summer holidays in Cachagua and to write often.

Suddenly, Santi strode out of the trees with a determined step. He walked past Sofia, pulled the delicate Eva into his arms and kissed her so ardently on her pretty pink lips that the other girls had to turn away in embarrassment. They held each other vigorously, the way lovers do when they don't want to part. They kissed with the intimacy of two people familiar with each other's bodies. Sofia felt the blood plummet from her head to her toes, and the world spin about her. When they wrenched themselves apart, Eva climbed into the car and disappeared down the long avenue of trees. Santi waved until she was nothing more than a glint on the horizon, then he walked up to Sofia.

'Don't ever lie to me again,' he said steadily. 'Do you understand?' Sofia opened her mouth to respond but nothing came out but air. She strained her neck to prevent the tears from falling and dared not blink in case one broke free and revealed her shame. Then he smiled at her and shook his head. 'You're very naughty, Chofi.' He sighed, putting an arm around her neck fondly. 'What am I going to do with you?'

Chapter Ten

———————

When Santi broke the news at the end of the summer holiday that he was leaving to study in America for almost two years, Sofia fled the room in tears. Santi ran after her but she shouted at him to leave her alone. Fortunately, he knew better than to do as she asked and followed her out onto the terrace.

'You're going in a month? How come you didn't tell me before?' she said, turning on him angrily.

'Because initially I was going to go in September when my courses start, but I want to travel for six months first and then for a few months afterwards. Anyhow, I knew you'd be upset.'

'But I'm the last to know. I am, aren't I?' she sobbed crossly.

'Yes, you are. I suppose. I don't know. No one else is very interested,' he said, shrugging his shoulders.

'Two years?' She wiped away the tears that made glistening tracks down her dusty cheeks.

'Well, almost two years.'

'How many months exactly?' She sniffed.

'I don't know.'

'Well, when do you come back?'

'The summer after next. October, November — I'm not sure yet.'

'Why can't you study here like everyone else?'

'Because Papa says it's essential to live abroad. I'll improve my English and get a good qualification.'

'I'll help you improve your English,' she said meekly, smiling sadly through the blur that made him look like a fuzzy shadow.

Santi laughed. 'That would be interesting,' he mused.

'Will you come back for the holidays?' she asked hopefully.

'I don't know.' He shrugged his shoulders again. 'I want to travel and see the world. I'll probably spend the holidays travelling.'

'You mean not even for Christmas?' she gasped, suddenly feeling empty inside at the prospect of living two years without him.

'I don't know. Probably not. Mama and Papa will come and see me in America.' He watched his cousin sink onto the floor and almost cry a puddle onto the paving stones. 'Chofi, I'll come back. Two years isn't such a long time,' he said softly, surprised at the violence of her reaction.

'It is. It's for ever,' she stammered. 'What if you fall in love and marry an American? I might never see you again.'

Santi laughed and placed an arm around her, pulling her against him. Sofia closed her eyes and wished that he loved her like she loved him, then he wouldn't go away and leave her.

'I'm hardly going to get married at eighteen, am I? That's silly. Anyway, I'll marry an Argentine. You don't think I'd leave Argentina for ever, do you?'

Sofia shook her head. 'I don't know. I don't want to lose you. I'm going to be stuck here with Agustin and Fercho with no one to defend me. They'll probably stop me playing polo altogether now.' She sniffed and nuzzled her face into his neck. He smelt of ponies and that musty male smell that made her want to stick her tongue out and lick his skin.

'I'll write to you,' he suggested.

'You promise?'

'I promise. Long, long letters. I'll tell you everything. And you must write to me and tell me everything, too.'

'I'll write every week,' she replied resolutely.

Sitting there in his arms she realised that her feelings had gone beyond the affection one might feel for a brother, even a special one, and trespassed into something much deeper and forbidden. She loved him. She hadn't really sat down and thought about it before, but with the scent of his body clinging to her nostrils, with the feel of his skin against hers and his breath on her forehead she knew that the reasons for her possessiveness were because she loved him. She didn't just fancy him – she loved him. Yes, she loved him with all her heart and soul. Now she understood.

For a frightening moment she almost lost herself and told him. But she knew it was wrong. She also knew that he loved her like a sister so there was no point revealing to him her dark longing when it would only bewilder him or at worst send him running in the opposite direction. So she sat pressed against him and he remained ignorant of the force that sent her heart pounding into her ribs like a maddened bird throwing itself against its cage in its barely restrained yearning to fly out and sing.

Santi returned to his house pale and confused and told Maria how upset Sofia was that he was leaving. 'She was in tears. I couldn't believe it. She was shattered,' he related in bewilderment. 'I knew she'd be upset, but I had no idea she'd be *that* upset. When I left her she just ran off.'

Maria immediately rushed over to find her cousin and bumped right into Dermot playing croquet with Antonio, Soledad's husband who maintained the estate. When she told him why his granddaughter had taken flight he put down his mallet and lit his pipe. Dermot loved his granddaughter with an intensity that he had once felt for his own daughter. To him she was more radiant than the sun. When he had arrived in Argentina after the death of his wife it had been little Sofia who had kept him from yearning to join her. 'She's an angel in disguise,' he would say, 'one of God's little angels.'

Grandpa O'Dwyer drove up to the ombu tree in the *carro* with Antonio at the reins. He felt more comfortable with Antonio and

Jose than he did with his daughter's adopted family, in spite of his inability to communicate in anything else but gesture. Sofia was sitting at the top of the tree with her head in her hands. When she saw her grandfather step unsteadily down from the cart she put her head in her hands again and cried even louder for his benefit. He stood at the foot of the tree and called at her to come down.

'Nothing will come of crying, Sofia Melody,' he said, puffing on his pipe. She thought about it a while and then slowly descended. When she reached the bottom they both sat down on the grass in the gentle morning sunshine. 'So, young Santiago is going to America.'

'He's leaving me,' she moaned. 'I was the last person to know.'

'He'll come back,' he said kindly.

'But he's going for two years. Two years! How will I live without him?'

'You will,' he said sadly, remembering his lovely wife. 'You will because you have to.'

'Oh Grandpa, I'll die without Santi.'

Grandpa O'Dwyer puffed lazily on his pipe and watched the smoke waft up and dissolve into the air. 'I hope yer mother doesn't know about this,' he said seriously.

'Of course not.'

'I don't think she'd be very pleased. You'd heap a whole lot of trouble on yer young shoulders if she were to find out.'

'What's wrong with loving someone?' she asked defiantly.

Grandpa O'Dwyer's mouth curled up at the corners. 'Santiago's not someone, Sofia Melody – he's yer first cousin.'

'So what?'

'So a lot,' he replied simply.

'Well, it's our secret now.'

'Like my liquor,' he chuckled, licking his pale lips.

'Exactly,' agreed Sofia. 'Oh Grandpa, I want to die!'

'When I was yer age I loved a beautiful girl, just like you. She meant the world to me, but she disappeared to London for three years. Now Santiago's only going for two. But I knew that one day, if I waited, she'd come back to me. Because do yer know something, Sofia Melody?'

'What?' she asked sulkily.

'Everything comes to those who wait.'

'No, it doesn't.'

'Have yer ever tried?'

'I haven't had to.'

'Well, I waited. And do yer know what happened?'

'She came back, fell in love with you, and married you. Right?'

'Wrong!' Sofia raised her head curiously. 'She came back and I realised that suddenly I didn't want her no more.'

'Grandpa!' she laughed. 'What did you say comes to those who wait?'

'Wisdom. Time gives you the opportunity to stand back and be objective. Wisdom doesn't always bring the expected or it wouldn't be worth the wait, would it, if you already knew what it was going to tell you? Those years of waiting gave me wisdom. When she came back I chose not to have her. I had learned that she wasn't the girl for me after all. Lucky for you I didn't marry her because then I would never have married yer grandmother.'

'I'd like to have known my grandmother,' Sofia said wistfully.

Grandpa O'Dwyer sighed deeply. Not a day went by when a simple flower or the song of a bird didn't remind him of his Emer Melody. She was everywhere he looked, and the memory of her generous, kind expression helped him stagger through yet another day without her.

'I'd like you to have known her too,' he gulped and his eyes misted. 'She would have loved you, Sofia Melody.'

'Am I like her?'

'You don't look like her, she looked more like yer mother. But you have her charisma and charm.'

'You miss her, don't you, Grandpa?'

'I miss her. Not a moment passes when I don't think about her. She was everything to me.'

'Santi's everything to me,' she said, drawing him back to the problem at hand. 'He's everything to me and I've only just realised. I love him, Grandpa.'

'He's everything to you now, but yer young.'

'But Grandpa, I don't want anyone but Santi. I never will.'

'You'll grow out of him, Sofia. You wait. Some handsome Argentine will come and sweep you off yer young feet just like yer father swept the young Anna Melody off hers all those years ago.'

'No, he won't. I love Santi,' she argued emphatically.

Dermot O'Dwyer chuckled out of the side of his mouth, puffing at the same time on his pipe. He looked into her petulant face and nodded.

'Fair play to yer, Sofia Melody. Then wait for him. He'll come back. He's not going for ever, is he?' As always, Grandpa O'Dwyer couldn't help but humour her. There was nothing in the world that he would deny her. Not even Santiago Solanas.

'No.'

'Then have some patience. It's the patient cat that catches the mouse.'

'No it isn't, it's the quick cat that catches the mouse,' she said, her face opening into a small smile.

'If you say so, me darlin'.'

At the beginning of March when the leaves were just beginning to curl up at the edges and the long summer holiday that had lasted from December had almost drained away like sand in an hourglass, Sofia stood at the front of Chiquita and Miguel's house to say goodbye to Santi. In the lengthening shadows of the humid summer evening she remembered what Grandpa O'Dwyer had told her. Like a patient cat she would wait for him. She wouldn't look at another boy. She would remain loyal to him for ever.

The last few weeks of the holiday had been hard for Sofia. She had to dissemble when her impulses caused her face to flush and her hands to sweat whenever she was in the presence of Santi. She had to bite her tongue when she found the words 'I love you' balancing precariously on the end of it, ready to spill out in a moment of thoughtlessness. She had to hide her feelings from the rest of the family when she wanted to cry openly in the face of the void that would be left once he had gone.

Santi took care not to talk about his adventure when he was with her; he didn't want to reduce her once more to tears. He had been touched by her unrestrained display of affection. He felt proud like a hero of war departing for another battle while his womenfolk howl and tear their hair out for him. He knew he wouldn't miss her. Of course he would write to her, she was like an adoring little sister and he would write to his mother and Maria as well. But America awaited him with the promise of adventures and long-legged women of easy virtue. He couldn't wait to taste America. Besides, Sofia would be there when he got back.

At last Santi strode out of the house with Antonio following behind with his bags. He embraced a tearful Maria and shook hands with Fernando who was secretly pleased to see him go. Fernando watched his brother's departure with relish. Everyone loved Santi. He was good at everything, charmed everyone, made people laugh – he sailed through life with the ease and grace of a sleek ship while Fernando felt more like a tug-boat. He had to work hard and in spite of his efforts achieved little. Hence the older he got the less he tried. Yes, he was not sorry to see his brother go. He was positively delighted. Without Santi around to eclipse him, perhaps he might feel the sun on his face for a change. Panchito sat in the arms of old Encarnacion, too young to understand or care. When Santi hugged Sofia he promised her again that he would write.

'You're not still angry with me, are you?' he asked, grinning at her fondly.

'Yes. But I'll forgive you when you come back,' she replied and swallowed back her tears. He had no idea how he moved her. He was oblivious to her stomach that lurched when he touched her, to her heart that skipped when he smiled at her, to her blood that swam in her cheeks when he kissed her. To Santi, Sofia was a little sister. To Sofia, Santi was everything and now he was going there was barely any point in breathing. She only breathed because she had no choice. Like Grandpa O'Dwyer had said, she'd live because she had to.

Miguel and Chiquita climbed into the car and shouted to Santi to hurry. They were running late. He waved at them all from the back seat. Fernando retreated into the house. Maria and Sofia stood watching the car until it had long disappeared out of sight.

The next few days passed by very slowly. Sofia mooched around in a sulk that not even Grandpa O'Dwyer's dry humour could alleviate. Maria followed her like a happy dog, her cheery smile and jolly jokes serving only to irritate the lonely heart of her friend who wanted to be left alone to mourn. The holidays were drawing to a close and with them the long summer days and all that went with them. Finally Maria decided she had had enough of her cousin's grouchiness.

'For goodness' sake, Sofia, snap out of it,' she said when her cousin had refused to play tennis with her.

'Snap out of what, Maria?'

'Moping around like someone's died.'

'I'm sad, that's all. Aren't I allowed to be sad?' she asked sarcastically.

'He's only your cousin. You're acting like you're in love with him.'

'I am in love with him,' Sofia replied shamelessly. 'And I don't care who knows it.'

Maria was shocked. 'He's your first cousin, Sofia. You can't love your first cousin.'

'Well, I do. Got a problem with it?' she asked challengingly.

Maria sat in silence for a moment. Overcome with a jealousy she couldn't recognise, she jumped to her feet and shouted at Sofia: 'You should grow up! You're too big for childish crushes.

Anyhow, Santi isn't in love with you. If he was he would never have fancied Eva, would he? Can't you see that you're making a fool of yourself? It's scandalous to be in love with a member of your own family. Incest. That's what they call it – incest,' she said angrily.

'Incest is brother and sister. He's my cousin,' retorted Sofia crossly. 'Well, you obviously don't want to be my friend any more!'

Maria watched helplessly as her cousin stormed out of the room, slamming the door so loudly behind her that the painting to the right of it fell to the floor and broke into small pieces.

Maria dissolved into angry tears. How could Sofia be in love with Santi? He was her *cousin*. It just wasn't right. She sat and thought about it, turning it over and over in her mind, trying to make sense of her own feelings of jealousy and isolation. They had always been three, now suddenly, in a word, they were two and there was no room for Maria.

Back in Buenos Aires for the start of the school term, Sofia still refused to speak to Maria. They sat in the car in icy silence while Jacinto drove them to school and Sofia made sure she didn't even look at her cousin during class. Maria had had fights with Sofia before, all of which she had lost. Somehow Sofia was able to sustain a feud longer than was normally possible between such close friends. She had a talent for being able to switch off her emotions when it suited her, and appeared to thrive on the drama. She deliberately avoided Maria during the breaks, laughed loudly with her friends and shot her cousin mean stares.

Maria was determined not to weaken. After all, she hadn't started the fight. Sofia had baited her. She wasn't going to let her get away with it. For the first few days she tried hard to ignore her. At night she quietly cried herself to sleep, unable to fully understand her pain. But during the day she discreetly went about her work while Sofia managed to get all the other girls to avoid her too. She had a compelling charisma that drew people to her. Once their classmates learnt of the fight they all scuttled over to Sofia's side of the room like frightened rabbits.

After a week Maria couldn't bear the frost any longer. She felt miserable and alone. She buried her pride and wrote a note to her friend: *Sofia, please let's be friends again.* Sofia perversely enjoyed making her cousin suffer. And she was most certainly suffering. When she received no reply, Maria wrote another note: *Sofia, I'm sorry. I should never have said the things I did. I was wrong and I apologise. Please let's be friends.'*

Sofia, who was rather enjoying the attention, turned the note over and over, deciding what to do next. Finally, when Maria broke down in tears in the history class she realised she had gone too far. Sofia found her in the break crying on the steps. Sitting down beside her she said, 'I don't love Santi any more.' She didn't want Maria sneaking on her to anyone. Maria's tear-stained face smiled at her gratefully and said that it wouldn't matter if she did.

Chapter Eleven

Buenos Aires, 1958

Soledad heard Sofia crying and hurried to her room. Gathering the two-year-old child into her arms she held her sobbing body against her breasts and talked to her reassuringly. 'It's only a bad dream, my sweet,' she said and Sofia responded by clinging on to her with her hot arms and legs. Soledad looked closely at the child's plump olive skin and hazelnut eyes and noticed how thick her dark lashes were as they glistened with tears. 'You're a real beauty, aren't you? Even when you're crying,' she said, and kissed her damp cheek.

Anna only seemed interested in her daughter when she was asleep. As a small baby she had been unable to tolerate her plaintive cries, sending her back to Soledad whenever she did so much as whimper. Paco, who had never taken much interest in his sons as small children, could scarcely take his eyes off her. He would run upstairs the moment he returned from work to say goodnight or to read her a bedtime story. Sofia would sit on his knee, work her body into his until it was comfortably curled against him, then rest her head against his chest and suck her thumb. Soledad was astounded. Señor Paco didn't seem the type to be sweet with small children. But Sofia wasn't just any child. She was his little girl and at two years old she had already ensnared him in her web of charm.

Soledad enjoyed her weeks in Buenos Aires. Having been brought up in the countryside the city was new and exciting for her. Not that she went out much. She was too busy looking after Sofia. But she would sometimes go to the shops leaving Loreto, the maid who lived in the apartment, to care for the child while she was out. Paco had asked Soledad to spend some time in the city with Sofia, who had taken to crying out for her in the middle of the night. 'She needs you, Soledad,' he had said. 'And so do we. It upsets us to see her distressed.' Of course Soledad had accepted immediately, even though that meant leaving Antonio sometimes for a whole week at a time. Still, she always returned with the family at the weekends to continue her job as normal. 'Do you want to sleep in my bed?' she asked the sleepy child. Sofia nodded before resting her head against Soledad's heavy bosom and closing her eyes.

Soledad descended the stairs with care, the sleeping child in her arms. Señor Paco is home very late, she thought, noticing his briefcase and cashmere coat draped over the chair in the hallway. He had missed saying goodnight to Sofia. When she reached the hall she heard their voices behind the closed door to the sitting room and in spite of her instincts that warned her against spying, she stopped to listen. They spoke in Spanish.

'. . .Well, where did it come from?' Anna snapped angrily.

'Business, it's not what you think,' Paco replied coolly.

'Business? Why on earth did you need a hotel in this city when you have a perfectly good apartment? For God's sake, Paco, I'm not a fool!'

There followed a heavy silence. Soledad didn't move, she stood as still as if she were a piece of hall furniture; she barely breathed. Her heart beat though, in fact, it accelerated fiercely. She knew she was listening to a conversation that was private. She knew she should turn and walk away, carry Sofia off to her room and pretend she hadn't heard anything. But she couldn't. She was too curious; she had to know what they were talking about. She heard pacing.

Señor Paco must be walking the room; she heard the cold sound of shoes on wood and then the soft sound of the carpet, back and forth, and the occasional sniff from Señora Anna. Finally Paco spoke.

'Okay, you're right,' he said sadly.

'Who?' sobbed Anna.

'No one you know, I can assure you.'

'Why?' Soledad heard Anna get to her feet. She then heard the sharp tapping of her heels, as she must have walked across the floorboards to the window. Once again there was a tense moment of silence.

'A man needs to be loved, Anna.' He sighed wearily.

'But we loved each other, didn't we? At the beginning?'

'We did. I don't know what went wrong. You changed.'

'*I* changed?' she retorted severely. '*I* changed? I suppose then all this is *my* fault? I drove you into her arms, did I?'

'I'm not saying that.'

'Then what are you saying? You changed too, you know!'

'Anna, I'm not saying it's your fault. We're both to blame. I'm not excusing myself. You wanted to know.'

'I want to know why.'

'But I don't know why. I fell in love with her. She loves me back. You stopped responding to me years ago, what do you expect?'

'I suppose you're going to tell me that this is some sick Argentine custom, husbands taking mistresses when they get bored with their wives.'

'Anna.'

'Well, then it's exclusive to your family, is it? It's in the blood,' she snapped scornfully.

'What are you talking about?' he replied slowly. Soledad noticed the tone of his voice change; it descended a note.

'Your father and his . . . mistress.' She was about to say 'whore', but instinct cautioned her against going too far.

'Don't bring my father into this. This is about you and me, it's got nothing to do with Papa.' Paco was stunned, wondering how exactly she knew.

'I just hope you don't teach Rafael and Agustin to do the same. I don't want them breaking hearts the way you do.'

'I can't talk to you when you're like this,' he said, exasperated. Soledad heard him making his way towards her and turning swiftly she scuttled across the hall. But he strode out and slammed the door behind him before she had time to disappear.

'Soledad,' he said sternly. Blushing deeply she bowed her head and turned to face him. This is the end, she thought. Why was I so stupid? She would have to pack her bags and leave. She sniffed miserably. 'Bring Sofia to me,' he ordered. Soledad shuffled over without meeting his eyes.

'My dear Sofia,' he said in a soft, honey voice as he kissed his daughter's hot forehead. She seemed to respond to his touch even in sleep. 'You love me, don't you? And I love you, you don't know how much,' he whispered.

Soledad noticed his face had transformed into an expression of tenderness; she noticed too that his eyes glistened. She stood there while he stroked his daughter's face, feeling awkward, awaiting his reproof. But none came. He caressed the child's cheek, then, picking up his coat, he made for the door.

'Are you going out?' she heard herself ask, then wished she hadn't; it was none of her business.

Paco turned to her and nodded gravely. 'I won't be back for supper – and Soledad?'

'*Sí*, Señor Paco?'

'What you have heard this evening must not be mentioned to anybody, do you understand?'

'*Sí*, Señor Paco,' she replied emphatically, flushing guiltily.

'Good,' he said, and he closed the door quietly behind him.

Soledad glanced at the sitting-room door before making her way through the kitchen to her quarters. She knew she shouldn't have been eavesdropping, but once she had recovered from the shock she began to piece together their conversation. So, Señor Paco was having an affair, she thought to herself. It didn't surprise her. Most men took lovers every now and then, and why shouldn't they? However, this didn't seem to be about sexual gratification, but about love. If Señor Paco had stopped loving Señora Anna then that *was* serious. She felt desperately sorry for her mistress. She felt sad for both of them.

Anna remained in the sitting room, slumped into an armchair, too weary and miserable to move. She wondered what to do next. Paco had admitted to having an affair but he hadn't suggested he'd stop seeing the other woman. She had heard him leave. Running straight back to *her*, whoever she was. She didn't want to know. She didn't trust herself. She'd be quite capable of rushing over and stabbing her in a fit of anger and despair. She thought of Aunt Dorothy. This was probably a penance for jilting Sean O'Mara. Maybe her aunt had been right all along, perhaps she would have been happier if she had married him and never left Glengariff.

The weeks that passed were bleak and unhappy. Paco and Anna didn't discuss the matter again and nothing seemed to have changed, only the water froze over and communication ceased altogether. Anna watched Paco's relationship with Sofia with bitterness. Every caress wounded her; it might just as well have been her daughter who was the other woman in his life. He spent more time with her than he did with his wife and he enveloped her with love that had once been hers, shutting Anna out completely. Anna spent her time with her sons, soaking up their affection like a plant in the desert. She found it hard to love Sofia, who was somehow connected to Paco and her misery. The child even took to whining when she was in her mother's arms as if she sensed the ill-feeling there, whereas she warmed to her father's embrace, shamelessly grinning as if to say, 'I love him and not you.' Anna could barely watch without hurting inside.

Anna thought she had never felt such unhappiness. Earlier that year, her father had sent her a telegram telling her that her mother had died. When he had arrived at her door she had tried to find her mother's love in her father's embrace but he too had been swallowed up by the little enchantress that Sofia had become. They were strangers. The bond that had once sealed their love for each other had been worn apart by the years of estrangement.

She missed her mother more than her father, whom she watched roam about the farm like a lost dog. She remembered Emer's mellow laughter and the light in her gentle eyes. She remembered the smell of soap and lavender that enveloped her like an ethereal cloud and in her mind she raised her mother onto a pedestal that she had never been close to in life. She didn't recall the woman whose sad old face had melted into a river of tears that autumn evening they had embraced for the last time. The mother she needed right now was the woman who had dried her tears when her cousins had teased her in Glengariff, the mother who would have stopped the world from turning had it put a smile on her daughter's face. She missed her mother's unconditional love. As a grown-up, love had become so hard to keep.

Anna allowed Soledad to assert herself more in the nursery with young Sofia. The boys were now five and seven and at school, so she found she had more time on her hands. She needed more time to herself. Anyway, she thought, Sofia is perfectly happy with Soledad. Anna took to painting and built a small studio out of one of the spare rooms in their apartment in Buenos Aires. She wasn't very good, she could see that. But it was a distraction from domestic life and allowed her to spend time on her own without questions. Paco never entered her studio. It was her sanctuary, a place she could call her own, a place she could hide in.

Paco was deeply hurt that his wife had found it necessary to mention his father's affair with Clara Mendoza. It didn't surprise him so much that she knew, for at the time many people had known, but it surprised him that she could stoop low enough to use it as a weapon to hurt him. He watched her warily and asked himself whether their romance in London all those years ago had really happened at all. It was as if he had fallen in love with a sweet young woman and had brought a bitter one back to Argentina with him by mistake. He imagined the *Ana Melodía* of his memories sitting forlornly beside the fountain in Trafalgar Square and wondered whether she was still there. His heart ached for her. He still loved her.

One day in mid-spring, Anna was out walking over the plains with Agustin. It was very warm and the wildflowers were beginning to burst open and paint the *pampa* with colour. To their delight they spotted a couple of young *vizcachas* sniffing each other in the sun, their furry brown backs glistening in the light. Anna sat down among the long grasses and pulled her five-year-old son onto her knee.

'Look, darling,' she said in English. 'Can you see the rabbits?'

'They're kissing each other,' he said.

'We have to be quiet and still, or we'll frighten them away.' They sat and watched the creatures jump around playfully, every now and then looking about them as if they sensed they were being watched.

'You don't kiss Papa any more,' said Agustin suddenly. 'Don't you like him any more?'

Anna was stunned by the question and troubled by the anxious tone in his voice.

'Of course I do,' she replied emphatically.

'You're always fighting and shouting at each other. I don't like it,' he said and suddenly began to sob.

'Look, you've frightened away the rabbits,' she said, trying to distract him.

'I don't care. I don't want to see the rabbits any more!' he cried. Anna held him closely and tried to reassure him.

'Papa and I sometimes fight, like you and Rafael, or you and Sebastian. Do you remember that fight you had with Sebastian?' The child nodded slowly.

'Well, it's nothing more than a small fight.'

'But Sebastian and I are friends again now. You and Papa are still fighting.'

'We'll make up, you'll see. I promise, we'll make up. Now, dry yer tears and let's see if we can spot an armadillo to tell Grandpa,' she said, gently drying his face with her shirt sleeve.

As they walked back to the house she decided she simply couldn't live like this. It was unbearable for her, it was unbearable for the family. It wasn't fair that their misery should filter down to their children. She looked at Agustin's now smiling face and knew she couldn't disappoint him.

As she approached the house Soledad came running out, her face wet with tears. Oh God, thought Anna in panic, gripping Agustin's small hand. Not Rafael, please not Rafael.

'What is it?' she asked hoarsely as her maid approached, white with anguish.

'Señora Maria Elena!' gasped Soledad.

Anna burst into tears with relief. 'What's happened?' she sobbed.

'She's dead. Señora Maria Elena is dead.'

'Dead? Good God! Where is my husband? Where is Paco?' she asked.

'At Señor Miguel's house, Señora.'

Anna handed Agustin over to Soledad and ran through the trees to Miguel and Chiquita's house. On entering she found the whole family together in the sitting room. Her eyes searched through the crowd for Paco. But she couldn't see him for people. Chiquita saw her and walked hastily over to meet her. Her face was swollen from crying.

'Where is Paco?' Anna asked croakily.

'On the terrace with Miguel,' she replied, pointing to the French doors. Anna squeezed past her relations whose miserable faces were now no more than a blur, until she reached the doors to the terrace. She peered through the glass and saw Paco talking to Miguel. He had his back to her, so he didn't see her approach. Miguel acknowledged her sadly before tactfully retreating back inside. Paco turned to see his wife's pale face looking at him plaintively.

'Oh, Paco. I'm so sorry,' she said and felt the tears spilling onto her cheeks. He looked at her coldly. 'How did it happen?'

'A car crash, she was on her way down here. Hit by a truck,' he replied flatly.

'I can't bear it. Poor Hector, where is he?'

'At the hospital.'

'He must be devastated.'

'He is. We all are,' he said, averting his eyes.

'Paco, please.'

'What do you want me to do?' he asked impassively.

Anna gulped back a sob. 'Let me in,' she said.

'Why?'

'I want to comfort you.'

'You want to comfort me,' he repeated as if he didn't believe her.

'Yes. I know how you must be feeling.'

'You don't know how I'm feeling,' he replied scornfully.

'You're the one who's having an affair, I'm prepared to overlook that. Forget it. Make a new start.'

Paco looked at her and frowned. 'Because my mother's died?' he said.

'No, because I still care about you,' she replied anxiously, blinking at him.

'Well, I'm not prepared to forget what you said about my father,' he retorted angrily.

She looked up at him, stunned. 'Your father? What did I say about Hector? I love Hector.'

'How could you stoop so low as to throw his affair at me as if it's some family tradition?' he said bitterly.

'Oh Paco. I only said that to hurt you.'

'Well, you succeeded. Are you happy now?'

'Agustin asked me why I don't like you any more,' she said softly. 'His little face was pale with fear. I didn't know what to say. Then I thought about it. I *do* like you. I've just forgotten how to love you.'

Paco looked into her watery blue eyes that shone with self-pity and his heart softened. 'I've forgotten how to love you too,' he said. 'I'm not proud of myself.'

'Can't we try and repair the damage? It's not all gone, is it? Can't we wander down those London streets again and recapture that magic? Can't we remember?' she said and her pale lips quivered.

'I'm sorry, Anna,' he said, shaking his head. 'I'm sorry I hurt you.'

'And I'm sorry I hurt you too,' she said and smiled weakly. She gazed at him with solicitous eyes.

'Come here, *Ana Melodía*. You're right, I do need your comfort,' he said and slowly pulled her into his arms.

'Is it over?' she said after a while. 'Can we try again?'

'It's dead,' he told her and kissed her forehead with a tenderness she thought she'd never experience again. 'I never stopped loving you, *Ana Melodía*. I just lost you, that's all.'

Maria Elena was buried in the family tomb in town after a sad and stirring service in the church of *Nuestra Señora de la Asunción*. She had been loved by everyone. In fact, there weren't enough seats in the church to accommodate the large number of people who wanted to come to pay their respects so the townspeople had to spill out into the square. Fortunately it was warm and the sun shone down brazenly as if no one had told it that Maria Elena had died.

Anna watched Paco's hands shake as he read the lesson and found herself crying all over again. She thanked God that He had made it possible for them to love each other once more. She traced her eyes over the icons beside the altar and found comfort in them. If I was deeply unhappy, she thought, this church and the good Lord would be where I would go for consolation. When it was Miguel's turn to read she noticed Chiquita wilt like a flower. It had been a terrible shock for everyone, but no one suffered as much as Hector. He seemed to age in a matter of hours, literally melt away in front of their very eyes. He was inconsolable. The strength was sapped out of him. The grief corroded his life like a waterfall of pain, battering his nerves and the canyon that had become his broken heart. He died a year later.

In the years that followed, Anna and Paco's lives returned to normal. They watched their children grow and delighted in them as parents should. They talked to each other again, but they never found London in the Argentina they built together. Paco had given up his mistress, Anna tried hard to be a good wife, but the roots of their problems remained even though the tree looked stronger.

Chapter Twelve

Santa Catalina, 1973

It was late when Sofia crept into her grandfather's room. The winter moonlight dusted the darkness with a pale blue light as she stopped at the end of his bed and looked down at him. He was snoring loudly, but to Sofia there was something comforting about the noise he made. It reminded her of her childhood, making her feel cherished and secure. She could smell the sweet remains of his pipe, embedded in the curtains and furniture after many a puff. The window was open and the wind rattled along to the rhythmic rise and fall of his breathing.

Sofia did not want to wake him, but she wanted him to wake up. She knew she shouldn't be in his room in the middle of the night; her mother would disapprove if she found out. Anna had been horrid to Sofia that day. She didn't like it when her father indulged her daughter. She accused Dermot of spoiling the girl and did her best to overrule him. But Grandpa O'Dwyer had promised Sofia a leather belt with a silver buckle carved with her initials. Anna had said he was wasting his money, that Sofia wouldn't appreciate it. She said that Sofia never looked after her things. Threw them on the floor expecting Soledad to pick them up and tidy them away.

If he _had_ to buy her anything at all, it should be something sensible – like literature, or piano music. Paco had inherited his mother's piano; Sofia barely used it. It was time the girl put her mind to something, finished something. She had no concentration: she started projects and then lost interest. Yes, Anna decided, studying the piano would be better for her than spending all her time up that ridiculous tree. All young ladies of her class should paint and play music, read good English literature and know how to run a household. Girls shouldn't spend all day riding ponies and climbing trees.

'Encourage her to do something sensible, Dad,' she suggested. But Grandpa O'Dwyer wanted to buy Sofia a belt just like he'd promised.

That was why Sofia was in his room. She wanted to tell him that she would love his belt and look after it, because she loved him and it would always remind her of her dear grandfather. Her mother had never understood her fondness for her grandfather, but Sofia and Dermot had a deep affection for one another that united them in an unspoken bond.

She shuffled awkwardly. Coughed. Shuffled again. Finally, Dermot O'Dwyer rolled his big frame onto his back. He narrowed his eyes, believing Sofia to be a leprechaun or some ghoul and put a hand up in alarm.

'It's me, Grandpa – Sofia,' she whispered.

'Jesus, Mary and Joseph, girl. What are you doing, standing at the end of my bed? Are you my guardian angel watching over me while I sleep?'

'I think you've scared your guardian angel away with your snoring,' she laughed quietly.

'What are you doing, Sofia Melody?'

'I want to talk to you,' she said and shuffled her feet again.

'Well, don't stand there, girl. You know the floor is full o' crocodiles waiting to eat yer feet. Get into bed.'

So Sofia climbed into bed with her grandfather – another thing her mother would strongly disapprove of. At seventeen years old she shouldn't be getting into bed with an old man. They lay side by side 'like a pair o' statues on a tomb'. She felt his body next to hers and was suddenly overcome with affection for him.

'What d'you want to talk about, Sofia Melody?' he asked.

'Why do you always call me that?'

'Well, yer grandmother was called Emer Melody. When yer mother was born I wanted to call her Melody but yer grandmother wouldn't hear of it. She could be right stubborn when she wanted to be. So we called her Anna Melody O'Dwyer. Melody being like a middle name.'

'Like Maria Elena Solanas.'

'Exactly like Maria Elena Solanas, God rest her soul.'

'But my middle name is Emer, not Melody.'

'You'll always be Sofia Melody to me.'

'I like it.'

'You have to like it. That's the way it is.'

'Grandpa?'

'Yes?'

'You know the belt?'

'I do.'

'Well, Mama says I won't look after it. But I will. I promise I will.'

'Yer mother's not always right about everything. I know you'll look after it.'

'So can I have it?'

He squeezed her hand and let out a wheezy laugh. 'You can have it, Sofia Melody.'

They lay there staring up at the shadows that danced on the ceiling as the cold winter wind blew in through the curtains and skipped across their hot faces with icy feet.

'Grandpa?'

'What now?'

'I want the belt for sentimental reasons,' she said shyly.

'For sentimental reasons, eh?'

'Because I love you, Grandpa.' She had never said that to anyone before. He lay in silence a moment, moved. She blinked into the darkness wondering how he would respond to this sudden outburst.

'I love you too, Sofia Melody. I love the bones of you. You better go off to sleep now,' he said quietly, his voice faltering mid-sentence. Sofia was the only person who had the power to rock his sentimental old heart.

'Can I stay?'

'As long as yer mother doesn't find you,' he whispered.

'Oh, I'm up long before her.'

Sofia awoke feeling cold. A shiver ran right the way down from her head to the end of her big toe. She wriggled closer to her grandfather for warmth. It took a moment before she realised that it was he who was making her cold. He was as cold and stiff as a dead fish. She sat up and looked down at his bristly face. His expression was one of joy. If he hadn't been cold and stiff she'd have thought he was about to burst into one of his wheezy chuckles. But his face was like a mask; there was nothing behind it and his eyes were open, staring vacantly up into nowhere.

She pressed her hot face next to his and pulled it against her. Fat tears tumbled down her cheeks, bouncing off her nose onto his, until her whole body shook with violent sobs. She had never felt such misery. He was gone. But where? Was there a heaven? Was he now with Emer Melody in some beautiful place? Why did he die? He was healthy and full of life. No one had been more alive than her grandfather. She rocked back and forth, cradling his big frame in her arms, until her jaw ached and her stomach hurt from crying. Panic seized her as she tried to recall the last words he had said to her. The belt, they had talked about the belt. Then she had told him she loved him. She wailed at the recollection of that tender moment. Once she had started to wail she was unable to stop herself, until her wailing woke everyone in the house. At first Paco thought it was an animal being killed outside his window by a vicious prairie dog. But then he recognised the voice of his own daughter as she choked on her breath before letting out another loud cry.

As her brothers, Rafael and Agustin, and her mother and father ran to her aid she remembered his last words. 'As long as yer mother doesn't find you.' He had always been her accomplice.

They had to prise him from her. She then clung to her father. The shock of finding her grandfather dead suddenly hit her like the slap of a cold hand and she shivered uncontrollably. Anna allowed the tears to flow freely. She sat on the edge of the bed and ran her thin hand over his brow. Taking off the gold cross that hung about her neck she pressed it to his lips.

'God keep you, Father, and bless you. May He grant you entry into the Kingdom of Heaven.' Then looking up at her family she asked to be given time alone with him. Rafael and Agustin shuffled out. Paco kissed his daughter's forehead before leading her gently away.

Anna Melody O'Dwyer drew her father's lifeless hand to her face and kissed it sadly. Pressing her lips into his rubber palm she cried not for the corpse that lay inert before her, but for the father she had known growing up in Glengariff. There had been a time when she had shared his heart with her mother, before Sofia had crept in there like a cuckoo and squeezed her out. He had probably never forgiven her for leaving Ireland to marry Paco all those years ago, or at least for never returning — not even once.

Having lost her he had replaced her in his affections with his granddaughter who seemed to combine all that he had loved in Anna with all that was lovable in Sofia as a unique human being. She had seen it; first in Paco and then in her father. Sofia had stolen them both. But she didn't ask herself why because she was afraid of the answer. Afraid to admit that maybe Paco had been right. Perhaps she *had* changed. How else was it that she had managed to alienate the two men she loved more than anyone else in the whole world?

But instead of reflecting on herself, Anna gazed down at all that was left of a cantankerous old man and searched his features for the father she had lost somewhere over the years. And now it was too late to reclaim him. Too late. She remembered her mother telling her once that the two saddest words in the dictionary were 'too late'. Now she understood. If he would only breathe again she would show him how much she loved him. In spite of the years that had corroded the ties that had bound them, in spite of life that had somehow forced a wedge between them, she really had loved him with all her heart, and yet she had never told him. He had been more of a nuisance to her, like an untrainable, mangy dog that she had found herself constantly apologising for. Yet he had been a tormented soul, happier descending into madness than facing the reality of a life without the warm love of his wife. His madness had been an anaesthetic to numb him against his growing desolation. If only she had taken the time to understand him. To understand his pain. 'Oh God,' she prayed, squeezing her eyes closed, releasing a glistening tear that caught on her long pale eyelashes, 'just let me tell him that I loved him.'

To show how much she had loved him, Anna organised for him to be buried on the plain, among the ponies and birds, in the long wild grass under a crooked eucalyptus tree. Antonio and the boys from the stables helped dig the hole and Padre Julio stammered a few prayers and gave an agonising address beneath the bleak winter sky. But his stammer had always amused Grandpa O'Dwyer, so in a way it was fitting.

The whole family had come to pay their respects. With bowed heads they mumbled the prayers and with downcast faces watched as the coffin was lowered unsteadily into the ground. As the last of the earth was patted down, the clouds suddenly parted and a bright ray of sunshine burst forth, flooding the early winter plains with a strange warmth. They all looked up in surprise and delight. Anna crossed herself and thanked God for delivering her father to Heaven. Sofia watched the light with a heavy heart and thought how dark the world had suddenly become. Without Grandpa O'Dwyer even the sunshine seemed muted.

Chapter Thirteen

Brown University, 1973

Santi ran a hand up the inside of Georgia's dress to discover she was wearing stockings. He felt the rough lace with his fingers and then the smooth, silky skin of her thigh. His heartbeat quickened with anticipation. He pressed his mouth to hers and tasted the sweet peppermint of the packet of gum they had shared when they had left the dance together. He had been impressed by her forwardness. She lacked the inhibition of well-bred Argentine girls and there was a coarseness about her which he found appealing.

Her kiss was eager. She seemed to relish his strong young body, clawing his skin with her long red nails, licking the salt that mingled with his own scent. She smelt of expensive perfume and he could taste the powder on her skin when he ran his tongue down her body. Her belly was round and plump. When he fiddled with her suspender belt she coolly pushed him away saying in her deep, chocolate voice that she preferred to make love with her stockings on, and proceeded to slip out of her black panties.

He opened her legs, which she then voluntarily opened even wider and he knelt between them, smoothing his hands over her hips and thighs. She was blonde, a natural blonde he noticed, looking at the tidy triangle of hair that revealed to him her charms.

She watched him with brazen eyes, enjoying him admiring her. For the next two hours she showed him how to caress a woman, slowly and sensually, and gave him more enjoyment than he thought possible. By two in the morning he had come enough times to prove that Georgia really was a fantasy of the bedroom, and she had come with the ease of a woman comfortable with her own body.

'Georgia,' he said, 'you're not for real. I want to hold you all night to ensure you'll still be here in the morning.' She had laughed, lit a cigarette and promised him they would do nothing for the whole weekend except make love. 'Long, slow and passionate, right here in Hope Street,' she had said. She told him how much she loved his accent and made him talk to her in Spanish. 'Tell me you want me, that you love me – let's just pretend,' she said. So he told her, *'Te quiero, te necesito, te adoro.'*

When they were spent, their bodies aching from their pleasure, they slept. The lights of the occasional car bathed them momentarily in gold, exposing naked limbs that were limply draped over each other. Santi dreamed. He was in the Ancient History class with Professor Schwartzbach and there was Sofia. She sat with her long dark hair tied into her usual plait, knotted with a silky red ribbon. She was wearing jeans and a lilac shirt which enhanced her glowing tan. She looked beautiful, smooth, dark and glossy. She turned to him and winked, her mahogany brown eyes smiling capriciously at him. Then suddenly she was Georgia, sitting naked, grinning at him. He was embarrassed that she was naked in front of the whole class, but she didn't seem to mind. She gazed at him sleepily. He longed for Sofia to come back, but she had gone. When he awoke, Georgia was between his legs. He looked down at her to make sure that it was Georgia and not Sofia. His body relaxed when he saw her lustful blue eyes looking up at him.

'Honey, you look like you've seen a ghost,' she laughed.

'I have,' he replied and allowed himself to drift on the sensual sensation of her tongue working its magic on him again.

Santi had spent the first six months of his two years abroad travelling extensively around the world with his friend Joaquin Barnaba. They went to Thailand where they trawled the red-light district in search of entertainment and whores. Santi had been appalled as well as fascinated by the things women could do with their bodies, things that he wouldn't have been able to invent even in his most lurid dreams. They smoked cannabis in the Cameron Highlands of Malaysia and watched a sunset that turned the hills to gold. They travelled to China where they walked along the Great Wall, admired the Hall of Supreme Harmony in the Forbidden City and discovered to their disgust that the Chinese really do eat dogs. They backpacked their way through India where Joaquin vomited outside the Taj Mahal before spending three days in bed with dehydration and diarrhoea. They rode elephants in India, camels in Africa and beautiful white horses in Spain.

Santi sent postcards back to his family from each country he visited. Chiquita despaired that she was unable to contact him. For six whole months he was in places where they could not reach him, and moving on every few days without knowing where he was going. They were all relieved when at the end of the winter they received word that he was in Rhode Island finding a place to live and registering for his courses, which included Business Studies and Ancient History.

For the first few days at Brown, Santi stayed in a hotel. However, when he attended his first lecture on campus he met a couple of affable Americans from Boston who were looking for someone to share their house in Bowen Street. By the end of the lecture, given by an ancient professor with a small mouth hidden behind a thick white beard and an even smaller voice that gobbled up the ends of his words, they had discovered almost everything there was to know about each other and had become the best of friends.

Frank Stanford was short but strong, with broad shoulders and well-defined muscles, the sort of young man who made up for his lack of height by working out in a gym to ensure he was as toned as possible and by endlessly practising games such as tennis, golf and polo so the girls would overlook his stature and admire him for his accomplishments. He was immediately impressed with Santi, not only because he came from Argentina, which was in itself immensely glamorous, but because he played polo and no one played better polo than the Argentines.

Frank and his friend Stanley Norman, who preferred to sit in a corner smoking cannabis and strumming his guitar to throwing around a tennis racket or polo mallet, invited Santi back to Bowen Street to show him their house. Santi was impressed. It was typical American East Coast with tall sash windows and imperious porch in a street lined with leafy trees and elegant cars. Inside, it was immaculately decorated with newly painted walls, pine furniture and navy blue and white upholstery in stripes and checks.

'My mom insisted she do it up for me,' said Frank casually. 'She's one of those mothers who's vastly overprotective. As if I'd mind. I mean, look at the place – it should be in a magazine. I bet it's the grandest house in the street.'

'We don't have house rules, do we, Frank?' Stanley asked in his slow Boston drawl. 'We don't mind chicks.'

'Yeah, we don't mind, we only request you bring back her sisters if they're cute. Know what I mean?' Frank winked at Stanley and chortled.

'I imagine they're cute here,' said Santi.

'With your accent, buddy, you won't have any problems. They'll love you,' Stanley assured him.

He wasn't wrong. Santi was chased by the best-looking girls on campus and it didn't take him long to realise that they didn't want to marry him, they just wanted to sleep with him. In Argentina it was different. You simply couldn't sleep around; women demanded more respect. They wanted to be courted and they wanted to get married. But at Brown Santi made his way through them like a strawberry picker. Some he put in a basket to keep for later and others he ate straight away. In September and October he spent weekends with Frank and his family at Newport where they played tennis and polo. Santi became a hero with Frank's younger brothers who had never seen a real Argentine polo player before and was worshipped by Josephine Stanford, Frank's mother, who had seen many Argentine polo players before, but none so handsome.

'So, Santi – that's short for Santiago, isn't it?' said Josephine, handing him a glass of Coke and wiping her face with a white towel. They had just completed their third set of tennis against Frank and his younger sister Maddy. Santi nodded. 'Frank tells me you're just doing a one-year course, is that right?'

'That's right. I finish in May,' he replied, sitting down on one of the garden chairs and stretching his long brown legs out in front of him. His white shorts accentuated the rich honey colour of his skin and Josephine tried not to allow her eyes to linger there.

'You go back to Argentina after that?' she asked, attempting to ask mother-type questions. She sat down opposite Santi and smoothed her short white tennis skirt over her thighs with elegant fingers.

'No, I'm going to travel a bit, then return home at the end of the year.'

'Oh, that'll be nice. Then you start all over again in Buenos Aires.' She sighed. 'I don't know why you don't just do the university thing over here.'

'I don't want to be away from Argentina for too long,' he told her earnestly. 'I'd miss it.'

'That's nice.' She smiled sweetly. 'Do you have a girlfriend back home? I'll bet you do.' She laughed, winking at him flirtatiously.

'No, I don't,' he replied, putting his lips to the glass and draining it thirstily.

'Well, I am surprised at you, Santi. A handsome boy like you. Still, better for my American sisters, I suppose.'

'Santi's a bit of a hero on campus, Mom. I don't know what it is about Latin men, but girls go mad for him,' Frank joked. 'I have second choice – crumbs from the rich man's table.'

'Bullshit, Frank. Don't believe him, Mrs Stanford,' said Santi, embarrassed.

'Please, call me Josephine. Mrs Stanford makes me feel like a schoolmistress and I wouldn't want to be one of those. Goodness no.' She dabbed her blushing face with the towel again. 'Where's Maddy? Maddy!'

'Here, Mom, just getting myself a drink. Do you want anything, Santi?' she asked.

'Another glass of Coca Cola would be good. Thank you.'

Maddy was dark-haired and very plain, having inherited her father's somewhat unfortunate looks instead of her mother's thick auburn hair, golden skin and bewitching vixen face. Maddy had a large nose, small puffy eyes, which looked like she had only just woken up, and the sallow, pimply skin of a teenager living off fast food and sweet drinks. Josephine would have liked to encourage Santi to take her daughter out, but she was wise enough to recognise that her Maddy wasn't pretty enough or interesting enough for Santi. Oh, if I were only twenty years younger, she thought to herself, I'd take him upstairs and drain him of all that excess energy. Santi watched Josephine through narrowed eyes and wished she wasn't the mother of his best friend. He didn't care how old she was. He knew she'd be fantastic in bed.

'So, Santi. What about introducing my Frank to a nice Argentine girl. You have sisters, don't you?' asked Josephine, crossing one long white leg over the other.

'I have one, but she wouldn't really be Frank's type. She's not smart enough for him.'

'Cousins then. I'm determined to have you in our family somehow, Santi,' she giggled.

'I have a cousin called Sofia. Now she would be better.'

'What's she like?'

'Spirited, difficult, spoilt, but very beautiful and would play polo better than him.'

'Now that's a chick I'd like to meet,' Frank said. 'How tall is she?'

'Oh, about your height. She's not especially tall, but she's got charisma and charm, and she always gets what she wants. You'd have your hands full with her, that's for sure,' he said proudly, conjuring up Sofia's defiant face and remembering it fondly.

'What a babe! When can I meet her?'

'You'll have to come out to Argentina. She's still at school,' Santi told him.

'Do you have a picture?'

'Back at Bowen Street, I do.'

'Well, I think it's worth a trip just to see her. I like the sound of . . . what did you say her name was?'

'Sofia.'

'Sofia. I like the sound of Sofia.' He mused. 'Is she easy?'

'Easy?'

'Would she sleep with me?'

'Frank, darling, not in front of your mother,' chided Josephine, waving her hand in front of her as if to clear the air of his foul words.

'Well, would she?' he persisted, ignoring his mother who was just showing off to his new friend.

'No, she wouldn't,' Santi replied, feeling uncomfortable talking about Sofia in this way.

'I bet she would with a little persuasion. You Latins might have the charm but we have the persistence.' He chuckled. Santi didn't like the competitive look in his eyes and wished he hadn't mentioned Sofia.

'Actually, I know a girl who would be much better for you,' he said, backtracking frantically.

'Oh no. I like the sound of Sofia very much,' insisted Frank.

When Maddy returned with another glass of Coke, Santi sipped at it unenthusiastically. He suddenly felt very protective of his cousin and wondered how he was going to stop Frank from flying out to meet her. It was just the sort of thing Frank would do. He was rich enough to go anywhere and bold enough to try anything.

Once back at university he found another letter from Sofia in the mailbox. She had written every week as she had promised.

'Who's that from?' asked Stanley curiously. 'You get more letters than the post office.' He was strumming a Bob Dylan tune on his guitar.

'My cousin.'

'That wouldn't be from my Sofia, would it?' said Frank, emerging from the kitchen with a couple of bagels and smoked salmon for tea.

'I didn't think you were back,' said Santi.

'I'm back. D'you want some, they're good?' he said, chewing on a bagel.

'No, thanks. I'm going to read this upstairs. Mama's letters tend to be long.'

'I thought you said it was from your cousin,' said Frank.

'Oh, did I? I meant my mother.' He wondered why he was lying over such a trivial matter. Frank would soon forget about Sofia with all the girls at Brown.

'Hey, Jonathan Sackville is throwing a party tonight. Want to come?' said Frank.

'Sure,' replied Stanley.

'Sure,' replied Santi, retreating into the hall.

Once upstairs in the privacy of his room he read Sofia's letter.

Dearest favourite Cousin Santi,

Thank you for your last letter, though it has not escaped my notice that your letters are getting shorter and shorter. This is not on. I deserve more. After all, I'm writing very long ones myself and I'm busier than you are — remember, you don't have a mother like mine, forcing you to study all the time. I'm well, I suppose. Yesterday was Papa's birthday so we all had dinner at Miguel's house. It's so hot, you cannot imagine. Agustin actually hit me last week. We had a row about something. He started it, of course, but guess who got the blame? So I threw his entire wardrobe in the pool, even his prized leather boots and mallets. You would have laughed had you seen his face. I had to hide with Maria as I really thought he was going to kill me. Would you miss me, Santi? Oops, must go, Mama's coming up the stairs and she looks very angry. What do you think I've done now? I'll leave you guessing and tell you in my next letter. If you don't write soon, I won't tell you and I know you're dying to know.

    A big kiss,
    Sofia.

Santi chuckled as he read her letter. When he folded it away in his drawer with her other letters and those from his parents and Maria he felt a faint twinge of homesickness. But it only lasted a second before it was smothered by the thought Jonathan Sackville's party.

Jonathan Sackville lived a few blocks away from Bowen Street in Hope Street and was renowned on campus for giving the best parties with the prettiest girls. Santi didn't really feel like going, his spirits were unusually low, but he knew it was better than sitting around moping over letters from home. So he showered and dressed.

When Santi, Frank and Stanley arrived at the house Jonathan was standing in the doorway with an arm around two simmering redheads, swigging from a bottle of vodka.

'Welcome, my friends. The party's only beginning,' he slurred. 'Go on in.'

The house was vast and literally throbbing with loud music and the feet of about 150 people. They had to squeeze their way down the corridor to get to where the drinks were, through a crowd of people packed so closely together they resembled a buzzing hive of bees, jostling against each other and shouting above the music.

'Hey, Joey!' exclaimed Frank. 'Santi, you know Joey?'

'Hi, Joey,' Santi said flatly.

'Hey, Joey! What's up? Where's the beautiful Caroline?' Frank asked, looking over Joey's shoulder for his sister.

'Dive in if you dare, Frank. She's in there somewhere.'

'I'm going in, guys. Don't wait up!'

Santi watched Frank disappear into the swaying mass of sweaty bodies.

'This is giving me a headache. I'm going home to Dylan and Bowie,' Stanley said. He always sounded spaced-out even when he wasn't. 'Life's not meant to be a roller coaster. This is way too noisy – way, way too noisy. You want to come and chill out with me?'

'Yeah, let's go.' Santi was wishing he had never come. It had been a complete waste of time.

Once outside in the cool October air Santi was able to breathe again. The night was clear and starry, and he was reminded of those sultry summer nights gazing up at the sky from under the ombu tree. He hadn't missed his home once, so why was he suddenly feeling homesick?

'You leaving too?' came a thick voice from behind them. They both turned.

'Yeah, we're leaving. Want to join us?' said Stanley, looking her over and liking what he saw.

'No,' she replied then grinned at Santi.

'Do I know you?' he asked, studying her pale features in the street lights.

'No, but I know you. I've seen you around. You're new.'

'Yes, I am.' He wondered what she wanted. She was wrapped in a short red coat with slim legs half concealed within a pair of shiny leather boots that reached up to her knees. She shivered and stamped her feet.

'The party's too noisy for me. I feel like going someplace quiet and warm.'

'Where do you want to go?'

'Well, I was going home, but I don't want to be alone. Do you want to come and keep me company?' she asked, then smiled disarmingly.

'I gather you're not inviting me,' Stanley said resignedly. 'I'll see you when I see you, Santi.' He wandered off up the street.

'What's your name?' he asked.

'Georgia Miller. I'm in my second year. I've seen you on campus. You're from Argentina, right?'

'Right.'

'You miss it?'

'A little,' he replied truthfully.

'I thought so. You were looking a bit forlorn in there.' She slipped her hand through his arm. 'Why don't you come back to my house? I'll help you forget your home.'

'I'd like that, thank you.'

'Don't thank me, Santi. You're also doing me a favour. I wanted to go to bed with you the first time I saw you.'

Once in the warm light of Georgia's house Santi was able to see her clearly. She wasn't beautiful, her face was long and her sharp blue eyes set too far apart – and yet she was sexy. Her lips were asymmetrical but sensual and when she grinned she did so with only one half of her mouth. She was blessed with a mass of thick blonde curls, which bounced like a cheerleader when she walked, and when she took off her coat Santi felt his loins stir at the sight of her swollen breasts, slim waist and long shapely legs. She had the body of a porn star and she knew it.

'This body gets me into a whole lot of trouble,' she sighed, sensing him watching her. 'What do you want to drink?'

'A whiskey.'

'That bad, eh?'

'What is?'

'Your homesickness.'

'Oh, no it's not really. I'm fine about it.'

'But it gets you sometimes when you least expect it, doesn't it?'

'It does.'

'A letter perhaps, or sometimes a smell or music,' she said wistfully.

'How do you know?'

'Because, Santi, I'm from the South. Can't you tell?'

'The South?' he asked blankly.

'Georgia,' she said.

'Of course. I'm afraid your accent just sounds like everyone else's to me.'

'That's okay, handsome. Your accent doesn't sound like anyone else's to me. In fact, it's the nicest accent I ever heard. So you can talk as long as you wish and I'll just listen and swoon.' She laughed throatily. 'I just want you to know that I understand what it feels like, you don't have to pretend with me. I'm right there with you. Now, here's your whiskey, let's light a fire, put some music on and we'll both forget about our homesickness. Is that a deal?'

'That's a deal,' said Santi, watching her bend down to arrange the logs.

'Forget the fire, Georgia from Georgia, let's go upstairs,' he said suddenly, noticing the lace tops of her stockings and a flash of black panties momentarily revealed beneath her mini-skirt. 'There's only one way to forget about home and that is to lose ourselves in each other,' he added huskily, draining his whiskey glass.

'Well, come on up then. I'm aching to get lost in you,' she replied and taking his hand she led him up the stairs to her bedroom.

Chapter Fourteen

Santa Catalina, December 1973

Chiquita had hardly slept at all. It had been a humid night. She had tossed and turned restlessly in her airless room, listening to the regular snoring of her husband, Miguel, who lay large and hairy by her side. It wasn't due to the humidity, however, that she had found sleep an unattainable luxury that night, nor due to the nightmare that woke little Panchito and sent him crying to her bedside. It was due to the fact that her son Santi was returning home the following day after two years away, studying in America.

He had written often. She had awaited his weekly letters with excitement and read them with joy mixed with sadness for she missed him terribly. She had seen him only once for the spring break back in March. He had proudly shown his parents the campus, his house on Bowen Street where he lived with his two friends and they had driven out to the coast at Newport for a few days to stay with his friend Frank Stanford and his charming family. Miguel was delighted that he even managed to play polo and seemed to play most weekends. He was now nineteen, almost twenty, and seemed to be more of a man than the boy she had waved goodbye to that sultry March evening.

Chiquita and Anna spent many long evenings sitting out on the terrace, looking into the faraway distance, discussing their children in detail. Anna suffered so much from her daughter's outrageous behaviour. She had hoped that with time Sofia would calm down; in fact she felt she had only got worse. She was insolent and rebellious. She answered back and even called her mother names in flashes of temper that seemed to come from nowhere.

At seventeen she was more independent and obnoxious than ever. She was doing badly in her schoolwork, failing everything, coming bottom of the class, except in essays in which she excelled because she could indulge the imaginary world of her dreams. Her teachers lamented her lack of concentration and her deliberate efforts to disrupt the class for everyone else. They didn't know what to do with her either. On weekends at Santa Catalina she'd disappear on horseback and not return for hours. She didn't think to tell her mother where she was going. Often she'd return home after dark, missing her dinner on purpose.

The last straw had been when Anna had found out that Sofia had bribed the chauffeur to take her to San Telmo, the old part of the city, instead of school, where she had spent the best part of a week taking tango lessons with an ancient Spanish sailor called Jesus. Anna wouldn't have found out had the schoolmistress not telephoned to wish Sofia a speedy recovery from glandular fever.

When she confronted Sofia she had simply stated that she had grown out of school and wanted to be a dancer. Paco had laughed and praised her for her initiative. Anna had been furious. But Sofia had become so used to her mother's anger it no longer touched her. She would have to think of another way of controlling her daughter. It didn't help that she was both beautiful and charming; it was due to those qualities that she was allowed to get away with everything. Chiquita tried to explain gently to her sister-in-law that she was very much like her mother. But Anna would shake her red head in despair and hear none of it.

'She's too charming for her own good. She wraps everyone around her little finger – her father especially. He does nothing to back me up. I feel like a monster. I'm the only one who tells her off. She'll end up hating me if I'm not careful,' she said, sighing heavily.

'Perhaps,' Chiquita suggested helpfully, 'if you gave her more rein, more freedom, she wouldn't pull so hard at the bit.'

'Oh Chiquita, you sound just like my father.' Why, she thought, does this family have to bring everything back to horses!

'He was very wise.'

'Sometimes. Most of the time just plain irritating.'

'You miss him, don't you?' ventured Chiquita. She never really spoke to her sister-in-law about her parents. Anna wasn't comfortable talking about Ireland.

'In a way I do. What I miss is not the father who came out to Argentina, but the father I grew up with in Glengariff. Somehow our relationship changed. Maybe I changed, I don't know.' She lowered her eyes. Chiquita watched her face in the warm evening light and thought how incredibly beautiful she was, but how bitter she had become.

'I miss him too,' she said.

'It's partly thanks to him that Sofia is so spoilt. I never spoiled her. Neither Paco nor my father could ever see beyond the charm.'

'That Solanas charm!'

'That cursed Solanas charm!' repeated Anna, then laughed. 'My mother had charm too. Everyone loved her. Poor old Aunt Dorothy was fat and ugly – my mother took all the looks. Aunt Dorothy never married.'

'Whatever happened to her?' asked Chiquita.

'I don't know. I'm ashamed to say we lost touch.'

'Oh.'

'I know it was mean of me, but she was so far away . . .' Her voice trailed off. She felt guilty. She didn't even know if her aunt was dead or alive. She should have tried to find her when Grandpa O'Dwyer died, but she couldn't face it. Better she didn't know. What you don't know doesn't hurt, she thought, brushing the matter aside.

Chiquita longed to ask her about her other aunts and uncles, for she knew she had come from a big family from Grandpa O'Dwyer's stories, but she didn't dare. Instead she brought the subject back to Sofia.

'I'm sure Sofia will grow out of this behaviour. It is just an adolescent phase.'

'I'm not so sure.' Anna couldn't admit it to anyone but she saw more of herself in her daughter than she cared to let on. 'You know, Chiquita, what worries me most about Sofia is that if I do give her more rein as you suggest, she may run completely wild. I don't want the rest of the family to say I have bred a savage.'

Chiquita laughed sympathetically; she wasn't capable of thinking ill of anyone.

'Anna, everyone loves Sofia, she is a free spirit. My Santi and Maria adore her, everyone forgives her everything. It is only in your eyes that she does wrong; in everyone else's she can do no wrong at all. Anyway, what does it matter what other people think?'

'It matters terribly to me. You know what they're like. There's nothing people like more than to gossip.'

'Some people, yes, but they don't matter,' said Chiquita, watching her sister-in-law. After so many years Anna still felt she didn't fit in, she still felt inferior, that's why she worried so much about what other people thought of her children. She so desperately wanted to be proud of them. Their successes reflected on her, as did their failures. She felt compelled to prove her worthiness all the time. She could never relax.

Chiquita wanted to tell her that it simply didn't matter. Class didn't matter. Everyone loved Anna; she was part of the family. They loved her the way she was; her insecurities were part of her, part of the reason they all loved her. At first when she had arrived at Santa Catalina all those years ago they saw her as a gold digger who wanted to marry Paco for his wealth and status. She didn't fit in. But once she had gained her confidence the shy deer turned into a proud tiger who won the respect of everyone.

Chiquita longed to tell Anna that Sofia was rebellious because Anna doted on her sons. She so obviously lived for Rafael and Agustin. If they had behaved as outrageously as Sofia did, Anna would have taken pride in the flamboyance of their characters instead of trying to subdue them with discipline. She would have been delighted to see her own defiance reflected in them and have encouraged them with love. Instead she was jealous of her daughter's place in the family. Jealous that Sofia was such a large presence. Whether she was hated or loved no one could claim indifference. But Chiquita had tried before and her comments served only to draw attention to Anna's feelings of inadequacy. She had learnt not to refer to it.

'Anyway,' sighed Anna to Chiquita's relief, 'enough of Sofia, her ears must be burning and that wouldn't be very good for her at all. Now Rafael and Agustin are different people altogether. I believe Rafael is quietly dating Jasmina Peña – you know, Ignacio Peña's daughter. Now that would be a good match,' said Anna, breathing in through her nose with self-importance. 'He thinks I don't know, but I often hear him on the telephone. Of course I wouldn't mention it to him, he'll tell me in his own good time. He tells me everything, not like his sister who's like a thief in the dark . . .' She caught herself bringing the conversation back to Sofia again. 'You must be so excited that Santiago's coming home,' she said, suppressing the need to complain further about Sofia. 'I can't imagine how you survived Christmas without him.'

Chiquita shook her head forlornly. 'It was terrible. Of course, I tried not to show it for the sake of the others, but you probably noticed. It just wasn't the same. I love it when all of us are together. Anyway, he wanted to go to Thailand and travel around. He's been everywhere. I don't think there's a single continent he hasn't been to in the last year and a half. It's been a wonderful experience. I think you'll notice a big change in him. He's a man now,' she said proudly, recalling the spring break when she had realised that the child he had once been was gone for ever. His voice was low and gravelly, his chin dark with stubble, his eyes deeper due to experience and his physique strong and powerful like his father's. She noticed too that his limp was now barely noticeable. 'I can't believe he is coming home,' she sighed happily.

Santi was due home in the middle of December, in time for the long summer break which lasted from December until March, after which he would start a five-year course at the university in Buenos Aires. He had missed one Christmas, Chiquita had been determined that he should not miss another. She had quietly counted the days, not wanting to wish her life away, but she could hardly help herself living for that day.

On the morning of Saturday 12 December, having not slept at all during the night, she rose with joy in her heart. Opening the curtains the sunshine looked somehow more radiant than normal and the flowers more delicate. She busied herself going over Santi's room again, placing a vase of fresh roses on his bedside table. The house was filled with excitement. Panchito ran around the ranch in a frenzy with his little cousins and the children of the *gauchos* and maids who lived on the farm. Fernando disappeared off on horseback, awaiting his younger brother's return with mixed emotions, sensing the old feelings of jealousy and resentment emerging once again from their long sleep. Miguel had left early for the airport in the Jeep, leaving his wife distraught with impatience to arrange the lunch and Maria, not wanting to get in her mother's way, ran over to Sofia's house the minute she had finished her breakfast.

She found Sofia sitting on the terrace with her family surrounded by cups of tea, *medias lunas* and *buñuelos*.

'*Hola* Maria, *qué hacés?*' she shouted when she saw her cousin approach.

'*Buen día*, Anna, Paco . . .' said Maria, happily bending down to kiss each one.

'Your mother must be so excited,' said Anna, knowing exactly how she'd feel were it Rafael or Agustin returning home.

'Oh, you can't imagine, she didn't sleep a wink last night. She's been into his room a dozen times to make sure it's perfect.'

'Santi won't even notice,' said Agustin, buttering a *media luna* and dipping it into his tea.

'Of course he will, he'll notice everything,' replied Anna enthusiastically. Maria pulled up a chair as Soledad emerged from the kitchen with another cup and saucer.

'Miguel?' asked Paco, without looking up from the newspaper.

'He left early to pick Santi up from the airport.'

'*Bueno*,' he replied, then getting up mumbled that he was off to Alejandro and Malena's house for cocktails.

'Bit early for a drink, eh Papa?'

'At Alejandro and Malena's all day is drink time, Sofia.' And he wandered off, his grey hair glistening in the sunshine.

'So Sofia, I bet you can't wait to see Santi,' enthused Maria, pouring herself a cup of tea. 'I wonder what he's going to look like? Do you think he'll be at all different?'

'If he's grown a beard or anything silly like that I'll kill him,' she replied happily, her eyes sparkling with excitement.

'He won't recognise Panchito, he's so grown up now – he'll soon be playing polo with the big boys.'

'And girls,' added Sofia, glancing over at her mother from under her brow. Sofia knew it displeased Anna to see her daughter race up and down the pitch with the men and she enjoyed tormenting her. Why, when Maria was so dignified and feminine, was Sofia such a boy? Anna simply couldn't understand it. 'Hey, Rafa, the first thing Santi will want to do is play a game,' she said naughtily. 'Shall we get one together for him?'

'You're irritating Mama, Sofia, give her a break,' he responded absentmindedly, engrossed more in the Saturday papers than in the girlie chitter-chatter of his sister and cousin. Anna sighed in a manner that was only ever for Sofia's benefit, a long-suffering sigh with a shaking of her head.

'Sofia, why don't you see how things go. He'll have so much to tell us all,' she suggested tightly. Then, remembering Chiquita's advice, she thought she'd give it a try and added weakly, 'Actually, why shouldn't Santi enjoy a game with you, Sofia? I'm sure he won't want to sit talking to us all afternoon.'

'Really?' Sofia replied slowly. She looked quizzically at her mother, who simply smiled back at her and resumed eating her breakfast. After a while the two girls got up from the table and ran off into the house leaving the adoring Soledad to clean up after them.

Once in Sofia's floral pink room they fell onto the large bed, crumpling the freshly pressed linen spread and kicking their *alpargatas* onto the floor.

'Can you believe that?' crowed Sofia.

'What?'

'Mama – she said she didn't mind me playing polo!' She shrugged her shoulders.

'That's a first.'

'Yes, it is. I wonder why?'

'Don't wonder, Sofia, just enjoy it.'

'I will. Of course it won't last.' She sighed. 'Wait until I tell Santi.'

'How long have we got? Hours!' grumbled Maria, looking at her watch.

'I'm so excited I can hardly contain myself,' enthused Sofia, her well-defined face blushing through her tan. 'What am I going to wear?'

'Well, what have you got?'

'Oh, not much. All my smart things are in Buenos Aires. I always wear jeans or *bombachas del campo*.' She threw the wardrobe doors open. 'See!' The cupboard revealed little more than neatly folded piles of T-shirts and sweaters and rows of hanging denim jeans.

'Right, let's have a rummage,' said Maria helpfully, delving further. 'What are we going for, then? What's the look of the day?'

'Something like you,' Sofia said, after a moment's thought.

Maria was wearing a pretty dress that reached down to her ankles, trimmed with lace and ribbon matching the ribbon in her long dark hair.

'Like *me*?' she replied in astonishment, crinkling up her nose. 'But I've never seen you in a dress like this.'

'Well, there's always a first time. Look, Santi is coming back after two years and I want to wow him.'

'Save your wows for Roberto,' replied Maria with a smile.

Roberto Lobito was tall, bronzed, blond and had enough charm to date anyone he wanted. A close friend of Fernando's he belonged to the Lobito clan of La Paz, the neighbouring *estancia*. Not only did he play a six-goal handicap on the polo field, he was also a crowd-puller. If Roberto Lobito was playing, all the girls on the farm, and most probably the neighbouring farms as well, would crawl out from under their romantic novels to watch him play.

Sofia herself had never been interested. Even when he had chatted her up that time after the *Copa Santa Catalina* or the other time when he had cantered over to her and tapped her on her bottom with his polo mallet, she simply hadn't cared. To Roberto that had made her different from all the other girls who blushed and stammered when he talked to them. There was no challenge in that. Sofia talked to him, joked with him, but he could tell she didn't fancy him and that made the chase all the more exciting.

After her row with Maria, Sofia had thought it a good idea if she dated someone to lure her cousin off the scent. No one else suspected her covert feelings for her cousin except Maria, and the only way to convince her that she had grown out of her childish crush had been to seem passionately in love with someone else. She didn't fancy anyone, so it hadn't really mattered who she chose. Her pride meant that whoever she decided on had to be the best-looking guy around, so she had chosen Roberto Lobito.

It was easy. Instead of saying 'no' and laughing off his advances, she had allowed him to kiss her. It was a disappointment. Not that she had expected the *pampa* to shake, but a tremor would have been good. When his wet mouth had smooched on hers, his tongue playing with her not so enthusiastic tongue, she had pulled away in disgust. She simply couldn't keep this up for too long. But then an idea had come to her. She closed her eyes and let him kiss her again. This time she had imagined it was Santi's lips on hers, his hands around her waist, his chin scratching her skin. It had worked. Suddenly her heartbeat had quickened, her face had flushed and the *pampa* had quivered, almost. Anyhow it had been better than looking at Roberto Lobito's eager face an inch away from hers.

Not a minute of those twenty months had passed when she had not been thinking about Santi and longing for the day of his return. When he had left she had felt her whole world collapse about her. Santa Catalina just wasn't the same without him. As she became Roberto Lobito's girlfriend to the world, in her heart she became Santi's secret lover – although there was a big difference: she never slept with Roberto Lobito. As she grew from a child into a woman she realised that her feelings had also grown into something else, something far more dangerous. She spent hot nights tossing in her large bed blushing at the sensual thoughts that entered her head. She often awoke in the early hours of the morning, her limbs aching with wanting him so much. She would lie frustrated under the sheets not knowing how to relieve herself from this oppressive heat. She knew these thoughts were sinful, but after a while she was so used to them they ceased to frighten her, but comforted her instead. So she indulged them.

At the beginning she felt guilty and it was hard to get Padre Julio's kind but disapproving face out of her thoughts. But after a while Padre Julio found better things to do than watch over Sofia's nocturnal adventures and he disappeared altogether. Telling no one of her desires she guarded them closely, and her secret entertained and diverted her from missing him so much. In her heart she felt close to him even though he was miles away. And his letters, filled with memories of home and details of his new world, kept her going for days.

Sofia pulled out a white sundress and held it up against her.

'What about this one?' she asked. 'Mama bought it for me in an attempt to lure me off the polo field and out of jeans. I've never worn it.'

'Well put it on, let's have a look. Funny, I can't imagine you in a dress,' repeated Maria, frowning apprehensively.

Sofia slipped the white cotton dress over her head, struggling to draw it over her chest and bottom. It was held up by two thin straps and structured to the hips before falling away from the body almost to the ground. In spite of being too tight around the hips it exhibited her small waist and broad, athletic shoulders in a manner that was almost brazen. Her swelling breasts pushed at the bodice without inhibition and gave the impression that with the slightest movement they might tear the material and burst forth. She flicked her long shiny plait out of the back and stood expectantly in front of the mirror.

'Oh Sofia, you look beautiful,' Maria sighed with genuine admiration.

'You think so?' she replied bashfully, turning to see how it looked from the back. She did indeed look lovely, although slightly uncomfortable; not used to wearing a dress she felt a little vulnerable and oddly demure — strange how a change of look seemed to be accompanied by a change of personality, she reflected with amusement. However, she was pleased.

'I can't wear my hair like this, I always have it like this. Can you put it up for me?' she asked, suddenly swept up by the novelty of it all, wanting the change to be total and dramatic. Maria, still stunned by the transformation, sat Sofia at her dressing table and proceeded to pin her long dark locks onto the top of her head.

'Santi won't recognise you,' she laughed, clenching the pins between her teeth.

'Neither will anyone else,' Sofia commented, barely able to breathe in her bodice. She played impatiently with the box of pins and ribbons as they laughed at the thought of everyone's reactions.

The only reaction, however, that Sofia was interested in was that of her favourite cousin whom she hadn't seen for two long and painful years.

Finally the day of his return had arrived and all that waiting and longing now seemed to her to have passed in a moment. Once Maria had pinned up her hair, Sofia took one last look at herself in the mirror before setting off to Chiquita's house to await the arrival of the young hero.

'What are we going to do till midday?' said Maria as they walked through the trees to her house.

'God knows,' shrugged Sofia. 'Perhaps we can help your mother.'

'Help Mama? I can't believe there is anything left for her to do!'

Chiquita was wandering around her flowerbeds tending to the watering in an attempt to keep her impatience at bay. The tables for lunch had been set by Rosa, Encarnacion and Soledad and the drinks were cooling in ice buckets in the shade. As the two girls approached she looked up and smiled broadly. She was a slender, elegant woman with style and good taste that permeated everything she did. At once she recognised the new Sofia and putting down her watering can approached her joyfully.

'Sofia, *mi amor*, I can't believe it is really you. You look fantastic. Your hair suits you so well like that. I imagine Anna must be thrilled you're wearing the dress she bought you. You know we chose it together in Paris.'

'Really? Well, that's why it is so pretty then,' replied Sofia, feeling a lot more confident now that her beloved aunt had approved.

The three of them sat out on the terrace in the shade of two parasols, chatting away about nothing and everything, occasionally glancing at their watches to see how much longer they had to suffer the wait. After a while Anna arrived. In a pale blue dress and sunhat she looked ghostly but beautiful in a pre-Raphaelite sort of way. Paco arrived next with Malena and Alejandro and their children, followed shortly by Fernando, Rafael and Agustin. As soon as her brothers laid eyes on Sofia they couldn't resist but tease her mercilessly.

'Sofia's a girl!' goaded Agustin, looking her up and down in amusement.

'No, really. What gives it away, *boludo!*' she retorted sarcastically and for once her mother, thrilled that at last her daughter looked decent and pretty, silenced them with a sharp lashing of her tongue. The rest of the family arrived in small groups until they all waited together, drinking wine amid the smoke-filled air of the *asado*.

As usual the packs of skinny dogs greedily sniffed the ground around the barbecue. Panchito and his little cousins ran after them squealing each time they managed to pull a tail or pat a furry head without their mothers noticing and sending them in to wash their hands.

Finally, Sofia noticed a small cloud of dust gather in the shimmering distance and slowly approach.

'Hey everyone, there they are!' she announced. 'There they are!' And with that an expectant silence descended upon them all as they turned their attention to the cloud of dust.

Chiquita held her breath, not wanting to bring bad luck by hoping too much, expecting any second for the car to turn the other way and to be disappointed. No one noticed one of the dogs steal a sausage from the barbecue. Panchito, now six years old, ran after it oblivious to the arrival of his brother whom he barely remembered anyway. Sofia felt her heart thumping against her ribcage as if it were struggling to free itself from its confine and burst out along with her suffocating breasts. She felt the palms of her hands grow damp with excitement and suddenly wished she had worn jeans and a shirt the way he would have remembered her.

The cloud got bigger and bigger as it approached until the glimmering steel of the Jeep twinkled through the dust, turned the corner and rattled down the avenue of trees towards the ranch.

When it finally halted under the shade of the eucalyptus trees out jumped a taller, broader and more dashing Santi, in a pair of ivory chinos, a sky-blue open-neck shirt and brown leather loafers. The young American had returned.

Chapter Fifteen

Santiago Solanas arrived to a welcome party such as he had never seen before. He was suddenly surrounded by his cousins, brothers, aunts and uncles who all wanted to kiss him, embrace him and ask him dozens of questions about his adventures abroad. His mother smiled through her tears with joy and relief that her son had returned safely to the bosom of his family.

Sofia watched him descend the Jeep and saunter over in the unique way that he walked, confident, slightly bow-legged from having spent his life on a horse, with his slight but detectable limp. He embraced his mother with genuine tenderness. She seemed to dissolve into his arms. He was broader and heavier than he had been the summer before he departed for America. He had left a child and returned a man, Sofia mused, biting her lower lip anxiously. She had never before felt nervous in his presence, and yet suddenly she was overcome with a shyness that was new to her. In her dreams she had unwittingly cultivated a sensual, intimate relationship with him that, although contrary to reality, had become a reality for her that she was now unable to reverse. She couldn't look at him without blushing. He, of course, knew nothing of it, and when he saw her, embraced her with the same brotherly love as he always had done.

'Chofi, how I missed my favourite cousin,' he breathed into her softly perfumed neck. 'You look so different, I hardly recognised you!' She lowered her eyes apprehensively. He, noticing her awkwardness, frowned in confusion. 'I think my Chofi has blossomed into a woman while I've been away,' he said, giving her a playful squeeze. Before she could reply, Rafael and Agustin pushed her to the side and patted their cousin on his back with rough affection.

'*Che*, good to have you back!' they exclaimed merrily.

'It's good to be back, I can tell you,' he replied, his large green eyes searching the crowd for Panchito. Chiquita, sensing this, hurriedly scoured the terrace and fields for her youngest, eager for everything to be just perfect for her Santi. Finally Miguel appeared round the corner of the house with a squeaking and writhing Panchito dangling happily over one of his big shoulders.

'Ah, there you are, you naughty rascal,' his mother said cheerfully. 'Come and say hello to your brother.' At this request the little boy went quiet and putting a chubby finger in his mouth allowed his mother to take his hand and lead him over to where Santi was waiting for him.

'Panchito!' Bending down, Santi swept the bashful child into his strong arms. 'Have you missed me?' he asked, ruffling the little boy's sandy hair. Panchito, who looked very much like his brother, opened his green eyes as wide as he could and studied Santi's face with fascination.

'What is it, Panchito?' he asked, kissing his smooth, tanned face. The little boy laughed mischievously and after much coaxing buried his head in Santi's neck and whispered something to him. 'Ah,' laughed his brother, 'you think I'm as hairy as Papa, do you?' And Panchito ran his hand over his brother's bristly chin.

'Hey, Panchito, are you going to let me give Santi a hug too?' said Maria, putting her arms around both of them. Fernando took longer in coming forward; when he did he felt his chest constrict with resentment, but did his best to disguise his awkwardness. He had watched his brother arrive to a hero's welcome and had hated every moment of it. It sickened him. All he had done was study in a different country, what was the big deal? Pushing his jet-black hair out of his eyes he looked up at Santi from beneath a heavy brow and managed a thin smile. Santi pulled him into his arms and patted him on the back like an old friend. Old friend? They had never been friends.

'How I missed the Argentine *asado!*' sighed Santi, tucking into his *lomo* and blood sausages. 'No one cooks meat like an Argentine.' Chiquita glowed with pride, having taken so much trouble to prepare everything just the way he liked it.

'Show everyone how you speak English like an American,' Miguel said proudly. He had been impressed when he had heard his son talking with the Stanford family back in the spring. As far as he could tell, he didn't sound any different from the rest of them.

'Yes, I spoke English all the time. All my courses were in English,' he replied.

'Well, are you going to show us your English or not?' asked his father, pouring himself some more wine from a crystal decanter.

'Well, what do you want me to say? *I'm glad to be home with my folks and I missed you all,*' he said in perfect English.

'Oh, *por Dios*, spoken like a true American!' declared his mother, clapping her small hands together proudly. Fernando almost choked on his *chorizo*.

'Anna, you must be relieved now you have someone else to talk to in your own language,' said Paco, raising his glass to his nephew approvingly.

'If you call that my own language,' she replied with mock disdain.

'Mama speaks Irish, that's hardly pure English either,' said Sofia, unable to resist.

'Sofia, when you don't know what to say, sometimes it is better not to say anything at all,' her mother replied coolly, fanning herself under her hat.

'What else did you miss while you were in America?' asked Maria.

Santi thought for a while before replying. He gazed into the half distance, recalling those long nights dreaming of the Argentine *pampa*, the smell of eucalyptus and the vast blue horizon, so wide and so distant that it was difficult to tell where the earth ended and the sky began.

'I'll tell you exactly what I missed. I missed Santa Catalina and everything that goes with it,' he said. His mother's eyes misted over and she smiled at her husband who responded with equal tenderness.

'Bravo, Santi,' he said solemnly. 'Let's raise our glasses to that.' And they all raised their glasses to Santa Catalina, except for Fernando who smouldered in silence.

'May it never, ever change,' said Santi wistfully, glancing momentarily at the strange but beautiful young woman in the white dress who looked at him with limpid brown eyes, and wondered why he felt so uncomfortable in her presence.

With Latin sentimentality the lunch was punctuated with emotional speeches, encouraged along by the constant flow of wine that swelled the senses. The boys, however, found this display of family tenderness a little excessive and tried hard to suppress their laughter. They only wanted to know the calibre of girls in the States and how many Santi had slept with, but they tactfully left their questions until later when they were alone with him on the polo field.

In despair Sofia threw herself into her room and slammed the door behind her. She almost tore the dress off her body in frustration. Santi had hated her new look, and on reflection so had she. He had completely ignored her. Who was she trying to be? She felt so ashamed. She had looked a fool in front of everyone.

Rolling the dress into a tiny ball she shoved it at the back of the cupboard behind her sweaters and vowed never to wear it again. Hurriedly she pulled on her jeans and polo shirt and picked the pins out of her hair, hurling them onto the floor as if they had been the cause of his indifference. Sitting in front of the bedroom mirror she brushed her hair with angry strokes that hurt her head. She then plaited it, tying it as usual with a red ribbon. Now I feel like Sofia, she thought to herself, and wiped her tear-stained face with the back of her hand. With a determined step she strode out into the sunshine and hurried towards the pony lines. Never again would she try to be what she wasn't.

When Santi saw her approach he was relieved to see that it was the familiar, puerile Sofia who was striding towards him with her unique duck's gait. The arrogance of her walk amused him and he smiled at the sudden twinge of nostalgia that caused his stomach to lurch. He had felt slightly uneasy when he had first laid eyes on her in her white dress and grown-up hairstyle, although he hadn't really understood why. She had looked like a ripe peach bursting with sensuality yet there had been something about her that had placed her beyond his reach. She wasn't his old friend any more, but someone new. He couldn't help noticing either her newly rounded figure beneath the dress that went transparent when the sun shone behind it, and her shiny brown breasts that underlined her growing up and growing away. She wasn't a bit the Sofia he had remembered.

Before he could dwell on it any more she came bounding up to him. It still disturbed him that she had flowered into a woman. He somehow longed for the child she had been when he had left. But once they started chatting the familiar mischievous sparkle in her eyes returned and he was relieved to find that the person inside the new voluptuous body was in fact his beloved cousin after all.

'Papa lets me play all the time,' she said cheerfully as they walked over to the pony lines.

'And *Tía* Anna? How did you manage to get round her?'

'Well, you won't believe it, but this morning she actually suggested I play polo with you.'

'Is she sick?'

'She must be. Certainly not entirely *compos mentis*,' she laughed.

'I enjoyed your letters,' he said and smiled down at her, recalling the hundreds of long epistles, written in her messy, careless scrawl on pale blue airmail paper.

'I enjoyed yours. You sounded like you had a really incredible time. I was quite envious actually. I'd love to go away.'

'You will one day.'

'Did you have lots of girlfriends in America?' she asked masochistically.

'Lots,' he replied casually, and his hand grabbed the back of her neck fondly. He squeezed it a little too enthusiastically. 'You know, Chofi, I'm so happy to be back, I can't tell you. If I was told now that I would never leave Santa Catalina again I would be the happiest man alive.'

'But didn't you like America?' she asked, remembering the tone of his letters which all suggested that he had lost his heart to it.

'Sure I did, I had a great time, but you only realise how much you love something when you leave it for a while. When you return you see it in a totally different light because you are suddenly able to stand back and see it the way it is. All the things you previously took for granted you suddenly love with such intensity, because you know what it is to be without them. Do you know what I'm saying?'

She nodded. 'I think so,' she replied, but she clearly didn't for she had never left Santa Catalina like he had.

'You take it for granted, don't you, Chofi? Do you ever stop and look at it in all its beauty?'

'Yes, I do,' she replied, not sure whether she really did or not. He looked at her with a wry smile, the crow's feet at the ends of his eyes extending and deepening as he did so.

'I learnt a valuable lesson while I was away. My friend Stanley Norman taught me.'

'Stanley Norman?'

'*Sí*. I have to tell it in English, it won't work in Spanish.'

'Okay.'

'It's a little story about "the precious present".'

'The precious present.'

'It's a true story about a little boy who lived with his grand-parents. His grandpa was a serene and spiritual man who told him wonderful stories. One of the stories he told his grandson was about the "Precious Present".' Sofia thought of Grandpa O'Dwyer and suddenly felt sad. 'The child was so excited about it and would always ask his grandpa what exactly this present was. The old man told him that he would find out all in good time, but that it was something that would bring him a lasting happiness such as he had never experienced before. Well, the little boy kept his eyes peeled and when he was given a bicycle for his birthday which made him very happy indeed he thought that this must be the "Precious Present" his grandpa had described. But by and by he grew bored with his new toy and realised that it couldn't be the Precious Present because his grandpa had told him that it would bring him lasting happiness.

'Well, the little boy grew into a young man and he met a lovely young woman with whom he fell in love. At last, he thought, this is the Precious Present that will bring me lasting happiness. But they fought and grew restless and in the end went their separate ways. So the young man travelled and saw the world and in every new place he thought that he had at last found true happiness, but he was always looking to the next country, the next beautiful place, and found that his happiness never lasted. It was as if he was searching for something unattainable, but searching nonetheless. And this made him very sad. Then, having married again, having had children and finding that he *still* hadn't discovered the Precious Present that his grandpa had told him about, he became very disillusioned.

'Finally, one day his grandpa died and with him died the secret of the Precious Present – or so the young man thought. He sat down miserably and recalled all the happy moments he had shared with his wise old grandpa. And then it dawned on him, after all those years of searching. What was it about his grandpa that made him so satisfied, so contented and so serene? What was it about him that made you feel like the most important person in the world when you talked to him? Why was it that he created such a peaceful atmosphere around him and passed it on to everyone he met? The Precious Present wasn't a present after all in the material sense of the word. It was in fact the here and now, the present, *el momento – ahora*. His grandfather had lived in the moment, savouring every second. He wasn't existing in the tomorrow, for why waste your energy on something that might never happen? And he didn't dwell in yesterday because yesterday is gone and doesn't exist any more. The present is the only reality and in order to attain lasting happiness one has to learn to live in the here and now and not worry or waste time thinking about anything else.'

'Hey, *vamos chicos!*' shouted an agitated Agustin, already cantering around the field stick and balling.

'What a divine story,' Sofia said, thinking how much Grandpa O'Dwyer would have liked it. That was part of his philosophy.

'Come on, Chofi, we'll play together again – we play well that way, don't we?' he said, breaking away from her to mount his pony. Sofia watched him canter off into the field. His story had made a deep impression on her.

Santi was thrilled to be playing with his brother and cousins again on the farm that he loved so much. He was filled with a bursting energy and *joie de vivre*, and felt at that moment that he could conquer anything and anyone. He cantered around the field aware of every smell, every colour and everything that belonged to Santa Catalina and inhaled it all in long, deep breaths. He loved it like a person. As the match began he was firmly existing in the moment, not wanting to hasten the arrival of tomorrow or think about yesterday.

Sofia was playing with Santi, Agustin and Sebastian. On the opposing team played Fernando, Rafael, Niquito and Angel. It was a friendly match though not without the usual competitiveness that arose when all the family played together. Their shouts echoed across the field as they roared up and down, sweating with exertion in the heavy, damp air.

Paco enjoyed watching his daughter play; in her he saw his own aggressive love of the game reflected, and was proud of it. She was the only girl he knew who played to such a high standard. Sofia embodied all the qualities that he had recognised in Anna when he had first met her, although Anna disagreed with him whole-heartedly. According to her, she had never been nearly as daring or outrageous as her daughter; those qualities she could only have inherited from him.

The cousins were used to Sofia's presence on the field and no one minded. They had tolerated her participation in the match against La Paz that time because they had won, but they prevented her from ever playing in a match again. They knew they could treat her like a man but other players who were unused to playing with a woman just couldn't bring themselves to act naturally around her. Therefore Paco agreed it wasn't right that she should alter the tone of the match. She was allowed to play only with her cousins. For Sofia, she didn't care as long as she played. For her polo was more than a game, it was liberation from all the constraints imposed upon her by her mother. On the field she was treated like everyone else. She could do what she wanted, shout and scream, vent all her fury, and what's more, her father applauded her.

The late-afternoon sun cast long, monstrous shadows which seemed to have a life of their own as they fought one another like medieval lancers on the grass. Once or twice Fernando nearly rode his brother clean off his pony, but Santi just smiled happily at him and galloped off. Santi's smile made Fernando feel even more irritated. Didn't he realise that his aggression had nothing whatso-ever to do with the game? He'd push him harder next time. At the end of the match they gave their ponies, glistening with sweat and snorting froth, back to the grooms who had been milling around the pony lines in their *bombachas* and berets.

'I'm going to the pool for a swim,' announced Sofia, wiping her forehead which was damp and itchy from where her hat had been.

'Good plan, I'll join you,' said Santi, jogging over to her. 'You've improved your game since I last saw you. No wonder Paco lets you play all the time.'

'Only with the family.'

'Quite right too,' he approved.

Rafael and Agustin joined them and, patting Santi firmly on the back, mobbed around with him like they used to. Everyone had forgotten now that he had been away and life continued as it always had done.

'See you at the pool!' Fernando shouted to the others, as he gathered his *tacos* together and piled them into the back of the Jeep. He watched his brother wander off with his cousins and wished he would just disappear back to America. Things were fine without him, but now everyone would worship Santi again and place him back up on that darned pedestal. He swallowed his feelings of inadequacy and climbed into the driving seat. Sebastian, Niquito and Angel made their way in the opposite direction to their houses which were situated at the other side of the park, signalling that they too would meet at the pool.

Sofia undressed in the cool darkness of her room, wrapped herself in a towel and then made her way through the trees to the pool. Sunk into a small hill surrounded by tall plane trees and poplars, the water glistened seductively in the soft light of evening. The scent of eucalyptus and cut grass hung in the still, humid air and Sofia, remembering Santi's words, gazed at the beauty surrounding her and savoured it. Dropping her towel she dived naked through the mirrored surface that lay before her flat and glossy, a fine playground for the large number of flies and mosquitoes that skated about on top of it. After a while she heard the deep, gruff voices of her cousins and brothers as they approached, and then the loud roar of Sebastian's moped, and suddenly the tranquillity that she had been enjoying was shattered and lost.

'Hey, Sofia's naked!' announced Fernando when he noticed his cousin's shimmering body beneath the water.

Rafael shot her a disapproving look. 'Sofia, you're too big to skinny dip,' he complained, throwing off his towel.

'Oh, don't be such a spoilsport!' she shouted back, not in the least bit disconcerted. 'It's lovely, I know you want to.' And she laughed wickedly.

'We're all cousins, what does it matter?' said Agustin, shedding his shorts and diving in naked. 'She's got nothing worth seeing anyway.' He spluttered when he came up for air.

'I'm just thinking of my sister's dignity,' persisted Rafael anxiously.

'She lost that a long time ago. With Roberto Lobito. Ha!' laughed Fernando, dancing around the edge, his white bottom contrasting with his brown legs and back, before he too dived into the water.

'All right, but don't blame me when Mama gives you the bollocking of a lifetime.'

'Who's going to tell her?' she laughed and splashed around with the boys. Santi stepped out of his shorts and stood naked by the water's edge. Sofia couldn't help but allow her eyes to scrutinise his body as he remained without inhibition, hands on hips. Unable to stop herself her gaze rested in wonderment on that part of him that had always been insinuated but never revealed. There she lingered for a moment transfixed. She had seen her father, brothers and cousins naked before but there was something about Santi's nakedness that won her admiration. There it hung, proud and majestic before her, somehow bigger than she had expected. Then something pulled her eyes back to his face and she saw that he was watching her. His expression was clouded with anger. She frowned at him, trying to work out his thoughts. He then dived in, slicing the water with a noisy splash in an attempt to force from his mind the image of his cousin rolling naked with Roberto Lobito.

Conscious that he was in her vicinity, Sofia swam about

pretending not to notice him and splashed half-heartedly with the others. She tried to work out why he could possibly be angry with her. What had she done? Anxiety stole her enthusiasm and she felt depressed.

Suddenly Rafael alerted them to the arrival of Anna, who with an irritated expression was marching purposefully up to the pool.

'You'd better duck, Sofia,' he whispered urgently. 'I'll get rid of her as quickly as possible.'

'I don't believe it!' she gasped. 'That woman's a plague.' And pressing herself up against the wall her brother pushed her head under the water.

'Hola, boys — have you seen Sofia?' Anna asked, her eyes darting from one to the other.

'Well, she played polo with us and then made her way back to the house. We haven't seen her since,' Agustin replied earnestly.

'She's not here,' said Sebastian. Anna then noticed that they were all naked and a splash of colour stung her pale cheeks.

'I should hope not,' she replied tartly, though it wouldn't have surprised her. Then smiling at them all from under her sunhat she told them to send her daughter home if they saw her. Once she had gone Sofia arose to the surface, spluttering and gasping for air, then dissolved into coughs and laughter.

'Close one, boluda,' chided Rafael angrily. 'You just don't know when to stop!'

Santi watched her from the other end of the pool and felt a stab of jealousy he was unable to explain. He suddenly didn't want her swimming naked with all the boys. He wanted to slap her for dating Roberto Lobito. Of all the men she could have chosen, why had she chosen him?

Chapter Sixteen

The following day Santi awoke feeling foolish. He had allowed his feelings to flare out of control. Why should he care who she dated, he asked himself. Then he explained his rage by persuading himself that he was only protecting her like a brother would, or in her case, should. But then he thought of her writhing naked in the arms of Roberto Lobito and was so overcome with nausea he had to sit down. Damn it! She could date anyone *except* Roberto Lobito.

Roberto was a couple of years older than Santi and considered himself the biggest catch since Rhett Butler. He swaggered about the farm as if he owned the place, and to top it all he drove a flashy car imported from Germany. The importation duties were so vast it was virtually impossible to bring over such a car, but Roberto's father had managed it. He hated Roberto Lobito. Why had he targeted his Sofia?

It was hot and sticky by the time he got out of bed. His excitement at being back at Santa Catalina had dissipated and now all that remained was the bitter taste of last night's revelation. He dragged himself out onto the terrace to find Maria having breakfast in the sun. He casually asked her how long Sofia had been seeing Roberto, pretending that he thought it a perfect match.

'They make a very good-looking couple – a polo-playing couple.

I doubt there are many men who can boast about that,' he said, his throat constricting with inner rage.

Maria, insensitive to her brother's true feelings, said that they were really keen on each other. In fact, they had spent most weekends together at Santa Catalina for the last eight months. A real item. Santi changed the subject; he couldn't bear to listen to it. It made him feel like throwing up. Put him off his breakfast.

He decided to go and chat to Jose, find out how the ponies were. Perhaps take one out for a practice. Anything rather than find Sofia and Roberto together. He could just see them laughing and God forbid – kissing. He felt lower than he had ever felt. He wanted to return to America, run away from a jealousy he was incapable of defining.

Chatting to Jose distracted him momentarily, but once he was on a pony, galloping around the field after the white ball, Santi's thoughts once more returned to Sofia. He hit the ball with great force, each time imagining it to be the head of Roberto Lobito. But, as hard as he hit it, he was unable to crack it.

After a while he noticed he was being watched. Sofia was sitting on the fence, quietly observing him. He tried to ignore her and managed to do so for a while. But finally he cantered up to her, his heart beating fast with adrenaline. He would tell her exactly what he thought of her Roberto Lobito.

She smiled as he approached. A nervous smile. She knew he was angry and she had spent all night in the stifling humidity trying to work out the reason why. She swallowed anxiously as he neared her, trying to repress the churning feeling that had turned her belly to liquid.

'Hola,' she said, then waited for him to speak.

'What are you doing?' he asked coldly without dismounting. His pony snorted in the heat and shook his head.

'Watching you.'

'Why?'

She sighed and looked hurt. 'What's the matter?' she asked miserably.

'Nothing. Why, should there be anything the matter?' His pony shuffled, then snorted again with impatience. He sat back in the saddle, looking down at her loftily.

'Don't play games with me, Santi. We know each other too well for that.'

'Who's playing games? I'm just pissed off, that's all.'

'What have I done?' she asked. He clicked his tongue as if to say, Come on, now who's playing games. 'You're upset that I'm dating Roberto Lobito?' she volunteered.

'Why would I care?' His expression hardened at the mention of Lobito's name.

'Because you do care.'

'What's it got to do with me who you date?'

'Well, it seems to have a lot to do with you,' she replied. Then, exasperated, she hopped down from the fence. 'You're right. It's got nothing to do with you,' she said, and shrugged her shoulders as if she no longer cared.

Suddenly Santi dismounted and grabbed her by the arm as she began to walk away. Dropping the reins of his pony he pushed her up against the tree, took her neck in one hand and pressed his hot lips to hers. It all happened so fast that when he pulled away, mumbling an apology, she wondered if it had, in fact, happened at all. She wanted to tell him that it was okay. She wanted more than anything for him to kiss her again.

As he mounted his pony she held the reins for a moment to stop him galloping off and said in a trembling voice, 'Every time Roberto kisses me I imagine it's you.' He looked down at her, his face no longer angry, just anxious. He shook his head, wishing that he hadn't heard her.

'Dios, I don't know why I did that!' he said and cantered off.

Sofia was left at the fence like a stunned rabbit. Rooted to the spot she watched him gallop off into the middle of the field without looking back. Unconvinced that he had actually kissed her she traced her lips with a shaking finger. They were still wet and still quivering. Her belly fluttered even more and her legs felt light as if they belonged to someone else. She wanted to run after him, but she didn't dare. Santi had kissed her. She had dreamed of this moment, except that in her dreams it had lasted a lot longer. But it was something. It was a start. When she was finally able to walk away she skipped unsteadily through the trees with a heart brimming with hope. Santi was jealous of Roberto Lobito. She laughed happily, unable to believe it was real and that she wasn't dreaming. Could it be possible that Santi might love her back? She didn't know for sure, but what she did know was that she had to break it off with Roberto as soon as possible.

When Sofia called Roberto Lobito at his *estancia*, La Paz, and told him that she couldn't be his girlfriend any more there was a heavy silence while her words sunk in. He had never, *ever* been chucked before. He asked her if she was all right, she couldn't possibly be well. She replied frostily that she was fine. It was over.

'You're making a huge mistake,' he said. 'Just remember what I say. When you come to your senses and want me back, I won't have you. Do you understand? I won't take you back.'

'Good,' she replied, and hung up.

Sofia thought that by finishing with Roberto Lobito she would make Santi happy. Yet he wasn't happy. He still ignored her and it seemed that their friendship was gone for ever. What about the kiss? Had he forgotten? She hadn't. Whenever she closed her eyes she felt his lips on hers. She couldn't confide in Maria. She couldn't let her know how she felt. So she complained to Soledad. Soledad was always there for her. Not that her advice was of any use, but she always gave Sofia her full attention, listening with an expression of sympathy and adoration. Sofia told her that he was ignoring her. Not including her like he used to. She sobbed into her maid's spongy bosom that she had lost her best friend in the whole world. Soledad rocked her gently in her arms and told her that boys of Santi's age wanted to hang out with other boys or girls they were in love with. As Sofia fell into neither category, she must be patient.

'He'll come back when he's grown up a bit,' she promised. 'Don't you worry, *gorda*, you'll find another boyfriend and then you won't care at all about Señor Santiago.'

Fernando was furious at this latest turn of events. How could Sofia finish with Roberto Lobito? Roberto was his closest friend. If she had ruined his friendship he would never forgive her. Didn't she realise that every woman who met him wanted him? Did she realise what she was giving up? Selfish bitch. She was only thinking of herself, as usual.

Fernando made a point of inviting Roberto Lobito to the farm at every possible opportunity for two reasons. One, because he worried that Sofia might have put him off coming at all, or worse put him off being friends with Fernando. Two, because it amused him to watch Sofia squirm uncomfortably when she saw him about the place – call it revenge on behalf of his friend. In fact, he maliciously flaunted Roberto around the *campo*, intent on showing Sofia what she was missing. She had slighted Roberto, therefore she had indirectly slighted him. Roberto didn't resist and took advantage of Fernando's loyalty by making a point of flirting outrageously in front of her as if to show her that he didn't care for her any more. He did care.

Sofia found his antics tiresome and retreated into her own world, taking a pony out for rides, or going for long solitary walks across the *pampa*. Maria followed her friend around when she allowed it, aware that there was something she wasn't telling her. This saddened Maria who tried desperately to ingratiate herself with her cousin, smiling brightly when inside she felt heavy and excluded. Sofia had sulked in the past but never for too long. Maria had always been her accomplice, her ally against everyone else. Now Sofia seemed to want to be alone.

At first, Santi found it easier not to be around Sofia. Embarrassed that he had allowed his impulses to flare out of control he resolved that it was better not to see her until he had managed to convince himself that he was sick or something – anything rather than in love with Sofia. He couldn't be in love with Sofia. It was like being in love with Maria. Incestuous and wrong; of that he was certain. When he remembered the kiss, he cringed inwardly until his stomach scrambled into a thick knot. 'Did I really kiss her?' he asked himself during the torturous nights that followed. 'God, what was I thinking? What must she think of me?'

He groaned, hoping that by ignoring the situation it would go away. He convinced himself that she was too young to know her mind. He should be more responsible. After all, she looked up to him and admired him. He knew that. He was older than her and knew the consequences of such a liaison. He told himself over and over to grow up and get over it.

He hung about with the boys, moving around the farm in a pack like the dogs, searching for some novelty or other. Yet, he spent the whole time expecting to see Sofia at the pool or on the tennis court, only to find himself fighting his disappointment. It was easier when she was around. At least he knew where she was. He knew they couldn't be lovers. Their families would never allow it. He could imagine the lecture from his father. The one that started, 'You have a bright future . . .' And he could see his mother's appalled expression in his mind's eye. But his body ached for Sofia in spite of his reasoning, wearing him down little by little. Finally he could fight no longer. He had to talk to her. He had to explain himself. He had to tell her that his kiss had been no more than a moment of madness. He'd tell her he thought she was someone else – anything rather than tell her the truth, that he was tormented by his growing love for her and saw no possibility of it abating.

Maria was on the terrace playing with Panchito and one of his little friends from the farm when Santi asked her whether she had seen Sofia. She said she hadn't a clue where Sofia was and grumbled that she had grown into a stranger these past few days. Chiquita emerged from the house with a basket of toys and told Santi to go and make up with Sofia.

'But we haven't had a fight,' he protested. His mother gave him a look as if to say, 'Don't think I'm a fool.'

'You've ignored her ever since you got back, and she was so excited about seeing you. Maybe she's upset because of Roberto Lobito. Do go and sort it out, Santi.' Maria took the basket from her mother and emptied its contents onto the tiles. Panchito squealed in delight.

Santi found Sofia engrossed in a book under the ombu. Her pony was snoozing in the shade. It was very humid. Looking up at the sky he could see black clouds making their way in over the horizon. When she heard him approach she put her book down and looked up at him.

'I thought I'd find you here,' he said.

'What do you want?' she asked aggressively and then wished she hadn't sounded so angry.

'I came to talk.'

'What about?'

'Well, we can't go on like this, can we?' he said, sitting down beside her.

'I suppose not.'

They sat in silence for a while. Sofia remembered his kiss and wished he would kiss her again.

'The other day . . .' she began.

'I know,' he interrupted, trying to find the words that he had rehearsed but they eluded him.

'I wanted you to.'

'You said,' he replied, feeling the sweat collect in feverish beads on his forehead.

'So why did you ride off like that?'

'Because, Chofi, it can never be. We're cousins – first cousins. It's too close. What would our parents say?' He placed his head in his hands. He despised himself for his weakness. Why couldn't he just tell her, decisively, that he didn't feel anything more than brotherly affection for her and that his actions had been a big mistake?

207

'Who cares what they say? I never have. Who'd tell them anyway?' she said brightly. Suddenly the impossible seemed quite possible. He had said they shouldn't, not that he didn't want to. She put her arm around him and rested her head on his shoulder. 'Santi, I have loved you for so long.' She sighed happily. Those words, so often said silently in her head, were now uttered from the depth of her soul. He pulled his head out of his hands and put both arms around her, nestling his face in her hair. They sat a while, pressed tightly together, listening to the other's breathing, wondering where to go from there.

'I've tried to convince myself that I don't care for you,' he said at last, feeling lighter with the unburdening of his conscience.

'But you do care,' she said joyfully.

'Unfortunately I do, Chofi,' he said, playing with her plait. 'I thought of you so much while I was away.'

'Did you?' she whispered, dizzy with pleasure.

'Yes. I didn't think I'd miss you at all, but I surprised myself. I cared about you even then but I didn't understand my feelings until now.'

'When did you realise you loved me?' she asked shyly.

'It wasn't until I kissed you. I didn't understand why I minded so much about you dating Roberto Lobito. I guess I just didn't want to think about it too hard. I was afraid of the answer.'

'I was surprised when you kissed me.' She laughed.

'No one was more surprised than me, I can assure you.'

'Were you ashamed?'

'Very.'

'If you kissed me again, would you feel ashamed?' she asked and grinned at him, daring him to try it and see.

'I don't know, Chofi. It's . . . well, complicated.'

'I hate it when things run smoothly.'

'I know you do. But I don't think you understand what a kiss between us might mean.'

'Yes, I do.'

'You're my uncle's daughter,' he lamented.

'So what?' she said light-heartedly. 'Who cares? What matters is we like each other, we make each other happy and we are learning how to live in the present. What could be a better test?'

'You're right, Chofi,' he conceded and she noticed that he had suddenly turned serious again. She withdrew from his embrace and looked at him, searching his face for his expression. He raised his rough hand and ran it slowly down her cheek, tracing her tremulous lips with his thumb. For a long moment he searched deeply into her brown eyes as if attempting to fight his impulses one final time. Then he surrendered to a desire far greater than his reasoning and, with uncharacteristic force, he pulled her to him and placed his soft, wet mouth onto hers. She caught her breath as if she had suddenly been ducked underwater. She had imagined this scene so many times and yet she hadn't anticipated the light sensation that turned her stomach to foam and the tingling feeling in her limbs. This certainly wasn't the kiss of Roberto Lobito, whose efforts now seemed very contrived in comparison with Santi's. Fighting for air, she pulled away, suddenly confused by the fevered rush of her emotions. Then she recognised the longing in his eyes and in the pounding of her heart and she gave him her lips once more. In that moment she knew what Santi's story had been all about, and she was aware that she was truly existing in the moment, savouring every new sensation. With a tenderness that caused her belly to flutter, he kissed her temples, her eyes and her forehead, holding her small face in his hands, caressing her skin with loving fingers. She felt consumed by him, enfolded in his arms, lost in the intoxicating scent of his skin. Neither of them noticed the inauspicious clouds gathering darkly above them. Utterly absorbed in each other, they failed to feel the first drops of rain that soon turned into a heavy deluge, pounding onto their bodies as they crouched against the trunk of the tree for shelter.

Chapter Seventeen

The next few days passed in a blissful haze of illicit, stolen moments. Life on the farm went on as usual but for Santi and Sofia every minute was sacred. Every moment alone was dedicated to hurried kisses, behind closed doors, trees or bushes, in the pool when they were sure they wouldn't be discovered. To them Santa Catalina had never before vibrated with such intense beauty and radiance.

The pair would disappear up the dusty tracks on horseback to lie under the shade of the ombu and celebrate the dawn of their love with tender kisses and gentle caresses. There Santi would pull out his penknife and they would entertain themselves for hours carving their names and secret coded messages in the soft, green branches. Climbing as high as they dared into the enchanted kingdom of the most ancient tree in Argentina they would watch the kaleidoscope of ponies snorting and grazing peacefully in the arid fields below. Able to see for miles they could detect the comings and goings of the *gauchos* on horseback wandering lazily up the tracks in the distance, clad in their traditional *bombachas*, leather boots and silver coined belts. In the evening, which was their favourite time, they would sit on the fragrant grass gazing out onto the vast horizon and wallow self-indulgently in the melancholy of the sunset.

Everything filled Sofia with joy. Even the smallest, most

insignificant task, like scattering Soledad's breadcrumbs on the grass for the birds, gave her pleasure and she glowed because Santi loved her. She felt her heart would explode with the intoxicating, overwhelming love she felt for him. She worried that people would notice because she no longer walked but skipped, she no longer talked but sang, she no longer ran but danced. Her whole body vibrated with love. She understood why people would do anything for it; even kill for it.

Above all, Sofia's relationship with her mother improved. She became a new person, helpful, attentive and unselfish.

'If I didn't know any better, I would say that Sofia is in love,' her mother said one morning at breakfast after Sofia had been unusually agreeable about giving Panchito some extra English lessons.

'She *is* in love, Mama,' replied Agustin nonchalantly, stirring his coffee.

'She is?' Anna cried happily. 'But who on earth with?'

'With herself,' interjected Rafael quickly.

'Don't be unkind, Rafael. She's being very agreeable at the moment. Don't spoil it by antagonising her.'

What interested her far more than Sofia was the beautiful Jasmina, Rafael's girlfriend, whose father, the celebrated Ignacio Peña, was the most successful lawyer in Buenos Aires. Coming from such an illustrious family, she would make a good wife for Rafael, an addition to the family of whom Anna could be proud. In fact, she had known the girl's mother for a short time; Señora Peña was a devout Catholic and they met occasionally at Mass when they spent weekends in the city. Anna had made a mental note to attend Mass more often. Befriending Señora Peña would most certainly render her influential in her son's future.

'For God's sake, Agustin! What do you think you were doing, telling Mama that Sofia's in love? Have you no sense at all?' Rafael said gruffly when their mother had left the breakfast table.

'Lighten up, Rafa. I was just telling her the truth,' he protested.

'Sometimes it's better to lie.'

'Come on, it's only a crush.'

'You know what Mama's like. You remember her reaction to Joaco Santa Cruz marrying his first cousin?'

'Sofia is hardly going to marry Santi. Poor girl. He's just humouring her like one would humour a puppy.'

'Whatever. But think next time before you go opening your big mouth.'

The love affair between Santi and Sofia went undetected by the majority of those on the farm. Anyone who suspected anything, like Rafael and Agustin, put it down to an adolescent crush and thought it quite charming. There was nothing unusual about the amount of time the two spent together. They did nothing out of the ordinary. Yet between them there passed looks and gestures that had a secret significance only to them. They dwelt in a dreamy world that ran parallel to everyone else's but differed in vibration. They felt they were living on an idyllic plane where nothing could touch them, least of all damage their love. They were dwelling in the precious present and nothing else mattered.

The polo matches continued and yet Sofia didn't care so much if she played or not. Her mornings with Jose dwindled and she spent more time with Soledad in the kitchen baking cakes which she would then proudly take over to Chiquita's house for tea. She ceased to fight with her mother but asked her advice about make-up and clothes. This filled Anna with happiness and she rejoiced in the certainty that her daughter must at last be growing up. There were no more skinny dips, or shameless displays of capriciousness, and even Paco, who never seemed to notice them anyway, admitted that his daughter was changing for the better.

'Sofia!' shouted Anna from her bedroom. It was raining outside, heavy, constant and unrelenting. She closed the windows with a grimace and sighed irritably as she noticed a large puddle of water on the carpet. 'Soledad!' she cried. Sofia and Soledad both entered her bedroom at the same time.

'Soledad, please clean up this dreadful puddle. You must close all the windows of the house when it rains like this. Goodness, you'd think the world was about to end, looking out there,' she complained. Soledad wandered off slowly in the direction of the kitchen to fetch a bucket and sponge. Sofia flopped onto her mother's bed with a pot of pink nail varnish.

'Do you like this colour?' she asked in English. Her mother sat on the bed and took a good look at it.

'My mother hated me wearing nail varnish. She thought it looked cheap,' she recalled and smiled wistfully as she remembered her.

'Well it is, that's why it's sexy,' laughed Sofia, opening the bottle and applying it.

'Good God, girl, it'll look a mess if you put it on in a rush. Here, give it to me. There, nothing like someone else's steady hand.' Sofia watched as her mother held her hand in hers and carefully painted on the varnish. She couldn't remember the last time her mother had given her so much attention. 'I've got a favour to ask you, Sofia,' she said.

'What is it?' Sofia asked reluctantly, hoping it didn't involve drawing her away from Santi.

'Well, Antonio is arriving in town from Buenos Aires on the four o'clock bus. I wonder if you could ask Santi to be a dear and go and pick him up in the truck. I know it's a bore, but Rafa and Agustin can't go.'

'Oh, that's fine. He won't mind. We can go together. Anyway, what's Antonio been doing in Buenos Aires?' Sofia asked casually, trying to hide her excitement. They could spend all afternoon together by the lake, just the two of them. She hoped Maria wouldn't want to come.

'Poor old thing, he had to go into the hospital. It's his hip again.'

'Oh, right,' she responded absentmindedly. She was already by the lake with Santi.

'Thank you, Sofia, it's very sweet of you. I just can't bear to go in this rain.'

'I love the rain!' she laughed.

'That's because you didn't grow up with it like I did.'

'Do you miss Ireland?'

'No. I was thrilled to leave and now – well, I've lived here for so long, I wouldn't belong if I went home. It would be like a foreign country to me.'

'I'd miss Argentina,' said Sofia, holding up one hand and admiring her nails.

'Of course you would. Santa Catalina is a very special place and you belong here. It's your home,' replied her mother, surprising herself. She had always resented her daughter for fitting in when she had found it so hard to feel accepted in her adopted country. She looked across at Sofia's radiant face and felt a new emotion. Pride.

'I know. I love it. I wish I didn't have to go back to Buenos Aires,' she sighed.

'We all do things we don't want to do. But more often than not they're for the best. You learn that as you get older.' Anna smiled softly and screwed the lid back on the little flask of varnish. 'There. You now look like a prize tart,' she joked.

'Thanks, Mama!' exclaimed Sofia in delight.

'Don't smudge them now.'

'Must go and tell Santi about his errand,' Sofia announced, jumping off the bed and disappearing down the corridor, passing Soledad, puffing from having climbed the stairs, weighed down with buckets and brushes on her way to tackle the puddle.

Santi was delighted at the chance to spend the afternoon with Sofia. Rather meanly, they decided not to tell Maria, who was playing with Panchito in the sitting room with her mother and her mother's friend Lia. Dashing through the rain, they arrived at the truck breathless with excitement and wet to the skin. They left the farm at half past two in order to give themselves some time together before Antonio's large frame would climb in between them at four. Side by side they rattled up the driveway, splattering mud up the side of the vehicle as they left the ranch. Santi turned on the radio and they both hummed along to John Denver. Sofia placed her hand on his damp knee as he drove. Neither needed to talk, they enjoyed each other's company in silence.

The *pueblo* was deserted. A rusty car lurched its way around the square in front of them at an infuriatingly slow pace. The few shops like the hardware store and the food store were closed for the afternoon siesta. An old man sat on the bench in the middle of the *plaza* under a battered brown hat as if he hadn't noticed it was raining. Even the dogs had scurried off for shelter. As they passed the church of *Nuestra Señora de la Asunción*, they looked for the usual gaggle of gossiping old ladies dressed in black, 'crows' as Grandpa O'Dwyer had always called them, but even they had retreated in out of the deluge.

They drove slowly through the village. The road around the square had been covered in tarmac a few years before, but all the other routes were still dirt tracks. Once past the square it wasn't long before they were on the open road that ran alongside the lake. Finding a secluded spot under some trees, Santi pulled up.

'Let's go and walk in the rain,' suggested Sofia, climbing down. They held hands and laughed as they ran from the shelter of one tree out into the rain, then dived for cover under another tree when they couldn't take the downpour a moment longer. Checking that they were quite alone, for it was not easy to pass unnoticed in a village of that size, especially for a Solanas whose family were very well-known by most of the inhabitants, Santi pushed Sofia up against a tree and kissed her neck. He then pulled back and looked down at her. Her hair was soaking. He wiped it off her face, revealing her glowing pink cheeks and hearty smile. She had a big, generous mouth. He loved her mouth, the way it could go from sulky to smirky in a moment. It was always inviting even when it was quivering with rage. The rain dripped through the leaves in large, heavy drops but the air was thick and humid so they welcomed them. He placed his hands around her waist and pulled her against him. She could feel his excitement through his jeans.

'I want to make love to you, Chofi,' he said, looking steadily into her eyes.

'We can't.' She laughed throatily. 'Not here. Not now.' She laughed to hide the fear that made her lips tremble and turn pale. She had wanted Santi to make love to her from the moment she had realised that she loved him, two years before. But now it was really going to happen she felt afraid.

'No, not here. I know a place,' he said, taking her hand and pressing his wet lips into her palm without releasing her anxious eyes from where he held them securely with his. 'I'll be gentle, Chofi. I love you,' he said and smiled kindly down at her.

'Okay,' she whispered, lowering her eyes, nervous of what was to come.

Santi led her by the hand to the musty shelter of an old boathouse that stood low and squat by the edge of the lagoon, among the long grasses and rushes where herons and spoonbills made their nests. Once inside out of the rain they lay laughing at their boldness on top of a pile of empty sacks made out of rotting hessian. The light entered through cracks and ragged holes in the wood, casting shimmering shafts onto a dusty boat that lay neglected on its side, like a beached whale dragged up out of the water. They listened to the rat-a-tat tapping of the rain on the tin roof and breathed in the stuffy air that smelt of oil and sweet, decaying grass. Sofia snuggled up to Santi, not because she was cold, but because she was shivering with nervousness.

'I'm going to make love to you very, very slowly, Chofi,' said Santi, kissing her temple and tasting the salt.

'I don't know what to do,' she ventured softly. Santi was moved by her fear. Here was the girl he loved more than anyone else, stripped of her petulance and her arrogance. Stripped to her sweet core. The Sofia no one else knew but him.

'You don't need to know what to do, my love. I will love you, that's all,' he replied in a deep, reassuring voice and smiled at her fondly. To reduce her fear he balanced himself on one elbow and ran the other hand down her face, tracing her tremulous lips with the tip of his finger. She smiled nervously, embarrassed by the silent intimacy of his actions and the strength of his eyes that bore through hers into her soul. She didn't speak. She didn't know what to say. She bowed to silence in awe of the magnitude of the moment.

Then he lowered his lips and kissed her with tenderness on her eyes, her nose, her temples and finally her mouth. He ran his wet tongue over the inside of her lips and explored her teeth and gums until his mouth was pressed heavily onto hers, consuming her entirely. She inhaled unsteadily as his hand ran under her wet T-shirt and felt the gentle shudder of her belly and the soft rise of her breasts. He pulled the shirt over her head and saw her naked torso, pale and shivering in the misty light that entered between the rotting beams. He kissed her neck and her shoulders while his fingers ran over the downy little hairs on the surface of her belly, over the stiff strain of her nipples, round to the small of her back that lifted off the ground in response to his touch. He teased her breast with his tongue until the pleasure turned to pain that somehow ached in another place far from where his mouth was, between her legs. Yet, she didn't want him to stop, it was a pain that was at once excruciatingly uncomfortable and exquisitely pleasurable.

Finding the buttons on her jeans he undid them one by one and she wriggled out of them, dragging with them her white panties until she lay before him, trembling at her own nakedness. He watched her expression as he gently caressed her. Sofia's cheeks were red and shiny and her eyelids made heavy by the awakening of her senses. She hovered tenuously on the brink of womanhood. This fragile balance between the child and the woman gave her a rare beauty that glowed through her skin like the golden light of autumn. Then his hand descended into the very secret place that she alone had discovered during those sultry nights when her longing for him had given her no choice but to explore her sexuality herself, solitary in the darkness. Then she had imagined her fingers were his. But her fingers hadn't been like his at all but poor substitutes to ward off the frustration of those long months of waiting. They found her now and she let out a deep sigh.

For a while she lost herself in pleasure. Santi watched the small beads of sweat collect in the valley between her breasts and on the surface of her proud nose. She had closed her eyes and allowed her legs to flop open in a way that suggested she was unaware even that she had done it. Unable to withstand the strain of his own desire Santi sat up, pulled his shirt over his head and threw off his jeans. Sofia returned from that faraway place and opened her eyes wide at the sight of his maleness, different from that time by the pool because it was now awake and impatient. Santi placed her hand upon it. She didn't resist but scrutinised it with the curiosity of a scientist, running her hand up and down, turning it over, marvelling at the weight of it.

'So this is what drives you men, is it?' she said, before dropping it carelessly onto his belly. Santi chuckled. Shaking his head he took her hand again and showed her how to stroke it properly. Then he fumbled in the pocket of the jeans he had cast aside and withdrew a square piece of paper. He told her it was important to take precautions. He didn't want to get her pregnant. She laughed as she helped him put it on.

'Poor thing, what if he's afraid of the dark?' she said as her inexperience served only to hinder the operation rather than help it.

'You're a hopeless pupil,' he complained laughingly pushing her hands away and doing it himself.

Sofia closed her eyes expecting a sharp pain to sear through her body as he entered her, but none came. Instead her body was filled with warmth and drained of any remaining anxiety. She clung to Santi and discarded her innocence with the enthusiasm of the newly converted. Santi had had sex countless times in America but with Sofia he made love for the first time.

When they emerged into the light the rain had stopped and the sun was breaking through the cloud causing the lake to glisten like well-polished silver.

'Antonio!' Sofia suddenly remembered the purpose of their journey. 'We mustn't forget to collect him.'

Santi looked at his watch; they still had another quarter of an hour. 'I want to spend every last minute of it kissing you,' he said, pulling her into his arms again.

Once Sofia had tasted the forbidden fruit she wanted more. It wasn't easy to find secluded places on the farm away from the *gauchos* and large throng of cousins and friends, but as Grandpa O'Dwyer had always said, 'Where there's a will, there's a way,' and the uncontrollable will of Santi and Sofia would have found water in the desert.

As it was still the long summer break, they were down on the farm all the time. They discovered that by day it was almost impossible to make love without the fear of discovery ruining their enjoyment. Occasionally during the siesta when the grown-ups disappeared into the coolness of their rooms to sleep off the copious amounts of food and wine they had consumed at lunchtime, they were able to sneak off into the spare room in the attic of Sofia's house, which was far from her parents' bedroom and rarely used. There they would love one another in the languid heat of the afternoon, amid the scents of jasmine and cut grass and the singing of the many different types of bird that gathered in the trees outside, attracted by the promise of Soledad's breadcrumbs. Or they would escape from their bedrooms at night when the rest of the farm lay sleeping and make love under the starry sky and the all-seeing moon.

They would talk about the future – their future. A future that was as unattainable as the clouds above them. But neither cared that their dreams were mirages, forged in the rosy optimism of their love. That a life as man and wife at Santa Catalina was an impossible wish. They drifted on the clouds all the same, knowing that one thing was for certain; they would love each other for ever.

Chapter Eighteen

At the end of February Sofia awoke feeling nauseous. Perhaps she had eaten something slightly off the night before. Recovered by the afternoon, she forgot all about it until the next morning when she was violently sick.

'I don't know what's the matter with me, Maria,' she complained over the bowl of butter and flour that she was mixing for Panchito's birthday cake. 'I feel fine now, but I felt like death this morning.'

'Sounds like morning sickness,' joked Maria, winking at her cousin without noticing the sudden pallor that had drained her face dry.

'Another immaculate conception,' Sofia replied with an unsteady smile. 'I don't think I'm reverent enough.'

'Well, what did you eat last night, then?'

'And the night before,' she said, trying to laugh when she wanted to cry at the thought that perhaps she was pregnant. They had been conducting their affair for no more than six and a half weeks and Santi had always taken great care to use protection. Sofia knew, because she had become rather efficient at putting the condoms on for him. She pushed the thought to the back of her mind, certain that she was overreacting. 'It's probably Soledad's rice pudding,' she said, feeling herself again.

'You get rice pudding?' Maria exclaimed enviously, greasing the cake tins. 'Encarnacion!' she shouted. The old maid shuffled into the kitchen with a basket full of washing.

'Sí, Señorita Maria?'

'How long do we leave it in for?'

'I thought Señorita Sofia would be a professional cake-maker by now. Bake for twenty minutes, then have a look at it. If it's not ready, another ten. No, no, Panchito!' she cried as the small child skipped into the kitchen. 'Come with me – there, take my hand. Let's go and see if there's a dragon on the terrace.' And she led him out into the sunshine.

'What are dragons?' asked Sofia.

'Lizards. Panchito thinks they're dragons.'

'Well, they are, I suppose. Small dragons.'

Maria watched her cousin lick the bowl. She noticed how glossy Sofia looked. She had scrunched her hair up onto the top of her head with a rubber band, wisps had come loose around her face and neck, sticking to the sweat on her skin. She still managed to look beautiful even in a cook's grubby apron.

'What are you looking at, *gorda?*' Sofia grinned fondly at her cousin.

Maria smiled back. 'You're very happy at the moment, aren't you?' she said.

'Yes. I'm happy here with you, cooking in your kitchen.'

'But you're getting along much better with Anna.'

'She's not all bad, the old stick insect.'

'Sofia! She's beautiful!'

'Too thin,' she replied wryly, offering Maria the bowl.

'I wish I was too thin,' lamented Maria, suddenly deciding not to help her cousin lick the bowl after all. Sofia placed it in the sink for Encarnacion to wash up.

'Maria, you're perfect. You don't want to be thin. You're feminine, glowing, healthy, curvy and beautiful. You're all woman, girl!' They both laughed.

'You are ridiculous, Sofia.'

'No, I'm honest. I'll always tell you the truth. You're lovely just the way you are.'

Maria smiled gratefully. 'You're very special to me, Sofia,' she said sincerely.

'You're my best friend, Maria, you're special to me too.' The two girls hugged each other, both amused and touched by their sudden display of tenderness.

'Shall we put the cake in then?' said Sofia, releasing her. She picked up the tin that was brimming with thick brown cake mix and sniffed it hungrily. 'Mmmm, smells heavenly!'

Dios! Put it in quick, or it won't be ready in time.'

Chiquita had invited all Panchito's little friends from the neighbouring farms for his surprise birthday tea. The afternoon sun turned the terrace to a warm pink hue as the children ran around with chocolate faces and sticky hands followed by the dogs who swiped pieces of cake from their fingers when they weren't looking.

Fernando, Rafael, Agustin, Sebastian, Angel and Niquito dropped by for a moment to grab some cake and biscuits before wandering off into the park to kick a ball around. Santi lingered longer. He watched Sofia as she chatted to her mother and aunts under the shade of an acacia tree. He loved the way she always moved her hands dramatically when she talked, the way she looked up from under her thick brown lashes as if she were about to reveal something shocking but was just awaiting her moment in order to get the optimum reaction. He could tell she knew she was being watched because the corners of her mouth twisted into a self-conscious smile. Finally she glanced over at him. He blinked twice without changing his expression. Sofia returned his message and grinned so broadly he had to caution her with a look. She allowed her eyes to remain and lovingly caress his face and lips. He turned away, afraid that someone might notice and hoped that she had had the sense to do the same. But when he turned back she was still looking, her head leaning on one side, her smile wistful. Maria busily helped the children to sandwiches and sweets, cut the cake, picked up spilt cups of orange juice and ran after the dogs when they sniffed their way too close to the food. She was far too occupied to notice the tender glances between her brother and cousin.

Later that night, Santi and Sofia sat on the bench under the veranda of his house. Secretly they held hands in the darkness. When he squeezed her hand twice that was a message like their blinking. It meant 'I love you'. She squeezed it back until it became a game to see who could outsqueeze the other. His family had all gone to bed, the house was still, the air cooler than before. Autumn was closing in, ushering out the sultry nights with its fresh yet melancholic wind.

'I can smell the change,' said Sofia, snuggling up to Santi.

'I hate the end of summer.'

'Oh, I don't mind it. I like the dark evenings in front of the fire,' she said and shivered.

He drew her in close and kissed her forehead tenderly. 'Imagine what mischief we could get up to in front of Mama's fire,' he murmured.

'Yes! You see, winter's not so bad.'

'Not with you. Nothing's bad with you, Chofi.'

'I can't wait to spend a winter with you, and a spring, and another summer. I want to grow old with you,' she said dreamily.

'Me too,' he told her.

'Even if I grow as *loca* as Grandpa?'

'Well . . .' He hesitated, shaking his head in jest.

'I have a lot of Irish blood in me,' she warned him.

'I know, that's what I'm worried about.'

'You love me because I'm different from everyone else. You told me so!' She laughed and nuzzled her nose under his chin. He gently pulled her face up and stroked her cheek.

'Who couldn't love you?' He sighed and lowered his lips onto hers. She closed her eyes and enjoyed the warm, familiar feel of his mouth and the spicy scent of him as he kissed her.

'Let's go to the ombu tree,' she suggested and he smiled at her knowingly.

'To think you were an innocent child a couple of months ago,' he mused, kissing the end of her nose.

'And you were the devious seducer,' she replied.

'Why, Chofi, is everything always my fault?' he joked.

'Because you're a man and it's chivalrous to take the blame for my misconduct. You have to protect my honour.'

'Honour indeed. What's left of it!' he smirked.

'I have plenty of honour left,' she protested, grinning broadly.

'How could I have been so careless? Let's go immediately to the ombu so I can get rid of it once and for all,' he said and, taking her by the hand, they disappeared into the darkness.

The following morning Sofia awoke to the same nagging nausea she had felt the two previous mornings. Running to the bathroom she threw her head down the loo and proceeded to vomit up all of Encarnacion's supper. After brushing her teeth she ran into her mother's room. 'I'm ill, Mama, I've been sick!' she said, dramatically falling onto her mother's large white bed.

Anna placed a hand on her daughter's forehead and shook her head. 'I don't think you've got a temperature, but I'd better call Dr Higgins all the same. It's probably just a bug.' She hurried off to the telephone.

Sofia lay on the bed and suddenly terror gripped her heart. What if she was pregnant? She couldn't be, she thought, dismissing it again. Not once had they made love without condoms. Besides, it was scientifically proven that condoms were ninety-nine per cent safe. No, she simply couldn't be pregnant. But fear cast a dark shadow over her soul and as much as she tried to push the thought away, she trembled at the possibility that she might belong to the unlucky one per cent.

Dr Ignacio Higgins had been the Solanas' family doctor for years and had dealt with everything from Rafael's appendicitis to

Panchito's chickenpox. He smiled at Sofia reassuringly and after chatting to her about her holidays proceeded to examine her. He asked her questions, nodding knowingly at every answer she gave. When his old, crinkled face frowned gravely and the grin was replaced by an expression of the deepest concern she felt her heart accelerate and wanted to cry.

'Oh, Dr Higgins, please don't tell me it's serious,' she begged, her large hazel eyes filling with water because she already knew the answer. Why else would he have asked her about her periods?

Dr Higgins took her hand in his and caressing it affectionately with his thumb, he shook his head. 'I'm afraid, Sofia, you are pregnant.' He knew she was unmarried. Having been the family doctor for so many years he also knew how the family would react to a pregnancy outside of marriage, especially in a child as young as seventeen.

His words knocked the air out of Sofia and she felt her stomach plummet like it did sometimes when the car went over a large rise in the road. Her father used to tell her that she had lost her tummy. She wished she *had* lost her tummy. She slumped back weakly against her pillows. That cursed one per cent, she thought bleakly, watching those long afternoons of loving swirl away like water down a drain.

'Pregnant! O *Dios*, are you sure? What am I going to do?' she choked, biting her nail. 'What am I going to do!'

Dr Higgins tried his best to comfort her, but she could not be comforted. She watched her future disappear into a thick black void in front of her very eyes and there was nothing she could do to bring it back.

'You must tell your mother,' he suggested once she had calmed down a bit.

'Mama? You've got to be joking,' she replied, turning pale. 'Well, you know what she's like.'

The doctor nodded his old head compassionately. He had been in this situation countless times; young girls devastated by the seed growing in their ripe bodies, when such a miracle of nature should be something to celebrate. His familiarity with this situation in no way diminished his ability to be touched by it. His grey eyes misted like those foggy Irish days of his ancestors and he wished he could reverse the pregnancy with a pill.

'You can't do this on your own, Sofia, you must have the support of your parents,' he told her.

'They'll be furious – they'll never forgive me. Mama will kill me. No, I can't tell her,' she said hysterically, her smiling mouth reduced to a miserable arch that trembled inconsolably.

'Well, what can you do? They'll find out somehow. You can't hide a child growing inside you.'

She placed her hand instinctively on her belly and closed her eyes. It was Santi's child inside her. She was carrying a part of him. This was without doubt the worst moment of her life, and yet she felt a warmth inside. She dreaded to think what her parents would do. Yet she had no choice: they had to be told.

'Can you tell her for me?' she asked sheepishly.

He nodded. That was normally the way it was done. This thankless task was one of the doctor's many duties and one of the most sorrowful. He hoped they wouldn't blame the messenger as so many fraught parents often did.

'Don't worry, Sofia, it'll be all right,' he said kindly, getting up. Then turning to her, he added, 'Can you not marry this man, my dear?' But he recognised the insensitivity of his question as soon as he had said it, for why else would she be so unhappy?

Sofia shook her head in misery and, unable to reply, broke down in sobs. She dreaded her mother's reaction. She had no idea what she was going to do. How could she have been so unlucky? They had done everything to ensure that this didn't happen. She waited in terror. She had so often baited her mother for fun by missing school, or sneaking off to a nightclub with a young man without her permission, but those were minor and laughable in comparison to this. This time her mother's wrath would be well-deserved and terrifying. If she found out about Santi, she might well kill them both.

The door flew open and in marched her mother, her face as white as Christ in one of El Greco's creepy paintings. Her lips trembled with fury and Sofia recognised the disappointment in her eyes.

'How *could* you?' she cried in shrill Irish tones, her face turning purple with anger. 'How could you? After all we have done for you. What is the rest of the family going to think? The shame of it. What were you thinking? Why did you let it happen? It's bad enough that you . . . that you . . . out of marriage,' she stammered, 'but to get pregnant! I am so disappointed in you, Sofia.'

She collapsed into the chair and lowered her eyes as if to look at her disgraced daughter revolted her. 'I brought you up in a house where God's laws are respected. May He forgive you.'

Sofia made no reply. They both sat in silence. The blood sapped from her mother's cheeks like a recently slaughtered pig and her opaque eyes gazed out of the window as if she might see God among the dry plains and humid sky. She shook her head in despair.

'Where did we go wrong?' she asked, wringing her hands. 'Did we spoil you too much? I know Dad and Paco treated you like a little princess, but I didn't.' Sofia stared at the patterns on the quilt, trying to make sense of them. The situation was too surreal to take seriously. It simply couldn't be happening to her. 'I have been too strict – that's it, isn't it?' continued her mother miserably. 'Yes, I was too strict. You felt trapped, that's why you had to break all the rules. It's my fault entirely. Yer father always told me to be more lenient, but I couldn't. I didn't want the family to accuse me of being a bad mother, along with everything else . . .'

Sofia could hardly listen to the ranting of her mother without feeling disgusted. If it were Maria, Chiquita would be sweet and understanding, she'd want to help and look after her, but here was her mother blaming herself. Typical Irish Catholic – she'd be donning a sackcloth and ashes next! She longed to tell her to get down from her cross, but she could see that now probably wasn't the most sensible time to say it.

'So who's the father? Who is it? *Dios*, who could it possibly be? You haven't seen anyone except yer family.'

Sofia watched in dreadful anticipation as her mother slowly worked it out for herself. Her expression gradually changed from self-pity to disgust and she writhed with revulsion.

'Oh my God, it's Santi, isn't it?' she gasped, her curt Irish accent biting into the word 'Santi' with distaste. 'I'm right, aren't I? My God, I should have seen it coming. Why didn't I see it coming? Yer disgusting – both of you. How could he have been so irresponsible? He's a man now – how could he have seduced you, a child of seventeen?' Then she burst into tears. Sofia watched her impassively and thought how ugly she looked when she cried.

'I should have guessed, I should have noticed you both sneaking around like thieves with yer dirty secret. I don't know what we're going to do. The child will probably be mentally ill as you're so closely related. How could you be so devious? I must tell yer father. Don't leave the room until I come back!'

And Sofia heard the door slam behind her. She wanted desperately to run to Santi and tell him, but for once she hadn't the strength to disobey her mother. She lay there unmoving, awaiting her father.

As it was in the middle of the week, her father had to drive down from Buenos Aires. Anna couldn't tell him what the problem was over the telephone so he had to wait in suspense, his stomach churning with worry, until he arrived at Santa Catalina. Anna informed him immediately and they sat down to discuss the situation for over two hours. After a weary battle Paco had to give in to his wife, who had managed to convince herself that the child would be mentally ill. Sofia would have to terminate the pregnancy. When he finally entered his daughter's room he saw her lying asleep, curled into a pitiful ball, on her bed. He felt his heart break as he approached her. In his eyes she was still his little girl.

Sitting on the edge of her bed he ran a tender hand through her damp hair.

'Sofia,' he whispered. When she opened her eyes he was looking at her with such love she threw her arms around him and cried like a child into his chest.

'I'm sorry, Papa, I'm sorry,' she sobbed, shaking with shame and fear. He held her close and rocked her back and forth, rocking himself to ease his pain as well as hers.

'It's all right, Sofia, I'm not angry. I'm not angry. It's all right, it's going to be all right.'

It felt reassuring to be in his safe embrace. All the responsibility she passed over to him with a deep sense of relief.

'I love him, Papa.'

'I know you do, but Sofia, he's your cousin.'

'But there's no law against marrying your first cousin?'

'That's not the point. We live in a small world, and in our world marrying your first cousin is seen to be like marrying your brother. It's shameful. You can't marry Santi. Besides, you're very young. It's just an infatuation.'

'It's not, Papa. I love him.'

'Sofia,' he said gravely, shaking his head. 'You can't marry Santi.'

'Mama hates me,' she wept. 'She always has.'

'She doesn't hate you – she's disappointed, Sofia. And so am I. But your mother and I have discussed it at length. We will do what is best for you, trust me.'

'I'm so sorry, Papa,' she repeated tearfully.

Sofia padded sheepishly into the sitting room where her parents awaited to inform her of their decision. She sat down on the chintz sofa, her eyes lowered. Anna was perched stiffly on the window seat, her legs tightly crossed under her long dress. She looked pale and wan. Paco, his face drawn with worry, paced impatiently up and down the room. He looked older and greyer than before. The doors to the corridor and the dining room were shut firmly. Rafael and Agustin, anxious to know what the icy atmosphere was all about, had been told to disappear. So they had reluctantly wandered over to Chiquita's house to watch television with Fernando and Santi.

'Sofia, your mother and I have decided that you simply cannot keep the child,' her father began gravely. Sofia swallowed hard and was about to speak but he silenced her with a wave of his hand. 'You will go in the next few days to Europe. Once you have . . .' He hesitated, struggling with the idea of a termination that would weigh heavily on his conscience, being, as it was, against his faith and principles. 'When you are well again you will study there rather than here at the University of Buenos Aires as planned. This will give you, and Santi, time to get over this infatuation. You can then come home. No one must know about this, do you understand? It will be our secret.' He deliberately kept from her the information that she would stay with his cousin Antoine and his wife Dominique in Geneva and study at a school in Lausanne so there would be no chance of Santi finding out and following her there.

'You will not bring shame upon our good family name,' added her mother tightly, considering what this sort of scandal could do to the future prospects of her sons. She recalled bitterly the recent happy moments she had shared with her daughter and the growing sense of pride she had felt. Those moments made the disappointment all the more severe.

'You want me to have an abortion?' Sofia repeated slowly. Her hand rested on her belly and when she looked down she saw that she was shaking.

'Your mother . . .' began Paco.

'Oh, so it's you!' she said, turning viciously on her mother. 'You know you'll go to Hell for it! You're meant to be a good Catholic. Where have all your principles gone? I can't believe your hypocrisy. You make a mockery of your own faith!'

'Don't speak to your mother like that, Sofia,' her father said in a tone she had rarely heard him use. She looked from one parent to the other through the eyes of a stranger. She no longer knew them.

'The child will be insane, Sofia. It isn't fair to bring a child like that into the world,' her mother replied with forced calmness. Her voice softened and she added with a weak smile, 'It's for your own good, Sofia.'

'I won't abort it,' she told them stubbornly. 'My child won't be insane. You're so worried about the family reputation. It's got nothing to do with the health of my child. You think no one will find out? That's a joke.' She laughed scornfully.

'Sofia, you're angry now, but you'll understand in time.'

'I'll never forgive you for this,' she said and crossed her arms defensively in front of her chest.

'We're only thinking of you. You're our child, Sofia, and we love you. Trust me,' said her father.

'I thought I could,' she responded flatly.

Abortions were for whores. They were dirty and dangerous. What would Padre Julio say if he found out? Would she be damned to eternal Hell? Suddenly she wished she had listened to his sermons instead of dreaming about sex and Santi. Having thought that religion was for weak-minded people who needed direction like Soledad, or for fanatics like her mother who used it only when it suited her, she now feared that there really *was* a God and that He would punish her for what she had done. While she had been dreaming, religion had crept in through her subconscious only to surface and torment her at the very time she was most in need of its comfort.

'I have to say goodbye to Santi,' she said finally, staring at the patterns on the wooden floor.

'I don't think we can allow it, Sofia,' replied her mother coldly.

'I don't see why not, Mama. I'm already pregnant!'

'Sofia, don't speak to me like that. This is no laughing matter. It is very, very serious. No, you cannot see anyone before you go,' she said resolutely, smoothing her hands down the skirt of her dress.

'Papa, this is not fair. What harm can it do to see Santi?' she pleaded, pushing herself up from the sofa. Her father thought about it for a while. He walked over to the window and looked out onto the *pampa* as if the vast horizon would grant him an answer. He couldn't look at his daughter. His guilt was too great. He knew he should stand up to his wife, but he also knew that if he did, he would lose her for ever. Things had been so much better. He knew that this wasn't so much about Sofia's affair as his own affair back in 1956. Both he and Sofia had betrayed Anna's trust. He could tell that was what she was thinking; he could see the hurt in her eyes. It was about Anna's nagging feelings of isolation. But he had no choice, he had to agree.

'I think your mother is right, Sofia,' he said at last without turning around. 'You'll go with Jacinto to Buenos Aires tomorrow morning. Why don't you run along and pack your things. You'll be away some time . . .'

Sofia heard his voice crack but she felt no pity. 'I will *not* go without saying goodbye to Santi,' she shouted, her face red with frustration. 'You're not thinking of me, you're thinking of your stupid family name and reputation. How can you put that above the feelings of your own daughter? I hate you, I hate you both!' She ran out of the room onto the terrace. She didn't stop running until she reached the privacy of the trees. Leaning against the bark she sobbed at the injustice of the world, and looking around at her beloved Santa Catalina she felt nothing but hatred.

Back in the kitchen she could hear her parents fighting in the sitting room. Her mother was sobbing loudly and shrieking at her father in English. She didn't wait to listen.

'Soledad,' she hissed.

The maid looked up from her cooking to see Sofia tearfully standing in the doorway. 'What is it, what is it?' she replied in her gentle voice as she rushed over to embrace the young woman who would always be a child to her. She held her tightly although Sofia was now taller than she was.

233

'Oh Soledad, I am in such trouble. Will you do something for me?' Her eyes, that only a moment ago had been matt, now glittered with the excitement of a plan. She ran over to the sideboard and grabbing a pencil scribbled a brief note.

'Give this to Santi as soon as you can. Don't tell anyone, or show it to anyone, do you understand?'

Thrilled to be involved in a secret, Soledad, winked and put the note in her grubby apron pocket.

'I will go right now, Señorita Sofia. Don't you worry, Señor Santiago will have this letter in his hand in a second.' And she bustled out of the room.

When Rafael and Agustin arrived at Chiquita's house they told their cousins with great excitement that Sofia was in trouble again.

'She's had it coming to her for weeks,' Agustin sniggered gleefully.

'That is so untrue,' said Maria. 'Your mother was saying only a few days ago how well they're getting on. Don't be so unkind.'

'How long do you think they'll be?' asked Santi uneasily.

'Not long. Knowing Sofia, she'll run off with her bags packed,' Rafael said, switching on the television and flopping down onto the sofa. 'Maria, will you be an angel and get me a drink?'

'All right,' she sighed. 'What do you want?'

'A beer.'

'One beer – anyone else?'

Santi stood by the window looking out, but all he saw was his own reflection in the glass staring anxiously back at him. They all sat in front of the television but Santi wasn't watching. After half an hour he could wait no longer and he left the house in great haste. Just as he was crossing the terrace he saw Soledad, red-faced and sweating, striding purposefully through the trees towards him.

'Soledad, what are you doing?' he asked when she reached him. He felt uneasy.

'*Gracias a Dios, gracias a Dios*,' she replied, crossing herself in agitation. 'This is a letter from Señorita Sofia – she told me to give it to you and no one else. It is a secret, you understand? She is very upset, very upset. She's crying. I must go to her.' She dabbed nervously at her forehead with a white hanky.

'What is wrong with her?' he asked, sensing the seriousness of the situation.

'I don't know, Señor Santiago. I don't know anything. It is in the letter.' And before he could say another word she disappeared like an apparition into the trees.

Once in the light of the veranda he opened the note. *Meet me under the ombu tree at midnight*, was all it said.

Chapter Nineteen

———

Sofia had long since stopped crying. Lying on her bed she waited with the patience of someone resigned to her fate. Time passed very slowly, but she knew midnight would come eventually. She watched the plants swaying in the wind outside her window and they had a strange hypnotic effect that dulled her pain.

Finally she got up, collected the torch from the kitchen and, like a prisoner of war, made her escape. She crept like a puma with silent steps through the darkness to the ombu tree. With a contracted heart she hurried through the park as if her very life depended on it. She was strong with resolve but weak in the face of her inevitable destiny. She felt she was acting a part in a tragic school play, and although the drama appealed to her she couldn't quite reconcile herself to the reality of it.

The walk to the tree seemed much longer than usual. She quickened her steps. As she neared the ombu she noticed a small yellow light, Santi's torch, dancing in mid-air like a giant glow-worm as he paced up and down with impatience.

'Santi!' she gasped, falling into his arms. 'Santi, they know, they've found out, they're sending me away.' She stammered, afraid she wouldn't have time to tell him everything before they were discovered.

'What? Who knows? How?' he asked, confused. He had known

something was wrong from the urgent tone of her note, but he had never expected this. 'Calm down, no one's going to find us here. It's okay,' he said, trying to sound strong when he felt conquered by the powers of Fate.

'No, it's not. They're sending me to Switzerland – they're sending me away. *I hate them!*'

'How do they know?'

Sofia was about to tell him in her usual impulsive way that she was pregnant, but stopped herself. Her parents had told her not to tell anyone. They had been very specific. She feared that if she told Santi he would be unable to keep it to himself. He would probably stride into the house like a cowboy, guns smoking, and demand his rights as the father of the child. There was no telling what her parents might do then. She was still required to do their bidding by law. They could send her away and prevent her from ever returning. While she was in Argentina she was at their mercy. No, she couldn't tell him now, she decided. She would write to him from Geneva when her parents were too far away to do anything about it. So, struggling against her longing to share her sorrow she resigned herself, for the time being, to carry the truth alone.

'They know,' she conceded, 'and they're furious. They're sending me away to get over you.' She sobbed miserably, searching his eyes through the dark for confirmation of his affection but all she could make out were two dark holes.

'But Chofi, let me talk to them. They can't send you away. I won't stand by and let them send you away!' he whispered fiercely, determined to beat the forces that were trying to separate them.

'Oh, I wish you could, but they won't listen to you. They're just as angry with you as they are with me. You wouldn't believe the things my mother has said to me. I think she's thrilled to be getting rid of me.'

'I'm not going to let them take you from me. What will I do without you? I can't be without you, Sofia!' he hissed, his voice a plaintive cry in the dark.

'Oh, Santi, just accept it. We have to.'

'This is ridiculous,' he spat angrily. 'They don't have any proof. How come they're so sure? Who saw us?'

'I don't know, they didn't tell me,' she said, ashamed that she was able to lie with such ease.

'I'll come with you,' he said brightly. 'I'll leave with you. Let's go and start a new life together far from here. Let's face it, we would have had to in the end anyway. There's no future for us here.'

'You would leave Santa Catalina for me?' she said, choked by the ferocity of his devotion.

'Yes, I would. I've left before. But this time I won't come back,' he said gravely.

'You can't,' she sighed, shaking her head. 'You love Argentina as much as I do. You couldn't leave and never come back. Besides, your parents would be mortified.'

'We're in this together, Chofi. I won't let you take all the blame. For God's sake, it takes two to have an affair. So let me be banished with you.'

'But your parents?' she said, imagining the extent of Chiquita's sorrow.

'I'll do what I want. I don't need my parents' permission to leave the country.'

'I need mine to leave the country,' said Sofia miserably.

'Okay. So go along with your parents' plan. I'll come later and find you,' he said, holding her upper arms so tightly she winced.

'Santi – you really would lose everything for me?'

'I'll do anything for you, Chofi.'

'But your future is here. If you come with me, how can we ever return? You can't defy your family if you aren't prepared to abandon them for ever.'

'Then I'll abandon them for ever. I love you. Don't you understand, my future is with *you*. You're not some fleeting fancy, Chofi. You are my life.' And as he uttered those words he realised that she was, indeed, the force that drove him. It took a situation like this for him to realise the depth of his love, the extent of his need. Without her everything that he cherished at Santa Catalina would disintegrate like a body deprived of the breath that sustains it. She was the life force that fed everything. He knew that now with as much certainty as he knew he wasn't going to lose her.

'Okay. If you're serious, let's make a plan,' she said, her heart beating back to life again. 'Once I'm in Switzerland I'll write to you and tell you where I am. Then you can come.' They both smiled at the simplicity of their plan.

'Okay, but they may try to intercept our letters. We have to be prepared for everything. Say I confide in Maria – you can write the letters to her,' suggested Santi.

'No,' Sofia said immediately. Then, more gently, 'No. We can't trust anyone else but ourselves. I'll get someone else to write the address – I'll send them from another country if I have to. Don't worry, I'll write lots of letters. They can't intercept them for ever, can they?'

'I love you,' he murmured, and although she couldn't see the expression in his eyes she could feel his emotions as if they were phosphorescent vibrations radiating from every pore, enveloping her like hot tentacles, pulling her closer.

'And I love you,' she sobbed and fell on him, kissing him. They clung to each other, afraid that once apart, Fate would separate them and they would never find each other again. For a long while they wept in silence; only the constant clicking of the crickets filled the emptiness that engulfed them.

'Let's make a wish,' he said finally, pushing her away and delving into his pocket.

'What?'

'I want to wish that one day, we'll be able to stand here together, perhaps as much older people, to begin the rest of our lives together as an accepted couple.'

'You don't believe in wishes.' She laughed bitterly.

'It's a last resort, Sofia. I'll try anything once.'

'The rest of our lives then. Let's carve our names,' she whispered. 'Just an S for Santi and an S for Sofia.'

They both stood and gripped the knife together, Santi's large, rough hands covering hers. She noticed his were trembling. When they had finished they shone the torch on their initials and wished.

'You won't forget me, will you?' he croaked into her neck and she breathed in the familiar scent of his skin and closed her eyes, willing the precious present moment to last for just a little longer.

'Oh Santi, wait for me. It won't be long, please wait for me. I'll write, I promise. Don't give up on me,' she sobbed, straining her eyes in the darkness to lovingly take in every detail of his face so that she could imagine it later when she was thousands of miles away.

'Chofi, there are so many things I want to say that I should have said before. Let's run far away from here and marry.' Then he laughed bashfully. 'This isn't exactly an ideal moment, but if I don't ask you I'll regret it for the rest of my life. Will you marry me?'

She smiled at him in the way that a mother might indulge a child. 'Yes. I'll marry you, Santi,' she said sadly and kissed his agitated face, wondering if such a thing were possible with so much against them.

'Don't forget to write,' he said.

'I promise.'

'*Bueno*, my darling, until we see each other again. And we will, so let's not be sad.'

After holding each other one last time they made their way back to their houses in silence, their hearts throbbing with the belief that they would eventually be reunited.

Chapter Twenty

One moment Sofia was there, the next she was gone. Maria ran over to her cousins' house when her mother told her the news and demanded an explanation. Her aunt looked red-eyed and weary. She explained that Sofia had gone to visit friends in Europe before studying at a finishing school. She would be away some time. She had done very badly in school, which had been due to too many distractions in Buenos Aires, so she had been sent off in disgrace. Anna apologised that she hadn't given her time to say goodbye. It had been a last-minute thing.

Of course Maria didn't believe her. 'Can I write to her?' she asked tearfully.

'I'm afraid not, Maria. She needs to be away from everything that was distracting her here. I'm sorry,' Anna had replied, closing the conversation by pursing together her pale lips and walking out of the room. When Maria noticed that her mother no longer sat taking tea on the terrace with her aunt she knew something had happened between their two families.

The weekend after Sofia had inexplicably disappeared from the ranch, Paco went for a long ride with his brother Miguel to explain to him what had happened. It was early morning, the long grass glistened in the pale light and an occasional *vizcacha* hopped sleepily across the plain. Paco and Anna had decided not to reveal that

Sofia had been pregnant. They could not risk the scandal getting out. So he told Miguel only that Sofia and Santi had fallen in love and embarked on a sexual relationship.

Miguel was appalled. He felt humiliated that his son could stoop to such a level. It wasn't so bad that the two cousins had fallen in love – these things happened! But to have a sexual relationship was irresponsible and unforgivable. He blamed his son. 'He's older and should know better,' he said.

When they returned a couple of hours later Miguel was ashen with rage. He marched into the house and confronted Santi immediately.

'This is to remain within the walls of this house. Do you understand?' he barked, his fists clenched with fury.

Chiquita burst into tears when she heard. She knew what it would do to their family – that it would put a strain on her relationship with Anna. She felt guilty that it was her son who had committed the offence. She also felt desperately sorry for Santi, although she shared that sentiment with no one.

Miguel and Chiquita knew that Sofia was in Geneva with their cousins and they agreed with Paco and Anna that it had to be kept secret in order for the two lovers to get over their infatuation. They needed time without contact. They would make sure Santi wasn't able to write to Sofia. In spite of his pleas they withheld her whereabouts from him.

Anna was so upset she withdrew completely. Keeping herself busy in the house and garden she refused to see anyone. She felt so ashamed and thanked God that Hector wasn't around to witness her humiliation. Paco told her gently that life had to go on, she couldn't hide away for ever. But this only led to arguments, which always ended with Anna stalking out in tears and then refusing to talk to him at all.

After a couple of weeks she decided to write to Sofia in a calm tone, explaining why she had sent her to Europe. *It won't be long, my love, before you are back at Santa Catalina again, and all this mess will be forgotten*, she wrote affectionately because she felt guilty. After the third letter Sofia still hadn't replied. Her mother couldn't understand it. Paco also wrote; the difference was that he continued to write long after his wife had given up. 'If she doesn't respond, what can I do? I'm not going to waste my ink. She'll be home before too long,' she said angrily. Months passed and there was still no reply; not even to Paco.

Chiquita had attempted to see Anna, but she must have seen her coming and retreated into the house. She had telephoned a few times but Anna had refused to speak to her. It wasn't until Chiquita wrote a letter, begging to talk it through, that Anna weakened and allowed her to visit. At first the atmosphere was raw. They sat opposite each other, their bodies stiff as if ready at any moment for fierce confrontation, and talked about the most mundane things, like Panchito's new school uniform, as if everything was normal, yet watching each other warily through glassy eyes. They were unable to sustain the charade for long. At last Chiquita collapsed like an empty sack and began to weep. 'Oh Anna, I'm so desperately sorry. It's all my fault,' she sniffed, reaching out to her sister-in-law with solicitous arms. Anna wiped away a tear from her own cheek.

'I'm sorry too. I know what a minx Sofia can be. They are both to blame,' she said, longing to blame it all on Santi, but knowing that Sofia must take her share of it.

'I should have seen it coming – I should have noticed,' grieved Chiquita. 'I just thought nothing of them spending time together. They always have. We weren't to know that they were being irresponsible when they were alone together.'

'I know. But the important thing is that Sofia spends a few years away from home without contact with anyone. By the time she returns they will have grown out of it.'

'They'll probably feel very foolish,' said Chiquita hopefully. 'They're young. It's puppy love.'

Anna stiffened. 'That wasn't the behaviour of puppies, Chiquita.

The physical act of love is as far from puppy love as one can get – let's not forget that,' she said coolly.

'You're right, of course. One mustn't make light of it,' Chiquita agreed sheepishly.

'Santi is the one with sexual experience. Sofia, in spite of all her sins, was still a virgin and would have been one on her wedding night. God help her.' Anna sighed melodramatically. 'Now her husband will have to accept her as she is. Used goods.'

Chiquita wanted to remind her sister-in-law that it was the 1970s. That sex was seen differently now than in their day. The 1960s had seen the most monumental sexual revolution. But according to Anna, that revolution had happened in Europe and hadn't reached Argentina. 'European women can reduce themselves to the level of the common tart,' she had once said sharply. 'But my daughter will be a lady on her wedding night.'

'Santi is indeed the one with the sexual experience. He's also the man and I completely accept responsibility. I cannot apologise enough. In fact, he must come and apologise in person,' said Chiquita, prepared to do anything to mend their fraying relations.

'I don't want to see Santi at the moment, Chiquita,' Anna replied frostily. 'You must understand that my nerves are raw. I can't face my daughter's seducer right now.'

Chiquita's bottom lip quivered and she clamped her teeth together in order to restrain herself from violently defending her son. But she kept quiet in order to make peace with Anna.

'We are both suffering, Anna,' she conceded diplomatically. 'Let's suffer together and not hurt each other with accusations. What's done is done and we can't turn back the clock, although I would do anything to be able to.'

'Yes, so would I,' she replied, thinking of the life that had been squandered. 'May God forgive me,' she said in a low voice that seemed to come from the bottom of her throat. Chiquita frowned. Anna had almost whispered it and the other woman wasn't sure if she had intended her to hear it or not. She smiled and lowered her eyes. At least they were able to talk, but it was an arduous conversation. When Chiquita returned to her house later she lay down on the bed and fell into a tormented sleep. They might have opened the lines of communication, but she knew it would take years for their relationship to return to normal.

Agustin and Rafael were told that Sofia had developed a crush on her cousin and had been sent abroad to get over it. Their father made light of it, but the brothers knew that if it was serious enough for their sister to be sent to Europe it must have been more than just a crush. Rafael, in defence of his sister, confronted Santi and blamed him for being so irresponsible. He was older, had lived abroad, he shouldn't have encouraged her. She was barely more than a child. He had ruined her future. 'When she comes back, I don't want you anywhere near her, do you understand?' he said. He didn't know, of course, that she didn't intend to come back and that Santi was preparing to fly over to join her just as soon as he received word.

Agustin enjoyed the scandal. He thrived on the intrigue and gossip and enjoyed lying on the grass analysing the situation with his cousins Angel, Sebastian and Niquito. He went out of his way to be close to Santi, hoping that he would open up and tell him the details of their affair. Was it an affair? Did they really sleep together? What had his parents said? What was he going to do when Sofia returned? Did he love her? But much to his disappointment, Santi didn't reveal anything.

Fernando was delighted that his brother was in trouble. He'd finally fallen off his pedestal with a most satisfactory crash. He wasn't the golden hero any longer. In fact, Fernando couldn't have been happier, for he had always been irritated by Sofia, showing off all the time, intruding into their polo games, hanging around with Santi, the pair of them looking down their smug noses at everyone else. They deserved it. Talk about killing two birds with one stone. He felt six inches taller.

As much as he tried to hide his misery, Santi's pain showed all over his face. His limp got worse. He cried when he was alone at night and waited impatiently for a letter so he could go and join Sofia. He needed to be reassured that she still wanted him, now that she was far away. He wanted to reassure her too that he was waiting for her. That he loved her.

When Maria finally found out that her brother and cousin had been lovers she screamed at her mother: 'How could you not tell me, Mama! I had to hear it from Encarnacion! I'm the last person to know. Didn't you trust me?'

Furious with her uncle and aunt, she avoided them. She blamed her brother for getting her friend into such a terrible situation, and waited for a letter apologising for not saying goodbye and for not confiding in her. She was astounded that she hadn't suspected anything, but when she reflected on the summer she remembered sadly that she had always been the spare part in their relationship. Santi and Sofia had often excluded her, leaving her to play with Panchito while they went off on horseback, or sloped off to play tennis without her. She had grown so accustomed to it over the years that she hadn't even noticed. She had always been grateful to be included and had accepted it meekly when they had brushed her off. It didn't surprise her at all that she hadn't noticed. No one had noticed.

Sofia had always been devious, but Maria never thought she'd be the victim of one of her plots. She recalled their argument a couple of years before when Sofia had confessed to her that she was in love with Santi. Perhaps if she had listened and tried to understand, Sofia might have confided in her now. She resigned herself to the fact that it was partly her fault that her cousin had kept it from her. But she still felt angry and jealous and neither emotion diminished over the weeks while she waited for a letter.

A month later, when finally a letter arrived at their home in Buenos Aires, it was not addressed to Maria, but to Santi. He had paced the hall every morning with the misery of a caged bear, hoping for a thin blue envelope to release him from his desolation.

Miguel had instructed Chiquita to go through the pile and take out any letters that might be from Sofia before Santi had a chance to find them. But Chiquita's heart had softened, watching her son decline further and further into his unhappy, solitary world and so she had deliberately begun to let them sit on the table just long enough for Santi to see them before she descended the stairs to do what her husband had instructed.

Santi was grateful to his mother but they never spoke about it. Both pretended they had not noticed. Every morning he flicked through the letters, mostly addressed to his father, and watched his hope fade away with each letter that he rejected. What Santi and Chiquita didn't know was that Maria went through the post in the entrance hall every morning on her way to the university, before the porter took it up to their apartment.

When Maria saw the letter she picked it up and studied the handwriting. It wasn't Sofia's writing and it had been posted in France, but it was definitely from Sofia. Who else did he know in France? It was obviously a love-letter and it was obviously written and posted in such a way as to prevent anyone from discovering it. They were once again excluding her. She felt she had been slapped in the face. The hurt grabbed her by the throat and she gasped for air. She was too angry to cry. Jealousy overpowered her and consumed her until she ached to scream out at the unfairness of it all. Hadn't she been a good friend to Sofia? How could she so callously turn her back on her like that? Wasn't she her best friend, after all? Didn't that count for anything?

Maria crept into her bedroom with the letter and locked the door. She took off her shoes and lay on the bed tucking her feet in behind her. She spent a long while looking at it, wondering what to do. She knew she should give it to Santi, but she was so angry that her fury blinded her. She wasn't going to let them get away with it. She wanted them to suffer like she was suffering. Ripping open the envelope she pulled out the letter within, and immediately recognised the messy scrawl of her cousin. She read the first line. *To my love,* it said. Without reading the rest she turned over the page to confirm that Sofia had signed it. She had. *My heart beats with the anticipation that you will soon be here with me. Without that promise, I don't think it would beat at all.* Then she had signed it simply, *Chofi.*

So, Maria thought bitterly, Santi is going to go and join her. He can't leave, she raged silently, he can't leave too. Not both of them. That means that they are planning to run off together and never come back. What will Mama and Papa think? They'll die of grief. I can't let this happen. Santi will regret it for the rest of his life. He'll never be able to return to Argentina — neither of them will. Her heart quickened as she devised a plan. If she burnt the letter, Sofia would believe he had changed his mind. She would endure her three years in Europe; by then she would have grown out of the infatuation anyway, and then come back as planned. Whereas, if Santi followed her there now, neither would come back, ever. She couldn't bear to lose them both.

Maria wrote Sofia's address in her diary, writing backwards in case Santi were to come snooping, and put the letter back into the envelope. She didn't read the rest. She couldn't put herself through the torture of reading the details of their affair, not even to satisfy her curiosity. She walked solemnly out onto the balcony with a box of matches. Lighting the envelope she let it burn into a flowerpot, until there was nothing left besides a small mound of featherlight ashes that she pressed into the earth with her fingers. Then she slumped onto the tiled floor, dropping her head into her hands and finally allowed the tears to break and fall freely. She knew she shouldn't have burned the letter but they would all thank her in the end. She wasn't just doing it for herself, or for them, but for her parents whose hearts would break if Santi left them for ever.

She hated Sofia, she missed her, she longed for her. She missed her moods, her petulance, her sharp wit and irreverent humour. She felt so hurt and betrayed. They had grown up together and shared everything. Sofia had always been selfish, but she had never shut her friend out before. Not like this. She couldn't understand why Sofia hadn't written to her. She felt she didn't matter: she wasn't important. It sickened her to think that she had been nothing more than a loyal puppy, following Sofia around, never really appreciated. Well, she'd done it now. Sofia would hurt just as much as she was hurting. Now she would know what it felt like to be treated as if she didn't matter. When she later reflected on what she had done, she felt a terrible guilt and vowed never to tell anybody. When she looked at her reflection in the mirror she didn't recognise herself any more.

When another letter arrived, not long after the first, Maria felt her stomach lurch with guilt. She hadn't expected Sofia to write again. Hastily she hid it at the bottom of her bag and later condemned it to death by fire like the last one. After that she stalked the post every morning with the cunning of a professional thief. Trapped by her previous deceptions she would have been unable to stop even if she had wanted to.

Weekends weren't the same once Sofia left. All that remained after her parting was a bitter residue and an animosity between the families that threatened to destroy their much-cherished unity. The summer faded as the winter set in. The air smelt thickly of burning leaves and damp earth. The atmosphere on the farm was one of melancholy. Each family retreated into itself. The Saturday *asado* was washed away with the rain and soon the burnt ground where the barbecue had been became nothing more than a puddle of muddy water symbolising the end of an era.

As the weeks dragged on into months Santi became more and more desperate for some sort of communication from Sofia. He wondered whether she was being prevented from writing to him. All part of the strategy to get over him, no doubt. His mother was sympathetic but realistic. He must get on with his life, she said, and forget about Sofia. There were plenty of other girls about. His father told him to stop 'moping around'. He had got himself into a mess: 'It happens to us all at some stage in our lives; the trick is to push through it. Bury yourself in your studies, you'll be glad later on that you did.' It was obvious that they were both deeply disappointed in him, but there was no point in making the boy suffer more than he was already suffering. 'We've punished him enough,' they said.

Sofia filled his every moment, whether he was lying in tormented sleep or out galloping angrily across the plain. He spent every weekend on the farm, retracing their steps, running his hand nostalgically over their symbol in the trunk of the ombu tree. He would torture himself remembering her until he would crumble like a child and cry until he had no more strength left in him to sob.

In July of that year Juan Domingo Perón, President of the Republic of Argentina, died after only eight months in office, following his return from exile the previous October. Whether loved or hated Perón had been in the public eye for thirty years. His body was not embalmed and the funeral was simple according to his own instructions. His second wife, Isabel, became President and the country spiralled into decline. Intellectually challenged, she relied on her Machiavellian adviser, former policeman and astrologer, José Lopez Rega, nicknamed 'El Mago' (the Wizard), who claimed he could raise the dead and speak to the Archangel Gabriel. He even mouthed Isabel's speeches as she gave them, claiming that the words came directly from the spirit of Perón. But the blood was gushing out of the country and neither Isabel nor Lopez Rega could stop it. The guerrillas broke into revolt only to be met with the death squads of El Mago. Paco predicted that it wouldn't be long before their President was overthrown.

'She's a night-club dancer, I don't know what she's doing in politics. She should stick to what she's good at,' he grumbled.

He was right. In March 1976 the military deposed Isabel in a coup and put her under house-arrest. With General Videla at their head they proceeded to launch a bloody war on anyone who opposed them. People suspected of subversion or anti-government activity were rounded up, tortured and killed. The Great Terror had begun.

Chapter Twenty-One

Geneva, 1974

Sofia sat on the bench overlooking the deep blue lake of Geneva. Her eyes, fixed somewhere amid the faraway mountains, were red and sore from crying. It was quite cold although the sky was the most magnificent cornflower blue. She sat huddled in her cousin's sheepskin coat and wool hat and shivered. Dominique had told her to eat. What would Santi think if she returned to Argentina a poor version of the woman he had said goodbye to? But she didn't feel like eating. She would eat once he replied to her letter.

Sofia had arrived in Geneva at the beginning of March. It was the first time she had been to Europe. She was immediately stunned by the differences between her own country and Switzerland. Geneva was meticulously tidy. The streets were clean and smooth, the shop windows framed with gleaming brass, their interiors luxuriously decorated and scented. The cars were glossy and modern and the houses free from the kind of blemishes that a turbulent history had bestowed on the buildings of Buenos Aires. Yet in spite of all its order and polish Sofia missed the mad exuberance of her home city. In Geneva the restaurants closed at eleven whereas Buenos Aires only awoke at that time and continued to buzz until well into the small hours. She missed the froth of activity, the noisy cafés, the street parties and entertainers, the smell of diesel and burnt caramel and the sound of barking dogs and screaming children that were all part of the ambience of the streets of Buenos Aires. She found Geneva quiet. Polite, cosmopolitan, cultured but quiet.

Sofia had never met her father's cousin Antoine and his wife Dominique before, although she had heard her parents speak of them. Antoine was her father's second cousin; she knew all about him from her father's stories of his 'London days', when they had enjoyed the city together like two hounds on a hunt, and Anna had told her that she had lived with the couple in Kensington during their engagement. Sofia seemed to recall that Anna hadn't taken to Dominique – she found her too 'over the top', whatever that meant. Dominique had never liked Anna, she recognised an opportunist when she saw one, but she warmed to Sofia the minute she laid eyes on her. So like Paco, she thought happily.

To Sofia's relief, Antoine and Dominique turned out to be the most delightful couple she had ever met. Antoine was large and humorous and spoke English with a very heavy French accent. At first she thought he was putting it on to make her laugh. She certainly needed a laugh when she arrived. But it was genuine and he enjoyed her amusement.

Dominique was a woman in her forties. She was curvaceous with a candid, generous face and large blue eyes that opened very wide when she wanted to show interest in something. She tied her long blonde hair (which she was happy to point out wasn't at all natural) into a ponytail with spotted hankies. Always spotted hankies. Dominique told Sofia that she had met Antoine thanks to a spotted hanky, which he had handed to her from the row behind at the Opéra in Paris. Antoine had noticed her wiping her tears on the sleeve of her silk dress. From that moment on she always wore a spotted hanky in commemoration of that important day.

Dominique was loud and flamboyant, not only in the way that she laughed, for she sounded like a big exotic bird, but also in the way that she dressed. She always wore brightly coloured flowing trousers and long shirts she bought from an exotic shop called Arabesque in London's Motcomb Street. Every finger had a ring on it that sparkled. 'A good knuckle-duster in times of need,' she had said, before telling Sofia of the time she knocked the false teeth out of the leering mouth of a grubby flasher at Knightsbridge tube station. 'If he had been well-endowed I would have shaken his hand,' she joked. 'London is a strange place, the only place I've ever been flashed at or threatened. Always on the tube, too.' She added wryly: 'I remember a man, another grubby little man, who barely reached up to my navel. He looked up at me with these livid eyes and said "I'm going to fuck you". So I looked down my nose at him and told him, very firmly, that if he did and I found out about it, I'd be very, very, cross. He was so startled he jumped off at the next station like a scalded cat.' Dominique enjoyed being outrageous.

Sofia was dazzled by the violet and shimmering blue eye-shadows she used to enhance the colour of her eyes. 'What's the point of using natural colours? Nature can do that by itself,' she had laughed when Sofia asked her why she chose such vivid colours. She smoked through a long black cigarette-holder like Princess Margaret, and painted her fingernails blood-red. She was confident and opinionated and sassy. Sofia understood exactly why her mother hadn't liked her, for they were the very qualities that Sofia immediately admired. Sofia and Anna had rarely agreed on anything.

Antoine and Dominique lived in opulent splendour in a large white house on the Quai de Cologny, overlooking the lake. While Antoine spent long hours working in finance, his wife wrote books. 'Lots of sex and murders,' she replied with a grin when Sofia had asked her what she wrote about. She had given her one to cheer her up. It was called *Naked Suspect* and was appallingly bad; even Sofia with her inexperience of good literature could see that. But it sold well and she was always running off to sign copies and give interviews. The couple had two children in their teens – Delfine and Louis.

Sofia had trusted Dominique right from the moment she had shown sympathy for her situation. 'You know, *chérie*, years ago I had a roaring affair with an Italian. I loved him with all my heart, but my parents said he was not good enough for me. He owned a small leather shop in Florence. In those days, I lived in Paris. My parents sent me to Florence to study art, not men – but I can tell you, *chérie*, I learned more about Italy with Giovanni than I would ever have done in a classroom.' She had laughed, a deep throaty laugh. 'And now I cannot remember his second name. It was a long time ago. What I am trying to say, *chérie*, is that I know how you are feeling. I cried for a month.'

Sofia had now cried for more than a month. She had lain on Dominique's white damask bedspread one rainy afternoon and told her everything, from the moment Santi had arrived back home that summer to the moment he had kissed her goodbye under the ombu tree. She had lost herself in her memories and Dominique had sat back against the pillows chainsmoking, listening sympathetically to her every word. She had left out no details, describing their lovemaking without blushing. She had read Dominique's novels, so she knew there was little that would shock her.

Dominique had supported Sofia right from the start. She couldn't understand why Anna and Paco hadn't allowed the two to marry and have their child. If she had been Sofia's mother she wouldn't have stood in their way. There must be more to all this, she thought, and blamed it on Anna. 'So unlike Paco,' Antoine had said when Dominique had recounted Sofia's story.

Then they had discussed the baby. Sofia was adamant that she would keep it. 'I have told Santi about the baby in my letter. I know he will want me to have it. He'll make an adorable father. I'll take it back to Argentina. It will be out of their control then. We'll be a family and that's the end of it.'

Dominique was encouraging. Of course she shouldn't abort the child. What a barbaric thing to do. She would help her through it – she'd be proud to. It would be their secret until Sofia decided she was ready to tell her family. 'You can stay as long as you like,' she had said. 'I will love you like my own daughter.'

At first it had been quite exciting. Sofia had written to Santi the minute she had arrived and Dominique had inscribed the envelope for her with wholehearted enthusiasm. Dominique had then taken her shopping up the rue de Rive to celebrate and bought her the latest European fashions. 'Wear these while you can. You won't fit into them for long,' she had laughed.

They had gone skiing on weekends in Verbier where Antoine had a beautiful wooden chalet nestled in the mountainside, looking down the valley. Louis and Delfine brought friends and the house was filled with laughter and games in front of the flickering flames of the large open fire. They had posted the letter across the border with much ritual, pleased that no one would suspect a postmark from France. While Sofia missed Santi, she imagined him receiving her letter and scribbling back immediately. They calculated the time it would take for him to write to her and the time it would take for the letter to reach her. She waited excitedly for it to arrive. When the two weeks they had anticipated turned into a month, then two, her mood declined until she simply wasn't able to eat or sleep and she began to appear tired and pale.

Sofia had filled her days with the various courses that Dominque had set up for her. Courses in French, courses in art, courses in music, courses in painting. 'We must keep you busy so you don't miss your home or think too much about Santi,' she had said.

Sofia had allowed them to absorb her because they provided her with some sort of spiritual relief. The music she chose to play on Dominique's piano was heart-wrenching, the paintings she painted were dark and melancholic, and she vented her tears in the face of such ethereal beauty when she studied the paintings of the Italian Renaissance. As she waited for Santi's letter or for his presence that she felt sure would appear as a surprise on their doorstep, she used art to find expression for her misery and her hopelessness. She had written again, and again, in case he hadn't received the first letter, but still no word came from him. No word at all.

She looked out over the lake and wondered whether Santi had been appalled by her pregnancy. Perhaps he didn't want to know. Maybe he thought it was just better for everyone if he forgot about her and got on with his life. And what about Maria? Had she forgotten her too? Sofia had wanted to write to her; in fact, she had started a couple of letters but each time she had scrunched up the paper and thrown it into the fire. She felt too ashamed. She didn't know what to say. Sofia looked about her, at the small fragile flowers poking out through the melting snow. Spring was on its way and she had a child growing inside her. She should be happy. But she missed Santa Catalina, the hot summer days and their humid siestas in the attic where no one had been able to reach them.

When she returned to the house Dominique was frantically waving at her from the balcony, a blue envelope in her hand. Sofia ran up the road. Her depression lifted. Suddenly the clean air filled her lungs and she savoured the taste of spring. Dominique was smiling broadly, her white teeth glimmering against her scarlet lips.

'I was so tempted to open it. Hurry! What does it say?' she said, impatient with excitement. Finally the young man had written. Sofia would smile again.

Sofia grabbed the letter and looked at the writing on the front. 'Oh!' she groaned in disappointment. 'It's from Maria. But perhaps she's written for him since they probably forbade him to write to me.' She tore open the envelope. Her eyes scanned the lines of neat, flowery writing. 'Oh no!' she wailed and burst into tears.

'What is it, *chérie*, what does it say?' asked Dominique, alarmed. Sofia flopped onto the sofa while Dominique read the letter.

'Who is Maxima Marguiles?' she asked angrily.

'I don't know,' sobbed Sofia, heartbroken. 'Maria says he is going out with Maxima Marguiles. How can he – so soon?'

'Do you believe your cousin?'

'Of course I do. She was my best friend – after Santi.'

'Perhaps he's going out with someone else to show his family that he doesn't care any more about you. Perhaps he is acting?'

Sofia took her head out of her hands. 'Do you think so?'

'He's clever, isn't he?'

'Yes, and I went out with Roberto Lobito for the same reason,' she said, brightening up.

'Roberto Lobito?'

'Another story,' she replied, waving her hand in the air, not wanting to be distracted from talking about Santi.

'Did you tell Maria about your affair with Santi?' Dominique asked. Sofia felt her stomach sink with guilt. She should have told Maria.

'No. It was our secret, I didn't tell anyone. I couldn't tell anyone. I always told Maria everything – but this time . . . well, I just couldn't.'

'So, you don't think Maria knows,' Dominique said steadily.

'I don't know,' Sofia replied biting her nail in agitation. 'No, she can't know, because if she did she wouldn't want to hurt me by telling me about Maxima. She would also have mentioned our affair in her letter. We were best, best friends. I imagine then she doesn't know.'

'Well, Santi will hardly have confided in her then, would he?'

'No, you're right.'

'Okay, if I were you, I would wait until you receive a letter from Santi.'

So Sofia waited. The days lengthened into summer until the sun had melted all the snow and the farmers let their cows out of their sheds to roam freely amid the mountain flowers and long grasses. By May she was four months pregnant. Her belly was round but the rest of her was thin and gaunt. Dominique's doctor told her that if she didn't eat she would damage her child. So she forced herself to eat healthily and drink plenty of fresh water and fruit juices. Dominique worried about her constantly, praying that Santi would write, damn him! But no letter came. Sofia still hoped long after Dominique had given up hoping. She would sit for hours on the bench looking out across the lake, watching winter melt into spring, spring flower into summer and finally summer die into autumn. She felt a part of her die with it. Her hope.

It was only later when she felt less emotional and able to look at things more objectively, that it occurred to her that if Maria had known her whereabouts then Santi most certainly would have known, too. She realised that he could easily have written to her, but he hadn't. He had betrayed her, for whatever reason. He had made a conscious decision not to communicate. Sofia tried to console herself by justifying his betrayal with many different reasons that might have given the desperately love-sick Santi no other option but to let her go.

On 2 October 1974 Sofia gave birth to a healthy baby boy. She wept as she held him to her breast and watched him feed. He had dark hair like her and his eyes were blue. Dominique told her that all babies were born with blue eyes. 'Then his will be green like his father's,' Sofia said. 'Or brown like his mother's,' added Dominique.

The birth had been difficult. She had screamed as the pain had viciously wrenched her womb apart. Gripping Dominique's hand until it had drained of blood, she cried out for Santi. In those intense moments where struggle gives way to relief and finally joy, Sofia had felt her heart empty with her womb. Santi didn't love her any more and the withdrawing of his love cast a shadow over her soul. She felt she had not only lost her lover, but the only true friend she had in the world. She sank once more into despair.

The delight she felt when she first held her child momentarily filled the void Santi had left. She ran her hand down his mottled cheek, stroked his angel hair and breathed in the warm scent of him. As he fed she played with his tiny hand that clutched hers possessively and refused to let it go, even once he had fallen asleep.

He needed her. She took great pleasure in watching him fill his little stomach with her milk. Milk that would sustain his life and make him grow. As he sucked on her breast she felt a strange pulling sensation in her belly that delighted her. When he cried she felt it in her solar plexus even before she heard it. She would call him Santiguito, because if Santi had been there that is the way he would have wanted it – Little Santiago.

After the initial joy of loving her new baby, Sofia's vision once more darkened and her future seemed to hold nothing to brighten it. It was then that she experienced a crisis of confidence. She was consumed by an icy panic that seemed to squeeze the air out of her lungs and make it difficult for her to breathe. She wasn't capable of looking after a small baby on her own; she didn't know how to. Not without Santi, not without Soledad. When she opened her mouth to scream, nothing came out but a long, silent cry. She was alone in the world and she didn't know how to face it.

Sofia thought of Maria often. She yearned to share her misery with her friend, but didn't know how to. She felt guilty. If Maria knew, which by now Sofia felt she most certainly did, she would feel betrayed. She knew for sure when no more letters arrived. Sofia felt so cut off from all that had been familiar to her. As much as she tried to love Geneva, it represented nothing but pain. Whenever she looked out of her hospital window, over those shimmering mountains in the distance, she thought about what she had lost. She had lost the affection of both Santi and Maria. She had lost her much-cherished home and all that was familiar to her, everything that had made her feel loved and secure. She felt abandoned and alone. She didn't know where to go from there. Wherever she went, however far away, she couldn't run away from herself and the deep sense of bereavement she carried inside her.

After a week in the hospital, Sofia brought her baby home to the Quai de Cologny. She had had a lot of time to think while she had lain in her hospital bed. It was no easy decision to come to, but it was plain that Santi didn't want them. She couldn't return home to Argentina, and she certainly wasn't going to Lausanne as her parents had planned. At first, back in March, they had both written to her, attempting to explain themselves. Her father had written more often. But Sofia had never written back, so their letters had dried up. She supposed they thought that things would get back to normal once she returned home. But she wasn't ever going home.

She explained to Dominique that she couldn't bear to be in Argentina if she couldn't have Santi, and Geneva was too quiet for her to build a future there. She was going to put her roots down in London.

'Why London?' asked Dominique, deeply disappointed that Sofia and little Santiguito were going to leave her. 'You know you can stay here with us. You don't have to go.'

'I know. But I need to get away from everything that reminds me of Santi. I love it here with you. You and Antoine are the only family I have now. But you have to understand, I want to make a new start.' She sighed and lowered her eyes. Dominique saw that the child before her had grown into a young woman since she had become a mother. Yet, she didn't glow with that post-natal radiance normal in young mothers. She looked sad and oddly evasive.

'Mama and Papa met in London,' she went on, 'I speak the language and I have a British passport thanks to my grandfather who was from the north of Ireland. Also, London is the last place they would come looking for me. Geneva or Paris would be their first choices, or Spain, of course. No, I've made up my mind. I'm going to London.'

Sofia had always been fascinated by London. Having been to the English school of San Andres in Buenos Aires, she had learnt about England's kings and queens, the beheadings and the hangings, the pageantry and the ceremony that went with the monarchy. Her father had promised to take her one day. Now she would go alone.

'Chérie, what are you going to do in London with a small baby? You cannot bring him up on your own.'

'I'm not taking him with me,' she replied, her eyes fixed on the Persian rug beneath her feet. Dominique was unable to hide her shock. Her eyes bulging like a frog's, she stared at Sofia's pale face in horror.

'What are you going to do with him? Leave him with us?' she stammered angrily, sure that Sofia must be suffering some sort of post-natal depression.

'No, no, Dominique,' Sofia responded wearily. 'I want to give him to a nice, kind family who will look after him as their own. Perhaps a family who have wanted a child for a long time . . . please find such a family, Dominique,' she pleaded, but her expression was one of resolve.

Sofia was drained of tears. She had no more left to shed. She had reached a drought and her heart was numb. Antoine and Dominique sat her down to try to convince her otherwise. It was raining heavily outside, mirroring her own inner misery. Santiguito slept peacefully in his cot, wrapped in an old shawl of Louis'. Sofia explained that she couldn't be with this child who reminded her every time she looked at him of Santi and his betrayal. She was too young. She didn't know how to cope. Her future seemed like a big black hole that she was spinning towards without control. She didn't want her baby.

Antoine sternly told her that this was a human being she was talking about. She was responsible for him. He wasn't some toy one could simply give away. Dominique told her gently that she would forget about Santi, that her child would develop a personality of his own and no longer remind her of him. But she didn't listen. If she left now it wouldn't hurt so much to be separated from him; he was a mere baby. If she stayed any longer she would never be able to let him go and she *had* to let him go. She was too young to look after him and he couldn't be part of the new life she felt compelled to begin. She had made up her mind.

Dominique and Antoine spent long hours discussing what Sofia should do while she was out of the house walking Santiguito up and down the lakeside in his pram. Neither of them wanted her to give the child up for adoption; they knew she would regret it for the rest of her life. But Sofia was young and unable to see that far ahead. With her inexperience, how could she have possibly known that those nine months of carrying him and few weeks of loving him would tie him to her in an indestructible bond?

In the hope that by talking to a doctor she might come to her senses, Dominique and Antoine sent her to a psychiatrist. Sofia obliged them by going, but stated very firmly that she wasn't going to change her mind. The psychiatrist, Dr Baudron, a small man with silver-grey hair smoothed back off his face and a chest that looked to Sofia like that of a fat, happy pigeon, talked to her for hours, making her analyse moment by moment the last year of her life. She told him everything impassively, as if she were sitting up in the corner of the room on the ceiling, watching herself recount the moments that had led her to his office with the mouth and voice of someone else. After endless, futile talking, Dr Baudron told Dominique that either she was in a state of trauma or she was the most controlled human being he had ever met. He would have liked more time, but his patient had refused to see him any more. Sofia was still in her ship, undeterred by the delay, navigating her way to London.

Once Sofia had managed to convince her cousins that she wasn't going to change her mind, there were papers to sign and people to see in order to legally give her child up for adoption. Dominique was devastated. She tried to tell Sofia that she would regret it, maybe not now, but later. Sofia didn't want to know. Dominique had never met anyone more stubborn in her life and for a moment she sympathised with Anna. When she didn't get her own way Sofia wasn't quite the angel she had thought she was. She had a violent temper, sulked and then folded her arms in front of her, settling her face with an expressionless veneer that no amount of cajoling could break through. Not only was she stubborn but she was proud. Dominique longed for Sofia to pack her bags and take the child back to Argentina with her; after the initial shock and scandal the storm would abate and they would both be accepted again. But Sofia didn't want to go back. Ever.

While she waited for the adoption process to be completed the reality of leaving her son grew more intense as each day passed. Now she knew she was leaving she treasured every moment with Santiguito. She could barely look at him without weeping; she knew she would never know him as a grown man, have no input into the shaping of his character or his destiny. She wondered what he would look like as a small child. She held his tiny body against hers and talked to him for hours as if by some miracle he would remember the sound of her voice or the scent of her skin. Yet, in spite of the pain of leaving him she knew she was doing the right thing for both of them.

Reluctantly, Dominique and Antoine gave her some money to help her get started in London. Dominique suggested she stay a few nights in a hotel before finding a flat to rent. The couple took her to the airport to see her onto her flight.

'What shall I tell Paco?' Antoine asked gruffly, trying not to show his emotions. He had grown tremendously fond of Sofia, but he couldn't help resenting her for her ability to be so cold. How she could give up her child was something he was unable to understand. Delfine and Louis were the best things that had ever happened to him.

'I don't know. Tell them I decided to make a new life, but don't tell them where.'

'You will go home eventually, won't you, Sofia?' asked Dominique, shaking her head sadly. Sofia watched her long, ethnic earrings swing about her neck. She would miss her cousins. She swallowed hard in order to maintain her composure.

'There is nothing left for me in Argentina. Mama and Papa cast me away as if I meant nothing to them at all,' she said, and her voice trembled.

'We've been through all of this before, Sofia. You must forgive them or your bitterness will eat away at you and bring you nothing but unhappiness.'

'I don't care,' she replied.

Dominique took a deep breath and hugged her cousin who had become a daughter to her – though no daughter of hers would ever be this stubborn. 'If you need anything, anything at all, you can always call. Or come back. We are here for you, *chérie*. We will miss you, Sofia,' she said and held her tightly and allowed her tears to wash away her make-up.

'Thank you. Thank you both,' sobbed Sofia. 'Oh dear, I didn't want to cry. I'm such a cry-baby. What's the matter with me?' She sniffed and wiped her face with the back of her hand. She promised to keep in touch. She promised to call if she needed anything.

Holding tiny Santiguito for the last time she felt his soft head against her lips and breathed in his warm baby smell. She could barely leave him and almost changed her mind. But she couldn't stay in Geneva, to be reminded every second of her misery. She had to start again. She gazed down into his dear little face and held it there, taking a mental picture to carry with her and remember for always. He returned her gaze, his shiny blue eyes watching her curiously. She knew he would never remember her, he probably couldn't see her clearly anyway. She would disappear out of his life and he would be ignorant of ever having known her. She pulled herself up and silently willed herself to go forward. Running a finger down Santiguito's temple she turned, picked up her bag and disappeared through passport control.

Once on the other side she swallowed hard, held her head up and stopped crying. She was starting again, a new life. As Grandpa O'Dwyer always used to say, 'Life is too short for regrets. Life is what yer make of it, Sofia Melody. It's the way yer look at it. A glass is either half empty or half full – it's all a matter of attitude. A positive mental attitude.'

Chapter Twenty-Two

_____

Santa Catalina, 1976

Two years had gone by without a word from Sofia. Paco had spoken to Antoine who had explained that she had left without revealing where she was going to stay. Sofia hadn't wanted them to know where she was, not even which country she was in, but Antoine considered the whole thing wholly out of proportion. So he told Paco that she had simply said she wanted to lay her roots down in London.

Anna was devastated that Sofia had not gone to school in Lausanne as planned and desperately wanted to contact her daughter to beg her to come home. She worried that Sofia might decide never to return. Had she been too harsh? She told herself that the child had needed discipline – that's what parents were for. What had she expected, a mere pat on the wrist? 'Don't do it again, dear.' No, she had deserved every bit of it. Surely she understood that. But it was all behind her now, it was in the past. Dominique had assured her that Sofia had 'dealt with her problem'. How could the child hold a grudge for so long? It had all been for the best. She'd thank her one day. But not even to communicate? Not even a letter, nothing. After all the letters they had written her. Anna felt like a monster. She convinced herself that Sofia was going through an 'unfortunate' phase and would eventually return. Of course she would return, Santa Catalina was her home. 'She's as stubborn as her grandfather was. A true O'Dwyer,' Anna lamented to Chiquita. But inside her heart ached with the nagging regularity of someone who knows she has done wrong but cannot admit it, even to herself.

Chiquita had watched Santi grow thin and pale. She worried that his limp was giving him trouble, but he wouldn't communicate with her. He was there in body but his mind was in another place. Like Anna she hoped that her child would return. Fernando was at university in Buenos Aires, studying engineering. He was also going through a difficult stage. Staying out after curfew, losing his ID card, getting into trouble with the police. There were stories of people being arrested and disappearing. Sinister stories. She worried that he was mixing with irresponsible young socialists who plotted to overthrow the government. 'Politics isn't a game, Fernando,' said his father gruffly. 'You get into trouble, it'll cost you your life.'

Fernando rather enjoyed the attention. Finally his parents were noticing him. He basked in their concern and took to telling exaggerated stories of his exploits. He almost willed himself to get caught by the police so that his parents would be forced to demonstrate how much they cared for him by the effort and energy they put into getting him out. While his father got angry his mother cried with relief that he had returned unharmed. He enjoyed pulling her emotional strings; it made him feel loved. He watched Santi occupy the house like a spectre. He came and went and made very little noise. Fernando hardly noticed him. He lost himself in his studies and grew a beard, so he lost himself in the mirror too. How fortune had turned on him, thought Fernando gleefully, and all because of Sofia. They deserved each other.

Maria had broken down into deep sobs when her mother told her that Sofia had gone to live in London and had left no forwarding address. 'It's all my fault,' she had wailed, but she wouldn't say why. Her mother had comforted her as best she could, reassuring her that she'd come back eventually. Chiquita felt helpless; all of her children were so unhappy. Only Panchito smiled all the time and seemed content.

In November 1976 Santi was nearly twenty-three years old, but he looked much older. He had finally resigned himself to the fact that Sofia was never coming back. How the lines of communication could have failed he just didn't know. They had planned it so carefully. After having waited for her letters in the apartment, he had thought that perhaps his father was taking them from the porter as he left the building for the office every morning, so Santi had taken to getting up early and going through the post at dawn. But still there was no letter from Sofia. Nothing.

Finally he had confronted Anna. At first Chiquita had told Santi to stay out of his aunt's way. Anna had specifically told her that she didn't want to see him. So Santi had done as he was told and made sure he didn't bump into her. But after about two months, when he was maddened by the silence in the mailbag, he strode into her apartment in Buenos Aires and demanded to know where Sofia was.

Anna was sitting with the cook talking through recipes for the following week's meals, when Loreto appeared at the door to the sitting room, red-faced and trembling, to announce that Señor Santiago was in the hall, demanding to see her. Anna told Loreto to tell him that she wasn't there, that she had gone out and wouldn't be back until late, but she returned, apologetically, saying that Señor Santiago wouldn't go until Señora Anna returned, even if he had to spend the night on the floor. Anna relented, dismissed the cook and told Loreto to bring him in.

When Santi appeared at the door, he looked more like a shadow than a man. His face was black with misery and his eyes livid with fury. He wore a beard and had grown his hair long. He no longer looked handsome but decadent and menacing. In fact, Anna thought he looked more like Fernando, who had always appeared slightly sinister, ever since he had been a boy.

'Come and sit down,' she said calmly, hiding the tremor in her voice behind a steely veneer of control.

Santi shook his head. 'I don't want to sit down. I won't be staying long. Just give me Sofia's address and I'll leave,' he said in a monotone.

'Now listen to me, Santiago,' Anna said sharply. 'How dare you demand my daughter's address when you are the man guilty of stealing her virtue.'

'Just give it to me and I'll go,' he repeated, determined to avoid a scene. He knew what his aunt was like. She had reduced his mother to tears many times. 'Please,' he ventured with forced politeness.

'I won't give you her address, because I don't want you two to see each other again, or communicate. What do you hope for, Santiago?' she said icily, smoothing back her shiny red hair that was scraped into a knot at the back of her head. 'You don't think you can marry, do you? Is that what you want?'

'Just give it to me, damn you! Who she chooses to see is none of your business,' he snapped, losing his composure.

'How dare you talk to me like that! Sofia is my daughter. She was no more than a child – a minor. How do you think I feel? You stole her innocence,' she accused furiously, her voice ascending a few notes.

'Stole her innocence? God, you've always been so melodramatic, Anna. You don't want to think of her enjoying it, do you.' Anna's face twitched nervously. 'She *did* enjoy it. She enjoyed every moment of it because she loves me and I love her. We made love, Anna. Love. Not sex, not sordid, dirty sex, but beautiful love. I can't expect you to understand, you don't look capable of enjoying love like Sofia. You're too dried up with bitterness and resentment. Well, don't give me the address then. But I'll find it. I'll find it and Sofia, and I will marry her in Europe and never come back. Then you'll wish you hadn't sent her away.'

He didn't wait to be ordered out, but left hastily, slamming the door behind him. After that brief collision Chiquita and Miguel had berated him for his rudeness and Paco had confronted him, albeit in a calmer manner, and had explained to him why he wasn't able to write to Sofia. Santi had been too distraught to notice the hurt in his uncle's eyes and the greyness that had not only destroyed the colour of his hair but had also deprived him of the golden skin of his happier days. They were both broken men. But Santi couldn't give up. Sofia had told him never to give up.

For two and a half years he had tormented himself with possible scenarios. Perhaps she had written and the letter got lost. What if she had been waiting for a letter from him? Oh God, what if she *had* written? He worried himself into a state of total despair until Maria's conscience could bear the guilt no longer and she confessed.

It was a dark, drizzly winter's night. Santi stood outside on the balcony, gazing down onto the noisy streets of the city, eleven stories below him. As if in a dream he watched unblinking as the world continued oblivious to his pain. Maria stepped out to join him, her lips pale and trembling. She knew she had to tell him. If she didn't he might just throw himself to his death and then she'd never forgive herself. She stood beside him and looked below at the cars that lit up the street with their bright lights, blowing their horns for no apparent reason as Argentines always do. She turned to look at his shadowy profile that continued to stare down without noticing that she was beside him. Without knowing that she was about to confess her darkest secret.

'Santi,' she said, but her voice failed her, the word escaping in no more than a whisper.

'Leave me alone, Maria. I need to be alone,' he said, without taking his eyes off the long drop below him.

'I need to talk to you,' she replied, this time putting more force behind her words.

'So talk,' he said brutally, without meaning to be unkind. His unhappiness had made him insensitive to anybody else's feelings, as if he were the only human being to suffer.

'I have a confession. Don't be angry, let me explain wh-wh-why I did it,' she stammered, the tears already running down her face in anticipation of his reaction. He slowly turned his head and looked at her with heavy eyes.

'Confession?' he said flatly.

'Yes.'

'What confession?'

Maria gulped and wiped the tears from her cheeks with a shaking hand. 'I burnt Sofia's letters to you.'

When Maria's words reached his understanding, all Santi's anger, misery and frustration coiled with such force that he was unable to control himself. He pulled his hand back and brought it down onto the railing with a loud thud. He picked up one of his mother's flowerpots and threw it against the wall where it shattered, splattering the wall with mud. Then he turned and looked at his sister with loathing. Fat tears tumbled down her cheeks. 'I'm sorry,' she repeated over and over, trying to touch him. 'How can I make it up to you?'

'Why?' He shouted at her, stepping back from her. 'Why did you do it, Maria? It's not like you! How could you?'

'I was hurt. Santi, I was hurt. She was my friend too,' she replied, desperate to get through to him. But he just stood over her, staring at her. 'Santi. Please forgive me. I'll do anything.'

'My God, Maria. You of all people. *You!* I can't believe you would be so vindictive.' He gasped, shaking his head in complete astonishment. Maria watched him tremble with fury. He looked so old for a man so young. She had done that to him. She would never forgive herself.

'It was a mistake. I hate myself. I want to die!' she moaned. 'I'm sorry. I'm so sorry.'

'How did you find the letters?' he asked in bewilderment.

'I retrieved them from the porter on my way to the university.'

'God, Maria, you're devious. I never thought you were like that.'

'I'm not. I'm really not. I just couldn't bear you to leave. Not you as well as Sofia. I thought of Mama and Papa and the suffering they would have to endure and I just couldn't let you do it.'

'So you read the letters.'

'No. I just read the last few lines.'

'What did they say?'

'Something about longing for you to go to her in Switzerland.'

'So she had expected me to come. She must think I betrayed her,' he whispered for his anxiety had left his throat constricted, like the neck of a hanged man.

'I thought she would come back. I thought she'd come back to find that you'd both grown out of it. Then things would be the same again. I never thought she'd leave for good. Oh Santi, I never thought she'd leave for good. I wish I'd never done it.'

'So do I,' he choked, sinking onto the wet tiled floor and dropping his face into his hands. His whole body shook with violent sobs. At first he pushed his sister away when she tried to comfort him. But she persisted and after a few attempts he allowed her to wrap her arms around him and they cried together.

It took two years for Santi to forgive his sister completely. When he clubbed together with Fernando and a couple of Fernando's guerrilla friends that cold July night to rescue their sister from the sinister Facundo Hernandez, he suddenly saw beyond himself and his own pain. He woke up.

Maria fell in love with Facundo Hernandez in the autumn of 1978. She had just celebrated her twenty-second birthday. Facundo was tall and swarthy, being of Spanish blood. He had dark brown eyes with long black lashes that curled out like spiders' legs. He was a young officer in the military – part of General Videla's army – and wore his smart new uniform with pride. Facundo worshipped the General with the enthusiasm of a new recruit and strutted about the streets of Buenos Aires with an air of self-importance that pertained to all those in the military at that time.

General Videla had seized power in March 1976 with the aim of terminating the chaos of the Perónist years and restructuring Argentine society. The government launched a bloody war on its opposition, arresting all those suspected of subversion. Houses were broken into in the middle of the night, suspects dragged from their beds never to be seen again. It was a time of great fear. The 'disappeared' reached perhaps as many as 20,000 and left no legal trail behind them. They simply vanished.

Facundo Hernandez believed in democracy. He believed the military were laying foundations for an eventual 'democracy' which, in their own words, would 'suit the reality and needs and progress of the Argentine people'. He was a small cog in this big machine that was going to reform his country. The torture and murders were, he told himself, an unavoidable means to this end, and the end justified the means.

Facundo Hernandez first laid eyes on Maria Solanas one Sunday morning in April when she was walking in the park in Buenos Aires with a friend. It was a warm day, clear skies shone resplendent over the city and the park was full of children playing in the sunshine. He followed her while she ambled slowly along the path. He liked the way her hair gleamed and fell thickly down her back. She was full. He liked full women. He liked their round bottoms and round thighs. He watched her bottom move as she walked.

Maria and Victoria sat down at one of the small tables and ordered a couple of Colas. When Facundo Hernandez introduced himself and asked if he might join them, they were suspicious and explained nervously that they were waiting for a friend. '*Un amigo*' they said, a male friend. But when he recognised Victoria and claimed to be a friend of her cousin Alejandro Torredon they relaxed and introduced themselves. Maria immediately liked Facundo. He made her laugh. He made her feel attractive. He paid her lots of attention and practically ignored her friend. Still wary of him she declined to give him her telephone number but agreed to meet him at the same time the following day in the park.

Soon their walks turned into lunches and finally dinner. He was charming and intelligent. She found him very amusing. He had an irreverent sense of humour and loved to make fun of people. He had a way of noticing everyone's foibles. The woman leaving the Ladies' with her skirt hitched into her panties. The old man talking at the next-door table oblivious to the piece of food stuck on his cheek. There was something to laugh at in everyone. Maria found him so attractive she laughed at his jokes. Later she would find them cruel.

He kissed her for the first time in the dark street outside her apartment. He kissed her with tenderness and told her he loved her. Once he had watched her disappear into the hall he decided that this was the woman he would marry and later told Manuela, his regular whore, reassuring her that his marriage wouldn't change their relationship. 'No one looks after me like you do, Manuela,' he grunted as she took him in her mouth.

At first Maria thought she deserved it. A small disagreement and he slapped her around the face. She was stunned, apologetic. It was her fault; she had been too outspoken. She should show him more respect. She loved him. She loved the way he held her, talked to her, kissed her. He was generous, he bought her clothes. He liked her to dress in a certain way. He got upset if she met him wearing baggy sweaters. 'You have a beautiful body,' he would say. 'I want everyone to see what I have and die of jealousy.' He told her he was proud of her. If something wasn't done the way he liked it, he hit her. She accepted his punishments believing that she deserved them, longing for his approval. After he hit her he would cry, cling to her, promise her he would never hit her again. He needed her. She was the only one who could save him. So she continued to see him because she loved him and wanted to help him.

She would meet him in the afternoons at his apartment in San Telmo. When he said he didn't want to make love to her, because like herself, he was a good Catholic and intercourse was for the procreation of mankind, she was flattered and touched. He didn't want to spoil her, he said, but he was happy to touch her and caress her. But intercourse must wait until they were married. Maria hadn't told her parents about Facundo or introduced him to them. Later she would look back and recognise that she knew, somewhere in her subconscious, that her family wouldn't approve of Facundo Hernandez.

Chiquita watched her daughter come home with bruises. Sometimes a cut lip, a purple cheekbone. Maria told her it was nothing. She had merely fallen in the street. Tripped down the stairs in the university building. But the bruises appeared with more frequency and Chiquita spoke to Miguel. Something had to be done.

One evening in late June, Fernando followed Maria to Facundo Hernandez's apartment in a seedy building with no character or charm. He watched her climb the stairs and let herself in. Walking around the back Fernando climbed onto the wall and jumped onto the balcony of the first floor. It was easy. He hauled himself up onto the next floor and peered in through the window. The sun reflected off the glass and made it difficult to see in. But once his eyes adjusted he could see past his own reflection into the room beyond.

The man looked like he was devouring his sister. He didn't make love to Maria. He just mauled her neck and felt her breasts through her tight shirt. Then he pulled away sharply and hit her. He shouted at her, something about wearing a brassière. 'I thought I told you not to wear one.' She was crying. Apologising. Trembling. Then he was down on his knees, kissing her, cuddling her, until they were clinging to each other, rocking.

Fernando was appalled and felt the bile rise in his stomach. He had to lean back against the wall for a while, breathing deeply, before he could resume his stake-out. He wanted to burst in through the glass and wring the bloody man's neck. It was his sister he was abusing! But he knew it would achieve nothing. He had to be patient and watch.

Fernando didn't leave it at that. He followed the man to the brothel. Found out his name and that he was an army officer. He didn't need any more information. He was the enemy. He had to be taught a lesson.

When Fernando told his parents they were devastated. Chiquita couldn't understand why her daughter hadn't told her, why she hadn't asked for help. 'She's always told me everything,' she said tearfully, shaking her head in disbelief. Miguel wanted to kill him for abusing his little girl. Fernando had to physically restrain him from reaching for his gun.

Fernando felt heroic; it was he who had found out who the man was, followed him, stalked him. He was the one in control of the situation and his parents were grateful. They needed him, relied on him. He told them not to worry, that he was going to deal with it himself, and to his surprise and delight they agreed. For the first time he saw pride in their eyes when they looked at him. He had gained their respect and it felt good.

Santi, imprisoned for the last four years in his own gloomy world, at last broke his bondage. At first Fernando didn't want him involved. This was his moment and he wanted to bask in the glory alone. But when he saw how full of admiration Santi was for him he relented. 'You can come,' he said gravely, 'but you have to do it my way. No questions.' Santi agreed. Fernando saw that he was grateful, humble even. Fernando knew that it was going to be dangerous, but he was ready. He felt stronger than he had ever felt before.

The two brothers sat and discussed Maria. In the darkness under the stars, looking down from the balcony onto the busy streets of Buenos Aires, they talked about their childhood. When Fernando felt the first twinges of a bond developing with his brother he barely noticed; it crept up on him when he was too busy talking to Santi as an equal – an equal with a common cause.

They waited their moment, then together with two guerrilla friends of Fernando's they stole into Facundo Hernandez's apartment in the middle of the night. Breaking the curfew, risking their lives. With their faces covered in black stockings they pulled the terrified man out of his bed. Tied him to a chair and beat him until he arrived at the frontier between this life and the next. He begged to live. Fernando told him that if he ever went near Maria Solanas again, spoke to her or communicated with her in any way, they would return to finish the job. Facundo gasped with fear before passing out.

Chiquita talked to her daughter. It wasn't easy. In the cosy security of her bedroom Chiquita told Maria what she knew, of his beatings and his whore. Maria tried to defend him, saying they were mistaken – Facundo had never hit her, ever. Emotionally she backed into a corner and scratched anyone who came near her. She accused them of spying on her. It was her life – she could see who she wanted. They had no right to get involved.

It took a long time, but with Fernando and Santi's help they gently wore her down until she hung her head and shook like a child. 'I love him, Mama. I don't know why, I just do,' she cried. As the evening drew in they talked and talked, Miguel, Chiquita, Santi, Fernando and Maria, all together in that small room, united. Maria looked around her and took comfort from their loyalty and love. Worried, Chiquita left her daughter asleep in their matrimonial bed and called the doctor to come and take a look at her. Dr Higgins was unavailable so he sent someone from his practice. A gentle young man called Eduardo Maraldi.

Slowly, life at Santa Catalina returned to normal. The winter months finally thawed and gave way to the lengthening days and budding flowers. The scent of fertility filled the air and the birds returned to announce the arrival of spring. Past wounds began to heal over and resentment dissipated with the winter mists. Santi opened his eyes and began to see the world again; it looked different somehow. It was time to shave off his beard.

Chapter Twenty-Three

Eduardo Maraldi was tall, lanky and intellectual. He had a long sensitive nose and grey eyes that betrayed his every emotion. If it had not been for his small, Trotsky-style spectacles, they would have declared his feelings to anyone who got close enough to look into them. When he first visited Maria she was immediately struck by the soft voice that belied his tall frame, and the gentle way he placed his hands on her when he examined her.

'Tell me, where does it hurt?' he asked her and she found herself playing down her pain for fear of upsetting him. She was used to doctors who were coolly detached, doctors who didn't get too involved with their patients.

By the second visit she was telling him all about Facundo. Things she hadn't even told her mother. Like how he'd force himself on her when he was drunk – he had never wanted to have sex with her, he had wanted to save her virginity for their wedding night, but he had run his hands over her body and when he had been drunk he had hurt her. She told Eduardo how he had made her touch him in a way that she had found distressing. How he had made her do things she didn't want to do. How he had frightened her and won her love at the same time. Encouraged by Eduardo's unassuming smile and kind expression she told him things she never thought she'd tell anyone. Suddenly, responding to his sympathy, she started to cry. He placed his arm around her and without overstepping that fine line that separates doctor from patient, he did his best to comfort her.

'Señorita Solanas,' he said after she had calmed down a little, 'physically your wounds will heal until they disappear altogether and no one would ever know you had been hurt. That is not the problem.' She looked up at him quizzically. 'It is your mental scars that I worry about. Is there anyone you can talk to at home?'

'I haven't talked about it really with anyone.'

'What about your mother?' He recalled the slim, affectionate woman whom he had met on his first visit to her house.

'Oh, I talk to her. But not like I talk to you,' she replied and blushed. She lowered her eyes.

'You need to be looked after and loved,' he said. She flushed a deeper red and hoped he hadn't noticed. He had and he also felt hot under his collar.

'Oh, I have a very loving family, Dr Maraldi.'

'Those mental scars will take a long time to heal. Don't expect miracles. You may suddenly get depressed for no apparent reason. You may find it difficult to start a new relationship. Just be patient and remember that you have been through something that will have affected you more than you realise.'

'Thank you, Doctor.'

'If you need to talk, you can always come and see me,' he suggested. He hoped that she would.

'I will. Thank you.'

When she left his surgery, Eduardo splashed his face with cold water. Had he spoken out of turn? Had he scared her off? He wanted to tell her that *he* would look after her, but he couldn't ask a patient out. It was unprofessional. Oh, how he hoped she'd come back.

Maria wished Sofia were around. She would have been able to talk to her frankly about all of this. She missed her. She thought of her often, wondered what she was doing, who she was with. She had tried to write again to explain, but Dominique had sent the letter back with a note of her own, telling her that Sofia had gone to live in London and that she had no idea of her address. Well, Maria wasn't that stupid. Sofia had obviously told her that she didn't want her family to know where she was. She really had cut herself off – and it was all her fault. The guilt she felt weighed heavily on her heart. She half wanted her cousin to come back so she could explain, and half never wanted to see her again because she felt too ashamed. She knew she would never find a friend to replace Sofia.

During the next two months Maria thought of Eduardo more often than she had expected to. The images of Facundo slowly receded in her mind and Eduardo's long, angular face took his place. She hoped he'd call, but he never did. She knew she could go and see him, under the pretence that she needed to talk, but she worried that he might see through her. She doubted he had thought of her once since their last meeting.

Then the strangest thing happened. God, or whoever controls our destinies, realised that if He didn't intervene these two self-effacing creatures would never find each other again. So He placed Eduardo in the middle of the street as Maria was wandering absentmindedly down it with her basket of books, on her way back home after a lecture at the university. Not looking where she was going, she bumped right into him. They both apologised at the same time before they raised their eyes and recognised each other.

'Señorita Solanas!' he exclaimed and his misery lifted. The last two months had dragged by as he had plunged himself into depression for no reason at all. Suddenly, his spirits jumped out of their socks and he smiled wider than was normally comfortable.

'Dr Maraldi,' she laughed in surprise. 'This is such a . . .'

'Coincidence. Yes, isn't it!' He chuckled and shook his head in awe of his luck.

'Please call me Maria,' she said, her face aflame.

'I'm Eduardo. I'm not your doctor today.'

'No, no you're not,' she replied and giggled foolishly.

'Do you want a coffee or something?' he asked, then added quickly, 'You probably don't have time.'

'Oh, I'd love to,' she said just as quickly.

'Good. Good,' he stammered. 'I know a nice café a couple of streets from here. Here, let me help you with your bag,' he insisted. She let him take her basket, which was really quite heavy due to a new hardback history book she had bought, and they wandered slowly down the street. Eduardo made sure he walked on the outside.

Café Calabria was cool and not very busy. Eduardo chose a table in the corner by the window and pulled out her chair. When the waiter ambled over Eduardo gave him their order and asked for two *alfajores de maizena*. 'Oh, I really couldn't!' protested Maria, worrying about her figure. Eduardo looked at her and thought how truly beautiful she was because of her luscious body. She reminded him of a ripe peach. Maria noticed his expression behind his glasses and heard herself adding, 'Well, all right, just this once.'

Their coffee lasted through lunch and tea and they didn't leave until six in the evening. Maria told him all about Sofia; she confessed everything. He understood all her actions and had an explanation for every one. He seemed to have a deep knowledge of psychology. She told him of her cousin's relationship with her brother and trusted that he would never tell anyone.

'I did a terrible thing,' she explained sadly. 'I burnt Sofia's letters. I wish I hadn't, I'll never forgive myself. Because now I've lost my best friend and I almost lost my brother.'

Eduardo looked at her, his face full of compassion. 'You thought you were doing the right thing. The path to Hell is paved with good intentions,' he said and chuckled kindly.

'I know that now.'

'You shouldn't have done it. But we learn much more from unhappy times than we do from happy ones. With every sadness there is always something positive just around the corner. Perhaps one day when Sofia is happily married with five children, she'll come to you and thank you. Who knows? The important thing is not to torment yourself about it now. There's no point crying over something that is done and irreversible. Look forward,' he advised, taking off his glasses and cleaning them with the napkin.

'So you don't think I'm evil?' she asked and smiled shyly.

'No, I don't think you're evil. I think you're a good person who made a mistake and — well, we all make mistakes,' he said, reassuring her. He wanted to tell her that he thought she was a beautiful person on the inside as well as on the outside. He wanted to love her enough to erase any trace of hurt or guilt or pain. He knew that he could make her happy if she would only give him the chance.

Eduardo told Maria that he had almost married. When she asked him why he had changed his mind, he replied truthfully that there was something missing. A spark, a connection. 'Call me an incurable romantic,' he said, 'but I knew I could love someone more than I loved her.'

Since that afternoon they had spent long hours on the telephone, gone on a few dates to the cinema and dinner before he attempted to kiss her. She knew he was taking it slowly and was grateful even though she had wanted him to kiss her that afternoon in the café. He arrived with a small bunch of wildflowers to pick her up. He then drove her to a restaurant on *La Costanera* overlooking the river where they gazed at each other through the candlelight and talked without pause. After the dinner he suggested they walk a little by the waterside. She knew he was going to kiss her and she suddenly became nervous and quiet. They walked along in silence for a while until the silence became too arduous to bear. Finally he took her hand and held it firmly, then he stopped walking and took her other hand, swinging her around to face him.

'Maria,' he said.

'Yes?' she replied.

'I . . . I've wanted to . . .' It was agony. She wished he'd just kiss her and get it over with.

'Eduardo, it's okay. I *want* you to,' she whispered finally, then caught her breath at her boldness. He seemed relieved that she had given him her consent. Momentarily she feared it would be unpleasantly awkward but then as he placed his warm hand on her face and his trembling lips on hers he kissed her with a confidence she didn't think he possessed. Later when she told him this he smiled proudly and informed her that she gave him the belief that he could do anything.

Chiquita and Miguel had been aware of every outing with Dr Maraldi. They had sat up in bed at night discussing the romance. Chiquita prayed every night before she went to bed that he would look after her little girl and make her forget the horrendous Facundo. She prayed so hard that sometimes she would wake up with her hands still firmly pressed together. When they announced their engagement at the end of the summer Chiquita muttered a silent word of thanks before embracing her daughter tearfully.

'Mama, I don't know why I deserve this,' Maria said later when she was alone with her mother. 'He's everything I could possibly want. He's kind, and funny, and eccentric. I love him because of the way his hands shake when he handles fragile things, because of the way he stammers when he's nervous, because of his humility. I'm so lucky. So, so lucky. I only wish Sofia were here to see me. She'd be happy for me, I know she would. I miss her, Mama.'

'We all miss her, dearest. We all miss her terribly.'

Chapter Twenty-Four

London, 1974

Sofia arrived in London in mid-November 1974 with a flagging spirit. She took one look at the grey sky and drizzle and yearned for her homeland. Her cousin had made a booking for her at Claridges. 'It's just next to Bond Street,' she had said brightly, 'the most glamorous shopping street in Europe.'

But Sofia didn't want to shop. She sat on her bed staring out of the window at the relentless rain that seemed to float down from the sky. It was cold and damp. She didn't want to go out. She didn't know quite what to do, so she called Dominique to tell her that she had arrived safely. She could hear little Santiguito crying in the background and her heart ached with longing for him. She recalled his little fingers and perfect toes. When she put down the receiver she went over to her suitcase and rummaged inside. She pulled out a piece of white muslin and pressed it against her nose. It smelt of Santiguito. She curled into a ball on her bed and cried herself to sleep.

The hotel was very grand, with tall ceilings and beautiful plasterwork on the walls. The staff were charming and looked after her every need as Dominique had said they would. 'Just ask for Claude, he will take care of you,' she advised. Sofia had found

Claude, a small, portly man with a shiny bald head that resembled a table-tennis ball. When she had mentioned her cousin Dominique's name, Claude's head had swelled red, right to the shiny plateau on top. Dabbing his forehead with a white hanky he had told her that if she needed anything, anything at all, she must not hesitate to ask. Her cousin was a very good client of the hotel, the most charming client, in fact. It would give him great pleasure to do her the favour.

She knew she should look for a flat, a job, but she hadn't the energy. So she went for long walks around Hyde Park, getting to know this new city. If her heart hadn't felt so heavy she would have enjoyed the freedom of exploring London without a parent or bodyguard shadowing her everywhere she went. She was able to go anywhere, talk to anyone, without suspicion. She wandered up the streets, peering into shop windows that glittered with Christmas decorations, she even visited a few galleries and exhibitions. She bought an umbrella from a small shop in Piccadilly; it would become her most useful purchase.

London was so unlike Buenos Aires. It didn't really feel like a city at all, more of a large town. The houses were low and the roads lined with trees and perfect, smooth pavements, twisted and turned so one had no idea where one was going to end up. Buenos Aires was constructed on a grid system of blocks; one always knew where one was going to end up. To Sofia, London was as shiny and neat as a polished pearl. Her own city looked grubby and crumbling by comparison. But Buenos Aires was home and she missed it.

After a couple of days she began to look for a flat. On Claude's advice she spoke to a lady called Mathilda at a rental agency in Fulham who found her a small, one-bedroom apartment in Queen's Gate. Pleased with her new flat, Sofia went out shopping for things to put in it. It was fully furnished but she wanted to make it her own, her little fortress in this foreign land. So she bought a bedcover, rugs, china, vases, coffee-table books, cushions and pictures.

Shopping made her feel better and she ventured out in spite of the frightening wave of bombs that hit London at that time. One actually went off in Harrods and one outside Selfridges. But Sofia didn't have a television and didn't bother to buy the papers – she heard all the news she needed from the taxi drivers who were the jolliest group of men she had ever met. London taxis were shiny and spacious and the buses were adorable, like models from a toy town.

'Foreign, are you?' asked one taxi driver in an accent that made it hard for her to understand what he was saying. 'Not a good time to come to London, luv. Don't you get the news where you come from? Those bloody Unions seem to be runnin' the country. There's no proper leadership, that's the problem. The country's in free-fall. I told my wife, I said, "The country's going to the dogs. What we need is a good sharp shock." ' Sofia nodded blindly. She didn't know what he was talking about.

Sofia gradually warmed to London with its handsome policemen in funny hats, the guards outside St James's Palace who never moved, and the little townhouses and mews; it was like nothing she had ever seen before. A doll's city full of doll's houses, she thought, remembering her mother's book on England with all those quaint photographs. She hung around outside Buckingham Palace only because she wanted to know what everyone else was doing there with their noses pressed to the iron gates. She discovered the Changing of the Guard, which so enthralled her she had to return the following day for a second viewing. She starved her heart of thoughts of Santi and Argentina and of little Santiguito until it gave up the fight and numbed itself into submission. She wouldn't torment herself any longer.

When her money began to run out she embarked reluctantly on the search for a job. Unqualified, she started by trawling around the shops. They all wanted someone with experience and as she had none they simply shook their heads and saw her to the door. 'There's so much unemployment,' they sighed, 'you'll be lucky if anyone wants you.' After three long weeks of looking without success, Sofia became desperate. Her money was disappearing and she had to pay the rent. She didn't want to call Dominique. She had been kind enough and Sofia couldn't bear to be reminded of her son.

One day, feeling downhearted, she wandered into a bookshop on the Fulham Road. A kind-looking man wearing glasses was sitting behind a pile of books, humming along to the radio. She told him she was looking for work but everywhere she had tried needed people with experience and she had none. She imagined things were busy, as it was the Christmas season. The man shook his head, said he was sorry, but they didn't need any more staff. 'It's only a small shop, you see,' he explained. 'However, they do need help next door at Maggie's. You could try there. You see, they're not looking for experience.'

She wandered back out in the cold. It was getting dark. She looked at her watch. It still surprised her how early it got dark in England. It was only three-thirty. Maggie's, it turned out, was a hair salon. Sofia recoiled. She certainly wasn't desperate enough to stoop to *that* level. So after looking in through the foggy window she walked on by, bought herself a hot chocolate at a café and sat gazing into her cup. After a while she watched the other people around her. Some had been out Christmas shopping; their bags brimmed with shiny packages. They all chatted away, oblivious to her. She placed her hands around the mug to warm them and hunched over the table. She suddenly felt very alone. She didn't have a single friend in this country.

Oh, how she missed Santi – and she missed Maria, too. Maria had been her best and most treasured friend. She longed to talk to her and communicate what she was going through. She regretted never having written to her. She regretted never having confided in her. She imagined Maria must be as sad and as lonely as she was. She knew her friend. But it was too late now. If only she had written a year ago. But if she hadn't known how to begin a letter then she certainly wouldn't know how to begin one now. No, she had missed her moment. She had not only lost her lover, but the woman who, albeit of a more gentle and timid nature than herself, had understood her and supported her through everything. They had spent their whole lives together, and now it was over. A fat tear plopped into her hot chocolate.

Outside, the street bustled with people; everyone had somewhere to go. A tea party perhaps, a job, friends to see, family to drop in on. She had no one. No one cared about her here. She could die on one of these cold, unfamiliar pavements and no one would notice. She wondered how long it would be before someone found out who she was in order to notify her family of her death. Probably weeks, months, that is if they would bother at all. She possessed a British passport thanks to her grandfather, but she didn't belong in this place.

She paid the bill and left. On her way down the street she passed Maggie's again, and decided to turn back and take another look. She pressed her face up to the window and peered in. A tall, lanky man was cutting a woman's hair, stopping every now and then to use his hands to illustrate his story. A young blonde girl sat at the desk answering the telephone. She had to control her laughter in order to take the bookings. Just then the door opened, sending out into the street the strong smell of shampoo and perfume.

'Can I help you?' asked a red-headed woman of about fifty, poking her head out into the street. She wore scarlet lipstick like Dominique and had painted the most hideous shade of lime green above her eyes with an unsteady hand.

'I hear you're looking for someone to help?' replied Sofia tentatively.

'Jolly good. Come on in. I'm Maggie,' she said once Sofia had stepped into the warm interior of the salon.

'Sofia Solanas,' she replied. The man had stopped telling his story and turned to look at her. His snake-like eyes traced her features, taking in her clothes, mentally scrutinising her from top to toe. He sniffed his approval.

'Very nice, Sofia. *Very* nice. I'm Anton. Anthony really, but Anton sounds more exotic, don't you think?' he said and then laughed before mincing over to the cupboard to pull out a large pot of gel.

'Anton's a real character, Sofia. Just laugh at his jokes and he'll love you, sweetie. Daisy does, don't you, dear? And he loves her.' Daisy smiled warmly and extended her hand from behind the desk. 'Now, it's ten till six, sweetie, helping out. That's sweeping, washing hair and keeping the place tidy. I can't pay you any more than eight pounds a week, tips on top. Is that all right? I think it's fair. Don't you, Anton?'

'Very generous, Maggie,' he gushed, filling his palm with what looked like green slime.

'But my rent is eight pounds a week,' Sofia protested.

'That's all I can do. Take it or leave it,' said Maggie, folding her arms in front of her large bosom.

'I rent too. What if we pooled our resources. I mean, if we shared?' suggested Daisy eagerly. She lived in a rundown flat in Hammersmith, and it took her ages to get into work in the morning. 'Do you live locally?'

'Queen's Gate.'

'No wonder your rent's so high. Where are you from, darling?' asked Maggie, who couldn't quite place her accent.

'Argentina,' she replied, and her throat tightened. She hadn't heard that word spoken aloud for so long.

'Lovely,' said Anton, who didn't know where in the world it was.

'Well, if you want a flatmate, I'd be happy to share.'

Sofia didn't like the idea of sharing. She had never had to share anything. But she was desperate and this Daisy had a nice face. So she agreed.

'Right – your first job can be to go and buy a bottle of good cheap wine, Sofia!' laughed Maggie, opening the till and pulling out some change. 'This is indeed cause for celebration – isn't that right, Anton?'

'A cause for celebration, Maggie,' he repeated, his hand flopping over on its wrist revealing well-manicured nails.

After a couple of weeks, this small salon became Sofia's new home, and Maggie, Anton and Daisy her new family. Maggie had left her husband and had started her own business to make ends meet. 'Silly girl,' said Anton, when she was out of earshot. 'He was very rich and *very* well-connected.' Anton lived with his boyfriend, Marcello, a dark, handsome, hairy-chested Italian, who occasionally came into the salon to drape himself over the leopard-print sofa and listen to Anton's stories. Maggie would open a bottle of wine and join him. But however much she fluttered those false lashes at him he had eyes only for Anton. Maggie flirted with the clients too. Most of them loved the attention. 'I sprinkle them with Maggie dust, sweetie, then send them back to their wives,' she'd say. Daisy and Sofia would laugh all the way home at her delusions.

Daisy was bright and witty, but most importantly she was warm. With a shock of thick blonde hair that fanned out behind her in tight, shiny curls and a chin that went into a cheeky point, giving her face the definition of a love heart, she was exuberant as well as kind. They shared the flat, small as it was, and everything that it contained. At first Sofia found it hard to share her space, but little by little she began to rely on her new friend. She needed her. The other girl took away the loneliness and filled the hollow space that had once belonged to Maria.

Daisy's parents were from the country – from Dorset, which Daisy pointed out on a map. 'It's green and hilly and very pretty,' she told Sofia, 'but provincial. I've always been attracted to the bright lights of the city.'

Daisy's parents were divorced. Her father, a builder, trawled the North Country for work while her mother, Jean Shrub, lived with her lover Bernard, by coincidence also a builder, in Taunton and worked as a beautician.

'I always wanted to do what she did, going around to people's houses and filing their nails. But once I qualified I tripped on my first job and poured wax over Mrs Hamblewell's dog, a total disaster, the poor thing practically had to be skinned. So I put down my manicure tools and came up here. Don't tell Maggie, but I might very well take it up again. Maggie's could use a beautician, don't you think?'

She always made jokes about her name, Daisy Shrub, introducing herself as, 'Daisy as in flower, Shrub as in bush.' She said it was lucky she wasn't a gardener; no one would ever take her seriously. Daisy rolled her own cigarettes that she'd sit and smoke out of the window in their flat as Sofia hated the smell, and they'd talk about their lives and their dreams. But Sofia's dreams were invented for Daisy's benefit; she could never reveal the truth of her past, not to anyone.

At Maggie's Sofia swept the floors, marvelling sometimes at the multicoloured hair she often found herself cleaning away. Anton loved dyeing hair. That was his favourite job. 'All the colours of the rainbow, duckie, so much choice.' He had a client, Rosie Moffat, who came in literally every fortnight for a new shade. 'She's been through them all. I'll have to start at the beginning again or give her stripes. *Such* a dilemma,' he complained.

Sofia also washed hair. That part of her job she didn't like so much at the beginning, as it ruined her nails. But after a while she got used to it and the men especially gave her big tips.

'Doesn't talk much about herself, does she, Anton?' said Maggie, lying on the sofa filing her talons.

'She's an adorable girl, though.'

'Adorable.'

'And hardworking. I just wish she didn't look so sad,' he said, pouring himself a glass of wine. It was half past six, time for a drink.

'She laughs at your jokes, doesn't she, sweetie?'

'Oh yes! But she still carries sadness around with her like some sort of hideous penance. Tragedy in motion, darling.'

'Darling, you're so poetical. You're not going to leave me to write poetry, are you?' She laughed and lit a cigarette.

'I *am* poetry, duckie, anyway I wouldn't want to put all those sweet little poets out of business, now would I?' He brought her an ashtray. She inhaled deeply, her shoulders relaxed instantly.

'Do you know why she came to London?'

'She never said. In fact, Maggie, we know sweet bugger-all about her, don't we?'

'I'm frightfully curious, darling.'

'Ooh, me too. Give her time. I'm sure she's got a gripping story to tell.'

As Christmas approached and the streets of London glittered and sparkled with decorations and fir trees, Sofia couldn't help but wonder whether they missed her back at home. She pictured them preparing for the festivities. She imagined the heat, the dry plains and those leafy eucalyptus trees until she could almost smell them. She wondered whether Santi ever thought about her, or had he forgotten? Maria had stopped writing to her after that painful letter she had sent back in the spring. They had been friends, best friends. Was it really that easy to forget? Had they all forgotten? When she thought of home she felt gutted inside.

Daisy returned to her mother for Christmas. She called to say that there was so much snow they weren't able to leave the house, so her mother was giving them all manicures and pedicures. 'I hope this goes on for weeks, we might get a new house out of Bernard.' Sofia was sad to see her leave — she had no family to go to and felt her friend's absence dreadfully.

Sofia spent Christmas Day with Anton and Marcello at Maggie's powder-pink house in Fulham. 'I love pink,' she gushed displaying her pink fluffy slippers as she showed Sofia around.

'I'd never have guessed,' laughed Sofia, but inside she felt dead. She noticed that even the loo seat was lilac. They opened bottles of champagne, Anton danced around the room in zebra-print bell bottoms with tinsel wrapped around his head like a Roman crown, and Marcello lay on the sofa smoking a spliff. Maggie had spent all day cooking with Sofia, who had nothing else to do except miss her home. They had all brought small presents for each other. Maggie gave her a box of nail varnishes Sofia knew she'd never use and Anton gave her a green vanity case, complete with mirror and pouch for make-up. She reflected on her poverty. She had belonged to one of the richest families in Argentina; now she had nothing.

After dinner and too much wine they sat by the fire, watching the flames lick the walls, transforming them from pink to orange. Suddenly Sofia dropped her head into her hands and wept. Maggie eyed Anton who nodded at her. She got down onto the floor and put a heavily perfumed arm around her.

'What is it, sweetie? You can tell us, we're your friends.'

So Sofia told them, omitting the part about Santiguito. That secret was too shaming to reveal to anyone.

'A man. Wouldn't it just be a bloody man!' complained Anton angrily, when she'd finished.

'You're a man, darling.'

'Only half, duckie,' he replied, draining his glass and pouring himself another. Marcello lay sleeping on the sofa, his mind floating somewhere amid the Tuscan hills.

'You're better off without him, sweetie,' Maggie said gently. 'If he couldn't even keep his promise and write to you, I'd say you're well rid of him.'

'But I love him so much it hurts, Maggie,' she sobbed.

'You'll get over him. We all do in the end, don't we, Anton?'

'We do.'

'You'll find some lovely Englishman,' Maggie said helpfully.

'Or Italian.'

'I'd steer well clear of those if I were you, darling. Yes, a nice Englishman.'

The following day Sofia awoke with a headache and a desperate yearning for her child. She curled into a small ball and sobbed into the muslin until her head felt it would split in two like a melon. She recalled Santiguito's small face, those clear, innocent blue eyes that had trusted her. She had betrayed him. How could she have been so callous? What had she been thinking? How could Dominique have allowed her to give away her precious baby, the life she had grown inside her? She held her belly and mourned the loss of her son; she suddenly feared she would never see him again. She had cried so much, the aching in her throat had become unbearable. Finally, she pulled the telephone onto the bed and dialled Switzerland.

'*Oui?*'

Sofia's heart sank when she heard the grumpy housekeeper's voice answer the telephone. 'Madame Ibert, it's Sofia Solanas in London. Can I speak to Dominique, please?' she asked hopefully.

'I'm afraid, Mademoiselle, Monsieur and Madame La Rivière are out of the country for ten days.'

'Ten days?' she asked, surprised. They hadn't said they were going anywhere.

'*Oui*, ten days,' she replied impatiently.

'Where have they gone?' she asked desperately.

'They did not say.'

'They didn't say?'

'No, Mademoiselle.'

'Did they leave a number?'

'No.'

'They didn't leave a contact telephone number?'

'Mademoiselle Sofia,' the woman said irritably, 'they did not say where they were going, they did not leave a number or an address. They said they would be away for ten days but that is all. I regret, I cannot help you. I am sorry.'

'I'm sorry too,' she sobbed, and put down the receiver. Too late, it was too late.

Sofia rolled into a ball once more and wrapped her arms about her. Putting her face against the muslin she recalled that the last time she had felt this kind of unhappiness had been when Grandpa

O'Dwyer had died beside her. She would never see Santiguito again. She would never see her beloved grandfather again either. It was so final, as if Santiguito had died. She would never, ever be able to forgive herself.

Chapter Twenty-Five

Christmas had been painful. Alone in her flat, Sofia had cried herself to sleep thinking of Santa Catalina and missing them all. Anton and Maggie had looked after her over the rest of the holiday, making sure that she wasn't left alone to spiral into depression. When the salon reopened, she was relieved to go back to work, and hoped that 1975 would prove to be a happier year for her. To this end, Sofia willed herself to look forward instead of backwards – after all, that's what her grandfather would have advised had he been alive. It seemed to help.

Dominique visited London regularly as Antoine was doing more business in the City than before. When she was with Dominique they'd eat in elegant restaurants and shop in Bond Street; Sofia was reminded of the life of privilege she had once had and she appreciated it, because the moment Dominique returned to Geneva her life would drop down to that of a normal working girl again.

The year passed swiftly. She made friends with Marmaduke Huckley-Smith, the bespectacled man who ran the bookshop. He introduced her to his friends, one of whom took her out every now and then, which was nice, but Sofia didn't fancy him. She didn't fancy anyone.

In their spare time, Sofia and Daisy would trawl the King's Road for bargains. The ethnic look was in fashion and Sofia indulged in long floaty skirts from Monsoon; Anton coloured her hair with thick streaks of red and straightened Daisy's hair one day when he was bored, which left the blonde girl barely recognisable, but striking. They went to the cinema once a month and to the West End where they saw *The Mousetrap*.

'You know the man who built this theatre was a rich aristo who fell in love with an actress. He built it for her. Don't you think that's incredibly romantic?' hissed Daisy from their seats.

'Maybe one of Maggie's lovers will build her a new salon. Now that would be something!' giggled Sofia.

Anton took them all to *The Rocky Horror Show* and embarrassed them by arriving in a rented pink Cadillac clad in suspenders and lace underwear, with Marcello mincing along behind him in a tiger-print trouser suit. Maggie was horrified and exclaimed that she hoped he would remember to change before work on Monday morning. Sofia remarked that all Marcello needed to complete the outfit was a long tail. The Italian replied dryly that if he showed her his 'tail' no other man would live up to the comparison.

Daisy managed to get cheap tickets for David Bowie who was playing at Wembley. Besides Bowie, Daisy had a crush on Mick Jagger and played his music very loudly in the salon, which irritated Maggie, who preferred the gentle tones of Joni Mitchell.

The bleak winter months slowly disappeared, taking with them Sofia's misery. As the streets filled with pink and white blossom, Sofia discovered a new state of mind – Grandpa O'Dwyer's positive mental attitude.

She threw herself into her work and Maggie raised her salary. Sofia enjoyed living with her friend Daisy and they spent many nights out at the Café des Artistes, laughing over their drinks. Daisy always drank beer, which Sofia found quite repulsive. Neither could she understand the greatest British love of all – Marmite. But it seemed to her she was in the minority. Everyone, it appeared, had grown up on Marmite. 'That's why we're so tall,' beamed Anton, who reached at least six foot three.

In August Maggie closed the salon for two weeks and invited them all to stay in her rented cottage in Devon, to enjoy the sea and the beaches. Sofia had a lovely time, although she did miss the sunshine, as it seemed to rain most of the time. She remembered her mother talking about of the hills of Glengariff and wondered whether they resembled the hills of Devon. They had picnics on the damp beach in their bathing suits, cowering under umbrellas as the wind blew sand into their sandwiches. But they laughed at each other's jokes and at Marcello who would never understand the madness of the English, shivering in thick velvet trousers and polo-neck sweater. 'Take me back to Tuscany,' he whined, 'where I can see the sky and know that there is a sun.'

'Oh, do shut up, Marcello, don't be so Italian,' mumbled Maggie, wolfing down a slice of chocolate cake.

'Careful, duckie, I love him because he's Italian,' Anton said, allowing his friend to snuggle up against him for warmth.

'Marcello's right,' said Daisy heartily. 'Look at us – the only people on these beaches are British. Aren't we ridiculous, sitting out here in the rain, on a cold summer's day as if we're in the South of France.'

'That's why we won the war, sweetie,' replied Maggie, trying to light a cigarette in the wind. Every time she struck a match it blew out. 'Oh for God's sake, someone – Anton, Sofia, I don't care who – light me a bloody cigarette before I lose my patience.'

'You didn't fight in the war, Maggie,' laughed Anton. 'You can't even light a ciggie.' He put the cigarette in his mouth and turning his back to the wind, lit it for her.

'I'm surprised at you, Anton,' she retorted dryly, 'you're more woman than man. You're very quiet, Sofia, have you lost your tongue?' She glanced at Sofia who sat huddled in a damp towel. She pulled an uneasy smile with pale blue lips that quivered in the cold.

'I'm afraid I take Marcello's side. I'm used to the beaches of South America,' she said through chattering teeth.

'Well, aren't you two grand,' Maggie smirked. 'Still, it'll be the making of you both. A dose of good British fortitude. That's why our armies are the best in the world. Fortitude, and no one has it like the British.'

'Well, you certainly have it, Maggie,' laughed Daisy. 'Sofia, I bet you never envisaged you'd be here when you were lying on those hot beaches in South America.'

'You're right,' she replied truthfully, but at least there was nothing about Devon that reminded her of home. On those cold, forlorn beaches she was in a completely different world.

Christmas 1975 was a happier time than the year before. Sofia spent ten days with Dominique and Antoine in their chalet in Verbier. Delfine and Louis had invited friends and once more the chalet vibrated with happy shrieks of delight as presents were opened and games played. Christmas lights glimmered in the crisp air and bells resounded up and down the valley. The weather was suspended in a magical limbo where the sun glowed every day in a cornflower sky that broke only after Sofia had departed for London. When she returned the New Year held a surprise that she could not have predicted.

Daisy had suggested they go to a club in Soho 'where all the actors hang out'. As Sofia loved the theatre, she thought it a wonderful idea and picked up an old patchwork skirt and floppy velvet hat at the market in Portobello Road to wear with the brown leather boots she had bought with Dominique in Geneva. She didn't have much money as it was almost impossible to save on her small earnings, but she felt she deserved a treat. A treat to symbolise the beginning of a new, more positive, era.

The club throbbed with merry people piling in out of the cold. The girls found themselves two seats at the bar as an exasperated couple left because they couldn't get anyone's attention to give them a drink. Looking around them Sofia and Daisy recognised at least two actors and a television presenter. Thanks to their youth and beauty, they had no difficulty finding someone to serve them.

The barman smoothed down his long black hair that he had tied into a neat ponytail, and appeared in front of them, his face spread into an oily smile.

By a quarter to midnight Daisy was in full flirt with a sweaty sculptor who had clearly had too much to drink. After dribbling down her low-cut blouse he spirited her away to the other side of the room. Sofia smiled at her and shook her head. Daisy didn't seem to mind who she kissed as long as he bought her a drink and gave her some attention. Sofia sat calmly watching the people around her. Everyone was merry, but she didn't mind being alone. She was used to it by now.

'Can I buy you a drink?' She turned to find a well-built, handsome man take the seat beside hers. She recognised him immediately from the play she had seen a few weeks before. He had been the lead in *Hamlet*, which he had acted out with great bravado. Personally, she thought he had *over*acted the part, but she didn't think he'd appreciate her advice at this particular moment. She nodded and asked for another gin and tonic. He raised his hand, masterfully summoning the barman who scuttled over immediately.

'A G and T for my friend, and a whisky for myself,' he said, then turned back to Sofia, resting his elbow on the top of the bar.

'My grandfather used to drink whiskey,' she said.

'A fine drink.'

'In fact, he was buried with his "bottle o' liquor",' she added, imitating his Irish accent.

'Why?'

'Because he was afraid the leprechauns might steal it,' she laughed. He gazed down at her and chuckled. She was certainly unlike anyone else he'd met before.

'Are you Irish?'

'My mother is Irish. My father's Argentine.'

'Argentine?'

'Yes, but of Spanish blood.'

'God!' he exclaimed. 'What brought you here then?'

'That's a long story,' she told him dismissively.

'I'd like to hear it.'

They sat talking over the loud music. Had he not shifted his stool nearer to hers and leaned in towards her to hear better, they would have had to shout. He introduced himself as Jake Felton. He spoke with a beautiful English accent, his voice rich and commanding.

'Sofia Solanas,' she told him.

'That would make a strong stage name. And *you* would make a delightful actress,' he said knowingly, allowing his eyes to devour her generous features.

'I saw your play.'

'You did?' he exclaimed and grinned. 'Did you like it? Don't tell me if you didn't,' he added jovially.

'I did like it actually. But you have to remember, I'm a foreigner, so I didn't understand a lot of the English.'

'Don't worry. Most English people don't understand Shakespeare either. Will you come and see me again? I'm in a new play starting in February at the Old Vic.'

'I might,' she said coyly and drained her glass.

When midnight was announced – five, four, three, two, one HAPPY NEW YEAR! – everyone raised their glasses and kissed their partners. Jake placed a hand on her face and kissed her. He would have landed on her lips had she not turned her face to give him her cheek. When he asked if he could see her again, she gave him her number.

To her surprise, Jake Felton called her the following week. On the first date he took her to dinner at Daphne's in Draycott Avenue. He knew Giordano, the flamboyant Italian who ran the restaurant, and was consequently given the best table in the room. At first, Sofia felt uncomfortable, as though she was betraying Santi. But then she reminded herself that it was Santi who had already betrayed her. She had to grow up, move on.

After a few months Jake and Sofia were seeing each other regularly. Maggie and Anton were speechless with admiration when they heard and were genuinely happy for their friend. 'Jake Felton. Dishy!' Anton had enthused, once he had recovered from the shock. Daisy had warned her to watch out – 'he's a real ladies' man,' she had said. Daisy had a lot of time to read the gossip columns in her job. Sometimes the telephone didn't ring for hours. Sofia responded that all Latin men were like that so she was used to it. Soon Sofia was watching him rehearse and meeting all his friends. Suddenly her small world in London sprang open and she found herself moving in circles that were altogether more thrilling and more bohemian.

When Jake made love to Sofia she preferred the lights to be on. She liked to look at him. He was flattered. She couldn't tell him that when she closed her eyes she thought of Santi. Jake was different from Santi in every way. But her body had been Santi's, he alone had entered it. As much as she tried to block him out, the feeling of a man inside her reminded her of him, and it reminded her of the child they had made together. She had to keep her eyes open to forget. Jake was tender and he excited her, but she didn't love him. He told her he loved her, that his world had changed because of her. That he had never been so happy, so fulfilled. But she was unable to respond with the same fervour. All she could do was tell him how fond she was of him, how comfortable she felt with him, how he had filled the void inside her.

Sofia would watch Jake rehearse in the evenings and later criticise his performance. She even helped him learn his lines when they were in bed together at night. He would suddenly spring up and launch into one of his soliloquies. In restaurants he'd beg to practise with her; 'You be Julia – go on!' he'd plead. So they'd sit reading the lines from memory across the table, their faces full of the expressions of the characters they were playing until their laughter would invade the scene and they'd collapse gasping for breath.

'But does he ever talk about *you*, duckie?' Anton asked one evening, after they'd been going out for about a month.

'Of course he does. It's just that his job is very important right now, that's all. It takes priority,' Sofia insisted. Anton sniffed his disapproval as he watched her sweep up the remaining clumps of hair from the floor.

'I don't like to be a killjoy, darling, but when I met him I thought him decidedly arrogant,' Maggie commented, tapping her cigarette ash onto the floor. Anton gathered up the towels and threw them into a tall wicker basket.

'He comes across as arrogant, because he's shy,' Sofia said defensively.

'Shy! If he was shy, darling, he wouldn't be throwing himself about like that on the stage,' she scoffed. 'Anton, do be a little gem and pour me another glass of vino. That's the only thing an old girl like me can look forward to these days.'

'Don't be a sourpuss, Maggie!' Anton chided her, then smiled sympathetically. 'You'll soon be devoured by some gorgeous hunk, won't she, Sofia?'

Sofia nodded. 'David Harrison, the man who produced Jake's play, has asked us down to his house in the country for the weekend,' she told them, putting the brush away and joining Maggie on the sofa.

'We know who David Harrison is, don't we, Maggie?'

'Yes, he's very famous. Had an acrimonious divorce about ten years ago – maybe more, I can't remember. Now *there's* a man for you, darling.'

'Don't be ridiculous, Maggie. I'm very happy with Jake.'

'Pity,' Anton said through pursed lips.

'Well, as you wish,' Maggie told her. 'Don't say I didn't warn you though when Jake runs off with his leading lady. They're all like that, actors. I've had a few myself. Wouldn't go down that road again if you paid me. Still, David Harrison's old enough to be your father . . . Mind you, there's nothing wrong with a nice, rich, older man, is there, Anton?'

'Tell all when you come back, won't you, duckie?' he said to Sofia, and winked at her.

Jake picked Sofia up from Queen's Gate on Saturday morning in his Mini-Cooper and then drove like a bottle fly down the motorway to Gloucestershire. He talked about himself all the way; he was having a small dispute with his director over a certain scene in the play. 'I'm the actor,' I told him, 'and I can tell you my character just wouldn't react like that. I know my character!'

Sofia remembered her conversation with Maggie and Anton and gloomily watched the frosty countryside race past her window. Jake didn't seem to notice that she was quiet, he was far too busy ranting on about his director. She was relieved when they arrived at David Harrison's sand-coloured house that stood at the end of a long drive, just outside the town of Burford.

David Harrison appeared at the door surrounded by two honey-coloured Labradors who wagged their thick tails at the sight of the car. David was of average height and slim with a full head of light brown hair, greying slightly at the temples. He wore small, round glasses and a big, amiable smile.

'Welcome to Lowsley, don't worry about your bags,' he said. 'Come and have a drink.'

Sofia followed Jake across the gravel towards him. The two men shook hands and David patted Jake affectionately between the shoulder-blades. 'Good to see you, Lothario.'

'David, this is Sofia. Sofia Solanas,' he said and Sofia extended her hand.

'Jake has told me an awful lot about you,' David said, shaking it firmly. 'It will be a pleasure getting to know you myself. Now come on in, don't stand on ceremony.'

They followed him into a large hallway. Each wall seemed to be covered with paintings of every size and there was not a surface that didn't carry unsteady towers of books. The rich wooden floor-boards were partly obscured by luxurious Persian rugs and large plants in china pots. Sofia liked the house immediately. It was warm with an overpowering smell of dogs.

David led them into the sitting room where four people Sofia didn't know sat smoking and drinking around a boisterous fire. It reminded Sofia suddenly of Chiquita's house at Santa Catalina and she suppressed the ache that always followed such recollections. They were introduced to the other guests: his neighbours Tony Middleton, the writer, and his wife Zaza, who owned a small boutique in Beauchamp Place, and Gilbert d'Orange, a French newspaper columnist and his wife Michelle, nicknamed Miche. Then they all sat down and resumed their conversation.

'So what do you do?' asked Zaza, turning to Sofia. Sofia cringed.

'I work in a hair salon called Maggie's,' she replied and held her breath, waiting for Zaza to smile politely but disdainfully before turning away.

But to her delight Zaza's painted green eyes opened very wide and she gasped, 'I don't believe it. Tony, darling. Tony!' Her husband broke off his sentence and turned to Zaza. Everyone stopped to listen. 'You won't believe it! Sofia works with Maggie!'

Tony grinned wryly. 'What a small world. Now Maggie was married to my second cousin, Viv. Good God, how is the old girl?'

Sofia was elated and in a few moments had everyone holding their stomachs with laughter as she imitated Maggie and Anton. David watched her from the drinks' cabinet and thought he had never seen anyone more lovely in his life. There was something tragic in her large brown eyes, in spite of her generous smile, and he wanted to gather her up and look after her. She was much younger than the others and yet had no trouble conversing with them. It was only when Zaza, who had clearly lost her heart to Sofia, innocently asked her about her home country that their guest went quiet for a while.

After lunch in the musty dining room, served by a rotund lady called Mrs Berniston, Gilbert and Miche disappeared off to their rooms for a siesta. 'That chocolate pudding and wine has made me *très, très fatigué,*' Gilbert said, taking his petite wife by the hand and leading her up the stairs. Jake decided to go jogging.

'Is that such a good idea after a heavy meal?' Sofia queried.

'I didn't go this morning and I'd like to do so before it gets dark,' he replied, running upstairs two at a time.

'Well, why don't we go for a walk? Then we'll get some exercise too,' suggested Zaza enthusiastically. 'Will you join us, David?'

The air was icy and yet the sun shone down warmly from a clear, cerulean sky. The gardens were wild though they eerily echoed the order of a past era when David's ex-wife, a fanatical gardener, had looked after them and loved them. The four of them, Tony, Zaza, Sofia and David wandered up the stone path that cut through the garden to the back of the house, laughing about how full and lethargic they felt after such a large lunch. The trees were bare and frozen due to the February frosts and the undergrowth wet and rotting beneath their feet.

Sofia gulped in the country air and realised it had been a long time since she had been in such a beautiful place. She remembered Santa Catalina in winter and thought that if she closed her eyes and breathed in the scents of damp earth, rich with the sweet smell of winter foliage, she could almost convince herself that she was there.

She liked David. He had that English nonchalance that so appealed to her foreign nature. He was very attractive in an intellectual way, not beautiful but handsome. He was strong, knew his mind, and was charismatic, yet his pale blue eyes had depth to them, revealing that he too had experienced life's struggles. When they walked down a small hill towards a cluster of stables, Sofia felt her heart lurch.

'If anyone wants to ride, I have a couple of horses,' David said casually. 'Ariella used to breed them. When she left, the stud farm was closed down and I had to sell off all the mares. It was tragic. Now I just keep a couple for my own amusement.'

Sofia found herself walking faster and faster until she had left the others behind on the hill. She felt her throat constrict as she fumbled the bolt on one of the stable doors. When the sound of rustling straw indicated that there was a horse inside she sniffed back her emotions. The smell of warm hay struck her at once and she held out her hand, smiling sadly as the animal's velvety muzzle nudged it curiously. She ran her fingers down his white face, all the time gazing lovingly into the horse's shiny marble eyes. It was only now, with the unique scent of horse clinging to her nostrils, that Sofia realised how much she'd missed them. She pressed the animal's head to hers and used its fur to wipe away her melancholy.

'Who are you?' she asked, stroking his ears. 'Aren't you beautiful. So beautiful.' She felt a tear on her lip and licked it away. The horse seemed to sense her unhappiness and puffed into her face. She closed her eyes and imagined she was home again. Leaning against her new friend and feeling his silky warm coat against her skin she was briefly transported back to the humid *pampa*. But it was all too real and she opened her eyes suddenly and blinked away the memory.

When David walked around the corner he saw Sofia's head buried in Safari's neck. He wanted to approach her and yet sensed the moment was a private one. Tactfully he led Tony and Zaza around to the other side.

'Is she all right?' hissed Zaza who noticed everything.

'I don't know,' David said, shaking his head anxiously. 'A curious girl, isn't she?'

'She didn't want to talk about her home when I asked her about it earlier,' Zaza noted.

'Perhaps she just misses it,' Tony said sensibly. 'She probably feels homesick.'

'David!' They all turned to see Sofia, running eagerly towards them. 'I need to – I mean I'd *love* to go for a ride. May I?'

Zaza and Tony continued their walk alone, leaving David and Sofia to saddle up the horses and embark on a long ride that wouldn't see them back before sundown. As Sofia and David cantered over the Cotswolds Sofia felt as if a constricting weight had been lifted off her chest. She was able to breathe again and she drank in large lungfuls of air. Her mind cleared; suddenly she knew who she was, she knew where she belonged. She felt she had come home, riding up there on those hills, able to see for miles the patchwork of fields and woods that undulated out before her like a rough sea of green. She smiled again; not just on the outside but she smiled broadly and genuinely on the inside. Her whole body was injected with an energy, a high she hadn't felt since she had last been at Santa Catalina.

David noticed the change in her immediately. Like an actor in a play she had discarded her costume and revealed the real person beneath. By the time they shut the stable doors and hung the tack up in the tackroom they were laughing like old friends do, from the pit of their bellies.

Chapter Twenty-Six

As Jake drove Sofia back to Queen's Gate she reflected on David's offer.

'I would dearly love to get this place going again,' he had said, referring to the stud. 'You obviously have a good understanding of horses. My ex, Ariella, bred racehorses. She produced top-class yearlings. When she walked out, that was the end of that – I sold them all except for Safari and Inca. I'd pay you, of course, and hire anyone you required. You wouldn't have to be stuck in the country all week, you could oversee it. The place is dead without people looking after it. It'll go to ruin before too long and I'd hate to have to sell the horses.'

Sofia recalled his phlegmatic tone. He was matter-of-fact, yet there had been a warmth in his expression. She found herself smiling as she remembered him. It was a nice idea but Jake would never allow it; he wouldn't want her to work out in the country. He was way too possessive, but Jake was all she had.

By April the play had been running for a couple of months when Sofia opened the door to Jake's dressing room to find him screwing Mandy Bourne, his leading lady, up against the wall. He had pulled down his trousers and what later stuck in Sofia's mind was his white bottom thrusting aggressively against a dishevelled, sweaty Mandy still in eighteenth-century costume. She had even stood there for a couple of minutes before they had noticed her. Mandy was grunting like a hungry pig, her face twisted into an expression of pain, but Sofia took it that she was enjoying it by the mewing sounds she made between grunts. Jake was murmuring, 'I love you, I love you,' in time to his thrusts and appeared to be arriving at the *moment critique* when Mandy opened her eyes and screamed. Jake buried his face in her flabby breasts and exclaimed, 'Christ!' when he saw Sofia standing stiffly in the doorway. Mandy had fled in tears.

There was no apology, no penitence. Jake had blamed Sofia, saying he had only slept with Mandy because he was unable to get through to her. 'You don't love me!' he had shouted accusingly.

Sofia had responded coolly, 'I have to trust you first.'

When she left the theatre that night she did so for the last time. She never wanted to see Jake Felton again. Picking up the telephone she hoped that David Harrison would remember the offer he had made back in February.

'You're leaving us?' cried Anton in despair. 'I can't bear it!'

'I'm going to set up a stud farm for David Harrison,' she explained.

'Devious man,' Maggie snarled, drawing on her cigarette.

'Oh Maggie, it's got nothing to do with that. Though, you *were* right about Jake Felton. Men — who needs 'em!'

'Ooh no, you're out of date! Maggie's taken a lover, haven't you, duckie? A client. I think her Maggie dust may have worked after all.' Maggie grinned a self-satisfied smile.

'Well done, Maggie. Oh God, I'm so sad to leave you all,' Sofia waited, 'but I won't be down at Lowsley all the time. We'll keep in touch.'

'You'd better. Anyhow, we'll hear all the gossip from Daisy. Just don't forget to ask us to the wedding.'

'Maggie,' laughed Sofia. 'He's too old.'

'Careful, I'm in my forties too, you know,' she replied, then added throatily, 'We'll see.'

Daisy was devastated that she was going. Not only because she would miss her friend, but also because, if things worked out for Sofia, she'd have to find someone else to share the flat with. She didn't want to share with anyone else. She and Sofia had become as close as sisters.

'So if you like it, you'll just move down there permanently?' she asked, horrified at the thought of being stuck in the country, however luxurious the house was.

'Yes, I love the countryside. I miss it,' said Sofia. Lowsley had awakened her dormant senses to her affinity with nature; now the smell of the city appalled her.

'I'll miss you. Who's going to do your nails now?' Daisy asked, pushing her bottom lip out grumpily.

'No one. I'll bite them again.'

'Don't you dare, just when I've got them looking so pretty.'

'I'm going to be using my hands for farmwork, so I won't need pretty nails any more,' laughed Sofia happily, anticipating days filled with horses and dogs and those endless green hills. The two girls embraced.

'Don't forget to call often and visit occasionally. I don't want to lost touch,' said Daisy, wagging her finger at her friend to hide her sadness. Sofia was used to leaving places, leaving people, making new friends. She was accustomed to it by now. She had taught herself to switch off her emotions in order to avoid hurting so she promised Daisy that she would call weekly, then she left, moved on. Like a nomad she looked ahead to the next adventure without dwelling too much on the human ties she was leaving behind.

Once Sofia was happily installed in a small cottage at Lowsley she realised she wouldn't be sad at all if she never went to London again. She had missed the countryside more than she had realised and now she had found it again she never wanted to let it go. She spoke to Daisy most days on the telephone and laughed at the latest gossip from Maggie's. She didn't have much time, though, to think of her old friends. She was too busy setting up David's stud farm.

He had said she could 'oversee' it. She had no intention of 'overseeing' it. She wanted to be as involved as possible and what she didn't know she would learn.

She found out from Mrs Berniston that when Ariella had walked out, they had had to close down the stables, making Freddie Rattray, known as Rattie, redundant. Rattie had been the stud manager, looking after the foals and running the farm. He was an expert, Mrs Berniston informed her. 'You won't find a better man than Rattie,' she said.

Sofia wasted no time in tracking down and hiring Rattie and his eighteen-year-old daughter Jaynie, with the help of Mrs Berniston who used to write regularly to Freddie's late wife, Beryl. As Beryl had recently died, Freddie was anxious to come back to Gloucestershire and take up his old life.

When David came down for the weekends he was greeted by Sofia's wide smile and infectious sense of humour. She always wore jeans and a T-shirt, often with the old beige jersey of his that she had borrowed and never returned, wrapped around her waist. The country air had changed her complexion; it now glowed with rude health and she let her long glossy hair fall about her shoulders rather than tying it back like she used to. Her eyes shone and her irrepressible energy made him feel younger in her presence. He looked forward to his time with her and felt heavy in spirit when he had to leave for London on Sunday evenings. He was pleased that she was making progress with the help of Rattie, whom she adored. 'He's so English – he's like a garden gnome from a fairytale,' she said.

'I don't think Rattie would be very pleased with that description,' David chuckled.

'Oh, he doesn't mind. I call him "the gnome" sometimes and he just smiles. I think he's so happy to be back, I could call him anything.'

Rattie was also a keen gardener and David was astounded by the transformation of his grounds in the short time he had employed them. Sofia was tireless. She awoke early and made herself breakfast in the big house as Mrs Berniston, who came three days a week to cook and clean, suggested she might as well use Mr Harrison's kitchen as the fridge was always full. Then she would take one of the horses for a ride across the hills before starting the day's chores in the stables.

Rattie knew everything about horses and she had a great deal to learn. As a child at Santa Catalina she hadn't even been required to put a saddle on a horse as everything was done for her by the *gauchos*. Rattie teased her, saying she was spoilt and he'd bring her down to size and she told him that he was only there because of her, so he should treat her with more respect. With his crooked smile and wise face he reminded her in a small way of Jose. She wondered whether Jose missed her, whether Soledad's gossip had reached him, whether he thought less of her.

Under Rattie's guidance they bought six top-class mares and hired two grooms to work with his daughter, Jaynie. 'It'll take time to get the place up and running,' he warned Sofia. 'The breeding cycle is eleven months, you see,' he said, wrapping his leathery hands around a cup of steaming coffee. 'Autumn is the time to look for stallions for our mares, stallions with good pedigree and conformation, you understand?' Sofia nodded. 'You want top-class racehorses, you need top-class stallions.' She nodded again with emphasis. 'In August and September you put in an application for a stallion – we do this by using a bloodstock agent. He'll negotiate with the owner of the stallion for a nomination. Now I've been out of it for a few years, but Willy Rankin used to be my man and I believe he still is.' He slurped another gulp of coffee. 'January the fourteen is the start of the season. That's when we take the mares off to the stud until they're scanned in foal.'

'When do they have their foals?' Sofia was trying to ask sensible questions; it all sounded rather more complicated than she had expected. She was glad Rattie knew what he was doing.

'From February to mid-April. Now that's a magical time. You

really see nature working right in front of your eyes.' He sighed. 'Right in front of your very eyes. Ten days after the foal is born and healthy, both foal and mare go back to the stallion.'

'How long do they stay there for?'

'Anything up to three months. Then once she's back in foal again we bring them home.'

'When do we sell them?' she asked, filling up the kettle and putting it back on the Aga.

'This takes a lot of learning, doesn't it?' he chuckled, noticing that she was growing tired of the details. 'A far cry from your life on the — what do you call it? *Pampa?*'

'The *pampa*, Rattie. You're right, though — I never did anything like this,' she added humbly, opening the jar of coffee granules.

'Well, if you love horses like you do, you'll soon learn,' he said kindly. 'Now in July, there's a lot of work getting the yearlings ready for the sales. You'll enjoy that time. Walking them out every day, teaching them how to wear a bridle, that sort of thing. Then the people who run the sales will come and inspect our yearlings to see if they're suitable for the top sales. The sales take place in October in Newmarket. Now that will be interesting for you. I think you'll enjoy that,' he said, handing her his empty cup to refill. 'I'll teach you everything I know, but you can't learn sitting here at a kitchen table. The learning's in the doing, that's what my father always used to say. "Enough talk, more do," he said. So, I'll stop talking now and we'll do. Is that all right with you, young lady?' he asked as she handed him back his cup, now full of thick black coffee, just the way he liked it. 'Lovely,' he said, taking it from her.

'I think that's just fine, Rattie.' Sofia didn't care so much for the details; as long as she was working with horses she felt at home.

The summer passed quickly. Sofia had made it to London only once. Maggie and Anton were furious with her at first and it had taken a lot of flattery to coax them out of their sulk. She had stayed only for an hour, as she was anxious to get back to her horses. They were grateful for her visit, but felt her slipping away and that saddened them.

By September David had begun to spend more time down in the country. He created another office in the study and hired a secretary to work part-time there. Suddenly his home had come alive again, vibrating with the voices of people and animals. But if David was honest with himself he had fallen hopelessly in love with Sofia and could hardly bear to be away from her. That was the reason he had hired her. He hadn't cared what she cost; he'd have paid any figure she'd asked. Employing her was the only way he could see her without courting her – and he was realistic enough to know that by confessing his feelings he'd only scare her away. As it was, twelve pounds a week and free board in the cottage was nothing compared to what he wanted to give her, which was a new name and everything he owned.

Sofia was delighted that David had decided to spend more time at Lowsley. He brought the dogs with him, Sam and Quid, who followed Sofia around all day, their adorable clown's eyes smiling at her lovingly. They spent long evenings walking in the garden talking, watching the long summer shadows shorten into autumn until the days began to recede and the nights close in. David noticed that she never talked about her home and he didn't ask. He couldn't pretend he wasn't curious; he wanted to know everything about her. He wanted to kiss away the troubles that he could feel simmering beneath her smile. In fact, he wanted to kiss her every time he saw her and yet he didn't want to frighten her off. He didn't want to lose her. He hadn't been this happy in a long time. So he never tried. Then just when Sofia was succeeding in forgetting about her past someone arrived at Lowsley to remind her of it.

David hadn't had a house-party weekend since the summer. He had been happy to be alone with Sofia, but Zaza had suggested she might be longing to meet people her own age. 'She is a very attractive young woman. Some man will snap her up before you know it. You simply can't hide her away,' she had said, without realising how much her words had hurt him.

David watched Sofia as she rushed about the estate and thought how happy she looked. Hardly the expression of someone aching to meet other young people. She seemed content with the horses. But Zaza had insisted, dismissing him with the words, 'It takes a woman to understand a woman.' After all, he was more or less twenty years her senior, hardly the right company for a girl of her age.

When Zaza and Tony introduced him to Gonzalo Segundo, a swarthy, unusually tall Argentine polo-playing friend of their son, Eddie, David took the hint and invited them all for the weekend. He hadn't anticipated Sofia's reaction.

'Sofia Solanas!' exclaimed Gonzalo, when they were introduced. 'Are you any relation to Rafa Solanas?' he asked in Spanish. Sofia was stunned. She hadn't spoken Spanish for a long time.

'He's my brother,' she replied hoarsely. Then took a step back as the sound of her own voice speaking her mother tongue brought all those suppressed memories clattering about her head like a falling pack of cards. She went pale before running out of the room in tears.

'Was it something I said?' asked Gonzalo, perplexed.

It wasn't long before David knocked on her door.

'Sofia, are you all right?' he said softly, knocking again. She opened the door. David walked in followed by Sam and Quid who sniffed anxiously at her ankles. Her face was wet from crying and her eyes were bloodshot and furious.

'How could you!' she shouted. 'How could you invite him down here without asking me!'

'I don't know what you're talking about, Sofia. Calm down,' he said firmly, trying to place a hand on her arm. She swiftly withdrew it.

'I will not calm down,' she retorted angrily. David closed the door behind them; he didn't want Zaza listening to this. 'He knows my family! He'll go back and tell them about me,' she sobbed.

'Does that matter?'

'Yes! Yes, it does matter!' she snapped and walked over to the bed. They both sat down. 'It matters very much to me,' she added quietly, blinking away the tears.

'Sofia, I don't know what you're trying to tell me. You can't expect me to know if you don't tell me. I thought you'd like to meet someone from your country.'

'Oh David.' She gulped and threw herself against his chest. Slowly he put his arm around her. She didn't flinch or push him away so he sat there and held her. 'I left Argentina three years ago because I had an affair with someone my parents disapproved of. I haven't been back since.'

'You haven't been back?' he repeated, not knowing quite what to say.

'I fought with them. I hate them. I haven't spoken to anyone in my family since then.'

'You poor old girl,' he said and found himself running a hand down her hair. He was too afraid to move in case the moment was ruined.

'I love them and despise them. I miss them, try to forget them. But I can't, I just can't. Being here at Lowsley has helped me to forget. I've been so happy here. And now this!'

David was mystified when she began to cry again. This time violent sobs vibrated out from deep within her being. He held her close and tried to comfort her. He had never seen anyone as miserable as Sofia was at that moment. She was crying so hard she could scarcely breathe. David panicked, he wasn't very good at this sort of thing and thought that perhaps a woman would be better equipped. But when he got up to fetch Zaza, Sofia held onto his jersey and begged him to stay.

'There's more, David. Please don't go. I want you to know everything,' she pleaded. Then she sheepishly told him about

316

Santi's betrayal and about Santiguito, omitting that Santi was her first cousin. 'I gave my baby away,' she whispered hopelessly and looked at him steadily. Falling into her stricken eyes he felt her pain. He wanted to tell her he'd give her children, as many as she wanted. He'd love her enough to match the love of her entire family. But he didn't know how to tell her. He pulled her into his arms and they sat in silence. In that tender moment David felt he loved her more than he thought it was possible to love anyone. When he was with Sofia, he realised how lonely he had been. He knew he could make her happy.

Sofia felt strangely better for having shared her secret with him, even if she had only told him half the story, and lifting her head up she looked at him through different eyes. When their mouths found each other neither one was surprised. In those few minutes Sofia had trusted him more than she had trusted anyone else except Santi. When David held her against him she forgot the rest of the world, and all that existed was Lowsley and the refuge she had built there.

Chapter Twenty-Seven

When David and Sofia returned to the drawing room everyone pretended that nothing had happened. Sofia thought how very British that was. Where she came from, everyone would be falling over each other to ask questions. Gonzalo and Eddie had obviously been told by Zaza not to add to her distress by mentioning it so they simply grinned at her and asked her about the horses.

Zaza lit a cigarette and sat back on the sofa, her narrowed eyes sliding from David to Sofia with suspicion. David has a bounce in his step which he is trying very hard to disguise, she thought to herself, exhaling smoke in a thin line out of the corner of her mouth. She watched Sofia. And her eyelashes are still wet from her tears, but her cheeks are glowing with an excitement she can barely suppress. Something is definitely going on here . . .

Gonzalo found Sofia irresistible on two accounts, she was tragic and beautiful. He had heard something of her in Argentina. Buenos Aires was a small town and a scandal like hers would have been impossible to keep secret. He tried to recall what it had been about. Hadn't she had an affair with one of her brothers and been banished to Europe? No wonder she didn't want to be recognised — the shame of it. But still, he thought, watching her wide smile and quivering lips, I could forgive her anything.

'Sofia, will you take me out on horseback?' he asked her in

Spanish. She smiled weakly, her eyes darting quickly to David who raised an eyebrow. Now she had declared herself to David she didn't want to be separated from him, even for a minute.

'Gonzalo wants me to go riding with him,' she said, hoping that someone would suggest a better plan.

'Good idea,' said Tony, chewing on his cigar. 'Eddie, why don't you go with them?'

'Yes, darling, do. The fresh air will do you good,' said Zaza, longing to be alone so she could interrogate David. Eddie, who slouched lazily in the armchair by the fire, had no intention of going out in the cold. It was a horrid drizzly day, and anyway it was obvious that Gonzalo fancied Sofia. He didn't want to get in his way.

'No, thanks. You both go together,' he said, his fingers delving into the box of fudge that sat temptingly on the table.

'Darling, you can't stay in all morning, you should work up an appetite for Mrs Berniston's lunch.'

'Well, you and Dad are staying in,' he retorted, digging his bottom further into the armchair. Zaza pursed her lips in frustration. Her interrogation would just have to wait.

David watched Sofia leave the room with Gonzalo and stifled a pang of jealousy. Although he knew Sofia went reluctantly, he couldn't tolerate the thought of her out there on those hills with a man from her homeland. A young, handsome man who spoke her language, understood her culture and related to her in a way that he would never be able to. When she had gone the room felt colder.

'What a genius you are, darling,' said Zaza, watching David carefully.

'How so?' he asked, trying to inject a humorous tone into his voice that he knew sounded flat.

'To agree to invite Gonzalo.'

'Why is that particularly clever of me?'

'Because they make such a delightful couple. Gonzalo and Sofia!' she laughed, then clamped the ebony cigarette-holder between her red lips and scrutinised his expression. He gave nothing away.

'Zaza, darling, there's no place for Cupid this weekend. The bloody man sent her up to her room in tears. Hardly the most romantic way to win a woman's heart,' interjected Tony.

'What was all that about?' asked Eddie, delighted that his father had opened the subject. They all looked at David. He sat on the fireguard and stoked the logs with an iron poker.

'She misses her home, that's all,' he replied cagily.

'Oh,' said Eddie, disappointed. Tony nodded sympathetically.

'Was that all?' persisted Zaza. 'What was it you said to her that put the smile back on her face?'

'Oh, I didn't put it back, she did. Once she'd got over the shock of it she talked to me about her home and then felt better,' he said unconvincingly, and winced. Zaza would see straight through that hopeless lie.

'I see. Well, she and Gonzalo will be able to get to know each other a little without us oldies watching their every move. Young people,' she sighed. 'Oh, to be young again.'

David's spirits sank. He was over twenty years older than Sofia. What had he been thinking of? Zaza was right, Gonzalo made a better match for her than he did. Perhaps she would realise that out there on the Cotswolds. She hadn't seen a young man of her age for months. She'll talk of her home and realise that Argentina is where she belongs, he thought gloomily. He could still feel her lips against his. He could still taste her. Had he exploited her during a moment of weakness? He shouldn't have allowed himself to kiss her, he should have resisted.

Changing the subject, he tried hard to talk as normal but his throat was tight and the words just didn't have their usual buoyancy. Zaza noticed the hurt behind his eyes and knew that she had gone too far. She had always loved David; even though she was perfectly happy with Tony she had always kept a little part of herself back for him. She had spoken with the mouth of a jealous woman and she hated herself for it. She attempted to lift his mood with amusing tales but they failed to make his laughter penetrate deeper than the lines on his face. She looked at the clock on the mantelpiece and longed for Sofia to come back and reassure him.

Gonzalo was an accomplished horseman. Sofia watched how he sat in the saddle, that typical Argentine slouch, that delicious confidence, that hateful arrogance, and her heart stumbled. They spoke Spanish and after a while she was rattling the words out with excitement and waving her arms expressively as Latin speakers do. She suddenly felt released from the constraints of having to hide her true self. She felt like an Argentine again and the sound of her voice, the feel of those words on her tongue, made her dizzy with happiness.

Gonzalo was funny, telling her stories that made her laugh. He was careful not to ask her about her family and she didn't volunteer any information. She seemed happier to listen to him. In fact, she couldn't get enough of him. 'Tell me more, Gonzalo,' she pleaded, soaking up his words with the enthusiasm of someone who has been deaf for a long time and suddenly hears again.

They walked through the mud that gathered in the valley under the trees, the horses' hooves squelching as they made their way towards the foot of the hills. The drizzle had now turned to rain that ran down their faces and seeped through their clothes. Once up on the hills they galloped across the top, laughing together as they enjoyed the wind in their hair and the motion of the horses beneath them. They rode for miles until thick fog gathered about them, appearing up from the valley as if from nowhere.

'What's the time?' Sofia asked, feeling her stomach ache with hunger.

'Twelve thirty,' he replied. 'Do you think you'll find your way back in this mist?'

'Of course,' she said jovially, but she wasn't sure. She looked about her; each direction looked the same. 'Follow me,' she said, trying to sound confident. They rode side by side through the whiteness, their eyes fixed on the receding patch of green that stretched out in front of them. Gonzalo didn't seem worried at all. Neither did the horses who puffed contentedly into the icy air. Sofia felt chilled and longed for the fire back at Lowsley. She longed for David, too.

Suddenly, they came across what seemed to be the grey stone ruins of an old castle.

'Does this look familiar?' asked Gonzalo, watching a twinge of concern mar her beautiful features. She shook her head.

'*Dios*, Gonzalo, I must be honest with you. I've never seen this ruin. I don't know where the hell we are.'

'So, we're lost,' he said dismissively and smiled broadly. 'Why don't we stay here until the fog subsides. At least we can get out of the rain.' She agreed and they both dismounted. They led the horses under cover and tied them to a stone. 'Come with me, we'll find somewhere sheltered,' he said, taking Sofia's hand and striding purposefully across the rubble. He was walking so fast, practically dragging her over the slippery stones, she had a hard time keeping up. Then she fell. She didn't think anything of it until she tried to get up. The pain in her ankle bolted through her leg and she collapsed with a whimper. Gonzalo crouched down beside her.

'Where does it hurt?' he asked.

'My ankle. Oh God, I haven't broken it, have I?' She winced.

'It looks more like a sprain. Can you move it?'

She tried feebly, only able to move it slightly. 'It hurts,' she complained.

'Well, at least you can move it a little. Now hold on, I'm going to carry you,' he said decisively.

'If you show the strain on your face, I'll kill you,' she joked as he placed his arms under her and lifted her off the ground.

'No strain, I promise,' he replied and carried her into the dark interior of the remains of one of the towers. Laying her down on the damp grass he took off his coat and placed it on the ground beside her. 'Here, sit on this,' he said, helping her to shuffle over without putting any strain on her foot.

'As if I'm not wet enough already.' She chuckled. 'Thank you.'

'If we take off your boot, we won't be able to get it back on again,' he warned.

'I don't care, the bloody thing hurts so much. Please take it off. If the ankle swells up we'll never get it off, and I'd prefer to ride home without it than in pain.' Gonzalo gently eased the boot off while Sofia sweated in agony, her face contorted and burning.

'There, done,' he said triumphantly, taking her foot in his hand and drawing it onto his lap. He carefully removed her sock to reveal the tender pink skin beneath it that looked helpless and exposed against the rough surroundings. Sofia breathed deeply and wiped away her tears with the sleeve of her coat. 'It's quite swollen, but you'll live,' he said, running his warm hand up her shin.

'That feels nice,' she sighed, leaning her head back against the stone. 'Down a bit – yes, there . . . ah,' she said as he gently massaged the arch of her foot. 'So much for Mrs Berniston's lunch,' she said sadly.

'Don't tell me she's a great cook.'

'The best.'

'I could do with a big, juicy piece of *lomo*,' he said, suddenly feeling very hungry.

'Me too, *con papas fritas*.' She smiled nostalgically. They then proceeded to list all the Argentine things they missed.

'*Dulce de leche.*'

'*Membrillo.*'

'*Empanadas.*'

'*Zapallo.*'

'*Zapallo?*' he echoed, scrunching up his nose.

'What's wrong with *zapallo*?'

'All right. *Mate.*'

'*Alfajores* . . .'

✻   ✻   ✻

Back at the house David gazed out into the mist and then at the clock on the mantelpiece.

'They've got stuck in the fog,' said Tony. 'I shouldn't worry. She's in safe hands. Gonzalo's as strong as an ox.' That's what I'm worried about, thought David bleakly.

'I'm hungry,' Eddie piped up. 'Do we have to wait for them?'

'I suppose not,' David replied.

'We mustn't let Mrs Berniston's lunch overcook,' said Zaza. 'I'm sure they'll be back soon. Sofia knows the hills very well,' she added helpfully.

'Not that well,' sighed David. 'Not in this bloody fog. It doesn't look like it's going to lift, either.'

'Oh, it will. Fog lifts very quickly in these parts,' Zaza said immediately.

'Darling, what do you know about fog?' Tony teased her.

'I'm just being positive. David's worried, can't you see?'

'Maybe I should go and look for them,' suggested David.

'Where on earth would you start? You don't even know where they've gone,' Tony commented. 'If it gets dark I'll come out with you.'

'You can't ride, darling,' said Zaza, nervously lighting another cigarette.

'I'll go in the Land Rover.'

'And get stuck in the mud?' added Eddie unhelpfully. Tony shrugged his shoulders.

'No, Tony's right. Let's have lunch. If it gets dark we'll all go and look for them.' David was happier now they had established a plan. He tried not to think of them out there, cuddling for warmth against the elements. He felt sick and unhappy. He knew the hills better than anyone – he'd find them. He hoped Sofia was all right. She was a good rider, but even good riders fall – and the stupid girl never wears a hat, he thought miserably. It's not the bloody *pampas*; in England people wear hats to prevent them from breaking their necks. He hoped she had taken Safari out; he was gentle and

324

wouldn't throw her. He couldn't be as sure about the others. With these images clinging to his thoughts he led his guests into the dining room for lunch.

Sofia let her mind drift across the *pampas* as she reminisced with Gonzalo and allowed his hand to massage the pain away in her ankle.

'Let's put your sock back on. I don't think we should let your foot get too cold,' he suggested after a while.

'But you're doing a fantastic job, Dr Segundo,' she joked.

'Dr Segundo knows what's best, Señorita.'

'Careful,' she warned as he began to thread her foot back into the sock.

'How does it feel?'

'Better,' she replied, surprised, as it didn't hurt as much as she had expected. 'You've got healing hands.'

'Not only a doctor but a healer, too – you flatter me,' he chuckled. 'There, as good as new. Any other ailments that need seeing to, Señorita?'

'None, thank you, Doctor.'

'What about your troubled heart?'

'Troubled heart?'

'Yes, your troubled heart,' he said seriously, and taking her face in his hands, his lips descended onto hers. She shouldn't have allowed him to kiss her, but the sound of his voice speaking Spanish, that inimitable Argentine accent, the riding boots, the smell of horses, the swirling fog that hid them from the world . . . she lost herself momentarily and responded. It felt nice but it didn't feel right. Pulling away she noticed the fog was subsiding.

'Look, it's clearing up,' she said hopefully.

'I'd like to stay here,' he told her softly.

'Well, I'm wet and cold and my foot hurts. Please take me home, Gonzalo,' she pleaded.

'All right,' he sighed. 'I hadn't noticed how cold and wet I was.'

Sofia suddenly yearned for David. He must be worried sick, she thought.

Gonzalo lifted her over the stones back to where the horses were tied up. 'I'll take your boot for you,' he said, settling her onto Safari. The ride back was long and precarious. Sofia got lost once again but, determined not to let on, she allowed Safari a free rein in the hope that he would know his way back. When he happily led them home she wondered why she hadn't done that in the first place.

'Right, I'm going to find them,' David decided, retreating from the window. It was almost dark and the pair still hadn't returned. 'Something's wrong. They need help,' he added irritably.

'I'll follow you in the Land Rover,' Tony offered. Eddie caught his mother's eye, but neither dared to speak. Lunch had been uncomfortable. David was more ill-humoured than Zaza had ever seen him; he had barely been able to concentrate on the conversation. He had kept looking out of the window, searching through the fog, as if Sofia and Gonzalo would suddenly appear out of it like they always did in the movies. Tony and Eddie hadn't noticed anything. Men are so insensitive sometimes, Zaza had thought crossly, as they discussed the West Indies cricket score as if nothing had happened.

David ran through the hall, grabbed his coat and boots and opened the door to find Gonzalo emerging through the fog with Sofia, wet and shivering, in his arms.

'What the devil happened to you?' he rapped out, unable to hide the exasperation in his voice.

'It's a long story, we'll tell you later. Let's get Sofia upstairs,' Gonzalo replied, ignoring David's offer to carry her from there.

'I've just twisted my ankle,' said Sofia as she passed him.

'Good God, what happened?' Zaza exclaimed. The pair looked like they'd been rolling about in the mud.

'Where's your room?' asked Gonzalo, taking Sofia up the stairs.

'Straight on,' she told him, looking about for David, but he wasn't following. Once in her room Gonzalo placed her gently down on the bed.

'You need help getting out of those wet things. I'll run you a bath,' he said.

'Don't worry, I'm fine. I can manage,' she insisted.

'Dr Segundo knows best,' he said, removing her boot.

'Please, Gonzalo, I'm fine, really.'

'Thank you, Gonzalo,' came a firm voice behind him. 'Why don't you get out of your wet things. You've been a hero, but even heroes have to take a break.'

'David!' breathed Sofia in relief. Gonzalo shrugged his shoulders and smiling at Sofia to show his reluctance he left the room.

'What the hell have you been up to?' he asked crossly and stalked into the bathroom to run the bath. Sofia heard the gush of water as he turned on the taps and suddenly felt weary.

'We got lost in the fog, but thanks to a ruined castle—'

'How in God's name did you get all the way over there?' he snapped.

'David, it wasn't my fault.'

'And what about the horses? Didn't you see the fog, or were you too busy with your new friend?'

'I didn't suggest we go riding. I didn't want to go in the first place. You could have stopped us.'

'Get out of your wet things before you catch your death of cold. I've run you a bath,' he said, making for the door. Sofia recognised his jealousy and she smiled softly.

'I can't do it by myself,' she said feebly. He turned around and Sofia thought his angry face looked adorable; she wanted to kiss his fury away.

'I'll call Zaza,' he said stiffly.

'I don't want Zaza. I don't want Gonzalo, either. I want you,' she said slowly and looked straight into his dejected eyes.

'You were gone for hours. I was worried,' he burst out. 'What was I to think?'

327

'You can't think very much of me if you imagine me hopping from one man to the next. Don't you trust me?'

'I'm sorry.'

'It's because he's Argentine, isn't it?' she said.

'And handsome and young. I'm over twenty years older than you,' he protested miserably.

'So?'

'I'm old.'

'And I love you. I'd love you however old you were. It makes no difference to me,' she said, struggling out of her clothes.

'Let me help you with this,' he said, walking over. He knelt in front of her and took her face in his hands and kissed her. His mouth was soft and warm and Sofia wanted to curl up against him, but he eased her away. 'You're like a sodden dog,' he laughed, looking down at the wet patch that now discoloured his shirt.

He pulled her jersey and T-shirt over her head in one swift movement. She shivered. Her hair fell limply about her naked neck and shoulders in long, dripping tentacles. He kissed her again in an attempt to put some life back into her purple lips, but they trembled in spite of him. She unbuttoned her jeans and allowed him to gently remove them, taking care to pull the leg cautiously over her bad ankle. They were soggy and splattered with mud. 'My darling, you're freezing. Let's get you into the bath,' he said solicitously.

'What – in my underwear?' She laughed and unhooked her brassière. Her breasts were surprisingly plump for her slight body and covered in goosebumps, and her blood-red nipples stood out rigidly in protest at the cold. She wriggled out of her panties and extended her arms to him. He lifted her cold body off the bed and into the bathroom.

'You're beautiful,' he said and kissed her temple.

'And cold.' She pressed her face against his rough jawbone. 'Bubbles,' she sighed as he lowered her through the thick foam into the hot water below.

David sat on the chair and watched as the colour returned to her lips and cheeks, and her shoulders relaxed and sank into the water. Her swollen ankle throbbed as the blood pumped into it with renewed energy. She began to feel herself again. After wrapping her up in a large white towel, David laid her down on the bed and made to leave the room. But she stopped him.

'I want you to make love to me, David,' she said, tightening her grip about his neck.

'What about the others?' he said, smoothing his hand over her damp hair.

'They can look after themselves. I'm poorly, remember.'

'Exactly – and sex isn't good for your ankle,' he said.

'I don't make love with my ankle,' she giggled into his neck. He laughed too and kissed her again. Then he was making love to her, caressing her, touching her, enjoying her. To her delight she found that when she closed her eyes, David was all she saw.

Chapter Twenty-Eight

'I knew something was up that weekend we were down with Gonzalo,' Zaza said a month later. 'I could see it in your eyes, David. You are a hopeless actor.' She laughed throatily. He had called her that morning to invite her out to lunch as he was to be in town for a few days on business. 'I can barely tear myself away from Sofia,' he had said and then he had told her about their relationship. 'Poor Gonzalo was smitten,' she added from across the small table at the Ivy, putting the wineglass to her scarlet lips.

'I thought she would fall in love with him,' he said sheepishly.

'So did I, that's why I suggested you invite him in the first place. If I'd had a clue about your feelings for her, I would never have been so tactless. Will you forgive me?'

'You're wicked, Zaza, but I can't help liking you,' he chuckled and opened the menu.

'So what are you going to do?' she asked. 'Do you mind if I smoke?'

'Go ahead.'

'Well?'

'I don't know.'

'You'll marry her, of course,' she said and felt her throat stiffen.

'I don't know. Now, what are you going to have?' he asked, calling over the waiter. But Zaza wasn't so easily deterred when she had a mission. She ordered with haste and resumed her line of questioning.

'She'll want to get married. All girls do. What about Ariella?'

'What about her? We've been divorced for seven years.'

'Have you told Sofia about her? She'll want to know.'

'What is there to know about Ariella? She was my wife, a good gardener.'

'A bitch, an exasperatingly beautiful bitch,' said Zaza, spitting out the word 'bitch' with relish. 'She'll be furious when she finds out.'

'No, she won't. She's safely tucked away in France with her lover,' he said. Once he would have smarted at the memory of that smooth Frenchman who had lured his wife from him. It had nearly broken him. But now it was all in the past and he had Sofia whom he loved more than he had ever loved Ariella.

'She'll come back to stir up trouble, I bet. She'll start wanting you again now you love someone else. That's the funny thing about Ariella, she always wants what she can't have, and David, you'll be irresistible to her now.'

'You don't understand Ariella at all,' David said dismissively.

'Neither do you. It takes a woman to understand a woman. I understand her in a way that you never could. You see, she's devious. She likes a challenge. She likes to shock, do the unexpected. She likes to ripple the waters.' Zaza narrowed her eyes. 'She was always very good at rippling the waters. Of course, she could never ripple mine. No, I was someone she was always unable to crack. But she'll be back, mark my words.'

'Okay, enough about Ariella, how's Tony?' said David, moving to one side to allow the waiter to slide a plate of steaming sea bass in front of him.

'Your mother — has she met your mother?' said Zaza, ignoring him. She bent over to sniff the parsnip soup.

'No, she hasn't met my mother.'

'But she will, won't she?'

'There's absolutely no reason to subject her to Mother.'

'Well, I suppose she loved Ariella, didn't she? The right breed, the right parentage. Oxford-educated, bright and classy. She won't like an Argentine, she won't be able to say. "How nice, the Norfolk Solanas." She'll know nothing about her, won't be able to pigeon-hole her. God, darling, is she Catholic?'

'I don't know. I've never asked her,' admitted David patiently.

'God forbid – a Catholic! Not really much hope then, is there? Still, you're her only son. You'd imagine she'd enjoy your happiness, wouldn't you?'

'I haven't told her about Sofia, and I don't intend to. It's none of her business. She'd only be unpleasant. Why give her the opportunity?'

'It always amazes me that a dragon like Elizabeth Harrison could have produced someone as adorable as you, David. Amazes me, really.' She waved her spoon in the air as if it were a cigarette.

'So, now the inquisition is over, how's Tony?' he repeated with a smile.

As David walked back to his office through the cold November streets, he buried his gloved hands in his pockets and hunched his shoulders against the wind. He thought of Sofia and smiled. She hadn't wanted to come up to London, she preferred to stay with the dogs and horses in the country. Since the dreaded Gonzalo episode they had been blissfully happy, just the two of them. Friends had come and gone but they had relished their time alone together, riding out on the hills, walking through the woods, making love on the sofa in front of the crackling fire.

He loved the way she'd wander into his office while he was working and put her arms around him from behind, pressing her smooth face against his. In the evenings she'd curl up in front of the television, pulling both dogs onto the sofa with her, sipping a steaming cup of hot chocolate and nibbling biscuits while he read in the little green sitting room next door. At night she'd wrap her limbs around his until he got so hot he'd be forced to gently pull away without waking her. If he did wake her he'd have to resume his position until she had fallen asleep again. She needed to be close and secure.

Sofia hadn't spoken to Maggie and Anton for a few months. Daisy had kept in touch and had even visited a couple of times. She still worked in the salon and kept Sofia up to date with the gossip. Daisy had urged her to call Maggie. 'She'll think you've become too grand if you don't,' she had said. Maggie wasn't in the least bit surprised when Sofia told her about David.

'Didn't I say he'd seduce you?' she said and Sofia heard her inhale sharply. She always lit a cigarette the minute she knew she was going to be on the telephone long enough to smoke it.

'Yes, you did,' laughed Sofia.

'Dirty old man.'

'He's not an old man, Maggie, he's only forty-two.'

'Dirty man, then, sweetie.' She chuckled thickly. 'Have you met his ex yet?'

'The infamous Ariella. No, not yet.'

'You will. Exes always appear to put a spanner in the works,' she said and inhaled loudly again.

'I don't care. I'm so happy, Maggie. I never thought I'd love again.'

'One always loves again. It's a myth that there's only one man out there for every woman. I've loved several, sweetie. Several and they've all been a delight.'

'Even Viv?' asked Sofia archly, recalling Tony's second cousin.

'Even Viv. He was a big man – if you know what I mean. He never failed to satisfy me even when we hated each other. I hope David satisfies you,' she said.

'Oh, Maggie!'

'You're such an innocent, sweetie – well, I suppose that's all part of your charm. One of the reasons he loves you, no doubt. Don't lose that innocence, it's rare these days,' she said dryly. 'Are we going to see you sometime? Anton is pining like a dog.'

'I'll be up soon, I'm sure. Things are rather busy around here.'

'Before Christmas would be nice.'

'I'll try.'

Sofia lit the fire in the little green sitting room. When they were alone in the house the sitting room was cosier than the larger drawing room which really only came to life when filled with people. David had called twice while she had been out on the hills so she had called him back, feeding the dogs with her spare hand. She missed him. He had only been away for a night and a day but she was used to him now and the bed seemed large and cold without him.

The fire began to flicker merrily. She played a CD. David liked classical music so she chose one of his; it would give the impression that he was about the house and fill the silence. The evening was closing in, the light fading slowly into the winter mist. She closed the heavy green curtains and thought of Ariella. The house had obviously been decorated by her. It reflected a woman's taste. David wasn't the sort of man to take an interest in decoration.

Sofia wondered what she looked like. David hadn't told her much about his ex-wife, except that she had exquisite taste, an eye for art and a love of music. She was cultured and clever. They had met in their last year at Oxford. He hadn't ever been pursued by a woman before; in his world men had always done the chasing. But Ariella wasn't a woman to sit back and wait to be courted – she went out and got what she wanted. He hadn't been interested at first, he was quite keen on a girl on his literature course. But she persisted and finally they fell into bed. Ariella wasn't a virgin; she behaved more like a man when it came to sex, David had explained. They had married after about a year and divorced seven years later. That was ten years ago. Another life, he had said. No children, Ariella hadn't wanted a family. That was it.

Sofia hadn't asked any questions. It wasn't relevant and David didn't hound her with questions about her past. But now she was alone in the house she suddenly felt Ariella's presence in the chair covers and wallpaper. There were no photographs in picture frames as one might expect, but then the divorce had been acrimonious. After all, she had left him, not the other way around.

Sofia found herself opening drawers and searching through David's cluttered papers and books for photographs of his past. She didn't think he'd mind, he'd probably show them to her if he were there anyway. But she didn't want to ask him, she didn't want to look too interested. There's nothing worse than a jealous girlfriend, she thought. Anyhow she wasn't jealous, just curious.

Finally, at the bottom of a cupboard in his study she saw what looked like a dusty photo album. She pulled it out. It was heavy, bound in leather, chewed in one corner by a dog, no doubt. She opened it in the middle to make sure it was what she was looking for. When she saw a smiling David with his arm casually draped over the shoulders of a pretty blonde she closed the book, carried it into the sitting room, curled up on the sofa with a plate of biscuits and a glass of cold milk and started again from the beginning. Sam and Quid lay on the floor in front of the fire, their thick tails thumping onto the carpet contentedly, one eye on the plate of biscuits.

The first pages were of David and Ariella at Oxford, a cold picnic on hills somewhere. Ariella was very pretty, Sofia thought grudgingly. Her hair was flowing and almost white, her skin pale pink and her face long and angular. She wore a heavy coat of black mascara that accentuated the feline slant of her green eyes, and there was a sly expression on her surprisingly thin lips. She was beautiful and yet if you took each feature individually there was nothing remarkable, they just all fitted together rather well. It's only due to her white hair that she seems to stand out in all the photographs, thought Sofia, determined not to grant her charisma as well as beauty.

She turned the pages, smiling at photographs of David as a young man. He was skinny and raffish-looking then, before time and prosperity had rounded him off at the corners. He also had a head of thick sun-bleached hair that flopped over his forehead. David was always surrounded by people, always laughing, playing the fool, whereas Ariella was always demure, watching everyone quietly, and yet she seemed to glow in a strange way; one's eye was immediately drawn to her in each photograph.

Sofia searched for albums of their wedding and subsequent years together but found none. That one book seemed to be the only one he possessed. She was happy it was covered in dust, stuffed at the bottom of a cupboard he probably never opened.

When David returned a couple of days later, Sofia ran out to meet him with the dogs who jumped up leaving muddy paw-prints on his trousers. She kissed his face all over until he dropped his bag in the hall and carried her upstairs.

Sofia soon forgot about Ariella as she adorned the house with Christmas decorations. David, who usually spent Christmas with his family, decided it wasn't fair to force so many strangers on Sofia just yet and came up with a compromise. 'We'll spend Christmas in Paris,' he announced over breakfast. Sofia was astounded.

'That's not like you. Paris?' she gasped. 'What's come over you?'

'I want to be alone with you in a beautiful place. I know a small hotel by the Seine,' he replied nonchalantly.

'How exciting. I've never been to Paris.'

'Then I'll show you. I'll take you shopping in the Champs-Elysées.'

'Shopping?'

'Well, you can't spend your life in jeans and T-shirts, can you?' he said and drained his cup of coffee.

Paris enthralled Sofia. David travelled in style. They flew first-class and were picked up from the airport by a shiny black car that drove them straight to their discreet hotel on the water's edge. It was a crisp morning. The sun shimmered in the pale winter sky and a thin layer of snow melted on the pavements and trees. The streets glittered with Christmas decorations and lights and Sofia pressed her nose to the window and looked out in excitement across the stone bridges that straddled the icy water.

As he had promised, David took her shopping. In his old cashmere coat and felt hat Sofia thought he looked both distinguished and handsome. He'd stride into each shop, take a seat and give his opinions as Sofia tried things on for him. 'You need a coat,' he'd say, 'but that one's too short,' or, 'You need an evening dress – that looks stunning on you.' He even went as far as taking her into a lingerie boutique where he insisted she choose lace and silk to replace her cotton underwear. 'A beautiful woman such as you should be wrapped in beautiful things,' he said. He didn't let her carry any of the bags but organised for them to be sent back to the hotel that evening.

'David, you must have spent a small fortune,' she said over lunch. 'I really don't deserve it.'

'You deserve every bit of it and more, darling. We're only just beginning,' he replied, clearly taking pleasure in spoiling her.

When they arrived back at the hotel Sofia was delighted to find all their purchases neatly piled in their glossy bags in the sitting room adjoining their bedroom. David left her to unpack and wandered downstairs to 'have a look around'. Sofia pulled each item out of the tissue paper and laid them all across the sofas and chairs until the room itself looked like an expensive boutique. She then turned on the radio and listened to the sensual French music while she lolled in a steaming hot bubble bath. It was blissful. She had been so happy she hadn't thought about her home or Santiguito for many months, and she wasn't going to start now. At that moment the past ceased to chase her and allowed her to enjoy the present unharassed.

When David returned Sofia was at the door impatiently awaiting him in the new red dress he had bought her. It was cut low at the front, exposing a tiny part of her lace underwear at the cleavage then close-fitting almost down to the ground, revealing when she walked a stocking-clad leg through the slit up the side. She was taller due to her high heels and her hair was clean and loose, falling about her in smooth, shiny waves. He was stunned and the admiration in his expression caused her stomach to flutter with happiness.

After dinner in a small, elegant restaurant that opened onto the enchanting Place des Vosges, David helped her into her new coat and led her by the hand into the crisp night. The sky was alive with hundreds of tiny stars that trembled from far away and the moon so large and clear it took them both by surprise.

'You know it's Christmas Eve,' he said as they walked slowly across the square.

'I suppose it is. I haven't really celebrated Christmas since I arrived in England,' she said without self-pity.

'Well, you're celebrating it tonight with me,' he said and squeezed her hand. 'It couldn't be a more beautiful night.'

'It's stunning. Santa Claus will have no problem finding his way through the sky tonight, will he?' she laughed. They ambled around the icy stone fountain and gazed up at the sculpture that depicted a flurry of wild geese setting off into the night. 'It looks as if someone's clapped their hands and frightened them,' she exclaimed in admiration. 'Clever, isn't it?'

'Sofia,' he said quietly.

'It's amazing those top ones don't snap off, they look so fragile.'

'Sofia,' he repeated earnestly.

'Yes?' she replied, without taking her eyes off the sculpture.

'Look at me.' It was such an odd thing to say that she turned and looked at him.

'What's wrong?' she asked, but she could see from his expression that there was nothing wrong. He took both her gloved hands in his and looked at her tenderly.

'Will you marry me?'

'Marry you?' she repeated in amazement. For a fleeting second she saw Santi's anguished face and heard his voice resound weakly on the wind: *'Let's run away far from here and marry. Will you marry me?'* But then it was gone and David was standing over her, watching her apprehensively. She felt her eyes fill with tears and wasn't sure whether she was happy or sad.

'Yes, David, I will marry you,' she stammered. David visibly exhaled with relief and his face crumpled into a smile. He pulled a small black box out of his pocket and pressed it into her hands. She opened it carefully to reveal a large ruby ring. 'Red's my favourite colour,' she whispered.

'I know,' he replied softly.

'Oh David, it's beautiful. I don't know what to say.'

'Don't say anything. Put it on.'

She fumbled to remove her glove, giving the ring back to him so as not to drop it onto the glittering cobblestones. He then took her pale hand and slipped the ring on her finger before lifting it up to his lips and kissing it. 'You've made me the happiest man in the world, Sofia,' he said, his blue eyes shining at her with emotion.

'And you've made me complete, David. I never thought I'd love again. But I love you,' she said and placed her arms around his neck. 'I really do love you.'

Chapter Twenty-Nine

Santa Catalina, 1979

It was at the beginning of 1979 that Santi finally allowed himself to be loved again. It was also the year that Fernando's chickens came home to roost.

Chiquita would never forget the day they arrived at Santa Catalina to find their house broken into. She had only seen that sort of destruction in magazines. Other people's houses, other people's misery. It was always someone else's problem. But she had looked around at smashed furniture, broken glass, torn curtains. Someone had urinated on her bedspread. The house smelt of strangers. It reeked of menace. They had found Encarnacion, too old to withstand this sort of shock, wringing her hands in despair, her face twisted with terror, howling on the terrace. 'I don't know how they got in. I didn't see anyone. Who could do this?' she wailed. When Miguel and Chiquita heard that Fernando had been arrested they realised they were dealing with something much bigger than themselves.

Carlos Riberas, a friend of Fernando's, called them from a phone box to inform them that their son had been involved with the guerrillas and that he had been arrested. He couldn't tell them any more than that. He didn't know where they had taken him, or when he would be released. He wanted to add 'if they release him at all'. But he stopped himself. Fernando's parents obviously had no idea of his nocturnal activities. He hoped Fernando would be strong enough to resist naming his friends.

Miguel sank into a chair and sat so still he might have been turned to marble. Chiquita burst into tears. Wringing her hands and pacing the room she sobbed that she had no idea of Fernando's involvement with the guerrillas, not a clue. He had conducted his activities in total secrecy. 'I don't know my son!' she grieved. 'My own son is a stranger to me.'

Numbed by their sense of utter helplessness, the couple held each other. Both wished they had paid their son more attention; their anxiety over Santi's affair with Sofia had completely eclipsed Fernando. Perhaps if they had been better parents they would have noticed and been able to stop him in time. But now what?

Miguel and his brothers contacted everyone they knew in a position of power, but no one had any idea where Fernando was. They were told that he had probably been abducted by 'off-duty' security men – paramilitaries operating for the government. There was nothing they could do but wait. In the meantime they would continue to enquire as to his whereabouts.

The whole Solanas family waited. A dark fog collected over Chiquita's home, a fog from which she feared she might never be released. While she tearfully put her house back together again she kept telling herself that her husband's family had influence. They would never hurt a Solanas. Fernando would be returned to them and everything would be all right. It was probably a terrible mistake. Her son couldn't be involved with the opposition, not knowing the dangers. He just wouldn't put himself or his family through this. No, she convinced herself, there must be some mistake. Then more soberly she wished they had been able to prevent him from getting involved with those irresponsible young people. Hadn't Miguel warned him of the risks involved? Yes, she did remember something about that. Why hadn't they been more attentive? Once more she blamed herself.

Fernando sat miserably in an airless cell. A small window allowed enough light to illuminate the concrete walls and floor. There was no furniture. Nothing he could lie on. He had been beaten. He thought they had probably broken a couple of ribs, maybe a finger, he couldn't tell, it was too swollen. But he hurt all over. His face throbbed. He didn't know what he looked like, but he imagined he looked bloody and raw. They had abducted him while he walked along the street. A black car had pulled up on the kerb, the door had opened and two men in suits had walked out, grabbed him and forced him into the back seat. It had all happened in less than twenty seconds. No one noticed. No one saw.

With a gun pressed up against his ribcage, they had blindfolded him and taken him to an apartment block about thirty miles outside the city. Two days ago, three? He couldn't remember. Names, that's what they wanted, names. They said he was dispensable. They didn't need him. They had plenty of other people who would talk. He believed them. He had heard the screams echoing through the building. They could kill him and no one would care. They said his friends had betrayed him – so why protect them?

When he refused to talk they had knocked him unconscious. When he came to he had no idea how long he had been out. He felt disorientated and afraid. The fear hung so dense on the walls he could smell it. He missed his family and wished he were back home at Santa Catalina; his stomach literally lurched with longing. Why had he got involved with those stupid people? He didn't really care about his country like he pretended to. Why hadn't he just kept his head down like his father had told him to? He had felt so pleased with himself. Joining the guerrilla movement had made him feel important and powerful; it had given him a purpose, an identity. He hadn't told anyone close to him about it and he had wallowed in the pleasure his secret had given him. He was doing something worthy, or at least it had felt worthy at the time. It had been exciting. Rather like playing Cowboys and Indians – only the stakes were higher. He had joined clandestine meetings in the basement of Carlos Riberas's house. He had marched in demonstrations and handed out subversive anti-government leaflets. He did believe in democracy, but nothing was worth risking one's life for.

Fernando sniffed back his misery. He was a coward – he had even soiled his trousers. He had never before felt such pangs of despair; they seemed to tear at his insides – he could almost hear the ripping. If they kill me, he thought, let it be quick and painless. Please God, let it be quick.

When he heard the sharp, steely footsteps making their way down the corridor towards him, he was seized with panic. He wanted to scream but no sound escaped his dry, sticky mouth. The door opened and a man entered. Fernando shielded his face against the light that entered with him.

'Get up,' the man ordered. Fernando staggered to his feet; every move gave him pain. The man walked over to him and handed him a brown envelope. 'Here is a new passport and enough money to get you across the river to Uruguay. There is a car waiting for you outside. Once you're in Uruguay I don't ever want to see or hear from you again – understand? If you return you'll be killed.'

Fernando was dumbfounded. 'Who are you?' he said, looking into his face. 'Why?'

'That doesn't matter. I'm not doing this for you,' the man said tersely and escorted him out.

It wasn't until Fernando was safely across the border that he suddenly remembered where he had seen that man before. It was Facundo Hernandez.

When Chiquita heard Fernando's voice she wept with relief. Miguel took the telephone and listened to his son recount his experience. 'I can't come home, Papa, not until there's a change of government,' he said. His parents were devastated that he wasn't

343

coming home, but grateful that he was alive. Chiquita wanted to see her son, she wanted proof that he really was all right, and it took a lot of reassuring before she finally allowed herself to believe that he was telling the truth. It would take months for Chiquita's nightmares to subside. For Fernando, his experiences in that small, airless cell would haunt him for many years to come.

A couple of months after Fernando's departure, Santi met Claudia Calice. His parents had asked him to represent them at a charity dinner in Buenos Aires. Chiquita was suffering from stress and she felt unable to face the world so soon after her son's escape from what had been, most certainly, the 'jaw of death'. So Santi sat at the table, stifling a yawn, listening to the speeches and making polite conversation to the powdered lady on his right. He let his eyes float about the room, taking in the merry faces of bejewelled women, half listening to the monotone that irritated his patience like a buzzing mosquito hovering about his ear. He nodded at intervals so she was under the illusion that he was listening. Then his eyes settled on a smooth young woman, apparently doing the same thing, at a table the other side of the room. Like an accomplice she smiled at him sympathetically before turning to her neighbour and nodding attentively.

After the dinner Santi waited for the man on her left to leave his seat, then he crossed the room. She welcomed him by pulling out the chair and introduced herself. She whispered into his ear that she had watched him go pale with boredom. 'It has been dreadfully dull for me too,' she said. 'The man on my right is an industrialist. I had nothing to say to him. He didn't once ask me about myself.' Santi told her that he would like nothing more than to listen to her talking about herself.

In the weeks that followed, Soledad noticed that Santi had begun to smile again. She felt slightly possessive of him and didn't take to the sophisticated, laminated Claudia Calice who was becoming a regular visitor at Santa Catalina. She worried for

344

Sofia, although she hadn't heard from her since she had left in 1974. Claudia was brown and glossy, like a wet seal. She painted herself beautifully and her shoes were always highly polished, never scuffed. Soledad wondered how she managed to look so groomed all the time. Even in the country when it was pouring with rain her umbrella matched her belt. Whether she liked the woman or not it didn't really matter, her opinion didn't count, but she was grateful for one thing: this Claudia Calice was making Santi happy. He hadn't been happy for a very long time.

Soledad missed Sofia dreadfully, so much so that sometimes she cried out loud, worrying about her, hoping she was happy. She longed for her to write, but she never did. She didn't understand the girl's total lack of communication. Sofia was like a daughter to her. Why didn't she write? Soledad had asked Señora Anna if she could write a letter herself, just to let Sofia know she was cherished. It had upset her deeply that Anna had refused to give her the address. She didn't even say when the child would be returning home. Such was Soledad's distress that *La Vieja Bruja*, the old witch in the village, had given her a white powder to mix with her *Mate*, which she was required to drink three times a day; it seemed to be working. She found she was able to sleep at night and stopped worrying so much.

On 2 February 1983 Santi married Claudia Calice in the small church of *Nuestra Señora de la Asunción*. The reception was held at Santa Catalina. As Santi watched his bride walk down the aisle on the arm of her father he couldn't help but imagine that she was Sofia. His stomach lurched momentarily with longing. But then she was by his side, smiling up at him reassuringly, and he felt a surge of affection for this person who had shown him that it was possible to love more than one woman in a lifetime.

Chapter Thirty

'Maria, what was Sofia like?' Claudia asked one summer morning. Santi and Claudia had been married for over a year and yet she had never dared ask anyone about Sofia, and for some reason no one talked about her. Santi had told her about the affair. He had told her he had loved her, it wasn't some sordid sexual fling behind the pony lines. He hadn't hidden anything from her intentionally, but a woman's curiosity about the ex-lovers of her husband knows no bounds and Claudia's desire for more information was not yet satisfied.

'What *is* she like,' corrected Maria, not unkindly. 'She's not dead. She may well come back,' she added hopefully.

'I'm just curious, you understand,' Claudia said, appealing to Maria's common female bond.

'Well, she's not very tall, but she gives the impression that she is much taller,' began Maria, putting down the pile of photographs that were scattered about her on the red paving stones and looking out over the hazy summer plains. Claudia wasn't interested in how she looked. She knew how she looked. She had browsed through enough albums of photographs, studied the pictures that were scattered all over Paco and Anna's house in silver frames. She knew exactly what Sofia had looked like from a baby to a woman. She was lovely looking; there was no doubt about that. But she was more interested in her personality. What was it about her that had captured Santi's heart? Why was it that in spite of his efforts Claudia felt convinced that Sofia still possessed it? But she let Maria talk on; she didn't want to miss this opportunity. Having her sister-in-law all to herself without being surrounded by her husband, cousins, brothers, parents, uncles, aunts was rare. When she had spotted Maria sitting alone on the terrace that Saturday morning, quietly going through stacks of old photographs, she had seized the moment and hoped no one would appear around the corner to ruin it.

What she didn't realise was that Maria longed to talk about Sofia. She missed her. Although the feeling was now more of a dull ache provoked by certain associations that reminded her of her cousin, the years hadn't managed to erase the indissoluble bond that the two women had forged together over their childhood and youth. No one else wanted to talk about Sofia, and if they did it was almost in a whisper that they spoke, as if she had died. The only person Maria seemed able to reminisce with was Soledad, who spoke about Sofia in a loud, angry voice, not angry with Sofia, of course, but angry with her parents whom she believed had prevented her return. Now Claudia wanted to listen, Maria was only too eager to talk.

'Everyone talked about Sofia,' she said proudly, as if she were talking about a daughter. 'What would she be up to next? Was her mother unfair on her or was Sofia just plain difficult? Did she have a boyfriend or didn't she? She was so beautiful they were all in love with her. She always dated the best-looking men around. Roberto Lobito, he could have anyone but he couldn't tame Sofia. She used him and cast him aside like a polo ball. He'd never been chucked before. I bet it did him good. He was rather too pleased with himself.'

She laughed and then continued as if she were alone and talking to herself: 'Nothing frightened her. In that respect she was almost more like a boy. She didn't have girlie phobias like me. She loved spiders and beetles, frogs and toads and cockroaches, and she played polo better than some of the boys. She always fought with Agustin over that. She fought with everyone. She did it to rile them all, but she never meant it. She was just bored and wanting some amusement. She made them all furious, of course; she knew exactly how to aggravate each person – she knew their weak spots. Things were a lot more fun when she was around. Santa Catalina was a more exciting place when she was here. There was always trouble, excitement, laughter. Now she's gone it all seems rather bland – nice of course, Santa Catalina will always be that – but the sparkle has gone out of it. But she'll be back, just to make sure that no one forgets about her. That will be typical of Sofia. She always loved to be the centre of attention, and of course she always was in one way or another, by making people love her or loathe her. It didn't matter; she just needed to feel noticed.'

'Do you really think she will come back?' asked Claudia, biting a piece of dead skin from the side of her long painted nail.

'Of course she will,' Maria replied emphatically. 'I know she will.'

'Oh.' Claudia nodded and pulled a weak smile.

'She loved it here too much to leave it for ever,' Maria said and began to sort through the photographs again. She swallowed hard. Sofia couldn't leave them for ever, could she?

'What are you doing?'

'I haven't had the time lately to stick all these into books. It's quiet this morning, so I thought I'd start sorting through them.' Then Maria noticed one of Sofia and picked it up. 'There, that's a typical photograph of Sofia,' she said and gazed at it sadly. 'That was the summer she left.'

The summer she was in love with Santi, thought Claudia bitterly. She took the photograph from her sister-in-law and looked into the brown, radiant face that seemed to grin triumphantly out at her. Claudia saw a certain complacency in her smile. She was dressed in a pair of tight white trousers and brown boots, sitting on a pony holding a mallet casually over her shoulder. Her hair was pulled back into a ponytail. Claudia hated horses and didn't much like the countryside either. The fact that Sofia had loved both to distraction made her dislike them even more.

The effort Claudia had made before they married to pretend she enjoyed them had been a complete waste of time. She found out one afternoon when Santi had taken her riding. Sitting stiffly on the pony, utterly miserable, she had finally dissolved into a fit of angry sobs and confessed to hating the very sight of horses. 'I never want to ride again,' she had sniffed.

To her surprise, Santi had almost seemed happy. He had taken her home, put his arms around her and told her that she never had to go near another pony as long as she lived. She had been relieved at first that she no longer had to continue pretending, but later she wished he hadn't been so delighted. Ponies, riding, the countryside – they were part of Sofia's territory and Claudia believed Santi wanted to keep them exclusive to her. 'Was Santi always particularly close to Sofia?' she asked carefully.

Maria looked at her in alarm. 'I don't know,' she lied. 'You should ask Santi.'

'He never talks about her,' she shrugged and lowered her eyes.

'Oh, I see. Well, they were always close. He was like an elder brother, you see, and Sofia was like my sister.' Maria suddenly felt uncomfortable, as if the conversation was beginning to spin out of her control.

'Do you mind if I look through some more?' asked Claudia, tactfully changing the subject. She sensed she was perhaps being too inquisitive. She didn't want Maria going back and telling Santi.

'Here, why don't you look through these – I've already sorted them,' Maria offered, relieved, and handed one of the neatly marked piles to Claudia. 'Don't muddle them with the rest, will you?'

Claudia sat back in the chair, placing the photographs on her lap, and Maria stole a glance at her while she didn't know she was being looked at. She was only a couple of months older than Maria, but she seemed much older. Sofia always said that people are born a certain age; she claimed to be eighteen and said that Maria was in her twenties. Well, if that were the case, she would probably have said that Claudia was forty. It had nothing to do with her face, which was a rich, smooth, brown colour, she was naturally beautiful, but more to do with the way she dressed and behaved. She had offered to teach Maria how to use make-up to her advantage. 'What I could do with your face,' she had said tactlessly. Maria was too nice to take offence. She didn't want to be painted with those rich colours like Claudia, and anyhow Eduardo would hate it. She wondered whether she slept in it, and if she didn't she wondered if Santi recognised her in the morning. She was dying to ask, but didn't dare. There had been a time when she could have asked him anything, but things had changed – only subtly, but they had changed.

No one had understood why Santi had married Claudia. They liked her enough, for she was pleasant, kind, pretty, but the couple didn't seem to have anything in common. Like oil and water they didn't gel. Chiquita had warmed to her immediately, but that was only because she was relieved that he had married at all. She was happy to see her son smile and move on. Oddly enough, the one person Claudia had really bonded with was Anna. They were both cool in temperament and both hated horses. They spent a lot of time together and Anna had taken trouble to make her feel welcome.

'What are you looking at?' Claudia asked suddenly, without taking her eyes off the photographs. Maria feared she had been aware all the time of being evaluated.

'I'm just curious, you paint yourself so beautifully,' she replied helplessly.

'Thank you. I did offer,' she said and smiled down at Maria.

'I know. I think I might have to take you up on it.' Maria smiled back weakly.

* * *

'*Dios*, what do you look like?' exclaimed Eduardo in horror when he saw his wife enter for dinner with the face of a salesgirl behind the counter selling Revlon.

'Claudia's given me a lesson,' she replied feebly, blinking at him with long, heavy black lashes.

'I wondered what you two were doing locked in there,' he said, taking his glasses off to clean them on his shirt. Just then, Claudia appeared behind Maria wearing a long black dress, held up by two delicate silver straps.

'*Mi amor*, you look lovely,' said Santi, standing up to kiss his wife. He had barely seen her all day.

'Don't you think you should change out of your jeans for dinner?' she hissed. 'You smell of horses.'

'Mama won't mind. If she's not used to me now, she never will be,' he told her and sat back down again. Claudia squeezed in beside him although the armchair wasn't designed for two. He ran a hand down the back of her hair.

'*Mi amor*,' she complained, 'can't you wash your hands if you're going to touch me? I'm all clean.'

He grinned mischievously and pulled her back and hugged her. 'Don't you like the sweat of a red-blooded man?' he teased.

'No, I don't,' she laughed grudgingly, sitting up and shaking him off. 'Please Santi, I want you to touch me, all I ask is for clean hands.' Santi got up reluctantly and disappeared out of the room. After five minutes he returned cleanshaven and in a new set of clothes.

'Better?' he said, raising an eyebrow.

'Better,' she replied, making room for him on the armchair.

Dinner was out on the terrace in the light of four large hurricane lamps. Miguel, Eduardo and Santi discussed politics while Chiquita, Maria and Claudia discussed them. Chiquita enjoyed her new extended family and watched their animated faces in the warm glow of the lamps. She always carried a quiet sorrow in her heart for Fernando, miles across the river in Uruguay, but they had been to see him often.

Fernando was still tormented by his experience. He had let his black hair grow long; at least it was clean and shone like a crow's wing. She remembered with nostalgia the long summer holidays of his boyhood, when life was innocent, when the games he had played had finished at bedtime. Now he was a long way from home, on a beach, living the life of a stray dog. It wasn't the same as having him at Santa Catalina but she realised that she should be content that he was alive and not worry about trivial things.

Panchito, now a lithe seventeen-year-old, spent as much time as he could in other people's houses with cousins and friends of his own age. Chiquita encouraged him to invite friends home in an attempt to make it more interesting for him, but if he wasn't shining on the polo field he was elsewhere and much of the time she didn't even know where he was or whom he was with. She barely saw him.

'What was Miguel like when you met him?' asked Claudia.

Chiquita laughed. 'Well, he was tall and . . .'

'Hairy,' interjected Santi helpfully. They all laughed.

'Hairy. But not as hairy as he is now.'

'Was he lupine, Mama? Did he chase you and carry you off to his lair?'

'Oh Santi, you are ridiculous sometimes.' She smiled and her eyes twinkled happily.

'Well, did you, Papa?'

'Your mother was being chased by everyone. I happened to be the lucky one,' he said and winked at Chiquita across the table.

'You were both very lucky,' said Claudia diplomatically.

'Luck had nothing to do with it. I had to make sacrifices to the ombu,' he chuckled.

'The ombu?' Claudia was confused. Maria glanced at Santi and noticed the muscle in his jaw tighten. He pulled a packet of cigarettes out of his pocket and lit one.

'Don't tell me Santi hasn't taken you to the ombu?' said Chiquita in surprise. 'When he was a boy he spent all his time at the very top of that tree.'

'No, you haven't. What's so special about it?' she asked, directing her question to Santi, but he didn't respond, he just blew the smoke out of his mouth in silence.

'We used to make wishes there. We thought it was magic, but it isn't really. It's nothing special,' Maria said quickly, making light of it. She felt Eduardo's leg press against hers in support.

'It *is* a very special tree,' Miguel said gruffly. 'It's part of our youth. As children we played there, as grown-ups we dated there. In fact, without being indiscreet, the ombu is where I first kissed your mother.'

'Really?' said Maria. No one had ever told her that.

'Absolutely. To your mother and me it's a very special tree indeed.'

'Santi, will you take me there? I'm all curious now,' Claudia said.

'I'll take you there sometime,' mumbled Santi hoarsely. His face appeared deathly white in the flickering light of the candles, accentuating his features grotesquely.

'*Mi amor*, are you all right? You've gone very pale,' Claudia said in concern.

'I'm feeling a little dizzy actually. It's the heat. I've been in the sun all day.' He stubbed out his cigarette before getting up from the table. 'No, you stay and eat,' he said to his wife. 'I'll be fine, I just need to walk around a bit.'

Claudia looked dejected, but pulled her chair in and placed her napkin neatly back on her lap. 'Whatever you like, Santi,' she replied tightly and watched him disappear into the darkness. Once more she heard Sofia's laughter taunting her from out of the black empty space that surrounded them.

Santi walked across the *pampa* to the ombu. There was enough light from the clear, starry sky for him to see his way without stumbling, but he knew that terrain without it. Once at the tree he climbed it to the top then sank onto a steady branch and leant miserably back against the thick trunk. He felt a throbbing in his throat as if his collar were too tight, but his collar was undone. He placed a hand there in an attempt to loosen the clamp. His chest also felt compressed and uncomfortable. He tried to breathe deeply, but succeeded only in taking in jagged, shallow breaths. His stomach churned with nausea and his head ached. He looked out into the night and remembered how he used to sit there with Sofia, gazing up at the planets and stars that glimmered above them. He wondered if she could see the same sky and whether she looked up at it and still thought of him.

Suddenly he began to sob. He tried to control himself, but the sobs spilled out from deep within him. He hadn't cried for a long, long time. Not since Sofia had left him raw and broken all those years ago. He had thought that finally he had found happiness with another woman. Claudia made him smile, she sometimes even made him laugh. She was warm and soft to make love to, kind and considerate to live with. She was undemanding and uncomplicated. She did everything she could to please him and only lost her temper occasionally. She was cool, her emotions were controlled, but that wasn't to say she didn't feel. She felt everything, she was just careful what she revealed. She was quiet and dignified. No one could say she wasn't beautiful. She looked after herself. So why the hell did he long for the chaos, the selfishness, the passion of Sofia? Why, after all this time, almost ten years, did she still have the power to bring him to his knees to cry like a child?

'Damn it, Chofi!' he shouted out into the damp night air. 'Damn you!'

Claudia wanted to start a family. She was desperate for a child. But he just wasn't ready. How could he bring a child into the world when he was still hoping Sofia might come back? If he made that commitment to Claudia it would really be a commitment for life. Marriage should be for life, but children were irreversible. He still hoped that one day Sofia might return to him and he wanted to be ready. Everyone thought he had forgotten about her, but he would never forget. How could he forget when her face loomed out from every corner of the *estancia*? Memories of her clung to every part of the ranch, to every piece of furniture. There was no getting away from her, and yet somehow he didn't want to; she tormented him and gave him comfort at the same time.

When he returned to the house Claudia was waiting for him, sitting on the bed in her night-dress, her face taut and anxious. She had removed all her make-up; without her lipstick her face was drained of colour.

'Where did you go?' she asked.

'For a walk.'

'You're upset.'

'I'm fine now. I needed some air, that's all,' he said and began pulling his shirt out of his trousers and unbuttoning it.

Claudia watched him steadily. 'You went to this ombu tree, didn't you?'

'Why do you think that?' he asked, turning away.

'Because that's where you always used to go with Sofia.'

'Claudia . . .' he began irritably.

'I saw Maria's photos – there were lots of you up that tree with Sofia. I'm not accusing you, *mi amor*, I want to help you,' she said, reaching out to him, but he continued undressing, throwing his clothes onto the floor.

'I don't need help and I don't want to talk about Sofia,' he said flatly.

'Why not? Why don't you ever talk about her?' she asked, her voice suddenly unfamiliar.

He looked at her rigid features. 'Would you prefer it if I talked about her? "Sofia this, Sofia that" – is that what you want?'

'Don't you understand that by *not* talking about her she hangs over us like a ghost. Every time I get close to you I feel her slipping in between us,' she said and her voice trembled.

'But what do you want to know? I've told you everything.'

'I don't want you to hide her from me.'

'I'm not hiding her from you. I want to forget her, Claudia. I want to build a life with you.'

'You still love her?' she said suddenly.

'Where is all this coming from?' he asked in confusion, sitting down on the bed beside her.

'I've been patient,' she said unsteadily. 'I've never asked about her, I've left that part of your life alone.'

'So why are you insecure about her now?' he asked gently, taking her hand in his.

'Because I feel her everywhere. I feel her in the silences when people pause for breath. Everyone's afraid of talking about her. What did she do that makes people so furtive? Even Anna doesn't talk about her. It's as if she's dead. Not talking about her only makes her bigger, more threatening. I feel her taking you away from me. I don't want to lose you to a ghost, Santi,' she said and she swallowed hard, unused to baring her emotions.

'You're not going to lose me. Not to anyone. It was over years ago.'

'But you still love her,' she ventured again.

'I love the memory, Claudia. That's all,' he lied. 'If she were to come back we would both have changed. We're different people now.'

'Promise?'

'What do I have to do to convince you?' he asked, drawing her into his arms. But he knew.

He suddenly pulled her against him and kissed her deeply, his tongue sliding over her teeth and gums, pressing his lips firmly against hers. She caught her breath. He had never kissed her like that before, not with such urgency. He threw her back across the bed and pulled her silk night-dress up to her belly. He looked at the soft undulation of her stomach and ran his hand over it, staring at it in silence. She opened her eyes and noticed the strange look that had come over his face. When she caught his eye and frowned his features softened. He grinned at her as she tried to work out his thoughts but then his face was buried in her neck and he was kissing and licking her until she cried out in pleasure. His hands moved firmly between her legs and on her breasts, his touch confident and vigorous, and she writhed as he made her feel sensual in a way she had never allowed herself to feel before. Then he opened his trousers and released himself. Pulling her legs apart he entered her.

'But you're not protected?' she asked, her face red and wanton.

'I want to plant a seed, Claudia,' he replied breathlessly, looking at her seriously. 'I want to build a future with you.'

'Oh Santi, I love you,' she sighed happily, wrapping her arms and legs about him like an octopus, pulling him against her. Now you'll let me go, Chofi, thought Santi silently. Now I really will forget you.

Chapter Thirty-One

England, 1982

' "Ribby stared with amazement — Did you ever see the like! So there really was a patty-pan? . . . But my patty-pans are all in the kitchen cupboard. Well, I never did! . . . Next time I want to give a party — I will invite Cousin Tabitha Twitchit!" ' Sofia said softly and closed the little book by Beatrix Potter.

'Again,' Jessica said sleepily, without taking her thumb out of her mouth.

'I think one's enough, don't you?'

'*The Tale of Tom Kitten?*' she suggested hopefully, snuggling further into Sofia's lap.

'No, one's all you're getting. Give me a hug,' she said, wrapping the child in her arms and kissing her smooth pink face. Jessica clung to Sofia, not wanting to let go.

'What about the witches?' she asked as Sofia tucked her into bed.

'There aren't any witches, certainly not here anyway. Look, this is a special magic bear,' she said, tucking the teddy into the bed with her. 'If a witch comes anywhere near you this bear will cast a spell that will make the witch disappear into a puff of smoke.'

'Clever bear,' the child said happily.

'Very clever bear,' Sofia agreed, then bent down and kissed her forehead tenderly. 'Good-night.' When she turned to leave she saw David standing quietly behind the half-open door, watching her through the gap. He smiled at her pensively. 'What are you doing?' she whispered, slipping out of the room to join him.

'Watching you.'

'You are, are you?' she laughed. 'Why's that?'

He pulled her into his arms and kissed her brow. 'You're a natural with children,' he said huskily.

She knew where this conversation was leading. 'I know, but David . . .'

'Darling, I'll go through it with you, you won't be by yourself.' He looked into her fearful eyes. 'This is our child we're talking about. A little bit of me and a little bit of you, the one thing in the world that will be a part of both of us and belong exclusively to us. I thought that was what you wanted.'

She led him down the corridor, away from the child's bedroom. 'I love children and one day I would like to have one – lots. A bit of you and a bit of me, it's the most romantic, wonderful thing, but not yet. Please David, give me time,' she asked.

'I don't have time, Sofia. I'm not getting any younger. I want to enjoy a family when I'm young enough to be able to,' he said, feeling his stomach reel with the strange sense of *déjà vu*. He'd had this conversation countless times before with Ariella.

'Soon. Very soon, darling, I promise,' she said, pulling away from him. 'I'll be down in a minute. Tell Christina that her daughter is tucked up in bed and ready for her to go and say good-night.'

Sofia closed her bedroom door behind her. She stood still for a moment to be certain that David hadn't followed her. The landing was quiet and still; he must have gone back downstairs to deliver her message to Christina. She walked over to the bed and, lifting up the bedspread, ran her hand under the mattress. Then she pulled out a grubby white square of muslin – Santiguito's muslin. She settled on the floor and crossed her legs. She brought the cloth up to her nose and closed her eyes, breathing in the musty smell that was once Santiguito's. Now the years had discoloured it and many a handling had worn away both the scent and the material. It looked more like a rag; if one didn't know better it would be thrown out with the rest of the rubbish. But Sofia treasured it as the most important of all her possessions.

When she held it against her face it was like pressing a button on a movie projector. She would close her eyes and watch the images of her baby that were as fresh and vivid as if she had only just seen him the day before. She'd remember his minute feet, each perfect toe pink and soft, his fluffy hair, his smooth, smooth skin. She'd remember the feeling he gave her when he sucked on her breast, the glazed look that came over his face as he filled his little round belly. She remembered everything, she made sure she remembered everything. She'd replay the tape over and over again so as not to forget a single detail.

She and David had been married for four years and all anyone wanted to know was when they were going to start a family. It was none of anyone else's business, Sofia thought crossly. It was between her and David although for some reason Zaza felt she had special status. Sofia had snapped at her a couple of times but she was as tough as an old piece of leather with a skin as thick, and she hadn't taken the hint. Only David, Dominique and Antoine understood her reasons for not wanting a child. Dominique and Antoine had flown over for her wedding, a quiet registry office affair, but they hadn't wanted to miss it. Since Geneva they had become better parents to her than she believed hers had ever been. When she thought of Anna and Paco, which she tried not to do very often, she only seemed able to recall their pale faces, now almost icy green in her recollections, telling her to pack her things for her long exile. Dominique called her often, always under-standing, always supportive. She remembered her birthday, sent her presents from Geneva, postcards from Verbier and seemed to sense when things weren't too good for she always telephoned at just the right time.

'I want a baby, Dominique, but I'm afraid,' Sofia had confessed the day before.

'*Chérie*, I know you're scared, and David understands your fears. But you can't cling onto a memory. Santiguito isn't real. He doesn't exist any more. Thinking about him can only bring you pain.'

'I know. I keep telling myself that, but it's like I've got a block somewhere. The second I imagine my stomach all big and heavy I panic. I can't forget the misery it brought.'

'The only way you will forget is by having a child with the man you love beside you. When that child brings you so much joy, you'll forget about the pain Santiguito brought, I promise you.'

'David's so sweet. He doesn't talk about it much, but I know he's thinking about it all the time. I can see it in his eyes when he looks at me. I feel so guilty,' she said, sinking back against the pillows on her bed.

'Don't feel guilty. One day you'll give him a baby and you'll make a happy family together. Just be patient. Time is a wonderful healer.'

'*You're* a wonderful healer, Dominique, I feel better already,' laughed Sofia.

'How is David?' asked Dominique. She was pleased that Sofia had fallen in love and put the past behind her, almost.

'The same as always. He's made me very happy. I'm so lucky,' she said truthfully.

'Don't worry, you're young, you have masses of time for children,' Dominique said kindly, but she understood David's fears and sympathised wholeheartedly.

Sofia had lived the last five years consciously. She had never taken her life with David for granted. She had never for a moment forgotten the misery that lurked like a black fog over the first few years of her exile, partly obscuring some of the events that had been too painful to leave in the open. Santi had taught her to live in the present; David had proved to her that it could be done. Her love for her husband was solid and unwavering. He was confident and masterful and yet she had discovered beneath his reserve a vulnerability that endeared him to her. He very rarely told her he loved her, it wasn't his way, but she knew he did and how much. She understood him.

Sofia had the misfortune of meeting her mother-in-law, Elizabeth Harrison, only once. David had introduced them a week before the wedding at the Basil Street Hotel for tea. He had said it was best to meet on neutral ground – that way, his mother wouldn't be able to intimidate her or cause a scene.

It had been a brief and awkward meeting. An austere-looking woman with stiff grey hair, thin purple lips and bulbous watery eyes as unsympathetic and as shallow as a grave, Elizabeth Harrison was someone used to getting her own way, and making everyone around her as unhappy as she was. She had never forgiven David for divorcing Ariella, whose appeal lay more in her pedigree than in her personality, nor had she forgiven him for using his money to produce plays when she had encouraged him to work in the Foreign Office like his father. She had sniffed her disapproval when she heard Sofia speak with a foreign accent and stalked out as best she could with a walking stick when Sofia had told her that she had worked washing hair in a salon called Maggie's in the Fulham Road. David had watched her go without running after her to beg her to come back. That had irritated her more than anything else. David didn't need her and didn't seem to care for her. She pursed her bitter lips and returned to her cold empty mansion in Yorkshire thoroughly dissatisfied with the meeting. David had promised Sofia that she would never have to see her again.

As much as Sofia lived consciously in the present the past had a spiteful habit of suddenly rearing out of nowhere, triggered by some vague association that pulled her thoughts back to Argentina. Sometimes it was simply the way the trees cast long shadows over the lawn on a summer's evening, or if the moon was particularly bright, the way it caused the dewy grass to glitter like rhinestones.

Sometimes it was the smell of hay during harvest-time or burning leaves in the autumn. But nothing brought it all back like eucalyptus and Sofia had barely been able to cope with their honeymoon in the Mediterranean because of the humid weather and eucalyptus trees. She had felt her heart contract and a longing consume her until she had scarcely been able to breathe. David had held her and hugged her until the feeling had passed. Then they had talked. She didn't like to talk about it, but David had insisted that bottling things up was a bad habit and he had made her go over the same events, time and again.

The two occasions that Sofia kept going back to were her parents' rejection and the day she left Geneva and little Santiguito for ever. 'I can remember it as if it was yesterday,' she'd sob. 'Mama and Papa in the sitting room, the atmosphere heavy and unpleasant. I was so scared. I felt like a criminal. They were strangers, both of them. I had always had a very special relationship with my father and suddenly I didn't know him any more. Then they banished me. They sent me away. They rejected me.' And she'd cry until the motion of her sobbing had released the tension in her chest and she'd be free to breathe again. The distress of leaving Santi was something she was unable to speak about with her husband for fear of hurting him. Those tears she shed inwardly and secretly, unwittingly allowing the grief to entrench itself deep within her being and fester.

After they had married Sofia hadn't really thought much about Ariella. Once or twice she had been mentioned, like the time Sofia had gone through the attic in search of a lamp David said she'd find there and had discovered a pile of Ariella's paintings stacked up against the wall under a dustsheet. She hadn't minded. David came up to look at them then threw the sheet over them again. 'She was rather good at painting,' was all he had said and Sofia hadn't been very curious. She had found the lamp she wanted, carried it down the stairs, closing the door on the attic. She hadn't been up there since and Ariella hadn't featured any further in her thoughts. A society party in London was the last place she expected she would meet her.

Sofia was nervous of parties. She didn't want to go, but David insisted. She couldn't hide away for ever. 'No one knows how long this war is going to go on for – you'll have to brave the world sometime,' he had said. When Britain had declared war on Argentina in April over the Falkland Islands Sofia had felt desperately torn. She was an Argentine and as much as she had sealed away that part of her life, she had always been sure of what she was – an Argentine through and through. Every headline stung, every cruel remark hurt. They were her people. But there was no use in defending them on this side of the Atlantic – the British wanted heads on sticks. David suggested kindly that she keep quiet unless she wanted hers on a stick too. It was difficult not to launch small skirmishes when people were so tactless – at dinner parties when boorish men thumped their fists down on the tables, deriding the 'bloody Argies'. The Argentines became 'Argies' and there was nothing complimentary about that name. Having been unaware that the Falkland Islands existed everyone suddenly had an opinion.

Sofia had to dig her nails into the palms of her hands to stop herself from giving them the satisfaction of upsetting her. Only afterwards would she curl up against David and sob into his chest. She wondered how her family were coping back at home. She wanted to fly the flag from the rooftop at Lowsley and shout as loudly as was humanly possible that she was an Argentine and proud of it. She hadn't relinquished her nationality. She hadn't deserted them. She was one of them.

The party was a dinner dance on an unusually sultry May evening. Given by Ian and Alice Lancaster, old friends of David's, it was the sort of party everyone talked about for months before and discussed for months after. Sofia had spent a small fortune in Belville Sassoon on a pillar-box red strapless dress that subtly sparkled against her olive skin. David had been sufficiently im-pressed not to be concerned about the price and smiled proudly as he noticed all the other guests casting their eyes over her admiringly.

Normally at these events the couple would go their separate ways, neither one worrying about the other. But Sofia was afraid someone might ignite a conversation about the war, so she took David's hand and followed him apprehensively around the room. The women were heavy with diamonds and stiff hairstyles, sharp shoulder pads and alarming make-up. Sofia felt light, though underdressed, in a simple solitaire that sparkled against her naked brown chest. A birthday gift from David. She noticed people whispering as she passed and conversations stall as she approached. No one mentioned the war.

A pale blue and white striped marquee had been erected in the garden behind the Lancasters' mansion in Hampstead. Extravagant displays of flowers spilled out over every table like leafy fountains, and the tent glowed in the light of a thousand candles. When dinner was announced Sofia was relieved to discover that she was on the same table as David – the hosts' table. As she sat down she winked across at David to reassure him that she was happy. He seemed to know the powdered lady on his left, but the seat to his right remained empty.

'Good to see you again!' exclaimed the man seated to Sofia's left. He was bald with a round, sunny face, thin lips and pale, liquid eyes. Sofia glanced at his name card. *Jim Rice.* She had met him before. He was one of those unremarkable people one meets all over the place but can never remember their name.

'Nice to see you again, too.' She smiled, silently trying to work out how she knew him. 'Where was the last time I saw you?' she asked casually.

'Clarissa's book launch,' he replied.

'Of course,' said Sofia, wondering who Clarissa was.

'God, who is that?' he said suddenly, throwing his eyes across the room to the tall, willowy woman who was sliding gracefully past the tables toward them. Sofia clamped her jaw together for fear that if she left it open it might never close. The exquisite creature in a simple white dress was unmistakably Ariella. Sofia watched her near the table. She also noticed that the chair to David's right had still not been filled. Please God, no, she prayed, not next to David.

'Isn't that Ariella Harrison, David's ex?' said the man to her right. 'What a cock-up,' he muttered as Ariella greeted a dumb-founded David and sat down next to him.

'George,' said Jim in a warning tone, trying to prevent the approaching *faux pas*.

'Bloody hell, a mother of a cock-up!' the other man gloated, licking his lips. Then turning to Sofia he asked, 'Do you think Ian and Alice did it on purpose?'

'*George!*'

'Good to see you, Jim. Cock-up, eh?' he repeated, pulling a face and nodding knowingly at him.

'George, can I introduce you to Sofia Harrison, David Harri-son's wife. George Heavyweather.'

'Shit,' said George.

'I thought you'd say that,' Jim sighed.

'I am most terribly sorry. Really. What an idiot.'

'Don't worry, George,' said Sofia, with one eye on George Heavyweather, who had now turned the colour of a pepper, and one eye on Ariella.

Ariella looked stunning in the flattering light of the candles. Her white hair was pulled back into a tidy chignon, accentuating her long neck and sharp jawbone. She looked remote, but beautiful. David leant back in his chair as if he wanted to increase the space between them, while Ariella leant in towards him, her head tilted to one side, apologetic. David nodded towards Sofia and Ariella looked over and smiled politely. Sofia managed to smile back weakly before turning away in time to hide the fear in her eyes.

'I'm sorry about George. Tactless fool. Never has been one to think before he speaks. You can always rely on George to put his foot in it. He's got a bloody big foot, too,' said Jim, slurping his wine. 'Last time he went up to Duggie Crichton and said, "I'd like to screw that dirty blonde over there, sure she'd be game," before he realised she was Duggie's new bird. Made a total ass of himself. Tactless fool.'

Sofia laughed graciously as he embarked on another story about George. She watched the body language between David and Ariella warm up and become friendlier. She hoped Ariella would choke on her salmon or spill red wine down her immaculate white dress. She imagined their conversation: 'So, that's the little Argie. How sweet she looks, like a little puppy.' She hated her. She hated David for being so nice to her. Why didn't he stand up and refuse to talk to her? After all, she had left him. She looked across at Ian Lancaster who was heavily into a conversation with a pink, skinny lady to his right. She looks like she's been hanging from the ceiling of someone's chalet drying out like a piece of *Bundnerfleisch*, she thought wickedly before laughing politely again at Jim's story.

The dinner seemed to be played out in slow motion. Everyone seemed to eat, drink and talk at an unnecessarily slow pace. When finally coffee was served and cigarettes lit, Sofia was desperate to go home. Then Ian Lancaster launched an attack on the Argentines and Sofia froze in her chair like a stunned animal.

'Bloody Argies,' he said, drawing in his cigar with flabby, blistered lips. 'Cowards, the lot of them. Running away from British bullets.'

'We all know that fool Galtieri only attacked our territory in order to distract his people from his hopeless domestic policy,' scoffed George. Jim rolled his eyes.

'Now hold on,' said David. 'Aren't we all a bit bored with discussing this war?' He looked over at Sofia, bristling across the table.

'Oh, yes. Sorry. Forgot you married an Argie,' their host continued viciously.

'An Argentine,' said Sofia crossly. 'We're Argentines, not Argies.'

'Still, you attacked British territory, you have to face the consequences – or run away,' he added and laughed unkindly.

'They're children. Fifteen-year-old conscripts. Are you surprised they're terrified?' Sofia said, fighting her indignation.

'Galtieri should have thought about that before he stumbled in. Pathetic. Utterly pathetic. We'll blast them into the sea.'

Sofia looked helplessly at David who raised his eyebrows and sighed. The table went silent; everyone looked down at their plates in embarrassment. The neighbouring tables, who had all been listening to Ian's attack, waited to see what would happen next. Then a small voice seeped into the pause.

'I have to commend your graciousness,' Ariella said silkily.

'Graciousness?' Ian replied uncomfortably.

'Yes, graciousness,' she repeated slowly.

'I don't know what you mean.'

'Oh, come on, Ian, don't be bashful.' She laughed prettily.

'Really Ariella, I don't,' he said, getting irritated. Ariella glanced around to make sure that everyone was listening. She liked a good audience in moments such as these.

'I want to commend your diplomacy. Here we are, in the middle of a war against Argentina and you and Alice have chosen to use the colours of the Argentine flag for your tent.' She looked up at the thick blue and white stripes. Everyone followed her and looked about them. 'I think we should all raise our glasses. I only wish we were all so gracious. Here we are, deriding Argentina and its people when we are in the presence of one of them. Sofia is an Argentine and I'm sure loves her country as much as we love ours. How tragic that we all have so little refinement as to call them Argies and cowards when she is a guest here at your table, Ian. Your guest, at your table. What a shame the good grace you started with when you chose these colours for your tent has been swallowed down with your wine. But I want to raise my glass to your sense of diplomacy and occasion all the same, because the thought is there. They always say it's the thought that counts, don't they, Ian?'

Ariella raised her glass before bringing it to her pale lips. Ian choked again on his cigar, the blood swelled to his face where it throbbed a horrible shade of purple. David looked at Ariella in astonishment along with the rest of the table and those in the vicinity. Sofia smiled at her gratefully, swallowing her fury with a gulp of red wine. 'Now, Sofia, would you accompany me to the powder room? I think I've had enough of some of the company at this table,' said she lightly, standing up. The men leapt to their feet, nodding at her in respect, their mouths agape. Sofia walked over to the other woman, holding her head as high as she was able. Ariella took her hand and led her past the tables of speechless guests to the door. Once outside, Ariella began to laugh.

'What a pompous idiot,' she said. 'I need a cigarette, how about you?'

'I cannot thank you enough,' said Sofia who was still trembling. Ariella offered her the packet. Sofia declined.

'Don't thank me. I enjoyed every minute of it. I've never liked Ian Lancaster very much. I could never see what David saw in him – and think what his poor wife has to suffer! Night after night, all that huffing and puffing, with his red face and cigar breath. Yuck!'

They wandered over to a bench and sat down. The tent glowed from the inside and the noise had flared up again, like dying coals of a fire revived with bellows. Ariella lit her cigarette and crossed her legs.

'You have no idea what an effort it was to be dignified. I wanted to throw my wine in his face,' said Ariella, holding the cigarette between her long fingers garnished with manicured pink talons.

'You were very dignified. He was speechless and furious.'

'Good. How dare he!' she exclaimed, drawing the smoke into her lungs.

'They all do, I'm afraid. I didn't want to come tonight,' Sofia said sadly.

'This must be a horrid time for you. I'm sorry. I'm full of

admiration that you came. You're like a gazelle in a field full of lions.'

'David wanted to come,' she replied.

'Of course. As I said, I never understood what he saw in that hideous man!'

'I don't think he'll see much in him after tonight,' laughed Sofia.

'He won't. He'll probably never speak to him again.' She blew the smoke out of the side of her mouth and studied Sofia's face from beneath her heavy black lashes. 'David's very lucky to have found you. He's a different person now. He's happy, fulfilled. He looks young and handsome. You're very good for him. I'm almost jealous.'

'Thank you.'

'We were very bad for each other, you know. Very bad indeed,' she said, flicking her ash onto the grass. 'He was grumpy with me all the time and I was demanding and spoilt. I still am. I regret that I hurt him, but I'm happy that we went our separate ways. We would have destroyed each other if we'd stayed together. Some things just aren't right. But you and David . . . I can see when a partnership is going to work. You've mended his heart in a way that I would never have been able to.'

'You're being hard on yourself,' said Sofia, wondering why she had ever felt threatened by Ariella.

'I never liked his friends, either. Zaza was a complete pain. She wanted David for herself. I'd watch that one if I were you.'

'Oh, Zaza's nosy and interfering, but I like her,' insisted Sofia.

'She hated me. There, you see. You and David are made for each other. Although, we now have a mutual hatred of Ian Lancaster in common.' She laughed.

'We certainly do,' sighed Sofia. 'I thought you lived in France?'

'I did, with Alain, the lovely Alain,' said Ariella and laughed bitterly. 'Another one that didn't last. I don't know,' she sighed heavily, 'I don't think I'm made to be constant.'

'Where's Alain now?'

'Still in Provence, still a struggling photographer, still roguish and vague. Very, very vague. I don't think he's noticed I've gone.'

'I can't imagine anyone not noticing you, Ariella.'

'You would if you knew Alain. Anyway, I think I'm better off without men, without attachments, without commitment. You see, I'm a gypsy at heart, always have been. I paint and travel, that's my life.'

'I saw one of your paintings in the attic at Lowsley. It's very good,' Sofia said.

'You sweet girl. Thank you. I should come and retrieve it. Maybe we could have tea.'

'I'd like that.'

'Good.' She smiled. 'I'd like that very much. Are you and David going to have children?'

'Perhaps.'

'Oh, do. I love children – other people's children. I never wanted to have children myself, but David longed for them. We used to argue about it all the time. Poor David, how I made him suffer. Don't leave it too long, David's not getting any younger. He'll be a wonderful father. He wants to be a father so much.'

When she heard these words, Sofia sat back and looked up at the stars. She thought of all those young men dying on the hills of Las Malvinas. They all had mothers, fathers, brothers, sisters, grandparents to mourn them. She remembered her father explaining death to her as a child; he had said that every soul became a star. She had believed him. She still believed him; at least she wanted to. She gazed up at all the souls that glimmered in the silent infinity. Grandpa O'Dwyer had told her that life was all about preservation and procreation – that life must be nurtured with love for it can't survive without it. She had David to love but suddenly, staring up at the millions of souls above her she realised that the whole point of loving was to create more and more love. She decided then that she was finally ready for a baby. Santiguito might just as well be one of those stars, she thought sadly to herself, for I will never see him again. She recalled Dominique's advice and knew that she had to let him go.

Chapter Thirty-Two

The most satisfactory aspect of liking Ariella was the extent to which it tormented Zaza. Sofia derived enormous pleasure from relating Ariella's triumphant speech to her and watching her screw up her interfering nose in disdain. It had been over a month since the party, but Zaza's curiosity about Ariella was insatiable and she made Sofia recount the story over and over every time she saw her.

'How can you like her? She's a bitch!' gasped Zaza, lighting two cigarettes by mistake. 'Blast,' she exclaimed, throwing one into the empty fireplace. 'Did I really do that?'

'But she was fantastic. The cool way she squashed Ian Lancaster into the ground . . . She was so dignified yet ruthless – you should have seen her. You know he apologised to me afterwards? The little worm. Of course I was very gracious. I wasn't going to lower myself to his level, but I don't ever want to see him again,' she said haughtily.

'And David really has vowed never to see him again?'

'It's over,' she replied and ran a finger across her neck in a mock execution. 'Over.' She laughed. 'Ariella came to pick up her paintings last week and stayed not just for tea but for the whole night. We talked and talked, I didn't want her to leave.' She watched Zaza squirm.

'And David?'

'Let bygones be bygones.'

'Quite incredible. Incredible.' She sighed, chipping off a piece of scarlet nail varnish that had begun to peel. 'You are eccentric, both of you.'

'Oh goodness, look at the time. I've got an appointment before meeting David at the office at four,' said Sofia, looking at her watch. 'I really must be going.'

'What's the appointment for?' asked Zaza, then checked herself. 'I mean, you're all right, aren't you?'

'Oh yes, fine. Just the routine dentist and hygienist,' Sofia said nonchalantly.

'Okay. Give David my love,' said Zaza, scrutinising Sofia from beneath her heavy green eyelids. Dentist my ass, she thought to herself. She wondered whether it might really have something to do with a certain gynaecologist.

Sofia arrived at David's office at four-thirty. She was trembling and pale yet she smiled with the restraint of someone with an enchanting secret. The secretary swiftly put the telephone down on her boyfriend and greeted the boss's wife enthusiastically. Sofia didn't wait to be announced but walked straight into her husband's office. He looked up from his desk. Sofia leant back against the door and smiled at him.

'Oh God, you are,' he said slowly, his face crumpling into an anxious grin. 'You really are? Please tell me you really are.' He removed his glasses with a shaking hand.

'I am,' she told him and laughed. 'I don't know what to do with myself.'

'Oh, I do,' he said, springing to his feet and striding over to her. He gathered her into his arms and held her tightly against him. 'I hope it's a little girl,' he breathed into her neck. 'A miniature Sofia.'

'God forbid,' she giggled.

'I can't believe it,' he sighed, pulling away from her and placing his large hand on her belly. 'There's a little human being in there, growing a bit every day.'

'We can't tell anyone for a couple of months — just in case,' she cautioned him. Then she remembered the expression on Zaza's face. 'I had lunch with Zaza at her house. I pretended I had to go to the dentist. But you know Zaza. I think she's a little suspicious.'

'Don't worry, I'll fend her off,' he said, kissing her forehead.

'I would like to tell Dominique, though.'

'Very good idea. You must tell anyone you like.'

Sofia didn't suffer the usual morning sickness. In fact, to her surprise she felt incredibly well and boisterous. David flustered around her not really knowing how to cope but wanting to be involved and supportive. Where her last pregnancy had been a miserable experience, this time was altogether different. She felt so full of joy that Santiguito's memory receded into the mists of her mind. David spoiled her with attention. He bought her so many gifts that after a few weeks she had to tell him not to buy any more as she was running out of places in the house to put them. She talked to Dominique every day, and the latter promised to come over at least once a month.

After the couple's three-month silence was broken, Sofia was besieged by vans full of flowers and gifts from excited friends and relations of David's. As she was unable to ride in her condition Sofia took up the piano again, taking lessons three times a week with a lively octogenarian whose face reminded her of a tortoise. She made regular visits to her gynaecologist in London and spent hundreds of pounds on items for her baby that she simply couldn't do without. Certain that she was going to have a girl she chose the most feminine things she could find and asked Ariella to paint all the Winnie-the-Pooh characters skipping across the walls of the baby's bedroom. 'I want it to be a light, happy room,' she said. Ariella's artistry was such a success that she ignited a trend that took her all over Gloucestershire with her paintbrush and E.H. Shepard's illustrations to copy.

In February an exuberant Zaza arrived for tea with a carload of her children's old baby clothes. She sat down on the sofa as near as possible to the fire and lit a cigarette with a gleaming silver lighter that Tony had given her for Christmas.

'Darling, it's so cold in this house. What's happened to your heating?' she complained, shivering.

'I'm boiling hot all the time. I think it's all part of being pregnant,' said Sofia, who sat perfectly comfortably in a sleeveless polo-neck.

'It might very well be, but what about the rest of us? Really, I'm surprised David doesn't put his foot down.'

'David's an angel. He had to run out last Sunday and get me a jar of olives. I had a terrible craving. I just had to have them.'

'Yuck, I've never much liked olives. How ghastly,' Zaza grimaced. 'Now, let's open this case and I shall show you my booty. No darling, not you. You sit where you are and let me do the heavy work,' she added bossily when Sofia tried to help lift it onto the coffee-table. Zaza unzipped it with care, holding the zipper between the pad of her thumb and the knuckle of her forefinger to avoid breaking a nail.

'These were Nick's,' she said, holding up a pair of red velvet trousers. 'Adorable, don't you think?'

'Perfect for a two-year-old boy,' laughed Sofia. 'This is going to be a girl.' She placed a hand on her swollen belly.

'You don't know,' said Zaza. 'That lump looks like a boy. I remember, mine was that shape when I had Eddie. Dear little thing he was.'

'No, I know it's going to be a girl. I sense it.'

'Whatever it is, as long as it has ten fingers and ten toes it really doesn't matter.'

'It does to me,' Sofia said, wishing silently for a girl. 'This is sweet,' she added, pulling out a tiny white dress. 'Now this *is* for a baby girl.'

'That was Angela's. So pretty. Of course, they grow out of these things far too quickly.'

'You're very kind to lend them to me,' said Sofia, holding a miniature pair of blue shoes.

'Don't be silly. I'm not *lending* them to you – I'm giving them to you. I don't need them any more.'

'What about Angela? She may need them one day.'

'God – Angela!' she huffed. 'She's going through that hideous adolescent stage. She says she doesn't like men and that she's in love with a girl called Mandy.'

'She's probably only doing it to irritate you,' said Sofia knowingly.

'Well, it's working. Not that I'm worried about Mandy.'

'You're not?'

'No, I've fancied women in my time – not that I've touched one since school. But Angela's so moody with it. She's rude and disrespectful, spends all our money and then asks for more, as if the world owes her a living. Or at least that we do. Give me ten Eddies any day. The rate Angela's going, she won't be needing these,' she said, stuffing her red talons into a couple of knitted bootees. 'No, I'm relying on Eddie to one day make me a granny, but not for many years, I hope. I'm really far too young and glamorous to be a granny. Seen Ariella lately?'

'Not for a while, she's busy painting.'

'That room is something of a wonder to behold. She's very talented,' said Zaza, raising her thin eyebrows and nodding in admiration.

'She's coming for the last weekend in March,' Sofia informed her. 'Why don't you and Tony come too? David would love to have you both. I've got my surrogate parents, Dominique and Antoine coming over as well. It'll be great fun. You'd adore Dominique.'

'Oh, I don't know. Ariella and I never did get on. I've never liked her,' she mumbled hesitantly.

'That was years ago. You're both different people now. If I can love Ariella then surely you can too. Please come. Being pregnant is all very well, but I can't ride and have very little to do except practise my scales for the tortoise. I need good company,' she pleaded.

Zaza thought about it for a moment. 'Oh, go on, twist my arm,' she said happily. 'I'd love to. It'll give me a break from Angela. They can have the whole bloody house to themselves.'

'Then that's settled. Good,' said Sofia.

As March was slowly driven out by an impatient spring that scattered the garden with snowdrops and early daffodils, Sofia's belly swelled with the growing blessing inside her that decided to jump about whenever she wanted to be still. Sometimes she could see a little fist mould itself for a moment in her skin as the baby kicked and punched in its eagerness to come out into the world. Sometimes it danced to the hesitant music of her piano playing until the tortoise, Harry Humphreys, would look so afraid as to almost hide his face in his shell while her shirt moved around mysteriously beside him. David liked to place his head on her tummy and listen to the baby shuffling around in the amniotic fluid. They spent long hours discussing what they thought she would look like, what features of theirs she might inherit. 'Your rich brown eyes,' said David, kissing Sofia's eyelids.

'No, your beautiful blue eyes,' she said, kissing his.

'Your nose.'

'That I agree with,' she laughed, kissing his larger nose fondly.

'Your mouth,' he said, placing his on her lips.

'Of course,' she agreed . . . 'But your brains.'

'Naturally.'

'My body.'

'I should hope so if she's a girl. Your horsemanship. Your daring.'

'Your sweet nature instead of my stubbornness.'

'And your pride.'

'All right, don't rub it in!'

'Your funny walk.'

'It's not that funny.'

'Yes, it is — you walk like a duck,' he said and she laughed.

'Do I?' she said coyly. But she knew she did and she knew how attractive it was. Santi had accused her of putting it on to get attention; he had said it made her look self-satisfied and arrogant. But she didn't put it on, she had always walked like that.

'If it's a boy . . .'

'It won't be a boy. I know she's a girl. A little girl,' she said emphatically.

'Another Sofia, God help us!'

She threw her arms about his neck and kissed the soft skin beneath his ear. He held her tightly and hoped for her sake that their child would be a little girl and that she would be as adorable as his wife.

Ariella arrived first. She could barely conceal her fury when Sofia told her that Zaza was coming. 'Well, I'll suffer with good grace,' she said condescendingly as David carried her suitcase up to her room. Sofia was helping her unpack by giving instructions from the bed when the dogs barked announcing the arrival of a car. Sofia looked out of the window and waved at Zaza and Tony.

'David's down there,' said Sofia, settling back onto the bed again.

'Let's leave them to it, shall we?' suggested Ariella. 'It's always strange coming back here and not owning it. It's a beautiful house. I can't think what possessed me to leave,' she joked.

'Well, I'm glad you did, so please don't change your mind.'

'Oh all right, if you insist.'

Just then the dogs trotted in followed by David, Tony and Zaza.

'Darling Ariella, it's been so long,' gushed Zaza, pulling her scarlet mouth into an artificial smile.

Ariella smiled back coolly. 'Years, actually. How have you been? Still with Tony, I see,' she said, watching Tony and David wander on down the corridor.

'Oh darling Tony, I know a good thing when I see one,' Zaza said and laughed nervously. 'You look well, Ariella,' she added. She could call Ariella lots of things but she couldn't deny her the luminous beauty for which she was so famous.

'Thank you. So do you,' Ariella replied politely, running a slender white hand through her angel hair.

'That room, you are clever. It's brilliant,' Zaza said, referring to the baby's bedroom.

'I've been somewhat inundated with requests. I can hardly keep up,' Ariella told them.

'Well, darling, clever you. Clever, clever you. I never knew you painted so well.'

'Cartoons aren't my *métier* actually, but it's new and I like new things.'

'Yes,' said Zaza.

Sofia showed Zaza to her room, leaving Ariella to finish her unpacking.

'Darling, you never told me how exquisite she is,' hissed Zaza, when they were out of earshot.

'You've known her for years.'

'Yes, but she's got more beautiful. She never, well – glowed like that. She did glow, yes she did, but differently. She's incredible. Much nicer than I remember,' she chattered excitedly.

'Good,' said Sofia, watching Zaza's control slip into a childish exuberance.

Dominique and Antoine arrived last of all. Their plane had been delayed and they descended from the car dishevelled and exhausted but not without humour.

'Antoine has promised me my own jet,' said Dominique as she entered the hallway, pushing past the dogs. 'He says I never have to travel commercial again. It's far too stressful and ruins my looks.'

'She is right,' Antoine declared in his heavy French accent. 'If I buy one, why not ten, then all her friends can enjoy them too.'

Sofia waddled over to embrace them, as much as was physically possible. 'I'll be able to get closer in a few weeks,' she joked, breathing in the familiar scent of Dominique's perfume.

'When is the baby arriving?' asked Antoine.

'*Cher* Antoine, I've told you countless times – only ten days to go. Any moment now.'

'I hope you're ready to roll up your sleeves, darling,' said Zaza to David. 'It could come at any moment.'

'I'm ready to roll up mine,' Tony interjected jovially. 'I've already delivered two of my own although I'm slightly out of practice.'

'That's not the only thing that requires practice,' said Zaza under her breath.

Ariella grinned and glanced at Tony; it didn't surprise her. He looked like the sort of man who was more at home smoking a cigar with the other codgers. Her attention was diverted as Quid stuck his nose aggressively into her crotch.

'For goodness' sake!' she wailed as she tried to push him away. He forced his nose further in, wagging his tale wildly.

'Quid, stop,' ordered David in amusement. '*Quid!* Sorry, Ariella, he's not used to such fragrant women. Come on, Quid, behave. You shouldn't treat ladies like that, it's not gentlemanly behaviour.'

'For goodness' sake, David, can't you learn to talk to your dogs properly?' Ariella complained. 'They're not people. Honestly,' she sighed, brushing down her trousers and marching across the hall to the drawing room.

Once there, she slipped out of her shoes and curled up on the sofa, pulling her feet up from the floor to avoid the dreaded Quid who eyed her lasciviously from David's feet. Dominique, dressed in large, floppy green trousers and a bright floral cardigan that reached down to her knees, perched on the fireguard, her hands playing with the beads that hung about her neck like shiny red beetles. Zaza stood the other end of the fireguard, striking a pose, or so Sofia thought. She held her cigarette high in the air where it smoked at the end of the black ebony holder. Her short brown hair was sleek, cut into a severe bob and her narrow green eyes surveyed the room from their lofty height. She watched Ariella warily, taking care not to let her guard down. Ariella had a tongue as sharp as a shark's tooth and as bloodthirsty, she reminded herself. David, Antoine and Tony stood by the window discussing the garden.

'Fancy shooting some rabbits?' suggested David. 'The garden's full of the damn pests.'

'Don't be mean,' shouted Sofia from the bed. 'Poor little things.'

'What do you mean, poor little things? They eat all the bulbs,' David objected. 'What do you say?'

'All right,' said Tony.

'*Comme vous voulez,*' Antoine shrugged his shoulders.

The following day was mild for March. The sun shook off the winter fogs and blazed enthusiastically, pleased to be out. Ariella and Zaza appeared for breakfast elegantly clad in mild country colours. While Zaza's green tweed trousers and jacket were stiffly new, Ariella's pleated tweed skirt ensemble had belonged to her grandmother and had softened and faded with the years. Zaza glanced at Ariella enviously, while Ariella smiled with the contentment of someone who knows they always look immaculate whatever the occasion.

David took the key from a small drawer in the hall and opened the gun cabinet. He chose one for himself and a couple for Antoine and Tony. They had belonged to his father who had been a keen shot in his day and were all elegantly engraved with the initials *E.J.H.* for Edward Jonathan Harrison.

Sofia wrapped herself in a sheepskin coat of David's and grabbed a long stick from the cloakroom to keep the dogs in check. As they gathered on the gravel at the front of the house Dominique appeared in a bright red coat, yellow and blue striped scarf and white tennis shoes.

'You'll scare all the animals away dressed like that,' Tony said, cheekily, looking at her in mock horror.

'Except the bulls,' beamed Ariella. 'I think you look marvellous.'

'*Chérie*, perhaps you should borrow a coat of Sofia's?' Antoine suggested kindly.

'You can if you like,' said Sofia, 'but I'd rather you came like that to warn them all of the danger.'

'If Sofia wants me in red, she shall have me in red,' Dominique decided. 'Now let's go. I need a good walk after all that toast and scrambled eggs. No one cooks breakfast like the English.'

They walked up the valley towards the woods. Every few minutes the men would indicate to the women that they had seen a rabbit and everyone would have to stop and remain very still until they had shot it. Tony, who had missed everything, turned to the four women and hissed, 'If you would all stop talking I might shoot something.'

'Sorry, darling,' said Zaza. 'Pretend we're not here.'

'For God's sake, Zaza, they can hear your voices in Stratford!'

The party moved on up the path like a slow train stopping at every station. Sofia kept the dogs under control by patting them on their backs every now and then with the stick and saying, 'Heel!' which they seemed to understand. Once the rabbits had all been either frightened away by the gunfire, or Dominique's coat, David and Antoine tucked their guns under their arms and called it a day. Tony, who had still missed everything, furiously looked about for something to shoot. Finally he aimed at a plump, low-flying pigeon, pulled the trigger and watched in delight as a few feathers sparked into the air. The bird flew on.

'That'll come down,' he said triumphantly.

'Yes, it will,' said Ariella, 'when it's hungry.'

'Right, that's it,' huffed Tony. 'I've had enough of this. Let's walk on and get some exercise. A couple of us need to talk less and walk more.' He turned to Ariella who was laughing so hard she had to hold on to Zaza for support. 'Women,' sighed Tony. 'They are so easy to amuse.'

By Sunday Zaza and Ariella were firm friends yet the balance of their friendship was uneven. Zaza, still wary of Ariella, was very much in her thrall. She laughed at all her jokes and glanced at her after she had spoken to check her reaction. Ariella was more amused by Zaza than impressed. She enjoyed the power her beauty gave her and took pleasure in watching it dazzle Zaza like a fox in torchlight. Sofia watched their dynamic with amusement and loved Ariella all the more for playing with Zaza so effortlessly.

As Sofia wandered down the upstairs landing that evening, she heard Zaza and Tony arguing in their bedroom while they packed their cases to leave. She stopped to listen.

'For God's sake, don't be so pathetic. What on earth for?' Tony was saying, his voice patronising as if he were talking to his daughter.

'Darling, I'm sorry, I can't expect you to understand,' Zaza told him.

'Well, how can I? I'm a man.'

'It's got nothing to do with being a man. David would understand.'

'You're just showing off,' said Tony.

'I didn't want to discuss it in this house,' hissed Zaza, obviously afraid of being overheard. Sofia felt briefly guilty.

'Well, why did you bring it up then?'

'I couldn't help it.'

'You're being very childish, you know. You're no better than Angela, the pair of you.'

'Don't put me in the same basket as Angela,' snapped Zaza crossly.

'You want to run off to France with Ariella, Angela's in love with a girl called Mandy — what's the difference?'

'The difference is that I'm old enough to know what I'm doing.'

'I give it a month. Go and try it out if you want to, but she'll spit you out when she's bored . . .'

Just then Sofia experienced a sharp pain in her womb. She cried out as she leant against the wall for support. Tony and Zaza came out of their room to see what the noise was and ran to her aid.

'Oh God, it's the baby!' declared Zaza excitedly.

'It can't be,' gasped Sofia. 'It's not due for another ten days. Ouch!' she cried, bending over.

Tony ran down the stairs shouting for David while Dominique and Ariella rushed out of the drawing room into the hall. Antoine followed Tony and bellowed down the corridor for David. David, who was cleaning his guns, wandered out of the gun cabinet to find his wife being helped down the stairs by an anxious-looking Zaza. He dropped his rag and strode to her side. Sam and Quid sprang about in excitement hoping they were about to be taken for another walk.

'Dominique, get her coat. Where are my keys?' he stammered, feeling his pockets. 'Are you all right, darling?' he said, taking Sofia's other arm. She nodded to make him feel better.

'It's okay, you can take mine,' said Ariella, holding her keys out, watching Quid warily.

'Thank you. I owe you one,' David replied, grabbing them.

'I don't think you do,' she said as Quid trotted towards her with a determined look in his eyes.

Dominique helped Sofia into her coat. 'I'm coming with you,' she said. 'Antoine, you're going back to Geneva alone. I'm staying.'

'As long as you like, *chérie*,' he replied and shrugged his amiable shoulders.

'Quid, Quid, *no!*' shrieked Ariella, looking about for David, but he had left the front door open behind him and the sound of tyres on gravel indicated that she would have to fight the dog on her own. 'It's just you and me, doggie!' she hissed. 'And I take no prisoners!'

'How unusual,' commented Zaza. 'First babies are always late.'

Chapter Thirty-Three

Sofia was frightened. It had nothing to do with giving birth. Nor was she even afraid that her child might be in danger. She knew everything was all right. She knew her child had just lost patience with the wait, and she didn't blame it. So had she. But she was afraid she might, after all, have a boy.

'Where's Dominique?' she asked anxiously as they wheeled her into the delivery room.

'Waiting downstairs,' David replied shakily.

'I'm frightened,' she choked.

'Darling . . .'

'I don't want a boy,' she said tearfully. David held her hand tightly. 'If it's a boy, what if he's like Santiguito? I don't think I could bear it.'

'It'll be all right, I promise,' he said reassuringly, pretending to be strong. He had never felt this nervous before, his stomach was skipping all over the place. Sofia looked so unhappy and he was powerless to help her. He didn't know what to say. Besides, he was feeling faint himself. He fought his nausea by focusing on comforting his wife. But Sofia continued to fret. She saw Santiguito's small round face looking possessively into hers. How could she love another child? Perhaps she shouldn't have got pregnant in the first place.

'I'm frightened, David,' she said again. Her mouth was dry, she needed a drink.

'Don't worry, Mrs Harrison. First-time mothers are always a little apprehensive. It's only natural,' the nurse said kindly.

I'm not a first-time mother! cried out Sofia in her head. But before she could think any more about Santiguito she was pushing and screaming and squeezing David's hand until he winced and had to pry her nails out of his palm. The last birth had been long and painful. To her surprise this baby slid out into the light of the hospital lamps with the speed and efficiency of someone anxious to leave the place they came from and arrive. The child's arrival was welcomed by a sharp smack and signalled by a shrill cry as it inhaled for the first time a gulp of life-sustaining air.

'Mrs Harrison, you have a beautiful little girl,' the doctor said, giving the baby to the nurse.

'A girl?' sighed Sofia weakly. 'A girl. Thank God.'

'That was quick!' David said heartily, trying to cover up the emotion that stuck in his throat like cottonwool. 'Very quick.'

The nurse laid the baby, now wrapped in a white muslin square, onto the mother's breast so that Sofia could hold her and look into her mottled red face. Accustomed to overwhelmed parents she turned away tactfully to allow the father to say a few proud words to his wife.

'A little girl,' he breathed, peering over the muslin to take a look. 'She's the image of her mother.'

'Honestly David, if I look like this I may as well give up now,' she joked weakly.

'Darling, you were so brave. You've performed a miracle,' he whispered, his lips trembling at the sight of the tiny human being that twitched in her mother's arms.

'A miracle,' she repeated, kissing her new baby's damp forehead tenderly. 'Look how perfect she is. She's got the tiniest little nose – it's as if God forgot to give her one and stuck it on at the last minute.'

'What shall we call her?' he asked.

'I know what *not* to call her.'

'Elizabeth?' he said and laughed.

'What was your father's mother called?' Sofia asked.

'Honor. What about your mother or grandmother?'

'Honor, I like that name. Very English. Honor. Just Honor,' she said, watching her baby with shiny eyes.

'Honor Harrison . . . I like it too. Mother won't – she hated her mother-in-law.'

'So we have something in common after all,' Sofia commented dryly.

'I never thought you'd have anything in common with Mother.'

'Honor Harrison you will be beautiful, talented, smart and witty. You'll have the best of both of us and we'll love you for ever.' She smiled happily up at David. 'Tell Dominique I want to see her. I have someone here I wish her to meet.'

After Dominique, the first visitors were Daisy, Anton, Marcello and Maggie who piled in on the second day weighed down with flowers and presents. Anton came with his scissors to trim Sofia's hair and Maggie had brought her manicure set to paint her nails. Marcello draped himself over a chair and sat in silence, mute but beautiful as if he were being painted. Daisy perched on Sofia's bed gazing adoringly into the cot beside her.

'We're the Three Wise Men, sweetie,' said Maggie. 'Bearing gifts to give the new Messiah. Though it appears we're not the first,' she added, looking at the bouquets and gifts that were scattered about the room.

'There are four of you,' pointed out Sofia.

'No, Marcello doesn't count. He's barely there at the best of times,' she replied.

'We're here to pamper Mummy,' Anton declared, brushing her hair. 'I don't know what it's like giving birth, duckie, but I once saw a documentary on telly and it nearly did me in.'

'Anton, I don't know why you care – you'll never have to go

through it,' Sofia said contentedly, watching the pieces of dark hair fall about her like feathers.

'Thank God — can you *imagine* all that screaming and wailing,' Maggie joked pulling out a purple varnish. 'If men had babies, even half-men like Anton, the preciousness would be intolerable. Not to mention the noise. Let's hope science never advances that far, at least not in my lifetime.'

'Not purple, Maggie, what about a pale pink?' Sofia said.

'*Natural?*' Maggie squirmed, appalled.

'Yes, please. I'm a mother now,' Sofia replied proudly.

'That'll wear off after a while, that new mother business. After a few weeks of screaming you'll want to shove her right back again. I know because Lucien drove me to distraction. I almost served him up with the Sunday roast. Believe me, you'll be gasping for your old independence, sweetie. As soon as you want purple nails and green hair, Anton and I will be ready, won't we, Anton?'

'We certainly will, Maggie. People are so dull these days, all they want are highlights. Highlights! What's exciting about *highlights?*'

'So how are you, sweetie? Bruised, I imagine. I'm surprised you can sit down.' Maggie grimaced. 'I still haven't recovered from having Lucien over twenty years ago. The body never goes back, sweetie. That's the sadness. Viv worshipped me for my body until I had Lucien. Then he started looking around for someone firmer and tighter in all the right places. They say you're like a rubber band and spring back into shape. Well, it never happened to me. There's nothing rubber about my body. I used to be able to touch my toes but now I can't even see them, I wouldn't know where they were. I put that down to childbirth. Yes, I blame Eve. If it had been that coward Adam who had eaten the apple from God's tree we wouldn't be fat and flabby now, would we?'

'Speak for yourself, Maggie. Sofia's in perfect shape,' said Daisy, smiling broadly at her friend. 'How do you feel? Is it really as bad as Maggie says?'

'Maggie always exaggerates,' she said, grinning at Maggie. 'It was very easy, actually. David's hand is a bit sore, mind you, but apart from that he's very happy and proud. So am I.'

'Where is the lovely David?' said Anton fruitily. 'I've always had a bit of a warm spot for hubby.' He glanced at Marcello who hadn't moved since he arrived.

'He'll be back later. Poor thing, he's shattered,' Sofia replied.

'She's so sweet,' enthused Daisy, peering again into the cot. 'She's like a little mouse.'

'Darling, you shouldn't call her a mouse. Mothers always think their babies are beautiful,' said Maggie in reproof. 'I thought Lucien was beautiful until he grew up.'

'If you're going to use an animal try to be a *little* more imaginative, duckie. Mouse is very run of the mill,' said Anton, standing back to admire his handiwork.

At that moment the door swung open. Elizabeth Harrison stood in the doorway. Her hooded eyes darted about the room searching the strange faces for Sofia, her scraggy neck wobbling like a turkey's from beneath her determined chin.

'Is this Mrs Harrison's room?' she barked. 'And who are all these people?'

Sofia glanced at Maggie who was blowing her nails dry.

'It's the wicked witch of the North,' she hissed.

Maggie looked up. 'Are you sure? Looks more like one of Anton's friends in drag.'

'I've come to see my grandchild,' the woman said without acknowledging her daughter-in-law. She hobbled angrily across the room. 'This is a hospital, *not* some ghastly salon.' She sniffed censoriously.

'You could do with a haircut, duckie,' said Anton, sucking in his cheeks as she passed him. 'You know that look is very passé, it shows your age.'

'Good God, who are you?' She recoiled. 'Who *are* these people?'

'They're my friends, Elizabeth. Anton, Daisy, Maggie and . . . well, ignore Marcello, he doesn't want to be talked to, just admired,' she said and giggled under her breath. 'This is my mother-in-law, Elizabeth Harrison.'

Elizabeth shuffled past Marcello, putting as much distance between his chair and her person as was humanly possible in such a small room. She bent over the cot. 'What is it?'

'She's a little girl,' replied Sofia, pulling the cot towards her protectively. She didn't want her mother-in-law getting too close, she might give the child bad luck.

'Name?'

'Honor,' Sofia beamed jubilantly.

'Honor?' Elizabeth said crossly. 'What a ghastly name. Honor indeed.'

'It's a beautiful name. We've called her Honor in honour of David's grandmother, your late mother-in-law. He was very fond of her, he tells me.'

'Honor's the name of an actress, or a singer, don't you think Anton?' Maggie said naughtily.

'Certainly a performer, Maggie,' Anton added for good measure.

'Where's David?' Mrs Harrison demanded.

'Out,' Sofia replied coldly. He probably knew you were coming, you horrid, smelly old trout, she thought to herself.

'Well, tell him I came,' she said before resting her bulging eyes on Sofia. She looked her over thoughtfully. 'David's my only son,' she told her in a deep voice that croaked due to the mucus in her lungs. 'And this child is my only grandchild. I would have preferred him to marry someone from his own country and class. Ariella was perfect, only David couldn't see that, the fool – just like his father. But you have given him a child. I would have preferred a boy, but you will have a boy next time, to carry his name on. I don't like you and I like your friends even less. But you have given my son a child so you have something in your favour at least. Tell David I came,' she repeated before leaving the room. Then as they were about to erupt into a vicious commentary the door swung open and she reappeared in the doorway.

'Oops, she's forgotten her broomstick!' Anton said.

'Or forgotten to cast a spell,' Sofia added.

'You may also tell David that I will not call the child Honor. He'll have to think of something else.' Then the door closed and she was gone.

'What a pleasant woman,' Daisy said sarcastically.

'What I could do with her hair,' Anton tut tutted.

'I wouldn't bother, sweetie,' said Maggie, 'she'll be dead before too long.' Then to everyone's surprise Marcello moved.

'Porca miseria!' he said languorously. 'She's been dead for years.'

When David arrived later that afternoon, Sofia was breastfeeding. He stood at the end of the bed and watched her. They smiled at each other in silent understanding. There were no words to adequately express David's awe of the power of nature and he didn't want to spoil the moment by bringing such a scene down to earth with commonplace syllables. So he stood, his expression tender, almost melancholic, and watched the mysterious bond between mother and child. Sofia gazed into the face of her baby enjoying every movement she made, marvelling at the exquisite perfection of her features.

When Honor had finished feeding, Sofia wrapped her tightly in her muslin and placed her gently back in her cot to sleep. 'I can hardly bear to put her down,' she murmured, running a finger over her baby's velvet head.

'I have some surprising news,' David said, sitting on the side of the bed and kissing her.

'So do I,' replied Sofia. 'But you first.'

'Well, you're never going to believe this. Zaza has left Tony and run off to Provence with Ariella.'

'You're right – I don't believe it!' gasped Sofia, astounded. 'You know, I did overhear Tony and Zaza arguing in their room last weekend, but I didn't really understand what they were talking about. Now it all fits into place. Are you sure?'

'Tony just called and told me.'

'What did he say?'

'That they had run off together. He said she'd be back within the month when Ariella had moved on to something else to divert her.'

'Was he angry?'

'No. Not angry, more like irritated. He says Angela's appalled and furious that her mother has outdone her. She's declared that she's not really in love with Mandy — she never was, apparently. In fact, she's in love with a boy called Charlie. Eddie, on the contrary, appears to have taken it in his stride.'

'That doesn't surprise me much,' said Sofia.

'Anyway, Tony says he doesn't mind her running off to experiment. He'll be there to pick up the pieces when it all goes wrong, which inevitably it will. Ariella's just playing with her for her amusement. Like a sly white cat with a big, juicy mouse. This must be giving her a lot of pleasure. She never did much care for Zaza.'

'Do you think they'll get in touch?' asked Sofia, dying to hear more.

'Absolutely. They'll want to congratulate you. So what is your news?' he asked, taking her hand and stroking it.

'The mother-in-law from Hell showed up here this morning,' she said.

'Oh,' replied David warily.

'Guess who was here when she came?' Sofia asked, grinning mischievously.

'I don't know — who?'

'Anton, Maggie, Marcello and Daisy.'

'Oh God!' He sighed. 'She must have been horrified.'

'She was. She says she doesn't like the name Honor so you'll have to think of something else, as if I don't have any say in the matter.'

'According to her, you don't.'

'We scared her off, I think.'

'Don't worry. Leave her to me,' said David, resigned to the fact that he would now have to call his mother to fight another trivial battle in their ongoing war. A silly war bred from her inability to control him and nurtured by a growing bitterness that ate away at her spirit like an insatiable phantom. A war that would see an end only with her death. He imagined his poor father trembling in the skies anticipating her storming up there one day like a moody black cloud to join him.

The telephone rang.

'Zaza!' Sofia exclaimed excitedly into the receiver. David raised an eyebrow.

'Darling. Well done, you! A little girl, I hear. Such a pretty name. You must be over the moon,' enthused Zaza.

'I am. We're so happy. How are you? Where are you?' she asked impatiently, more interested in hearing Zaza's news than in reporting her own. She was now becoming bored with repeating the story of Honor's birth to each friend who called.

'I'm in France.'

'With Ariella?' said Sofia.

'Yes. I suppose Tony's been on the blower to David. Typical. It must be all over London by now.' She sighed melodramatically.

'No, I don't think so. David's very discreet,' insisted Sofia, winking at her husband.

'Oh,' said Zaza, sounding disappointed. 'Well, Ariella's here and wants to talk to you. We're having a lovely time.' She gushed, 'Thinking of you and your baby. Send my love to David. I can't talk to him now, Ariella's here.' She lowered her voice. 'You know what I mean.'

'I know, I'll tell him. Pass me over to Ariella,' said Sofia and heard Zaza shouting for her in a voice that skipped on her name: *Ari-ellaaaa!*

'Sofia, congratulations,' said Ariella calmly.

'What are you up to?' asked Sofia seriously.

'Oh, taking a break,' she replied casually.

'When are you going to come back?'

'Once I've amused Alain enough to win back his attention. Then I'll send Zaza home to Tony. She'll be able to spice him up a bit by then, I should imagine.' Ariella laughed lightly.

'You're wicked,' said Sofia who was clearly amused.

'Not wicked. I'm doing them both a favour. Zaza needs an adventure. Tony needs a new Zaza. Zaza needs a new Zaza, believe me.'

'I should watch my back,' laughed Sofia.

'Don't worry, you're not my type. You're far too clever. No, you wouldn't be any fun at all.'

While Sofia slept that night she dreamed. She was sitting up in her hospital bed talking to Ariella and Zaza who were trying to convince her to leave David and join them in Provence. She was shaking her head, laughing, saying no she wouldn't and they were laughing too, telling her how much she would love it. Then the door swung open and in walked a woman dressed in black. She was bent and crooked, resembling a crow, and she hobbled as she walked as if she were dragging a foot behind her. She smelt, for Ariella and Zaza recoiled, holding their noses before disappearing into nowhere. Then, suddenly, the woman was reaching into the cot and grabbing her child. Sofia was screaming, holding on to Honor, desperate not to let her go. The woman was so ugly and deformed she didn't look like a human being at all, more like a bat. She was saying. 'You promised to give up your child. You can't change your mind now.' Then she turned into Elizabeth Harrison, staring at her with those watery, bulbous eyes that swam about in the sockets like oysters.

The nurse shook Sofia to wake her. She was very distressed, sweating and screaming for help. When she awoke she stared at the nurse with large, frightened eyes as she took a while to realise that she was, in fact, awake and not trapped within the nightmare.

'Are you all right, Mrs Harrison? You were having a bad dream,' the nurse said compassionately.

'I want my husband,' sobbed Sofia. 'I want to go home now.'

The following day David came to take Sofia home. Once more installed within the safe walls of Lowsley Sofia forgot about her dream and the strange witch who had tried to steal her child away. She sat by the fire with Sam and Quid wagging their thick tails, chatting happily to Hazel, the nurse, who was holding Honor in her arms, gently rocking her as she slept. David worked in the office next door and Sofia thought how pleasant it was that life had returned to normal. Then she cast her thoughts to Zaza and Tony and wondered whether life would ever be the same again for them.

Chapter Thirty-Four

———————————

Honor crawled around the dining-room table in the furry lion costume that Sofia had bought her at Hamleys, roaring fiercely at her friend Molly who ran ahead of her, squealing in mock terror. The other children who had come for Honor's third birthday party were in the kitchen with Sofia, clinging shyly to their mothers' legs. But Honor wasn't afraid of anything. She would often disappear for ages only to be found by her anxious mother, lying tummy down on the grass, studying a caterpillar or a slug that happened to inspire her curiosity. She was fascinated by everything, especially nature, and confident that if she wandered off for long enough, her mother or nanny would eventually find her.

Today was a very special day, her mother had said. It was her birthday. She could sing 'Happy Birthday' and often did at other people's birthdays, but today she wouldn't have to sing it because all her friends would sing it to her. Then she could blow out the candles, something she loved doing, and often did on other children's cakes, much to her mother's embarrassment as the child would disintegrate into tears and matches would have to be found in order to light the candles again. Today was a celebration of three years of joy that she had given Sofia and David as much as an excuse for their daughter to enjoy her own party with all her friends.

Sofia's heart had expanded over the past three years like the universe. Grandpa O'Dwyer had always said that the purpose of life was to create more and more love. Sofia thought he'd be very proud of her as her heart was literally throbbing with it. She loved her daughter more with each dawn, more with each change that occurred as she grew and developed her own, very strong, personality. She'd spend long hours drawing with her, reading to her, taking her out across the fields for walks or sitting her on her small pony, Hedgehog, and leading her up and down the path which led to the woods. Honor was curious and fearless. She would carry her friend, Hoo, the blue silk hanky that David had given her, wherever she went and Hoo made her feel secure. If Hoo got lost the house had to be systematically searched until he appeared, usually behind a sofa or under a cushion, and was returned to his anxious friend who couldn't sleep without him.

'Honor!' shouted Hazel as best she could, which wasn't much at her age. She had arrived at Honor's birth, hired for a month, but had ended up there for good after David and Sofia had begged her to stay on full-time. She had taken it as a compliment and agreed, having grown immensely fond of Honor and her parents in the short while she had known them.

She had later celebrated her decision when she had met the roguish Freddie Rattray, the widower who ran the stud farm with the help of his daughter Jaynie. Sofia called him Rattie, but Hazel couldn't bring herself to be so informal although everyone else seemed to call him Rattie as well. To her he was Freddie, but only after he had begged her not to call him Mr Rattray. 'That makes me sound so old,' he had said. 'Freddie makes me feel that at least I'm only halfway over the hill. I don't want to see the other side for a good many years.'

Hazel had laughed demurely, running a damp palm over her shiny white hair that was pulled into a neat bun at the nape of her neck. She seemed to spend a lot of time taking Honor down to see the horses and often accompanied Freddie when he took the child for a walk on Hedgehog. Sofia, usually quick to detect a growing affection such as theirs, was too busy watching her daughter to notice the tender looks and flirtatious laughter that resounded from the stables.

'Honor, tea-time!' shouted Hazel, walking into the dining room to find the two girls skipping happily round and round as if imagining their own merry-go-round. She caught Honor as she galloped past and helped her out of her lion costume. Honor had specifically asked to wear a 'pretty dress' for her tea-party. Sofia had laughed at her early sense of occasion. 'Now, let's go and see what Mummy has made for tea,' she said.

'Chocolate Crispies!' cried Honor, her blue eyes widening with glee.

'Chocolate Crispies!' copied Molly, stomping after her.

In the kitchen, Sofia was helping the other mothers seat their children. Johnny Longacre was crying, having been hit by Samuel Pettit, and Quid had already licked little Amber Hopkins's face – which her mother considered extremely unhealthy. She was rushing about like a wasp trying to find a clean cloth with which to wipe the child's face.

'Honor, sweetheart, come and sit down,' Sofia said calmly amid the chaos. 'Look, aren't those sandwiches clever? They're in the shape of butterflies.'

'Can I have a Chocolate Crispie, please?' Honor asked, stretching her hand out to take one.

'No, not until you've had your Marmite sandwich,' said Sofia, grimacing as the smell of Marmite clung to her fingers.

'Sofia, can you please remove your dog? He's trying to eat Amber's sandwich,' said Amber's mother in exasperation. Sofia asked Hazel to put Quid in the study, out of trouble. 'You may as well put me there too,' she laughed. 'I'm in such deep trouble you can barely see me.'

'Sofia, Joey didn't get a marshmallow. There don't seem to be any left. Marshmallows are his favourites,' said Joey's mother, her plain face creasing up apprehensively, afraid that her beloved boy might have to go without. Sofia thought she looked like one of the eggs that Honor drew faces on at breakfast.

Just then the kitchen door opened and in stepped Zaza, dressed in pale brown suede trousers and tweed jacket, her lips painted into a red scowl as she saw the kitchen full of screaming children and their over-anxious mothers.

'Good God, what is going on in here?' she gasped in horror when Sofia clambered over a howling child to greet her. 'If these are Honor's friends I just hope she gets more discerning as she grows older.'

Zaza, it turned out, had lasted six weeks in Provence with Ariella and later Alain. 'I knew when I was no longer wanted,' she had told David. 'Alain was adorable, though very vague – he barely noticed us most of the time. Still, Ariella's besotted by him, and after I had served my purpose I left them to it and came home.' Then Tony had told her that she had returned a much more interesting woman, whatever that meant, and he was considering sending her back for a refresher course the following year. Sofia had been pleased things had returned to normal. She had been surprised at how much she had missed Zaza.

'This party is turning into a nightmare,' Sofia sighed, watching the children stuffing themselves with chocolate. 'One of them is going to throw up any minute, I just know it.'

'Not over my suede trousers or I'll wring his little neck,' said Zaza, stepping back.

'Why don't you go and sit in the drawing room, it's safer in there,' suggested Sofia.

'Actually, I came to tell you that Tony is throwing me a birthday party for my fiftieth this summer.' Zaza smiled broadly. 'I don't know whether I should be celebrating or committing suicide – still, it'll be a summer lunch-party and we'd love you both to come.'

'Of course we'll come. It's not as though we have to go very far, is it?' she laughed.

'Now if you don't mind I might go and sit this one out. Come and find me when it's all over, or at least when they've all washed their hands and faces.'

Back at the tea-party, Honor's face was mottled with pieces of chocolate and cake. Her fair curly hair was studded with Smarties, put there by a sweetly enamoured Hugo Berrins, who was now flicking jelly at the other children, not so sweetly. Sofia rolled her eyes and leant back against the sideboard with Hazel.

'Do you think Honor will ever look the same again?' she said wearily. She had noticed she's been feeling very tired recently.

Hazel smiled and placed her hands on her wide nurse's hips. 'If it weren't for that little monkey,' she said, pointing to Hugo Berrins, 'she'd look as clean as if she'd just been bathed. I'll take her straight up once they've all gone and wash it all away.'

'She has enjoyed it, though, hasn't she?'

'She loves being the centre of attention. No one loves being adored more than Honor.'

'Oh dear, I know where she gets that from,' laughed Sofia wryly.

Finally the mothers wrapped their children in their heavy coats and led them out into the March evening, shouting to Sofia, 'See you at school on Monday.' Sofia waved them off, delighted to see them go and determined to do something different for Honor's fourth birthday. 'I don't think I can cope with this again next year,' she said to Hazel. 'Perhaps we'll just have a small tea-party.'

'Oh, you'll go through it again, Mrs Harrison. It always used to surprise me how mothers would put themselves through that sort of chaos year after year. But the little ones love it, don't they?' Hazel took a sleepy Honor by the hand and led her up the stairs to be bathed. Sofia kissed her little nose, which was the only part of her face not covered in chocolate and jelly, before crossing the hall in search of Zaza.

Zaza was beside the fire listening to music, smoking a cigarette and reading a book on Argentine *estancias*.

'What's that?' asked Sofia, sitting down beside her.

'It's a book called *Estancias Argentinas* – I thought you might like it,' said Zaza.

'Where did you get it?'

'Eddie gave it to me. He's just come back. He's had a wonderful time playing polo out there.'

'Really,' said Sofia impassively.

'What a beautiful book. Was your house like these?'

'Yes, exactly like those.'

'You know, I think Eddie was playing with a friend of yours,' said Zaza. 'In fact I know he was, because Eddie said they talked about you. In fact, they're over here now, in England. He's a professional. He said he knew you.'

'Who was that?' asked Sofia, not sure that she wanted to know.

'Roberto Lobito,' replied Zaza, narrowing her eyes and watching for Sofia's reaction. Eddie had said that Sofia had apparently had a scandalous affair with someone her parents had disapproved of and that is why she had left. She wondered who that man might have been. Sofia relaxed her shoulders and Zaza crossed Roberto Lobito off the list of suspects.

'Oh, him,' she said and chuckled. 'He was always a good player, even then.'

'He's married – an exquisitely beautiful woman. They're over here now until the autumn, I believe. I hope you don't mind but I asked them to my party.'

'Right,' said Sofia. Zaza blew the smoke out of her nose then waved her hand in front of her to push it away from Sofia who hated cigarettes.

'I don't think I've seen a more beautiful woman than Eva Lobito,' she sighed, taking another deep drag.

'Eva Lobito?' Sofia recalled Eva Alarcon from all those years ago and wondered if it was the same person. She had only ever known one Eva.

'What does she look like?' she asked curiously.

'White-blonde hair – like an angel's. Long face, olive skin. Pretty

laugh. Very graceful, long legs, heavy English accent. Charming.'
There was no doubt about it, that description belonged exclusively
to Eva Alarcon, and Sofia was going to see her again, and Roberto,
after all these years. She knew that to see them would bring back
happy memories, trailing in their wake that inevitable melancholia,
but she was curious and her curiosity was stronger than her anxiety.
She longed for the party like one longs for a drink, knowing the
headache and sickness that will surely follow.

Sofia pulled Honor onto her lap and wrapped her arms around her,
hugging her, as was their bedtime ritual, and kissing her pale,
flawless skin.

'Mummy, when I'm big I will be just like you,' the little girl said.

'Will you?' Sofia smiled.

'Then when I'm bigger I will be just like Daddy.'

'I don't think so.'

'Oh yes I will,' she said with certainty. 'I will be just like Daddy.'

Sofia laughed quietly at the child's understanding of a person's
evolution. When she slid between the sheets at nine-thirty, David
stroked her forehead and kissed her. 'You've been very tired
recently,' he commented.

'Yes – I don't know why.'

'You don't think you could be pregnant, do you?'

Sofia blinked up at him hopefully. 'I hadn't thought about that.
I've been so busy with Honor and the horses, I haven't been
counting days. Oh David, you could be right. I hope so.'

'Me too,' he said, bending down to kiss her again. 'Another
miracle.'

Chapter Thirty-Five

Sofia sat on the squat stump of a tree that once dominated the hills. It had been felled by a vicious October wind the winter before. Nothing is invincible, she thought. Nature is stronger than all of us. She looked around at the luminous June morning and enjoyed the splendour of another ephemeral dawn. Placing her hand on her belly, she marvelled at the miracle that was growing inside her, yet her heart shuddered with sadness knowing her family were ignorant of the life she had made for herself across the waters. Nervously, she recalled Roberto Lobito and Eva Alarcon as she had known them, now well over ten years ago, and tried to picture them as they would look today.

What worried her more than seeing them was *not* seeing them. If they decided at the last moment not to attend Zaza's party, the disappointment would be enormous. She had mentally primed herself for this afternoon and her curiosity had increased over the last few months. Having come to terms with the fact that she was going to hear news from home, the thought of that news being denied her was unbearable. She was desperate to know what had become of Santi.

She arrived home in time to have a bath and prepare herself for Zaza's lunch-party. She spent an hour trying on outfits, watched in bewilderment by Sam and Quid who wagged their tails at whatever she put on. 'You're no help at all!' she said, throwing another ensemble onto the bed. When David appeared at the door Sofia had her back to him and was furiously struggling to pull a dress down over her hips. He watched her for a moment before the dogs gave him away.

'I'm fat!' she grumbled, angrily flicking the dress across the room with her foot.

'What's the matter?' he asked, hugging her from behind. They watched their reflection in the mirror.

'I'm fat,' she said again.

'You're not fat, darling, you're pregnant.'

'I don't want to be fat. I can't fit into anything.'

'What do you feel most comfortable in?'

'My pyjamas,' she replied sulkily.

'Okay, wear your pyjamas,' he said and kissed her before wandering into the bathroom.

'Actually, that's not a bad idea,' she said happily, pulling out a pair of white silk pyjamas from the chest of drawers. When David walked back into the room, Sofia stood before him in the drawstring trousers and T-shirt. 'David, you're a genius,' she beamed, admiring her reflection. David nodded, wading through the clutter of shoes and dresses to get to his cupboard. Sam and Quid sniffed their approval.

Tony had erected a white marquee in the garden in case of rain, but as the day was clear and hot the guests stood outside in the sunshine, in floral dresses and suits, drinking glasses of champagne and Pimms and admiring the rambling rusty-bricked manor and flowers that spilled over in abundance wherever one cast one's eye. Zaza darted over to embrace David and Sofia before running after one of the waiters who had emerged prematurely from the house with a tray of smoked salmon.

Zaza did not have a style of her own, but was canny enough to recognise good taste when she saw it. She had spent thousands of Tony's hard-earned pounds hiring decorators and landscape gardeners to transform their home into one which rightly deserved to adorn the pages of *Homes & Gardens*. Sofia appreciated the aesthetic perfection of Pickwick Manor but thought Zaza tried too hard. No sooner was she sucked into the throng of people than Sofia's eyes fearfully searched the faces for Eva and Roberto.

'Sofia, lovely to see you again,' chortled a strange man, bending down to kiss her. His breath smelt of an unpleasant *mélange* of salmon and champagne. She stepped back and frowned up at him blankly. 'George Heavyweather,' he said in a tone that betrayed his disappointment at her lapse of memory. 'Now, surely you can remember where we met?' he asked playfully, nudging her with his elbow.

Sofia sighed irritably, recalling the tactless oaf she had sat next to four years before. 'Ian Lancaster's dinner,' she replied impassively, looking past him into the crowd.

'Absolutely. God, it's been a long time. Where have you been hiding yourself away? You probably haven't noticed that the war's over!' he said and chuckled at his lame joke.

'Excuse me,' said Sofia, shelving her manners. 'I have just seen someone I would prefer to talk to.'

'Oh, yes – well, fine,' he stammered jovially, 'we'll hook up later.' Not if I can help it, thought Sofia as she was promptly swallowed up by the crowd.

Sofia and David had arrived late. After Sofia had spent the best part of half an hour unsuccessfully hunting the grounds for Eva and Roberto she resigned herself sadly to the reality that they had obviously decided not to come. Finding a bench under a shady cedar tree away from the crowds, she sat down despondently. Time was crawling by so slowly. She wanted to go home and wondered if anyone would notice if she quietly slipped away.

Then: 'Sofia?' came a warm husky voice from behind her. 'I've been looking for you.'

'Eva?' gasped Sofia, standing up and blinking in surprise at the elegant white-haired woman who floated into focus.

'*Hace años!*' she breathed into Sofia's neck as she kissed her affectionately. Sofia's head spun as she inhaled Eva's cologne, the same lemon scent she had worn twelve years before. They both sat down.

'I thought you weren't coming,' said Sofia in Spanish, taking Eva's hand and holding it tightly as if she were afraid she might disappear if she let go.

'We were late. Roberto got lost,' Eva explained and laughed prettily.

'It's so good to see you. You haven't changed,' Sofia said truthfully, her gaze washing over Eva's perpetual youth with admiration.

'Neither have you.'

'When did you marry Roberto?' she asked. 'Where is he?'

'He's in the crowd somewhere. We married three years ago. I went to live in Buenos Aires when I finished school and met Roberto at a party. We have a baby, who's also called Roberto — he's heavenly. Ah, you're pregnant,' she said, placing her free hand on Sofia's barely noticeable belly.

'I already have a little girl of three,' she replied and smiled as Honor's face emerged clearly through the fog that had mysteriously clouded her head while she had been talking to Eva.

'*Cómo vuela el tiempo!*' sighed Eva nostalgically.

'Time certainly does fly. It's been twelve years since we met that summer. Twelve years. Seeing you now, it could have been yesterday.'

'Sofia, I can't play games with you and pretend I don't know why you left Argentina and that you haven't been back. If I pretend, our friendship will not be an honest one,' Eva said, her pale blue eyes probing Sofia's questioningly. She placed Sofia's hand between her long honey-coloured fingers and pressed it expressively. 'I beg you to go back,' she said softly.

'I'm happy here, Eva. I'm married to a wonderful man. I have a daughter and another child on the way. I can't go back now. I

407

belong here,' Sofia insisted in alarm. She hadn't expected Eva to bring up the past so suddenly.

'But can't you at least pay them a visit – let them know you're okay? Put the past behind you. So much has happened in the last decade – if you leave it any longer you might leave it too long. You might never be able to connect with them again. They are your family, after all.'

'So tell me then, how's Maria?' Sofia asked, directing the conversation away from a subject Eva could never understand.

Eva withdrew her hands and placed them in her lap. 'She's married,' she replied.

'To whom?'

'Eduardo Maraldi, Dr Eduardo Maraldi. I don't see Maria very often, but when I last saw her she had two children, I think, with perhaps another on the way, I can't remember. Everyone's having children at the moment, it's difficult to keep track. You know Fernando is in exile in Uruguay?'

'Exile!'

'He got mixed up in the guerrilla warfare against Videla. He's okay, and he could have come back to Argentina when the government changed, but to be honest I think he was so shaken up by his experience – they tortured him, you know – that he now lives and works in Uruguay.'

'They tortured him?' gasped Sofia, horrified. She listened to Eva recount the story as she knew it, how Miguel and Chiquita's home had been broken into, how Fernando had been kidnapped and somehow miraculously escaped into Uruguay. Sofia sat petrified by what she heard, regretting that she hadn't been there to lend her support.

'It was hideous,' continued Eva gravely. 'Roberto and I went and stayed with him once – he has a house in Punta del Este, on the beach. He's a different man,' she said, reflecting on the sullen young man who now lived like a hippy writing articles for various Uruguayan newspapers.

'And Santi? Is he all right?' Sofia asked anxiously, wondering how all this had affected him.

'He's married. I've seen him a bit about town. He's still dashingly handsome.' Eva blushed. She hadn't forgotten his kisses. She traced a long finger across her lips absentmindedly. 'His limp is worse for some reason and he has aged. But it suits him. He's still the same old Santi.'

'Who has he married?' asked Sofia, trying to disguise the tremor in her voice lest it betray her. She averted her eyes and cast them out somewhere into the half distance.

'Claudia Calice,' Eva said, her voice lifting at the end of the name enquiringly.

'No, I never knew her. What's she like?' Sofia asked, struggling with that familiar emptiness that now threatened to engulf her once again. She was crushed by the news that he had committed to someone else, and she recalled once more that moment under the ombu tree when he had begged her to run away and marry him. The ghostly resonance of his words still echoed through the corridors of her memory.

'She's very elegant. Dark, glossy hair. Very groomed. Typically Argentine,' said Eva, unaware of Sofia's unremitting attachment. 'She's charming. She's quite social, more at home in the city than in the country. I don't think she likes the country. At least, she confided to me once that she hates horses. She said she had to pretend to Santi who as we all know, lives for them.' Then Eva added in a more gentle tone: 'You didn't know he had married?'

'Of course not. I haven't spoken to him since – well, since I left,' she replied hoarsely and lowered her eyes.

'Surely Santi can't be the reason you haven't been back?'

'No, no. Of course not,' Sofia said a little too quickly.

'Haven't you communicated at all?'

'No.'

'Not even to your parents?'

'Especially not to my parents.'

Eva sat back against the bench and studied Sofia's features in amazement. 'Don't you miss it?' she asked, aghast. 'Don't you miss *them*?'

'I did at the beginning. But it's incredible how you can forget when you're this far away,' she lied forlornly. Then added, 'I have made myself forget.'

They sat in silence, Eva pondering on possible reasons for Sofia's exile and Sofia reflecting sadly on Santi and his life with Claudia. She tried to picture him older, with a heavier limp but she could not. In her mind he was as she had left him, eternally youthful.

'You know Agustin now lives in America, in Washington? He married an American,' said Eva after a while.

'Really? And Rafa?' Sofia asked, trying to sound interested, but all she could think about was Santi and she longed for Eva to talk about him again.

'He married Jasmina Peña years ago. Not long after you left, in fact. Now they are blissfully happy. I don't see much of them. They spend most of their time at Santa Catalina as he looks after the farm. I always liked Rafa, he was somehow safe when all the others were baying for blood. He could always be relied on, not like Agustin,' she said, recalling Agustin's unwelcome attention. While he had been in Buenos Aires he had earned himself something of a reputation, taking girls out, sometimes running a few at the same time. He was the sort of young man mothers warned their daughters about and later girls warned their girlfriends about. No wonder he had married an American, thought Eva. A whole new patch to play around on.

'Is Santi happy?' asked Sofia suddenly, biting her lower lip.

'Yes, I think so. But you know what it's like, people marry, have children and somehow you lose touch with them. I see them every now and again, but Roberto and I travel so much. His polo takes him all over the world and I go with him. I'm rarely in Buenos Aires and I haven't been to Santa Catalina since Fernando left. Fernando and Roberto were so close, now we don't seem to have time to see even him. But when I last saw Santi it was at a wedding in the city,' she recalled.

'Will you tell me about it?' asked Sofia, risking exposing her feelings for a glimpse of Santi. Eva looked at her curiously. She knew Sofia had been sent away to get over an infatuation she had had for her cousin, but Eva had no knowledge of the depth of feeling between them. How could she have known that within, Sofia still wept silently for Santi, that like a balloon she had let him go only to find that he drifted eternally among the clouds in her memory.

'*Bueno*, it was the wedding of a cousin of Roberto's. They have a beautiful *estancia* not far from Santa Catalina, about two hours from Buenos Aires. I had never met Claudia before, but she and Santi had been married for about two years. Yes, it must have been well over two years because they married in 1983, I think, and it was last summer. Santi was stressed out, anyway — there was a *mala honda* between them; they had obviously had a disagreement because they barely spoke to each other. Claudia spent all her time with the little children. She's very good with children. I noticed that they all followed her around like the Pied Piper of Hamelin. I also love children; at that time Roberto and I were trying for a baby. I suspect they were trying too, because they had been married a couple of years and she was so obviously wanting them.

'Anyway, I talked to Santi,' Eva told Sofia. 'He still plays a lot of polo, not professionally like Roberto — actually, I don't think he likes Roberto that much.' She smiled to herself, wondering whether his wariness of her husband might have been due to the fact that he may have wanted her for himself. She remembered once again his kiss and a pink glow diffused across the apples of her cheeks. 'I don't think this is a very good example, because I know he's happy. He's very happy with Claudia. They must have been having a bad day. He was distracted. But he couldn't have been more charming. They both were. Your parents were there, too, by the way. I've always liked your parents, especially your mother. She's warm and kind.'

If Sofia had been listening she would have frowned at that description of her mother, but she was in the clouds with her balloon, thinking about Santi.

'I just don't understand why you can't go back,' Eva said urgently. 'The most difficult part would be seeing everyone again, but after the initial "hellos" surely things would return to normal. I know they'd all be so happy to see you again.'

'Ah, there's Roberto,' said Sofia as Roberto came striding up towards them. He had aged a little. His good looks were undermined slightly by a heavy jaw that seemed to pull his mouth down with it. But he was still handsome.

'I see you've met my wife,' he said, running his hand down Eva's long white hair.

'We had met once before.'

'I've never been in love with anyone like I'm in love with my wife,' he said pointedly. 'She's made me a complete man.'

Sofia smiled. He had always been transparent, she thought as he tried to indirectly tell her that their romance all those years ago had meant nothing. He needn't have bothered; it had meant nothing to her either. After a while she couldn't think of anything else to say to him.

Eva and Roberto watched Sofia walk off towards the tent, where the buffet lunch was being served.

'She's still very beautiful,' Eva said. 'She's a strange girl, you know. Imagine leaving your home like that, without even a word. What sort of person can do that?'

'She was always as stubborn as hell,' Roberto shrugged. 'She was spoilt and independent. Fercho couldn't stand her.'

'Well, she was sweet to me. She really made an effort that time I stayed at Santa Catalina. I'll never forget that. I'm very fond of her – I'm fond of her whole family.'

'Are you going to tell them you saw her?' he asked.

'Of course. I'll tell Anna. I don't want to stir things up, it seems to be a sensitive subject.' Then she added thoughtfully: 'I might be wrong, but I suspect she still cares for Santi. She asked me lots of questions.'

'After so many years? I can't believe it's possible.'

'Oh, it's possible. You don't think she refuses to go back because of him?'

'No. Fercho said she fell out with Anna and Paco and blamed them for making her go to Geneva. He said she was just making a point and that she'd go back in the end. When things get boring over here, she'd go back to put the wind up them at Santa Catalina. Believe me, I know Sofia. She's not capable of a quiet life. She's always caused trouble and she's not going to change now, however wonderful her husband is.'

'Roberto, you're being unkind,' Eva said, shaking her head. 'I'm going to tell Anna that she's well and happy. I think I might get her address from Zaza, then at least Anna can write to her if she wishes to. It's all so unnecessary,' she sighed, standing up. 'I'd never leave you for anything in the world,' she added, embracing him.

'*Amorcita*, you wouldn't leave me, because I wouldn't let you,' he smirked and kissed her. Eva watched Sofia over Roberto's shoulder as she left the tent with a man who must be her husband. They were both carrying plates of chicken and salad. A troubled expression clouded Eva's placid face as she thought of the suffering that Sofia's exile must cause her and she was determined to put an end to it.

Eva's intentions were good ones – but she had underestimated the recipients of her goodwill. When Anna received a letter from Eva, recounting the conversation she had had with Sofia and embellished with details of Sofia's life in England, she turned the attached address over and over in her long white fingers. Eva hadn't anticipated that mother might perhaps be as stubborn as daughter.

Anna had been deeply wounded by her daughter's rejection.

413

Why on earth should she be the one to fly the white flag first? Why, Sofia hadn't even called during the Falklands War, she hadn't called to tell them they were grandparents – she hadn't called, *ever*. She knew where they were, their numbers hadn't changed, and now she expected them to extend the olive branch to her. Well, life wasn't that easy.

Did she think they were heartless? Did she think they didn't care? She had always been difficult and stubborn, but to disappear to the other end of the world without so much as a letter of explanation was very cruel. Paco had never recovered. He had aged, become more introverted. It was as if Sofia had died. Except death would probably have been preferable, understandable, less hurtful. At least they could have mourned her properly instead of the interminable misery of not knowing. Death isn't a rejection. Sofia's disappearance was a deep rejection. She had hurt the whole family, shaken the very foundations of it, and the splinters of their once-treasured unity were scattered across the plains, never to be recovered. No, it wasn't for Anna to make peace, but for Sofia. So she folded the letter away in the drawer which contained her most private things and decided not to tell Paco. He would only try to persuade her to contact their daughter and she didn't want to ignite another row about Sofia.

Chapter Thirty-Six

November, 1997

How strange it is that a person can love someone for a lifetime. That however far away they are, for however long, one can carry their memory in one's heart for an eternity. That is how it had always been for Sofia. She had never stopped loving Santi and little Santiguito. She knew she should not, and in many ways she had closed the book, written the last line, signed off. She had let them go. Like a treasure chest she had dropped them with all her secrets to the bottom of the ocean. But some things never die; they just go quiet for a time.

Sofia had left Argentina in disgrace in the autumn of 1974. She had never thought for one moment that it would be almost twenty-four years before she would return. She had never planned for it to be that way. She had never planned. But the years had somehow rolled on into decades and then one day her past beckoned her home.

Buenos Aires, 14 October 1997
Dearest Sofia,
I gather that you and Maria stopped communicating many years ago. That is why I am writing. There is no easy way to tell you this but Maria is

dying of cancer. I watch her fade each day — you have no idea how difficult it is to watch someone you love disappear little by little before your very eyes when there is nothing you can do to help. I feel quite useless.

I know your lives have taken you in different directions, but she loves you very much. Your presence here would be wonderfully healing. When you left us there was a dreadful void and a deep sadness we all shared. We never expected you to shut us out for ever. I regret that no one made more of an effort to convince you to return. I don't really know why none of us did. We should have — I blame myself. I know you, Sofia, and I know you will have suffered in your 'exile'.

Please, dear Sofia, come home, Maria needs you. Life is precious: Maria has taught me that, I only regret that it has taken me so long to write this.

With my fondest love,

Chiquita

Chiquita's letter burst the abscess that contained Sofia's repressed memories. In a fevered torrent of images they fell about her, dragging up bitterness and regret from their long hibernation. *Maria is dying. Maria is dying.* She turned those words around and around in her head until they were nothing but meaningless, empty syllables. But still they meant death. Death. Grandpa O'Dwyer had always said that life was too short for regrets and for hatred. 'What's gone is gone and what's in the past is in the past and should be left there.' She missed her grandfather. At times like these she needed him so badly. But she was unable to heed his advice when the past invaded her present through all her senses. She wished now that she had had the courage to return years ago. Eva had been right, she had left it too long. She was forty one years old. Forty one! Where had all those years gone? Now Maria seemed a stranger to her.

Sofia re-read the letter with a floundering heart. She wondered how Chiquita had found her. Looking at the envelope she noticed the address was correct, even down to the postcode. She thought about it, turning the letter over and over in her trembling hands.

Then she remembered; Eva must have obtained it from Zaza. Her stomach reeled. After all this time Argentina had finally found her. She didn't have to hide any more and she was grateful.

Eleven years had passed since she had sat under that cedar tree with Eva. Eleven years. How different things might have been had she listened to her and returned home as she had suggested, to let bygones be bygones. But now eleven more years of estrangement added on to the previous twelve made twenty-three years. A lifetime. Could the decomposition of relationships be reversed at such a late stage? Would they even remember her?

Sofia rode over the icy hills. The countryside looked as if it had been sprinkled with a pale blue glitter as the sun rose up behind the forest to melt the frost away. Above her the sky shimmered aquamarine, not a cloud in sight to mar its perfection. She reflected on the last ten years of her life. India had been born in the winter of 1986, giving Honor a little sister to play with, not that she had been very interested in the baby at first. But now they were firm friends and did everything together in spite of the three-and-a-half year age difference. Honor was independent and outspoken; India was quieter, more of a home-bird.

The years had passed swiftly. They had been happy years — sunny years. Yet beneath the fragile surface of her happiness lay the haunting memory of Santi. Rarely a day passed when something had not occurred to remind her of him. However fleeting the thought, however brief her acknowledgement of it, she still remembered him. And she still kept Santiguito's muslin under her mattress. More out of habit than attachment. She had two daughters to occupy her heart. Santiguito was lost somewhere out there in the world and she knew she would never find him. But she couldn't let go. The muslin was all she had left of him and in a strange way, it was all she had left of Santi. So it lay squashed between the bed and the mattress in spite of the little attention she gave it.

As Sofia galloped over the hills she was acutely aware of being alive. She thought about life. Life with all its energy, with all its emotion – with all its adventure. Maria was going to leave it all behind. Suddenly the past became incredibly important because there would be no future for her to share with Maria. Sofia wanted to cling onto it, but like sand in her hands the past slipped through her fingers leaving her with no option but to go forward. She had to go to her.

'I'm sorry that your cousin is ill, but I'm glad that something has finally happened to force you to see sense,' was David's reaction to the news. Sofia was reluctant to leave the children, but he insisted that he could take care of them himself; her trip was too important. She wanted to go and yet at the same time she worried about what she'd find there. David only knew half the story; he had no idea that the man she had loved and lost lived at Santa Catalina. Had he known, she doubted he would have been so happy to send her back. She wondered whether her decision not to tell him about Santi might have been influenced by a subconscious desire to keep the door open. For that very reason she decided not to tell Dominique she was going.

David insisted she pack at once. There was no time to waste deliberating on what it would be like once she got there. He told her to be practical. She was going back to see Maria, she shouldn't think any further than that. He accompanied her to the airport with Honor and India to whom airports suggested holidays and sunny climes, and bought her far too many magazines to read during the long flight. Sofia could tell he was feeling emotional. He always adopted a brisk tone when he was anxious, talked too fast, dwelt on unnecessary details.

'Darling, do you want a novel as well?' he said, picking up one by Jilly Cooper and turning it over to read the back.

'No. These magazines are quite enough,' said Sofia, thanking India who skipped up with a bumper packet of Snickers. 'Sweetie, I couldn't possibly eat all these. If you ask Daddy nicely he might let you choose something for yourselves,' she added, watching Honor making her way through a bag of chocolate raisins, which hadn't been paid for.

Leaving them was difficult. She lingered too long saying good-bye, which reduced India to tears with the stress of it all. At almost eleven years of age, she was still dependent on her mother and had never been separated from her for more than a couple of days at a time. Honor, who was fiercely independent and confident, put her arm around her little sister and promised to cheer her up in the car.

'I'm not going for long, sweetheart. I'll be back before you miss me,' said Sofia, pulling the tearful child into her arms. 'Oh, I love you so much,' she breathed, kissing her wet cheek.

'I love you too, Mummy,' sobbed India, hanging around Sofia's neck like a koala bear. 'I don't want you to go.'

'Daddy will look after you and it's the holidays soon. Lots to look forward to,' she replied, wiping the child's face with her thumbs. India nodded and tried to be brave.

Honor grinned as she kissed her mother and wished her a safe flight, drawing herself up like a grown-up and patting India on her quivering shoulder. David embraced his wife and wished her luck.

'Call me when you arrive, won't you,' he said, placing his lips on Sofia's for a long moment during which he silently prayed that she would be returned to him safely. Sofia waved at her small family before disappearing through passport control. India had managed to force a smile, but once her mother had gone, she disintegrated once more into tears. David took her by the hand and the farewell-party left the airport for home.

It was only when Sofia's was near landing in Buenos Aires that the reality of her situation began to sink in. It had been twenty-three years since she had last stood on Argentine soil. She hadn't seen any of her family for all that time, although she had heard through Dominique that her parents had desperately tried to track her down at the beginning. But Sofia had cut them all off completely. Having deeply resented them for sending her away she had, in a perverse way, enjoyed making them suffer. Dominique had protected her. But as time wore on she had found the longing for her homeland increasingly difficult to bear until she had had to admit to herself that pride was the only thing standing in the way of her return.

David had tried on countless occasions to encourage her to make a visit. 'I'll come with you, I'll be there by your side. We'll go together. You must let go of this bitterness,' he had said. But Sofia hadn't been able to do it. She hadn't been able to let go of her pride. She wondered now how her family were going to react when they saw her.

In her mind's eye she could still see and smell Argentina as she had left it all those years ago; she wasn't prepared for the change. But as the plane descended into the Eseisa Airport, at least the skyline of the city, bathed in the flamingo-pink light of morning, was still very much as she had last seen it. She was overwhelmed with emotion. She was coming home.

There was no one to meet her at the airport, but why should there have been? She hadn't told anyone she was coming. She knew she should have called, but whom? She had chosen to dispense with them all; there was no one she could have turned to – no one. In the old days she would have contacted Santi. Those days were gone.

The moment she stepped out into Eseisa Airport she drew into her nostrils that intoxicatingly familiar smell of caramelised, humid air. Her skin immediately felt damp and her senses swam in the stirring sea of her memories. She looked about her at the dark-skinned officials who stalked around the airport with great importance, bristling with authority beneath their starched uniforms. While she waited for her luggage she glanced at the other travellers, listened to their conversations in Spanish, with the bubbling Argentine accent, and felt that she was truly home. Shedding her English skin like a snake she slunk through customs like the *Porteña* she used to be.

On the other side bustled and jostled an ocean of brown faces, some with placards inscribed with the names of the people they were meeting, others with their children and even their dogs screaming and barking into the stifling air, awaiting relatives and friends returning from lands afar. Their dark eyes watched Sofia as she pushed her trolley through the crowd that parted like the Red Sea to allow her to pass.

'Taxi, Señora?' asked a black-haired *mestizo,* twisting the corners of his moustache with lazy fingers. Sofia nodded.

'Al Hospital Alemán,' she replied.

'De dónde es usted?' asked the man as he pushed her trolley out into the dazzling light. Sofia didn't know whether she recoiled because of the intensity of the sunshine or because her taxi driver had just asked her where she was from.

'Londres,' she replied hesitantly. She obviously spoke Spanish with a foreign accent.

Once in the back of the black and yellow taxi, she sat next to the open window, which she wound down as far as it could go. Her driver lit a cigarette and turned on the radio. His dry brown hands ran roughly down the cool figure of the Madonna that hung from the mirror before he started the engine.

'Do you follow football?' he shouted into the back. 'Argentina beat England in the World Cup of 1986. You must have heard of Diego Maradona?'

'Listen, I'm Argentine, but I've lived in England for the past twenty-three years,' she replied in exasperation.

'No!' he gasped, dragging the sound of the 'O' out of his throat in a long hiss.

'Yes,' she said firmly.

'No!' he gasped again in disbelief that anyone would want to leave Argentina. 'How did you feel during the war of Las Malvinas?' he asked, watching her face in the mirror. She would have preferred him to look where he was going, but the years of being British had refined her manners. If she had been a real Argentine she would have shouted at him rudely. He hooted loudly at a stalling car in front of him and overtook on the wrong side, showing his fist to the equally irate driver by sticking it out of the window and waving it furiously.

'*Boludo!*' He sighed, shaking his head and inhaling the cigarette that hung limply out of the side of his mouth. 'So, how did you feel?'

'It was very difficult. My husband is English. It was a difficult time for both of us. Neither of us wanted that war.'

'I know, it was between the governments, nothing to do with what the people wanted. That piece of shit, Galtieri – I was there in the Plaza de Mayo in 1982 with thousands of others to applaud him for invading the islands, then again a few months later baying for his blood. An unnecessary war. All that bloodshed, for what? A distraction. That's what it was, a distraction.'

As they weaved their way precariously up the freeway that took them straight into the centre of Buenos Aires, she gazed out of the window onto a world that looked to her like an old familiar friend, but wearing a new expression. It was as if someone had built over all her memories, polished away the rust that she had grown up with and loved so deeply. As they drove through the city she noticed the parks were beautifully clean and full of well-trimmed flowerbeds. The shop windows were framed with shiny brass borders and displayed the latest European collections. It looked more like Paris than a South American city.

'This place looks really amazing,' she said. 'It looks so . . . well, I suppose the word is prosperous.'

'You say you haven't been here for twenty-three years, *qué barbaridad!* You missed the Alfonsín years when inflation reached such heights I had to print a new price sheet every day, sometimes twice a day. It got to the stage where I asked for dollars, the only way not to lose money. You know, people lost their life's savings from one day to the next. Terrible. But now things have improved. Menem has been a good President. A good President,' he said, nodding his head in approval. 'The *austrál* was replaced by the *peso* – one *peso* to the dollar. Now that changed everything. We can depend on our currency again and have pride in it. One *peso* to the dollar – imagine that!'

'The streets look fantastic – look at those boutiques.'

'You should see the shopping malls. *Patio Bulrich* and now that fancy *Paseo Alcorta*. You'd think you were in New York. The fountains, the cafés, the shops. There's so much foreign investment now, it's incredible.' Sofia gazed out of the window as they passed a beautifully manicured park. 'Companies look after the parks – it's good advertising for them and means they're clean for our children to play in,' he said proudly.

Sofia's head swam as she breathed in the smell of diesel mingled with the shrubbery and flowers from the park and the sweet scent of chocolate and *churros* from the *kioscos*. She noticed a brown-skinned boy striding across the road towards the park with about twenty pure-bred dogs on leads trotting eagerly behind him. When her driver tuned into the football match between Boca, whom he obviously supported, and River Plate, Sofia knew she had lost him. When Boca scored he swerved so violently across the road that he would have crashed had all the other cars not done the same. Once more he stuck his fist out of the window and tooted his horn to the other cars to display his delight. Sofia watched the small porcelain Madonna swing from the mirror and after a while she found herself drawn into its hypnotic rhythm.

Finally, the taxi halted outside the Hospital Alemán and she paid him with unfamiliar *pesos*. There had been a time when you wouldn't have stepped out of the car until the driver had done so in case he drove off with your bags still in the boot, but Sofia was too eager to get out. She felt carsick. Her driver placed her two bags on the pavement then returned to his radio. She watched him rattle his way up the street and disappear into the swarm of buzzing vehicles.

Weary from her thirteen-hour flight and over-emotional, Sofia went right in, bags and all, and asked for Maria Solanas. When she mentioned her name the nurse frowned momentarily before nodding in acknowledgement.

'Ah, yes,' she said. She wasn't used to people using Maria's family name. 'You must be her cousin – she has spoken a great deal about you.' Sofia felt the colour rise in her cheeks, she wondered what exactly she had been told. 'You're lucky, she's going home this afternoon. You might have missed her.'

'Oh,' Sofia replied blankly. She didn't know what to say.

'You are very early – we don't usually allow visitors until nine a.m.'

'I have come all the way from London,' she explained wearily. 'Maria isn't expecting me. I'd like some time alone with her before her family arrive. I'm sure you understand.'

'Of course.' The nurse nodded sympathetically. 'I have seen your photos. Maria loves to show us photographs. You look . . .' She hesitated uncomfortably, as if suddenly aware that she was on the brink of making a *faux pas*.

'Older?' Sofia suggested helpfully.

'Perhaps,' the nurse mumbled and her cheeks glowed. 'I know she will be so happy to see you. Why don't you go on up – it's the second floor, Room 207.'

'How is she?' Sofia ventured, wanting to prepare herself a little before seeing her cousin.

'She is a very brave lady, and popular. Everyone has grown enormously fond of Señora Maraldi.'

Sofia made her way towards the lift. 'Señora Maraldi' – the name sounded alien to her and Maria suddenly drifted further out of reach, like a small boat disappearing into the mist. Back in England Sofia had tried to absorb the news of her cousin's illness, but it had seemed so far removed from her life that it hadn't touch her like it touched her now. The smell of detergent, the sound of her shoes on the shiny plastic floors that lined the long hospital corridors, the nurses striding purposefully up and down with trays of medicine, the gloom that always lingers in such places penetrated her understanding and suddenly she felt afraid. Afraid of seeing her cousin after all this time. Afraid she might not recognise her. Afraid she wouldn't be welcome.

Sofia hesitated at the door, not sure of what she would see on the other side. With some difficulty she assembled her flagging courage and entered. Through the early morning dimness she saw an unfamiliar figure lying under white sheets. She realised she had foolishly stumbled on some poor invalid sleeping peacefully in the shadows. Embarrassed, she mumbled a quick apology. But then as she was about to turn and leave, a small voice called out her name.

'Sofia?' She turned and blinked into focus. Lying on the bed was indeed her angelic friend, gaunt and grey, smiling over at her. Choked, she stumbled to her bedside and kneeling on the floor buried her face in Maria's outstretched hand. Maria was too overwhelmed to say any more, and Sofia was too moved to look at her. She stayed there for a long while, crushed by what she saw. Maria's illness had changed her; she looked so different Sofia hadn't even recognised her.

Sofia took a while to compose herself. Managing to look up at her cousin once, she only broke down again; all the while Maria remained calm and serene as Sofia abandoned herself to grief. Finally she was able to see her clearly. Pale and emaciated, Maria lay there smiling in spite of the ill fate that was sucking the life out of her.

'I so hoped you'd come back. I missed you so much, Sofia,' she whispered, not because she didn't have the strength to speak, but because the moment was too sacred to shatter with loud words.

'Oh Maria, I missed you too. You have no idea,' sniffed Sofia.

'How funny, you speak Spanish with an accent!' she exclaimed.

'Do I?' replied Sofia sadly. Another part of her home that she had lost along the way.

'Who told you?' asked Maria, gazing into Sofia's livid eyes.

'Your mother – she wrote to me.'

'My mother? I didn't even know she had your address. She must have kept it a surprise in case you didn't come. *Qué divina,*' she said, and smiled the small, grateful smile of a young woman who cherishes each kind gesture, for in the face of death love is the only comfort. 'You look so well.' She ran her hand down Sofia's cheek, wiping away the tears. 'Don't be sad, I'm stronger than I look. It's because I've lost my hair.' She grinned. 'I don't have to bother washing it now – such a relief!'

'You're going to get well,' Sofia insisted.

Maria shook her head sadly. 'I'm not going to get well, not now. In fact, I'm such a hopeless case, they're sending me home to Santa Catalina.'

'But there must be something they can do? They can't give up. You have so much to live for.'

'I know. My children for a start. I worry about them constantly. But they will grow up with love. Eduardo is a good man. Let's not sit here being all negative, there's no point. You have come home, that is all that matters. Right now I am so happy.' And her large eyes glittered with tears.

'Tell me about your husband. I feel I've lost you over the years. Please tell me about him.'

'Well, he's a doctor, he's tall and gawky and kind. I couldn't love any man more than I love Eduardo. He makes me smile on the inside. He's been so strong through all of this mess.'

'And your children?'

'We have four children.'

'Four!' exclaimed Sofia, impressed.

'That's nothing in this country, surely you remember?'

'I just can't believe your little body was able to produce so many.'

'It wasn't little then, I assure you. I was never little.' She laughed.

'I want to meet them all. I want to know them. They're my cousins too!'

'You will. You'll meet all of them at Santa Catalina. They come and see me every day. Eduardo will be here in a minute. He comes in the morning and after lunch and spends most of the evening with me. I have to tell him to go home, or back to work. He looks so tired. I worry about him. Worry about how he'll cope when I'm gone. In the beginning he was my rock, but now, in spite of my illness, I feel I'm his. I can't bear to leave him behind.'

'I can't believe how calm you are about dying,' Sofia said quietly and her heart flooded with love and sadness. Humbled by Maria's courage she reflected on her own selfish pride, the pettiness of which seemed churlish to her now. Oh, the frustration of hindsight that enables you to see the error of your ways when it is too late to make amends, she thought miserably. Neither dared talk about Santi.

'And what has become of the Sofia I grew up with? Who has broken your spirit?'

'Maria, you never used to be this strong. *Por Dios*, I was always the strong one.'

'No, you always pretended to be strong, Sofia. You were naughty and rebellious because you craved your mother's attention. She gave it all to your brothers.'

'Perhaps.'

'I've had my moments of despair, of fear, believe me. I've asked, "Why me? What have I done to deserve this miserable ending?" But finally you just have to go along with it, accept it and make your last days as happy as possible. I have put my trust in God. I know death is nothing more than a gateway into another life. It's not goodbye but farewell. I have faith,' she said serenely and Sofia believed that she had, indeed, found some sort of inner peace.

'So, you married a theatre producer?' said Maria brightly.

'How do you know?' Sofia asked in surprise.

'Because there was a feature on you during the Malvinas War in one of the papers.'

'Really?'

'Yes, an Argentine living in England during the conflict. There was a picture. We all saw it.'

'How strange. I thought of you all so much then. I felt I was betraying my country,' Sofia confessed, remembering that difficult time when she was torn between her homeland and the new home she had adopted.

'Look how English you are. Who'd have thought? What's he like?'

'Oh, he's much older than me. He's kind, very clever, a wonderful father. He treats me like a princess,' said Sofia proudly and pictured David's intelligent face.

'Good for you. How many children?'

'Two girls. Honor and India.'

'What beautiful names. Honor and India,' she repeated. 'Very English.'

'Yes, they are,' she replied and pictured India crying at the airport. She was debilitated momentarily by a pang of anxiety before Maria's questions brought her back to the present.

'I always knew you'd have something to do with the theatre. You were a prima donna from the moment you were born. Do you remember all those plays we put on as children?'

'I was always the boy,' laughed Sofia.

'Well, the boys never wanted to join in. How embarrassing!' She sighed. 'Do you remember making the grown-ups pay to watch us?'

'Yes, I do. What did we do with the money?'

'Well, it was meant to go to charity. I think we spent it at the *kiosco.*'

'Do you remember the time Fercho bribed Agustin to run naked through our finale dance?'

'Yes, I do. Dear Fercho. You know he's in Uruguay?' Maria sighed sadly.

'Yes, I do. I saw Eva Alarcon – you remember Eva, don't you?'

'Of course. She married your Roberto.'

'He was never my Roberto,' said Sofia defensively. 'Anyway, they were in England and filled me in a little.'

'Agustin's still in Washinton. He comes to visit about once a year although his wife doesn't like it much. Poor Agustin – if he's ever allowed to come home he does so alone. I don't think his wife is very nice. Agustin deserved better. But Rafa's here with Jasmina. He has such beautiful children. You'll love Jasmina.'

Maria told Sofia as much as she could about the past. She wanted to. She felt that perhaps by telling her cousin she would somehow feel included and then maybe the years wouldn't appear to have been so many, or so long. Sofia listened, often moved, sometimes amused, while her cousin recounted her life and the lives of her family from the moment that Sofia had been taken from them.

When she finished Sofia was still kneeling beside her bed clutching her cousin's bony hand in hers. Maria used to be curvaceous, 'womanly' Paco once called her. Now she was gaunt and had lost all her hair, but her smile held all those innocent moments they had shared at Santa Catalina and she longed so much to turn the clock back and relive them again.

'Sofia, all these years . . .' sighed Maria sadly.

'Oh Maria, I cannot begin to tell you.' Sofia silenced her with the wave of her hand.

'Sofia, I'm so sorry.'

'Me too. I should never have stayed away for so long. I should have . . .'

'Let me speak, you don't know the whole truth.' Maria's face was full of shame.

'What do you mean, Maria? What truth?'

Maria's hazelnut eyes, as large as marbles, shone with remorse. She swallowed hard, trying to control her emotions that grappled their way to the surface, dragging up the guilt that for years had plagued her conscience with poison.

'I lied to you, Sofia. I lied to you and I lied to Santi.' She turned her face away. She couldn't look at her cousin; she was too ashamed.

'How? What do you mean?' Sofia suddenly felt a cold draught slip in through the crack in the door and shivered. *Please not you, Maria. Not you!* She prayed silently.

'When I found out that you and my brother had been lovers I was so angry. You used to tell me everything and yet you had completely shut me out. I was one of the last to know and you were meant to be my best friend.' Large tears rolled down her cheeks, dropping onto her pillow.

'Maria, I couldn't tell you. I couldn't tell anyone. Just look at the reaction we received. There was no way anyone would have let me marry my first cousin. It was disgraceful!'

'I know, but I felt so left out, and then you went away. You never wrote. You just wrote to Santi. You never even bothered to drop me a line. It was as if I meant nothing to you. Nothing at all.'

Sofia suddenly realised what Maria was trying to say. 'You made sure he didn't get my letters, didn't you?' she said slowly, but her mind was in turmoil. She would never have believed it if Maria had not told her personally. It was so unlike her to be vindictive. Yet, she couldn't hate her. She was dying. She couldn't hate her.

'I saw how upset Mama was. She was inconsolable. We all felt betrayed. Saddened. It tore our family apart. Mama and Anna barely spoke for a year! And it was years, literally, before life went back to normal again. Santi had a bright future. Papa was desperate that he was going to throw it away because of you. So I wrote and . . .'

'Told me that he had fallen in love with Maxima Marguiles.' That letter had shattered all Sofia's dreams, like a mirror that had reflected her strongest desires, splintered into a thousand pieces. The following year in London had been the bleakest of her life. No wonder Santi had never written; he had been waiting to hear from her. He wouldn't have known where to reach her. He must have waited like she had, after all. *He hadn't stopped loving her.*

The weight of these revelations crushed her spirit and she sat on the floor mute with disbelief, gutted of any feeling at all. She had given away her child because she had believed he hadn't wanted them. But he had, he *had* wanted them. The last twenty-three years had been lived out in response to a misunderstanding, in response to a lie. Maria would never know what she had done.

'Please forgive me, Sofia. Please try to understand why I did it. I lied. He didn't even know a Maxima Marguiles. He was miserable without you.' Maria inhaled deeply and closed her eyes. How fragile she looked, and how tired. Her skin was sallow and lifeless; when her eyes were shut she appeared almost dead except for the gentle rise and fall of her chest as she breathed.

Sofia slumped onto the cool linoleum floor, recalling those long hours spent wishing and praying that he would come and find her. No wonder he had never come.

'But you could have returned, Sofia. You didn't have to run away for ever.'

'Maria, I never ran away! I was sent away,' Sofia snapped angrily.

'But you didn't come back. Why all this time? Please tell me it wasn't just because of me?' Maria opened her eyes and looked at her cousin imploringly. 'Please tell me it wasn't because of what I told you?'

'I didn't come back because . . .'

'You had everything here, everyone loved you, why did you throw it all away?'

'Because . . .' she choked desperately.

'Why, once time had diminished your feelings for each other, why didn't you come back? I've felt so guilty for so long. Please tell me it wasn't because you despised me. Why, Sofia, *why*?'

'Because if I couldn't have Santi I didn't want Argentina, or Santa Catalina. Without him there was nothing for me here.'

Maria looked at Sofia and her expression changed from self-pity to amazement.

'You loved my brother that much? I'm so sorry,' she said in a low voice.

Sofia could not speak. Her throat had constricted, leaving her numb with anguish. Maria gazed at her cousin with solicitous eyes.

'Then it is my fault,' she said sadly. 'I was wrong. I had no right to meddle in your life. I had no right to take your love away.'

Sofia shook her head and smiled bitterly. 'No one took it away, Maria. I shall love Santi until I die.'

Those words had scarcely had time to settle when the door swung open and in walked Santi. Sofia was still sitting on the floor. The sunlight now flooded into the room and she winced in the brightness. At first he didn't recognise her. He smiled politely, those familiar green eyes revealing a certain sadness they hadn't had before. The gloss of youth had been replaced with lines and creases that gave his face a ripe wisdom and charm. He too was heavier than he had been back then, but he was still Santi, the same, irreplaceable Santi.

Then a spark of recognition struck him in the face and his cheeks strung crimson before draining of colour altogether.

'Sofia?' he gasped.

'Santi.' Sofia wanted to run into his arms and bury herself in the familiar smell of him, but a petite, dark-haired woman entered the room behind him followed by a tall, thin man and she had no choice but to remain by Maria's side.

'Sofia, I want you to meet Claudia, Santi's wife, and Eduardo, my husband,' Maria said, detecting her cousin's discomfort. Nothing could have prepared Sofia for that moment. Although she had known for years that he had married, just like herself, in her dreams he was always there for her. Drowning in disappointment she pulled herself up. She shook hands with them, deliberately ignoring the Argentine custom of kissing. She just couldn't kiss the woman who had taken her place in Santi's heart.

'I must go, Maria,' she said, desperate to leave the room. She had to get out. She had to be left alone to think all this over.

'Where are you staying?' the dying woman asked, concerned.

'The Alvear Palace Hotel.'

'Perhaps Santi will take you to Santa Catalina, won't you, Santi?'

He nodded in bewilderment without taking his eyes of her. 'Sure,' he mumbled.

As Sofia passed him on her way out their eyes locked together for a second as they had done so many times in the past, and in them she recognised the Santi she had grown up with and loved. In that brief moment she realised that her return was going to bring her more pain than her departure had done twenty-three years before.

Chapter Thirty-Seven

Thursday, 6 November 1997

Sofia returned to the Alvear Palace Hotel emotionally depleted. Once in her room she shed her clothes, creased and sweaty from her journey, and fell into the shower. She let the water pound onto her skin and enfold her in mist. She wanted to lose herself. She wanted Santi's face to disappear into the steam. And yet the tears came as readily as the water and Santi's face clung to her thoughts. She knew she should stop but allowed herself the luxury of sobbing loudly and in private. When she finally emerged her skin was as wrinkled as a rhino's and her eyes sore from crying.

Sofia hadn't expected to see Santi. She didn't know when she expected she would see him, certainly not in her first hour of being in the country. Her nerves hadn't been prepared for the double shock. Maria's dying body had been enough without the appearance of the man she had never ceased to love. She had hoped to see him later, when she had had time to prepare. She must have looked terrible. She cringed. She had always been vain, and although their lives had taken different routes she still wanted him to want her.

From what Maria had told her, they both believed the other to have betrayed them. Now the truth was known, what was he thinking? Supposing he had waited until he truly believed she had forgotten him? Suppose he had been anticipating her return to find the years passing without a word. She could barely think about it without feeling sick with longing to hold him and tell him of the months she had awaited his letters, only to receive nothing and to give up completely. What wasted years. And now what?

She reached for the telephone. She wanted to speak to David, just to hear his voice. She sensed the danger in seeing Santi again and didn't trust herself. She was about to dial the number when it rang. She sighed and picked up the receiver.

'Señor Rafael Solanas for you in reception,' said the concierge.

'In reception?' News travels fast in Buenos Aires — her brother had found her. 'You had better send him up,' she replied.

Sofia threw on the white fluffy hotel dressing gown and brushed her wet hair back off her face. She studied her swollen eyes in the mirror. How could she expect Rafael to recognise her when she didn't even recognise herself. What was he going to say? She hadn't seen or heard from him in what felt like a lifetime.

He knocked, she waited. She stood a moment watching the door as if it was about to open all by itself. When he knocked again, this time impatiently, she had no choice but to open it. When he entered they stood and looked at each other for a brief moment. The years hadn't changed him. If anything, he had got better-looking. He was obviously happy and his happiness radiated about him like an aura that extended itself towards her and engulfed her. He smiled and threw his arms around her, lifting her off the ground. She felt like a child as her feet dangled off the floor. Involuntarily she responded with equal affection and embraced him. The gulf that time had assembled between them seemed to have existed only in her mind.

After a while they both laughed into each other's bodies.

'It's good to see you,' they stammered in unison and then laughed again. He took her hand and led her to the bed where they spent the next couple of hours sitting and just talking, about old times, present times and the lost years. Rafael was a very contented man. He told her about Jasmina, and how he had fallen in love with her back in the early 1970s, when Sofia was still at Santa Catalina. He reminded her that she was the daughter of the eminent lawyer Ignacio Pena. 'Mama was weak with delight,' he said. 'She had always admired Alicia Pena.' Sofia remembered her mother's snobbery with a cringe, but Rafael seemed to float above those trivialities as one can when one is truly happy. He had five children – the eldest was fourteen, the youngest only a couple of months. Sofia didn't think he looked old enough to have a daughter of that age.

'You know Maria is to be taken down to Santa Catalina this evening?' he said finally. Having avoided the subject they were cruelly jolted back to the present.

'I know,' she replied, feeling the pleasure of their reunion dissolve with the reminder of her morning visit to the hospital.

'I'm afraid she will die, Sofia, but it will be a relief for her. She has been so sick. In so much pain.'

'I feel guilty, Rafa. If I had known she was to have such a short life I would never have been so selfish. I wouldn't have stayed away so long. I wish I had come back sooner.'

'You had your reasons,' he said without bitterness.

'I wish I had shared her life. We were best, best friends. I feel such loss.'

'Life is too short for regrets, Grandpa used to say that. Do you remember?' She nodded. 'You're here now, aren't you?' He looked at her with tenderness and smiled. 'You don't need to go back to England. You're home now.'

'Oh, I'll have to go back at some stage, the girls will be driving David up the wall!'

'They're my nieces, my family, they must come home too, Sofia. You belong at Santa Catalina. You should all come out and live here.' He sounded just like their father, she thought.

'Rafa, it's impossible, my life is in England now. You know that.'

'It doesn't have to be. Have you seen Santi yet?'

Sofia felt her cheeks sting at the mention of his name. She tried to act natural. 'Yes, briefly at the hospital,' she said casually.

'Did you meet Claudia?'

'His wife? Yes. She looked . . . very nice.'

Her brother didn't notice how difficult it was for her to talk about Santi, let alone his wife. For Rafael, her affair with Santi was part of another life that they all once shared but which was now so long ago it no longer counted. He didn't suspect, not even for a moment, the love that burned with her every thought of Santi, as if with the long years that too had passed into distant memory.

'I am driving down to Santa Catalina this afternoon. Will you come?' he asked casually. She was relieved not to have to rely on Santi to take her. She wasn't ready to confront him yet.

'I don't know. I haven't seen Mama or Papa for years, they don't even know I'm here.'

'Then it will be a surprise.' He beamed cheerfully.

'Not a pleasant one, I suspect. But yes, I'll come. I'll come for Maria.'

'Good. We'll have a late lunch. Jasmina and the children are already on the farm. As it's a Thursday we had to take them out of school so they could be there when Maria arrives.'

'I so look forward to meeting them all,' she gushed, trying to sound enthusiastic.

'They'll love you, they've heard all about you.'

Sofia wondered what exactly they had heard. Before she left for the country later that day she called David. She told him she missed him, which was true, she did, and she suddenly wished he had flown out with her.

'Darling, you're better on your own. You need time alone with your family,' he said, touched to know she needed him. He didn't know how much.

'I don't know whether I want this after all,' she said, biting her thumbnail anxiously.

'Darling, you do, you're just scared.'

'You're so far away.'

'Now you're being silly.'

'I wish you were here. I don't want to do this alone.'

'You'll be fine. Anyway, if it's really that bad you can just take the next plane home.'

'You're right – I can, can't I,' she replied, relieved. If things got difficult she could simply leave – easy! After all, she'd done it before. David passed her on to her daughters who chatted away enthusiastically, unaware of the cost of the call. Dougal, the new spaniel puppy, had already eaten most of David's socks and had managed to chew his way through the telephone cord. 'It was a miracle your call got through at all!' giggled Honor. When Sofia replaced the receiver she felt much stronger.

Buenos Aires disturbed her. She felt like a tourist where once she had belonged. She knew every side street and watched the shadows of her past haunt the sidewalks and plazas replaying scenes from long ago. She wondered if Santa Catalina would evoke the same sensations and it troubled her. Once again she began to wish she had never come.

However, to her delight, the drive out to the countryside became increasingly familiar. They left the sprawling, cancerous city behind, passing fewer and fewer houses until they reached the long, straight roads of her youth that cut through the plains like old scars. She breathed again the well-known scents of her childhood. The sweet grass, the dust and the unmistakable, intoxicating eucalyptus.

When they arrived at the gates of Santa Catalina it was as if those twenty-three years had been no more than a dream. Nothing had changed. The smells, the sun filtering in lucid shafts through the avenue of maple trees onto the dusty drive, the skinny dogs, the fields full of ponies and as they approached even the house, her home, was the very same one she had left behind.

438

Nothing had changed.

They drew up outside the house and parked under one of the tall, shadowy eucalyptus trees. Sofia noticed a group of young children playing on the swings in the park; they recognised the car and came running towards them. They almost knocked Rafael over in their enthusiasm to embrace him. Sofia realised immediately that two of them were his children. The girl was blonde with a naughty expression on her face; her younger brother had auburn hair like his grandmother.

'Clara, Felix, say hello to *Tia* Sofia.'

The little boy squirmed with embarrassment around his father's legs so Sofia just smiled at him. The little girl, however, marched boldly up to her and kissed her. 'If you're my aunt how come I've never seen you before?' she asked, looking her straight in the eye.

'Because I live in England,' she replied.

'Granny lived in Ireland, you know. Do you know Granny?'

'Yes, I know Granny – she's my mother. You know, your father and I are like you and Felix, brother and sister.'

Clara narrowed her eyes and scrutinised her. 'Then how come no one's ever talked about you before?'

Sofia glanced at Rafael and from the expression on his face she could tell that little Clara was something of a menace.

'I don't know, Clara, but I can promise you they'll all be talking about me now.'

The child's eyes widened with the whiff of scandal and, grabbing Sofia's hand enthusiastically, she announced that her grandparents were taking tea on the terrace.

In a strange way this child, probably about ten years old, gave Sofia confidence. She reminded Sofia of herself at that age – spoilt and unpredictable. It struck her that these children's young lives were echoing her own childhood. She remembered how they used to play on the swings, ran around in groups just like them. Santa Catalina hadn't changed at all, it was only the people who changed as a new generation appeared and grew up there, like a play that evolved in front of a consistent backdrop.

Sofia followed Clara around to the front of the house. Later she would laugh when she remembered the expressions on the faces of her mother and father as they sat in the tranquillity of the long afternoon shadows gazing as they always did out onto the distant plains. A typical day on the farm, nothing unusual, nothing to disturb their routine or so they thought. The sight of them brought it all back and she confidently strode up to them.

When Anna saw Sofia she dropped her teacup onto the terracotta paving stones, shattering the china into large pieces. Her long white fingers shot straight to the necklace around her throat, which she twisted in agitation. She looked to Paco for guidance. Paco went very pink in the face and staggered to his feet. The sight of his sad eyes brimming with remorse was enough to stir Sofia's distant heart.

'Sofia, I don't believe it. Is it really you?' he asked huskily and shuffled forward to embrace her. As with Rafael, she felt herself respond with unchecked affection. 'You don't know how much we have longed for this moment. So much, we missed you so much. I am so happy you are home,' he said with genuine joy. Her father had aged so dramatically since she had last seen him that she felt the bitterness dissipate.

Anna remained seated. She wanted to embrace her child, she had imagined she would, but now suddenly her daughter stood before her with distant eyes, she didn't know what to do.

'Hello, Mama,' Sofia said in English. As Anna hadn't stood up to greet her daughter, Sofia didn't approach her.

'Sofia, what a surprise. I wish you'd let us know,' she said confused, then wished she hadn't said it. She hadn't meant it to sound like that. She anxiously smoothed back her rusty hair that she had tied into a severe bun at the nape of her neck. Sofia had forgotten how cold her blue eyes were. In spite of the many years that should have mellowed their differences, she felt no affection for Anna. She was a stranger to her. A stranger who reminded her of someone from her past who had been a mother to her.

'I know. There just wasn't time,' she replied coldly, not sure of how to interpret the woman's apparent indifference. 'Anyway, I came for Maria,' she added.

'Of course,' her mother replied, regaining her composure. For a moment Sofia was sure she saw disappointment set Anna's cheeks aflame, then spread in a hot rash over the diaphanous skin of her throat.

'Have you seen her yet? She is so changed,' Anna said sadly, casting her eyes across the plain as if she longed to be far away among the long grasses and beasts of the *pampa*. Away from this interminable human suffering.

'Yes, I have,' replied Sofia, chastened. She lowered her eyes and suddenly an overwhelming sense of loss caused her chest to compress. Maria had shown her how fragile human life was and how precarious. She looked down at her mother and her resentment softened.

At that moment Soledad rushed out to clear up the china followed eagerly by an over-excited Clara.

'You should have seen *Abuelita*'s face. She went white, and then she dropped her cup – *imagináte* . . .'

Soledad hadn't aged but she had expanded like a prize cow at a village *fête*. When she saw Sofia standing before her, those watery brown eyes liquified into a river of tears that cascaded down her face and into her wide smile that gaped in surprise. She pulled Sofia into her familiar bosom and sobbed uncontrollably. 'I don't believe it. Thank You, God. Thank You for bringing my Sofia back to me,' she cried.

Clara hopped up and down with excitement as the other children who had been playing with her on the swings stood around in bewilderment.

'Clara, go and tell everyone that Sofia has returned,' said Rafael to his daughter, who immediately strode up to her cousins and delegated the task to them. They shuffled off reluctantly, followed by a few bony dogs sniffing at their heels.

'*Tía* Sofia, everyone is very pleased to see you,' she grinned, as Soledad swept up the china with unsteady hands. Sofia sat down at the table — the same one that she had sat at so many times all those years ago — and pulled the child onto her knee. Anna watched her warily while Paco clutched his daughter's hand in his but could no longer find the words to speak. Both sat in silence but Paco's tears communicated with Sofia more than he could ever have in syllables. Rafael calmly helped himself to cake.

'Why is *Abuelito* crying?' whispered Clara to her father.

'They are tears of joy, Clara. *Tía* Sofia has been away for a very long time.'

'Why?' Sofia noticed she was directing her question at her.

'It's a long story, *gorda*. Maybe I'll tell you one day,' she replied and caught her mother's eye.

'That would be highly inappropriate, don't you think?' she said in English, but Anna wasn't chastising her. She was trying to display a sense of humour.

'I understood that,' laughed Clara, who was clearly enjoying the scene. The more she sensed intrigue the more she liked her new aunt.

Before the conversation could get her into more trouble people began to arrive from every corner of the farm. Groups of curious children, Sofia's nephews and nieces, Chiquita and Miguel — a very tall Panchito, and to her horror a beautiful, radiant Claudia. Sofia was touched by the welcome, the warmth of which she could never have anticipated or hoped for. Her Aunt Chiquita embraced her for a long time. In her eyes Sofia could see that she was grateful she had come home to comfort Maria through her last days. She looked tired and strained and wore a haunted expression on her face where there had once been a gentle beauty. Chiquita had always been serene, as if the cruel world had never invaded her benevolent existence. Maria's illness had all but broken her.

Sofia couldn't help but notice Claudia's grace; she was every-thing that Sofia was not. She was feminine, dressed in the sort of dress that Sofia had welcomed Santi back from America in, the one he had hated. Her long dark hair was loose and flowing and her face perfectly painted but not overdone. If Santi had tried to find a woman who least resembled her he couldn't have done a better job. Sofia wished she had made more of an effort to get her figure back after India was born.

Although Claudia kept her distance Sofia could feel her every move. She didn't know whether Santi had told her the whole story, but she jealously wanted her to know. She wanted her to understand that Santi had always been meant for her, that Claudia had been his second choice, a substitute. She couldn't bear to talk to her so she turned her attention to the children, but like an animal marking her territory Claudia bristled with mistrust beneath those cool, smiling eyes.

Sofia recognised one of Santi's sons immediately by the way that he walked. Slow, laid-back and confident. He must have been about ten years old. She whispered into Clara's ear and she called him over bossily.

'You must be Santi's son,' said Sofia, suffering a gnawing pain in her chest, for in this child she saw what could have been hers.

'Yes, who are you?' he replied arrogantly, sweeping his blond hair out of his eyes.

'I'm your cousin Sofia.'

'How come you're my cousin?'

'She's my aunt. *Tía* Sofia!' laughed Clara, taking Sofia's hand affectionately in hers and squeezing it.

The boy looked mistrustful and narrowed his large green eyes suspiciously. 'Ah, you're the one who lives in England,' he said.

'That's right,' she replied. 'Do you know, I don't even know your name?'

'Santiago.'

The colour drained from Sofia's face. 'That's a bit confusing, isn't it?'

'I suppose.'

'So what do they call you?'

'Santiguito,' he replied.

Sofia swallowed hard in an attempt to retain control of her feelings. 'Santiguito?' she repeated slowly. 'Are you a good polo-player like your father?' she croaked, watching him shift his weight from one foot to the other.

'Yes, I'm playing with Papa tomorrow afternoon. You can watch if you like.'

'I would like that very much,' she replied and he smiled tentatively, lowering his eyes. 'What else do you guys do? You know, when I was a child we used to make wishes in the ombu tree. Do you do that?'

'Oh no, Papa doesn't let us go there. It's out of bounds,' he said.

'Out of bounds, whatever for?' she asked curiously.

'I've been there,' whispered Clara proudly. 'Papa says that *Tío* Santi's angry at the tree because he made a wish once and it didn't come true. That's why he doesn't let us visit it. It must have been a very important wish for him to be so angry.'

Sofia suddenly felt nauseous and in need of space. She pushed Clara gently off her knee and walked briskly in the direction of the kitchen, bumping straight into Santi.

Chapter Thirty-Eight

———————

'Santi!' she gasped, blinking the mist from her eyes.

'Sofia, are you all right?' he said quickly. His hands held her upper arms more tightly than he meant to and his eyes searched her face as if probing her features for her thoughts.

'Oh, I'm fine,' she stammered, resisting the impulse to throw herself against him as if those twenty-three years had been but a blink in the eye of time.

'I gather you came down with Rafa. I called your hotel but you had already left,' he said, unable to disguise the disappointment in his voice.

'Oh yes,' she replied. 'I'm sorry, I didn't . . .'

'That's fine, don't worry,' he assured her. There followed an uncomfortable moment of silence during which neither could think of anything to say. Sofia blinked at him helplessly and he grinned back bashfully, feeling inadequate. 'Where are you off to at such speed?' he said finally.

'I wanted to see Soledad, I haven't really had a chance to chat to her. You remember how close we were.'

'Yes, I do remember,' he said and his sea-green eyes bore into hers like a light from a lighthouse beckoning her home.

That was the first mention of the past. She felt her throat go dry as she remembered sadly how it had been Soledad who had delivered her desperate note to him that night they had met for the last time. She felt herself sinking into his gaze. He was trying to communicate something without being able to find the words. She wanted to talk about the past – there were so many things she wanted to say – and yet now was not the moment. Sensing twenty pairs of eyes watching them from the terrace she once more cautioned herself against revealing too much. She saw the pain and years of loneliness etched in lines on his brow and around the eyes, and she longed to run her fingers over them and erase them. She wanted him to know that she had suffered too.

'I met your son – Santiguito. He's so like you,' she said, for want of anything better to say. His shoulders sagged with disappointment that their conversation had been reduced once more to the mundane. He suddenly retreated into indifference. A wall had at once been erected between them and Sofia didn't know why.

'Yes, he's a good boy, he plays a fine game of polo,' he replied flatly.

'He told me you are both going to play tomorrow afternoon?'

'It depends how Maria is.'

Sofia had been so blinkered by her own preoccupations she had completely forgotten about Maria; after all, she was the reason Sofia had come out.

'When are they bringing her home?' she asked.

'This evening. You will come over, won't you? I know she will want to see you.'

'Of course.'

He shuffled uncomfortably and looked down at the paving stones. 'How long are you staying?' he asked.

'I don't know. I came out to see Maria before . . . to spend some time with her. I haven't thought any further than that. I'm so sorry,' she said, instinctively touching his hand. 'This must be a horrible time for you.'

He withdrew and fixed her with distant eyes that only a moment ago had been welling with emotion. '*Bueno*, Sofia, I'll see you later,' he said, and wandered out onto the terrace.

Sofia noticed his limp had got worse. She watched him go a moment. She suddenly felt very lonely. She didn't go into the kitchen immediately but made her way instead to where her bedroom had once been, only to find that it was exactly as she had left it twenty-three years ago. Nothing had changed.

Her heart pounded with excitement. It was as if she had opened a door to her past. She wandered around picking things up, opening cupboards and drawers; even the lotions and scents she had used were still on the dressing table. What choked her most was the basket of red ribbons she had always worn in her hair. She sat before the mirror and held one between her fingers. Slowly she let her hair down until it fell over her shoulders; it wasn't as long as it had been back then, but she managed to plait it. She tied it with the ribbon and sat gazing at her reflection.

She ran her fingers over her face that had once glowed with the gift of youth. Now the surface was thinner, dryer and the lines around her eyes revealed the years of sadness and the years of joy. Every emotion was stamped into her features like a kind of physical passport displaying the many places she had visited in her life. The low places of torment and the high places of delight. The laughter, the tears, the bitterness and finally the humble resignation that comes when one realises that it is only futile and self-destructive to fight life. She was still good-looking, she recognised that. But youth is something that one takes for granted and is only appreciated when it is lost. She had been young once, young and brave and headstrong. She looked at the mirror and longed to jump through it into the past and relive it all again.

Every item in the room dragged her back to those languid days at Santa Catalina and she bathed in the wistful pleasure they gave her. In the cupboard every piece of clothing told a story, like a museum of her life. She laughed at the white dress she had worn for Santi's return that was still scrunched up in a ball at the back of the shelf and the stack of jeans she had worn every day. It was fascinating. Of course she couldn't have got into anything had she wanted to, she was no longer a size eight. But the shirts and sweaters would have fitted. She longed to put it all on and walk out onto the terrace.

'When we sent you away I always expected you to come back.' Sofia turned to find her mother standing uncomfortably in the doorway. 'So I left yer room as it was.' She spoke in English, it seemed a release for her to talk in her own language. She walked over to the window and ran her hand down the curtains. 'When you didn't return I couldn't bear to clear yer room out. There was always a chance that you might change yer mind. I didn't know what to do with yer things. I didn't want to throw anything away in case . . .' Her voice trailed off.

'No, everything's as I left it,' replied Sofia, sitting on the bed.

'Yes, it just happened like that. I have never had to move you out. Rafael has built a house, Agustin lives in the States, Paco and I are now alone. You can stay here as long as you want to. Unless you have somewhere else you would prefer to stay?'

'No, I hadn't given it any thought actually, so this would be very nice. Thank you.' Then she couldn't resist it so she added, 'Just like old times!' She turned and to her surprise, her mother's brittle expression softened and she detected the beginnings of a smile.

'Let's hope not,' Anna replied.

As she closed the door to her room and made her way over to Chiquita's house later that evening, Sofia recalled those idyllic days when her romance with Santi was still undiscovered and her mother and she were friends. That summer had been the happiest of her life. She remembered those days and her heart was filled once more with the secret hope that she could somehow relive them.

Maria was sitting up in bed in a pale blue night-dress. She looked celestial. Although she had no hair, her skin was as translucent as gauze and her sherry eyes shone with pleasure.

'It is just magic to be at home,' she enthused, pulling two of her smaller children to her and kissing their tanned faces lovingly. 'Eduardo, get Sofia the photo album, I want to show her the years she missed.'

Unlike the hospital the atmosphere was one of happiness. Chiquita's house was full of warmth, music and laughter, the sultry night bathed in the sweet scents of damp grass and jasmine. Santi and Claudia had no country house of their own so they stayed with his parents at weekends and during the school holidays. She could see why Santi had never wanted to leave. This house was his home, and the echoes of an enchanted childhood still reverberated off the walls.

Santi and Sofia barely exchanged words as she sat and talked the hours away with his sister and mother, but they were very conscious of the other's presence. The women laughed about the adventures they had had, one story striking the memory of another, and the years of separation slowly melted away. When they left Maria asleep in her brightly decorated room full of flowers Sofia felt as if they had never been parted.

'You know, Chiquita, it is so good to see Maria again,' she said as they entered the sitting room. 'I'm glad I came.'

'It has done Maria the world of good. She missed you so much. I think you have given her the will to live perhaps a little longer.' Sofia embraced her aunt. The fear and uncertainty of the last few months had eaten away at Chiquita's spirit and stretched her emotions to their limit. She was as fragile as a twig.

'You and your family are what Maria cherishes. *You* give her the will to live. Look how happy she is to be at home. Her final days will be peaceful and full of joy.'

'You're so right, my dear Sofia,' and then she looked at her through her tears and whispered, 'and what are we going to do with you, eh?'

'What do you mean? I shall return to my family, of course.'

Chiquita nodded with understanding. 'Of course,' she said gently, but she smiled and her eyes traced Sofia's features as if she were reading the feelings they betrayed.

449

Santi and Claudia were sitting quietly reading magazines. Panchito, now a strapping thirty year old, slouched on the sofa watching television. He reminded her of Santi as a young man. His legs were long and skinny, dangling over the armrest. He had a charisma that Sofia found engaging. Like Dorian Gray, Panchito looked like a younger, flawless image of his brother. His eyes were the same sea-green and yet they lacked the depth of his brother's. His face was unlined and smooth yet that too lacked the character of Santi's, whose face showed that he had suffered and survived.

Sofia looked at Santi and loved him more for his crumpled skin and melancholic eyes. He had once exuded a confidence that believed it could tame the ebb and flow of life and train it to do his bidding. Fate had taught him that one cannot conquer what is out of one's control; one can only learn to live in harmony with it. Santi had relinquished his arrogance the hard way.

'Santi, bring Sofia a glass of wine – white or red?' asked Chiquita.

'Red,' said Santi, automatically answering the question for her. Red had always been Sofia's favourite colour.

'Yes, thank you,' she replied in surprise. Claudia looked up from her magazine and watched her husband pour the wine. Sofia waited for the look of anxiety that was sure to follow, but it never came. If Claudia had minded she made sure she didn't show it.

'So, Sofia, how long will you be staying?' she asked, her apathetic blue eyes smiling a little too much in an attempt to hide the fear that trembled behind them.

'I don't know, I have no plans,' Sofia responded with a smile of equal sincerity.

'Don't you have children and a husband?'

'Yes, I do. David's busy with a play at the moment so he couldn't come. Anyhow, it would be hard for him, he doesn't know any of you and he doesn't speak Spanish. He's happy for me to stay as long as I want.'

'We all read about you in the papers,' enthused her aunt. 'Such a nice picture – you looked beautiful. I still have it somewhere. I'll pull it out and show you sometime. Yes, I must still have it somewhere.' Santi brought her the wine. Sofia caught his eye but he didn't respond. 'You should have been an actress. You were a prima donna even as a child,' recalled Chiquita, 'you were always attracting attention. I'm surprised your husband hasn't put you in one of his plays! You know, Claudia, she was quite the exhibitionist. I remember a play that was put on at San Andrés, Sofia, and you refused to take part because you weren't the lead. Do you remember, Santi? She must have cried for a week. You said you were better than everyone else.'

'Yes, I remember that,' he replied.

'She always got her way, Claudia. Poor Paco could never say no.'

'Nor could Grandpa,' Sofia admitted sheepishly, laughing a little. 'It used to drive my mother insane the way we'd gang up on her.'

'Now your grandfather – what an extraordinary man *he* was.'

'You know I still miss him. I miss his humour,' Sofia said wistfully. 'I'll never forget that time he was kept in the intensive care unit at the hospital in Buenos Aires, having contracted some highly infectious disease. God knows what he had, but whatever it was it baffled the doctors. I think it was some sort of amoeba. Do you remember, Chiquita?' she said.

Chiquita frowned and shook her head. 'I don't believe I do.'

'Well, the doctor said Grandpa was not permitted to leave his room. At one point, he wanted to go to the bathroom and after ringing his bell a couple of times to no effect, he left his room and wandered around the whole floor until he found the *baños*. On his return he noticed there was a sign on the door of his room stating that no one, under any circumstances, was permitted to enter without supervision – *highly contagious patient within* it said. Grandpa decided he couldn't possibly go in, as he'd be breaking the rules. So what do you think he did? He shuffled off around all the wards, infecting everyone he came into contact with, until he found a nurse to escort him back to his room. Apparently he caused a minor panic. Knowing Grandpa O'Dwyer, he would have done it on purpose. They always answered his bell after that.'

'They must have praised the day he left,' chuckled Santi, shaking his head. 'I remember the time you fought with Anna and packed your bags and came over to our house, declaring that you wanted Mama to adopt you. Do you remember, Sofia?' He laughed, the wine dulling his senses and loosening his muscles that ached from having to dissemble his emotions.

'I'm not sure I want to remember that, it's a bit embarrassing,' Sofia said awkwardly.

'No, it wasn't. Santi and Maria were thrilled. They encouraged it,' said Chiquita.

'What did my parents say about it?' she asked. She never did get to the bottom of that one.

'Well, let me think.' Her aunt sighed, narrowing her eyes. 'Your father . . . yes, Paco came over and got you. I recall he told you there were very nice orphanages you could go to if you didn't want to live at home. He said you were too much of a handful to sell to any of his family!'

'Did he really?' Sofia giggled.

'You were always a handful. I'm glad you've settled down,' Chiquita said fondly. All the time Claudia hadn't spoken. She had just listened.

'She used to play polo with the boys,' continued Chiquita, nodding her head.

'*Dios* — it's been years, literally. I don't know whether I'd remember how to play.'

'Could you play as well as the boys?' asked Claudia finally, attempting to join in.

'Not as well as Santi, but definitely as well as Agustin,' Chiquita said truthfully.

'I wanted to do whatever the boys did. They always seemed to have much more fun than us girls,' Sofia recalled.

'You were a sort of honorary boy, weren't you, Chofi?' smirked Santi. Sofia hesitated. That was the first time she had heard him call her 'Chofi'. Chiquita pretended not to notice, but Sofia knew she had as her eyes anxiously darted to Santi and then back to her. Of course Claudia kept her composure and sipped her wine as if her husband had said nothing unusual.

'Sofia was such a menace. I am so happy you have settled down, found a nice husband – I knew you would,' Chiquita said nervously, trying to fill the silence.

Claudia looked at her watch. 'Santi, we should say good-night to the children,' she said tightly.

'Right now?' he asked.

'Yes. They'll be so disappointed if you don't say good-night.'

'I really should get back to my parents. It's been a long day and I'm tired. I'll see you all tomorrow,' said Sofia, getting up.

Claudia and Santi stood up to leave. Santi didn't kiss her. He just acknowledged her awkwardly before leaving the room, followed by his wife. Chiquita kissed her tenderly.

'Talk to Anna, Sofia,' she said.

'What do you mean?' asked Sofia.

'Just talk to her. Things have not been easy – for any of you.'

Chapter Thirty-Nine

As Sofia wandered slowly back to the house she remembered the many times she had walked this stretch of land. This used to be her home. The smell of eucalyptus hung in the humid air and she could hear the ponies snorting in the fields. The crickets clicked rhythmically — for as long as there had been Argentina she imagined there had been crickets. They were as much a part of the place as the ombu. She couldn't imagine the *campo* without them. She breathed in the scents of the *pampa* and drifted on her memories and bittersweet echoes of her childhood.

By the time she reached the house she felt sick with nostalgia. She needed time to be on her own, to think. Having expected Santa Catalina to have changed, it was disturbing to find that it hadn't. She could have been a child again and yet here she was within the body of a mature woman, full of the experiences of another country, another life. Looking about her she realised that Santa Catalina was fixed in a time warp, as if the world outside had not touched it. She wandered up to the pool and walked around it. But the memories cascaded, persisted; everything she set her eyes upon pulled her back to the past. The tennis court where she and Santi had so often played loomed out at her through the darkness and she could almost hear their ghostly voices laughing and joking on the breeze.

Sofia sat by the water's edge and thought about David. She imagined his expression, his pale blue eyes, the straight aristocratic nose she so often kissed. She imagined those features she loved. Yes, she loved him, but not in the same way that she loved Santi. She knew it was wrong. She knew she shouldn't crave another man's arms, another man's lips, another man's caresses, and yet she had never ceased to love this human being who was in some strange way attached to her soul. She longed for Santi and her longing choked her. After twenty-three years the hurt was still as raw as it ever had been.

It was dark when she reached the house. She had calmed down, walked a bit, breathed deeply, all those wise things Grandpa O'Dwyer had taught her to do when her brothers had teased her, leaving her hoarse with fury. She wandered into the kitchen where Soledad greeted her with a taste of *dulce de leche* mousse before it had set. Placing herself in her usual seat at the kitchen table while Soledad cooked, they chatted as friends. Sofia had to distract herself and Soledad was the perfect distraction.

'Señorita Sofia, how could you spend so long away? You didn't even write to me. What were you thinking of? Did you think I wouldn't miss you? Did you think I wouldn't mind? Of course I minded. I felt dejected. I thought you had stopped caring. After all I did for you. I cried for years. I should have been furious. I should be furious now. But how can I be? I'm too happy to see you to be cross,' she said reproachfully, hiding her face in the steaming cauldron of *zapallo* soup. Sofia felt desperately sorry for her. Soledad had loved her like her own child and Sofia had barely given her a thought.

'Oh Soledad, I never forgot you. It was just impossible to return. I made my life in England instead.'

'Señor Paco and Señora Anna – they were never the same after you left. Don't ask me what happened, I don't like to pry, but things were never the same between them. You left and they fell apart. Everything changed. I didn't like the change; I didn't like the atmosphere. I longed for you to come back and you never even wrote. Not a word. *Nada!*'

'I'm sorry, that was thoughtless of me. Soledad, if I'm honest, and I've always been honest with you, it hurt to think of Santa Catalina. I missed you all so much, I couldn't write. I know I should have, but it was somehow easier to try to forget.'

'How can you forget your roots, Sofia? How can you?' she asked, shaking her grey head.

'Believe me, when you're on the other side of the world, Argentina seems very far away. I just got on with my life as best I could. I left it too late.'

'You're as stubborn as your grandfather was.'

'But I'm here now,' she said, as if in some way that might console her.

'Yes, but you won't stay. There's nothing for you here now. Señor Santiago is married. I know you, you won't stay.'

'I'm married too, Soledad. I have a family to go back to, a husband I adore.'

'But your heart is here with us,' she said. 'I know you. Don't forget, I raised you.'

'What is Claudia like?' she heard herself asking.

'I don't like to speak ill of anyone, least of all a Solanas — I'm the Solanas family's biggest champion. There's no one loyal like me; otherwise I would have left years ago. But as it's you I'll speak my mind. She's not a Solanas. I don't think he loves her. I think there's only one person he's ever loved. I don't want to know the details, I'm not one to pry. After you left he wandered around like a ghost. *La Vieja Bruja* said that his aura was dim. She asked to see him, she would have sorted him out but he has never had an interest in the hidden world. After that dreadful business with Señor Fernando, Señor Santiago began to invite Señora Claudia to Santa Catalina for weekends and he smiled again. I didn't think he'd ever smile again. Then he married her. I think if she hadn't come along, he would have given up. Thrown the towel in, just like that. But I don't think he loves her. I watch things – I see things. Of course, it's none of my business. He respects her; she's the mother of his children. But she's not a soulmate. *La Vieja Bruja* says you only have one soulmate.'

Sofia listened to her ramblings. The more she listened, the more eager she was to free him from his desolation. It amused her that Soledad knew so much. She must have heard the gossip from the other maids and *gauchos*. But she knew their gossip only guessed at the truth.

Rafael and his wife Jasmina joined Sofia and her parents for dinner on the terrace. Sofia was thankful for their company. Jasmina was warm and sensual, her full body exuded a ripe fertility that the cool Claudia lacked, and Sofia was grateful for her earthy humour. She had brought her two-month-old daughter with her in a shawl and proceeded to breastfeed her discreetly at the table. Sofia noticed her mother disapproved but tried hard to conceal her displeasure. Jasmina knew her mother-in-law well enough to see the signs, and had the intelligence enough to ignore them.

'Rafa doesn't want any more children – he says five is enough. I come from a family of thirteen – *imaginate!*' And she smiled broadly, her pale green eyes twinkling mischievously in the candlelight.

'Really, *mi amor*, thirteen just isn't practical these days. I have to educate them all,' said Rafael, grinning at her lovingly.

'We'll see. I don't see any reason to stop,' she laughed, opening her shirt a moment to check on her feeding child. 'When they are this small I lose my heart to them. When they get older they don't need you so much.'

'I disagree,' said Paco, placing his large, rough hand on Sofia's. 'I think if as a parent you build a loving home, your children will always come back to it.'

'You have children, don't you, Sofia?'

'Yes, two daughters,' she replied, leaving her hand under her father's but unlike the old days she was very conscious that it was there.

'*Qué pena* that you didn't bring them with you. Clara and Elena would have so enjoyed meeting them. They'd all be about the same age, wouldn't they, *mi amor*? And I would be thrilled for them to practise their English.'

'They should practise more with me, Jasmina,' said Anna.

'Yes, but you know children, you can't force them to do anything they don't want to do.'

'Perhaps you should be a little tougher,' she insisted. 'Children don't know what's best for them.'

'Oh no, I couldn't bear to upset them. After school hours they are at home, and home is for playing.'

Sofia could see that this was one conflict her mother was not going to win and she admired the sweet way Jasmina dealt with her. There was leather beneath the sugar.

Soledad took every opportunity to come out onto the terrace, to serve the food, to take plates away, to bring in the mustard, to fill the water jug, she even popped her head around the door twice under the pretence that she had heard Señora Anna ring the bell. Each time she grinned a wide, incomplete smile. After a while Sofia couldn't conceal her laughter and had to muffle it into her napkin. Soledad was obviously curious to watch her with her parents. She would later go and discuss their reactions with all the other maids on the farm.

At eleven o'clock Jasmina wandered home with her daughter, disappearing into the park like an angel. Paco and Rafael sat chatting among the flies and moths that had collected around the hurricane lamps. Anna retired to bed protesting that she was old when Paco tried to encourage her to stay. Sofia was happy for her to go as she didn't know what to talk to her about. She resented her too much to talk about the past and didn't want to involve her in the present out of spite. Once Anna had gone she felt surprisingly uplifted and found herself slipping into conversation with her brother and father just like the old days. With them she was happy to reminisce. At eleven-thirty she crept away to her room.

The following day Sofia awoke early due to the time difference. She had slept through the night, a dreamless sleep that even Santi had been powerless to interrupt. She was grateful for that. She'd been exhausted, not only by the flight, but by the emotion. But once she was up she was unable to lie still. She crept into the kitchen, where the white light of dawn illuminated the table and tiled floor. It took her back to those days when she would grab something to eat from the well-stocked fridge before skipping out to practise polo with Jose. Rafael had told her that Jose had passed away ten years before. He had gone and she had never said goodbye. Without Jose Santa Catalina was like a smile with a front tooth missing.

Taking an apple from the fridge she dipped her finger in the pot of *dulce de leche*. Nothing tasted as good as Soledad's *dulce de leche*. She made it from milk and sugar that she boiled on the stove. As much as Sofia had tried to make it in England for her children, it had never tasted the same. She put a spoonful on her apple and ambled out through the sitting room onto the terrace. It lay still and ghostly in the shadow of the tall trees, awaiting the sun to rise up and discover it. She bit into her apple and savoured the sweet toffee taste. Gazing out at the early morning mist that lingered above the distant plains she suddenly felt a strong desire to take a pony out and gallop through it. She marched across the park towards the *puesto*, the little cluster of shacks where Jose had always tended the ponies.

Pablo greeted her as she approached, wiping his hands on a dirty rag. He smiled, baring his crooked, black teeth. She shook his hand and told him how sorry she was that his father had died. He nodded gravely and thanked her shyly. 'My father was very fond of you, Señora Sofia,' he said and grinned bashfully. She noticed that he now called her 'Señora' instead of 'Señorita'. The name placed a distance between them that hadn't existed all those years ago when they had practised polo together.

459

'I was enormously fond of him. It's just not the same here without him,' she replied truthfully, looking around at the strange brown faces that stared at her through the windows.

'You want to ride, Señora Sofia?' Pablo asked.

'I won't play, I'll just gallop around a bit. Get the wind in my hair. It's been a long time.'

'Javier!' he shouted. A younger man ran out of the house in a pair of *bombachas*, the coins on his belt glistening in the pale light. *'Una yegua para Señora Sofia, ya.'* When Javier made towards a dark mare Pablo shouted at him, 'Not Azteca, Javier. La Pura! For Señora Sofia the best. La Pura *is* the best,' he said, grinning at her again.

Javier brought round a pale chestnut pony and Sofia stroked her velvet nose while he silently saddled her up. Once mounted she thanked him before cantering off into the field. It felt good. She could breathe again. The pressure that had been gathering in her chest and throat slowly receded and she felt her body relax with the gentle motion of the gallop. She looked over to Chiquita's house and thought of Santi asleep with his wife. She didn't know it at the time, he told her later, but he was there at the window, watching her as she rode across the plain, wondering how he was going to get through the day. With her arrival everything had changed.

Sofia didn't see Santi all day. When she arrived at his house to visit Maria, he had gone into town with his children only to return after she had left. Every car that drove down the track she hoped would be him. She tried not to care, but she couldn't help worrying that the time would crumble in her grasp and soon she'd be back in England again. She was desperate to see him on her own. She wanted to talk about the past – their past. She wanted to bury the ghosts for good.

Chapter Forty

Chiquita had asked Sofia to stay for dinner. Although Maria was unable to eat with them, she wanted Sofia to be close. 'I don't want to miss out on a second of your stay. Soon you'll be gone and who knows when I'll see you again,' Chiquita had said. As Sofia had dined with her parents the night before, she didn't think they'd mind.

Dinner was outside among the crickets and predatory dogs. Eduardo looked pale in the eerie glow of the candle lamps. He spoke very little and hid behind his fine round glasses. His grief was etched into the lines around his eyes, grief that even his glasses failed to disguise. Santi and Sofia reminisced with Chiquita and Miguel – once again Claudia listened with a small smile that ill-fitted her solemn face. She obviously didn't want to look too interested but neither did she want to be accused of being rude. So she sat demurely, eating the pasta with a fork, occasionally dabbing the corners of her mouth with a white napkin.

Sofia rarely used a napkin. Anna had always tried to encourage her daughter to 'behave more like a lady'. But Grandpa O'Dwyer had always defended her. 'What's in a napkin, Anna Melody? Personally I find my sleeve more reliable – at least I always know where it is,' he'd say. He complained that napkins spent most of their lives falling off knees onto floors. Sofia looked down at her lap — Grandpa O'Dwyer was right once again. Her napkin had disappeared under the table. She bent down to retrieve it. Panchito, who was sitting on her right, grinned at her before flicking it up with his foot.

Chiquita and Miguel were deeply proud of Panchito. He was tall and handsome with Santi's charm. His smile was very much like his brother's, in the way the lines creased around his mouth. It was easy to see how his brothers' turbulent lives had affected his. He had grown up the perfect child to compensate for his brothers. Having watched his mother literally shrink in the wake of Santi's scandalous affair and Fernando's hasty departure to Uruguay he had made every effort to make her happy. He was very close to Chiquita — they all were. She doted on them and they could count on her to put them above everything else. She allowed her children's lives to quite literally shape hers. They *were* her life and she lived for them.

Panchito played a nine-goal handicap on the polo field, and as much as it wasn't considered the proper thing to do professionally, his parents had allowed him to pursue it. They could hardly deny him a career in polo when his talent cried out for him to play. His mother was way too involved in his life. It was clear from their conversations that Chiquita didn't want her 'Panchito' to grow up. Most of the family now called him Pancho instead of Panchito ('little Pancho'). But to his mother he would always remain Panchito. He was the baby and she was still clinging onto his childhood; if she had opened her grasp she would have found that she had been clinging on to nothing but air. Her Panchito had flown her nest years ago.

Soledad had told Sofia that he was quietly conducting an affair with Encarnacion's daughter, Maria (named after Maria Solanas) who was not only married but had a daughter, the father of whom could have been almost anyone in the *pueblo*. 'A nice young man like Pancho doesn't want to go to a brothel. He's just learning the ways of women,' she had said in his defence. When Sofia looked at 'young Pancho' she imagined he'd been 'learning the ways of

462

women' from the moment he'd discovered what his penis had been made for.

During dinner Santi and Sofia talked with restraint. On the surface no one would have guessed the tension they both felt in their chests, the effort it was to act as if they felt nothing more than the warmth of an old friendship. They laughed when they wanted to cry and spoke calmly when they wanted nothing more than to shout, 'How do you feel?'

Finally Sofia kissed her cousins good-night. Claudia stood rigidly in front of the French windows, eager to leave the terrace and retreat into the house with her husband. 'See you tomorrow, Sofia,' she said smilingly, but her eyes remained distant.

It was at that moment that Santi thrust a piece of paper into Sofia's hand. He looked at her with an expression of longing and kissed her on her cheek. Claudia didn't notice because his back was facing her. She just stood there expectantly.

Sofia stepped out into the night, clutching the piece of paper to her chest. She was impatient to open the note but the minute she saw it crumpled and distressed she recognised it as the very note she had sent Soledad to give him twenty-three years before. She struggled with her emotions as she opened it and read the words again: *Meet me under the ombu tree at midnight.* Conquered once more by that now-familiar sense of regret, she clutched it to her bosom and walked on. She couldn't sit as she would normally have done in order to regain her composure – she was too agitated. She kept walking.

Santi's feeling hadn't changed. He had kept her note, cherished it. And now he delivered it to her with the same urgency and secrecy as she had sent it to him that terrible night. He wanted her. She had never stopped wanting him. She couldn't help herself. She knew it was wrong but she was unable to pull herself back. Her heart ached with the thought of what might have been.

*   *   *

She felt like a child again, breaking the rules. As she brushed and plaited her hair at her old dressing table Sofia could have been eighteen again. She was thousands of miles away and swept back into a life so removed from the one she shared with her husband and girls that it was almost as if she were living a fantasy in which they had no place. At that moment nothing mattered but Santi. It felt so right. Santi was part of her. He belonged to her. She had waited twenty-three years for him.

She was about to leave the room when there was a hesitant knock at the door. She looked at the clock. Quarter to midnight.

'Come in,' she said irritably. The door opened slowly. 'Papa.'

Paco stood hesitantly in the doorway. She didn't want to invite him in, she was anxious to get to the ombu. She couldn't bear to be late for Santi, not after having waited so long.

'I just wanted to make sure that you are all right,' he said gruffly, and his eyes flicked around the room as if he was nervous of looking into hers.

'I'm fine, Papa, thank you.'

'You know, your mother and I are happy you are home. You belong here,' he said clumsily. He looked frail as he stood there, uncertain of what to say. He had always known exactly what to say.

'A part of me will always belong here,' Sofia replied. Then she felt sorry that this gulf existed between them. That it was so easy for people's lives to change them. She walked up to him and embraced him. While she held him in her arms she glanced at her watch. There was a time when nothing would have distracted her from his love.

'Now, go to bed and get some sleep. We've got all the time in the world to talk. I'm tired, it's been a long day. We'll talk tomorrow,' she said, gently but firmly showing him to the door.

'*Bueno*, Sofia, I will say good-night then,' he whispered, disappointed. He had come to tell her something, something that had cast a shadow over his conscience for many years. But it would have to wait. He would tell her another time. Reluctantly he left the room. Once he had shuffled down the corridor she was aware of a tear that he had left on her cheek when he kissed her.

Sofia didn't need a torch that night; the moon was so phosphorescent it cast silver shadows over the grass and fields. It felt oddly surreal as she ran over them. She remembered the night she took the same route for her last meeting with Santi. It had been dark and ominous then. She could hear a few dogs barking in the distance and a child crying. It wasn't until she could see the silhouette of the ombu tree against the glittering navy sky that she began to feel afraid.

As she approached she slowed down to a hasty walk. She searched the tree for him but couldn't see him anywhere. She had imagined she would see the glow of his torch jumping around like the last time. That moment would be for ever engraved on her memory. But tonight he needed no torch and it was light enough for her to see the hands on her watch. She was late. Had he not waited? She went cold. She felt her throat constrict with impatience. Then suddenly from behind the tree he appeared like a black shadow. They stared at one another. She tried to work out his expression, but she couldn't see it clearly in spite of the moonlight. He must have been doing the same. And then instinct overcame them, releasing them from all rational thought. They fell upon each other, touching, smelling, breathing, crying. Their actions spoke where words could never have done justice to the years of longing and regret. She felt then that she had truly come home.

She didn't know what time it was when they finally lay fulfilled and delirious on the sweet grass, and she didn't really care. She was aware only of his hand playing with the strands of hair that had worked free from her plait. She breathed in the spicy scent of him and buried her face in his chest. She could feel his warm breath on her forehead and the roughness of his chin against her skin. She wallowed in the sensual pleasure of the moment. Nothing else mattered or existed for her but him.

'Talk to me, Chofi. What happened when you left?' he asked finally.

'*Dios*, I don't know where to start.'

'I have asked myself so many times, what could I have done?'

'Don't Santi, don't torture yourself. I went crazy asking myself those same questions and I still don't know the answers,' she replied, raising herself onto her elbow and placing her finger across his lips. He took her hand and kissed it, blinking up at her.

'Why did they have to send you away? I mean, they could have sent you to boarding school – anything, but sending you to Switzerland was a bit drastic, and then not knowing where to find you. . .'

Sofia watched his anguished face, those tormented green eyes searching hers for an answer. He looked as vulnerable as a child and her heart lurched for him.

'They sent me away, Santi, because I was expecting your child,' she said quietly, and her voice quivered. He stared at her in disbelief. 'Do you remember when I was ill? Well, Dr Higgins was sent for. Mama went crazy. Papa was more understanding but furious. There was only one thing to do as, of course, I couldn't keep the child. Our affair was improper; they could never have accepted it. Mama, naturally, was only worried that I would bring shame upon the family and that was more important than anything else. I think at that moment she saw the devil in me. I'll never forget it as long as I live.'

'Slow down, Chofi – you're babbling. What did you just say?'

'Darling Santi, I was pregnant.'

'You were pregnant with my child?' he stammered slowly, unable to take it all in. He then sat up abruptly and rubbed his forehead with the palm of his hand.

'Yes,' she replied sadly, sitting up and letting him draw her into his arms.

'Oh Chofi, why didn't you tell me?'

'Mama and Papa had made me promise not to tell anyone. They

sent me to Geneva to have a termination. They didn't want anyone to know. I was afraid that if I told you, you'd demand to come with me, demand your rights as the father, confront my parents. I don't know – I was afraid. I was frightened to go against their wishes. You should have seen them. They were different people that night. I decided to write to you once I was far away, when my parents would be unable to do anything about it.'

She couldn't tell him that she had had the child and then given him away. She was too ashamed. How could she tell him that she had regretted giving him up from the moment she had come to her senses that bleak winter morning in London. Would he believe her if she told him that not a day went by when she didn't think about Santiguito, wonder where he was and what he was doing? How could she tell him without sounding callous or flippant? That wasn't the way he remembered her. So she left him to assume that she had terminated the pregnancy, and suppressing the pain, she carried it alone.

'Maria,' he said flatly.

'It's a long time ago,' Sofia said quietly feeling it was wrong to criticise her cousin now that she was dying. He held her close and she knew that the fact that she had carried his child brought them irreversibly closer together. He was thinking of what might have been. She could feel his regret because it reflected her own.

'Is that why you never came back? Because you lost our child?' he asked into her hair.

'No. I never came back because I believed that you didn't want me, that you had moved on and found someone else. I didn't want Argentina without you. I reached a point where my pride prevented me from coming home. I suppose I left it too long.'

'Surely you trusted me?'

'I wanted to, but after a while I lost hope. You were so far away – I didn't know what you were thinking. And I waited. I waited for years!'

'Oh Chofi, you should have come back. If only you had come

467

back, you would have seen how I was pining for you. I was lost without you. Nothing was the same. I felt utterly useless. I didn't know where to find you. I didn't know where you were, otherwise I would have written.'

'I know that now. I didn't think for one minute that Maria might have destroyed my letters.'

'I know. As I didn't receive them, I couldn't write back. I didn't know where you were. Maria confessed to me years ago, but by then it was too late. I know at the time she thought she was doing the right thing. She has been torturing herself with remorse for years, that's why she stopped writing to you. She couldn't bring herself to tell you, or to face you.' He smiled bitterly. 'I can't believe we were beaten so easily,' he said hoarsely, shaking his head. 'I gave up in the end. I had to, or I would have been driven insane. I thought you had found someone else. Why else would you not have come home? Then Claudia came along and I faced the decision of making a life with her or waiting for you. I chose a life with her.'

'Are you happy?' asked Sofia slowly.

'Happiness is relative. I thought I was happy until yesterday when you appeared at the hospital.'

'Santi, I'm so sorry.'

'I'm happy now.'

'Are you sure?'

'I'm very sure,' he replied, taking her face in his hands and kissing her forehead. 'It hurts me to think of you suffering alone in Switzerland. I want to know what happened. We have years to catch up on. I want to share every minute of them with you. I want to feel that I know your life so well I could almost have been there with you.'

'I will tell you about Switzerland, I'll fill you in on everything.'

'You should get some rest.'

'I wish we could spend the whole night together.'

'I know. But you're back. I've dreamed of you coming back a hundred times.'

'Did you dream it would be like this?'

'No, I imagined I'd be furious. But when I saw you, it was like we had parted only yesterday. You haven't changed at all, not at all.' And he looked at her with such tenderness she felt the tears stinging the backs of her eyes.

'I love this old tree,' she said, turning her face away to hide her emotion. 'It's watched us grow up, it's seen our pain, our love, our pleasure. No one knows it all like this old ombu tree.'

He sighed deeply and squeezed her. 'I never let my children come here,' he said.

'I know, your son told me.'

'Silly, really. I just felt it had let me down. I didn't want my children to live in a fantasy world of magic and wishes like we had.'

She squeezed him back. 'I know, but for me it always meant more than that. It was our secret place. It was our little kingdom. To me, the ombu will always represent an idyllic childhood. It's at the very core of all my memories. Every one. You see, we've just given it another.'

He laughed with her and his sadness lifted. 'I suppose I've acted foolishly.'

'No, but I don't think it would do any harm to let your children come here. Remember how we loved to climb it?'

'Yes, you were pretty athletic in those days.'

'In those days! I could climb it now for a few *pesos*.'

And so they climbed it together. And when they reached the top they could see the dawn breaking on the horizon, its blood-red rays seeping into the night and turning it to gold.

Chapter Forty-One

Saturday, 8 November 1997

Sofia awoke at midday to the chorus of *chingolos* and for a moment she had the surreal feeling that the last twenty-three years had been nothing but a long dream. The scents of the *pampa*, the eucalyptus and humidity clung to her nostrils and she lay prolonging the mood for as long as she could sustain it. She was transported back to her childhood and she lolled in the pleasure of her memories. She had been afraid to confront her past for fear that by giving way to nostalgia her craving would consume her entirely. But now her fears seemed unfounded. She lay as if in a trance and allowed her mind to be invaded by the fleeting pictures of the first few chapters of her life – the pages turning so rapidly she was unable to focus properly on any one of them. Having held them back for so long they rushed at her; self-indulgently she allowed them life once more. She didn't want to get up. Her heart yearned for the past to become present and for Jose to be awaiting her at the stables with her mare and *taco*.

When she opened her eyes, the first thing she saw was her suitcase. But then she smelt Santi on her skin, on her lips and her hands, and she lay back and covered her face with them and breathed him in slowly, savouring every moment of recollection.

She had returned. Santi still loved her. But Maria was dying and she was suddenly jolted back to reality.

Breakfast had come and gone and it didn't occur to her that her father might have been sitting on the terrace longing for her to join him. Soledad told her later. But her thoughts were only with Santi. She felt sad she had missed her father, but only for a moment, then the feeling was gone and she was marching purposefully over to Chiquita's house. She passed Anna reading in the sun under a large hat. How little people's habits change, she thought. Anna looked up and smiled. She returned her smile a little awkwardly and waved. Her mother knew where she was going, there was no need to explain. She had slotted right back in again.

The melodies of Strauss reached her before she reached the house. The music poured joy into her heart and she almost skipped in the dazzling sunshine. Maria was out on the terrace under a blanket, her head discreetly hidden beneath a small floral sunhat. Sofia noticed her cheeks were showing the first signs of colour and her eyes shone with happiness. She held out her hand as Sofia appeared from round the corner.

'Sofia,' she said and smiled at her tenderly, her expression full of warmth.

'You look so much better,' she replied in delight and bent down to kiss her.

'I feel better.'

Looking down at her thin but radiant face Sofia was sure that she was going to live. She just couldn't believe that someone as good as Maria would be taken from them. Especially now that she had just discovered her again.

Chiquita was wandering around the house looking after her plants while Maria's younger children played on the swings with their cousins.

'The others are on the tennis court and lying by the pool,' said Maria. 'You can go and join them if you like.'

'Do you get tired with everyone fussing around you?' asked Sofia. She didn't want Maria to feel she had to talk to her.

'A little. I don't want everyone hovering around me waiting for me to die.' And she laughed sadly and lowered her eyes.

'You know miracles happen. You're looking so much better,' she ventured hopefully.

'I would love a miracle to happen. It would be a lovely surprise.' She sighed. 'I do feel better though. That hospital makes you feel like you've died already.'

'Let's not talk about it, Maria. Let's talk about the old days,' she suggested.

'No, I want you to talk to me about what you've been up to for the last twenty-three years. I'll close my eyes and you can tell me a wonderful story.' And so Sofia sat back in the chair and let Maria doze off as she chatted away about the life they should have spent together.

As usual on a Saturday there was an *asado*. The familiar smells of burning *lomo* and *chorizo* swam on the breeze and she watched as the whole family gathered together under the tall leafy eucalyptus trees. Maria had retreated into the house with her nurse, unable to eat with the rest of them. The noise would have been too much for her. Sofia had forgotten how noisy their *asados* were.

Nothing had changed except the familiar faces looked older and the new ones unfamiliar. Clara demanded to sit next to her new aunt. She took her by the hand and led her to the tables of dishes spilling over with food. She took great pleasure in telling her how it was done. First she was to go and choose a piece of meat from the barbecue – she could have any piece she wanted, Clara offered generously – then she was to help herself to salad and potatoes from the table. Sofia looked down at this precocious creature and momentarily felt a deep longing for her own daughters. Clara noticed her tender expression and grinned up at her quizzically, before skipping off to help herself to some food.

If Sofia had allowed herself to dwell more on the family she had left behind she would probably have listened to the small voice of her conscience, but there was simply no time and the small voice went unheard. Santi appeared with Panchito and all the while she talked to them over the barbecue she was conscious of every move and gesture Santi made. She hardly noticed what she herself was saying; the words had a life of their own and she left them to it.

Santi and Sofia could still communicate secretly without anyone else noticing, through the movements of their eyes. Gestures that were commonplace for everyone else had special meaning for them. She found herself living in a continuous state of *déjà vu*. Santi and Sofia were reliving the past whereas the people around them had all changed and moved on. Sofia felt the same, Santa Catalina looked the same, smelt the same and yet it *wasn't* the same. But Sofia wasn't ready to face that yet. While she was near Santi there was some semblance of normality.

Clara was fascinated by her. But like all children, she was only interested in talking about herself. She wanted to tell Sofia everything. She desperately wanted to impress her, to the extent of jumping down from the table and walking on her hands the entire length of it. Her mother simply laughed and told her to reserve her antics for after lunch when there was less chance of her food making a guest appearance. Sofia admired the calm manner in which she dealt with her child. Clara laughed and skipped back to her seat. Of course she couldn't resist but tell her a few stories of her own. She couldn't have hoped for a better audience. Her eyes wide with admiration, Clara gasped in delight and disbelief that Sofia, a grown-up, could ever have been so wicked. The distraction, however, only lasted a while before she was back on centre-stage again, the words spilling out so fast Sofia could barely understand them.

Sofia's attention was not completely reserved for Clara. She could let her chatter on, making the right noises at the right moments, while at the same time watching and listening to the other conversations around her. She was very aware of Claudia, starched and glossy in an ice-blue shirt and jeans. She knew Claudia was also aware of her. She caught her staring at her a couple of times but Claudia looked away immediately as if she were embarrassed to have been caught looking.

The topic of everyone's conversation was Maria. Chiquita was telling them all how much better she looked today and how there was no place like home to put the life back into her. Her small face expressed her hope but Sofia could see the hopelessness behind her eyes. Then they all began reminiscing. Sofia found it unsettling to sit and listen to conversations about things of which she knew nothing. Of course, when Clara's attention was diverted she was able to join in and laugh at their stories. But their old days were not hers and she experienced the odd sensation of being an outsider. On the one hand she felt that she had slotted right back into the place, but on the other hand she had missed out on so much she couldn't really connect with anyone except for Santi. Her cousins all wanted to know how she had spent the last two decades but her life was so far removed from theirs a few sentences satisfied their curiosity and then they had very little to say to each other. Only Santi and Sofia hadn't changed. Their dynamic was exactly as it had been twenty-three years ago. So when he offered to stick and ball with her after polo, she was relieved. Claudia could only look on helplessly. Santi declared that he would not be going to Mass either, he wanted to stay with his sister. But Sofia knew the reason behind it. She noticed a small frown surface across Chiquita's pale face. She guessed she must have known too, or at least suspected. She hadn't forgotten the past like Rafael, and Chiquita knew her son better than anyone.

Sofia disregarded the suspicious eyes and retreated to the coolness of her room to take a siesta. She could see from her window the older children making for the pool in their swimsuits. But she was too hot and sleepy from the wine and humidity to join them. She suddenly felt rather old. Being a grown-up at Santa Catalina was a first for her.

* * *

474

'Santiguito plays well, doesn't he?' Santi said proudly, as his son galloped up the field.

'He's just like his father,' replied Sofia.

'Takes you back, doesn't it?'

'Certainly does,' she said and watched as he cantered off, his naked brown back flexing as he lifted his *taco*. She longed to be the girl she once was and leap onto a pony but she was older now. She wondered if she would even remember how to play.

Sofia sat on the grass with Chiquita and much to her surprise Anna wandered up to join them. The atmosphere was slightly tense at first, but once Clara had found them, their attention was diverted from one another to her gymnastics instead. The three of them laughed together as the child jumped around like a little monkey.

'You know, Sofia, you were just like that,' said Chiquita, as Clara whizzed past them.

'Yes, you were,' agreed her mother. 'You were such a show-off, I didn't know what to do with you.'

'Was I awful?' she asked, pleased that Anna was joining in. She nodded tightly but Sofia noticed that she was making an enormous effort to be agreeable.

'You were difficult,' she conceded.

Sofia didn't find it easy to talk to her mother. There were many subjects they were unable to discuss, so they skimmed around them like a couple of ice skaters afraid of breaking through to the water below, to the demons they'd have to face there. In the back of Sofia's mind, her mother remained the person responsible for sending her away. She had cheated her of this. The life she could have had was in evidence all around her. She could never forgive her for that. So they chatted politely with the help of Chiquita who acted like a referee, changing the subject each time she felt they were scraping the surface a little too close to the water.

'What are your children like, Sofia?' asked Chiquita.

'Oh, adorable, of course. Very English. David is a fantastic father and spoils them terribly. They're his little princesses and can do nothing wrong in his eyes.'

'And in your eyes?' asked her mother.

'Well, they can be wicked as well as charming,' she said, smiling as she recalled their faces. 'Honor's wild like I was — quite uncontrollable actually — and India just likes being at home with the horses.'

'So now you know what I had to put up with,' said Anna, and she smiled at her daughter.

'Yes, I do. There's no magical potion with children, is there? They have their own personalities you can't control.'

'They certainly do,' she nodded and suddenly both women realised that, after all these years, they finally had something in common. They were both mothers.

'You're not watching, *Abuelita*,' Clara whined to her grandmother, before flinging herself into another handspring. Once more the conversation was diverted and Sofia was only too happy not to talk about herself. She didn't want to discuss England, and thinking about David and the girls just made her feel guilty.

After a while her mother wandered off and Clara lay with her back against her aunt's chest and dozed in the sunshine. Sofia talked with Chiquita about Maria; her aunt tried to ask her about herself but the conversation would inevitably revert back to Maria — Sofia wanted it that way. They reminisced about the old days and she was happy for they were her old days too.

Once the game was over, an inexhaustible Santi cantered over to them.

'Mama, be an angel and loan Sofia to me for a while.' He looked down at her and grinned. 'Let's get you a pony.'

'*Bueno*, Santi,' she replied, getting up. Then she made as if to say something else but stopped herself with a sharp intake of breath. 'No, nothing,' she muttered in response to Sofia's quizzical look. 'I had better go and check on Maria. I'll see you both later.' And taking a drowsy Clara with her she made off into the trees.

Santi accompanied Sofia to where Javier was waiting with La Pura. Sofia raised herself into the saddle with ease. Javier handed her a *taco* and with a twinkle in his eye Santi cantered off, hitting the ball out in front of him. It felt fantastic to be in the saddle once again, the wind in her hair, with that long-forgotten feeling of charging up the pitch after the ball. They laughed like old times as they raised their *tacos* and rode each other off.

'It is like riding a bicycle!' Sofia shouted in excitement, finding that she hadn't forgotten how to play after all.

'You're a bit rusty, *gorda*!' he taunted, flying past her.

'I'll show you – *viejo*!'

'*Viejo*? Old man? I'll get you for that, Chofi!' And he came charging back towards her. She turned her pony and cantered off the field towards the ombu. He knew where she was leading him and he played the game willingly. The fields passed her at great speed as she galloped over the long evening shadows and dewy grass. The vast sky glowed a misty orange as the sun hung low like a large, radiant peach. Santi caught up with her and they rode side by side exchanging smiles but speechless with happiness.

Finally they slowed down to a gentle canter and drew up under those familiar branches. The ponies trembled with excitement and stood breathing noisily in the shade as they dismounted. The crickets rattled away from their secret hiding places, and Sofia inhaled those unique Argentine features that she loved so much.

'Do you remember your story about the Precious Present?' she said and stretched with pleasure.

'Sure.'

'Well, I'm truly living in the present, right now, right here.'

'So am I,' he said softly, coming up behind her and putting his arms around her. They both stood watching the horizon as it slowly changed colour before them.

'I notice everything now. The crickets, this big sky, the flat plain, the smells. I realise now how much I've missed it.'

He kissed her neck, nuzzling his face against hers. 'I remember when I returned from America,' he recalled. 'Argentina seemed different. Or rather, it was the same, but I noticed everything. Saw it in a different way.'

'I now know what you meant.'

'Well, I'm glad I taught you something,' he joked, but they didn't laugh. Instead they stood for a while in silence. Although Sofia didn't want to face it at that moment, she knew in her heart that at some point she would have to leave it all again.

Finally, he turned her around. Gazing into his tender green eyes she felt she could see right into his soul and he into hers. She knew what he was thinking and understood the depth of his love. He looked sad, as love often makes one, and they both self-indulgently gave into the melancholia of their emotions. When he kissed her it was so totally absorbing that if they hadn't leant against the tree her legs would have failed her. He tasted of sweat and smelt of exertion and because they couldn't get his boots off they made love with them on. This is the way lovers do it, or adulterers, thought Sofia to herself. There was something raw about it. Perhaps because they had more to lose this time around, their moments together would be hasty and stolen. The innocence of youth had been replaced by a worldliness that Sofia found incredibly arousing – and tragic somehow.

'*Dios*, I could really do with a swim,' he said, doing up his trousers.

'What a fabulous idea. Do you think anyone will be up there?'

'I hope not.' He pressed the palm of his hand against her damp cheek and kissed her again. 'I feel whole again, Chofi,' he said and smiled down at her.

By the time they had taken the ponies back and skulked their way to the pool the sun had set. The humidity turned the air to sugar and carried in its damp particles the smells of eucalyptus and jasmine. To their relief no one was there. The pool lay before them in silence, the water undisturbed. Quietly they threw off their clothes, muffling their laughter as they struggled to relieve Santi of his boots. Gently, so as to make no noise, they slipped through the surface, coming together underneath in the murky darkness.

'Where will you say you've been?' she asked him after a while. Neither of them had any idea what time it was.

'Mama will know exactly where I've been. I'll tell the truth but leave out the illegal parts,' he smirked.

'What will Claudia say?' she laughed mischievously. But he shook his head anxiously.

'You know, I hate to deceive her like this. She's only ever been good to me.'

Sofia wished she hadn't mentioned her name. 'I know, I don't like to deceive David either. Let's not think about it. Remember the Precious Present?' she said brightly, but the moment had been spoiled. They swam for a while in silence, struggling with their consciences before sitting down on the paving stones to dry.

'G for guilt, right?' she whispered sympathetically.

'Right,' he replied, putting his arm around her and pulling her close. 'But no R for regret.'

'None?'

'None. Come early tomorrow, won't you?'

'Of course, but I want to spend as much time with Maria as possible. She's looking so much better than she did in the hospital.'

'She is. But Chofi . . .'

'Yes?'

'She's going to die.' His voice quivered.

'Miracles . . .'

'Happen, right,' he choked and Sofia pulled him close as he disintegrated into deep, heartfelt sobs. She didn't know the words to comfort him. There were no words And anyway, the words he wanted to hear she simply could not give him. So she held him to her chest and gave him time to cry out some of the pain.

'Santi, sweetheart, let it all out. You'll feel so much better afterwards.' She found herself quietly crying too, but with a restraint that made her throat ache. She knew if she let herself go she would be inconsolable – and what's more, her tears wouldn't be for Maria alone.

Chapter Forty-Two

When Sofia returned to the house it was late and her parents were waiting for her on the terrace with Rafael and Jasmina. She explained that she had better bathe and change and asked if she could call home. She didn't really want to, but she knew David would worry about her if she didn't.

'How is your cousin?' he asked.

'She won't make it,' Sofia replied sadly, 'but at least I'm able to spend some time with her.'

'Listen, darling, you can stay out there as long as you like. The girls are fine, everything's fine.'

'And the horses?'

'Nothing new. The girls are missing you, though.'

'I miss them too,' she said, ashamed that the turmoil in her heart had overshadowed her pining for them.

'Honor's the lead in the school play this year. She's absolutely delighted because the cast includes girls of seventeen and she's only fourteen. I'm afraid she's crowing rather too much.'

'I can imagine,' she replied.

'Here, she wants to talk to you,' he said. When Honor's voice chirped into the telephone, Sofia felt her throat ache with a combination of guilt and homesickness.

'Hi, Mum. I'm the lead in *The White Witch*,' she exclaimed with glee.

'I know, Daddy told me. Well done you.'

'I have to learn my lines. I've got so many. I've got more than anyone else in the whole play and I'm having a special costume made for me by Miss Hindlip and elocution lessons in order to learn how to project my voice.'

'You'll be busy then, won't you?'

'Very. I won't have any time to study.'

'Nothing new about that,' chuckled Sofia. 'How's India?'

'Dad says it's better that she doesn't talk to you because it makes her sad,' Honor announced in her elder-and-more-responsible-daughter tone of voice.

'I see. Will you give her a special kiss for me then? I miss you both very much.'

'You're coming home soon, though, aren't you?'

'Of course, sweetheart. Very soon,' Sofia told her, trying to hide her emotion. 'Will you pass me back to Daddy? A big kiss to you both.' Honor made a kissing noise down the telephone before passing it to her father.

'Is India all right?' she asked anxiously.

'She's fine. She misses you, that's all. But don't worry, she's absolutely fine. You sound very down, darling. I'm so sorry, I wish I could be there for you.' His voice was sympathetic but irritating. She felt edgy.

'Look, I'd better go. It's expensive. Give the girls all my love,' she said.

'Of course. And look after yourself, darling.'

For a moment Sofia felt uncomfortable. The call left a bitter residue. She felt duplicitous and hated herself for her ability to lie so convincingly. Thinking of the innocent, trusting faces of her daughters made her deceit all the more despicable. David had never been anything but kind. His kind voice and kind words made her feel lower and meaner than she had ever felt. But when she appeared on the terrace a few minutes later, changed and ready for dinner, England retreated once more into the background and she was dwelling in the Precious Present of the warm, humid night, breathing the same air as Santi.

Dinner was very pleasant. A couple of candle lamps lit the table and the melodies of Mozart's *Requiem* resounded through the open drawing-room windows. She liked Jasmina very much and they chatted warmly like old friends.

'We're living in a terrible limbo,' said Jasmina. 'For the children life goes on. They are back to school on Monday. I don't think they even know what's happening. But for us, waiting like this, our lives are suspended until the moment when Maria will be taken from us. And we don't know how long that will be.'

'What will you do?' asked Sofia. 'Will you return to Buenos Aires as usual?'

'No. The children will go back with Juan Pablo, the chauffeur, tomorrow night, but we will stay – and wait, I suppose.'

'I shall be sad when Clara leaves; we've become quite attached.'

'She'll be sad to leave you – I think she's got a bit of a crush.' And she laughed in her charming, feminine way. 'She'll be back next weekend. By then you might be fed up with her.'

'I don't think so. She's adorable.'

'Rafa says she's like you were at her age.'

'I hope she doesn't end up like me,' she joked sadly.

'I shall be proud of her if she does,' Jasmina stated emphatically. 'You know, Maria is so happy that you have come. She missed you. She spoke often about you.'

'We were very close. It's sad when life doesn't turn out as one hoped,' she said wistfully.

'It is always unexpected, but that is what makes it an adventure. Don't think of what you have missed, Sofia, think of what you have.'

At that moment Soledad entered with Sofia's favourite dessert, banana and *dulce de leche* crêpes.

'For you, Señorita Sofia,' she beamed proudly and placed it on the table.

'You are divine, Soledad. I don't know how I survived without this for twenty-three years,' replied Sofia, humouring her.

'You won't be without it again, Señorita Sofia.'

'How long are you planning on staying?' asked Rafael, not waiting but helping himself to a large portion of crêpes.

'I don't know,' she replied truthfully.

'She's only just arrived, *mi amor*, don't ask her when she's leaving,' chided Jasmina.

'You must stay as long as you like,' said Paco. 'This is your home, Sofia, you belong here.'

'I agree, Papa. I told her she should bring her husband and children out here.'

'Rafa, you know that's impossible. What would David do?' She laughed.

'That's not the point. You can't disappear for years, return and then leave us again!'

Sofia glanced across the table at her mother. Just as she did so, Anna looked up and caught her eye. Sofia tried to work out what she was thinking, but unlike her father Anna's expression gave nothing away.

'I'm flattered. Truly,' she replied and helped herself to dessert.

'Agustin left us for America — I don't know, young people these days,' said her father, shaking his silver head. 'In my day family stuck together.'

'In your day, Papa, the situation in this country was such that you *had* to stick together. You never knew when one of the family would be snatched from under your very nose,' Rafael said sombrely, remembering Fernando.

'Times were hard.'

'I remember as a child,' he continued, 'noticing that you were always neurotic about where we all were.'

'Kidnapping was rife. You worried us constantly,' said Anna. 'Especially Sofia, disappearing all the time with Santi and dear Maria.'

'So what else is new?' quipped Rafael and Sofia didn't know whether he was referring to the present or to her disappearing act all those years ago.

'I never knew why you used to worry so much, Mama. I just thought you were paranoid,' she said.

'No, you didn't. You just thought I was a killjoy. You gave me a very hard time, Sofia.' She spoke, without the slightest hint of humour, although she hadn't meant to sound quite so bitter.

'I'm sorry, Mama.' Sofia surprised herself because she meant it. She had never looked at herself through her mother's eyes before. But now she was a mother herself, she worried constantly about her daughters. A small flicker of understanding lit up in her mind. She looked across at her mother and felt sad.

Sofia retired early that night. She left them talking on the terrace, their faces illuminated in the dancing candlelight, their voices joining the gentle choir of crickets that filled the silence of the *pampa*, and she wandered through the moonlit courtyard of hanging pots of geraniums to her room. Once in bed she tried in vain to sleep. She yearned for Santi. She wondered how long they had together. She knew the moment would arrive when she would have to leave him. Or was there a chance that they could have a life together? Surely after all this time they deserved it? Her mind threw these thoughts about in an attempt to make sense of them.

Finally, she kicked off her sheets in frustration. She needed to see Santi. She needed to know that it wasn't all going to end now they had found each other again. She slipped into her dressing gown and crept out into the night. The moon was full and phosphorescent. Like a frog she leapt from shadow to shadow, her bare feet wet with dew. She didn't know how she was going to find him, or how she was going to wake him without waking his wife.

Once at the house Sofia wandered around it, staying close to the wall. Peering through the windows she tried to work out which was their room. Unlike her house, Chiquita's was built on one floor so she didn't have to fight with ladders or wrestle with wall plants. Most of the rooms were obscured by shutters — she'd forgotten about the Argentine love of shutters. Of course she couldn't see through them so had no way of knowing what or who was on the other side. She made her way around to the terrace and stood on the smooth paving stones not knowing what to do next. She was about to give up entirely when a small red light caught her attention from under the veranda. She looked more closely and saw that it was the end of a cigarette.

'I gave up smoking years ago,' said the voice on the other end.

'Santi! What are you doing out here?' She gasped in relief.

'This is my house — what are *you* doing here!'

'I came to see you,' she replied in a loud whisper, tiptoeing over to join him on the bench.

'You're mad,' he chuckled. 'But that's why I love you.'

'I couldn't sleep.'

'Me neither.'

'What are we going to do?'

'I don't know.' He sighed and stubbed out his cigarette. He pulled her close and pressed his unshaven face against hers. It prickled.

'I can't bear it all to end, not now that we've just found each other,' she murmured.

'I know — I've been thinking the same thing,' he told her. 'I wish we had run away together all those years ago.'

'Me too. If only . . .'

'Perhaps we were given one chance, and we failed to take it.'

'Don't say that, Santi. You make your own chances!' she hissed.

'You're really bad coming over here like this.' He rubbed her head affectionately. 'I just hope no one else finds it difficult to sleep.'

'You and I have always been in synch.'

'That's the problem. And it won't ever go away, no matter where we are in the world.'

'How long have we got, Santi?' she asked with forced calmness, not wanting to show how desperate she was.

'Claudia's taking the children to Buenos Aires tomorrow evening,' he replied, but whether he misunderstood her question on purpose she didn't know.

'So we'll have some time together?'

'She's finding it hard.'

'What?'

'You suddenly turning up.'

'Does she know about us?' asked Sofia curiously, secretly taking pleasure in the fact that she did.

'She knows that we were once lovers. I told her. Everyone knew. As you can imagine, it was difficult to keep a scandal like that quiet. I didn't want her to be in the dark about something that everyone else knew. I also wanted to come clean. She deserved to know. I wanted her to understand that it wasn't something sordid, that we loved each other. She filled a void in my life, Chofi. She made me happy at a time when I thought I would never be happy again.'

'What are you trying to say?' she asked slowly, but she knew. He kissed her temple and she felt his chest expand as he breathed in deeply.

'I don't know, Chofi. I don't want to hurt her.'

'Well, let's not think about it now,' she said bravely. She believed that if they didn't confront the situation there was still hope. 'We don't have to make any decisions. Let's just enjoy being together, with Maria.'

'*Claro* – we don't have to make any decisions,' he repeated. Sofia hoped the uncertainty was tormenting him as much as it was tormenting her.

When she crept back to her room dawn was already transforming the sky above her into a spectrum of blues and pinks. She averted her thoughts from the future, for she was too afraid to face what was inevitable.

Naturally, Sofia awoke late, but this time she knew exactly where she was. She slipped into a short sundress and walked purposefully out into a radiant morning. It was very hot under the unforgiving Argentine sun. She remembered how she used to spend most of the summer stretched out on the sunbed by the pool 'toasting'. She missed the heat living in England and had forgotten this uninterrupted cornflower-blue sky that now glistened above her.

When she appeared on the terrace Jasmina and Rafael were reading with Anna and Paco under parasols while their children lay on their stomachs drawing with their cousins. It was a tranquil scene and Sofia felt quite envious. Is this what it would have been like if she had returned? Could she and Santi have built a life with little Santiguito, after all? Momentarily her body ached with longing for him and for her two daughters. She wondered where her son was now. He'd be twenty-three years old, a young man. He wouldn't even recognise her if he saw her. They'd be no more than strangers.

Stifling that familiar pain she greeted her family and placed herself at the table. It wasn't long before Soledad appeared with tea, toast, *membrillo* and cheese. She noticed Jasmina's baby was lying asleep on her breast, partially covered in a pretty white shawl. She had one hand on the child's head while the other held her book. If she could paint, Sofia would have drawn her there like that, serene and beautiful like a Sorolla *Mother and Child*.

All the while she sat there Sofia yearned to be with Santi. She longed for the evening when Claudia would disappear to the city leaving them alone together. No one spoke. Each person seemed lost in their own small world and Sofia recalled those innocent days of her youth when she was a part of their world. She watched her mother, quietly reading in the shade under a sunhat; the sunhat was very much her trademark. Sofia couldn't remember what she wore in winter-time; her memories seemed only to be of summer. Paco was reading the Sunday papers through a pair of small round glasses that perched on the bridge of his large hooked nose. Sensing her scrutiny, he looked up and smiled at her. His eyes twinkled fondly. Yet Sofia didn't fit into this scene. Everyone had their place there in the sun. They all shared an easy familiarity where words weren't necessary. They belonged. Sofia had once belonged but now the memory of that belonging had faded and she couldn't remember what it had been like.

She sipped her tea in silence. After a while Clara skipped over to her to show off her picture. It was very good for a child of her age, full of bright colours and happy faces. Her strokes were bold and confident. Sofia admired it.

'Aren't you a good artist!' she exclaimed enthusiastically. Clara glowed with pride. 'Who taught you how to draw?'

'No one – I just like it. I'm top of the class at school.'

Sofia smiled down at the child's elfin face. 'Are you going to be an artist when you grow up?'

'No,' she replied with certainty. 'I'm going to be an actress.' And she grinned happily.

'I think you'll make a very good actress, Clara.'

'Do you think so?' she cried, hopping from one foot to the other.

'What's your favourite film?'

'*Mary Poppins.*'

'And who would you like to be – the little girl?'

'No. Mary Poppins. I know all the words,' and she started singing 'A spoonful of sugar . . .'

'You really do know all the songs,' laughed Sofia.

'Mama says it's a good way to learn English.'

'She's right, it is.'

'I'm going back to Buenos Aires tonight,' the child moaned, pulling a face.

'But you like school, and you'll be coming back next weekend, won't you?'

'You will be here?'

'Of course I will,' Sofia replied, not wanting to disappoint her. She didn't know when she would be leaving. She didn't want to think about it.

'Are you going to stay here now? Papa says you will.'

Sofia looked over at Rafael who lifted his eyes from his paper and grinned at her guiltily. 'I don't think I will be staying,' she said truthfully. 'Not forever. But you must come and stay with me in England. You'd like it there. The best theatre is in England.'

'Oh, I know all about England. Mary Poppins lived in London,' she said earnestly.

'Quite.'

'Look, there's the *carro!*'

Out of the trees rattled the horse and cart with Pablo at the reins. Sofia remembered years before taking a gentle tour of the farm with her grandmother. *Abuelita* Solanas had always said that one of the greatest pleasures in her life was to drive around the *pampa*, sitting comfortably on the worn leather seat of the carriage, gazing at the countryside about her. Every time they neared a hole in the track, she would instruct Jose in her small but firm voice to take care, and occasionally to stop the horses if she spotted an interesting bird or animal. She had told Sofia that when she was younger they used to ride into town in it. When Sofia had remarked that it must have taken hours, her grandmother replied that life had moved at a much slower pace in her day. 'Nothing like the way it rushes about now. You'll be old before you've enjoyed your youth,' she had said disapprovingly. However, Sofia recalled the romance soon wearing thin as she had longed for Jose to speed the horses up a bit. But her grandmother wouldn't have it any faster and was clearly enjoying the scenery – and greeting the passing *gauchos* who ambled by.

Paco wandered over to the sleek horses. He patted them with a firm hand and chatted to Pablo.

'Sofia, do you want to join me?' said her father.

'Me too, me too!' squeaked Clara, throwing down her drawing pad and skipping over to her grandfather.

'I'd love to,' she replied and walked over to join them.

Pablo dismounted and her father lifted Clara up with his large hands, like one would lift a small dog. They sat either side of him at the front and he gave the reigns to Clara, patiently instructing her how to drive. Sofia watched Pablo walk back through the trees. They waved to Rafael and Jasmina, and to Anna, who put down her book and smiled at them from under her hat.

'Are they watching? Are they watching?' hissed Clara as she turned the horses, her face full of concentration.

'They have eyes only for you, my dear,' said Paco, and Sofia recalled how that was just the sort of thing he used to say to her.

They trotted off into the park. Sofia couldn't help but feel a pang of regret as they headed off in the opposite direction from Chiquita's house. She was desperate to see Santi and it was difficult to keep her mind on anything else. Like with her grandmother all those years ago, the novelty subsided after a while and she wished she were elsewhere. Her father listened with patience as his granddaughter chatted away without drawing breath. Finally, when a gap arose in their conversation he turned his attention to Sofia.

'You used to love driving the horses,' he said.

'I remember well, Papa.'

'You played polo better.'

'I liked polo better,' she laughed.

'Do you remember *La Copa Santa Catalina*?' he asked and he grinned at the memory.

'How could I forget? Thank God Agustin fell or you would never have let me play.'

'You know I wanted to let you play from the beginning.'

'You did?'

'But I knew how much your mother hated you playing. She resented the fact that you belonged, Sofia. She never has.' He turned and held her eyes for a moment. She saw regret.

'She chose to live here,' Sofia muttered, turning away.

'Clara – look, the other children are on the swings,' said Paco, who could detect the child was tiring of this game now that she wasn't getting any attention. 'Why don't you go and join them?'

'Can I?' she asked brightly and when he drew the ponies to a halt she hopped down and skipped merrily over through the park to join her cousins.

Sofia could sense that her father wanted to talk to her on her own and she waited warily for him to begin. He urged the ponies on and the jingling sound of their harness filled the uncomfortable pause that followed.

'It wasn't easy, you know,' he said after a while, his eyes fixed on the route in front of them.

'What wasn't easy?' she asked, confused.

He sat pondering for a moment, rocking up and down with the motion of the cart. 'I love your mother. We've had bad times. You leaving and never coming back made her retreat into herself. I know she appears cold. She's uncomfortable with herself. You made that insecurity worse.'

'How do you mean?' she asked, surprised.

'She didn't fit in – you did. Everyone loved you. She found it difficult to love.'

'But she used to love me?' asked Sofia, and then looked upon the words with amazement, as if she hadn't said them.

'She still does. But . . .'

'Yes?' She watched his profile and saw in it the expression of a man about to reveal some terrible secret.

'I fear I am somewhat to blame for the . . . troubled relationship you have had with your mother,' he said gravely. 'I have wanted to tell you about it for a very long time.'

'How could you be? You always saw my side. You were always there for me. In fact you over-indulged me most of the time.'

'Sofia, when your mother was carrying you, things weren't easy between us.' He struggled to find the right words and Sofia sensed what was coming. 'Things were strained. I couldn't cope. We were both very unhappy.'

'You had an affair?' Sofia interrupted. His shoulders dropped; he was relieved, probably, that she had saved him from having to say the words himself.

'Yes,' he replied, and she could see that his remorse still tormented him. This seems to be some sort of hideous family pattern, thought Sofia to herself. God, what am I doing?

'When I fell in love with your mother,' Paco continued, 'I had never met anyone like her before. She was fresh, carefree – she had a naturalness about her that is difficult to describe. When I brought her to Argentina things began to change. She became someone else. I tried to hold on to her but she grew more and more distant. I found the person I had lost in the arms of another woman. She's never recovered from that betrayal.'

They sat in heavy silence. Sofia began to realise then why they had been so harsh on her when she had committed her sexual misdemeanour. By punishing Sofia, her mother was punishing her father for having loved someone else. Her poor father was too entangled in his guilt to dissent.

'How could she have blamed her child simply for having been born during a difficult time?' asked Sofia. 'I can't believe she hated me because I reminded her of your infidelity.'

'She never hated you, Sofia. She never hated you. She just found it difficult to bond with you. She tried. She was jealous of you because I loved you so unconditionally, as did your grandfather, Grandpa O'Dwyer. She felt you stole the two most important men in her life.'

'The two most important men in Mama's life were always Rafa and Agustin,' she said sourly. 'I don't think she tried at all.'

'She looks back on the past with deep regret.'

'Really?'

'She has longed for you to come home.'

'I didn't understand, Papa. I was a child when you sent me away. I felt so dejected. I didn't want to turn my back on you all, but I felt you had all turned yours on me. I felt so guilty that I had got myself into such a mess. You were so disappointed. I thought it would hurt less if I never saw you both again.'

'I'm sorry, *hija*. We can't turn back the clock. If I could, I promise you I would pay all the money in the world. But we have to live with our mistakes, Sofia. I have lived heavily with mine.'

'And me with mine,' she said hoarsely, and looked out over those humid plains.

'Shall I drop you off at Chiquita's house? Then you can go and see Maria,' he said, turning the horses back in the direction of home.

Once they arrived at Chiquita's house Sofia turned to her father. To her surprise she saw in his eyes that old familiar twinkle and for the first time since she had arrived, there was that easy unspoken communication between them. She had thought she would never feel it again. And yet as he smiled tenderly at her she found herself fighting her tears. When he touched her hand she felt she was once more a part of him. She reached forward and embraced him lovingly and without inhibition. And he held her close in the way he used to.

Chapter Forty-Three

Sofia watched Paco as he turned the cart around and headed back into the trees. As a child she had believed her parents to be united by something greater than themselves. It was their divine right as children that their parents were there for them, and although her relationship with her mother was strained, she never once suspected that things might have been difficult between man and wife. In fact, she had never troubled herself to think about anyone else; she had always been too busy feeling sorry for herself.

It was very hot, the midday sun shone mercilessly down and she squinted in the glare. It was also very humid. Her skin felt sticky and uncomfortable. She would have welcomed a shower or a swim. She remembered as a child this heavy air building up for days, culminating in a fantastically dramatic storm. Storms in the *pampa* are uniquely terrifying. As a child Sofia believed the heavens to be thundering with the footsteps of a hundred grey monsters playing out a fearful celestial battle above her.

She entered the house. It was soothingly quiet and still in the cool shadows out of the sunshine. It took a moment for her eyes to adjust. Then she heard the low hum of voices at the end of the corridor. She padded down towards Maria's room. One of the doors on the right was open but she didn't notice it until a firm hand grabbed her and pulled her inside. She caught her breath but before she could panic, Santi's mouth was on hers, smothering any cry that might have escaped had he not silenced her. He half dragged her back into the darkness. She could hardly take the situation seriously but her laughter was muffled by his warm, sensuous mouth. He too was sweaty.

'You said you were coming early – where have you been?' he whispered into her ear.

'I went for a ride in the *carro* with Papa,' she replied and then laughed as he kissed her neck. 'That tickles.'

'I've been waiting for you all morning,' he said ardently. 'You sure know how to tease!'

'Santi, I didn't do it to tease. Papa wanted me to join him. I'm really pleased I did.'

He ran his hands up her body under her dress. She squirmed with pleasure. 'It went well then?' he breathed into her hair.

'I feel close to him again, Santi. He didn't elaborate, typical Papa, but we understand each other again.'

He pulled her dress up to her waist and buried his face in her neck, pressing his hot body against hers. 'I want you now, Chofi,' he whispered, pushing her against the wall. It was cold against her back.

'We can't. Not under the same roof as Maria,' she protested weakly.

His fingers traced her body with the urgency of someone who knows they may be discovered at any moment, yet finds the thrill of that possibility too alluring to resist. Those familiar hands found their way to her secret places, and overwhelmed by his touch she was no longer able to speak or dissent. The only sound was his deep breathing and the rustle of her dress. She felt wanton. Being sexually aroused makes one reckless; she didn't care if anyone discovered them, for at that moment she wanted to cry out in delight. Santi made her feel young again. Vibrant, confident – the Sofia she had left behind with her memories. It felt exhilarating to be that person again. She writhed as his hands ran over her skin. He had a firm, shameless way of touching her body that she found unbearably arousing. He was excited by every part of her that made her a woman. He wanted to smell, taste and enjoy her in a way that was quite animal and blushingly uninhibited. As he made love to her against the wall nothing else existed but that small room.

'I can't go and see Maria like this,' she whispered breathlessly once it was all over.

'Shhhhh.' He placed a hand on her mouth and narrowed his eyes suspiciously. Footsteps. He pushed her against the wall without taking his eyes off hers. The footsteps came closer, lightly stepping down the corridor. Sofia hardly dared breathe. Her imagination had already conjured up the scene. The horror on the face of Claudia. The disappointment in the eyes of her father. Once more leaving in disgrace. Her heart hammered in terror. But the footsteps passed innocently by the door and continued out of earshot.

She fell limply against him. He breathed deeply and kissed her damp forehead.

'Lucky,' he whispered.

'*O Dios*, Santi. What are we doing?'

'What we clearly shouldn't be doing. Now let's get out of here.'

'But I want to see Maria,' she said truthfully. 'I came to see Maria, you know.'

He smirked at her and shook his head fondly. 'Well, you saw me instead. God, you look a sight,' he added lovingly. 'You can't be seen by anyone looking like that.'

'Where shall we go? We're bound to be seen by someone.'

He thought a while. 'Look, you run into the bathroom and clean up – your hair's all over the place. You look wonderfully sensual. I love you like that, but Maria will guess immediately. I'll meet you in her room.'

'Okay.'

'Right, let's check the coast is clear.' But he stood unmoving.

'Well, go on then,' she said.

He held her face in his hands and kissed her again.

'I don't want to go. Look,' he said, placing her hand on his trousers, 'I could do it all over again.'

She laughed quietly onto his chest. 'You fool, you can't go out like that either – we're stuck here!' They both laughed uncontrollably at the absurdity of the situation. They were in danger of getting caught and ruining everything and yet all they could do was laugh like a couple of schoolchildren. Finally he edged his way to the door and peered out.

'Come,' he hissed at her. Together they tiptoed down the corridor holding their breath, their laughter evaporated. As soon as they reached the next door she dived inside and into the safety of the bathroom. He walked on towards his sister's room.

Once in the bathroom, Sofia leant back against the door and breathed again. She could still feel Santi's hands on her body and her skin glowed with exhilaration. When she looked in the mirror she could see what Santi had meant. Her cheeks were red and her eyes sparkled. She looked louche and wanton. It gave her pleasure to see herself like that. She washed her face and tried as best she could to tidy herself up.

Maria was pleased to see her. Her brown eyes lit up when Sofia entered the room. Suddenly Sofia felt guilty that she had allowed herself to make love to Santi under the same roof as her dying cousin. It just didn't seem right. She sensed Padre Julio wagging his bony finger at her from his gilded seat in the heavens.

Santi was sitting languidly in an armchair sipping a glass of wine; there was no guilt in his expression. Eduardo sat at the end of Maria's bed. Claudia was nowhere to be seen, much to Sofia's relief. She greeted Santi as if she hadn't seen him since the day before. When she bent down to kiss him he squeezed her arm twice – that had always been a secret code between them. She squeezed him back.

Eduardo looked grey and in spite of his smile his eyes gave away his hopelessness. Her heart cried out for them both. How could she be enjoying Santi in the midst of so much sadness?

Maria was weak but happy. They all chatted together and no one mentioned her illness. They all wanted to hope that she was going to get better; no one wanted to face the harsh truth that she was slowing down. They talked about the children going back to school. Maria didn't want them to go but it was better for them that their lives assumed some sense of normality. They would leave with Claudia and her children. Sofia caught Santi's eye when Claudia's name was mentioned and she could detect that he was as eager for their time alone together as she was.

Maria tired easily. When her eyes began to droop they decided to leave her to sleep and moved onto the terrace. Claudia was sitting neatly on the bench under the veranda with her daughter curled up against her like an affectionate dog. Sofia smiled stiffly at her, expecting a frosty reception. To her surprise, the other woman's eyes revealed an anxiety they hadn't had before. She looked fearful. Claudia sat up and gently pushed her daughter off with a gesture. The others were all helping themselves to drinks and taking their time in coming out to join them. Sofia had to make some conversation with Claudia; it was unavoidable.

'So,' she deliberated, 'you're going back to Buenos Aires tonight.'

'Yes,' Claudia replied, lowering her eyes. There was an awkward pause during which Sofia shuffled about not knowing whether to stand or sit.

'Which school do the children go to? San Andrés?' she asked.

'Yes,' Claudia said unhelpfully.

'I went there.'

'I know, Santi told me.'

'Right.'

'Santi and I have a lovely relationship, he tells me everything,' she said defensively.

'I know. He told me how good you've been to him. You've made him very happy,' Sofia enthused through gritted teeth.

'He's been good to me – I couldn't ask for a better husband or father to my children.' And she fixed Sofia with steely eyes. 'He wants to stay here for Maria. He adores her. He will be inconsolable once she is gone – but life will go back to normal again. I suppose you will return to your family?'

'Yes, I suppose I will.' But Sofia wanted more than anything to stay.

'How do you find it here after all those years away?' the other woman asked, and a small smile of triumph appeared on her lips.

'It's like nothing's changed. It's amazing how one slots right back in again.'

'But have you – slotted right back in again?' Claudia asked silkily.

'Of course.'

'People change though, don't they? On the surface it appears as if it is still your home, but you probably feel an outsider in both places.'

'Not really. I don't feel an outsider anywhere,' Sofia lied.

'Well, you're lucky. It is very common. I'm surprised you feel at home. There are so many new faces – a new hierarchy. You're not part of the place any more. Santi told me how you used to dominate everyone's conversation at Santa Catalina; now no one talks about you at all.'

Sofia was stung by her bluntness and inwardly recoiled. 'I don't really want to be talked about, Claudia,' she replied icily. 'Maria is the reason I have come. We have a friendship you could never understand. What you think is irrelevant. My roots here run deeper than yours ever will.'

'But I live here, Sofia, and Santi is my husband. In the end you will leave and return to those you belong to. You don't belong here any more.'

At that moment Santi sauntered out onto the terrace followed by Miguel, Panchito, Eduardo and Chiquita. He at once noticed Claudia's pink cheeks and a look of concern swept across his face as his eyes darted from his wife to his lover.

'Will you stay for lunch, Sofia?' asked Chiquita. 'Or dinner, perhaps?'

'I'll eat now with my parents, Chiquita, but I would love to join you for dinner.' Then turning to Claudia she added, 'I don't suppose I'll see you later.' Claudia's neck flushed with inner rage as Sofia smiled at her with satisfaction. 'Have a safe drive to Buenos Aires.'

As Sofia walked through the trees she almost skipped with happiness. She felt victorious. Claudia was on the offensive. If she felt threatened by her, that must surely indicate that things weren't well between husband and wife. She filled the void I left, but now I'm back, Sofia thought triumphantly to herself.

It must have been about five in the afternoon when the cars departed for Buenos Aires. Rafael and Jasmina's children left with the chauffeur, Santi and Claudia's left with Maria's. As the dust settled behind them, glinting in the sunshine, Sofia skipped victoriously over to Chiquita's house.

After dinner with Santi's family they all sat outside on the terrace. In the humidity there descended upon them a heaviness of heart. They sat in the darkness watched by the hidden eyes of the animals of the *pampa* and talked openly about Maria. Sofia could barely look at Eduardo's gentle face. However, it was somehow cathartic to talk about her all together like that. For once they were realistic. She was not going to live for much longer. Miguel had called Fernando, who had decided to come back to Santa Catalina for the first time since his imprisonment to say goodbye to his sister. He would overcome his fear for her sake and perhaps let go of the shadows that haunted him.

Chiquita and Miguel sat holding hands for comfort. It was not going to be easy in spite of the months of preparation. It could be days, literally. In those moments Sofia felt very close to her cousins. They all shared a past; they all shared a love for Maria. Those things formed a bond between them. A bond that whatever was to happen subsequently could never be undone.

Later when the household had retreated to their beds, Santi and Sofia sat on the bench like the night before. They sat in silence. They didn't feel the need to talk. They were comforted by the fact that they were close. He held her hand and pulled her to him. Sofia didn't know how long they sat like that, but after a while her body ached in discomfort.

'I have to move, Santi,' she said and stretched. She felt stiff and sleepy – and melancholic. 'I should go to bed. I can hardly keep my eyes open.'

'I want to spend the night with you, Chofi. I need to be close to you tonight,' he said. She looked at his crumpled face. He was a big man, and yet tonight he looked vulnerable.

'We can't stay here,' she objected.

'I know. It's not appropriate. I'll come with you.'

'Are you sure?'

'Perfectly. I need you, Chofi. I feel so miserable.' She embraced him like a child and he clung to her. There was something touching about the way he hugged her. Her heart ached for him. 'There's nothing any of us can do,' he grieved. 'I feel so useless. And then I think, what if this happened to one of my children? How would I cope? How are my parents coping?'

'You cope because you have to. It hurts and it will never stop hurting, Santi. But you have to be strong. These things are sent to test us. We don't know why they happen, but God wants Maria back. We must be grateful that we have been loaned her for as long as we have,' she said, blinking away the tears. She reflected back on her words and thought how like her mother she sounded. In spite of all her rebelling she had absorbed more of her mother's philosophy than she had realised. 'Come on, let's go to bed. You're more emotional because you're tired. You'll feel stronger in the morning.'

They walked through the trees holding hands. They should have been elated that they were able to spend the night together, but instead their hearts felt heavy and empty with an inexplicable loneliness.

'I have never thought about death, you know. I have never had to face it. But it scares me. We're all so damn vulnerable.'

'I know,' agreed Sofia flatly. 'We're all going to go sometime.'

'I look into the faces of my children. What am I supposed to say when they ask me where she's gone? I don't know what I believe in any more.'

'That's because you're angry with God. I spent my childhood being angry with God simply because my mother was a fanatic; it irritated me. But now I do believe. There must be some purpose to all of this.'

'I have to be strong for Mama, but inside I feel weak and ineffectual,' he confessed miserably.

'You don't have to be strong in front of me, Santi.'

And he squeezed her hand. 'I'm glad you came – you came when I needed you most.'

Sofia closed the door behind her and walked over to the window to fasten the shutters and draw the curtains.

'Listen to the crickets,' she said. She felt nervous. They had made love before, but tonight it would be slow and intimate. She heard Santi approach behind her and then he slipped his arms around her waist and pulled her to him. Softly he kissed her neck. She lay back against him and closed her eyes. His hands slid under her shirt and she felt his roughened palms on the surface of her belly. It was humid and her skin was damp. Then his hands were on her breasts, so gently she could barely feel them. His bristle tickled her neck and she writhed in pleasure. She turned to face him and his mouth descended onto hers with the fervour of someone who wants to blot out the pain of the present and forget himself in the arms of a loving woman. At last they abandoned themselves to each other and in the secrecy of the night she shared him with no one.

'Am I old?' she asked him afterwards when she noticed him looking at her body.

'You? Never old,' he said tenderly. 'Just older.'

Chapter Forty-Four

Monday, 10 November 1997

Fernando felt the sweat trickle down his back as he disembarked from the ferry that had brought him across the muddy waters from Uruguay to Argentina. It had been almost twenty years since he had last stood upon Argentine soil. Twenty years since he had taken part in political demonstrations against the military government that had marched into power on 24 March 1976. Although the coup itself had been bloodless, the following five years had seen the disappearance of nearly 10,000 people. Fernando had almost been one of them.

He looked back across the brown waters and remembered his escape all those years ago. Terrified and defeated, he had vowed never more to set foot in Argentina. He had seen too much violence to ever want to be that close to death again.

During that period, Fernando had learnt a great deal about himself. He didn't like what he had learnt. He was a coward. Not like those brave men and women who risked their lives and often sacrificed them for the good of their country, for democracy and for freedom. Who came in their hundreds to protest against General Videla and his henchmen in the Plaza de Mayo. They were the faceless heroes of Argentina's 'Disappeared', stolen from their beds in the middle of the night never to be seen or heard of again. Perhaps, he thought, it would have been better had he vanished with them, perhaps to a watery grave at the bottom of the sea instead of running into hiding in Uruguay. If the police had only realised just how innocuous he really was, how his blatant parading and crowing was all for show, all to make him feel and appear important, all to make up for the years of living beside a brother whose light shone so brightly there was nowhere for Fernando to shine. Until he befriended Carlos Riberas and joined the underground guerrilla movement. That was a corner so dark he was able to shine all on his own.

Once in Uruguay he had bought a small, dilapidated house on the beach, grown a beard, grown his hair, barely washed except for the times he swam in the sea. He had lost all self-respect. He hated himself and so he tried to lose himself beneath the thick black hair that grew up around him like the thorny forest in the tale of Sleeping Beauty. Except there was no princess to wake him with a kiss. He avoided women. He wasn't good enough; why would anyone love him?

He had written articles for various Uruguayan magazines and newspapers, attempting to continue the fight from across the water. But he didn't need the money – his family made sure he had what he needed. In fact, he had more money than he deserved so he gave it away to homeless beggars who roamed the dusty streets in drunken stupors, clutching their bottles of liquor in brown paper bags. He didn't feel any better about himself, though. He just felt dead inside.

Then one night he had awoken after one of his usual nightmares with the sweat soaking into the mattress leaving it soggy like marshland, and decided that he couldn't bear the mental torture any more. He got up, packed a few items into a rucksack and locked the door to his house. For the next five years he travelled extensively around South America. To Bolivia, Mexico, Equador. From the Chilean lakes to the mountains of Peru. But wherever he went the shadow of his torment was always one step behind him.

Standing on the top of Machu Picchu, with only the heavens above him and the mists of the earth below, he realised he had nowhere else to run to. He had reached the top. He had only two choices: to continue up into the realm of the gods or to go back down again and learn to live with himself. It was a difficult choice to make. The mists swirled below him in a hypnotic dance, beckoning him to hurl himself into the sweet silence and oblivion that they promised. The silence of death. The oblivion that enables you to forget even yourself. He stared down at it, swaying on the edge of the world. Yet, that too would be running away. He'd be no better than before when he had run away from Argentina, no better than a deserter. It would be so easy, too easy perhaps. There's no merit in that, he thought to himself, there's nothing brave about dying like this.

He collapsed onto the grass and held his head in his hands. The most difficult thing in life is living, he thought miserably, resigning himself to the fact that there were probably a good number of years ahead of him. I can either live them unconsciously, like a spectre, waiting to die, or I can hurl myself at life and make it as good as it can be.

When he arrived back at his house the telephone was ringing. It was his father, who'd been trying to reach him for weeks. Maria was dying of cancer. It was time to go home.

When Fernando arrived in Buenos Aires he asked the chauffeur, who had been sent by his parents, to take him to the Casa Rosada in the Plaza de Mayo. He just wanted to drive around it once. He wanted to see whether it still haunted him like it did in his dreams. The government house, painted pink by mixing beef fat, blood and lime together, dominates the square, flanked by the *Banco de la Nación*, the *Catedral Metropolitana*, the *Consejo Municipal* and the *Cabildo*. It is a beautiful square lined with tall exotic palm trees, busy flower gardens and colonial buildings. But to Fernando it had become a dark and menacing square, the scene of so much disillusionment.

As the car approached the square Fernando felt the fear rise up from his belly and sit in his throat like a fat toad making it almost impossible to speak without croaking. Cold sweat collected in his clenched fists and his breathing became shallow and irregular. Yet once in the square, the summer sun shining innocently down upon the plants and flowers, Fernando felt his terror dissipate as if dispelled by God Himself. The shadows were gone. Argentina was now a democracy and he could smell it in the sweet air and see it in the carefree faces of the people who ambled by. He looked about at the city's new face and noticed how it prospered, how it smiled. The fear no longer hung heavy about him but fell off his shoulders like a worn-out coat no longer appropriate in the new, warmer climate. 'Enough,' he said to the chauffeur. 'Take me to Santa Catalina.'

Fernando's arrival was a momentous occasion for his family. Reminiscent of Santi's return after his trip abroad well over twenty years before, they all gathered on the terrace of their home squinting into the sunshine for the first sighting of Fernando's car. Except his arrival was awaited with sadness for he was returning to say goodbye to his sister.

'He's much changed, Sofia,' said Chiquita sadly. 'I don't think you'll recognise him.'

Sofia smiled at her aunt sympathetically. 'Do you think he's come back to stay?' she asked, making conversation. She didn't really care whether he came back or not. She glanced over at Santi who was talking to his father and Eduardo. Fernando's arrival was shaded with apprehension. Miguel had worried that he wouldn't return in time. Maria was fading fast. No one could remain still. They either shuffled their feet or paced the grass. Even the dogs lay panting in the shade with their tails heavy and unmoving.

When Fernando's car turned the corner and drove slowly up the drive with the dignity and sobriety of a hearse, the small gathering breathed with relief rather than joy. Fernando looked out of the window and felt his heart inflate with affection and sweet melancholia. This was where he had grown up. This is what he had sacrificed for so many years and it hadn't changed at all.

He stepped out of the car and into the frail arms of his mother. He embraced his father, Panchito, his aunts and uncles who all commented on his long hair and black beard. He was barely recognisable. When he saw Sofia he gasped with astonishment.

'I never thought I'd see you again,' he said, looking down at the woman who reminded him of a cousin he had once loathed. But they were both different people now, as if their childhood had been an extended play which had long since closed down, their roles discarded along with the script.

'It's good to see you, Fercho. I'm glad you've come home,' she replied, for want of anything better to say. She felt awkward. Fernando was like a stranger to her.

When he saw Santi he did something that surprised them both. He wept. In Santi he saw the friend who had set out that cold winter's night to punish Facundo Hernandez. Yet he cried not because Facundo had saved his life, nor because they had both saved Maria's, but because he looked into the honest green eyes of his brother and saw only the wasted years caused by jealousy, resentment and fear. He wept because he had come home and because he was home to stay. He looked behind him and the shadow was no longer there.

Chiquita led Fernando inside to see Maria. Santi caught Sofia's eye and they both knew that this was not a moment for them; Fernando needed time alone with his sister.

'Let's go into town,' he said solemnly. 'No one will notice where we are now Fercho's home.'

'He's so different. He's like another person – someone I never knew,' she said wistfully, following him through the trees.

'I know. He's different for us, too.'

'I should feel something for him, but I don't,' she said, reflecting on the fickleness of time that allows you to connect with some people after long years of separation and not with others.

'He's been through a lot, Chofi. He's not the same as he was. You'll have to get to know him all over again. So will I.'

When Fernando saw his sister he was humbled by her brave smile and sparkling eyes but devastated by the destruction the disease had caused. Her face was gaunt, the cheekbones sticking out, reminiscent of those harrowing photographs from the German prison camps of World War Two, and she had lost her hair which emphasised the shape of her skull that was only too apparent beneath the thin layer of skin that clung to it. But her spirit was so big it dwarfed her appearance and seemed to illuminate the room. She extended her bony hand and welcomed him home and he fell to his knees and kissed it, in awe of her courage and only too aware of the lack of his own.

'Look at you!' she laughed, her eyes smiling at him with tenderness. 'What have you done to yourself, Fercho?' Fernando was unable to speak. His lips quivered but no sound escaped them. His dark eyes filled with tears. 'I have this terrible effect on everyone who sees me. I reduce them all to shivering wrecks!' she said, but her humour was unable to hide the tears that began to well in her own eyes and fall down her sallow cheeks. 'You're a silly, silly fool,' she continued with a tremulous voice, 'to leave us for so long. What were you doing over there, when we who love you were all over here, missing you? Did you miss us too? Are you here to stay?'

'I'm here to stay,' he croaked. 'I wish I . . .'

'Shhh.' She silenced him. 'I have a rule now. No regretting. No remorse. No wailing and pulling out your hair because you wish you had done things differently. I've been through this with Sofia — silly fools the pair of you. In this house we live in the present and enjoy each other without looking back, unless it's to talk about the good old days. They were good, weren't they, Fercho?' He nodded mutely. 'Ah, do you remember that friend of mine you had a crush on – my schoolfriend, you must remember? Silvia Diaz, that was her name. You used to write her love letters. I wonder what's happened to her now.'

'She never fancied me back,' he said, smiling at the memory of those innocent days.

'Oh yes, she did. But she was shy. She used to read and re-read your letters during class. She read them out to me. They were very romantic.'

'I don't think so.'

'Oh, they were. *Very* romantic. You were a dark horse. We could never keep track of you. But Sofia and I once spied on you kissing Romina Blaquier in the swimming pool.'

'I knew you were there,' he confessed and grinned at her.

'You didn't show it.'

'Of course not – I enjoyed the attention.' He laughed.

'That's better. Laughter is healing, tears only make me sad,' she said and they laughed together.

Chapter Forty-Five

'Do you remember, we used to come here every Saturday night for Mass?' Sofia's voice echoed against the cold stone walls of the church of *Nuestra Señora de la Asunción*.

'Before going to the night-club,' chuckled Santi. 'Not very reverent.'

'I never thought of that,' she replied. 'To be honest, Mass was just a chore.'

'You used to snigger the whole way through.'

'Quite difficult to keep a straight face with Padre Julio stuttering and lisping.'

'He died years ago.'

'I can't say I'm sorry.'

'You *should* say you're sorry, you're in his church,' Santi said, laughing.

'You mean he might hear? I wonder if people stutter in heaven – you never hear of stuttering angels, do you?'

They wandered down the aisle, their *alpargatas* treading softly and silently over the stones. The church was very bare, not like the Catholic churches in the city. The altar stood in humble simplicity under a clean white cloth adorned with drooping flowers. The air was stale and the spicy scent of incense lingered as there was no open window through which it could escape. The sun streamed in through the stained glass behind the altar casting long beams of light onto the floor and walls, showing up the dust which, were it not for the sunshine, would have gone unnoticed. Icons of the Virgin Mary hung from the walls among the many statues of saints and candles that shone out of the gloom. The pews were as Sofia remembered them, austere and uncomfortable enough to stop one falling asleep during the sermon.

'Do you remember the wedding of Soledad's niece Pilar?' said Sofia with a smile.

'How could I forget?' replied Santi, hitting his forehead with the palm of his hand and laughing out loud.

'Padre Julio mixed her up with her sister and gave the whole address about Lucia!' They tried to muffle their laughter.

'It was only at the end when he blessed the happy couple Roberto and Lucia that anyone realised that the person he had just been describing had nothing whatsoever to do with Pilar!' she added, barely able to get the words out. 'How awful. She was so upset and all we could do was laugh!'

When they reached the altar silence washed over them like a spell. They instinctively stopped fooling around. There were two small tables on either side of the altar covered in candles of every size and shape. Their minds turned to Maria. Santi struck a match and lit one.

'For my sister,' he said and closed his eyes in prayer. Sofia was moved. Lighting one herself she also closed her eyes and silently asked God to preserve her cousin's life. She felt Santi's hand find hers and hold it for comfort. He squeezed it twice and she returned his message in the same code. They stood there for a while. She had never prayed so hard. However, her prayers weren't totally unselfish. As long as Maria lived she had an excuse to stay.

'I wonder whether God minds that we only turn to Him in distress,' Santi said quietly.

'I imagine He's used to it,' she replied.

'I hope it works.'

'So do I.'

'I don't have much faith that it will, though. I'd like to. I feel guilty that I come here as a last resort. I feel I don't deserve a miracle.'

'You've come. I don't think it matters that you've come as a last resort. You're here now.'

'I suppose. I never used to understand those people who came to church all the time. I think I do now. It gives them comfort.'

'Is it giving you some comfort?' she asked.

'Sort of,' he replied, and smiled at her wistfully. 'You know, I should have liked to marry you in this little church.'

'With Padre Julio stammering "W-w-w-w-ill y-you t-take S-s-s-s-Sofia . . ."'

He chuckled at her imitation. 'Nothing would have mattered, even if he had given the address about Fercho!' he said, pulling her into his arms and kissing her forehead affectionately.

She felt so loved in his embrace. The smell of him brought back memories of another time and she longed to hold onto the moment for ever. She hugged him back and they stayed like that for some time, neither of them feeling the need to speak. She felt dreadfully melancholic and yet at the same time she was happy because she was with him. She was aware that these moments were transient so she clung to them and lived them more intensely than she had ever lived.

'Did you ever confess to Padre Julio that we were lovers?' he asked, pulling away.

'Are you crazy? No! Did you?'

'No. Did you ever confess anything?'

'Not really, I made it all up. He was so easily shocked it was too tempting not to make things up.'

'You're really bad, you know!' he said and smiled a little sadly.

'I thought I wasn't as bad as I used to be until I showed up here. I have now exceeded my own limitations.'

'I should feel guilty – I did at the beginning. But I don't now. It feels so right,' he said, shaking his head as if his feelings were now out of his control and no longer his responsibility.

'It *is* right,' she insisted, taking his hand in hers. 'It should have been like this.'

'I know. I feel guilty that I don't feel guilty. It's terrifying how one can forget.'

'Claudia?'

'Claudia, the children. When I'm with you I don't think about them any more.'

'Same,' she replied. But it wasn't really true. Every time David's face surfaced with those of their daughters she made every effort to suppress them. They had almost given up trying. But David could be very persistent when he wanted to.

'Come on. Let's get out of this place before Padre Juan catches us,' he said, making his way up the aisle.

'We're doing nothing wrong. We're cousins, remember?'

'Chofi, I can't forget. I think God made you my cousin to punish me for something I did in a past life.'

'Or He's got a sick sense of humour!'

Once out into the sunshine they had to shield their eyes from the glare. Sofia felt giddy for a moment while her eyes adjusted to the light. The humidity was stifling.

'We're going to have one hell of a storm, Chofi. Can you feel it?'

'Yes, I can. I love storms, I find them very exciting.'

'The first time we made love was during a storm.'

'Yes, I remember. How could I forget?'

They walked out onto the plaza. The road was still a dirt track, unchanged since the days of their grandparents. It ran sleepily around the square which itself was lined with tall trees. She noticed they still painted the lower part of the bark with white *Cal* to keep the ants off. Small houses and shopfronts opened out into the sunshine, their shady interiors oblique behind dusty glass windows. The *boliche* was still in the same place on the corner. It was the café where all the *gauchos* would get together to drink *Mate* and play cards.

Paco used to spend every Sunday morning there, reading the papers over a cup of coffee; Sofia imagined he still did, being a creature of habit.

As it was the afternoon the shops were all closed for siesta and the plaza was still and quiet in the heat of the day. They wandered into the square to sit on one of the benches in the shade. They were about to sit down when a voice called at them from one of the other benches. To their horror and surprise it was the famous *Vieja Bruja*.

'*Buen día*, Señora Hoffstetta,' said Santi, nodding his head politely.

'I didn't know the Old Witch was still alive!' hissed Sofia through her smile.

'I don't think witches die,' replied Santi.

La Vieja Bruja sat hunched in a long black dress – no wonder she had been given the nickname Old Witch. As a child, she had found her terrifying, Sofia recalled. Her face was small and pinched, like an old walnut. Her eyes were as black as her teeth and you could smell her a mile off. She clasped in her long, knotted fingers a brown paper bag.

The cousins sat down and tried to ignore her, but all the while they were talking Sofia could feel the woman's eyes on her back.

'Is she still looking at us?' she asked Santi.

'Yes, she is. Just pretend she's not there.'

'I can feel her. I wish she'd go away.'

'Don't worry, she's not a witch, really.'

'Don't believe it. She makes the witches in storybooks look like Snow White.' They both laughed into their hands. 'She probably knows we're talking about her.'

'If she's a witch then she most certainly does.'

'Let's go. I really can't bear her!' So they stood up to go.

'Bah!' she screeched. They ignored her and hurried on. 'Bah!' she persisted. '*Mala suerte*. You had your chance. *Mala suerte*. Bah!' They both stopped and looked at each other in astonishment. Santi was on the point of turning to confront her but Sofia managed to grab him by the arm and pull him on. 'Twin souls. I see into your auras, twin souls! Bah!' she continued.

'*O Dios*, she's frightening me. Let's get out of here,' insisted Sofia and they walked at great speed.

'How dare she talk to us like that, the gossipmonger!' Santi said angrily. 'It's people like her who go around making trouble for everyone.'

'You know she really is a witch, there's no mistaking it.'

'Well, why doesn't she just piss off on her broomstick then.' They both laughed nervously.

Suddenly, just when they thought they had seen the last of her, she appeared before them, crooked and reeking, with the semblance of an oversized, hairy bat. She shuffled up to Sofia and thrust the brown paper bag into her unsuspecting hands. She held it with the revulsion of someone carrying a bag full of dripping entrails, it felt soft and damp in her fingers. She looked into the woman's black eyes and panicked, but *La Vieja Bruja* nodded at her reassuringly and closed her hands around the bag. She squirmed and stepped backwards in a vain attempt to be rid of her. *La Vieja Bruja* grinned and muttered her name 'Sofia Solanas' before disappearing back into the square.

Once safely in the truck, Sofia slammed the door and rolled up the window. She was shaking.

'What's in the bag?' Santi asked impatiently, beginning to find the whole situation amusing.

'I don't know why you're smirking, there's nothing funny about it. You open it!' she cried and thrust it at him. Slowly he opened it and peered inside with half an eye as if he expected to find something grotesque within. Then he laughed loudly with relief.

'Well, what is it?' she asked.

'You're not going to believe this! It's a sapling – an ombu tree, for you to plant.'

'An ombu tree? What on earth am I going to do with an ombu tree?'

'Well, it certainly won't grow in England.' He began to laugh again.

'What an odd woman. How old is she? I thought she was ancient twenty years ago,' she exclaimed hotly. 'She should be cold in her grave by now.'

'Why give you an ombu tree?' muttered Santi, frowning. 'I'm surprised she even knew who you were.'

He started the engine and Sofia was relieved when they left the town behind and headed back to Santa Catalina.

'What did she mean by twin souls?' she said after a while.

'I don't know.'

'She's right though, we are. But I don't think you need to be clairvoyant to see that. She's so creepy. The trouble is, people believe her,' she said angrily. 'Soledad for one.'

'Oh, and you don't?' he said and his mouth twisted into the beginnings of a smirk.

'Of course not!' she sniffed.

'Then why are we even discussing her? If you didn't believe her you wouldn't even bother thinking about her.'

'That doesn't make sense. I don't believe her, she's a nuisance and I don't think she should go around frightening people. I don't believe in witches.'

'But you believe in the magic of the ombu.'

'That's different.'

'No, it's not!'

'It is. She's a madwoman. She should be locked up. The ombu is something altogether different. The magic of nature.'

'Chofi?'

'Yes?' she said irritably. Then looked at him and noticed the beginnings of a smile tickle his face.

'Has the ombu ever made a wish of yours come true?' he said, his eyes concentrating on the road as if he needed something to distract himself from laughing.

'Yes, it has.'

'Which one?'

'I once made a wish that you would fall in love with me,' she replied and smiled triumphantly.

'I don't think that had anything to do with the ombu.'

'You know nothing about it!' she exclaimed. 'You just don't understand the power of nature and you know something, I'll bet you this sapling *will* grow in England.' She turned and caught him smiling. 'Are you laughing at me?' she complained. 'Stop the car.'

'What?'

'Stop the car. Now!'

He steered off the road and up a track to some trees that opened out into a field. He switched off the engine and turned to face her. His large green eyes and mischievous grin were irresistible. She felt her irritation lift.

'Look – she *was* creepy,' insisted Sofia.

'She certainly was. But what's the harm in saying we're twin souls?' he said, kissing her neck.

'She said we'd had our chance.'

'What does she know? She's only an old witch,' he chuckled, unbuttoning her dress.

As soon as his warm lips were on hers she forgot about the ranting of the old woman in the plaza. He tasted of salt and smelt of that uniquely Santi smell she loved so much. She climbed astride him, catching her breath as she negotiated the steering wheel and gear stick. He pulled up her dress and ran his hand over the tender skin of her inner thighs. They were tacky with sweat. He pulled her panties to one side and slid into her. Placing his hands in the small of her back he pulled her against him, guiding her movements. As they made love half dressed she felt once more the excitement of breaking the rules.

Chapter Forty-Six

_____

Back at Santa Catalina they fell into the pool. The afternoon sun hung low in the west, smouldering like a dying coal in the limpid sky. Mosquitoes hovered about the trees and grass and the scents of Antonio's roses and honeysuckle reached them across the water. Lying with their arms over the edge, gazing out over the fields, they talked about the things that had changed during the years that they had been parted.

'You know, I miss Jose,' said Sofia. 'Pablo's sweet, but I somehow connected with Jose.'

'He was a wise old bird.'

'Who's this Javier? He's very handsome.'

'He's Soledad and Antonio's son. Didn't she tell you?' he replied, surprised.

'Soledad's son? Are you sure?'

'Of course I'm sure. I can't believe she didn't tell you. She probably assumed you knew.'

'How awful. I've done nothing but talk about myself since the moment I arrived.'

'He's a bit of a hero.'

'Really, how come?'

Santi told her how Javier had been helping his father with the plants around the pool a few years before, while the family sat sunbathing and chatting on the terrace that circled the water. Clara and Felix had been playing quietly on the grass with their other small cousins. No one had noticed Felix crawling over to the edge of the water to feel it with his hands. Javier just happened to look into the pool to see what looked like a small grey blur sitting at the bottom, unmoving. He didn't waste a moment. He dived in to find the small object was little Felix. He pulled the child out of the water, gasping and spluttering for air. He saved his life. If it hadn't been for Javier, Felix would have drowned. Paco gave him a new saddle with his initials engraved on a silver plaque as a reward for saving the life of his grandson. No one ever forgot what Javier had done. Paco had always been especially fond of Javier.

The moment they finished their swim Sofia headed back to the house, straight into the kitchen where Soledad was preparing the dinner.

'Soledad, you never told me you had a son,' she said enthusiastically, endeavouring to make up for her previous lack of interest. 'He's so good-looking too.'

'Just like Antonio,' laughed Soledad.

'Well, more like *you*, Soledad,' said Sofia. 'I feel awful – I've seen him around the *campo* for the last few days and I've never said anything.'

'I thought you knew.'

'Well, I do now. Santi told me how he saved Felix's life. You must be very proud.'

'I am. We both are. Javier polishes his saddle every day. It's the most precious thing he owns. Señor Paco is a very generous man,' she said with reverence.

'Javier is well deserving of his generosity,' Sofia told her.

Sofia wandered off to her room where she ran a cool bath. As she undressed she thought of Santi and wondered what the future held. She thought of David, too, how he had rescued her at a time when she felt vulnerable and lost. He had been so good to her. She was relieved when Soledad knocked on the door. She needed to be distracted from the questions that invaded her mind whenever she found herself alone.

Soledad entered hurriedly. To Sofia's surprise her round face was pale and tearstained and she wrung her hands in anguish. Sofia immediately led her to the bed where she sat beside her, placing an arm over her large shoulders to comfort her.

'What's the matter?' she asked and watched as the other woman's big frame shook with sobs. Soledad tried to speak but cracked at every attempt, breaking down once more in tears. Finally, after much cajoling she said she had a secret she had been sworn to keep. 'But you're my Sofia,' she wept. 'I can't keep anything from you.'

Sofia wasn't really interested in her secret. She had kept many of Soledad's secrets in the past and none of them had ever been worth anything. But she hated to see her old friend so upset, so she listened to her secret to comfort her.

'It's about Javier,' Soledad began weakly.

'He's all right, isn't he?' asked Sofia, concerned, imagining he might be ill.

'It's not like that, Señora Sofia. We love him, Antonio and I. We've given him a good home, watched him grow up into a man. We're proud of him. You'd be pleased.'

'Then why are you crying? He's a good son. You're lucky.'

'Oh, I know, Señora Sofia. You don't understand.' She paused, took a deep, shuddering breath. 'Señor Paco told us not to tell anyone. We never did. We kept his secret for twenty-three years. We thought you'd come back sooner. We were only his guardians, we told ourselves. You've always been his mother.'

'What are you talking about, Soledad?' whispered Sofia.

'Please don't blame me. I only did what Señor Paco asked me to do. He brought your baby over from Switzerland. He said he wanted him to have a good home. That you'd come back and regret what you had done. He didn't want his grandson to be brought up by strangers.'

'Javier is my son?' Sofia said slowly. She felt strangely detached from her body as if her words were coming out of someone else.

'Javier is your son,' Soledad repeated and began to howl like a wounded beast.

Sofia got to her feet and stood by the window looking out onto the dusky *pampa*.

'Javier is Santiguito?' she asked, not wanting to believe it. She saw in the glass his little hands and feet, his small nose that she had kissed too few times. She tasted the salt in her mouth. She watched her reflection in the window contort with pain, until her eyes were so blurred she ceased to see anything at all.

'Señor Paco and I – and of course Antonio – are the only people who know about this. He didn't want Señora Anna to know. But it is your right. You are his mother. If you want to tell Javier I cannot stop you. Maybe he should know who his real parents are. That he is a Solanas.'

Chapter Forty-Seven

Sofia ran out into the park leaving Soledad howling alone in her bedroom. It was almost dark. She didn't know what she was going to say to him, but she had to see him, she had to tell him. After all, wasn't it every child's right to know who had carried him? She saw herself in her mind's eye throwing her arms around him and breathing into his body, 'My son, you are Santiguito, the son I thought I had lost, the son I thought I would never see again.' The tears had ceased and in their place she felt a strange lightness of being. It was intoxicating.

As she neared the shacks she could make out the red flames of a campfire. The twangy tones of a guitar reached her, then singing voices, getting louder and louder as she approached. She was dismayed to find a group of *gauchos* sitting around the fire, laughing and drinking, their brown faces illuminated by the skipping flames. She stopped short and stood behind a tree in order to watch them. They couldn't see her. She strained her eyes, searching their faces for her son. Then she saw him. He was sitting in the middle between Pablo and another man she didn't recognise, singing enthusiastically with the others. Every now and then he'd smile, his white teeth gleaming in the flickering light. She couldn't see him well enough to notice whether he looked like herself or Santi and was unable to remember his features from the few times that she had seen him. She narrowed her eyes in frustration, attempting to see better.

Suddenly a slim woman opened the door to her house and wandered out to join the group, carrying a tray of dishes. Sofia was able to make out a skinny dog bouncing around her heels. When she moved to get a better look the dog must have sensed someone in the trees for it started yapping. It scuttled towards her, its tail pointed straight up in the air like a wild boar, ready to attack. The woman looked over to where Sofia was standing. She said something to the men and a couple of them leapt to their feet, hands on their *facones*. Sofia had no choice but to come out from her hiding place. Ashamed to have been caught, she showed herself. She noticed a ripple of sobriety pass through them as the guitar was put down and they stopped singing.

Javier, already standing up, took his hand off his knife and came marching towards her. 'Good evening, Señora Sofia. Are you all right? Is there anything you want?' he asked politely, frowning at her curiously.

She watched him stride over. He was tall, had good posture, was broad like his father. He also walked a bit like Santi, his knees turning outwards, but then he had spent his life on a horse so that wasn't really surprising. As he came closer she noticed that he had dark hair like her. He stood before her, waiting for her to speak. She was about to tell him that she was his mother, but the words wouldn't come out. Her enthusiasm vanished. She looked behind him at the small gathering of his fellow *gauchos* and realised that he was happy there. He was happy not knowing. He possessed something that had eluded her for so many years; a sense of belonging. He belonged there at Santa Catalina. How ironic that he belonged there more than she did and certainly more than her mother ever had. Sadly she realised that it would be cruel and selfish to shatter everything he had grown up to believe in. She gulped back her words and smiled weakly.

'I used to come here a lot as a child when Jose was still alive,' she said, trying to start up a conversation.

'My mother tells me you've been away a long time, Señora Sofia,' he said.

'Yes, I have. You have no idea how much I missed it.'

'Is it true it always rains in England?' he asked, his mouth breaking into a shy grin.

'Not as much as you'd imagine. Some days are as clear and blue as they are here,' she replied, hoping he wouldn't notice how closely she was looking into his features.

'I have never left Santa Catalina,' he said.

'Well, if I were you I would keep it that way. I have seen many different parts of the world and I can tell you there is nowhere more beautiful than Santa Catalina.'

'Will you be staying? My mother hopes that you will.'

'I don't know, Javier,' she said, shaking her head. 'Your mother is an old sentimentalist!'

'I know.' He laughed.

'She's been a good mother to you, I bet.'

'She has.'

'She was good to me when I was a child too. She was my partner in crime.'

After a while Sofia could see he was anxious to get back to his friends. After all, she was his boss's daughter, they were from two different worlds. He would never talk to her as an equal. Humouring her was part of his job.

She watched him walk back before making her own way home through the trees. He was definitely her son. Although she couldn't make out the colour of his eyes in the darkness, she imagined they were brown. If they had been green like his father's, she believed she would have noticed them before. There was nothing extraordinary about his appearance. He was handsome and yet he had been brought up as a *gaucho*. He was very much a product of his surroundings. No, it wouldn't have been fair to tell.

When she returned to her room, Soledad was still sitting there. She sat hunched and defeated, her hands clenched in her lap. When she entered Soledad blinked up at her with the eyes of someone whose very reason for living has been snatched away from them. They were raw from crying and dull with grief. Sofia, too, felt bereft. But seeing Soledad like that reinforced her decision. She had done the right thing.

When Sofia told her that she hadn't been able to tell him, Soledad's face lit up from within and her shoulders that had been stooped with tension, now relaxed with relief. She wept again, but this time her tears were of happiness. She held Sofia to her bosom, thanking her over and over again for giving her back her son. She told her that not a day had gone by when she hadn't reminded herself that Javier did not belong to her, that she was merely a guardian, bringing him up as best she could until the day his real mother would return to claim him. But Sofia told her sadly that he was Soledad's son. It was irrelevant who had borne him.

'Javier even looks like you, Soledad,' she said, sitting next to her on the bed, allowing her old friend to place a comforting arm around her shoulders.

'I don't know, Señorita Sofia, but he is a handsome boy, that is true,' she said, suppressing a smile of pride, knowing there was no place for her pride in that small room.

'How did it happen?' Sofia asked curiously. 'How come no one noticed when you and Antonio suddenly got a child out of nowhere?'

'Well, Señor Paco came to see us in our house. He told us that we were the best people qualified to look after your baby because you and I had always been close. I nursed you when you were a baby, remember?'

Sofia nodded. She thought of Dominique and Antoine devising their plan to send Santiguito out to Argentina. She didn't resent them; in fact, they had given him the best home he could have had. The home she lost, he had found. She smiled bitterly at the irony.

'What did he tell you?'

'He told us that you would come back one day, but that you

were unable to look after the child yourself. I didn't ask any questions, Señorita Sofia, I didn't pry. I believed what he told me and did my best to bring up Javier the way you would have wanted.' Soledad sniffed and her voice trembled.

'I know you did. I'm not blaming you. I just need to know, that's all,' Sofia said calmly, reassuring Soledad with a squeeze of her clammy hand. Soledad took a deep breath and then continued.

'So we made up some story about a niece of Antonio's who had died, leaving Antonio instructions in the will to look after her child. No one questioned it – that sort of thing happens all the time. Everyone was overjoyed for us. We had wanted a child for thirty years. God had been kind.' Her voice was reduced to a throaty husk and a fat tear plopped onto her plump cheek. 'Then a week later Señor Paco arrived at our house in the middle of the night with little Javier wrapped in muslin. He was beautiful. Like the baby Jesus, with large brown eyes, like yours, and soft brown skin. I loved him the moment I saw him and I thanked God for His gift. It was a miracle. A miracle.'

'My father was the only person who knew besides you and Antonio, right?'

'Yes.'

'So how did he treat him? Was it difficult for him?'

'I don't know, Señorita Sofia, but he was always especially kind to Javier. The child used to follow him about the farm like a dog. They had a good relationship. But Javier was always a *gaucho*. He was happier with us than he was with your family. He didn't belong in the big houses, he felt out of place. So as he grew up a natural distance developed between them. But as I said, Señor Paco has always been especially kind to Javier.'

'What was he like as a child?' Sofia dared to ask, although she knew it would be painful to hear what she had missed out on.

'He was cheeky. He had your moodiness and Señor Santiago's talent. He was always the best at everything. The best on a horse, the best at his schoolwork.'

'I was never good at schoolwork,' said Sofia. 'That didn't come from me.'

'But he is his own person, Señorita Sofia,' Soledad added truthfully.

'I know – I saw it. I expected him to look like me, limp like Santi. I expected him to have that self-confidence, that Solanas look. You know what I mean? But he's totally himself. He's a stranger to me and yet I carried him for nine months and I bore him into the world. Then I deserted him,' she said, her voice trailing off. 'At least I will no longer be tormented by not knowing what has become of him. I'm happy he has you as a mother, Soledad. Because you were my mother, too.' Then she cried again against the bosom of her maid. She cried for what she had lost and she cried for what she had found and she didn't know for which she cried the most.

That night she could barely sleep. Dreams seemed to appear as much when she was awake as when she drifted into a shallow slumber. She dreamed of making love to Santi, gazing into his face which suddenly transformed itself into Javier's. She awoke in panic, turned on the light and waited for her heartbeat to slow down. She felt so alone. She longed to be able to tell Santi about Javier, but she knew the damage she would cause if she did. She wondered why Dominique had never told her. She wondered how differently things might have turned out had she managed to speak to her that time their sullen housekeeper had informed her they were out of the country.

In the beginning, she had been afraid to tell Dominique and Antoine that she had changed her mind because she couldn't bear them to know she had made a mistake. They had warned her, she hadn't listened. If she had voiced her regret sooner, perhaps they would have told her where he was. Maybe she would have gone back to live in Argentina. She might even have had a future with Santi, who knows. At least she was sure of one thing; her father had acted out of love and she was grateful. He had ensured Santiguito a good home, a loving family. He must have expected her to come home in the end. Now of course it was too late. Too late for everything.

Chapter Forty-Eight

Tuesday, 11 November 1997

The following morning, after spending some time with Maria, Sofia went to visit Grandpa O'Dwyer's grave. She placed some flowers against the headstone which was green with moss and mildew. She didn't imagine anyone came there very often, for the grave hadn't been tended in years. She ran her hand over the words cut into the stone and thought how little there was left for her now at Santa Catalina. She could almost hear her grandfather's voice reaching her from the grave, telling her that life was a training ground, it wasn't meant to be easy, it was designed to instruct. A harsh school it was indeed.

When she turned to leave, the ghostly figure of her mother appeared from behind the trees in a pair of floppy white trousers and a crisp white shirt. Her hair was flowing and fell about her shoulders in limp rust-coloured curls. She looked old.

'Do you ever come and talk to Grandpa?' asked Sofia in English as she approached. Anna, hands in pockets, walked over slowly and stood in the shade of the weather-beaten eucalyptus tree that protected the grave from the elements.

'Not really. I used to,' she said and smiled sadly. 'I suppose yer going to tell me that I should be looking after his grave.'

'No, not at all,' replied Sofia. 'Grandpa liked things wild and natural, didn't he?'

'He'll like yer flowers,' she said, bending down stiffly to pick them up to smell them.

'No, he won't,' laughed Sofia. 'He won't even notice!'

'I don't know. He was always full of surprises,' Anna said, pressing her nose against the flowers before placing them back by the headstone. 'Though he never did care much for flowers,' she added, remembering how he used to chop their heads off with the secateurs.

'Do you miss him?' Sofia asked tentatively.

'Yes, I do. I miss him.' She sighed and took a deep breath. Looking at her daughter she paused for a moment as if working out how best to say something. She stood with her hands in her pockets, her shoulders hunched slightly as if it were cold. 'I regret many things, Sofia. One of them is losing my family,' she said hesitantly.

'But Grandpa lived here.'

'No, I don't mean then. I mean . . .' She put her hands on her hips and shook her head. 'No, I regret running away from them.' Sofia noticed that her mother found it difficult to look her straight in the eye.

'Did you run away from them?' she asked, surprised. She had never thought of her mother's marriage in that way. 'Why?'

'Because I wanted a better life than the one they had given me, I suppose. I was selfish and spoiled. I thought I deserved better. You know, the funny thing about getting old is that you think with time pain and hurt will fade, but time is irrelevant. I feel the same now as I did forty years ago. I just look different on the outside.'

'When did you start to feel regret?'

'Very soon after you were born my parents came over to visit.'

'Yes, I remember you telling me.'

'Well, it was then that I realised, if you don't spend time with people you drift apart. I had drifted apart from my family. I don't think my parents ever got over that. Then I saw you making the same mistakes I had. I wanted so much to stop you. There you were, running away from yer family – and I thought you were just like yer father!'

'Oh Mama, I didn't want to stay away so long,' Sofia protested tearfully. How could she explain what had happened, how she felt? How could she make her mother understand?

'I know you didn't, girl, it's that damn pride of yours – and mine!'

'I suppose we're just as bad as each other, aren't we?'

'I regretted treating you so harshly.'

'Mama, you don't have to say all this,' interrupted Sofia, embarrassed that her mother was baring her soul. 'This isn't Confession.'

'No, I want to. You see, you and I just don't understand each other. But that's no reason not to be friends. Let's sit down, shall we?' she suggested.

Sofia sat down on the dry grass opposite her mother and thought how appropriate it was that Grandpa O'Dwyer was present for this conversation.

'When I married yer father, I thought it would be easy starting a new life in a beautiful country with the man I loved. But I was wrong. Things are never that simple and I suppose I was my own worst enemy. I can see that now. I guess as one gets older one does acquire a little wisdom; the wisdom of hindsight. That's something my father did teach me. He was right about a lot of things, but I didn't really pay him enough attention. I wish I had.'

Anna paused for a moment and shook her head. She had made the decision that she was going to make it up with her daughter, she couldn't allow herself to falter now. She breathed deeply and swept the hair that had fallen into her eyes behind her ear.

'Oh Sofia, I can't expect you to understand. One doesn't even understand one's own feelings, or where they come from, let alone trying to understand someone else's. But I just didn't fit in here. I never have. I tried to, but I just wasn't cut out for this life of horses and Latin temperaments. I found the society here very unforgiving, and as much as I tried to belong, I just never found I could. I didn't want to admit to myself that I missed those green hills of Glengariff, the moody face of my Aunt Dorothy and my sweet, sweet mother whom I just, well, abandoned.'

Anna's voice faltered, but she pushed on. Her eyes were locked somewhere in the middle distance and Sofia felt this soliloquy was as much for herself as it was for her daughter.

'I hope Mam forgives me in heaven,' she added in a low voice, looking up at the sky.

Sofia sat with her eyes wide, afraid that if she closed them, the moment would be lost. She had never heard her mother talk like this before. If she had been this open when Sofia was growing up, perhaps they could have been real friends. Then Anna surprised even herself.

'I was envious of you, Sofia,' she conceded. That was as honest as a person could be, and Sofia felt a tightening in her throat.

'Envious?' she croaked.

'Because you made it all look so easy. I wanted to clip your wings and prevent you from flying because I couldn't fly,' she said hoarsely.

'But Mama, I wanted you to notice me, so I behaved badly. You only ever saw my brothers,' Sofia said, but her voice sounded more like a cry.

'I know. I couldn't bond with you. I tried.'

'I so wanted you to be my friend. I used to watch Maria with Chiquita and long for us to be like that. But we never got close. When I went to live in London I wanted to hurt you. Both of you. I knew if I didn't come home you'd both be sad. I wanted you to miss me. I wanted you to realise how much you loved me.' Sofia's voice cracked on the word 'love'. She couldn't continue.

'Sofia – come here. Let me tell you how much I love you. How much I regret the past and how aware I am that this might be the last time I can make it up to you.'

Sofia shuffled around to where her mother was sitting, and placing herself next to her she allowed Anna to put her arm around her and press her face against hers. Sofia felt her mother's tears on her cheek.

'I do love you, Sofia. You are my daughter.' She laughed sadly. 'How couldn't I love you?'

'I love you too, Mama,' she sniffed.

'You know the greatest of all Christian teachings is that of forgiveness. So you and I must learn to forgive.'

'I'll try,' replied Sofia. 'And you must try to forgive Papa too,' she ventured.

'Paco?'

'Papa,' she repeated.

Anna pulled her daughter closer and sighed. 'Yer right, Sofia. I'll try to forgive him too.'

Later that day, Sofia went for a ride with Santi and Fernando. She reflected on what her mother had said. Looking around at Santa Catalina she felt she could begin to understand Anna's feelings of isolation, because Sofia was slowly realising that she didn't belong there either. How ironic it was that her mother's envy of Sofia's place at Santa Catalina had been the reason for their acrimony; now Sofia's own sense of isolation was the very cause of their understanding.

Sofia had to look on passively as Santi ordered Javier around. To him Javier was like Pablo, a servant, nothing more. He was kind but firm, as was the rest of her family. Fernando was a little gruffer, like his father, Miguel; it was their way. How could they have known that Javier was their flesh, their blood? She smiled at him as he saddled up her pony and brought it around for her to mount, and he smiled back. But his smile betrayed no more affection than he felt for anyone else in her family – less probably as he barely knew

535

her. He didn't see his colouring reflected in her own, his grin and gait mirrored in Santi; there was no subconscious bond that pulled the three of them together. She had dreamed that nature would enable him to see from whence he came, but that dream was nothing more than romantic wish-fulfilment. He had grown to look more like Soledad and Antonio. She wondered how different he might have looked had he grown up with her and Santi. She would never know.

'What did you do today?' asked Maria later that evening when she and Sofia found themselves alone on the terrace after dinner. She looked better and had been able to eat with them at the table under the stars. The humidity was oppressive. They all felt the storm edging its way in over the horizon.

'I visited Grandpa's grave,' Sofia replied. Maria smiled at her through the darkness. Sofia suddenly wished she hadn't reminded her cousin of death. 'How do you feel?' she added, changing the subject.

'Better, actually. For the first time I don't feel ill. I feel well again. Perhaps your candles worked,' she said, referring to their visit to the church the day before.

'That would be nice. We prayed very hard,' Sofia replied hopefully. They sat in silence for a while. She was very aware that the others were leaving them alone to chat. She was grateful for this private moment with her friend.

'Sofia, what are you going to do?' Maria asked carefully.

'What do you mean?' she said, playing the innocent. But Maria could see through her in the same way that Santi could.

'You know what I mean. You'll have to go home in the end.'

Sofia swallowed hard. 'I know. But I can't think about it now.'

'You'll have to. You have a husband and two daughters. Don't you love them?'

'I do love them. I love them very much. They're just so far away.'

'Santi also has children and a wife whom he loves very much.'

'Not in the same way that he loves me,' she insisted in defence.

'But he can't have you. Don't you see? It's impossible.'

Sofia knew she was right but she didn't want to face the truth. Everything was so perfect. They were so happy together; she just couldn't imagine it coming to an end.

Maria took her hand in hers and held it tightly. 'Sofia,' she continued, 'it's all very well at the moment. You're both living in a dream. But what are you going to do once I'm gone? Santi will have to return to Buenos Aires, he has a business to run. Things will go back to normal and where does that leave you? What do you want — to run away together? To leave your families behind?'

'No! Yes! I don't know,' she replied in confusion.

'Sofia, I agree you're right together but it's too late now. I love my brother so much; I would give anything for you both to be happy. But you can't destroy the lives of those around you. You'd never be able to look yourself in the mirror again. You couldn't respect a person who was capable of leaving his children like that. Can you really build your happiness on other people's unhappiness?'

'I love him, Maria. I don't care about anything else. I wake up with him on my mind and fall asleep dreaming about him. I breathe him. I have to be with him. I just wouldn't want to live without him. I suffered so much when I left him all those years ago, I can't go through it again!'

'Do what you will,' conceded Maria kindly. 'Just think about what I've said.'

Sofia embraced her friend, so fragile and yet so brave. She felt a great surge of love for her. When she departed the first drops of rain were falling from the sky.

Chapter Forty-Nine

Wednesday, 12 November 1997

The thunder roared like an angry lion pacing the heavens. Sofia wanted to run over to Santi's house and curl up in his arms. The deluge fell in thick splashes against her window, rattling rabidly against the glass. She stood in the darkness looking out. It was very hot still. Every now and then a flash of lightning would illuminate her room with a shuddering silver blaze. She didn't feel afraid, she just felt sad.

Maria's words swam about in her mind and she could not free herself from them. Was it really impossible for her and Santi to be together? She had tried to get to sleep but the thunder mirrored the disquiet in her head and she tossed in anguish. Finally, she crept out into the rain and let the heavy drops fall upon her. She didn't mind getting wet; in fact she was grateful for it as the night was humid and sticky. She enjoyed the peace of the darkness, it had always had a strange allure for her. She lost herself in it. Pacing about the courtyard, she indulged in the sweet melancholy of her desolation. She loved Santi, but could she love him enough to let him go?

She looked at her watch under the light that swung in the wind above the door. It was three in the morning. She felt a shiver momentarily debilitate her body in spite of the heat. Suddenly she was gripped with panic. She sensed a terrible dread right in the core of her being. Something was wrong, she just knew it.

She found herself running through the rain and the wind to Chiquita's house. She didn't know what she was going to do once she got there. She just ran. The water poured down her face and soaked her night-dress to such an extent it clung to her body like weeds. Each time the thunder cracked she ran faster, leaping over the grass when the lightning struck. Once she reached the house she pounded on the door. When Miguel's face appeared, crumpled and anxious, she fell into his arms.

'Something's wrong!' she cried breathlessly. He looked at her in confusion but before he could say anything she pushed past him. Santi apeared from somewhere and suddenly the whole house was awake. When she entered Maria's room her fears were confirmed. Maria was dead.

Sofia was inconsolable. Miguel and Chiquita held each other as if their own lives depended on it. Panchito and Fernando sat slumped in chairs, weeping. Santi knelt on the floor by Maria's bed and stroked her hand, his face grey with resignation. Eduardo, who had been with her throughout, gazed out of the window as if in a trance. Sofia just stood there as her dreams disintegrated about her.

She took one last look at her friend. Maria was even more beautiful in death than she had been in life. Her skin was like porcelain and her expression was one of peace. Her decrepit body lay still and heavy and Sofia was very aware that it was nothing more than a shell, an empty house where she had resided, but now she was free of it. She was happy for her that she was finally released from the pain. She knew she was in another dimension where misery and illness could not reach her, but what of the rest of them?

Miguel kissed his daughter's forehead and then with Chiquita, Fernando and Panchito, they left Eduardo alone with his wife.

Santi walked up to Sofia, his face grey with despair. He pulled her into his arms and led her out into the corridor where they both abandoned themselves to grief. After a long while of weeping in silence he held her face in his hands and wiped away the tears with his thumbs. His eyes welled with tenderness.

'Where do we go from here?' she whispered, when she had controlled herself enough to speak.

He shook his head and sighed heavily. 'I don't know, Chofi. I just don't know.'

But *she* knew. Maria had been right.

After that, events passed in a blur. The funeral was a small, dignified affair during which Santi and Sofia barely exchanged glances. Claudia and the children had returned with Eduardo and Maria's children. There was no laughter. The rain had cleared but the sunshine failed to bring about gladness in anyone's heart.

Sofia sat with her parents on the uncomfortable seats of the church and Padre Juan gave a fluent address that moved them all to tears. More tears. She noticed her parents held hands and once or twice they exchanged tender looks. Their compassion moved Sofia who hoped that with the loss of Maria they might have found each other again. The heaviness weighed down upon them all as they bade farewell to a young woman who had had so much to live for. Sofia could barely look at Maria's family without feeling an indescribable sadness. Her children hadn't even said goodbye.

Maria was buried in the small tomb that belonged to the family, alongside her grandparents and other relatives who had gone before her. Sofia laid some flowers and said a small prayer for her. Once she would have looked upon this tomb as her own final resting place, but now she realised that she would be buried far away from here and there would be different faces at her funeral.

Claudia blinked at Sofia through her tears and she knew what she was thinking. It had all come to an end. There was no reason now for her to stay.

She embraced Chiquita and thanked her for sending her the letter. 'I'm glad you found me. I'm glad I came,' she said truthfully.

'I'm happy you came too, Sofia,' she replied. 'But I didn't send you any letter.'

If Chiquita hadn't sent her the letter, who had?

As they made their way back to the cars, a taxi drew up and out stepped a man Sofia recognised. It was her brother – Agustin. He strode straight up to Chiquita and Miguel, embraced them both and said how sorry he was that Maria had been taken from them. 'But I have come back,' he told Paco and Anna brightly. 'I have left Marianne and the children. I've come home.'

When he saw Sofia he greeted her with the politeness of a stranger. It was then that Sofia realised just how much those long years away had taken from her. They had changed her. She just didn't belong there any more.

Once back at Santa Catalina she called David.

'David, she's gone,' she said sadly.

'Darling, I'm so sorry,' his voice was full of sympathy.

'There's nothing here for me any more. I'm coming home.'

'Let me know when your flight gets in, I'll bring the girls,' he said gently.

'Oh yes, please bring the girls.' Suddenly she felt a tremendous wave of homesickness.

Sofia packed her bags and prepared herself for the long journey home. Santa Catalina seemed suddenly remote and aloof as if she wished to lessen Sofia's pain in leaving her. At five when the shadows began to edge their way into a cooler, more refreshing evening, her car drew up under the eucalyptus trees. She stood in their shade and bade farewell to her father.

'This is all very sudden. When will we see you again?' he asked gruffly in an attempt to mask his misery, but she could tell from his expression that he couldn't bear to see her go.

'I don't know, Papa. You have to understand that this is no longer my home,' she replied, fighting her emotions. 'I have a husband and two girls who are waiting for me in England.'

'But you haven't even said goodbye to anyone.'

'I haven't the strength. It is better that I go quietly – I don't think I've ever done anything quietly before!' she quipped in rather poor taste.

'You belong here, Sofia,' he said.

'I did once. And a part of me will always be here,' she replied and she noticed his eyes turn to the polo fields in the distance.

'Yes, it will.' He nodded and sighed deeply.

'Thank you, Papa,' she said and touched his hand. He turned to face her, unsure whether he understood what she was trying to say. 'You gave my child a home,' she added. 'Ironic, isn't it? He belongs in the home I lost.' Paco's eyes glistened as he searched for something to say. 'I know you did the right thing,' she told him hastily. 'I only wish I had come back with him. Then I would never have felt estranged from the people I love.'

Hearing those words, Paco pulled his daughter into his arms where he held her so forcefully she knew he was hiding tears that he did not wish her to see.

At that moment Anna appeared in the doorway like a spectre. The past twenty-four hours showed in the dark circles under her eyes. She looked tired and defeated.

'Mama!' exclaimed Sofia in surprise, reluctantly withdrawing from her father's embrace and wiping her cheeks with a trembling hand.

'I wish you would stay,' Anna said quietly, approaching her with a soft expression on her face. She walked out of the shadow into the sun and extended her hands to her. Sofia took them in hers. 'Maria is with God now,' she said.

'I know. She's with Grandpa,' Sofia said quietly.

'Will you call us?' asked Anna, and Sofia noticed her ice-blue eyes were melting.

'Yes. I would like you to know my children some day.'

'I would like that,' her mother replied. 'Your room will always be here for you, but I think it is time to clear it out, don't you?'

Sofia nodded, smiling back her emotion. In her mother's eyes she could see remorse, as if she were crying out from inside the shell of her body but unable to physically express her feelings. Sofia could sense her fighting with herself. Instinctively she made the first move for her. Placing her arms around her she pulled her thin frame towards her. Anna didn't resist. When she held her mother, Sofia felt a warmth radiate from her that she hadn't felt for many years. She remembered those few moments as a young child when her mother had drawn her into her arms and cherished her. She smelt the same and her scent unlocked the final door to Sofia's memories. She sensed the heaviness that comes from holding onto resentment for so long lighten its burden and release her. Perhaps, as Anna had suggested, they would both learn to forgive.

'I'm glad you came,' Anna smiled at her daughter, and suddenly Sofia remembered the letter. If Chiquita hadn't written it, then it must have been her mother. She had wanted her to come back after all. She must have written it signing it with the name of her sister-in-law for fear that if she had signed it herself, her daughter might not have come.

'The letter – it was you, wasn't it?' Sofia asked and grinned. 'Very cunning, Mama!'

'I can be cunning too, Sofia,' she chided her daughter. 'Ah, wait a minute, don't go yet. I have something for you,' she said with a sudden, uncharacteristic burst of enthusiasm. 'Something you should have had a long time ago. Wait while I go and get it.'

Anna retreated into the dark interior of the house. Paco noticed a bounce in her step that reminded him of the *Ana Melodía* he had lost somewhere way back, he couldn't remember when, and his lips trembled with the hope that maybe he would find her again. When she returned she held a red packet in her hands. She handed it to her daughter who turned it over curiously. She began to tear the paper.

'Open it in the car,' insisted Anna, placing a hand on the packet to prevent her from seeing what was inside. 'It's something to remember us by.' Sofia blinked at her mother but the fog in her eyes meant she could see little more than a blur.

Paco embraced his daughter for the last time, relieved that the secret he had kept for twenty-three years was now shared with her; there were no more secrets to drive a wedge between them. Sofia had thanked him for giving Javier the best home he could possibly have. He belonged at Santa Catalina.

Sofia hugged him back knowing that many moons would pass before she would hold him again. She took one more look at the place that had once been her home and realised that, although she had changed and moved on, it would live in her heart and in her memory, untarnished, like sepia photos of another, happier time. Maria would be there too, her radiant face smiling out through the plumbago and hibiscus.

Sofia climbed into the car and waved one last time at her parents, who after years of estrangement had finally come to know their daughter again. She tore open the red paper with impatience. What could her mother have possibly bought her? When she pulled out a black leather belt with the silver buckle engraved with her initials the blur melted into large, sentimental tears.

As Sofia drove up the avenue of tall trees, the house disappearing into the shadows, she said to the chauffeur, 'Turn left at the end here. There's one last place I want to go to before we hit the road.' And she directed him to the ombu tree.

Chapter Fifty

The car rattled along the dirt track as far as it could go. Once they reached the end she asked the driver to wait for her while she went the rest of the way on foot. The air was now cool after the storm and the grass greener from the rain it had so desperately needed. She walked with a heaviness of heart down the path she had taken so many times in the last few days. She felt empty of emotion, as if her nerves had simply shut down and refused to feel any more.

She reached the tree that had seen her through all her troubles. It stood majestic and proud, like a dear old friend who never judged but observed with a quiet understanding. She ran her hand over its trunk with affection and recalled happier times with Santi. Looking out over the fields she saw the *gauchos* playing polo in the distance, their tanned bodies shirtless in the heat. Javier was among them. She couldn't tell which one he was, but she knew he was there. There, where he belonged.

Suddenly she felt the presence of someone. She turned and saw the grim face of Santi. He looked just as surprised to see her as she was to see him.

'They said you had gone. I didn't know what to do with myself,' he exclaimed in torment and strode over to embrace her.

'I couldn't bear to say goodbye to you again. I just couldn't do it,' she mumbled, feeling an overpowering sense of desolation.

'I had just found you again,' he said miserably. 'I can't let you go.'

'It's impossible, isn't it? If only . . .'

'Don't,' he choked. 'If we start on the "if only" road we'll grind ourselves into the ground.' He nuzzled his face into her hair as if he wanted to hide from the inevitable.

'I wouldn't be the woman you love if I were capable of leaving my children,' she said sadly, remembering Maria's advice. She thought of Javier and the pain of having left him all those years ago still jarred at her conscience.

'I just want to breathe the same air as you.'

'But Maria was right. Our lives are so different now; we both have families we love. We can't destroy all those people.'

'I know. But I still keep trying to think of a way around it.'

'There is no way. I don't belong here any more.'

'You belong with me. We belong together.'

'It's a beautiful dream, a lovely "what might have been". But it's impossible. You know it's impossible.'

He nodded and sighed deeply in resignation. 'Then let me take an inventory of your face so I never forget it,' he said solemnly, running his fingers down her cheek. He kissed her eyes, 'soft and brown like sugar', he said, then he kissed her nose, her temples, her forehead, her jawbone telling her why he loved each part as he kissed it. Then he reached her lips. 'I'll never forget the feel of you, Chofi, or the smell of you.' And he tasted the salt of her tears as he kissed her.

They hugged each other. Looking into his sea-green eyes Sofia knew that in their very secret depths she would dwell, and at night, when fantasy and reality are one, she would appear to love him again. She kissed his lips for the last time and the taste of him stayed with her long after they had parted. She turned back once to see his lonely figure sitting at the foot of their tree. She waved and then she turned and walked away. That picture of him sitting alone under the ombu tree would later appear whenever she closed her eyes.

They said the ombu tree wouldn't grow in England. But I chose a place in our garden in Gloucestershire where the sun would set behind it and planted it all the same. It grew.

If you enjoyed
MEET ME UNDER THE OMBU TREE, here's
a foretaste of Santa Montefiore's new novel,
THE BUTTERFLY BOX.

Chapter One

Viña del Mar, Chile, Summer 1982

Federica opened her eyes onto a different world. It was hot, but not humid for the sea breeze carried with it a cool undercurrent from where it had dallied among the waves of the cold Pacific Ocean. Her room was slowly coming to life in the pale morning light that spilled in through the gap in the curtains, casting mellow shafts onto the floor and walls, swallowing up the remains of the night, exposing the regimental line of sleeping dolls. The constant barking of Señora Baraca's dog at the end of the street had left the animal with little more than a raw husk, but he still continued to bark as he always did. Some day he'd lose his voice altogether, she thought, which wouldn't be a bad thing; at least he wouldn't keep the neighbours awake. She had once tried to feed him a biscuit on her way to school but her mother had said he was probably riddled with all sorts of diseases. 'Best not to touch him, you don't know where he's been,' she had advised, pulling her six-year-old daughter away by the hand. But that was the problem; he had never been anywhere. Federica breathed in the sweet scent of the orange trees that floated upon the air and she could almost taste the fruit that hung heavily like lustrous packages on a Christmas tree. She kicked off the sheet that covered her and knelt on the end of her bed, leaning out through the curtains onto a world that wasn't the same as the one the sun had set on the day before. With the rising of the new sun a quiver ran through her skinny body, causing a broad smile to spread across her pale face. Today her father was coming home after many months travelling.

Ramon Campione was a giant of a man. Not only in stature – at well over six foot he was tall for a Chilean and tall for an Italian, which was where his family originated from – but in his gigantic imagination, which, like the galaxy itself, seemed never-ending and full of surprises. His adventures took him to the far corners of the earth where he was inspired by everything different and everything beautiful. He travelled, wrote and travelled some more. His family barely knew him. He was never around long enough for them to find the person behind the writing and the magical photographs he took. In the mind of his daughter he was more powerful than God. She had once told Padre Amadeo that Jesus was nothing compared to her father who could do so much more than turn water into wine. 'My papa can fly,' she had said proudly. Her mother had smiled apologetically to the priest and rolled her eyes, explaining to him quietly that Ramon had tried out a new contraption in Switzerland for flying off the mountain on skis. Padre Amadeo had nodded in understanding but later shook his head and worried that the child would only get hurt when her father toppled, as he surely would some day, off the tall pedestal she had so blindly placed him upon. She should focus such devotion on God not man, he thought piously.

Federica longed for it to be time to get up, but it was still early. The sky was as pale and still as a large, luminous lagoon and only the barking dog and the clamour of birds resounded against the quiet stirring of dawn. From her bedroom she could see the ocean disappearing into the grey mists on the horizon as if the heavens were drinking it up. Her mother often took them to Caleta Abarca beach, as they didn't have a swimming pool to cool off in, although the sea was almost too cold for bathing. Sometimes they would drive to the small seaside village of Cachagua, about an hour up the coast, to stay with her grandparents who owned a pretty thatched summerhouse there surrounded by tall palms and acacia trees. Federica loved the sea. Her father had once said that she loved the sea because she was born under the sign of Cancer whose symbol was a crab. She didn't much like crabs though.

After a long while she heard footsteps on the stairs then the high-pitched voice of her younger brother Enrique, nicknamed Hal after Shakespeare's 'Prince Henry'. That had been Ramon's idea – although his wife was English she had no interest in literature or history unless it was about her.

'Darling, you're dressed already!' Helena gasped in surprise as Federica jumped across the landing and into Hal's bedroom where she was dressing him.

'Papa's coming home today!' she sang, unable to remain still even for a moment.

'Yes, he is,' replied Helena, taking a deep breath to restrain the resentment she felt towards her absent husband. 'Keep your feet still, Hal darling, I can't put your shoes on if you keep moving.'

'Will he be here before lunch?' asked Federica, automatically helping her mother by opening the curtains, allowing the warm sunshine to flood into the dim room with the enthusiasm that belongs only to the morning.

'He'll be here sometime before noon, his flight gets in at ten,' she replied patiently. 'There, sweetie, you look very handsome,' she added, smoothing back Hal's black hair with a soft brush. He shook his head in protest and squealed before wriggling off the bed and running out onto the landing.

'I put on my best dress for him,' said Federica, following her mother down the stairs with buoyant footsteps.

'So I see,' she replied.

'I'm going to help Lidia cook lunch today. We're making Papa's favourite dish.'

'What's that then?'

'*Pastel de choclo* and we're making him *merengon de lúcuma* as a welcome home cake,' said Federica, flicking her straight blonde hair off her shoulders so that it fell thickly down her back. She had pushed it off her forehead with a hair-band, which along with her small stature made her appear younger than her six years.

'Papa's coming home today,' said Federica to Hal as she helped her mother lay the table.

'Will he bring me a present?' asked Hal, who at four years of age remembered his father only for the presents he gave.

'Of course he will, sweetie. He always brings you presents,' said Helena, placing a cup of cold milk in front of him. 'Anyway, it's Christmas so you'll be getting loads of presents.' Federica supervised Hal while he dipped his spoon into the tin of powdered chocolate and dropped it into his milk. She then grabbed the cloth from the sink to mop up the chocolate that hadn't quite made it to the cup.

'Fede, the croissants are ready, I can smell them beginning to burn,' said Helena, lighting a cigarette. She looked anxiously at the clock on the wall and bit her lower lip. She knew she should take the children to the airport to pick him up as other mothers would. But she couldn't face it. The awkward drive from Santiago Airport to the coast, all the while making conversation as if everything was positively rosy. No, it would be much better to see him at home, the house was big, more space for them to lose each other in. How silly, she thought bitterly, they had lost each other a long time ago somewhere in the vast distances they had placed between themselves. Somewhere in the faraway lands and imaginary characters that seemed so much more important to Ramon than the people in his life who were real and who needed him. She had tried. She had really tried. But now she was empty inside and tired of being neglected.

Federica buttered a croissant and sipped her iced chocolate, chattering away to her brother with an excitement that made her voice rise in tone, irritating the raw nerves of her mother who stood by the window blowing smoke against the glass. Once they had been in love, but even hate was an expression of love, just a different face. Now Helena no longer hated him, that alone would have been a good enough reason to stay. But she felt indifference and it frightened her. Nothing could grow out of that. It was a barren emotion, as barren as the face of the moon.

Helena had made a life for herself in Chile because she had believed, as did her daughter later, that Ramon was God. He was certainly the most glamorous, handsome man Polperro had ever seen. Then his article had appeared in *National Geographic* with photographs of all the old smugglers' caves and crumbling castles Helena had shown him, and yet somehow the photographs were suffused with a light that didn't belong to Nature. There was something mystical about them that she couldn't put her finger on. Every word he wrote sung out to her and stayed with her long after she had turned the last page. Now she recognised the magic as love, for it had followed them for the first six years, converting even the most mundane things, like filling the car up with petrol, into a magical experience. Their lovemaking had pertained to another plane far above the physical and she had believed that the power was within him and in him alone. Only after it had gone did she realise that the connection had been cut – like electricity, their 'magic' had been caused by the two of them and ceased the minute one of them felt disenchanted by it. Once it had gone it was gone for ever. That kind of sorcery is of high energy but low life span. At first they had travelled together, to the far corners of China, to the arid deserts of Egypt and the wet lakes of Sweden. When she became pregnant with Federica they returned to settle in Chile. Their 'magic' had followed them there too where the white powder coast and pastoral simplicity had enchanted her. But now it echoed with the emptiness she felt within her own being because the love that had filled it had drained away. There was no reason to stay.

She was tired of pretending. She was tired of pretending to herself. She longed for the drizzly, verdant hills of her youth and her longing made her hand shake. She lit another cigarette and once more eyed the clock.

Federica cleared away her breakfast, humming to herself and skipping around the kitchen as she did so. Hal played with his train in the nursery. Helena remained by the window.

'Mama!' shouted Hal. 'My train is broken, it's not working.' Helena picked up her packet of cigarettes and strode out of the kitchen, leaving Federica to finish clearing up. Once the table was wiped and the crockery washed up she put on her cooking apron and waited for Lidia to arrive.

When Lidia bustled through the gate she saw Federica's small eager face pressed up against the glass, smiling broadly at her.

'*Hola*, Señorita,' she said breathlessly as she entered the hall. 'You're ready early.'

'I've even cleared away the breakfast,' replied Federica in Spanish. Although her mother spoke excellent Spanish they had always spoken English as a family, even when her father was home.

'Well, you *are* a good girl,' Lidia wheezed, following the child into the kitchen. 'Ah, you angel. You've done all the work,' she said, casting her dark eyes over the mixing bowls and spoons already laid out on the table.

'I want it all to be perfect for Papa,' she said, her cheeks aflame. She could barely contain her impatience and suppressed her desire to run by skipping instead of walking. That way the nervous feeling in her stomach was indulged a little but not too much. Lidia struggled into her pink overalls then washed her swollen brown hands. She suggested Federica do the same.

'You must always wash your hands before cooking, you don't know where they've been,' she said.

'Like Señora Baraca's dog,' giggled Federica.

'*Pobrecito*,' Lidia sighed, tilting her round head to one side and pulling a thin, sympathetic smile. 'He's tied up all day in that small garden, it's no wonder he barks from dawn till dusk.'

'Doesn't she take him out at all?' Federica asked, running her hands under the tap.

'Oh yes, she takes him out occasionally, but she's old,' Lidia replied, 'and we old people don't have as much energy for things like that.'

'You're not old, Lidia,' said Federica kindly.

'Not old, just fat,' said Helena in English, walking into the kitchen with Hal's toy engine. 'She'd have much more energy if she didn't eat so much. Imagine carrying that bulk around all day, no wonder she wheezes all the time.'

'*Buenos días, Señora,*' said Lidia, who didn't understand English.

'Good morning, Lidia. I need a knife to mend this blasted train,' said Helena in Spanish, not even bothering to force a smile, however small. She was too anxious and impatient to think of anyone else but herself.

'I wouldn't worry about that, Don Ramon will be home soon and he can fix it. That's men's work,' said Lidia cheerfully.

'Thank you, Lidia, that's very helpful. Fede, pass me a knife,' she said edgily. Federica handed her the knife and watched her walk out again.

'Oh, it's so exciting that your Papa is coming home,' enthused Lidia, embracing Federica fondly. 'I'll bet you didn't sleep a wink.'

'Not a wink,' she replied, looking up at the clock. 'He'll be here soon,' she said and Lidia noticed that her small hands trembled when she began to cut the butter up into pieces.

'Careful you don't cut yourself,' she said gently. 'You don't want your Papa to come back to a daughter with only seven fingers.' She laughed, then wheezed and coughed.

Helena, who was usually very deft at mending things, broke the engine. Hal started to cry. Helena pulled him into her arms and managed to cheer him up by promising him another engine, a bigger, better one. 'Anyway, this engine was old and tatty. What use is an engine like that? The train looks much better without his engine,' she said and thought how much she'd like to be a carriage on her own without an engine. She lit another cigarette. The doors to the garden were open, inviting in the gentle sea breeze that smelt of oranges and ozone. It was too hot to be sitting in suburbia, they should be down on the beach, she thought in frustration. She wiped her sweating brow with her hand then looked at her watch. Her throat constricted. His plane would have landed.

Federica and Lidia buzzed about the kitchen like a couple of bees in a flowerbed. Federica loved to be included and followed Lidia's instructions with great enthusiasm. She felt like a grown-up and Lidia treated her as one. They chatted about Lidia's back pain and her stomach cramps and her husband's verruca, which was giving him a lot of trouble. 'I'm afraid of putting my feet where he's put his,' she explained, 'so I wear a pair of socks even in the shower.'

'I would too,' Federica agreed, not sure what a verruca was.

'You're sensible like me,' Lidia replied, smiling down at the skinny child who had a manner well beyond her years. Lidia thought she was far too grown-up for a child of almost seven but one only had to look at her mother to understand why. Helena gave her so much responsibility, too much probably, that the child would be quite capable of running the entire household without her.

When Helena entered the kitchen the smell of *pastel de choclo* swelled her senses and her stomach churned with hunger and tension combined. Federica was drying up while Lidia washed the utensils and mixing bowls. Helena managed to grab the remains of the cream before Lidia's podgy hands pulled it into the soapy water. She scraped her finger around the bottom of the bowl and brought it up to her pale lips. 'Well done you, sweetie,' she said, impressed. She smiled at her daughter and stroked her hand down her shiny blonde hair. 'You're a very good cook.' Federica smiled, accustomed to her mother's changeable nature. One minute she was irritable, the next minute she was agreeable, not like her father who was always cheerful and carefree. Helena's praise delighted Federica as it always did and her spirits soared until she seemed to grow an inch taller.

'She's not only a good cook, Señora, but she's a good house-keeper, too,' said Lidia fondly, the large black mole on her chin quivering as her face creased into a wide smile. 'She cleaned up all the breakfast by herself,' she added in a mildly accusing tone, for Señora Helena always left everything to her daughter.

'I know,' Helena replied. 'What I would do without her, I can't imagine,' she said nonchalantly, flicking her cigarette ash into the bin and leaving the room. She walked upstairs. She was weary. Her heart weighed her down so that even the stairs were an effort to climb. She walked along the cool white corridor, her bare feet padding over the wooden floorboards, her hand too disenchanted even to deadhead the pots of pale orchids as she passed. In her bedroom the white linen curtains played about with the silk breeze as if they were trying to open all by themselves. Irritably she pulled them apart and looked out across the sea. It lay tremulous and iridescent, beckoning her to sail away with it to another place. The horizon promised her freedom and a new life.

'Mama, shall I help you tidy your room?' Federica asked quietly. Helena turned around and looked at the small, earnest face of her daughter.

'I suppose you want to tidy it up for Papa?' she replied, grabbing an ashtray and stubbing her cigarette into it.

'Well, I've picked some flowers . . .' she said sheepishly.

Helena's heart lurched. She pitied her daughter for the love she felt for her father in spite of the long absences that should have made her hate him. But no, she loved him unconditionally and the more he went away the happier she was to see him when he returned, running into his arms like a grateful lover. She longed to tell her the truth and shatter her illusions, out of spite because she wished she still shared those illusions. She found the world of children so blissfully simplistic and she envied her.

'All right, Fede. You tidy it up for Papa, he'll love the flowers, I'm sure,' she said tightly. 'Just ignore me,' she added, wandering into the bathroom and closing the door behind her. Federica heard her switch on the shower and the water pound against the enamel bath. She then made the bed, scenting the sheets with fresh lavender like her grandmother had shown her and placed a small blue vase of honeysuckle on her father's bedside table. She folded her mother's clothes and placed them in the old oak cupboard, rearranging the mess that she found there until all the shelves resembled a well-organised shop. She opened the windows as wide as they could go so that the scents of the garden and the sea would spirit away the dirty smell of her mother's smoke. Then she sat at her dressing table and picked up an old photograph of her father that grinned out at her from behind the glass of an ornate silver frame. He was very good looking with glossy black hair, swarthy skin, shiny brown eyes that were honest and intelligent and a large mouth that smiled the crooked smile of a man with an irreverent sense of humour and easy charm. She ran her thumb across the glass and caught her pensive expression in the mirror. In her reflection she saw only her mother. The pale blonde hair, the pale blue eyes, the pale pink lips, the pale skin – she wished she had inherited her father's dark Italian looks. He was so handsome and no doubt Hal would be handsome just like him. But Federica was used to getting a lot of attention because of her flowing white hair. All the other girls in her class were dark like Hal. People stared at her when she went into Valparaíso with her mother and Señora Escobar, who ran the sandwich shop on the square, called her 'La Angelita' (the little angel) because she couldn't believe that a human being could have such pale hair. Helena's best friend, Lola Miguens, had tried to copy her by dying her black hair blonde with peroxide, but had lost her nerve half way through so now she walked around with hair the colour of their terracotta roof, which Federica thought looked very ugly. Her mother didn't bother to look after herself like Chilean women who always had long manicured nails, perfect lipstick and immaculate clothes. Helena bustled about with her hair scrunched carelessly up onto the top of her head and she usually had a cigarette hanging out of her mouth. Federica thought she was beautiful when she made an effort and judging by old photographs she was once very beautiful indeed. But recently she had let herself go. Federica hoped she would make an effort for her father.

Helena stepped out of the bathroom followed by a puff of steam. Her face was pink and her eyes sparkled from the moisture. Federica lay on the white damask bedspread and watched her mother dress and prepare herself for her husband's return. Helena could smell the lavender and the ripe scent of oranges and refrained from lighting another cigarette. She felt guilty. Federica was so excited she quivered like a horse in the starting gate while *she* awaited Ramon's return with trepidation and the secret knowledge that any moment now she'd gather together her courage and leave him for good. As she painted her face she watched her daughter in the mirror while she didn't know that she was being watched. She stared out of the window across the sea as if her father was arriving by boat and not by car. Her profile was childish and yet her expression was that of a grown woman. The anxious expectation in her frown and on her trembling lips betrayed too much awareness for a child her age. She worshipped her father with the devotion of a dog, whereas Hal worshipped his mother who, Helena felt, was more deserving of his love.

When Helena was ready, in a pair of tight white trousers and T-shirt, her hair scrunched up on her head, still damp and knotted, she sat on the bed beside her daughter and ran a damp hand down her face.

'You look lovely, sweetie. You really do,' she said and kissed her innocent brow affectionately.

'He'll be here soon, won't he?' said Federica softly.

'Any minute,' Helena replied, masking the tremor in her voice with a deftness that came from years of practice. She got up abruptly and hurried down the stairs. She couldn't smoke in the bedroom, not after Federica had prepared it so lovingly, but she was in desperate need of a cigarette. Just as she reached the bottom, her espadrilles landing on the cold stone tiles of the hallway, the front door swung open and Ramon filled the entrance like a large black wolf. Helena gasped and felt her stomach lurch. They stared at each other, wordlessly assessing the frigid estrangement that still grew up between them whenever they found themselves together in the same room.

'Fede, Papa's here!' Helena shouted, but as impassive as her features were her voice croaked with repressed emotion. Ramon's dark brown eyes pulled away from the stony countenance of his wife in search of his daughter whom he heard squeal with delight from the landing before the soft patter of her small feet scurried across the floorboards and skipped down the stairs two at a time. She jumped past her mother and into her father's sturdy embrace. She wrapped her thin arms around his bristly neck, nuzzling her face into his throat and inhaling the heavy, spicy scent that made him different from everyone else in the world. He kissed her warm cheek, lifting her off the ground and laughing so loudly she felt the vibration shake against her body like an earthquake.

'So you missed me!' he said, swinging her around until she had to wrap her legs about his waist to stop herself from falling.

'Yes, Papa!' she laughed, clinging on as her happiness almost choked her.

At that moment Hal ran into the hall, took one look at his father and burst into tears. Helena, grateful for the distraction, ran to him and picked him up in her arms, kissing his wet cheek. 'It's Papa, Hal darling, he's come home,' she said, trying to boost her voice with a bit of enthusiasm but her tone was dead and Hal sensed it and cried again. Ramon put his daughter down and walked over to where his son was weeping in his mother's arms.

'Halcito, it's Papa,' he said, smiling into the child's frightened face with his large, generous mouth. Hal buried his head in Helena's neck and wriggled closer against her.

'I'm sorry, Ramon,' she said flatly, sensing his disappointment but secretly taking pleasure from the child's rejection. She wanted to tell him that he couldn't expect his children to love him when he took no part in their lives, but she saw Federica's love set her cheeks aflame and the admiration shine in her pale, trusting eyes and knew that it wasn't entirely true. Nevertheless, he didn't deserve his daughter's love.

'I've got a present for you, Hal,' he said, walking back to his bag and unzipping it. 'And I've got one for you too, Fede,' he added as his daughter placed an affectionate hand on his back as he rummaged around for his gifts. 'Ah, this is for you, Hal,' he said, walking over to the little boy whose eyes opened wide at the brightly painted wooden train that his father waved in front of him. He forgot his fear and held his hands out. 'There, I thought you'd like that.'

'I broke his engine today,' said Helena, making an effort for the sake of the children. 'That couldn't have come at a better time, could it, Hal?'

'Good,' Ramon replied, retreating to his case.

'Now where's yours, Fede? I've got you a very special present,' he said, looking up at her expectant face. He felt her hand on his back again. It was so typical of Federica who always had to have some sort of physical contact to feel close. His hands burrowed deep into the bag that was filled not with clothes but with notepads, camera equipment and souvenirs from faraway countries. Finally his fingers felt the rough surface of tissue paper. He pulled it out, taking care not to knock it against the hard metal of his equipment. 'Here,' he said, pressing it into her trembling hands.

'Thank you, Papa,' she breathed, unwrapping it carefully. Hal had run off into the nursery to play with his new train. Helena lit a cigarette and smoked it nervously, leaning back against the banisters.

'So how are you?' he asked without approaching her.

'Fine, you know, nothing's changed,' she replied coldly.

'Good,' he said.

Helena sighed wearily. 'We have to talk, Ramon.'

'Not now.'

'Of course.'

'Later.'

Federica unwrapped the paper to discover a roughly carved wooden box. It wasn't pretty. It wasn't even charming. She felt the tears prick the backs of her eyes and her throat constrict with disappointment. Not because she wanted a nicer present, she wasn't materialistic or spoilt, but because Hal's present had been so much more beautiful than hers. She understood his presents as a reflection of his love. He couldn't love her very much if he hadn't even bothered to find her a pretty gift.

'Thank you, Papa,' she choked, swallowing back her tears in shame. 'It's very nice.' But she didn't have the strength to rebel against her emotions. The excitement had been too much, now the disappointment threw her into a sudden low and the tears welled and spilled out over her hot cheeks.

'*Fede, mi amor,*' he said, pulling her into his arms and kissing her wet face.

'It's nice,' she said, trying to sound grateful and not wishing to offend him.

'Open it,' he whispered into her ear. She hesitated. 'Go on, *amorcita,* open it.' She opened it with a shaking hand. The little box might have been plain on the outside, ugly even, but inside it was the most beautiful thing she had ever seen, and what's more it played the strangest, most alluring tune she had ever heard.